VENTURE
SCIENCE FICTION

– a new publishing imprint to bring you the very best in adventure SF. Time travel, galactic empires, alien invasions – all the traditional elements that have made science fiction the most exciting form of literature of the 20th century. In Venture SF, we'll be bringing you novels of action adventure – no short stories, no fantasy, no boredom. If action adventure SF is your type of reading, then Venture SF is for you – every book published by us will be the first appearance in paperback in the UK. We'll be publishing one new book every month – Start collecting them now!

VENTURE SCIENCE FICTION SERIES

Series editors, Rog Peyton and Rod Milner

VENTURE
SCIENCE FICTION

THE TIMELINER TRILOGY

Richard C Meredith

ARROW BOOKS
VENTURE SF

Arrow Books Limited
62–65 Chandos Place, London WC2N 4NW

An imprint of Century Hutchinson Limited

London Melbourne Sydney Australia
Johannesburg and agencies throughout
the world

First published in one volume 1987

Printed and bound in Great Britain by
Anchor Brendon Limited, Tiptree, Essex

ISBN 0 09 951690 X

BOOK ONE
AT THE NARROW PASSAGE

This book is dedicated to the memory of
H. Beam Piper and to the Paratime Police,
to Verkan Vall, to Tortha Karf, to Hadron
Dalla, and to all those who guard the
multiple worlds.

Contents

CONTENTS

At the narrow passage there is no brother, no friend.

—ARABIAN PROVERB

Some billion years ago, an anonymous speck of protoplasm protruded the first primitive pseudopodium into the primeval slime, and perhaps the first state of uncertainty occurred.

—I. J. Good, *Science,* February 20, 1959

1
France, Line RTGB-307,
Spring, 1971

It was spring in France when I contracted to kidnap Imperial Count Albert von Heinen and his wife.

It was a spring that had been too long in coming, and the bitter winter that had come before it had frozen all of western Europe and brought the war to a virtual standstill until the weather, in its own fickle way, finally began to warm and allowed us to return to the bloody games we were being paid to play.

The trenches in which we lived were very old and deep and muddy and cold when those first spring days came suddenly, almost unexpectedly, and though warm breezes blew across France, the trenches still remained cold, down deep in them, and it seemed that they would never dry out.

Trenchfoot was rampant. Most of us who hadn't come down with frostbite or pneumonia or one of the other diseases of the trenches that winter, finally gave in to that disgusting flesh rotting that I guess has been feared by foot soldiers as long as men have fought wars.

At least I had been lucky so far. We had a small stove in our dugout—the one I shared with Tracy and two subalterns—and I had kept my boots and socks more or less dry most of the time, and even though my feet stank a good deal more than I liked, they hadn't begun to rot. I was grateful for that, though that was just about all I was grateful for. Maybe I was getting a little bitter even then.

Above the intricate mazes of trenches, beyond our most remote lookout post, on the broken, muddy surface of the ravaged earth, the barbed wire still hung just as it had all winter, now rusty and even more forbidding than when we had first strung it the autumn before. Fragments of clothing—Imperial gray, they had once been—here and there a high-crested Prussian helmet, a rusting rifle with a broken bayonet, the barren, whitened bones of Imperial horses enduring the rain and snow and frigid winds that had blown across France during the winter. These were the silent, solemn reminders of the few foredoomed Imperial attacks that had taken place since the first winter snows came down and locked us into our positions.

At first the Germans had not seemed willing to admit that a British colonial division had set up housekeeping just a few miles from Beaugency. That was too damned close to their staff headquarters!

And during the first winter storms, and during the lulls between them, the Sixty-fourth Imperial Hussars, mostly on foot because of the terrain, had thrown a few feeble, bloody attacks at our lines. They had failed, as their commanders must have known they'd fail, but the attacks had been in the grand Prussian style, if for no other reason than to appease and glorify His Imperial Majesty, Franz VI, by the Grace of God, Emperor of the Romans.

Ha!

Well, during that bitter winter, suffering more from the weather than from the activities of the Imperials, the Second, Fourth and Ninth New England Infantry had sat on its collective ass a few miles southwest of Beaugency in our old, much-used trenches, a few hundred yards south of the River Loire and a mile to two from a battered little village whose name I don't know to this day.

But, as I said, spring had finally gotten around to coming, spring of the Year of Our Lord Nineteen Hundred and Seventy-One, by the Christian calendar used locally, the thirty-second year of the Great War, the War to End All Wars, they said. And with spring had come a renewal of the fighting and the end of my current contract with the Kriths.

Cannon had begun firing from the vicinity of Beaugency, the German equivalent of our two-and-a-half, three- and four-inch howitzers, from the Imperial artillery battalion that sat there. And big guns fired back from the south, British four-inchers answering the Germans.

Rifle and machine-gun fire crackled intermittently along the lines. Now and again there was the muffled roar of a hand grenade or a mortar shell lobbed into either our trenches or theirs. And occasionally a German or a British head would be foolish enough to show itself above the trenches and would promptly get itself blown apart, steel helmet or no steel helmet.

Off to the east, nearly every morning an hour or so after dawn, a flight of British airships moved north, bombers for the most part, bound for the Imperial encampments in the area of Fontainebleau, the railyards that led to Paris and what industry still functioned in the French city. They would unload their crude bombs on Fontainebleau and then return home, those of them that hadn't been blasted apart by Imperial antiairship guns.

At times we hoped that some of the airships might even get as far as Paris itself, to begin bombing the Imperial household that we had heard was setting up spring quarters in what had once, long years before, been the capital of France, the City of Lights. But we knew, when we stopped to think about it, that our—the British—airships stood a snowball's chance in hell of getting much beyond Fontainebleau. Between that city and Paris the Germans had ring after ring of antiaircraft guns that could knock down the fastest airship that the British Empire could put into the sky.

German-occupied Paris would hold out, and would keep on holding out until the British infantry marched right up to the gates of the city and took it from the Holy Roman Emperor, and that was a thing that in the spring of 1971 seemed very unlikely, no matter what the Kriths did to help. Well, short of nuclear weapons, that is, but I damned well knew that the Kriths weren't going to put nuclear weapons into the hands of the British. Hell, the British didn't even know there was any such thing—at least that's what I believed then.

As I said, it was spring of 1971 and I was a captain of the British Infantry, American Colonial Forces of His Britannic Majesty, King George X. More exactly, I was the commanding officer of Company B, Fourth Virginia Infantry.

My name then was Eric Mathers and I was supposed to have been from the city of Victoria, Province of Virginia, in the British North American Colonies, sometimes known collectively as New England. The men under me, colonials themselves, believed it, but that wasn't surprising since the Kriths had given me a damned good schooling in what

Virginia was like in this Timeline, or at least the area of North America that they call Virginia here, which isn't exactly the same geographical area as *your* Virginia. I spoke and acted like any other good Virginian, a loyal subject of George X and the British Empire.

The truth was somewhat different. I had never been in *their* Virginia in my life. I was simply a mercenary soldier in the pay of the Kriths, but that made me no less a good soldier for King George. The interests of King George and the Kriths happened to coincide, which was damned fortunate for George and his empire. So it seemed at the time, at least.

But then I was pretty ignorant in those days.

2
Change of Command

On the morning when all this began to change I was late rising. I didn't do that very often—sleep late—but a group of us had consumed a great quantity of gin the night before and my head ached like hell and I was halfway sick to my stomach and, as they say, RHIP —Rank Hath Its Privileges. I was exercising those privileges, what there were of them, when Tracy came stumbling into the dugout, urging me to get the hell out of bed and into my uniform.

I waved him away sleepily, but threw back the cover and gingerly put my feet on the burlap-covered earthen floor, carefully testing the ability of my legs to support me.

"Blast it all, Eric," said Lieutenant Hillary Tracy— whose real name was Darc HonGlazz, but that was in another world. "Get your arse out of that bloody bed. The muckin' colonel's coming round."

Yes, Tracy really talked that way. Well, of course, it was customary, almost necessary for us to mimic the speech of the British we served under, but I thought Tracy was carrying it a little too far.

"Cheerio, old son," I mumbled, mimicking Tracy more than the British, and discovered to my surprise that I could stand up.

I glanced once around the dugout, saw nothing that was new, wished vainly for a hot bath, and then reached for my pants, which hung on a peg driven into the earthen wall beside my bunk.

The dugout that had been the home of Tracy, myself, and two other officers for the past four and a half months was small and dark and damp, a cave hacked out of the French soil a year or two earlier by another band of British soldiers when they had held this area before. When the Imperial Germans had taken the trenches from us the previous spring, I supposed some of their officers had lived here, though it didn't look as if they had done much to improve it. They had just existed here until fall, when we had come in and driven them back out again. I wondered whether Germans or British would be living here after the next big offensive or counteroffensive or countercounter-offensive or whatever the hell the next battle would be called at headquarters. That's the kind of war it was.

There were four bunks, little more than field cots; a table; three folding chairs; a box that served as the fourth chair; a rickety wooden table that the Germans had built the spring before; an old, battered, cracked potbelly stove of prehistoric British origin; three carbide lanterns; innumerable sandbags; and four footlockers. The dugout's single entrance was covered by a moldy, moth-eaten old blanket that still, somehow, carried the Imperial German insignia. The ceiling was supported by rotten boards, beer-barrel staves, a hodgepodge of bits and pieces of wood placed there to support the soggy earth above. Below, the cold, damp, half-muddy floor was covered with burlap sacking, some British, some Imperial, and even some that might have been of native French origin. Come to think of it, that might have been the only thing in the dugout, save for the earth itself, that was French. But then, there was very little of France left anywhere after thirty-two years of war.

But the dugout was home. All the home that Tracy and I had anywhere. We were both Timeliners.

"Hurry it up, Eric," Tracy said. "The colonel's aide just rang up to say that the colonel is coming round with our replacements."

"Replacements?" I asked, coming awake at last, activating certain artificial circuits of my body that would bring me to a level of awareness known to few men.

"Bloody well right," Tracy said in all seriousness.

"Oh, cut it out," I said. My head was still aching.

"Cut out what, old boy?"

"That bloody damned accent."

"We've got to stay in character."

"You're overdoing it."

Tracy snorted through his broad nose but didn't reply. "Now what's this about replacements?" I asked, finally pulling on my trousers, British issue, heavy woolen winter uniform, a dull, sick olive that was as unpleasant a color as I could think of that morning.

"That's all I know, old boy," Tracy said. "The aide just said that the colonel was coming round with our replacements first thing."

"Then where are we going?"

"Haven't the foggiest."

I found a poplin shirt that was relatively clean, though perhaps not neat enough to suit the colonel, but since it was the best I had, it would have to do. I pulled it on, stuffed it into my pants and said to Tracy, "I can't say that I'm too surprised."

"No, I'm not either," Tracy answered, finally sitting down on his bunk and fumbling for a cigarette. "Our contracts are about up anyway, y'know."

"Well, this assignment's been a waste of time," I said, more to myself than to Tracy.

Tracy nodded a vague reply, struck a match, lit his cigarette, said, "Aren't you going to shave, old boy? You look absolutely ghastly."

I peered at my face in the fragment of mirror that hung on the earthen wall between our bunks, frowned, nodded. "You're right. I guess I'd better."

I wished desperately for an antihangover, but that hadn't been invented here yet. I'd just have to suffer, though I cut back on my awareness circuits so that I didn't feel quite so uncomfortable.

"There's hot water on the stove," Tracy said. "Tea too. Want some?"

"Yes, if you don't mind."

"Righto."

I would have preferred something stronger than tea, but then tea doesn't smell on your breath as strongly as gin, and I rather doubted that there was very much gin left after the night before anyway, considering the way we'd put it away.

I fumbled in my footlocker, found my razor and soap while Tracy poured me a cup of tea and brought it and a basin of steaming water over to me. He sat them on my bunk.

"Thanks," I said.

"I do wonder where we'll be going now," Tracy said as I worked up some lather in my shaving mug.

"Your guess is as good as mine."

I smeared my face liberally with lather, stropped my razor a few times across the belt, and then began scraping the stubble off my chin. Being fair and blond doesn't prevent me from having a very heavy, very tough beard that's hideously difficult to remove after a bad night.

Outside the dugout, through the yard of earth that separated us from the surface and through the tunnel that connected us to it, I heard the roar and whine of the big howitzers firing from our rear. A shell or two passed over us, headed for the Imperial trenches a few hundred yards away. It wasn't much, just a few rounds to let the Imperials know that the British Army was awake and still as nasty as ever.

"Anything else going on this morning?" I asked Tracy.

"Nothing much, so far as I know. Heard that there was a bit of action along the river about dawn. A German patrol coming down, I suppose. Lost their way and stumbled into the Ninth's trenches."

"Any prisoners?"

"Not so far as I know. Didn't ask."

"Doesn't matter."

I scraped away at my chin and speculated about the news that Tracy had awakened me with. So we were being replaced. Well, it was about bloody time that the Kriths realized that we were wasting our time in these filthy trenches. We had muddled along for four and a half months now, Tracy and I, waiting for the weapons to arrive that we were supposed to show our men how to use. Some new rifle, I understood. Something that would give the British a little more firepower, a little more accuracy. Nothing very startling, mind you. Nothing too much in advance of the current local technology, just enough for everyone to believe that it was a British development, a weapons breakthrough that would help, maybe, to change things, to turn the tide of history against the Holy Roman Empire, as Ferguson's breechloader had turned the tide of history against the American insurrectionists nearly two hundred years before—a pivotal point in this Timeline's history.

But the rifles had never arrived, for some reason that was never explained to me. The Krithian weapons supervisor Kar-hinter seldom took the time to explain anything that wasn't absolutely necessary. And we who were supposed to test the rifles in combat, we two Timeliner officers leading a company of American colonials, had sat in our dugout and waited and killed time and told dirty stories and played cards and drank gin when we could get it and shivered through the winter.

Now it seemed that the Kriths had given up playing this particular game with us and were going to pull us out of here and give us another assignment. I wondered whether it would be in this Timeline.

In a way I hoped it would be in another Line. I'd lost the little finger and part of the ring finger of my left hand during a fracas the autumn before, and I would have liked to have an opportunity to get new ones grafted on. But you can't do things like that in a Timeline as backward as this one was.

At last I finished with my face and splashed away the remaining soap, inspected myself for cuts, found that I had been luckier than usual and hadn't cut myself—I never had got used to shaving with a razor. I dried my face on a more or less clean towel Tracy had thrown on my bunk and drank about half the steaming cup of tea, scalding my tongue.

"How soon's the colonel supposed to be here?" I asked.

"Don't know. Anytime, I suppose."

"No time for breakfast?"

"I doubt it."

I shrugged and then found my jacket, a tight-fitting woolen garment of the same sickening green as the pants, distinguished only by the captain's bars on its collar.

"Hand me my pistol, will you, Tracy?" I asked as I buttoned my jacket.

Taking the pistol belt from the peg where it hung, Tracy handed it to me.

It was an awkward belt to wear and the pistol in the holster was big and ugly and efficient. The seven-shot, .62 caliber Harling revolver was the standard sidearm for Brittish officers There and Then, and it was a damned big pistol. I had grown to like the feel of it on my hip and hoped that whatever our next assignment was, I would be allowed to carry it. A .62 caliber slug is big and messy, especially when propelled by the 200 grains of powder in the standard issue cartridge. It certainly wasn't a sporting weapon. It had been designed to do just one thing—kill men, and that it did very well.

"How do I look?" I asked Tracy.

"Halfway human."

"That's an improvement, I take it?"

Tracy nodded.

"Any more tea?" I asked.

"Yes, I think so. Want me to look?"

"No, I'll...."

" 'Tention!"

The voice was Tracy's. He was sitting so that he could see the dugout's "door" and could see the figure who was shoving the blanket aside and stepping into the man-made cave.

As I snapped to my feet and turned, I saw him too. Colonel Woods.

"As you were," Woods said gruffly.

I relaxed, said, "Good morning, sir."

"Morning, Mathers, Tracy," the colonel replied in the clipped fashion that I suppose was natural to him.

Woods held the flap open until the other two men accompanying him came into the dugout. As I expected, one of them wore captain's bars and the other was a lieutenant. Our replacements.

Colonel Woods quickly made the introductions. The captain was a tall, slender Floridian named David Walters. The lieutenant was a shorter, stockier man named Carl Boland. He was a Virginian, the same as I was supposed to be.

"Spot of tea, Colonel?" Tracy asked once the three newcomers had seated themselves at the table—in the three chairs. I guessed that left the box for me and Tracy would just have to stand.

"No. Just had a cup," Woods answered. "No time, anyway. Must get back to headquarters."

Walters and Boland accepted Tracy's offer, and he began to rummage around for two fairly clean cups. .

"Sorry to come in on you so abruptly, Mathers," Colonel Woods went on to say. "Orders y'know."

"Yes, sir. Of course."

"You and Tracy will have till noon to get your gear together and introduce Walters and Boland to your men. A signaler will come then to accompany you to brigade headquarters."

"Brigade, sir?" I asked.

Woods nodded, shrugged, then pulled a mimeographed sheet of paper from his pocket and handed it to me. "Orders just came round this morning."

The orders were quite explicit. We were relieved of our commands as of 0900 and were to report to brigade at 1300.

"Brigade is sending a man round for you," Woods said. "Understand that HQ's been moved or some such. You'll have to wait for him."

"Yes, sir." Odd, I thought. Were we going to brigade at all? Probably not, but Woods wouldn't know that. He would never really know what became of us.

I knew for a fact that Woods wasn't a Timeliner; he was exactly what he was supposed to be. He knew nothing, suspected nothing of the existence of the Kriths or of the fact that men from other universes were here helping him and his British Empire wage war against the Holy Romans.

Nor did either Walters or Boland seem to be other than what they claimed. They gave no indications and we Timeliners have a thousand secret ways of letting other Timeliners know of our presence.

No, it appeared that the Kriths had given up on this one rather minor aspect of their master plan for this Line. They had something else in mind for Tracy and me. We'd learn what that was soon enough, I suspected.

"Well, must be shoving off," Woods said abruptly, rising. He offered his hand to me. "Been nice knowing you, Mathers, Tracy. You'll both get good reports from me."

"Thank you, sir," I said, shaking his hand.

After briefly clasping Tracy's hand, Woods turned,

ducked out under the flap that covered the dugout's door and vanished.

I turned back to my replacement.

"Well, Walters," I asked, "ready for me to show you around a bit?"

3
Kearns

Long before noon I had completed all the introductions, said all my good-byes, and packed what gear I had.

After a trip to the latrine, Tracy and I sat down on the bunks that had, a few hours before, been ours, and waited for the man to come who was to lead us to "brigade headquarters," whatever that might be this time.

Walters and Boland, after saying their good-byes to us, had gone to mess, so Tracy and I were alone when the sergeant came into the dugout, snapped to attention and saluted.

"Captain Mathers, sir?" he asked.

I nodded. "This is Lieutenant Tracy."

"I'm Sergeant Kearns, sir." Then he paused, his face relaxing. "Are we alone?"

"Yes, we are."

As I answered, Kearns deliberately placed the tip of his right thumb against the tip of his right ring finger. It was one of *our* signals. I replied by performing the same gesture with my left hand, though since most of my left ring finger was missing, I used the middle one. Tracy signaled with a similar gesture.

"*Ca kasser a Shangalis?*" Kearns asked, which loosely translated means: "With your permission, I shall speak in Shangalis." It was actually an abbreviated form of the complete sentence "*Retam ca kasser a rir nir paredispo Shangalis?*"

"*Swen ro,*" I replied.

The man who had called himself Kearns smiled, sat down on one of the vacant bunks and dug into his pocket for a cigarette.

"You don't mind if I smoke, do you?" he asked, still speaking Shangalis.

"No, not at all," I replied in the same language, the language that some believe to be the native tongue of the

21

Kriths; I doubt it, though. There are too many Indo-European roots in the language, too many *human* words. It's probably something the Kriths picked up far to the Temporal East and carried with them as they moved West. At least it looks that way to me, but I'm certainly no language expert. I'm just a hired gun, but men who know more about such things than I do have come up with that theory, and since the Kriths have never denied it, I assume that it might well be true.

"Care for a smoke?" Kearns asked, offering the pack to me.

"Might as well," I answered, accepting the offered pack and knocking one of the brown-paper cylinders out into my hand.

Then I looked up abruptly, peering into Kearns' eyes. It wasn't a *local* brand, and by local I mean from this universe. It was a Toltec-Line weed, from a long way East.

"I assure you that it's okay, Mathers," Kearns said suddenly when he realized that I was staring at him. "I just got in this morning, and I'm supposed to be leaving as soon as I take you to the meeting place. Only you two will see them."

I suppose that it was none of my business, Kearns' having brought in Outtime cigarettes. That wasn't my responsibility. The Kriths were running the show, and if they wanted to let Kearns do it, then it was their business. I told myself to forget it.

While I passed the pack on to Tracy and then lit my own cigarette, I took the time to study unobtrusively this man who had come to take us to our meeting with the Kriths. He was tall and slender, what they called wiry in build, though quite strong-looking. He was rather dark, but there seemed to be enough north European blood in his veins to prevent anyone from wondering whether he really belonged in the British Army. And then there were some far more exotic types fighting in the trenches of France under the Union Jack: Amerinds from the Indian Nations of middle North America; dark-skinned Punjabis from East India; South Sea Islanders from the Polynesian Colonies and the Aussie Commonwealth; and a host of others. No, Kearns, whatever he was other than European, would go unnoticed among the motley crew that fought for the British Empire.

His face was made of sharp angles, craggy planes like a half-finished piece of sculpture, and bore what appeared to be the scars of battles fought a long, long When from Here and Now. Still, there was something more to that face then just its simple ugliness, something strange and remote, something that seemed even more remote than just the cultural differences between him and me, though I could not guess from what Line he had originally come. I can't say that I instantly disliked the man, but there was something about him that put me on edge, and it was not until a very long time afterward that I even began to have an inkling of what it was.

"What's this all about, Kearns?" I asked, still speaking Shangalis.

"Damned if I know," he answered. "They just told me to come in and get you two."

"Where are we going?" I asked. "I mean, where are you supposed to take us?"

"The village a ways back," he said. "If you're both ready, we can go now."

"I suppose I am. Tracy?"

"Righto."

"Sorry," Kearns said as he rose to his feet, "but you'll have to carry your own gear. I wasn't allowed to bring anyone else to help."

"Okay," I said, hefting the haversack that carried all my worldly possessions, fifty pounds of nothing very much. A Timeliner learns to get along with very little more than himself and the clothes on his back. "Let's go."

4
Kar-hinter

Around the village the land was flat, without trees, except near the river where the ground was too marshy for plowing and the poplars and willows, those that had survived the shelling of the bloody summer before, still grew as they pleased, now beginning to bud in anticipation of summer. I wondered how many of those few trees would still be standing when the next spring came. It was not a pleasant thought.

The village itself stood not far from the Loire, a quiet, slowly winding river that must once have given a sensation of peace and gentleness to the now-ravaged countryside. I had been told that last spring the Loire had turned red with the mingling of British and Imperial German blood, and from the looks of the river's bank, craters that the winter rains and snows had not yet obliterated, I rather suspected that it was true.

There were only two streets in the village, unpaved, crossing at right angles, one running from the ford of the river where a bridge must have stood at one time, though there were few traces left of it now, the other road paralleling the river, running a few hundred yards from its bank, back far enough to remain on solid, dry ground, curving away from the river at times and then back closer at others. The two roads met in the village, crossed, and then ran on their ways, leaving what had once been a sleepy little human habitation. But the spring and the summer of the year before had done their damage to the village, as well as to the country.

The crossroads had been the center of life of the village, when it had had a life. A few buildings still stood, and there was enough left of some of them to tell what they had once been: the church, Roman Catholic, of course—years of British protection and then occupation had never been able to make any fundamental changes in the religious views of the French, though they had accepted the British with good enough grace, considering; a blacksmith shop, half-burned to the ground, though the forge and anvil were still visible through the wreckage, and a few rusting tools; what had once been an inn, its sign still hanging on one hook, weather-worn and fading—though the image of a wild boar was still fairly recognizable, the French words that had once been written below it were now nearly obliterated; a store of some sort, probably a general merchandise store, I guessed; a few other buildings that had lost their identity; and empty, broken-windowed houses.

I suppose I must have paused for longer than I should have, looking at the ruins and speculating about their past—a weakness of mine; I had once, very long ago, intended to be a historian—and it was Kearns' harsh voice that finally made me realize that we had more urgent business to attend to.

"Let's go," he said curtly. "Kar-hinter is waiting for us."

It was the first time that Kearns had said the name of the Krith that we were to meet. I hadn't thought of asking before, assuming that he wouldn't know, and also knowing that it wouldn't make a hell of a lot of difference anyway.

Kar-hinter, I repeated the name in my mind. He was the Krithian weapons supervisor for this Line, an old Krith who had been my chief on several assignments before, including the one I was just completing. He wasn't so bad to work for, even if he was a bit taciturn. I rather liked the old beast; well, better than I liked most Kriths, at least.

Now I don't want you to get the idea that I disliked the Kriths then. I didn't. Not at all. Nor did I particularly like them as individuals. I admired them as a race and appreciated what they were doing, but they were, by and large, a rather repulsive-looking bunch that I had never really learned to like in all the years that I had been working for them. But Kar-hinter, well, he was okay. For a Krith.

And please don't accuse me of racial prejudice or xenophobia, not until you've heard my story, at least.

I obeyed Kearns' urgings and follow him through the village, my feet squelching in the mud that even by the middle of the day had not dried very much. It would take several warm, clear, sunny days for the mud that lay over the whole of the Touraine to become solid earth again.

We passed through the center of the village and went on down the muddy road that led out of the town and toward the now-barren landscape beyond. Off in the distance, sheltered by two or three naked-limbed trees, stood a house that was virtually intact, its damages nearly repaired, the windows boarded over, smoke rising from the remains of a chimney.

"That's it. Over there," Kearns said, apparently realizing that I had noticed the house.

"Kar-hinter's there?" I asked.

"Kar-hinter and a British general named Asbury," Kearns answered.

It was then that I saw the British staff car parked beside the house, half-hidden by naked bushes that grew beside the house, by bare vines that in the summer must have covered the house with leaves and clusters of grapes. This was the wine country of France, or it was in other places and had been here once, when France had had the time to make wine, when foreign armies weren't ripping it apart.

By this time you may have gathered that I wasn't altogether happy with the way I made my living. I had outgrown a lot of the misplaced idealism that had led me into it in the first place, but then it was a living, and the only one I knew. It was often a dirty, nasty job, but, like they said, somebody had to do it.

Two men in British uniforms flanked the house's front door, tommy guns held across their chests, standing ramrod-stiff and staring off into space like automatons. Each wore the double chevrons of a corporal, which meant something in the British Army. Men like them had built the Empire, I said to myself, almost admiring their stance, though I myself was not that kind of soldier. I sometimes wonder if I was ever any kind of soldier at all. But I got by. Most of the time. At least I'm still alive as of this writing, and that's saying something.

The two guards came to attention as we approached, saluted me and Tracy across the receivers of their weapons, and one of them said, "May I help you, sir?" He was addressing me since I was the ranking officer.

Kearns answered for me: "Captain Mathers and Lieutenant Tracy to see General Asbury." He produced a sheet of paper from a breast pocket and handed it to the corporal who had spoken.

The corporal relaxed his grip on his tommy gun, took the paper, glanced at it, then back to me. "Certainly, sir. The general is expecting you. Go right in." He handed the paper back to Kearns, gave me another salute across his weapon.

The other corporal turned, opened the door, and I entered the house, Tracy and Kearns behind me.

The first room we entered was empty, though the floor was littered with paper and debris left behind when the former occupants had fled.

"In here," a voice called from another room.

In the next room there were three beings, two of them human, and enough furniture to make the place look as if it were habitable.

A large oak table occupied the center of the room, and a gas lantern sat in its middle. Below the lantern lay a map, but from the distance I could not tell what the map was of. Six chairs of assorted sizes and shapes sat around the table. There was a bed, a sofa, a cabinet on which sat a bottle of wine and some glasses, and three overstuffed easy chairs completing the furniture. A picture of Jesus hung on the wall, holding open His robes to expose a radiant heart. I suspected that the picture belonged to the former occupants of the house, not to any of the present ones.

One of the men was Sir Gerald Asbury, Brigadier General in His Britannic Majesty's Army. I had seen his picture often enough—he had been something of a hero the previous spring when the Touraine, or part of it, was recaptured from the Imperial Germans—though I had never before met him in person. He was a short, stocky, redheaded man, with a huge cavalry mustache, the stereotype of a British officer, but despite that, a bold and imaginative man, so I had been told. I rather liked his looks.

The other man I had met before. His name was Pall, and his nearly seven-foot frame was all muscle. His swarthy face was expressionless, as always, as he stood behind Kar-hinter, his hands hanging at his sides. He was dressed in a harshly-cut black uniform, without decoration save for the ugly energy pistol that hung on his left hip. He was Kar-hinter's bodyguard and one of the deadliest beings I had ever met. I don't know what Timeline he came from, but I don't think I'd care to visit it, not if it's inhabited by very many like him.

The third occupant of the room I knew also. That was Kar-hinter himself. A Krith.

I suppose that this is as good a time as any to describe the appearance of the Kriths, and since Kar-hinter was a fair representative of his race, at least the males of the race, I'll describe him.

Kar-hinter stood six-foot-four or so in his bare feet, which were always bare, as was the rest of him. Always. His coloring was brown tinged with green, a color that might have been olive had it been a little greener, but wasn't quite. I have seen Kriths who were a sable-brown and some who were a true olive. Their skin coloring varies within these ranges, though there seem to be no racial distinctions as there are supposed to be with human beings.

His head was big and almost egg-shaped and somewhat lumpy-looking. He had no hair on his head, or on any part of his body, and his skin was a not-quite-shiny satin surface. His eyes were enormous, brown, liquid, equipped with two sets of eyelids, but without distinct pupils, irises, or anything else. They were like big brown marbles. I'm quite sure that they don't work anything at all like our eyes and of course, it was impossible to tell just where he was looking. A reflection of light on the moist balls gave the impression of pupils, but it was not so.

Below his eyes was a row of tiny openings that dilated with heartbeat regularity. These were the nostrils of a Krith and all they had of a nose. The mouth below the nostril row was, like the eyes, enormous. Kar-hinter's lips were thick, heavy, moist, and hungry-looking. When his mouth opened, you could see rows of sharp, fanglike teeth. Kriths are primarily carnivorous and live mostly on a diet of uncooked meat, I understand.

Along the sides of Kar-hinter's face, running from about where his temples were to the middle point of his jaws were two rows of feathery membranes that twitched in the air like a fish's gills. These functioned as ears and as something more, though I'm not quite sure what.

He had virtually no neck, his head seeming to sit right on top of his broad, muscular shoulders. The arms that dropped from the shoulders were remarkably human, as were the five-fingered hands that grew from the slender wrists.

His chest was broad with prominent, almost feminine nipples. His stomach was flat, well-muscled, and flowed smoothly into his pelvic region. And it was there that you could see that Kar-hinter was very obviously a male.

His legs, in proportion to his long torso, were short and thick and terminated in wide, webbed feet. A short, prehensile tail grew from his buttocks and twitched aimlessly in the air as he rose to greet us.

Kar-hinter, as I said, was absolutely naked. He wore no decorations, no instruments, not even a watch, nor did he carry a pouch to hold personal belongings. I had never seen a Krith wearing anything at all. Whatever they carried with them was locked inside their huge heads, and that was enough. More about that later.

One more point about the Kriths: I assume that there are two sexes to their race—else why would Kar-hinter have the masculine equipment he had?—but in all the years that I had been working for them I had never seen a female Krith, nor had I ever heard of anyone who had. They refused to discuss the matter with humans. Krithian sex life was a complete mystery to the people who worked for and with them.

I gave both Sir Gerald and Kar-hinter a British salute, which they both returned, though Kar-hinter seemed to have a mocking expression on his alien face.

"Please be at ease, gentlemen," Sir Gerald said. "Sit down, won't you?"

"Thank you, sir," I said in English.

"I am Sir Gerald Asbury," the British general said, "and, I say, you might as well drop the formalities. I am quite aware of who and what you fellows are. And the men outside"—he gestured toward the front of the house—"are yours as well. I am the only *local* here."

I nodded, took off my cap and dropped it onto the couch

near me. After unbuttoning my coat, I took one of the chairs that the general indicated.

"Greetings, Kar-hinter," I said awkwardly, since I never did know quite what to say to a Krith.

"Hello, Eric," Kar-hinter said, clasping his hands behind his back. "And you, Hillary, and you, Ronald." The last was directed at Kearns. "Please, do all of you sit down and make yourselves comfortable. You, as well, Sir Gerald."

When we were all seated, Kar-hinter gestured to Pall, who got the bottle of wine and five glasses from the cabinet behind the Krith. He poured wine into each of the glasses and passed them around without speaking. I noticed that be poured none for himself. Then he returned to his statue-like position behind his master.

"Again, gentlemen, please make yourselves comfortable," Kar-hinter said. The Krith spoke local English without trace of an accent, a policy which the Kriths prided themselves on, though at times it must have been quite difficult. Their speaking mechanisms aren't made much like ours, but they do a damned good job with them anyway.

"I am sure that you are wondering why you are here," he said when we had each taken a sip from our glasses—the wine was excellent.

Tracy and I nodded, though Kearns didn't seem concerned at all. He had said before that he was going Out-time later on in the day, but for some reason I felt some doubts about that, though I didn't know why.

"Good wine, is it not?" Kar-hinter asked. "French, though not local. Pall acquired it from a few Lines East of here where they are not plagued by war. Not just yet, at least. Please, drink up. I brought this bottle especially for this meeting, and I would hate to see it go to waste."

Obediently we drank our wine and waited for Kar-hinter to get around to telling us why we were here. Kriths don't hurry very often, though they certainly expect it of humans when it's necessary. Well, that's what they paid us for. And I rather liked the pay. I could never have made that kind of money back in my Homeline.

"Now," Kar-hinter finally said after he had Pall refill

our glasses, "let me tell you about it. Or, rather, I shall let Sir Gerald begin. Sir Gerald, please."

"Yes, certainly," the British general said awkwardly, reaching for the map that lay on the table and then pushing it back, apparently deciding that it wasn't time for it yet. "To get straight to the point, gentlemen, Royal Intelligence has reason to believe that the Imperial Germans are working on something called an atom bomb. Kar-hinter assures me that you fellows know of such weapons, Outtime, that is."

"Yes, we do," I replied.

"Our scientists seem to have suspected that such a weapon is possible, but they are a very long way from developing it. Kar-hinter tells me that it is basically quite a simple thing."

Right then I was hardly listening to Sir Gerald's words. I was too stunned by what he had said. The Imperials building atomic weapons! It was fantastic. They were still three or four or even five decades from *that*. Hell, the locals hadn't even developed a really decent radio yet.

"Nevertheless," Sir Gerald was saying, "the Germans seem to have gotten somewhere with the idea. Seems they have a rather bright group of young scientists working for them, developing the theories of some fellow named Eisenstein or something. He has been dead for years, I'm told, but he left some rather impressive theories that weren't published until a few years ago, and then only in the Holy Roman Empire. The book fell into our hands only a few months ago. And then we began getting reports that the Imperials were actually trying to build such a bomb."

Kar-hinter waved Sir Gerald to silence with a careless, unconscious gesture of one accustomed to command.

"It is not necessary to tell you," Kar-hinter said, facing the three of us, "what atomic weapons in the hands of the Holy Roman Empire would do to our efforts here. They could, of course, if produced in sufficient quantities, put the Imperial Germans in command of this entire Line, even with their primitive delivery systems—and we certainly cannot afford that." He paused. "Please go on, Sir Gerald."

"Yes, of course," the British general said. "Well, as soon as we learned of the German efforts, we sent intelligence teams in to gather more detailed information." Sir Gerald paused reflectively for a moment, then continued. "The first two teams failed to report back. The third team did come back, rather badly mauled, I must say, but with *some* information." Sir Gerald paused again.

"Yes?" I asked.

"The Imperial Germans have a plant on the Baltic, near Königsberg, actually on the Gulf of Danzig," Sir Gerald went on slowly. "It's very well hidden and extremely well guarded. We are not exactly sure what they're doing there, but it is in some way connected with the atom bomb project. That is all we know." The British general looked at Kar-hinter.

"Thank you, Sir Gerald," Kar-hinter said. "As you might suspect, His Majesty, King George, ordered that this information be turned over to us. When we learned of the Imperial efforts to build nuclear weapons, we gave His Majesty a simplified explanation of just what they are. His own physicists were able to confirm this to his satisfaction.

"Sir Gerald was then put in charge of the British operation to prevent the construction of the bomb, with our technical advice. We *do not* wish nuclear weapons in this Timeline at this stage." The Krith looked at Sir Gerald. "As much as we admire and respect the British Empire, we are in no position to give them nuclear weapons, nor will we assist in their local production. Considering the world conditions on this Line, we cannot tolerate nuclear weapons. I hope you understand, Sir Gerald."

"Of course," Sir Gerald said without conviction. "It has been explained to me several times."

"Very good," Kar-hinter said, imitating a human smile without much success. "Will you proceed, please, Sir Gerald?"

"There is very little more to tell," the British general said. "We have made three attempts to gain entry into the Baltic plant. All have failed miserably. Considering its location within the Empire, it is, of course, impossible for us to get a large force near it, even by sea. Nor, I doubt, would it do us much good. As I said, the plant is well guarded: there are several regiments of infantry stationed within a few miles of the plant, and the Third Imperial Fleet is presently situated at Gdansk. The emperor is taking no chances of our getting anywhere near it. And, of course, we have now put him on guard."

"Then I assume you're planning a cross-Line attack?" I asked Kar-hinter.

"Ah!" Kar-hinter exclaimed, then made another of those expressions that were supposed to be smiles. He motioned to Pall to refill our wineglasses, scratched himself thoughtfully in an intimate place, and finally spoke. "It has been considered." He looked at Sir Gerald. "What Eric is asking, Sir Gerald, is whether we will establish a force in an alternate Timeline where the area is uninhabited and then skud the force into the plant and destroy it."

"Well, I was thinking of simply skudding a bomb across," I said.

"As I said, such things have been considered," Kar-hinter said, "though if we were to do so we would probably skud a spy in first to see exactly what they are doing there. But, ah, no. To answer your question, we will not do that. We are already interfering with this Line a bit more than is wise, or so the Tromas in the Homeline tell us. They will allow a cross-Line venture only after we have tried all other avenues. If all else fails, then we will be allowed to cross-Line at the Baltic plant. As I said before, this Line is not to be allowed nuclear weapons under *any* circumstances." He glanced at Sir Gerald.

"I'm sure you know best, Kar-hinter," Sir Gerald said, though he didn't seem to really mean it.

"Then what?" I asked.

"Now it seems," Kar-hinter said, belching politely and raising his winelgass, "a very fortunate set of circumstances has arisen that may allow us to gain all the information we need without ever approaching the Baltic plant." Kar-hinter, like a second-rate actor, paused dramatically.

"And what's that?" I asked on cue.

"The Imperial Germans have placed Count Albert von Heinen in charge of the atomic project. As well as being a distant cousin of the emperor, he is a highly trained engineer—for this Line—and has made himself an impressive record as a military field commander. Quite a young man, as well, I understand."

"Now it seems that Count von Heinen is presently visiting Beaugency. I am not sure why, but as I said, he is a man of many talents. Just why he is in Beaugency is of no great moment. The fact that he is here is of great importance to us. We shall kidnap him."

Kar-hinter paused again, finished his glass of wine, placed the empty glass on the table with a flourish. As he continued to speak, he paced back and forth at the head of the table, his short tail whipping in the air.

"Von Heinen will be spending the night in a villa just north of Beaugency. His American wife is with him, I understand, so we shall take her when we kidnap him. It may be that she can give us some additional information."

"I don't follow you," I said.

"The wife?" Kar-hinter asked. "An American, I said. Doesn't that mean anything to you, Eric? Ah, well, let me tell you. The Countess von Heinen, née Sally Beall, is the daughter of the late Archer Beall. What does that mean to you?"

"The ARA leader?" Tracy asked, speaking for the first time since the conversation began.

"Exactly, my dear Hillary," Kar-hinter said. "The late Mr. Beall, killed recently in the New York riots, was one of the major leaders of the American Republican Army, as well as president of the Mad Anthony Wayne Society. A very, very important man in American revolutionary circles."

Sir Gerald's red face showed obvious anger at the mention of the Bealls. As a loyal British officer—though he was, I believe, born in the American colonies—he was properly outraged at the rebels in America who were causing so much trouble during the war, siding with the Imperial Germans by their very presence, draining desperately needed troops from the European war.

"Beall's daughter married Von Heinen for purely political reaons, I am told," Kar-hinter said. "To cement German and American rebel relations, so to speak. But her capture will be merely a by-product of the main effort—an in-depth interrogation of Count von Heinen."

In-depth interrogation, Kar-hinter had just said. Mind probe! Now just how in hell were they going to pull that off, I wondered.

"Let me outline the plan, gentlemen," Kar-hinter said,

scratching his more intimate parts again. "We will go into greater detail later. But for now, the high points. You, Eric"—Kar-hinter pointed a finger at me—"assuming that you wish to take out a new contract, will lead the kidnapping party. At approximately midnight you will take four boats into the Loire, row upstream across the German lines and into Beaugency."

"How do we get across the German lines?" I asked. "You make it sound awfully simple."

"For you, it shall be," the Krith said. "Just after dark the British right flank will launch an attack against the German positions east of Beaugency and sweep toward the city. By midnight the whole British right will be entangled with the Germans. Then, just before you start up the river, a squadron of airships, laden with fire bombs, will proceed across the British right toward Beaugency. It is a suicide mission, I will admit"——Sir Gerald bit his lower lip but did not comment—"but it should do well in putting the city, or a good portion of it, to flames." Kar-hinter paused, smiled, belched. "Then, Eric, with all this going on to your right, with the Imperials so preoccupied with the battle, you should be able to pass up the river in the darkness and confusion with little difficulty."

Finally Sir Gerald could contain himself no longer.

"I must protest, sir!" he exclaimed.

"You have protested before, Sir Gerald," Kar-hinter said calmly. "You have protested straight to Buckingham Palace."

"I bloody well have!" Sir Gerald almost yelled. "And mucking little good it's done. But, sir"—he addressed the naked, alien Krith as a superior officer—"I just cannot condone sacrificing hundreds or thousands of British lives, not to mention a whole squadron of airships, just to allow a handful of men to—to . . ."

"Sir Gerald," Kar-hinter said firmly, his tail lashing sharply behind him, "please restrain yourself. You have registered your complaints."

Sir Gerald muttered something else under his breath and then was silent.

"When you reach the villa," Kar-hinter went on as if Sir Gerald had never spoken, "you will kidnap the count and his wife."

"And then what do we do with them?" I asked.

"There will be a skudder waiting for you," Kar-hinter said slowly.

"Now wait a minute," I said. "You told us that cross-Line movement had been forbidden."

"Yes," the Krith said, "for the Baltic plant. But this action will not be *direct* interference, so to speak. You will take Von Heinen and his wife cross-Lines to a designated place where there will be an interrogation squad waiting for them. They will probe the count and his wife, and then you will return them to this Line and release them. They will be conditioned to believe that they escaped from you—and no one will be the wiser for it."

"I don't understand it," Tracy said. "Cross-Lining in the Baltic is forbidden, but it isn't here. Why?"

Tracy should have known better than to even ask.

"Because it *is*," Kar-hinter said firmly. "You will do as you are told within your contracted terms."

"Why the bloody hell can't you just skud them or whatever it is you do right into the villa?" Sir Gerald asked angrily.

"It *must* be done as I have outlined it, Sir Gerald. This is the only way it may be allowed. There are reasons that I would find impossible to explain to you."

I could well understand Sir Gerald's mystification. Countless times in the past I had run up against the same sort of thing from the Kriths. I don't suppose we can ever understand their reasons for doing things the way they do them. They just don't think the same way we do.

Kar-hinter looked at Tracy and then at me, scratching himself thoughtfully. "There is one final matter to settle, gentlemen," he said. "Your present contracts are about to expire, and they certainly do not cover an operation of this nature. I have new contracts which I beg you to consider. You are the best men available for this job, and I would consider it a personal honor should you accept."

With this he pulled two sheets of paper from a folder lying on the table and handed one to Tracy and the other to me.

I read over my copy quickly and smiled to myself when I came to the part about the pay and the benefits offered for this job. All things considered, it was one of the best contracts the Kriths had ever offered me.

When I looked up, I saw that Tracy was smiling too.

"I take it that you accept?" Kar-hinter asked.

Without replying I signed my name on the bottom of the contract, thumbprinted it, and handed it back to Kar-hinter. Tracy did the same.

"Thank you," Kar-hinter said with a nonhuman smile-thing on his face.. "That will be all for the time being. Food will be brought to you shortly. I suggest that you rest now. There are bunks ready for you in the back room. At nightfall the remainder of your party will arrive, and we will go into the plans in more detail. Do you have any further questions now?"

"I have one," Kearns said, speaking for the first time.

"Yes, Ronald?" Kar-hinter asked.

"When do I leave?"

"When Eric, Hillary, and Sir Gerald leave," Kar-hinter answered slowly. "You shall accompany them to Beaugency. You are to be their skudder pilot."

Kearns just smiled, nothing more, as if he had known all along that he would be going with us.

Kar-hinter then nodded politely to Sir Gerald, to the rest of us.

"You will excuse me, gentlemen," he said. "I have work to do. I shall be back by dark." He left the room with the black-uniformed Pall at his heels.

Then we waited for our meal.

5
The Lines of Time

I suppose that Kar-hinter's intention in giving us so much wine was to make us sleepy, to force us to rest some before the activities of the coming night. Though, of course, that might not have been his intention at all. You can only guess at what a Krith's purposes really are.

Still, if that was his idea, it worked. Three glasses of strong wine on an empty stomach—for I hadn't eaten all day—had almost put me to sleep when a mess steward came in with three tins of beef hash, bread, and tea. It wasn't a particularly tasty meal, but it was nourishing and filling, and I felt much better after eating, and even sleepier.

As Kar-hinter had said, there were beds in the back room of the house, old metal-framed beds, worn and rusty, but supporting thick down mattresses. It had gotten quite warm by afternoon, and the golden French sunlight streamed in between the boards that covered the windows, illuminating the motes of dust that swam in the air like galaxies of stars.

Tracy and Kearns fell asleep almost at once, and I lay back, half-dozing as the afternoon came and slowly passed, moving toward night, not at all concerned about what Kar-hinter had planned for us. I had been through worse often enough not to be concerned. What would happen would happen. You can call it Greek fatalism, if you like.

I don't know where Sir Gerald went. Shortly after Kar-hinter and Pall left, the general got into his staff car, saying that he would be back before dark, and drove off. I sort of suspected that he was going somewhere to make another complaint about the Krithian plans, but I doubted that it would do any good. Apparently the plans for the British attack against the fortified German positions had come straight from the top, the General Staff or maybe from the king himself. I was sorry that it had to be that way—so many lives expended just to get us into the villa where Von Heinen was staying, but it had to be that way. There wasn't a damned thing I could do about it, and I didn't think that Sir Gerald could do any more.

So I rested and half slept and did something that was midway between remember and dream. Fragments of images, half-forgotten events, a girl's name, a glimpse of a childhood a long way and a long When from Here and Now. A blond Greek boy who was big for his age and had a way of getting into more trouble than he should have. At least I considered myself Greek, even if my blood was half-Saxon and I had been born on an island that is called Britain in a lot of Lines.

And I remember how my father had been hanged for treason by the governor of North Ionnia and a girl named Kristin had been raped by a gang of the governor's bullies and how I joined an underground student group in college and nearly got myself hanged before the general revolution broke out—backed by the Kriths, thought I didn't know that until later—and how the Kriths, when it was all over and we had won, asked me if I wanted to join the Time-liners. My family was dead. Kristin had committed suicide. Why the hell not?

And I remembered another girl named Marissa in one of the Carolingian Lines and how she had died terribly slowly and terribly painfully and how I had made the man who killed her die even more slowly and more painfully because I had loved her and would have quit the 'Liners and married her and settled down if it hadn't been for that goddamned war.

And I thought about the month I had once spent in one of the Rajaian Timelines—trying to forget about it all. That was a hedonistic Line where machines did the work of men and left people with nothing to do but spend their lifetimes in pursuit of pleasures of one sort or another. And while I was there, I had tried just about all of them, except for some that were even a little too perverted for me. Like the three girls and the trained monkey and the goat who all got together and. . . . Well, never mind that.

But what I thought about mostly, for some reason, was

the Kriths, who and what they were, and why. My thoughts weren't in any kind of order, but I'll try to present them as if they were. Maybe you can understand a little bit of it.

Who exactly are the Kriths? Friend, I don't know. I'm not even sure that they know themselves. They come from some Line a long, long way to the T-East, so far across the Whens that men hadn't even evolved on Earth. Whether the Kriths were even natives of Earth I don't know, but I sort of doubt it. Or if they are they came from a Line that branched off from ours millions of years ago, back when the first mammals were developing, for there are some fundamental differences between them and the mammals of our Lines that would take millions of years to produce. More likely, I thought, they came from another planet, a lot of Whens closer than a sixty-or-seventy-million-year old split.

Kriths are totally unable to do anything with machines. This is a fact—or at least I thought it was then—and I'd seen it proved countless times. They could never have developed spaceships, but with their built-in Line-skudding ability they could easily have come across someone who *had* developed spaceships, men or some other beings, and in those come to Earth. Hell, I know that doesn't sound much more likely than their having evolved here. So let's drop the subject. I don't know When and Where they came from, but they are. And the fact that they are is very important. Maybe one of the most important things in all the universes.

Let me tell you about *that*. Given a nearly infinite number of universes—at least I'm told that the number is nearly infinite, if that means anything, all beginning back when the first universe was created, if it ever was created. But the Lines are there, stretching East and West further than any Krith has ever gone, extending almost forever. I've seen a few hundred of them myself, but that's nothing, absolutely nothing. But to get back to the point I was trying to make: Given an almost infinite number of Timelines, just about anything is possible. Even Kriths.

The Kriths have a nervous system that isn't very much like ours. Oh, they have a brain, of course, three of them in fact. One is for, well, *thinking,* conscious thoughts like those you and I think. The second is for involuntary actions, the general running of the body, and it's located somewhere in the chest area so that a Krith can go on living for a hell of a long time with its head blown off, and I've seen it happen. Of course without his head a Krith isn't good for very much, but that's the way things are.

The third brain isn't really a brain at all; it's more a series of nervous ganglions extending the length of the spine, but well inside the body cavity, pretty well protected. What this setup was first evolved for, I don't know. I can't even guess, but then I have no idea what kind of environment the Kriths evolved in. Maybe it was originally a protection against, well, magnetic fields or something, or maybe it was a means of radio communications—for they do have that or something like it. As I said, I don't know why it ever started evolving. I just know where it led.

It led to cross-Lines.

The Kriths have their own built-in skudder. They can, at will, cross the Timelines from one universe to another.

Impossible? Damned near, maybe, but not quite. They exist and they do it.

I don't know whether they evolved intelligence before or after they developed their skudding ability. Maybe they both developed together. I suspect that maybe you can't have the ability to skud without a rational faculty to guide it, but that's only a guess. And sometimes I wonder just how rational the Kriths are. I mean, they can talk and think and act rationally, but they have no mechanical ability at all. They can't even build their own shelters. In other ways they're bright enough, so I don't know. I suppose they had to sacrifice a great deal to develop skudding to the level they they have.

Anyhow, they did learn to skud, and they began jumping across the Lines, into the parallel universes. I don't know what they found to the East of wherever they started, but to the West they found men.

At first the Kriths didn't interfere with humans. They just dropped in, so to speak, saw things they liked, and finally found a means of communicating. Shangalis was developed, either by them or by men, and a cross-Line language was born.

At some point men began to investigate the Kriths' means of skudding, but whether the Kriths prompted them to do it or whether men did it on their own, I don't know. Probably both in different Lines. And eventually men built skudders and the Kriths began to use them with human pilots. When the Kriths used their own built-in mechanisms to cross the Lines, all they could take with them was their own physical bodies. If they wanted to take anything else —men, machines, weapons, books, tapes—they had to have mechanical help. They got it when men built skudders and the Kriths took advantage of them.

So, a long, long way East of here, cross-Line trading began to take place, cultures of parallel worlds began to mingle, merge, change, and a whole new kind of civilization was built.

Still, all this doesn't explain much, doesn't explain, for example, why a mercenary soldier from a Europo-Macedonian Line was fighting a war in a Romano-British Line. Let me try to explain that to you.

Time travel is impossible.

I mean, travel into the future or the past. A lot of places have tried it, and they have always failed. It simply can't be done. Don't ask me why. I'm not mathematician. It just can't be done.

However, they tell me there is a way that communications from the future to the past can take place. It's pretty complicated and awfully costly, but it can be done. At least the Kriths have said it can and has been done. But you can judge for yourself.

A long way East, so the story goes, there's an Indus Line where technology developed early and reached a high level some hundreds of years ago. They had even got so far as building spaceships and exploring the nearer stars. It was there that the first future-to-past communication was attempted. The Kriths were in on it, so I'm told; they helped finance it by bringing in a great deal of Outtime wealth and materials to try the experiment.

A huge transmitting station was built on the Moon. From what I've been told it was the biggest transmitter ever constructed in any Line, more watts of energy than would be needed to run a dozen high-level-technology worlds. They tell me that the energy of the sun was somehow drained to power the station—and I don't mean by solar cells or something like that. They tapped the sun and poured its energy directly into the station.

This transmitter, though, was never connected to a real antenna. All its power was fed into dummy loads, huge chunks of the lunar surface converted into resistors just to drain off the transmitter's power. They set up this monstrous station and burned up half the Moon just to get rid of the power it produced.

All this was done just to get a standing wave on a huge bank of solid-state devices. A gigantic quasi-modulator was fed by the power, and it just sat there and waited . . . but not for long.

The idea goes something like this, as well as I can explain it: The signal is generated, and it exists and will continue to be generated and continue to exist for centuries. The quasi-modulator will be—is—was waiting for a signal to be fed back to it from the future.

They tell me that there are certain activites of subatomic particles that get cause-and-effect backward. A thing, they say, can happen *before* the cause of it takes place. They go on a to say that if a radio signal is existing in a certain type of solid-state quasi-modulator it can be affected by this backward effect and cause, that a whole chain of these backward effects and causes can happen in this quasi-modulator.

Now it's like this. Somewhere way in the future they decide it's time to send a message back to the past. They feed this message into the quasi-modulator—and somewhere down in the subatomic particles, down even below where the radio energy is bouncing around, this effect-before-the-cause chain will begin. The cause has happened, but a nanosecond before that the effect had already taken place; this effect had, even prior to that, been the cause for another effect even another nanosecond before, and so on. Backward through time the effect and then the cause, the effect and the cause, until it finally gets back down the chain of time to the beginning.

Okay, now you can forget all that. The Kriths say it works, and you can take their word for it if you like. I once did.

So, the Indus Line people built this station on the Moon, drove all this power into it and sat back and let it operate for the next half million years, if that's what it would take to get a message coming the wrong way in time.

Well, even before the station had gotten up to full power, a message came in. From the future!

Translated into local English the message read something like this:

FROM THE YEAR 7093 [which is about two thousand years from now by the reckoning of time in that Indus Line]. GREETINGS. WE HAVE WAITED UNTIL THE LAST POSSIBLE MOMENT TO SEND THIS BACK TO YOU. BUT WE KNOW THAT WE CAN WAIT NO LONGER. WE ARE DOOMED. WHILE THERE IS STILL TIME LET US TELL YOU WHAT HAS HAPPENED TO US ALL.

THERE IS A CIVILIZATION OF BEINGS ON THE FAR SIDE OF THE GALAXY. THEY ARE TOTALLY ALIEN, INIMICAL TO ALL THAT IS HUMAN AND KRITH. THEY HAVE BEEN BIDING THEIR TIME, AWARE OF US, BUILDING A GREAT ARMADA OF INTERSTELLAR WARSHIPS TO COME AND DESTROY US ALL.

WHY THEY HATE US WE DO NOT KNOW. NOR DO WE KNOW HOW TO FIGHT THEM.

HUMANITY AND KIRTH STAND ALONE AGAINST THE ALIEN HORDES THAT ARE COMING TO DESTROY US. AND WE ARE ALL BUT DEFENSELESS AGAINST THEIR WEAPONS.

ALL THE WORKS OF OUR GREAT MUTUAL CIVILIZATIONS SHALL PERISH UNLESS. . . .

And there the message ended. That was all there was of it. And it was the only message ever received.

The station is still in operation to this day—assuming it's all true—beaming its power into the Moon, and I suppose that it will continue to operate until the day two thousand years from now when it is destroyed—if the future is not changed.

But that one message came through. The aliens are coming to destroy us, mankind and Kriths together.

Across the Lines six more stations were built, beaming their power into the future. And each one received substantially the same message, asking for help from the past.

Crazy, isn't it?

The first time I was told the story I went out and got myself senseless drunk and got laid by the ugliest old whore in North New Ardhea.

But, to go on—the final analysis was this: All across the Lines there exists this same menace two thousand years away. A menace that will totally destroy everything human and Krithian unless something is done to stop it. That's when the Kriths really got started. They decided to do something about it. They decided to change the future, to change the message being beamed backward in time.

Using the sociodynamics of the Haldian Lines, they began to move across the Timelines, mostly to the West where men could, perhaps, someday be strong enough to fight the invaders, and began to build worlds that could meet and withstand the aliens.

They would move into a Line, the Kriths and the Haldian sociodynamicists, and analyze where the current trends would lead in two thousand years, what kind of world would be there to meet the invaders. Then they set about making the necessary changes to meet the countless invasions of the future.

Guided by their own strange logic and the sociodynamics of the Haldian Timelines, the Kriths would bring in what forces were necessary to make the changes, aiming the Lines in the direction of maximum strength in the distant future. They used sociologists, anthropologists, scientists of a hundred kinds to add, to subtract, to build, and to change, and they used mercenary soldiers where necessary.

Mercenary soldiers like me.

Now the world in which the British and the Holy Roman Empires battled was a fair example of how they worked. Haldian sociodynamicists said that without outside help the Holy Roman Empire would defeat the British within a decade. Before the century was out, it would consolidate its hold on the Western Hemisphere and then turn to face the growing Nipponese Empire. The twenty-first century, by local reckoning, would be devoted to another war between the Holy Romans and the Nippons, which would ultimately lead to nuclear warfare that would destroy both empires and most of the rest of civilization.

It would take a thousand years for even a primitive agricultural society to redevelop and at the end of the two-thousand-year span allotted to us the inhabitants of this Line would probably have barely reached the level of ancient Rome, local history. Hardly a match for the invaders.

On the other hand Haldian sociodynamics indicated that a victory by the British would ultimately lead to a mutual coexistence with the Nipponese, the eventual rise of republican forms of government within the next three hundred years, a falling apart of the old empires, and the gradual rise of a peaceful, united world with a high degree of technology.

By the end of the two thousand years *this* culture would have colonized a good chunk of the galaxy and be in position to more than take care of itself against the invaders.

So there Tracy and I and a few hundred other Time-liners were, with a handful of Kriths, helping the British defeat the Holy Romans and create this better world.

That's the sort of thing I believed then, and that's what I thought about as I waited for the sun to set and for Karhinter to return and prepare us for our mission—the kidnapping of Count Albert von Heinen and his wife.

I had no idea what else was going to happen before that mission was over.

6
Up the Loire

The moon had set early that night, and had it not been
for the flashing of cannon along the British right and the
answering flashes of Imperial German artillery and the red
glow in the east where the city had already begun to burn,
it would have been a night of pitch blackness, unbroken
even by stars, for a low cloud covering had moved in
shortly before nightfall, forewarning us of the rainstorms
that the meteorologists had predicted for tomorrow's dawn.

At times we could see airships moving in and out of the
clouds to the east, their bellies lighted by the glow of the
city burning under them, by the flames of their own bombs
exploding, and by the fainter flashes of Imperial cannon
and antiairship weapons. And once or twice as we watched
we saw an airship burst into flames, its catalyzed hydrogen,
impervious to flame most of the time, but still unstable and
liable to explode when the proper degree of heat was
reached, bursting out, lighting the undersides of the clouds
with a brilliant glow. Then the fireball would begin to fall
apart as the hydrogen was consumed. And I wondered how
soon the Kriths were going to help the British "invent"
heavier-than-air craft.

But we had little time to watch what was happening or
to wonder about things. We were in the boats, in the dark
river, in the shadows of the willows and the poplars, and
we were quietly paddling toward the cables and chains
that the Imperials had laid across the river to prevent
just such a venture as ours.

The lead boat held three British soldiers: a sergeant and
two privates, dressed in rubber swimming garments,
equipped with cutters and saws to' hack a path for us
through the cables and chains. Those three were really
what they appeared to be—simple British soldiers given an
assignment that they didn't fully understand, but about

which they asked no questions. Not of us, at least, we officers.

I was in the second boat, sitting in the front position, a paddle in my hands dipping softly, quietly into the dark water, moving us forward, while we listened. My own senses, augmented by artificial electrobiological systems, were at their peak and more acute than those of other human beings who did not have the Timeliner modifications.

Behind me sat General Sir Gerald Asbury, dressed now in the uniform of a common solider, with only a glint of metal on his collar to betray his rank. He too held a paddle and alternately dipped it right and then left and then back to the right again. Behind him sat Ronald Kearns, our skudder pilot, showing no emotion at all. Though he was a Timeliner like myself, I could not fathom what was going on in his head, though that is not strange in itself, for Kearns or whatever his real name was was probably from a world as different from mine as mine was from the one in which we both now found ourselves.

The third boat held Tracy and the two corporals who had been guarding the house in which we had met with Kar-hinter.

In the final boat there was another corporal and two privates, at least that is what their British uniforms said they were, though like the rest of us, save for the three in the leading boat and Sir Gerald, they were men from worlds other than this, men who moved across the parallel branches of time fighting a war for the Kriths that would not end for two thousand years.

We Timeliners have a lot of history in front of us.

"How much farther do you think it is?" I heard Kearns ask.

"A good distance," Sir Gerald answered. "We are still a mile or two short of the German lines, as best I can estimate, and the villa is a good five miles beyond that."

"Several hours then?" Kearns asked.

"At the rate we're going, yes," Sir Gerald whispered back. "We will be doing very well for ourselves to have the count in our hands by dawn."

"We'll have him before dawn," I said over my shoulder,

"I hope so, Mathers," said Sir Gerald.

"I know damned well, sir," I replied. "We don't have any other choice."

"It's your show," Sir Gerald whispered bitterly. "I'm just an observer."

I said nothing, for it was true. This wasn't a British patrol. It was strictly Krithian and Timeliner. The poor British were only causing a distraction for us, a bloody, nasty, costly distraction that Sir Gerald hated with all his guts. I can't say that I blamed him.

It seemed like hours, though it could have been no more than a few minutes later, when the sergeant in the lead boat held up his arm and signaled for us to stop. Not that I could really see his arm even with my aug-mented·retinas; it was only a shade of blackness some-how slightly distinguishable from the other shades of blackness along the river.

We slowed in midstream and carefully turned our boats toward the shore, up to the marshy ground, in close to the trees that grew on the water's edge. And there we stopped and waited, silent, hardly breathing, listening to the distant sounds of war and the closer sounds of Ger-man sentries marching along the edge of the river.

Then there were two soft, watery sounds, not quite splashes, more like the sound of two heavy bodies slowly lowering themselves into the river, down under the water. There was silence as the sergeant and one of the privates swam underwater up to where the first set of cables lay across the river.

There was nothing to do but wait and wish for a ciga-rette and know that I couldn't smoke one and then chew on my lip and recite an old Greek poem my father had taught me and think about women and wonder what was going to happen when we finally did get to the villa— though that sort of thing, long experience had taught me, was a complete waste of time. I'd do whatever I had to do when the time came, and that's all there was to it.

We were still a mile or two from Beaugency and the two bridges that spanned the Loire there, if they were still intact, and aerial photographs hadn't been too clear about one of them; it might be half lying in the water for all we knew.

Beaugency was an old town, I understood, or rather

the name was old. The present town was relatively new, for this part of France, having been built from the ground up around the turn of the nineteenth century. The earlier city by that name had been a few miles farther up the river but had been burned during the Peasants' Rebellion in the late 1700's that tried to overthrow the French monarchy and had very nearly succeeded before the British stepped in on the side of the royalist defenders of the crown and helped put down the rebellion with the same deadly Ferguson breechloaders that had stopped the American rebels two decades before.

The old Beaugency had been a stronghold of the rebels during the last stages of the rebellion. When their main forces had been crushed by the royalists and their British allies, the shattered armies had somehow converged on the Touraine and finally retreated into Beaugency. It was the last major rebel fortress to fall and the angry, victorious king had ordered that the city, like Carthage nearly two thousand years before, be leveled and salt sown upon the earth where it had stood.

The survivors of Beaugency, those who weren't beheaded or hanged under the king's eyes, were allowed to settle along the river a few miles from the spot where the old city had been. The new Beaugency had gradually grown up there—and that is the city toward which we moved or had been moving before we had stopped to wait for the cutting of the cables.

All this is of absolutely no importance, of course. It was just one of the bits of information I had picked up while we sat in the trenches during the long, cold winter.

At last we heard the movement of water again, the soft splashing of careful, highly trained swimmers returning to their boat. Again I saw the sergeant, once he had got his dripping body back into the boat, give me a hand signal; this one for us to follow.

Back out into the river we rowed, though not as far from the shore as we had been before. From here on we would have to do our best to avoid being seen, though I doubted that very many Germans were peering down into the river that night. There was too much going on to the east for them to worry much about the river.

After a while we passed the trenches and the last of

the cables that had lain across the river. Soon the Germans would discover that they had been cut, but it would not be soon enough for them to do very much about it. We hoped.

Then we came to the parts of the city that lay along the river. The main sections of the city had grown up to the east, away from the river, and that is where Beaugency's industry had been and that is where the Imperial forces were camped most thickly and that is where the bombs fell.

I had halfway expected to see refugees streaming toward the river, trying to cross the bridges or perhaps swimming the river itself, but there were none. Maybe there were no civilians left in Beaugency and the Germans who retreated from the battle—that would only be the wounded now—would be going north, not west. Karhinter had known pretty well what he was doing when he sent us up the river.

The first bridge showed no sign of damage, though about all I could really see were the two guardhouses on either end of the bridge and the two sentries who paced back and forth between them and threw occasional, disinterested glances down into the water. I doubt that they could see a thing in the blackness that surrounded us.

We passed the bridge without incident and came to the second about half a mile up the river, the one that the aerial photographs had indicated might be damaged. It was.

At one time a blast had struck the bridge on its extreme right, blowing it completely apart. The spans of twisted, rusted metal drooped down to the water and rested on the river bottom. Half the river was blocked to navigation. We were forced to cross over to the left bank and proceed there along the side.

There were no guards visible there. The Germans must have been fairly confident that no one would get this far up the river without being detected, I thought.

Soon the center of the city was behind us and even the glare in the sky was falling off to our right rear. We were well behind the Imperial lines—and without detection.

Funny, I should have known by then that the time to

be most careful in war is when you feel sure that you've accomplished something. That's when you get careless and when the enemy is most likely to do something deadly.

It came suddenly, without warning.

A light flashed above us from the riverbank. An instant later a second light came from the other bank. The two beams met on our lead boat. And a German machine gun opened up on it.

For an instant I was tempted to switch my body to full combat augmentation, to speed up my actions and reflexes to five times their normal speed—for that had been built into me too—but I did not. Full combat augmentation, though it makes a man the most deadly fighting machine in all the known universes, also drains a man's metabolism at an astonishing rate. And I knew that I would need all my strength when we reached the villa. I did not will those electrobiological circuits into operation.

One of the men in the lead boat came to his feet, a tommy gun in his hands, aimed toward the nearest of the spotlights. The tommy began to chatter within a second of the barking of the German gun, and its first slug must have hit the spotlight's lens. But even as the light was going out, the British soldier's body was cut in half by the machine gun's rain of bullets.

Then the boat seemed to come apart, two more bodies tumbling out as rifles from both sides of the river began to fire.

I grabbed up the rifle that lay in the boat beside me, swung it up, and pulled off a shot at the second spotlight. I heard another Enfield crack in unison with mine, off to my rear. Tracy had been just as quick as I.

The other German spotlight went out.

We dropped our rifles, all of us in the three remaining boats, grabbed our paddles and began paddling like mad up the river. We had only a few minutes of darkness, at best, before the Imperials brought up another light. We all knew that we'd better make the most of it.

It was still totally dark in the river and I'm sure that the Germans on the bank couldn't see us, but they could hear us, and they could fire in our direction. I just hoped that their hearing wasn't good enough to pinpoint us all, and I thought that echoes from the buildings along the river would aid us. My main fear was that one of our own men would be foolish enough to fire back, revealing our positions with the flashing of his weapon. I should have known better. All these men were experienced mercenaries—not heroes.

The river curved slightly, carrying us away from the spot where the machine gun was set up, though it continued to fire into the water around us until we finally got out of its range. The rifles, however, moved along as easily as we did and continued to pelt the river around us. More than once I heard the whistle of a bullet that missed my head only by inches.

"Ach!" came a sudden expletive from directly behind me. "Bloody hell!" It was Sir Gerald's voice.

"What is it?" I asked, hoarsely whispering.

"I'm hit," Sir Gerald said weakly.

"Where? How badly?"

"Right thigh," he gasped. "Don't know how bad. Really doesn't hurt much yet."

"Give it time," I said. "Is the bone broken?"

"Don't know."

"Kearns," I whispered, "see about it."

I heard movement behind me, Kearns slipping into position to investigate the general's wound with the tips of his fingers. Now I had to paddle the boat alone.

"Not too bad," Kearns' voice said a few moments later. "It's going to hurt him, but I don't think it got the bone."

"Can he walk on it?" I asked.

"If he has to."

"My God, man," Sir Gerald gasped, "I don't even know. . . ."

"If you have to, you'll walk on it, *sir*," Kearns said slowly, bitterly. "Or I'll blow your bloody head off."

"What are you saying?" Sir Gerald asked in a pained voice.

"I'm saying you're not going to slow us down when we hit the ground," Kearns said as if speaking to a child. "Mathers?"

"Yes?"

Kearns was silent.

"Oh!" I said, realizing what he meant. "I'm sorry, Sir Gerald, but you'll have to walk on that leg or surrender yourself to the Imperials."

That was enough for Sir Gerald; he said nothing more.

"Kearns, help me. I can't handle this boat alone."

But already I heard the splash of Kearns' paddle in the water.

By now the city was thinning, gaps appearing between the lower, smaller buildings and the light of the burning portions of the city was beginning to play on the water. In a few more moments the riflemen on the shore would be able to see us.

"Right," I whispered to Kears. "Head for the right bank."

We began to cut toward the center of the river, out to where we stood a better chance of being seen, but I figured that it was a chance we had to take.

The men in the boats following us must have been able to see us well enough to realize what I had in mind, for they began cutting out toward the middle of the river and then toward the right bank.

My boat had passed the midpoint of the river and was nearing the darkness of the right bank, Tracy's boat was now no more than a yard or two behind mine, and the final boat was very close to his, though I could barely see it. The Imperials on the left bank had momentarily lost us in the confusion, and we dipped our paddles silently, carefully, to try to avoid detection.

Then a brilliant explosion from the burning portion of the city lighted the river, revealing us.

"Balls!" Kearns muttered.

A voice screamed something in German from the bank.

Rifles and submachine guns began chattering, lacing the river with shot, here and there a tracer showing the paths of their bullets—many of them were very close to their targets.

"Let 'em have it!" I yelled back, grabbing up my rifle and hoping that inertia would carry the boat the rest of the way to the bank.

Kearns' tommy gun began to fire only seconds after my rifle. To my surprise Sir Gerald, who had been silent, fumbled with his Enfield for a moment, then placed it to his shoulder and began to snap off shots with a marksman's ease. He seemed to have forgotten about his wound, for the moment at least.

From a quick estimate of the number of rifle and submachine-gun flashes from the now-distant left bank I guessed that there were about fifteen Germans there. There seemed to be none on the right bank now, and I wondered why, though I thought that now and then I could hear small-arms fire from the vicinity of the broken bridge and I wondered if the British had overrun the German trenches and driven the Imperials that far back into the city.

But I didn't take much time to think about that sort of thing. I was far more worried about the fifteen or so firing from the left bank.

In a few seconds the brilliant light of the explosion passed, and the river was again plunged into darkness, save for the flickering red glow that reached it through broken buildings and naked trees. Then the Germans could see us no better than we could see them, and that was only by the flashes of our weapons.

Suddenly, unexpectedly, the boat's prow bumped against something solid. I spun around, felt forward, and my hands met slimy stone, the bank of the river and the stonework that had been built there.

"We're there," I gasped, grabbing the stone as best I could and pulling the boat in closer. The river's current turned us around so that the boat's side bumped against the old, slimy stones.

"Kearns," I said, "out! Help Sir Gerald."

"But I. . . ." Sir Gerald began to protest.

"Out!" I said and then turned my attention back to the far shore, slipping a fresh clip into my Enfield.

I heard Kearns' harsh breathing as he clambered around me and out of the boat onto the uncertain footing of the stones.

"Take my hand," he said.

"Be careful, you fool," Sir Gerald gasped.

"Shut up and get out," Kearns snapped, hauling upward on the general's arm.

Sir Gerald came to his feet awkwardly, gasping under

his breath, but British enough not to cry out from the pain.

He came out of the boat, half falling onto the stones, struggling and then with Kearns' help stumbling up the sides of the slippery stone steps to drier ground.

The boat began to slip away from the shore. I slung my rifle across my shoulder, grabbed the stones with both hands, pulled the boat back against the bank. Then, barely able to keep my footing as the boat tried to pull out from under me, I half stepped, half jumped onto the slimy stonework. For a moment I almost fell back into the water, dropped to a crouch, grabbed for a handhold, and then pulled myself up to where Kearns and Sir Gerald stood. Even as I reached his side, Kearns had begun to fire again toward the distant bank.

The second and third boats came up against the stones, and the men tumbled out. One man did not get out of the final boat, and his body was still in it when it began to pull away from the bank, bumping against the stones and then moving out into the current.

"Come on," I said. "We've got to get a couple of miles up the river and then cross back over. The villa's on the other side."

"Oh, shit!" someone muttered under his breath. A few of us fired parting shots at the Germans on the far bank and then we moved away from the river into the dark ruins of the city.

7
The Villa

The villa had been built in the early part of the century, back in the days before the war. Then France had been, in theory at least, a free and sovereign nation, though in reality it had been little more than a British satellite.

When the bloody Peasants' Rebellion of 1789–93 had been put down by the remnants of the French nobility and the British Army and the king restored to his throne mainly by British aid, France had been unable to sever all ties with its British allies. Normandy and Brittany had been ceded outright to the English throne by a grateful French king, but the king had not bargained on the redcoats who remained stationed near Paris and half a dozen other French cities to, as the British claimed, "guard the person of the rightful King of France."

When Louis XVI died in 1803, at the age of forty-nine, and was succeeded by Louis XVII, the British found a faithful servant in that weak-willed monarch. For the remainder of his reign Louis XVII was more than happy to allow British troops to protect him from his own people.

A string of other Louis' followed, none with the will or power to try to throw off the British occupation. A brief attempt was made, however, by the Duke of Gascony in 1868, but since no Joan of Arc stood at his side, the duke found the only reward for attempting to free his nation was a cell in the Tower of London and the hangman's noose.

By the beginning of the twentieth century local France accepted its vassalage to England perhaps not unwillingly, realizing now the growing power of the reborn Holy Roman Empire and the inability of France alone to maintain its independence from the German Empire, even more hungry for continental land than Britain.

The villa itself had been built by the Earl of Kent as a summer retreat on a parcel of land deeded to an ancestor of his by the grateful Louis XVI after the putting down of the Peasants' Rebellion.

Sitting on the bank of the Loire, five miles or so north of the center of the new Beaugency, the villa's ground covered perhaps fifty or sixty acres, half of it devoted to vineyards, for the Earl of Kent had had a great weakness for French wines, and half to stables, for he had also had a weakness for racing horses, mainly those of British Arabia.

The main house was an enormous, rambling, gingerbread structure, all frills and lace and useless ornamentation, three stories of rococo ugliness that the late Earl of Kent must somehow have found attractive.

Half a dozen outbuildings, servants' quarters and such, ringed the main house, half protecting it from attack, half hiding it from the beautiful countryside in which it had been built. The stables and their related buildings were located some distance from the main house and as far as we knew they were now used as garages for German motorcars. A company of elite, handpicked grenadiers inhabited the servants' quarters, and Intelligence had told us that there were six black-booted bodyguards living on the villa's main floor. Just where Count von Heinen and his wife were dwelling in the house, we did not know, though we believed that they and the guards were at present the villa's only inhabitants. Von Heinen, according to reports, had a passion for privacy. He had been warned against it—this morning he would learn why.

There were eight of us who came shivering out of the Loire into that cold predawn drizzle in the spring of 1971. Sir Gerald and a Corporal Land who had been in Tracy's boat were wounded, though neither very seriously. Sir Gerald's bleeding had stopped, and despite the agony in his leg, he had come to realize that the wound was not as bad as he had feared. Using his rifle as a crutch, he could hobble along and with his other hand use his .62 Harling if necessary. The corporal had a flesh wound in his left forearm, and after allowing a cursory examination and the application of dry bandages, he waved us away, saying that he had fought with wounds a hell of a lot worse.

We stopped in the shelter of a poplar grove a good hundred yards from the first building beyond the boathouse, unwrapped our weapons, checked them for dryness, and then got out our gas masks.

The corporal from the final boat sat his heavy pack on the ground and with the aid of Tracy's sheltered flashlight removed half a dozen gas grenades designed to be fired from our Enfields.

Kar-hinter had given us a weapon that had not yet been used in battle—at least not in this Line. It was a newly developed nerve gas, so we were told, and would stun and render unconscious for periods of two to three hours anyone exposed to it. It was claimed to be a British development, but I doubted it. I believed that Kar-hinter had it imported just for this one operation, though he had covered his tracks well. The grenades *looked* like British issue.

The corporal passed two of the grenades to me, two to Tracy, and kept two for himself. We each fitted one grenade onto our rifles, clipped the other to our belts. Then we all pulled our gas masks over our faces, cleared and checked them, and began moving toward the villa.

Halfway there, carefully concealing ourselves behind trees and bushes, we split into three groups: the corporal with the gas grenades and one man, Tracy and a private named Starne, and Sir Gerald, Kearns, the wounded Corporal Land, and myself.

"Okay," I whispered, "get yourselves into position, hold, and wait until you hear me fire. Then go into augmentation, and let them have it."

The others nodded, except for Sir Gerald who seemed puzzled at my reference to augmentation, and we moved apart.

Most of the buildings were dark. One of the servants' houses was lighted, two windows showing the yellow light of a gas lantern and the forms of two gray-clad Imperials sitting at a table, apparently playing cards and drinking something—German beer, I guessed. The yard immediately before the villa was lighted by two gas lamps that bracketed the main entrance. A German staff car sat in the glare of the lamps, and two men sat in the car, one of them smoking a long black cigar. A single light burned on the second floor of the main house, off in what I thought to be the west wing. It was my guess that there we would find the count and his wife. They were my own special targets.

Kearns was at my side, Corporal Land assisting Sir Gerald a few feet behind us, as we slowly, carefully circled the house, came in from the dark rear.

At last, within rock-throwing distance of the house, I signaled for Sir Gerald to sit down and wait until we had cleared the house. He made an effort to protest, then seemed to think better of it and slowly sat down, assisted by Land.

Giving the general a brief parting handshake, I signaled Kearns to circle back around the house. Land and I moved in closer.

I don't know why I hadn't thought of it before, but I had the second grenade on my belt, and it would probably do us a lot more good if it were on the end of Land's rifle. I slipped it off my belt, handed it to him, and pointed toward a window in the east wing, bottom floor. He got the message. We parted.

I wondered where the six bodyguards were sleeping, but I had no way of knowing. We would just have to hope that wherever they were, they would run into the gas once hell began to break loose in the villa. I figured they probably would. They wouldn't be expecting it.

Now I was at the window near the center of the rear wall and pressed my face against the cold panes of glass and tried to peer inside. There was total darkness. I only hoped that I wouldn't be firing into a closed pantry.

It seemed that there had been plenty of time for the others to have got into position. Kearns would now be standing in the shadows a few feet from the staff car, the safety off his tommy gun, a full clip in it. Tracy would be near a window of the servants' quarters where a light had shown, perhaps watching the two Imperials playing cards and drinking beer and probably wishing that he could have a stein himself. I did too. But later. Much later.

The time had come. There was no point in waiting.

I stepped back a few paces to be clear of flying glass, aimed the rifle and its heavy grenade at the window, snapped off the safety, squeezed the trigger.

The rifle seemed to explode with a tremendous roar in the stillness, though I knew that the grenade had muffled its sound. And the breaking of glass seemed just as loud, as did the pop! of the exploding grenade.

I willed electrobiological circuits into operation. All my senses and responses increased fivefold. Sounds slowed and shifted toward the bass; what light I could see became redder. The world seemed to be moving with slow motion now.

For a long, dragging instant it was still again, but only for an instant. A man yelled, his voice a rumble, a rifle fired, its sound like a distant cannon's boom, and was answered by another rifle from the servants' quarters. A voice sounded inside the villa, guttural German, and a light on the first floor flickered on.

"Come on," I yelled as well as I could from inside the gas mask, leaping toward the door that was a few feet off to my right. I kicked at it savagely twice before the latch sprang and wood splintered and the door swung inwards. Then I leaped into the house; Land was behind me, moving as rapidly as I in his augmentation.

Now I could see the room from which the light came, down a long corridor; at the end of it was a parlor or sitting room. A half-naked bull of a man stumbled to his feet in slow motion like a character in a dream, clutching for his submachine gun, swearing, yelling.

He never had a chance. I squeezed the trigger of my Enfield, firing from the hip, and opened a great hole in the man's left breast. He seemed to float back, stunned by the impact, but hung onto his submachine gun, slowly fighting to bring it up. I worked the bolt of my rifle, cursing its awkwardness when my reactions were so fast, threw another shell into the chamber and squeezed it off as the submachine gun in the dying man's hand came to languid life, emitting a trail of bullets my eyes could almost see individually that chipped plaster from

the hallway and ceiling. But the German suddenly lost
his face as my bullet and Land's both plowed through
flesh, bone, brains.

The gas was slowly drifting up around us, pale white
in the light from the parlor, drifting down the corridor
terribly slowly as a predawn breeze blew in from the
open door behind us.

There was a second man in the parlor, wearing only
the underclothing he had been sleeping in, and his eyes
were still dazed by sleep when I jumped into the doorway—no more than a blur to his eyes—and put a bullet
in his chest and another into his stomach. His dying
gurgle was a deep, bass rumbling and his slow-moving
hand tried to grab for the pistol that lay a few feet from
where he fell across a heavy oaken table, his blood terribly red against the old, dark wood.

I felt almost sorry for the man. He had probably
never even had a chance to see me.

There was a crashing from the front of the house as
Kearns kicked open the door, cautiously sprayed the entrance hall with submachine-gun bullets, then came on
in, yelling for blood. He had already left two men dead
behind him.

Land and I met him in the huge living room, an oak-
paneled, fireplaced stadium of a room.

I cut out my augmentation and signaled for the others
to do the same. The world shifted back into normal time
and I felt a sudden, brief weakness. A human body can't
operate like that for very long.

"Where are the rest of them?" Kearns' muffled voice
asked through his mask.

"Damned if I know," I said.

We split up, moved through the house, Kearns and
Land searching for the remaining bodyguards, I for
the stairs that would lead up to the second floor.

It didn't take me long to find them. Big as they were,
they were hard to miss even in the dark.

Right at that moment I should have augmented again,
but I didn't. I was too confident, I suppose.

I dropped my rifle on the sofa in the enormous hall at
the base of the stairs, pulled a flashlight from its clip on
my belt with my left hand, the heavy Harling with my

right. I flashed the light up the huge, broad stairs—and stumbled back as a pistol bullet cut along my left ribs.

"*Halten Sie!*" a voice called from the darkness above me.

I flashed the light up, saw a naked man standing at the head of the stairs, and shot him down. The heavy Harling slug seemed to lift him upward and throw him backward.

I was reeling back, cursing the pain in my side, thinking that somehow I ought to know the man who even now was tumbling down the stairs, smashing against the rungs of the banister, grabbing for a handhold on them, stopping his fall, reaching for the pistol that had tumbled down the stairs with him.

Holding the light on him and trying to forget about the pain in my side, I went up the stairs two at a time and realized who he was. Count Albert von Heinen.

He lay still when I reached him, blood oozing from a wound in his stomach, looking up at me, fire and hatred in his eyes, foul German curses on his lips.

Out of my own pain I hit him across the mouth with the back of my left hand, still holding the flashlight, and wondered how many of his teeth I was breaking.

"Shut up!" I told him.

Somewhere a woman was screaming, shrilly, hysterically.

"Mathers?" Kearns yelled from the darkness below.

"Von- Heinen's up here," I yelled back, pulling my gas mask off my face, letting it hang by its straps around my neck. "I shot him, but he's still alive. Watch him. I'm going on up."

I heard Kearns' heavy feet on the stairs below, but I didn't look back. I went on up to the room at the head of the stairs where the light shone and a woman screamed.

The door was standing open, and the woman was too terrified to try to stop me.

She stood with her back against the wall near a rumpled bed that was virtually surrounded by mirrors. She was as naked as Von Heinen, short, beautifully rounded, with the dark skin and dark eyes of the people of Mediterranean France. Lovely as she was, she certainly wasn't the count's blond American wife.

"Don't move," I told her and then repeated it in both German and my broken French.

She didn't, other than to sob hysterically, her hands at her throat, making no move to cover her exposed body.

There was no one else in the room, but then I hadn't expected there would be.

I slipped the flashlight back into my belt, crossed over to where the woman stood rooted in fear, grabbed her hands away from her throat, and slapped her twice with all the force I could muster.

"*Sei ruhig, stille!*" I told her. "*Wo ist Gräfin von Heinen?*"

"Here!" a voice said in English from behind me.

I spun, looked into the barrel of an Imperial automatic, calculated my chances if I went into augmentation now, shrugged and let the Harling drop from my fingers. I wasn't worried.

Sally Beall von Heinen was a beautiful woman, dressed in a thin, revealing gown that hid very little of her and I could not help wondering why the hell Von Heinen wanted to bundle with the sobbing girl near me when he had a wife like this one.

Heavy feet had come up the stairs at a run, were now slamming down the hallway. Countess von Heinen turned, found herself facing Kearns' tommy gun, faltered for a moment, fired wildly, hitting nothing.

I jumped, my fist coming down heavily on her right arm, grabbing her waist with my left arm, pulling her to the floor. I didn't need augmentation for this.

She struggled, fought, spat, scratched, clawed for my face, cursed, grabbed for the gun she had dropped, her gown tearing open. I didn't have time to appreciate the view. I threw a fist into her jaw, snapping her head back. She barely moaned as she lost consciousness.

"You okay?" Kearns asked after he pulled his gas mask off.

"I'll live," I said, rising to my feet and gingerly touching my injured side. "Von Heinen?"

"He needs attention, but I've seen men live for days with worse."

Gunfire rattled from below.

"Land's found the rest of 'em," Kearns said.

"Stay here. Watch them."

I grabbed up the Harling from the floor, jerked out my flashlight, and headed back down the stairs, pulling my gas mask up and switching back into combat augmentation.

By the time I reached the ground floor the firing had stopped, but I could still hear the low rumble of movement. I ran down another hallway, into a room where a gas lantern sputtered feebly, its glow red. Land leaned against the wall, his uniform dripping blood, his chest a series of ragged holes, a grim, bitter smile on his face. He had lost his gas mask somewhere.

He feebly pointed toward the four men in the room, sprawled across the bloody beds and floor. One had the top of his head blown away, and another had a great hole where his stomach should have been, and both were very dead. I couldn't see the other two very well, but they weren't moving either.

I cut out my augmentation and Land quit grinning and slid down the wall, leaving a wide red swash, and then he lay still. I didn't need to feel his pulse to know that he was dead too. I just wondered how he had lived as long as he had cut apart as he was.

As I turned and went back toward where Kearns was guarding the count and his wife, I heard a few ragged shots from outside the building, but by the time I had climbed the stairs and pulled my mask off again they had all ceased. I just hoped that the last shots had been fired by our boys.

Kearns and I found a robe to put on Countess von Heinen, covering her body and the torn gown, and then we tied her hands behind her back. Leaving her to regain consciousness as she would, we carried Von Heinen himself back up the stairs and laid him on the rumpled bed.

"Put a compress on that to try to stop the bleeding," I told Kearns. "I'll tie her up," pointing to Von Heinen's mistress who was returning to wide-eyed, fearful consciousness after having fainted during the fracas.

After tying and gagging the dark-haired girl—I hadn't bothered to find anything to put on her—I sat her in a corner and began searching for clothing for Von Heinen. We couldn't take him out naked as he was.

By the time we had finished dressing the count there were sounds coming from below.

I grabbed my pistol, moved cautiously to the head of the stairs, peered down. There was just enough light in the hallway for me to see three figures, two of them supporting the third between them.

"Hold it there," I yelled, fairly sure who they were.

"Eric?" Tracy's voice, muffled and distorted by his gas mask, called back.

"Up here."

"It's me, Starne and Sir Gerald."

"We've got Von Heinen and his wife. Come on up," I told him.

"Just let me rest, old chap," I heard Sir Gerald say.

They lowered him to the sofa where I had dropped my rifle earlier—now it seemed like hours—and came up the stairs.

"What about the others?" I asked.

"Not sure," Tracy answered, loosening his mask. "Dead I think."

Then I could see his face. He had a nasty gash across his cheek that ended where his mask had covered his mouth and nose. There was a rip down his left leg that looked painful, but not serious. Well, he and three others had wiped out nearly a full company of elite troops.

"You hurt?" he asked.

"Side grazed. I'm okay, just got careless. Land's dead, but Kearns doesn't have a scratch on him."

"He wouldn't."

We entered the bedroom where Kearns was pulling the German officer's boots on the count's feet.

"Is he—" asked the man named Starne who wore a British private's uniform.

"Stomach wound," I said. "He'll live, long enough at least."

Then Tracy noticed the naked girl tied and sitting in the corner.

"Who's she?" he asked, a wicked grin on his face.

"The Graf's playmate," I said. "They must have been at it when we came busting in. At least they were both naked and . . ."

"Let's get the hell out of here," Kearns said suddenly, reminding us all of why we were there.

We did exactly that, though Tracy looked almost wistfully at the dark-haired girl one last time as we started down the stairs.

8
Ambush

It was darker than ever when we carried the unconscious count out of the house. His wife, bleeding at the mouth, was walking with Tracy's pistol pressed into the small of her back. Sir Gerald, limping, assisted by Starne, brought up the rear.

The earlier drizzle had increased to a steady, soaking downpour, but we hardly noticed it.

"You're a lucky bastard," Tracy said to Kearns, who was carrying the German across his shoulder fireman fashion.

"No luck to it," Kearns said. "Just cautious."

"You didn't sound cautious," I said, "when you hit those two in the staff car."

Kearns laughed that odd laugh of his. We all laughed, even Sir Gerald. It was over, thank God, and the sudden release of tension brought us all easily to the point of laughter.

Von Heinen's wife did not speak; she only moved silently, mechanically as we forced her on. I would have expected a woman to yell, scream, go into hysterics as the dark-haired girl had, but Sally von Heinen did just as she was told, but nothing more. Then I reminded myself that she was the daughter of an American rebel leader and had probably been exposed to violence most of her life. In a way I was grateful to her. I think I would have knocked her teeth out had she behaved any differently.

We were a little more than halfway to the river when we saw the airship. It came down slowly, its propellers softly cutting the air, its engines muffled, its running lights out. We could see it only as a black cigar against the slightly lighter sky. Had it been day, though, we could have seen the Imperial German insignia along her gas bag, the flag of Franz VI that she flew. But that's the way it had been planned. Kar-hinter's plan.

The airship touched ground a few yards from the river, and men leaped out, driving pegs into the wet earth, hooking cables to them. Other men moved to the rear of the gondola, opened huge cargo doors, slid ramps to the earth, began rolling out a huge squashed sphere.

All of us, except for Countess Sally von Heinen and her unconscious husband, were familiar with the shape of a skudder, though it must have appeared very alien to her: a huge glasslike bubble mounted on a small, dark base, a craft never designed to move in space, only across the Lines of time.

"Mathers?" a voice called from the group of men who now stood around the skudder.

"*Natl,*" I answered in Shangalis.

"The skudder's ready. Want me to warm her up?" the man asked in the same language.

I glanced at Kearns in the rain and darkness. He nodded.

"Yes," I called.

"You're not Englishmen!" Sally von Heinen said, sudden horror in her voice. Maybe she was used to violence, I thought, but not to being kidnapped by men who spoke a language that was not of her world.

"We're not," I said. "Go on. Get in." I pointed her toward the skudder.

In a few moments we were all inside the craft and I pulled the hatch closed behind me. The man outside yelled, "Good luck," and I yelled back my thanks.

"Have you ever skudded before, Sir Gerald?" Tracy asked in English.

"No," the injured British general said breathlessly.

"Then brace yourself," Tracy said, laughing. "You're in for an experience."

"Everybody ready?" Kearns asked harshly.

"We're ready," I said, glancing over at the still-unconscious count.

By this time it dawned on me that his wife had shown absolutely no concern over his condition, but then he had been in bed with another woman when we burst into the villa. And I remembered Kar-hinter's having said that theirs was a marriage of politics. It made a little more sense to me now. Virgin wife? I wondered. And thought that if she were, it was a terrible waste.

Kearns' hands moved across the controls, making final adjustments, bringing the generators up to full potential, setting the destination indicators for about a dozen Lines to the East, one where gas and bacteriological warfare had nearly extinguished human life in Europe before the Kriths and Timeliners could enter to alter the course of that world's history.

"Okay," Kearns said. "Here we go."

An invisible hand came up and grabbed my genitals, jerking down, then snatching at my guts, moving up to stir my stomach with a lumpy club.

Flicker!

For an instant I saw lights in the direction of the villa and perhaps men moving there in this next-door world, but I wasn't sure.

Flicker!

Total darkness.

Flicker!

"It's far more interesting in the daytime," Tracy told Sir Gerald, who was too busy being sick to listen.

Flicker!

A dozen times that hand inside my abdomen jerked and pulled and twisted. Sir Gerald once muttered something I couldn't understand and Von Heinen groaned in his unconsciousness.

Flicker!

Then it all stopped, and I sat still for a minute trying not to be sick myself. Skudding sometimes got me that way too.

The night was still as dark as ever, the same clouds lay over this world as lay over the one we had left behind us; the same rain fell; the same trees grew on the same riverbank a few yards away; the same villa stood on the rise above us—or almost the same villa. The one in this world was not as well cared for as the other, inhabited only by rats and the bones of the very last Earl of Kent and his family who had died of a bitter, flesh-rotting disease as biological war swept across Europe.

But it wasn't the villa I was looking for. It was rather a prefabricated hut that stood no more than a dozen yards beyond the villa, and beside it a craft that was a larger version of our own craft, but one designed to carry cargo as well as passengers.

"Everybody out," Kearns said. The skudding didn't seem to bother his stomach.

I rose to my feet, trying to pull Von Heinen erect. Kearns came back to help me.

I don't know what it was that bothered me. I can't even now put my finger on it, but I had the strange, uneasy feeling that something was very wrong. Maybe it was the fact that no one had come out of the hut to greet us, but that shouldn't have bothered me. Maybe it was the fact that everything was too quiet, even for Here. I'm not sure, but I know I *felt* something.

Tracy opened the hatch, jumped to the ground. Starne followed him, and they waited while Kearns and I maneuvered the unconscious Imperial count into position and then took his weight between them as we passed him down. Then we followed.

"Tracy," I said, "you and Starne help Sir Gerald and go on. Kearns and I will bring these two."

Kearns hefted the count onto his shoulder, while the others, supporting the British general between them, started toward the hut.

They didn't get halfway.

Suddenly the whole area was illuminated.

"Son of a . . ."

A voice said very loudly in English, "Hold it where you are!"

I shoved Countess von Heinen back toward the skudder with a savage gesture, grabbed for the pistol on my hip, switched into combat augmentation. Kearns unceremoniously dumped the count, unslung his tommy gun. Starne broke into an augmented run toward the hut, and Tracy lowered Sir Gerald to the ground before going into augmentation.

Rifles chattered from behind the lights. Starne fell in mid-stride, clawing at his chest. Tracy staggered, cursed in Shangalis, jerked up his own pistol, fired, staggered toward the hut, and then fell in his own blood.

Whoever was firing at us had reactions just as fast as ours and that was a little frightening.

The whole night was ablaze with gunfire. *We* aimed for their spotlights. *They,* whoever they were, aimed for us.

Sir Gerald, perhaps unnoticed by our attackers, rolled over in slow motion, languidly pulled his pistol free, and fired off two shots as quickly as a nonaugmented man could—one put out one of the lights and the other brought an agonized yell—and then took a bullet between his eyes. He'd died in the old tradition. I wonder if he went to school at Eton—"The battles of Britain . . ." or however that goes.

Then a barrage of automatic-weapons fire splattered against the dome of the skudder behind me, some ricocheting away, some penetrating. Though the bullets seemed slow to my accelerated senses, they weren't, but I didn't stop to think about the damage done. There was no time.

I grabbed Sally von Heinen, momentarily cut out my augmentation. "Get him in the skudder!" I pointed toward her husband.

She looked at me defiantly.

"Get him in the skudder, or I'll kill you both."

Most of the gunfire from the ring of lights was now aimed at Tracy and Kearns, who had crawled toward the meager cover of a bush a few feet away. Tracy was trying to pull himself up against the hut, very weakly, and he seemed to be on the verge of losing consciousness. But none of the bullets was coming in my direction now. They seemed afraid of hitting Von Heinen or Sally, or both—whoever the hell *they* were

I was back into combat augmentation and yelling, "Hold your fire or I'll shoot Count von Heinen," and wondering if they could understand my accelerated voice. I put my Harling to his head so they'd know I meant business. It may have been a poor maneuver, but it was the only thing I could think of at the time. And it worked.

They stopped firing.

"Kearns, get Tracy."

Kearns got up warily, looked around, then walked out into the lighted area, his tommy gun held at the ready.

He stopped for a moment where Sir Gerald lay, then rose, shook his head. He repeated the same action above the unmoving form of Starne and then went on to Tracy.

In a few moments he had Tracy on his feet, half carrying him, and together they staggered back to the skudder.

"Get him in," I said, then, with exaggerated slowness, gestured for Countess von Heinen to follow. A moment later I jerked the still-unconscious count up and somehow threw him into the craft.

"Don't any of you try anything," I yelled, "or they'll pay for it."

I slammed the hatch shut and told Kearns: "Get our asses out of here!"

"Where?"

"Back to where we came from, I guess," I said, suddenly at a loss. "Maybe the airship's still there."

"Okay," Kearns said, dropping into the pilot's seat, snapping switches.

Then we flickered out of that universe, the inside of the skudder smelling of ozone and burning insulation.

I cut out my augmentation and fell back, gasping for breath. I was totally drained of energy.

9
Pursuit

The airship was gone.

Up in the villa and the outbuildings the same lights still burned, and all was silent. There was no movement. In the short time that we had been gone there had been no change, save that the airship was gone. But it would be dawn soon, and someone would come. Imperials, of course. And we couldn't be there when they arrived.

I turned back to Kearns who still sat in the pilot's seat, cursing savagely.

"What is it?" I asked.

"This goddamned thing," he said, gesturing toward the skudder's controls. "It's just about had it."

"We've got to get out of here."

"Not in this skudder we won't."

I'd been afraid of that, afraid that each time we flickered from one Timeline to the next we might not make it, that the skudder's drive would break down. I suppose we'd been lucky to get as far as we had.

"It won't move?" I asked without hope.

"Not one more jump," Kearns said.

"Up in the stables," Tracy said weakly. "There're supposed to be motorcars."

"Kearns, go see," I said quickly.

"What's wrong with the one sitting in the front of the villa?"

"Nothing, unless you put a bullet through the block."

"I didn't," Kearns said coldly. "I was shooting at men, not motorcar engines."

"Then get it."

Kearns nodded agreement, climbed out of the seat, opened the hatch and jumped to the ground.

I glanced at Von Heinen, his wife and then at Tracy, who lay back on the seat, blood flowing down his left leg from a wound above the knee.

"How bad is it, old man?" I asked in English.

"Bloody painful, old top," Tracy said, trying to force a smile onto his face.

I knelt in front of him, felt the leg. The bone was broken and jagged.

"I could have told you that," Tracy said.

I pulled a knife from my pocket, snapped open the blade, cut a slit up Tracy's trouser leg, and then cut away the cloth above the wound.

"I'm going to put a tourniquet on it," I said. "Think you can manage with that?"

"I'd bloody well better."

"We'll bandage it and put a splint on it as soon as we can."

When I was finished, I turned back to Von Heinen, who was making the sounds of a man returning to painful consciousness. Opening his shirt, I checked the compress that Kearns had applied to the stomach wound. It was soaked with blood, but the blood was beginning to dry. Externally, at least, the count had stopped bleeding.

"He's not going to do us much good dead, old boy," Tracy said.

"He's not going to do us any mucking good at all unless we get him back behind British lines."

"How do you suggest we do that?"

"I don't know," I answered slowly. "We'll take the motorcar and see if maybe we can get back down into Beaugency. It may be that the attack has broken up the German lines enough for us to get through."

I stopped for a moment and listened. The staff car that sat in front of the villa coughed to life, sputtered, then began to run smoothly. From a great distance, to the south, I could hear the infrequent boom of a howitzer, occasional small-arms fire, but from the sounds the real battle was over. Exactly what the British had accomplished, I couldn't even begin to guess, other than get *us* through the Imperial lines. But unless we could get back through, even that wasn't going to do us much good.

I tuned back to Sally von Heinen.

"Who were those men?" I asked her slowly, coldly.

"What men?" she asked, her face showing nothing but hatred for me."

"Those men who tried to rescue you and the count."

"How should I know?" she asked. "I don't even know where we were."

"Shit!"

"What do you mean, Eric?" Tracy asked.

"There shouldn't have been anybody there but our people," I said, "in that Line. According to Kar-hinter, there wasn't supposed to be another human being alive within a hundred miles—and the surviving natives of the Line don't have spotlights, rifles, and combat augmentation."

"Then you mean they were Timeliners?"

"You got any other ideas?"

"No, but—*Timeliners,* Eric?"

"It has to be. I don't know who or why, but—hell, you've heard stories of renegades who steal skudders and go off plundering backward Lines. Maybe it was some of them."

"I've only heard stories."

"I know, but who else could it have been?"

Sally might have had something like a smug expression on her face. I couldn't be sure, but before I could question her, Kearns pulled the staff car up next to the skudder and jumped out, leaving the motor running, but without headlamps burning.

"Ready?" he asked.

"Get out," I said to Countess von Heinen.

She did, but carefully, facing the deadly little Imperial pistol that Kearns now carried, the same gun she had tried to kill him with back in her husband's bedroom.

I helped Tracy over the hatch and lowered him down to Kearns. Holding Tracy with one arm, the other leveling the pistol at Sally, Kearns helped the injured man into the back seat of the car

"You wait there, ma'am," Kearns said, then turned to assist me with the groaning count.

We would have got him out of the skudder—but we ran out of time.

A dozen yards up the slope toward the villa the air shimmered for a moment, sparkling like arcing electricity; then a shape formed out of the shimmering, a flattened egg of metal and glass—a skudder that didn't look like any skudder I had ever seen before.

I thought about going into augmentation, but didn't know whether my body could take it again just yet. I'd wait and see.

Pushing the count's wife back toward our skudder, Kearns jerked up his diminutive pistol and fired into the developing shape.

"Get back in there," I yelled to the woman, crouching in the open hatch, leveling my Harling at the new craft.

Our bullets, roaring loudly in the predawn stillness, ricocheted off the flattened egg. A hatch opened and first one, then two weapons began to answer ours.

"Get Tracy," I yelled to Kearns, who stood midway between our skudder and the motorcar.

"I'll never get him back in," Kearns gasped.

"Get in the car then," I yelled suddenly. "Get out of here."

"You're mad."

A bullet rang shrilly as it struck the metal base of our skudder. I thought about the energy pistol that ought to be stashed inside our craft and wondered if I could get it.

"Do it," I yelled back to Kearns at the same time. "Turn on your lights, make all the noise you can. Maybe they'll follow you."

"Crap!"

"Go on!"

Cursing again, Kearns jumped into the car, snapped on the electric headlamps, and finally, firing across the hood as he did, he started the motorcar into motion.

"Stay right where you are," I said to Sally.

Turning back to the count, I saw that his eyes were open at last. "Sprechen Sie—Hell, do you speak English?"

He nodded weakly.

"Then listen very carefully. I will kill you and your wife on the spot unless you both do exactly as I say."

"Very well," he gasped.

"Can you sit up?"

He struggled awkwardly, but finally was able to pull himself up into a half-sitting position.

I turned to look out the hatch. The woman was still standing where I had told her to, perhaps fearful of the pistol I carried, but more likely just wary of the rifle fire from the strange skudder that was aimed at the dwindling taillights of the German staff car.

Then something happened that I couldn't quite believe at first. The thing that I knew to be a skudder, knew to carry the men who had attacked us on that Timeline a dozen universes away, rose slowly from the ground, turned in the direction of the staff car, and began flying a few feet above the ground.

A skudder that flew? I had always been told that it was impossible. I don't really know why a jet engine or an antigrav couldn't be used in conjunction with a skudder, but that was supposed to be one of the laws of the energies that allow passage across the Lines Something about the nature of a probability field and its interaction with other forms of energy. It just wasn't supposed to be possible for a skudder to do anything but skud. But apparently what I had been told was wrong. I was seeing a skudder fly, though I couldn't determine what kind of propulsion it was using.

You know, I think that was the first time I had ever really had a doubt about the omniscience of the Kriths. But just the first.

Once I got over my astonishment I felt relief. It was a weak ruse—the staff car—but it seemed to be working. The men in the alien skudder must have assumed that we had all been able to get into the motorcar and they were going after it. I hadn't expected it to work at all, much less this well—the *whole* skudder chasing down the dirt road after the car.

"Stay where you are, Countess," I said, then gestured for the count to come after me.

"I don't know that I can do it, old boy," he said in excellent, British-accented, if gasping, English.

"You'd better, *mein Herr*, or I'll blow the top of your head off."

Before leaving the skudder, I went to its controls, opened an obscure panel and adjusted a dial and pushed a red button. You don't just leave inoperative Outtime devices lying around in a world where your presence is supposed to be unknown. We had about five minutes to get out of range before the skudder destroyed itself.

I reached under the control panel, pulled out the energy

pistol that was hidden there and shoved it into my belt; then I clambered out of the hatch, dropped to the ground beside the woman, said, "Help me. Both your lives depend on our getting away before your friends come back. If they come back, I'll kill you both before they get me. I promise."

I don't know whether I really meant it. I'm not very good at killing in cold blood, but I suppose I thought I would do it at the time. Maybe I would have. But they believed me and that was the important thing.

The woman seemed to feel some repugnance at touching the man who was, technically at least, her husband, but she did, struggling with his weakened body to the best of her ability. We finally got him to the ground, where he stood, leaning against the side of the skudder, gasping for breath.

"That wound's going to start bleeding again," I said, "but I don't suppose we can do much about that." I paused. "We're going to the stables up there." I pointed with my Harling. "There'd better be motorcars in there."

"I don't think he can make it," the woman said.

"He will if he wants to see the sun rise," I said, noticing the beginning of a glow along the horizon in the east. It was going to be daylight in a few minutes. Again time was running out. That seemed to be a habit of mine.

"Let's go," I said, supporting one side of the wounded man, while his wife supported the other. Together we staggered toward the stables, our feet slipping in the mud.

The destruction of the skudder, which took place before we were halfway to the stables, was unspectacular, even in early dawn. There was a flash of light and a subdued roar as the metal base and probability generator it housed were consumed. The paraglas dome crystalized and shattered and fell in tiny fragments onto the slag. There wasn't enough left for anyone ever to be able to tell what it had been, no one from this Line at least.

We went on, the three of us, toward the stables.

I had had little time to think of my own wound, but I became increasingly aware of it and of the exhaustion of my body from running under augmentation as we carried the man between us. With probing fingers of my free hand I found the flayed flesh, raw and burning when I touched it, the dried, crusted blood under the sodden fabric of my shirt. As I had thought, it was only a superficial wound and though it might hurt me some, unless it got infected, it wasn't going to be any real trouble. I'd worry about infection later. Once I was sure I was going to live long enough to have an infection.

It was halfway to broad daylight when we finally reached the stables. Von Heinen had lost consciousness again and the last few yards I had somehow carried him alone, keeping both my eyes on his young wife, suspecting that she would take the first opportunity I gave her to run like hell. I didn't give her the opportunity, so she didn't.

I lowered Von Heinen to the wet ground, pulled the Harling from its holster, told his wife to stay at his side and went up to open the nearest doors.

At first I thought the cavernous stables were empty, but farther down I found three motorcars, all decked out with the flags of Von Heinen's rank. A *Feldmarschall*, he was. And he had come to the villa in style, though I was afraid that he wouldn't leave it in the same fashion. Not this time at least.

Going back to where the woman stood beside the unconscious man, I slipped the pistol back into its holster, jerked him up, pulled him across my shoulder, took a deep breath, and said, "Go on. Get in the first car."

With resignation on her pretty face the young countess preceded me along the front of the stable to where the cars were parked.

"Can you drive?" I asked.

"No."

"I don't believe you," I said. "Get in front. Are the keys in it? Don't lie again."

"Yes, they are."

I dumped Von Heinen in the back seat, climbed in beside him.

"Okay, let's go."

The motorcar started at once, which was a pleasant surprise, considering the state of the art of motorcars in this Line.

"Wait a minute," I said. "Shut if off."

She did as I ordered while I jumped out of the car,

grabbed up a large tarpaulin that lay on the stable floor a few feet from where the car was parked.

"Now let's go."

The motor started again, though it coughed a couple of times first. She shifted into gear and slowly pulled out of the stable into the driveway that led back around the villa's main house.

"Head toward Beaugency for the moment," I said, and then had the strangest feeling that I was being watched. I peered back over my shoulder out of the car's rear window, and for a moment I thought I saw a figure standing in the stable, back in the deepest part of the shadow. It seemed to be a man, but beyond that I could tell nothing about him. I reached for the Harling, but when I looked again, I could see nothing. The figure, if it had ever been there, was gone now. Perhaps it was just my fatigued mind playing tricks on me. I wasn't sure.

"What is it?" Countess von Heinen asked.

"Nothing. Go on. Drive slowly." I forced myself to try to forget about the figure, but I still felt uneasy about it, though it was a strange sort of unease I can't quite define. "Be careful," I went on, "and don't do anything foolish. You've only got a few inches of stuffing between you and the barrel of this pistol. I'd hate to make a big hole in your lovely back."

"I know," she said slowly. "I'll do as you say."

"I'm sure you will."

We passed the main house where Kearns had casually dumped the bodies of the two sentries who had once occupied the staff car he now drove. I wondered where he was, and I didn't mourn the dead Imperials. If I were going to mourn anyone, it would be Sir Gerald Asbury and Land, who had been cut apart by a submachine gun inside that big house, and Starne, who lay dead in another universe near Sir Gerald, and a British sergeant and three other men dead in the river and men who. . . . Hell! I didn't have time to mourn anyone. Not yet. I had to stay alive now and try somehow to get Von Heinen back across the British lines to Kar-hinter.

We had no more than hit the main highway outside the villa's grounds when I saw Imperial German troop movements in the direction of the city. Battered veterans of last night's fighting, moving back to regroup and refit and wait for replacements. They looked tired, but they didn't look *beaten*.

"Turn around," I ordered.

"Here?"

"Now!"

She slowed the car, made a U-turn in the road and headed north.

"The first road you come to off to your left, take it."

"Where are we going?"

"How the hell should I know?"

10
Contact and Report

For most of the morning we traveled west in the falling rain, the feeble windshield wipers hardly allowing Sally vision to drive. We stayed on back roads, little more than muddy ruts between farm lands that had lain fallow as war swept back and forth across this part of France. The ruins of a village here and there, a pile of cold embers that had once been a house, a series of bomb and shell craters and sodden, abandoned trenches, and little else. It was my intention to stay far enough north of the current German lines to avoid much investigation.

Only once were we stopped by a roadblock: two gaunt, tired soldiers in Imperial gray, soaked to the skin by the night-long rain, manning a barricade across what once might have been a paved road, but was now hardly more than a muddy path.

"Go slow," I told my driver, wondering what the sentries would think of a lone woman dressed in a robe driving an Imperial staff car that flew the banner of a *Feldmarschall*. We'd see. "Smile and wink at them, but don't let them look too closely in the back seat. And remember, if anything goes wrong, neither you nor your husband will live to talk about it."

"I understand," Sally replied coldly.

Then I pulled the tarp over the still unconscious Von Heinen and myself, pushed the pistol against the back of the driver's seat and waited, the air under the tarp hot and damp, smelling of hay and horseshit.

"*Halt, bitte,*" I heard a distant voice say. It may have had an Austrian accent; I wasn't sure.

"*Guten Morgen, Zugsführer,*" Sally von Heinen answered.

"*Guten Morgen, Fräulein,*" the Imperial sergeant replied.

In German, she asked him to let her pass, please. She

83

was really in a great hurry. Her husband was expecting her by one o'clock this afternoon.

"Wie heissen Sie, bitte?" the sergeant asked politely.

"Gräfin von Heinen," Sally answered simply. She was playing it straight. She knew she had to.

"Graf von Heinen! Möge er lange leben!" the sergeant said patriotically. *"Jawohl! Vorwärts, bitte, gnädige Frau."*

"Danke," Sally said, forcing friendliness I suspected.

And that's all there was to it.

As we pulled away from the sentry post I began making plans. Before too much longer we would have to find a place to hide the car, a place of comparative safety where I could leave the count and his wife for a few minutes and try to contact Kar-hinter and bring him up to date. He was going to have to get in and pick us up soon, or the whole thing would have been so much wasted effort and wasted British blood.

That much settled in my mind, I turned my attention back to Sally and tried to get her to talk, but she was unwilling to speak to a man who had kidnapped her, shot her husband and God-alone-knew how many other Germans who were her allies.

At last I sat back in the rear seat, checked Von Heinen's bandage, wondered how long he would last, pulled a soggy cigarette from an inside pocket, lit it, felt my bladder demanding to be emptied, wondered how much longer I could stay awake, and looked across Sally's shoulder at the ravaged French countryside.

And I thought about the world in which I now found myself, a world very, very remote from the one in which I had been born.

As I said before, I am from a Europo-Macedonian Line and this one was a Romano-British Line, Anglo-European Subsector; to be exact RTGB-307. Our Timelines, Sally von Heinen's and mine, had split a long, long time ago. In my world Alexander III of Macedonia, called "the Great," had created the first and greatest world empire, an empire that before his death at the age of sixty-one had spanned all the civilized world and had survived its founder by more than a thousand years.

In the world of Sally Beall von Heinen, Alexander had

died young and his empire had never really come into being. In her world the Greeks had gradually declined in power and influence, leaving only a great cultural heritage. A little Italian village on the Tiber River had picked up the pieces of the Greek world, adding a few ideas of their own, and from that built an empire, one not so great as my Alexander's had been, or quite so enduring, but a great one nevertheless.

The empire of this city called Rome flourished and grew, a new religion called Christianity had sprung up, the empire had fallen—ever read a fellow named Gibbon?—and the Western world slowly devolved into barbarism.

I guess we Greeks never really had a chance without Alexander. Funny.

Anyhow, ten centuries or so after the collapse of Rome the nations of Europe had formed and Western civilization reached a peak it had not known for a thousand years; ships sailed from Europe to India, China, Nippon, and eventually—there was an explorer named Columbus in these Lines—the two unknown continents to the west; here they're called North and South America.

Nations rose and fell; empires were carved out of the New World and the Old.

By about the beginning of the eighteenth century after the birth of the Jewish Messiah they call Christ, Europe consisted of Britain, France, Spain, Portugal, the Holy Roman Empire, and assorted nations of lesser importance. Britain, France, and Spain had come out as the greatest of the European colonial powers, though by this time Spain was already in decline and France was no real match for England on the high seas.

Britain took most of France's North American colonies away after establishing some of its own, battled with Spain, but never really got too much of a foothold in South America, looked east to China, India and south to Africa.

There is a crucial historical period in the Anglo-European and Anglo-American Subsectors in the latter years of the eighteenth century, local time. That was when the American colonists attempted to throw off what they called British Imperialism, for Britain was then the center of a burgeoning empire, threatening to surpass anything this world had ever seen before.

In many Lines the North American succeeded and the United States of America—as it is called in most Lines—was born. In many others they failed. This was one in which they had failed, Sally's world.

By 1775 the American Rebellion was in full swing in Sally's world, and for a while it also seemed possible that the American rebels could beat the British and gain the independence they wanted. And they probably would have, in her world, had it not been for a certain Major Patrick Ferguson, a British officer, who invented a new kind of weapon—one that loaded from the breech, rather than from the muzzle. It was a rather crude weapon at first, and for a while it seemed that Ferguson would get no help from the British lords—but in one of those curious twists of history that create the Lines of Time, aid was given him, resources were put at his disposal, and Ferguson went on to develop his breechloader.

By late 1780 the weapon was perfected, even beyond Ferguson's earlier dreams, a weapon with a rifled bore that could fire faster and more accurately than anything anyone had ever used before. It was a gun that could put the American rebel marksmen to shame. And it did.

By the summer of 1781 shiploads of the new Ferguson breechloaders were crossing the Atlantic, with men trained to use them. For once the innate conservatism of the generals was broken, and the bloody art of warfare leaped forward a hundred years.

In the next two years the Americans were on the run, their foremost leaders dead; Washington, a hero who made a valiant last stand at Yorktown, had died as he had lived. Half the American Congress was captured, tried for treason, hanged in the streets of Philadelphia.

Of the American generals only Anthony Wayne, "Mad Anthony," ssurvived, to lead his battered, decimated troops across the Appalachians, where he held out for two more long, bloody years before he was finally pinned against the western Virginia hills and shot as a traitor, still cursing the British with his infamous eyes.

With the death of Mad Anthony Wayne the American

cause collapsed, and Britain was again the supreme ruler of North America east of the Appalachians.

France, which had lent aid to the American rebels, feared an invasion by the British, but the lords in London, worn out by the war in America, let the French peasants punish the government.

The Peasants' Rebellion in France might have succeeded, very nearly did succeed, and failed only because the British, seeing that they had much to gain by supporting the French monarchy, finally came to the aid of the embattled Louis XVI, and with the still-further improved Ferguson breechloaders the redcoats shot down the French rebels as they had shot down the American rebels.

Its continental position secure with the first years of the 1800's, the crown sitting firmly on the head of the King of England, Parliament subdued and reduced in power, Britain went on to expand its holdings in North America, sweeping as far west as the Mississippi River and down into Mexico to the isthmus of Panama. Indochina was British, as were North Africa, South Africa, and the islands of the Pacific. Britain was supreme on land and sea.

About this time, following years of decline, the Holy Roman Empire, ruled by Franz III, found a rebirth, a growth in wealth and importance on the continent of Europe as the Germans and their kindred finally united under their emperor. The specter of republicanism, which had haunted both Britain and France for so long, never bothered the Holy Roman Emperor. Republicanism was a dead issue in this world—the American Rebellion and the Peasants' Rebellion in France had proved that.

By the end of the nineteenth century most of the world was divided between four empires—British, Spanish, Holy Roman and Nipponese—and so it was into the twentieth—and the final clash between the British Empire and the Holy Roman Empire, in which I was now embroiled.

Well, I'm no historian, despite the ambitions of my youth. My facts and places and dates may be a bit confused, and I admit that even what I have told you is very sketchy, but basically that is how the world I was in had come to be the way it was.

By noon fatigue and the pain in my side were beginning to get the better of me. I knew that I could not go much farther without some rest, and I knew that I needed to talk with Kar-hinter.

At last, miles from any village or even any farm, I ordered Sally to pull off the road, drive back along a cowpath as far as she could get the car and stop.

It had finally stopped raining by now, though as yet we hadn't seen the sun. Still the day was getting quite warm.

"What are you going to do now?" Sally asked as she climbed out of the car.

I shook my head, trying to clear it of the fog that filled it, the cotton that seemed to be stuffed behind my eyes.

"Are you going to shoot us and bury us here?" she asked.

"Don't be stupid!"

"What's stupid about that?" she asked, standing outside the car, her hands on her hips, the robe she wore somehow making her look smaller than she was, a child dressed up in mommy's clothing. "You'll never get us to wherever you were trying to take us. So if you're going to save your own neck, you're going to have to kill us and go on without us."

"I'm not planning on that."

"Then what are you going to do?"

"Arrange for someone to pick us up," I told her sharply. "Now you untie those lengths of rope from the tarp in the back seat of the car." When she did not move, I made a motion toward the pistol in my holster and said, "Go on!"

The girl went back to the car, and I stood there watching her, almost admiring her, thinking that she reminded me a little of Kristin or the way Kristin would have been if she had lived to be Sally's age. She had only been seventeen when she died. I tried not to think about her.

Sally pulled the tarp out, untied several lengths of rope, and brought them to me. She turned around, placed her hands behind her back, and waited silently while I tied them.

"Sit down," I told her, then knelt and tied her feet. "I'm going to have to gag you, y'know."

"I know. Don't tell me you're sorry. I don't want to hear it."

"Okay. Look, that robe you've got on, well, it's probably going to get warmer this afternoon. You'll be miserable if you leave it on."

"You want me naked, is that it?"

"I don't give a damn what you've got on," I said angrily. "I was just thinking about your comfort."

"Thanks!"

"Look, you've got that gown on under it. That's something."

"Not much." She paused. "Hell, take it off. You can rape me with the robe on if that's what you're after."

"I'm not going to rape you."

"Why not?"

"Oh, shit, woman!" Then I paused, looked at her, laughed. "I'm too damned tired, for one thing."

I knelt beside her, untied the rope, waited until she had unbuttoned the robe, and helped her slip it off. Then I retied her hands, carefully avoiding looking at her. She had the kind of body that was hard not to look at.

Then I took a fairly clean handkerchief from my pocket, knotted it, slipped the knot into her mouth, and tied it in place with another length of rope. Finally I pulled her back to where she could lean against a tree in what looked like a fairly comfortable position.

Von Heinen was sleeping or unconscious—I couldn't tell which—when I heaved him out of the car, carried him to within a few feet of Sally and tied and gagged him. I didn't particularly like the idea of trussing up a man as badly wounded as he was, but I wasn't in any position to take chances with his waking up and somehow freeing Sally.

"I'll be back in a few minutes," I told Sally, "and I won't be far away, so don't get any silly ideas about making noise. I'd hate to have to get rough with you."

Sally, of course, didn't answer, but she didn't have to. The way she felt about me was clear enough from her eyes. She'd have cut my throat laughing if she got the chance.

I looked one last time at Von Heinen, wondered how much longer he could live in his condition and then followed the path on toward the stand of young woods that lay a few yards from the grove of trees where Sally and her husband lay.

The woods, which probably had been farmland not too many years before, lay a half mile or so from the road, what there was of the road. And there was very little likelihood of any traffic along it. It didn't look as if there had been another motorcar on it for days.

When I was satisfied that I was well out of the range of Sally's hearing unless I yelled very loudly, I stopped and doglike relieved myself against the trunk of a tree. I felt better when I walked a few feet away and began doing what I had come back there to do.

First I took off my coat and carefully spread it out on a fairly level spot of earth and then sat down on the coat. Taking what appeared to be a windproof cigarette lighter from my pocket, I pulled it apart. It wasn't a lighter. It was a block of gray plastic with three tiny jacks in one end.

Next I removed what looked like a British-issue knife from its sheath on my left hip, held the blade in my right hand, the handle in my left and gave the blade a counterclockwise twist. The handle popped free. Up inside the handle nestled several feet of exceedingly thin wire, a fingernail-size microphone, and an equally small earphone.

I unrolled the wire, plugged one end of it into one of the jacks on the block, and then looped it over a tree branch above my head. Finally I plugged the microphone and the earphone into the two remaining jacks and I was "on the air."

In this Timeline, operating radio was still in its earliest infancy, though the grapevine had it that the Kriths were about to help the British "invent" the vacuum tube. As it was, a few spark-gap transmitters and cat's-hair and crystal receivers were being used by experimenters who predicted the day when radio—or wireless telegraphy—would be used for communications all over the world.

None of those wild-eyed visionaries had any idea that on Earths other than their own radio had reached and far exceeded their most fantastic dreams.

This tiny unit was far from being the most sophisticated radio I had used, but it was the best Kar-hinter had seen fit to give me. It would do the job. Its transmissions would be received at the main Krithian-Timeliner base on this Line which was near the Butt of Lewis on the Isle of Lewis in the Outer Hebrides—most of it underground. And that is where Kar-hinter would probably be right about now.

Why code names were necessary, I had no idea. There was no one on *this* Earth using this frequency. But Kar-hinter had required them should radio communications be necessary.

"Red mobile to red leader. Red leader, this is red mobile. Come in, red leader."

I felt like an ass sitting there on the soggy ground in the middle of nowhere, speaking code names into a little gray box, but that's the way the game is played.

"Red leader, this is red mobile. Red leader. . . ."

There was a crackle from the phone within my ear.

"Red mobile," said a voice that I didn't recognize, but thought was human, "this is red leader station. Stand by."

"Red mobile standing by."

There was silence for a long while. I assumed that the human operator had gone to get Kar-hinter.

I was right.

"Eric?" asked the Krith's voice.

"Yes, Kar-hinter. Late, but reporting."

"Are you safe?"

"As of the moment."

"Count von Heinen?"

"Alive, the last time I looked. I don't know how long he'll last, though. What about Tracy and Kearns?"

"Safe. They managed to get through the Imperial lines just after dawn. Hillary is in a field hospital now. He will be fine the doctors say."

"Good. Did they tell you what happened?"

"Yes, but they could give no explanations. Can you?"

I had the uneasy feeling that someone else was listening to me. I looked around, saw no one, felt foolish, and chalked it up to my imagination. I was just tired and getting jumpy. That's all.

"No. It doesn't make any sense. I've never seen a skudder like the one they were in."

"Nor I, from the descriptions." The Krith paused for a moment. "Can you tell me where you are?"

"Somewhere in France."

"I expected no more. We will be able to get a fix on you soon, Eric, but I do not know how soon we will be able to come after you."

"You can get a fix and then skud in from an adjacent Line, can't you?"

"We will, just as soon as a skudder is available to us. The one you used was the only one in this part of France on any nearby Line."

"The one at the station?"

"Damaged beyond repair."

"How?"

"A heat weapon of some sort, perhaps a thermal grenade."

"How long will I have to wait?"

"I cannot tell you as yet. Is your position exposed?"

"Not really, but I don't feel too safe."

"Do you think you can find shelter nearby?"

"I may. We passed some abandoned farmhouses a few miles back."

"That may do if there are no used roads nearby. Do you have a motorcar?"

"Yes."

"Use it if you must go get to a place of shelter and then hide it so that no one is likely to see it. Then transmit to us again so that we can get an exact fix on your new location. Perhaps then I can tell you how soon we can come in to pick you up."

"Okay. Anything else?"

"No, Eric. Except, do what you can for Von Heinen. We need him alive."

"I know. I will."

"Very good, Eric. That is all then. Out."

"Red mobile, out."

I disconnected the radio, carefully stowed the component parts back in their hiding places and shook out my damp coat.

The trail I had followed from the place where I had left Sally and the count continued on through the woods, fainter, apparently unused in years, but it offered the slight possibility that it might lead to something, a house, a farm. I decided to follow it a little way.

A dozen times I very nearly lost the trail as it wound through the woods, obscured by the growth of trees and brush, but at last I passed through the wood and out into a meadow. On the far side of the meadow, on a slight rise that was topped by a grove of very old poplars, stood the ruins of what once might have been a nobleman's secret retreat.

The house had not been large when it had been whole, and now less than a third of it was intact. It did not appear to have been damaged by the war, only by time, for it had stood there alone for many years, perhaps unknown by any living person. The west end of the house—or rather, cabin—was still covered by a roof, and as I crossed the meadow, I thought that perhaps a room or two might still be habitable, for a short time at least.

I approached the house cautiously, the energy pistol in my left hand, the Harling still in its holster, and heard nothing save the sudden movement of some tiny animal as it made its way out of the back, darting into the brush. I peered in through an open door hanging on rusty hinges, looking as if it were ready to fall at the slightest breeze.

The single surviving room was filled with the litter of years: leaves, twigs, the droppings of animals who had passed through it. There was no furniture, save an old pallet in one corner that someone, perhaps a passing hobo or a teen-age couple looking for a place to make love, had made from old blankets and straw. The pallet too was covered with twigs and leaves and obviously had not been used for years. The fireplace, which must have been grand at one time, was cracked, falling apart, and its hearth was covered with ashes that had been cold for half a decade or more.

But it was a shelter, and it appeared safe enough. It would be as good a place as any to wait for Kar-hinter.

I went back for Sally and the count, not looking forward to carrying the injured man that far.

When I returned, Sally appeared to be asleep. I stood over her for just a moment, looking down at her lush body which was not really covered by the torn gown, and for an instant I thought about doing exactly what I had told her I wasn't going to do to her. She *did* look inviting. But, hell, I told myself, this certainly wasn't the time or the place—and certainly not with Sally von Heinen, who hated my guts.

And, as I said, she did remind me a little of Kristin, and I remembered how she had been raped when she was seventeen by a gang of savage thugs, and I didn't think I could bring myself to act the way those bastards had.

I shook her gently.

"Wake up."

Her eyes opened with a start.

"I'm going to hide the car," I said. "Then we're going to take a little walk."

She just sat there and looked at me and hated me.

And I can't say that I blamed her too much.

11
The Cabin

Count von Heinen was still breathing, if weakly, and his pulse was a faint, though steady, thump under my finger when we finally arrived at the ruins of the cabin. Once or twice as we made the short trip that seemed to me to be miles long, he had stirred, jerked fitfully as if attempting to awaken from his unconscious slumber. He hadn't quite made it, and I wondered if he would ever awaken again unless he received medical attention soon. The bullet had been in his stomach for something like nine hours now, and no aid had been given him other than Kearns' compress and bandages. If Kar-hinter expected to get him alive, he'd damned well better hurry.

Inside the cabin's single surviving room Sally brushed the accumulation of debris from the old, moldy, rotten pallet, and I carefully laid the count on it. Surprisingly enough the wound had not begun to bleed again during the time I had carried him to the cabin, and I was grateful for that.

As for myself, well, I didn't feel that I was in much better condition than he was. I ached in every muscle and joint, and the graze wound in my side was a burning flame, and I wanted nothing more than to lie down and sleep for a week or two. But that would have to wait until after Kar-hinter came.

"Sit down," I briskly told the count's wife and took a piece of rope from my pocket to retie her hands.

"Do you mind . . ." She started to ask, then stopped short.

"Mind what?"

"Well, I have to go to the bathroom."

"There's no indoor plumbing here," I told her, "but there's a big world outside. I doubt that anyone would mind your using it."

"You'd trust me to go outside alone?"

"No."

She sat there glaring at me for a moment, then asked, "You wouldn't take my word?"

"No."

"I'll wait."

"For what?" I asked her. "If you've got to go, you've got to go."

"With you watching?"

I shrugged.

After a while she said, "Okay," very bitterly, and I followed her outside the cabin where she squatted on the ground, filled with shame, and relieved herself.

"I hope you enjoyed that, you degenerate voyeur," she said as she rose.

"No, not particularly," I said. "It's just a biological function."

She spat on the ground in front of me.

Hell, even beautiful women are human . beings. I learned that a long time ago. And at about the same time I learned that it's nothing to be ashamed of, being a human being.

When we got back into the cabin, I asked her if she'd like to put her robe back on. Maybe she'd be less self-conscious.

"What haven't you seen by now?" she asked.

"Not much."

"I'll leave the robe off for a while."

"Okay," I said, "I won't tie your hands, but you'd better just sit quietly on the floor. I have something that I have to do myself."

Clearing a space on the floor I removed my coat and quickly reassembled the radio. Before, I had still been wary of letting her see it, but now I felt safe enough. Barring a catastrophe I couldn't foresee, Sally would never tell anyone about this device that was alien to her world. Kar-hinter would come—soon, I hoped—she would be taken to an interrogation station, and during the painless mind probe her memories of this event, in fact, of everything that had happened since the predawn hours when we burst into the villa, would be removed. She would have no memories of strange men with stranger machines to spread to the rest of her world.

Though by this time I already had the suspicion that Sally knew a lot more about Timeliners than she was willing to admit, maybe a lot that even I didn't know.

She didn't speak as I assembled the transceiver, nor did she speak as I began to broadcast in Shangalis.

"Red leader, this is red mobile. Come in, red leader."

"This is Kar-hinter, Eric," said a tinny voice from the earphone. "Have you found a place of shelter?"

"Yes," I acknowledged. "I believe we're safe enough here."

"How is the count?"

"Still unconscious," I told him. "He's in pretty bad shape. You'd better hurry."

"I am doing the best I can," the Krith said. "But I must wait my turn. Skudders seem to be much in demand across the Lines today."

"Don't you have priority?"

"A high priority, yes, but not the highest. There are more important Lines than this one, you know."

I halfway wondered whether he might be wrong about that.

"How soon?" I asked.

"As yet I do not know." He paused. "Keep broadcasting. We are taking a fix on you now."

Two, three, or more direction finders were now beaming in on my transmitter, determining the exact location of it in relationship to the base stations. With no other radio signals to confuse them and with the kind of gear they had, it shouldn't be difficult for them to locate my position quite closely.

"You are sure of your safety?" Kar-hinter asked.

"Fairly sure. No one seems to have visited this place in years."

"Very well. Leave your unit on. As soon as I know when we will be able to come in for you, I will let you know. That is all for now. Red leader out."

I sighed with frustration, but there wasn't anything more I could do. It would have to be up to Kar-hinter now.

"Very well. Red mobile out."

I removed the earphone and laid it and the microphone beside the tiny block of the transceiver. I would leave it on for a while, then check back with Kar-hinter. The power cell inside the plastic block was good for hours of continuous operation.

Then I looked at Sally.

During the whole operation she had watched me with interest, but without astonishment, as if this were something she had rather expected.

"Who are you?" she asked as I found a fairly comfortable place to sit, pulled one of my few remaining cigarettes from my pocket, and lit it with a real lighter. I laid the energy pistol on the floor beside me; it was uncomfortable stuck in my belt when I was sitting down.

"Captain Eric Mathers, Royal British Army, Colonial Corps," I said flatly. I did not really expect her to believe it.

"No," she said, shaking her head. "You're no Englishman."

"I'm an American."

"American!" She almost laughed. "That wasn't English you were speaking just now."

"It was code."

"It didn't sound like code to me. It sounded like a formalized language."

"Have it your own way," I said, somewhat annoyed at her cross-examination, but also glad that she had finally begun to speak. Perhaps if she continued to talk, I would be able to learn a little of what she knew. I was damned curious. Maybe she was, too. Maybe that's why she was talking.

"Where *are* you from?" she asked.

"Virginia."

"Where in Virginia?"

"Victoria."

She smiled. "Do you know George Carter?"

The name meant nothing to me. It had been mentioned in none of the training tapes that the Kriths had fed into me when building my phony background, but still I thought I'd play it safe, though I had little hope of fooling her or little reason to, now. It was a game.

"The name sounds familiar. I'm not sure."

"Surely, if you're really from Victoria, you've heard of George Carter."

"I'm not sure. I've been away from home for a long time."

"Really now, Captain Mathers. George Carter served as mayor twice; then he was arrested for high treason in '64 or '65. It was a very big thing at the time. It must have been in the papers all over the Empire."

"Mike Trimble was mayor in '64," I told her. That was true.

"He was mayor before Mike Trimble."

"I thought Joe—ah—Joe Knight was." I was on shaky ground now.

"No, George Carter."

I wondered. I wasn't sure. The tapes hadn't been that detailed. Maybe a George Carter had been mayor of Victoria once.

"Don't you remember?" she asked, still smiling a sinister little smile. "He escaped from the provincial prison in Buffalo in '69. They've been searching for him ever since."

"No," I said flatly, deciding that she was inventing the whole thing to trap me into an admission. I was going to play the game all the way.

"Okay," she said, the smile fading. "I made it up. But I still don't believe you."

"Well, if I'm not an American, what am I?"

"That's what I want you to tell me."

"Okay," I said, giving her a smile of my own. "I'm a part of an invasion team from Mars. We're going to take over your planet next Tuesday."

"Do you really want it?" she asked, somehow returning my smile.

"It's better than Mars." And that was true, too. I've been there.

"You don't look like a Martian."

I can't say that I could really understand this apparent change of personality in her. Now she was talking to me on an almost-friendly basis, carrying on this joke. But then I wasn't too concerned about it either. A girl like Sally is nicer to be friends with than enemies.

"I'm in disguise," I told her. "Really I'm twelve feet tall with eight eyes and a dozen tentacles."

"I almost believe you."

"You might as well."

Von Heinen stirred, seemed for a moment as if he would awaken, then settled back, returned to the twilight state of unconsciousness.

"How bad is he?" Sally asked.

"Bad. A few more hours like this, and no one will be able to help him."

"You want to keep him alive, don't you?"

"That's my job."

"Were you calling for help just then?"

"Yes."

"Who?"

"My fellow Martians. They'll be landing in a flying saucer in the meadow out there in a few minutes."

"Flying saucer?"

"Forget it."

"I wish I could forget all of this."

"Maybe you will."

"What do you mean?"

"Nothing. You don't seem overly concerned about your husband."

"Should I be?"

"It's customary."

"He's a pig," Sally said slowly, bitterly. "But I don't want to see him die. We need him." She smiled a bitter smile. "Anyway, I suppose he's yours now."

"We'll give him back."

"Will you?"

"Yes."

"When?"

"When we're finished."

"Finished with what?"

"We want to ask him some questions."

"About the bomb?"

I nodded. Sally knew that we knew about the Baltic plant, so she was making no effort to hide it from me. How much more did she know? I was beginning to understand why Kar-hinter wanted her too.

"He doesn't know anything," she said.

"We'll find out."

"Your pleasure. But why me? You didn't kidnap me

just because I happened to be there. You could have left me tied up as you did Françoise."

"Françoise?"

"Albert's bedmate."

"The dark-haired girl with the big . . . ?"

Sally nodded, so I didn't say anything more about Francoise's very obvious physical attributes.

"I would have taken her along if I could have," I said, imitating a leer.

"Albert told me she was *good*," Sally said. "A better piece than me, he told me once."

"Is that why you hate him?"

"Because of her? Her kind's a shilling a dozen."

"Then why?"

"I'll hate people for whatever reasons I want. Why did you take me?"

"You're Archer Beall's daughter."

"Oh," Sally said, "you're also trying to find out just how closely the ARA is working with the Holy Romans?"

I nodded, though I wasn't really sure what Kar-hinter did want to learn from her.

"You don't have to force that out of me," she said. "Closer than I want, but not as close as the count and his friends would like."

"That doesn't tell me much, except that you don't like the Imperials."

"You didn't have to kidnap me to find that out."

"I think I get this much of the picture," I said. "You don't much like having the Imperials as allies, but they're the best available."

"They've got the only game in town," Sally said. "The Nippons don't give a damn about what happens in the Western world, and Spain doesn't have what it takes to try to buck Britain."

"What happens when the war's over, if the Germans win?"

"That doesn't worry me too much."

"Shouldn't it?"

"No," she said flatly.

"You mean to say that you think the ARA can defeat them whereas it can't beat the British?"

"The war's not over yet, one way or the other."

"No, it's not," I agreed. "But it seems to me that a world ruled by Britain would be preferable to one ruled by the Imperials."

She laughed very bitterly. "The only thing worse than an Imperial pig is a British pig. I'd shoot myself before I'd side with them."

"You really hate the British that much?"

"I really hate the British—and anyone who works with them. Even Martians or whatever you are."

"I'm sorry."

"Like hell you are."

"I am."

"Shit!" From her the word was startling.

She turned away, and we were both silent for a long while. I guess I'd blown that one.

Early afternoon was slowly changing into late afternoon, and shadows were lengthening across the meadow below. The warmth of the day was passing suddenly.

I got up, built a fire in the crumbling fireplace that filled the room with smoke, carefully moved Von Heinen closer to the fire, and checked his pulse again.

"He's still alive at least," I said.

"Good." There was little conviction in her voice.

I picked up her robe and held it out for her. "You want this?"

She looked at me for a moment, then rose, took the robe from my hands, threw it across her shoulders, sat back down and muttered, "Thanks."

I went back to the radio, slipped the phone into my ear, and said into the mike in Shangalis, "Red mobile to red leader."

"Red leader station here," came an immediate reply, but the voice was not Kar-hinter's.

"Anything new?" I asked.

"Not yet. We have your position, but no skudder is available yet. Please be patient."

"I'll do my best, but I can't guarantee how long Von Heinen's going to live."

"I'll pass that on to Kar-hinter when he returns."

"You do that."

"Red leader station out."

"Red mobile out," I said with disgust and then added in English, "Screw you, Jack."

"You sound unhappy," Sally said as I pulled the phone out of my ear.

"Just getting impatient." I looked at her for a moment, decided that she was ready to talk again. "I don't suppose you happened to bring a box lunch with you?"

"No one told me it was going to be a picnic."

"Sorry. An oversight on my part."

I fished my last cigarette from my pocket, lit it with an ember from the fire, and felt very annoyed with everything.

"I'm tired and I'm hungry and my side hurts like hell and I'm on my last cigarette and I think one of my patients is going to die on me," I said slowly, "so, Countess von Heinen, I do wish you'd give me some straight answers."

"About what?"

"For example, who were those men?"

"What men?" The innocence on her face was thin, transparent. She knew exactly who they were.

"You know who I mean. The ones who tried to rescue you and the count."

"I have no idea."

"You're lying."

"Are you going to beat it out of me?"

"If I get annoyed enough, I just might."

"I wouldn't like that."

"I wouldn't either."

"You'd probably rather try to rape it out of me."

"Is that an invitation?"

"I thought those were standard tactics."

"Rape? What do you mean?"

She shrugged.

"Just tell me," I said.

"You know," she answered slowly, "my father was called a traitor all his life, and I've been called that more times than I can remember, but so help me God, Captain Mathers, I'm an amateur at the game of treason compared to you."

"Now what are you talking about?"

"You and your kind." She paused. "I've fought

against the rule of a foreign nation imposed on my land, and I'm called a traitor for it. But you—you and your kind are selling out the whole human race. What do they call that?"

"I don't know what you're talking about. Wait—you don't *believe* what I said about Martians?"

"No, not Martians, something infinitely worse."

Did she know about the Kriths? Was that what she meant? It didn't seem possible. That was the most carefully guarded secret on this planet. But then. . . .

"I'll be glad when they get you into interrogation," I said. "Then maybe I'll find out whether you're really crazy."

"I doubt that you'll ever find out very much that way, Captain Mathers. And I strongly suggest that you keep your hand away from both your weapons."

"Stay right where you are," a masculine voice said slowly in English, and it was a voice that wasn't Von Heinen's. "Don't turn around."

Then I heard a swishing in the air—and the universe exploded in the back of my head. The last thing I remember was the look of triumph on Sally's face as I slumped forward and lost consciousness.

12
Captive

Mostly there was redness and flickering lights and pain from the back of my head, and the universe had an unpleasant, nauseating tendency to spin. Somewhere a long, long way off I heard a voice speaking.

". . . got the radio on the air it wasn't much trouble to find you."

"I was wondering if you'd ever come," replied a voice that I recognized as Sally's. The other voice I tentatively identified as that of the man who had slugged me.

"I'm sorry it took so long." His voice spoke Sally's English with an odd, almost intangible accent that wasn't German. Like me, English wasn't his native tongue, but I couldn't tell what was.

"That's okay. What about Albert?" Sally asked.

"Mica says he stands a good chance of living if we can get the bullet out soon."

"Where are we going?"

"Staunton."

"Here?"

There was an odd accenting to the way she said the word, as if she were referring to some special kind of "here."

"We'll stay in this Paratime," the man said. "We won't shift Von Heinen unless his condition gets worse. But Mica believes that Sol-Jodala can fix him up in Staunton."

"I hope so," Sally said.

"I thought you hated him."

"We still need him."

"I suppose we do."

By this time I had worked up the courage to open my eyes. I was lying on a floor—or deck—of some kind of craft, behind a row of seats. Metal walls extended up about waist-high, then fused into a transparent roof that

105

formed a dome above. Through the dome all I could see was a reddish evening sky, and though I had the sensation of motion, I could not be certain that we were actually moving.

My feet and hands were tied, and the rope that bound my hands was in turn lashed to a cargo ring set into the metal deck on which I lay. I could move, but not much.

By lifting my head up as far as the pain would allow, I could see the tops of two heads above the seats in front of me. One was Sally's blondness, the other dark. The man, I assumed.

I could not see what was behind me, but I had the feeling that I was near the rear end of the craft—and I assumed that the craft was the egg-shaped alien skudder that I had seen before.

Where was Von Heinen? I wondered. Were Sally and the man the only other people in the machine? But then, I supposed they could have been traveling in more than one.

"What are you going to do with Mathers?" Sally asked after a long silence.

"I don't know yet," the man answered. "Take him to Staunton with us now. We'll let Mica decide what to do with him then."

"You don't expect to get any information out of him, do you?"

"Him? No, not really. I've seen his kind often enough before. He's tough enough to stand up under just about any physical torture and the sort of mind blocks the Kriths put on their hired hands are impossible to break without killing the subject. No, if he tells us anything—if he even knows anything we don't—he'll only give it to us because he wants to."

"Do you expect him to want to?" Sally asked.

"Not really. But you can never tell. Some of them will listen to reason, but not many."

"And if he doesn't cooperate?"

"I suppose we'll kill him," the man said matter-of-factly.

"I hope you don't have to," Sally said.

"For God's sake why? He shot Von Heinen and kidnapped you."

"He wasn't unnecessarily brutal about it. He just talked mean."

"You're getting soft, girl. Is that what love does to you?"

"Love?" Sally asked.

"Yes, you and Mica . . ." The man let his voice fade away as if he were realizing that he was making some kind of mistake that he really didn't understand.

The craft lurched slightly as if hit by a gust of wind, and then I was sure that we were in motion, physical motion. We weren't skudding, I was sure of that. You don't mistake *that* flickering for anything but what it is.

"No," Sally was saying, going on as if the man hadn't made his last comment. "I don't think he knows what he's doing. I mean, I believe he's sincere."

"Most of them are," the man said, "but the Kriths have them so brainwashed that they'll never come around. I'm sorry if you've taken a liking to him, Sally, but we'll probably have to kill him."

"Okay, old top," I said to myself, "you've just made yourself a dyed-in-the-wool convert to whatever brand of the One True God you're selling. I'll play your games if that's what it takes to keep me alive." And I meant to stay alive long enough to find out what the hell was going on.

"Do you think I'd better check on him?" Sally asked.

Where had all the hatred gone? I wondered. Was she one of those people who hates the enemy with a purple passion until he's beaten and then knocks herself out being kind to him when they've got him down? Okay, that would be all the better.

"No," the man was answering. "He'll be fine. I didn't hit him that hard. Just enough to keep him dazed for a while. Let him be. You'll have plenty of time to nurse his wounds when we get to Staunton, if that's what you want."

"Okay," Sally said.

"You just sit here and keep me company. We've got a long flight ahead of us. Care for some coffee? There's a flask and some sandwiches in the hamper there."

"Thanks," Sally answered. "I'm starving."

The sky above the flying skudder was growing darker

by the minute, turning from red to purple, and it looked as if stars would begin to appear soon. I wondered where we were and where we were going.

None of it made any sense yet. Sally and the man seemed to know all about the Kriths and Timeliners. But who were they, Sally and the man? Timeliners themselves? Of a sort, I gathered. But who? And why? And what were they doing here? And where did this machine come from? And why did they call me a traitor? Didn't they know what the Kriths were doing—trying to save humanity, a hell of a lot of humanities on various Earths, from an invasion in the future?

They must have known, I told myself. The man had spoken of encountering others like me, of trying to convince them of something. Surely they would have told them why the Kriths were spreading across the Lines, why we Timeliners fought for them.

But, since they must have been told, they apparently hadn't believed it. And what could I be able to say or do to convince them? Nothing, probably. So, when the time came, I'd put up a few feeble arguments to whatever it was that they were going to try to sell me, then pretend to go along with them. That might give me a chance to stay alive a while, learn something and then maybe get back to Kar-hinter with what I had learned.

If it worked out—which seemed sort of unlikely at the moment, what with my lying trussed up on the floor of some alien kind of skudder—if it worked out, it would prove to be a lot more than Kar-hinter had ever bargained for when he sent us out to kidnap the count and his wife.

Just what had I stumbled into?

I figured that was enough thinking for the moment. My head still hurt like hell, and my empty stomach was more than a bit uneasy, and I was exhausted. The only logical thing to do was get a little sleep.

So I did.

When I awoke, rain was splattering against the dome above me at a high velocity. I couldn't really see it or hear it well, but I knew it was rain. The dome was pitch dark, and I could see nothing beyond it.

In the front of the craft faint panel lights glowed, reflecting from the dome. The craft was quiet except for the hum of whatever propulsion it used and it was something I couldn't identify. It seemed to be nothing I had ever encountered before—and I had driven or ridden in just about everything from goat carts to grav cars to spaceships.

I heard a feminine sigh from the front and then the sound of motion, a body rising, straightening itself.

"I guess I fell asleep," Sally said.

"You needed it," the man answered. "You should have slept longer."

"How long has it been?"

"Oh, a couple of hours, I guess."

"Where are we?"

"Mid-Atlantic. We ought to be in Staunton by midnight."

"We've run into a storm," Sally commented.

"Not a bad one. Radar says we ought to clear it in ten minutes or so. I think your friend back there is awake."

"Mathers?"

"Yes, you want to go check on him?"

"Okay."

Again the sound of movement, then a flashlight bobbing as Sally walked the few feet back to where I lay. For an instant I could see her silhouetted against the panel lights, dressed now in what looked like a form-fitting flight suit. I hoped that I would be able to see it in better light.

Then the beam of the flashlight was in my eyes, and I had to blink.

"How are you?" Sally asked, kneeling beside me.

"I'd be okay if I could find the rest of my head," I said.

"Scoti," she said, calling back over her shoulder.

"Yes?" the man replied.

"I'm going to untie him and bring him up front. Is that okay?"

"Do you have a gun?"

"The one you gave me."

"Make sure he knows it and that you'll use it."

"I know," I said.

"Okay, Mathers, but watch your step. Sally's a good shot. And if that isn't enough, you can remind yourself that I'm just as fast as you are, maybe faster. Augmentation, you people call it."

"Yeah," I said.

Sally knelt, placed the light on the deck beside the ring around which my ropes were tied, and quickly loosened them. She then slipped the flashlight into a pocket, but I could see her silhouette as she rose, pulled a small pistol from another pocket, and said, "Get up slowly. Do exactly what I say."

"Yes, ma'am," I said, awkwardly stumbling to my feet, then biting my lip against the pain that throbbed in the back of my head. The way I felt I doubted that I could have gone into augmentation even if I'd wanted to.

"That way," Sally said, gesturing toward the front of the craft with her pistol. "Take the seat behind Scoti."

Scoti turned out to be a stocky, dark man with almond eyes, apparently an improbable blending of Italian and Nipponese, but then he could have been anything from any When for all I knew.

"Remember," Scoti said as I sat down behind him, glancing over his shoulder, "Sally won't hesitate to put a bullet between your eyes if you do the slightest thing out of line."

"I'll remember," I said, and I wondered whether she would. She might.

"Are you hungry?" Sally asked, taking a seat opposite me, leveling the small pistol at me.

In the light of the control panel I could see the cream-colored outfit she wore a little better. It was some sort of flight suit, as I had thought earlier, and apparently one made just for her unless the material from which it was made adjusted itself to whatever body wore the suit. It fitted her like a second skin, and that certainly wasn't bad on her.

"I think I could eat something," I said.

Sally nodded and, always keeping an eye on me, went forward to a hamper, extracted a thermal flask, a cup, and a plastic-wrapped sandwich. She came back to where I sat, loosened the ropes that still held my hands together, and handed me the sandwich. Sitting down again, she placed the pistol in her lap and poured me a cup of coffee.

"Thanks," I said.

There was no talking in the craft while I wolfed down the sandwich and coffee.

When I was finished, feeling more nearly alive, Scoti looked back at me for a moment, then said, "Let me spell it out, Mathers, so there's no mistake. We know who you are, what you are and why you're here. Kriths, skudders, Timeliners, we know it all. So you don't have to play any silly games about hiding it from us. Okay?"

"Who are you?" I asked coldly, looking across the top of my coffee cup.

"My name is Scoti Hauser Angelus," the craft's pilot said in the same tone. "I am from what you would probably call a Romano-Albigensian Timeline a long way to the Parawest of here, and I am here to prevent you and your masters from accomplishing your ultimate goals."

Well, I thought, he *had* come straight to the point. From the West, he had said. That was possible, perhaps even probable and why I hadn't thought of it before, I didn't know. The Timeline we presently occupied was about as far West as we and the Kriths had ever come in force. Of course there had been some explorations farther into the Temporal West, but not very far to my knowledge —there were hardly enough Timeliners and Kriths to do the job now, much less expend manpower exploring. Yes, for all we knew there could be another civilization with cross-Lining capabilities farther to the T-West, but why they should feel as they seemed to feel about Kriths and Timeliners I still had no idea.

I looked over at Sally.

"She's a *local*," Scoti said.

In a way I was relieved.

"Can you explain all this to me?" I asked.

"I think it's better if we don't even try for the time being," Scoti said. "Just wait until we get to our destination; then you can ask all the questions you want."

I finished my coffee, sat back in the seat, glanced at the ugly little pistol in Sally's pretty little hand, then looked up at the dome that covered the craft and at the stars that were beginning to break through the layers of cloud and tried to remember what I could of a place called Staunton.

The name, after I thought about it for a while, seemed
to have some special significance. I was sure that I had
heard of it before. It had been in the training tapes. A
tiny, many-legged creature scuttled through my mind,
knocking around pieces and bits of ideas, concepts, memories—and the proper pieces fell into place.

Staunton: (1) a town in Virginia, Shenandoah Valley
or that area, that had been the rallying point of the
American Republican Army during the uprising of the
1920's. In '28 or '29, I couldn't remember which, British
regulars surrounded Staunton, boxed in the rebels and
held them under siege for thirty-seven days. Finally the
town caught fire; the rebels, half-dead of starvation, made
an attempt to break through the British lines and were
slaughtered. The British kept the town surrounded until
the fire had burned itself out and nearly all the inhabitants had perished. The cream of the ARA died in
Staunton, as did several thousand innocent civilians who
were caught in the town. It was a bitter memory for the
rebels and one that they weren't going to easily forget.

But that wasn't all there was to the name Staunton.
There was something else and I slowly dug it out.

Staunton: (2) rumor had it that somewhere in West
Florida the rebels had begun building a secret city. The
stories first began in the late fifties, as well as I could remember from the training tapes, and were quite common
for a few years. Most of the rumors were something to
this effect: somewhere back in the wilderness of southern
West Florida the ARA and the Mad Anthony Wayne
Society were building an underground city where they
would store arms, train troops and in general prepare for
the great uprising that would one day free America from
the British Empire.

Countless aerial searches had been made by the British
with absolutely no luck. Soldiers had gone into the West
Floridian forests and marched across hundreds of square
miles without finding any trace of this new Staunton.
Finally, in disgust, the British gave up and attributed
the whole thing to gossip, rumor, and just plain American
madness.

So there it stood.

But now I was ready to believe that there really was a

secret city, a hidden, unknown Staunton that was a hell of a lot more than the British had ever imagined, that was a base for Outtimers who were assisting the American rebels and the Holy Roman Empire.

Okay, I said to myself, we'll find out for sure soon.

Outside the craft the night was as dark as ever with no sign of a moon, though the stars shone brightly now that we had left the clouds behind us. Below, the Earth was a mass of unrelieved blackness, a nothingness. Then, very faintly, off to my left, south of the craft, I saw lights, a city on the horizon.

While I watched the lights, my mind still turning over all the information I had gathered since returning to consciousness, Scoti began angling the craft more to the south, in the direction of the city.

"I was a little off," he said to Sally. "That's Charleston down there."

Sally looked up, startled, as if she had been deep in thought. "Oh," she said, "I didn't realize we were so close to land."

"It's not as far as it was," Scoti said.

We passed directly over the mass of lights that was the chief harbor city of southern Virginia, Charleston, and lay near the borders of the provinces of Virginia and Florida, the way North America was laid out and subdivided in this Here and Now. Off to the right and left small masses of light lined the coast, revealing the shape of the shore where the sea ended and the American land began.

Soon, however, the coastal cities dwindled behind us and the darkness of the great and mostly undeveloped North American continent lay below us. We moved south and west, toward the forests of West Florida and the secret city.

I wondered what I was going to find there. And maybe I was a little bit frightened.

13
Staunton

I have no idea what time it was when we arrived at our destination. Earlier I had heard Scoti say something about midnight, but I'm not sure that's what time it really was when we got there. Whatever time it was, it was quite dark, though the night was pleasantly warm and crickets, frogs, things I couldn't identify sounded in the distance as I stepped down from the craft, Sally and Scoti each holding a pistol on me.

The grass-covered field itself was quite small and irregular in shape, perhaps a hundred feet long by twenty-five feet wide at its widest, but then it hadn't been designed for use by any conventional type of aircraft. One end of the field ended in a clump of trees, some real, some apparently artificial, that sheltered the hangar. Inside the hangar were two more craft something like the one in which I had just arrived. It was then that I realized that the craft I had been riding in was not the skudder that I had seen before, but a smaller one. The skudder that had carried the men who had tried to rescue the count and Sally was sitting inside the hangar, two or three yet unpatched bullet holes in its hull still revealing the battles of the night before.

I didn't have much time to look around right then. Scoti prodded me forward as half a dozen men and women, all dressed in the same sort of cream-colored flying suits that Sally and Scoti wore, came out of the hangar and toward us, flashlights in their hands.

"I am glad you made it, Scoti," said a tall, cadaverous-looking man when we were within speaking distance. He nodded to Sally, a strange, proprietary smile on his face. "I hope your ordeal was not too unpleasant."

"What about Von Heinen?" Scoti asked without waiting for Sally to reply to the other man.

"He is in the hospital," he answered, then turned to

look at me coldly, clinically as if I were a bug under a microscope.

"How is he, Mica?" Scoti asked.

"Very close to dying. Trebum is standing by with the other sautierboat in case he doesn't make it. Sol-Jodala will then cold-sleep him and try to revive him in Altheon."

"Don't you think you should go on and transfer him now if he's that bad?" Scoti asked.

"Sol-Jodala says to wait," the tall man said, "and in this case I must defer to them." Then he turned and looked at me again, something that I interpreted as contempt flickering across his face for a moment. Then he smiled, but it was a very artificial kind of smile. "Good morning, Captain Mathers. I trust that you had a pleasant trip."

"I'm afraid that you have the advantage of me, sir," I said with the same fake cordiality.

"Yes, in more ways than one," he said, his smile shifting to one of satisfaction, "but please forgive me. I am called Mica."

"Are you in charge here?" I asked.

"Yes, in some respects I am," Mica answered, the cold, bitter smile returning to his lips. "Why do you ask?"

"Just wondering."

Mica nodded to me, then turned to Sally.

"You must be exhausted, my dear," he said. "Go on to bed. You can fill me in on the background tomorrow." Without waiting for her to answer, Mica gestured to one of the men with him, who took Sally by the arm and led her off through the trees beyond the hangar. From the look on Sally's face the man was an old friend; she was home now, safe among those she knew and trusted.

"Scoti," Mica said, "take Captain Mathers to his quarters. G'lendal can check him, if that will satisfy her inquisitive urges, but I will wait until after breakfast to talk with him." He looked at me again. "It has been a very long day for us all, do you not agree, Captain Mathers?"

I nodded, but didn't speak. It was a rhetorical question anyway.

Pointing with a pistol toward a path that led into the woods in a direction opposite from the one that Sally had taken, Scoti told me to get moving. A second man followed close behind, a flashlight and another pistol pointed at the back of my head.

"Do you know where we are, Mathers?" Scoti asked.

"I have a pretty good idea."

"And do you know what this place is?"

"Your base, I suppose."

"Our major base in this Paratime."

I walked on, waiting for him to say something more, but apparently he had decided that there was little point in talking about it now. Time for that later, maybe.

"Take the next path to your right," Scoti said after a while.

In the darkness I could hardly see the path until I was on it, but Scoti had apparently known where it was long before we neared it. I had the feeling that Scoti knew his way around here pretty well—and that I would be a damned fool if I thought I could escape from him in the dark.

"Okay, hold it," Scoti said.

I stopped, looked in front of me. The man with the flashlight stepped around Scoti and me and illuminated a small structure in the darkness. It was a concrete cube, perhaps four feet high, concealed in clumps of bushes and trees that grew high above it, dark, heavy, towering long-leaf pines. In the side of the concrete structure was a metal door. The flashlightman opened the door by pressing his hand in a shiny spot and stood back, waiting.

"In," Scoti said, gesturing with his pistol as the door opened.

Ducking down, almost on my hands and knees, I entered the dark opening that immediately became lighted as my presence triggered some kind of mechanism. A staircase led downward from the door to a landing fifteen or so feet below. Beyond the landing I could see nothing.

"Go on," Scoti said, "but not too fast."

I went down the stairs, straightening up as soon as the ceiling got to a decent height, and at the bottom waited for Scoti and the other man.

Now I was standing at one end of a pale-green corridor that extended as far as I could see, finally dwindling in the distance to a vanishing point. Every few feet a bluish-white light burned in the ceiling, more than sufficient to illuminate the corridor. Off in the distance I heard or felt the operation of machinery, but what kind I could not even guess.

There was a door every fifteen or twenty feet on both the right and left, each carefully labeled with characters of an alphabet that I had never before come across in all my cross-Line travels, and I was struck again by the fact that I was dealing with people whose existence was not even suspected by Timeliners and Kriths. If I ever got out of it, wouldn't I have a report to turn in!

"Move," Scoti said, "straight ahead."

Since Scoti's gun looked as mean and ugly as ever, and since my head still hurt like hell and since I didn't know what else to do anyway, I moved as I was told, down the corridor to whatever it was that Scoti and Mica had in mind for me.

At regular intervals, which I guessed to be about a hundred feet apart, other corridors branched off this one to the right and left at 90 degrees. These other corridors were painted the same pale, hospital green and seemed to extend to the underground horizon. This was an enormous place here under the earth.

When we came to the third intersection, Scoti told me to turn left and keep going. I did, counting my paces as I walked.

At first we seemed to be the only ones in the vast, subterranean burrow, but when we had gone a hundred feet or so down the branch tunnel, a door opened before us. A pale blond young man stepped out, nodded to Scoti and the other man, and walked down the corridor in the direction from which we had just come. The fact that he was stark naked except for a wide green belt and a cap of the same color on his head aroused no comment from my captors and seemed to cause the young man no embarrassment. I shrugged.

We stopped for traffic at the next intersection. A man and a woman, both blacks, were coming down the corridor that crossed ours. They wore short, white, sleeveless gowns that reached to their knees. They stopped when they saw us, raised their hands in greeting.

"Good morning, Sol-Jodala," Scoti said.

"Good morning to you, Scoti, and to you, Nardi," the

man said with a clipped accent that sounded British but wasn't. "A prisoner?"

"Yes," my captor said. "A Krithian Timeliner working with the British."

"Not the man who kidnapped Sally and the count?" the woman asked, her voice almost identical to the man's.

They all seemed to act as if I weren't there or at least couldn't understand them even though they were speaking English.

"The same," Scoti answered.

The two peered at me for a moment with an animal-in-the-zoo-behind-bars look, then seemed to realize that I was a human being who was aware of them, nodded abruptly and turned back to Scoti.

"How is Sally?" the man asked.

"The poor girl's exhausted," he said, "but other than that she's okay. A few hours' rest will fix her up."

"We just looked in on the count," the woman said. "We believe that he will pull through. The crisis seems to be past."

"I'm glad to hear that," Scoti replied.

"Excuse us, please," the man said. "Morning meditations, you know." Again that pseudo-British accent, but it seemed natural.

"Of course," Scoti said. "Good day, Sol-Jodala."

"Good day," they answered together.

As they turned and started down the corridor, the oddness of it all struck me. The whole time they had not looked at each other or even seemed to recognize the existence of each other, yet they had alternated in speaking, first one, then the other, and now as they walked away I saw that their steps, the swinging of their arms, every motion was perfectly synchronized. Odd, I thought.

"Let's go," Scoti said. "It's not much farther."

Two intersections or so later we finally stopped. The door before which Scoti told me to halt was no different from any of the others and labeled in the same unintelligible alphabet.

Scoti fished a small metal cylinder out of his pocket, peered at one end of it while he twisted a movable band, then seemed to be satisfied and pressed the cylinder against a small white disk on the door. The door hummed and began to swing open.

For half an instant I had my chance. When Scoti stepped back to allow the door to open, it came between us. I stood more beside than in front of the other man and he was watching the door, not me, his gun lax in his hand. Augmentation or no, I'm sure that I could have grabbed the gun from him, shot Scoti before he realized what was happening and then the second man. But what if I did? Killing or escaping from these two just wouldn't have done me a whole hell of a lot of good. In less time than it took to think of it, I decided to play along with my original plan. I'd do as they said and pretend to accept whatever they wanted me to accept, and with my Krithian training and conditioning I believed that I could fool any lie-detection equipment anyone ever made or ever would make. Okay. Play it safe.

"In," Scoti said to me. Then to the other man, "Nardi, you keep an eye on him. I'll go tell G'lendal he's here, and then I'm going to get some rest. I don't think I've slept in three days."

To my surprise Nardi spoke. I had almost come to think he was mute. "Okay," he said. "You look beat."

"I am," Scoti said. "See you later." Then he turned to me. "Watch it, Mathers. I know you're no fool, but don't even think about acting like one.

"Thanks for the advice," I said and stepped through the open doorway, wondering just what was waiting for me inside.

The room was not small and ill-lighted and fitted out with torture devices as I had expected. Just the opposite. The room was a good twenty by twenty feet, pleasant and comfortable-looking. The furniture consisted of a bed, two easy chairs, a sofa, two unusual-looking lamps, two low tables, three landscapes on the wall, and a device that looked like some kind of intercom. Off to the left a door opened into what appeared to be a bathroom and another door led into a closet. A rather comfortable dungeon, I thought.

"Sit down, Mathers," Nardi said, gesturing toward the chairs and sofa. "Just take a load off your feet until G'lendal gets here."

I did as he said, realizing that despite the sleep I had got in the skudder, I was still pretty well worn out.

"You wouldn't have a cigarette on you, would you?" I asked.

Nardi, still standing in the center of the room, reached into his breast pocket, pulled out a partially crumpled pack of cigarettes, Players, local origin, and a book of matches. He tossed them on the sofa beside me.

"Go ahead," he said.

"Thanks. You want one?"

"No," he answered, sitting down on the bed, keeping his eyes on me.

"Who's this G'lendal, anyway?" I asked.

"She's our chief interrogator."

"Interrogator?"

Nardi smiled. "Oh, don't worry. We don't use rubber hoses and thumbscrews. She'll just ask you a few questions and see how you react to them."

"And if I don't react right?"

"Look, fella, Scoti didn't bring you here to torture you. Tomorrow, I guess, Mica will explain the whole setup to you. If you listen to reason and if G'lendal believes you, then you'll probably be put on probation. If not . . . well, if you're too damned hardheaded to see the truth when it's shown to you, that's your tough luck." He paused. "But as for right now all G'lendal's going to do is feel you out."

On the table beside the sofa where I sat was an ashtray and three worn books stacked on top of each other. I picked them up and glanced at their paper covers. The top one showed the picture of a Krith, a particularly ugly and unpleasant-looking Kirth at that, and the book's title was *The Greatest Lie*, by Martin Latham, subtitled *How Uncounted Human Beings Have Been Duped by the Kirths into Assisting Them in Their Conquest of Paratime*. The back cover, embellished with a full-length portrait of a naked Krith standing over a huddled man, went on to say something like: "Here, for the first time in a single volume, is Martin Latham's full story of the Krithian plot to conquer humanity. How their lies are created and how men are led to believe them. How Krithian lies are reinforced by distortions of reality. What

some men will do in the name of Krithian domination . . ."
and so on like that.

The second book was smaller than the first and not as badly worn. On its cover were only four words in letters at least an inch and a half high: *What Is a Krith?*

Good question. I'd like to know the answer to that one myself.

The final volume showed a full-color holograph of a beautiful nude woman standing against a background of Eden-like surroundings. It was called *Paradise in Paratime* and was subtitled *Rewards for the Ultimate Treason.*

Propaganda, all of it. And I realized that I was just beginning to encounter it. These people obviously believed, or wanted to believe, that the Kriths—and we Timeliners too—were a menace, and I knew that I was going to be pelted with it until I yielded or at least appeared to yield. I supposed that reading these books would be a part of my indoctrination. Okay, I'd read them.

Even though the cover of *Paradise in Paratime* intrigued me the most, I put it aside for *The Greatest Lie.* That one looked like the chief propaganda work—and as I later found out it was virtually the bible of the Paratimers—so I figured I'd better read it first and try to get my own lies in order.

I hadn't got beyond the title page when the door opened.

G'lendal, too, was a very pleasant surprise. I had expected a middle-aged, stocky, hard-faced policewoman type. She was anything but that.

At least twenty years old, but certainly no older than twenty-five, G'lendal was a diminutive ebony statue of Aphrodite straight from one of the more sensual cults of my own Line. About five feet tall, skin the color of black satin, hair long and black as interstellar space, a figure only partially hidden by the shimmering gown she wore, a figure whose proportions would have been impressive on a woman a foot taller than she was.

God, she's beautiful, I thought. Maybe the most beautiful woman I've ever seen in my life.

In her hand she carried a black case about the size and shape of a large overnight case.

"Good morning, Nardi," she said smiling.

"Hello, G'lendal," he replied, stumbling over his words as if he were as stunned by her as I was. "This is Eric Mathers."

I stood up.

"Good morning, Eric Mathers," she said, smiling, setting the case on the floor beside one of the chairs. "That's not your real name, is it?" There was no trace of an accent in the American English she spoke.

"No," I said as she sat down in the chair and I returned to the sofa.

"That's a name the Kriths gave you," she said. "There aren't any Kriths here. You can be honest with me. In fact, you must."

I looked at her for a long while without speaking.

"You know why I'm here, don't you?"

"I think so."

"Then let's be honest. You can start by telling me your real name."

Why not? I asked myself. There wasn't much point in pretending to be a British colonial when everybody knew I wasn't.

"Thimbron Parnassos," I said at last, and it was the truth.

"I think I shall call you Eric. It is easier to say."

"It's up to you."

"Now listen to me, Eric," she said earnestly. "We're not your enemies here unless you make us be. I only want to help you. Your whole life has been a series of lies and you had no way of knowing that you were being told lies. If you'll merely be open-minded about it, you'll see the truth."

"And what is this truth you want me to see?"

"That the Kriths are monsters determined to enslave the human race," she said slowly.

"That's kind of hard for me to swallow," I told her. "I've only seen them helping us."

"In due time it will all be explained to you. All I ask, all that any of us asks, is that you listen."

"Okay," I said. "I've been given to understand that if I don't, I'll probably get my head blown off."

"Probably," she said and smiled. "Now I'd like to run a

few tests on you just to establish some reference points."

"Tests?"

"To establish truth indices, you might say. Will you co-operate?"

"Would it matter if I didn't?"

"I would prefer to use as few drugs as possible."

"Okay, let's get on with it."

G'lendal smiled again. "Very good, Eric."

She rose from the chair, placed her case on the table beside the sofa. "First I'd like for you to take your clothes off and give them to Nardi," she said. "Then you may go into the bathroom and shave and shower, if you like. I'm sure it would make you feel better."

Nardi had a gun in case I didn't do as she said, so I undressed.

"Everything," she said, smiling when I got down to my shorts and paused for a moment. "I'm sorry if it embarrasses you, but it's necessary."

I nodded, unsnapped the shorts, and let them drop to the floor. I stood there as bare-naked as the day I was born, and it didn't seem to bother anyone but me. I suppose I'd been around the British too long.

"Roll them up and hand them to Nardi, please," G'lendal said, neither looking at me nor ignoring me as she opened her case and reached inside. "Your personal possessions—if you have any left—will be inspected and returned to you." She glanced over her shoulder at Nardi. "I assume that Scoti checked him," she said.

Nardi nodded. "He got all the dangerous stuff off him while he was unconscious." Nardi didn't look at me while he spoke. "He's an Augie, of course."

"Of course," G'lendal replied.

She had taken several small objects from her case and now held them in her hands.

"I assume that your augmentation control center is located between your shoulder blades?" she asked.

I nodded. I thought she could have found it easily enough even if I denied it.

"Hold still for a moment, please," she said. "This won't hurt at all, but it will render your augmentation controls useless."

She approached my naked back and pressed cold metal

against it. There was a short shrill buzzing, and I felt something dying within me, electrobiological circuits being killed. As she said, it didn't hurt—at least not physically. I felt as though I had lost a part of me.

"That's all there is to it," she said, stepping away. "You're an ordinary man now, Eric. Try to remember that."

I didn't speak.

"You may go shave and shower now," she said. "The bathroom is fully equipped."

When I came back into the room, my body still damp and my face still tingling from the odd shaver that seemed to dissolve my whiskers, a wet towel wrapped around my waist, G'lendal was assembling something on the table that I took to be a lie detector of some sort.

"Feel better?" she asked.

"Yes, some," I said, "but I could use some sleep." Though my senses were dulled from lack of sleep, G'lendal had dulled them even more by removing my augmentation. As she said, I was an ordinary man now, though I didn't resent her having done it. I would have done the same to an augmented captive.

"This won't take long," she said. "Then you can sleep as long as you like. Please take off that towel and sit down in this chair." She pointed with a long-nailed finger.

"You need any help?" Nardi asked.

"No, just stay where you are," G'lendal answered. Then to me, "Your wounds need attending to."

"I wouldn't object," I told her, feeling the tingling along my side from the bullet graze and the ache in the back of my head where Scoti had slugged me.

"Very well," the black girl said, fishing another kit from her case. "Hold still."

She sprinkled a bluish powder on the graze wound on my side and then covered it with a transparent adhesive bandage that seemed to melt into my flesh. I suppose that she did about the same to the back of my head, though I was unable to observe.

"That feel better?" she asked.

"Yes, I think so."

"Good," she said. "Now I'm going to tape some electrodes to your body. Don't be alarmed. They won't hurt."

I didn't answer, but then it seemed that I didn't need to.

From the thing on the table she carried a bunch of thin wires to where I sat, laid them across the back of the chair and began attaching the wires to my skin with a silvery-looking tape. One to each temple. One to each side of my neck. One on each shoulder. One above my heart. One just above my navel. One on each hip. One to the inside of each thigh. Even though her motions were smooth and professional, the touch of her woman's fingers excited me.

After she was finished, G'lendal stood behind me for a moment, tinkering with the lie-detection device. Nardi sat on the bed across the room watching me disinterestedly as if this were something he had seen a number of times before and wasn't too excited by.

"Now hold still just a moment," the black-skinned girl said.

Then something cold touched my left shoulder. There was a hissing sound and a sudden moistness entering my flesh.

"What was that?" I asked.

"Don't be alarmed," she said—I wasn't. "It was just a mild relaxer. I know better than to try to use any of the so-called truth serums on you Timeliners."

"Okay."

"Now I'm going to ask you a few questions," she said. "You can answer them any way you like. Right now you don't have to tell the truth unless you want to."

I'm sure that G'lendal knew that my training and conditioning, independent of my now inoperative augmentation circuits, could fool the lie detector, but she was going to try anyway. Okay, I thought, let's play your silly game.

"What is your name?" she asked.

"Thimbron Parnassos." My mind and body automatically gave the device a truthful response. But then it would have if I'd said Hieronymus Merganthaler.

"How old are you?"

"Thirty-three." Truthful response.

"When were you born?"

"2294 as we figure it at home. 1938 local time." Truthful response.

"Where were you born?"

"Sibyl, North Ionnia." Truthful response.

"Please equate that with some location in this Paratime."

"West Cheshire, England, near Hoylake." Truthful response—which it was.

Then—I supposed at the time that the sensation I felt in my mind was caused by the drugs she had injected me with. I still find it almost impossible to describe the feeling. It was, maybe, as if the top of my skull had been painlessly opened and someone were tickling my brain with a feather or maybe a very gentle puppy were sniffing at my gray matter. It was not really an unpleasant sensation, but it was one that I did not understand and that disturbed me.

"How long have you been in the hire of the Kriths?" G'lendal asked.

"Fourteen years."

"And what is your present position?"

"Mercenary soldier, absolute rank roughly equal to that of a colonel in the British Army."

"What do you think of the Kriths?"

"In twenty-five words or less?" I asked.

"In as many as it takes."

"Okay. Personally, I don't care for them. I mean, as individuals. There's something about them that I just can't bring myself to like. But what they're doing is good. It isn't just altruism—I'd suspect *that*. They're looking out for themselves, but to do that, they've got to help us humans. They're acting in their own rational self-interest to prevent their destruction by alien invaders two thousand years from now—and they're saving mankind in the process. How's that?"

"That's fine."

"How many words?"

"I didn't count."

The feathery tickling inside my head had now become a plucking: a chicken, gently at first, then with more force was pecking at my brain in search of kernels of corn. I didn't like it.

"Have you ever had doubts about their intentions?"

"Yes." Truthful response.

"Please explain."

"Well, I think anyone at some time or other will have a

few doubts about anything he believes. It's only human.
And I've had some vague, random doubts, but there's
never been any real reason for them. Everything the
Kriths have ever told me has been, sooner or later, supported by objective fact."

"Everything?"

"Yes, everything I can think of."

"What about the Cross-Line Civilization in the far
Temporal East?"

"What about it?"

"Tell me about it."

Suddenly I had a strange sensation of disassociation, as
if I had left my body for an instant and were now standing
or sitting to the rear of it looking at my own back. For
less than a heartbeat I saw the chair in which I sat, the
back of my injured head, my own naked shoulders, the
wires from G'lendal's lie detector trailing across the chair
to where they were taped to my body. Then it was over,
and all I felt was a vague swimming in my head.

"What about it in particular?" I was asking. "There's a
lot of ground to cover when you start talking about fifty
Lines that have blended into a single civilization."

"No," G'lendal said suddenly. "Forget about it. We'll
go on to something else." She paused for a moment. "Why
did you and your companions kidnap Count von Heinen
and his wife?"

"For information."

"What kind of information?"

"About nuclear weapons. We wanted Von Heinen so
that we could probe him about. . . ."

It happened again. This time more definitely and for a
longer period of time. I—the consciousness of *me*—was
sitting in a chair—no, on the sofa beside the lie detector,
watching the dials and meters and glancing frequently at
the back of my head. There was another consciousness
there with me, but I could tell nothing about it, other than
the fact that it was there.

I tried to will the eyes I looked through down at the
hands of the body I wore, but before I could tell whether
I was having any luck . . .

I was back in my own body.

"What the hell are you doing to me?" I demanded, leaping out of the chair and turning to face G'lendal.

"I'll stop," she said, her face just barely showing shock. Her hand snapped a switch.

"It's off now," she said, looking directly back into my eyes.

"What is that thing?"

"I can't tell you," G'lendal said. "I'm sorry. Please sit back in the chair, and I'll remove the electrodes."

I did as she said and a moment later felt her fingers on my temples and then sudden pull of hair as she jerked the tape away.

"It's a kind of mind probe, isn't it?" I asked.

"No, not really," she answered, pulling the electrodes from my neck.

But it was, I was sure. Not the kind of mind probes *we* used. Ours recorded the electromagnetic fields of the brain, interpreted them into words and symbols, recorded them on paper and tape, analyzed them with computers. Her machine, though, I thought, did something more direct. It actually entered the mind and dug for what it wanted, and in that way maybe it could bypass my conditioning. So it seemed to me at the time, anyway.

When G'lendal had finished removing all the electrodes she had taped to my body, she packed all her gear carefully in the case and turned to me one final time, saying, "For now, that will be all, but I will probably want to talk with you again."

I shrugged. I was in no position to argue with her, even if I'd felt so inclined. And, in truth, I didn't think I'd mind seeing *her* again at all.

"Good day, then, Eric," she said, and, with Nardi following her like a faithful dog, she left the room.

I was left alone, wondering what was going to happen next.

As it turned out, very little happened until the next day.

14
The Greatest Lie

When I awoke the next morning, it took me a few moments to orient myself and remember the bizarre series of events of the day before that had led me to captivity in this place called Staunton, somewhere under the earth of a place called Florida Here and Now.

It wasn't until I sat up that I noticed the tray of food sitting on a table beside the bed and the clothing draped across the end of the bed. Well, someone was thinking about me.

First I dressed in slacks and sport shirt of the local Line and then ate the still warm and rather conventional, by local standards, breakfast of bacon and eggs, coffee, orange juice, toast and jelly that had been provided for me.

Then I lay back on the bed and waited to see what was next. I had a long wait.

Since there wasn't much of anything else to do, I lit a cigarette and picked up the three books that had been left in the room. After looking at the inviting cover of *Paradise in Paratime* and deciding that G'lendal was even better looking than the lovely girl on the cover, I put it aside for *The Greatest Lie*.

The author, a fellow named Martin Latham, claimed to have been born in one of the Romano-Carolingian Lines where the Kriths had made their presence known quite some time ago. He told a little about his own Line—all of which seemed to be true since I had been there or to one very close to it—and then went on to tell how he discovered the "Lie," as he called it.

Since the "Lie" was one of the things that was stressed over and over again the whole time I was at Staunton, I might as well tell you about Latham's so-called discovery of it as well as I can remember it. I wish I had a copy of the book, and I'd give you this verbatim, but I don't. But it went something like this:

Latham showed an early inclination toward mathematics and technology. He had the soul of an engineer, but the mind of a pure research scientist and was ripe for the picking by the Kriths.

By the time he had finished the equivalent of secondary school the Kriths and their agents had already approached him about joining the Timeliners, with Academy instruction and training in skudder engineering. Latham jumped at the chance. And entered the Krithian Academy nearest his Homeline. While he was there, he showed such an amazing ability that he was allowed to do something almost unprecedented in the Academy: He took a "split major" in engineering—advanced electronics and skudder engineering—and graduated with honors in both fields.

The Kriths put him to work at once in one of their vast engineering labs in some unspecified, uninhabited Line. Latham loved his work. When he wasn't working on skudder design or tinkering with the most sophisticated electronic gear in all the Lines, he was spending his spare time reading anything he could put his hands on related to his fields and ultimately became interested in contratime communications. He requested that he be allowed to study the works of the Indus Line scientists who had actually established the contratime link that had informed the Kriths of the future menace of alien invasion. He was refused.

The story gets rather complicated and filled with cloak-and-dagger overtones along in here, but to simplify it, Latham's interest grew as he was more strongly refused the data he wanted. After a while he pretended that he had lost interest, though by this time he had become determined to learn everything he could about contratime communications, no matter what it took. Several years passed before he was able to lay his hands on the data he wanted.

One of his assignments led him cross-Lines to do some research in an area of the Lines through which skudders had always had some difficulty passing. On his way back to his base he was able to fake a malfunction in his skudder right in the middle of the Indus Lines. The defective skudder was examined by Indus technicians, and Latham was told that it would take some time to effect the repairs —his "faking" of a malfunction had been done well— and since no other skudders were available for his use, he would have to lay over for a few days—which is exactly what he wanted.

Latham managed to have dinner with one of his Indus colleagues and during the course of the dinner, by a stratagem I don't recall at the moment, he was able to steal the engineer's library access card, top-level. The next day Latham plugged into the planet-wide computer library and, pretending to be the engineer whose card he had stolen, asked for full data on the contratime experiments. The library produced a vast amount of data which Latham was given in the form of microdots which he hid on his person.

He secretly returned the library card to its owner, who had not yet discovered its loss, waited until his skudder was ready, and then returned to his base Line.

About half the information he had gotten from the Indus library was in Shangalis, while the remainder, and apparently the most important portion of it, was in the local Indus language. Before he could really get into it, he was forced to learn Indus in secret. This took him nearly a year, and more than once he was almost exposed, but finally Latham learned Indus and went back to his data.

According to his book, it didn't take him long to discover why the data had been kept from him. They were phony! The mathematics, while very complex and involved, led around in a circle and laboriously established nothing whatsoever. The experiments had been performed, the conclusions had been reached and the actual contact with the future had been . . . *faked!*

At first Latham didn't believe it. He checked and re-checked and re-rechecked his figures. And always came to the same final conclusions.

Stealing equipment from his own lab, he set up some of the experiments that the Indus scientists had performed —and their ultimate conclusions were validated. The whole theory of contratime communications fell apart. It just wouldn't work. Time was closed, forward and backward. The future could not talk to the past! It was that simple; the whole thing was a tremendous fraud!

Latham was in a quandary. What the hell was he going to do? Go to the Kriths? No, it was their plot, but for what reasons he couldn't even guess. Tell other humans? Who would believe him? And word would eventually get back to the Kriths—and then what would happen?

Finally, in desperation and fear, Latham stole a four-man skudder from the lab's skudder pool, removed the governor and the telltale from it, set its controls for the T-West and started out, intending to travel as far as the fully charged power cells would carry him, find men who had never been contacted by the Kriths, and tell them the whole story.

His skudder ran out of power in the Romano-Albigensian Lines, as he called them, far to the West of any Line that the Kriths and Timeliners had yet reached. There he found a civilization that had already developed their own skudders independently of the Kriths—and were moving East. He told them about the Kriths and the Timeliners and the "Lie" and that the Kriths were moving toward them.

The Albigensians began to prepare to meet the aliens—and save mankind from possible enslavement.

Well, in a large nutshell, that's the way the first part of Latham's book read.

Quite a story, but was any of it true? And if it was true, was that any proof that Latham was right? It seemed far more likely to me, giving it all the benefit of the doubt, that Latham had made an honest mistake—and had panicked. At least I saw no reason to believe one man whom I had never met, and who might not even exist, when all the evidence of my life pointed in just the opposite direction.

To hell with it, I said to myself, and got out of bed and began to pace the floor aimlessly, only to be interrupted by a peremptory knock on the door.

"Come in," I said, probably unnecessarily.

The door opened and the tall, thin, corpse-white form of the man called Mica entered the room, dressed now in a gray business suit of this Line.

"Hello, Captain Mathers," he said.

I nodded to him, lit the last cigarette in the pack that Nardi had left, and sat down on the end of the bed.

"I hope you slept well," Mica said, "and that your breakfast was agreeable."

"Yeah," I said between puffs of smoke.

"Please," he said, spreading his hands, "don't be angry with us. We are not your enemies unless you force us to be."

"Shit!"

"Come now. We can talk like rational men, can we not?"

"Okay, talk."

Mica was silent for a few long moments, his deep eyes scanning the room, then stopping at the open book on the table. "I see you have been reading Martin Latham's book," he said.

"Yes," I replied, thinking that if I were going to try to fool Mica and his gang into believing that I was swallowing their story I might as well begin now, but very gradually. It had better be believable. I didn't figure they'd be easy to fool.

"What do you think of it?" he asked.

"It's kind of hard to swallow, what I've read of it."

"How much have you read?"

"The first part, Latham's story of how he discovered the 'Lie' and you people."

"Ah," Mica sighed. "It is all quite startling to you, is it not?"

I nodded.

"It is as if, for example, an Englishman of this Paratime were suddenly told that there was no such place as China."

"Yes, sort of like that, I suppose."

"Let me go on," Mica said. "I would like to follow this analogy out. May I?"

"Why not?"

"Very well. Our hypothetical Englishman has been to America and the Continent, of course. He is a well-traveled man, and educated. He has met Chinese and seen pictures of China and knows fellow Englishmen who claim to have been to China—but he himself has never been there. *Still,* all evidence points to the fact that there is such a place as China. It never occurs to him to doubt for a moment the existence of China. Now what would happen," Mica asked, "if someone, in all seriousness, were to tell him that China does not exist?"

"He'd laugh in his face."

Mica smiled, nodded, then said, "Take this fantastic Cross-Line Civilization that you believe to exist far to the Temporal West. Have you ever been there, Captain Mathers?"

"No."

"Yet you know it exists. How?"

"Like your Englishman, I've seen pictures of it. I've spoken to people who have been there."

"Have you ever met anyone from those Lines? Any human natives, I mean."

I thought for a moment, honestly trying to rake up memories. "No, not that I can recall. I've met Kriths from there, though."

"No," Mica said, "let us ignore the Kriths for a moment. You have never met a human being who was native to those Lines. Now, the stories you have heard, the pictures, the tapes, the books you have read, could they have been faked? Could they have been lies?"

"Well, yes, I suppose they *could* have been. But it would have to be an enormous conspiracy to pull something like that off."

"Granted, but then, in the final analysis, all you have to prove that there *is* such a wonderful and beautiful Cross-Line Civilization is the word of the Kriths. Is this not so?"

"Yes, but not quite the way you mean it."

"Why not? Tell me, do you like the Kriths?"

"Yes and no."

"That is hardly an adequate answer, Eric. Do you know of a single Krith that you personally like as—well, as a person?"

"No, but then there are a lot of people I don't like either."

"Surely. But do you understand them? The Kriths? I mean, do they act from the same motives as human beings? Can you translate their thoughts into human terms?"

"No, not really. They don't think the way we do, I suppose, but then I don't think we should expect them to. They aren't people, but I trust them anyway."

"Why?"

"Well, they've never given me any reason not to."

"Ah," Mica sighed. "You're saying then that you have never *caught* them in a lie."

"I supposed you could take it that way."

"Then, in the final analysis, you believe in the Cross-Line Civilization simply because you have never caught the Kriths lying to you. That is hardly proof that they are *not lying*. All you can really be sure about is that, if they are lying, they are lying so well and so consistently that you have never caught them at it. Right?"

"I can't accept that."

"I do not expect you to at this stage." Mica paused. "Let us take Martin Latham. You have never met him, so you really have no reason to believe his words or even that he is a real person. He could be our 'Lie.' Is this so?"

"Yes, I suppose so."

"I have met him," Mica said, "and I believe him. Now you have my word that what Latham says is true, as opposed to the word of the Kriths that contratime communications exists. You must accept one of us on faith. Which will it be? You need not answer that yet. Not for a while, at least."

There was something almost sinister in his last sentence, but before I could comment, there was a gentle rapping on the door. Mica did not turn but called over his shoulder, "Come in." His eyes never left my face.

The door clicked, swung outward, and Sally and Scoti came into the room. They were both now dressed in the conventional clothing of this Line: Sally in a white blouse and a full green skirt; Scoti in a dark business suit. And more than ever Sally reminded me of Kristin.

"Good morning, Eric," Sally said. "How are you feeling?"

"Well enough," I answered, then nodded to Scoti.

"I hope you hold no hard feelings, old man," Scoti said. "For that bump on the head, I mean. I was just doing what I had to do."

I didn't answer.

"I have just been having a little chat with Captain Mathers," Mica said.

"And . . ." Scoti said expectantly.

"Calm yourself, Scoti," Mica said. "He is at least trying to be honest with us."

"That's all we ask, Eric," Sally said, sitting down on the sofa. "We don't expect you to give us any military secrets."

"I don't believe I have any you don't know about already," I said.

Sally looked so young and fresh and innocent that I found it hard to believe she was the same woman I had kidnapped—or tried to kidnap. She—well, I liked her.

"That doesn't matter," she was saying. "We just want you to listen to us and then judge for yourself what is true."

"Okay," I said. "I'll listen. I have a pretty good idea what will happen to me if I don't."

There was silence in the room for a few moments.

"Let me ask you a question," I said at last.

"Very well," Mica replied.

"Okay, suppose that what you're telling me is true. Suppose that there's really no Cross-Line Civilization and suppose that the whole contratime communications business is a fraud, then why are the Kriths going to all this trouble?"

Mica smiled, looked at the other two, then back to me.

"I was waiting for you to ask that, Captain Mathers," he said.

"So answer it."

"I wish I could."

That one sort of startled me. I had fully expected Mica and his gang to have a glib explanation of the Krithian logic behind the great plot they were postulating.

"I won't try to lie to you, Mathers," Mica said. "You are too intelligent a man for that. In all honesty we do not know why the Kriths are doing what they are doing. We know that they are telling the greatest lie in all history, in all the histories of all the Paratimes put together, but we really do not know why. We merely know that they are."

For a few moments I was at a loss for words. This wasn't working out as I had expected.

"Look at it this way, Mathers," Scoti said. "When you catch someone telling you a lie and you don't know why, you've got to assume that his purposes aren't good. It could be very dangerous to do otherwise, right?"

"Yes, I guess so."

"That is our assumption," Mica said. "We do not *know* that they mean mankind ill, but they are doing their best to profoundly alter the course of history in as many Paratimes as they can. They must have some reason, some logic of their own for doing it and all we can do is guess at what it is—and do what we can to stop it until we can learn why."

"Okay," I said. "If what you're saying is true, then I guess you'd have to act that way." For some reason I had the sudden feeling that Mica and Scoti honestly and truly did believe what they were saying. But then you never can tell about feelings, can you?

"We cannot tell you why the Kriths are lying, only that they are. And if you will let us, we will prove it to you," Mica said.

"Okay, prove it."

"That will take some time," Mica said, "but now I think you are going to let us have that time." He glanced at the watch on his wrist. "I have other responsibilities to attend to, but I'll see that additional books and tapes are sent to you. You can study them at your leisure. Is there anything else you would like?"

"Yes, some cigarettes, if you can get them."

"Of course," Mica said. "I will see to it at once." He rose. "Scoti, will you come with me?"

The other man nodded.

"I will see you later, Sally?" Mica asked.

"Yes," Sally said, glancing up at the tall, thin man, an expression on her face that I could not identify but that puzzled me. What was her relationship to him?

In a few moments the door closed behind the two men, and Sally and I were left alone in the room. It was a rather tense and awkward situation at first.

"I don't hold it against you," she said. "What you did. You were only doing your job as you saw it."

"I'm glad you look at it that way," I told her. "What about your husband?"

"Albert?" She smiled an odd smile. "He'll recover."

"You're glad of that?"

"I don't suppose it matters now. He won't be of much use to us anymore, it appears.

"Oh?"

"He was just a tool, as far as I'm concerned, and since it appears that the Kriths will find a way to destroy the Imperial nuclear project, we will just have to start another, without Albert."

I didn't go into it any further, either about Von Heinen or about the Kriths' destroying their Baltic plant. I was curious, but the answers could wait.

We were silent for a long while before I asked the next question.

"How long have they been here?"

"The Paratimers? Oh. . . ." She thought for a moment. "About fifteen years. They contacted my father when they first arrived. They've been working with us ever since."

"Who's this we?"

"The Mad Anthony Wayne Society."

"Uh-huh," I grunted. "What's their relationship to the Holy Roman Empire?"

Sally chewed on her lower lip for a moment. "Minor," she said after a while. "Only two years ago did they actually let them know who they were."

"Then the Holy Romans know about the Paratimers and the Kriths?"

"A little," she answered. "They haven't told them everything."

"Why?"

"They're on our side."

"Oh," I said, nodding. "And you also believe everything the Paratimers say?"

"Yes."

"Why?"

Sally smiled. "Now you sound like Mica interrogating one of our prisoners."

"I'm sorry, but I'm trying to learn what I can."

"I know. Yes, I believe them because, well, it makes sense to me, what I can see of it. They're human beings and the things you're working for aren't. That in itself seems reason enough."

"I suppose you've got a point there."

"Let me make another one, Eric."

"Go on."

"Our world is divided today between three, oh, call it

four, if you want to count Spain—our world is divided between these empires and not a one of them is worth a damn. I suppose, if I could really be objective about it, maybe the British are no worse than the Imperials, maybe even a little better since there are a lot of British people, some in the aristocracy, who don't approve of the way the king has treated the colonies. But, all in all, ninety percent of the human race is in a state not much better than slavery and the rest rule them, except for a few of us, like the ARA and the Mad Anthony Wayne Society, who still believe that people have the ability and, yes, the God-given right to rule themselves.

"Okay," she went on, "now look at what is happening. Who are your Kriths supporting? The British Empire. The greatest slaveowner in the history of the world—my world, at least. And who are the Paratimers helping? Us, the rebels who want to see an end to *all* slavery—the fact that we're working with the Imperials right now is only incidental to the whole thing. We'll take care of them once we've beaten the British. The Paratimers will see to that. But honestly answer me: Whose cause is more moral? The Kriths'? Or Mica's and Scoti's and the other Paratimers'?"

"On the face of it I suppose it looks right to you," I said. "But you can't see the whole picture."

"Can you?"

"Better than you can, I think."

"Then you tell me how it's moral to support tyrants. Or is your world ruled by a monarchy?"

I smiled. "No. My people are the ones who invented the republic in the first place, remember?"

"The Greeks?" Sally asked.

I nodded and then went on, "Well, if the Imperials are beaten by the British, your world stands a better chance of becoming free in the long run. If the Holy Romans win, you're in for a long period of tyranny and warfare that makes the present day look mild by comparison."

"How do you know?" she asked.

I paused for a moment. How could I answer her without falling back on the word of the Kriths? And, then, they hadn't figured on the Americans having an advanced technology behind them. Maybe my head was beginning to spin a little by then.

"You don't need to say it," she said. "You just have to accept the word of the Kriths, on faith, that that's the way it's going to turn out."

"Yes, I suppose so," I said defensively. "But I can show you the histories of other Lines where it has worked out exactly the way they said it would."

"That's still accepting their word. They wrote the books, didn't they, or at least supervised their writing?" She paused. "One of our great patriots was also something of a philosopher and once he said, 'A bird in the hand is worth two in the bush.' And at best your *bush* is only hypothetical."

"I don't suppose there's any point in trying to argue with you."

Sally smiled. "I don't want to argue with you, Eric. I want to be your friend."

"That's what everybody tells me."

She rose, smiled again. "I really must go. I'll come back to see you later."

"I'll be looking for you."

And then she was gone, and I was alone in the room again, and I wondered and wondered and wondered. . . .

A short time after Sally left, a panel in the wall below the intercom slid back revealing a receptacle in which sat two cartons of cigarettes, a stack of books and video tapes, and a small tape player and monitor.

Lighting a cigarette, I placed the tapes and books and player on one of the tables and scanned the titles on the tape boxes. Apparently Mica was giving me the whole propaganda story in one lump.

Well, I decided, I might as well get into it. If I were going to fool them into believing that I had swallowed their story, I had better learn my lines well. I spent the rest of the day reading books and viewing tapes.

15
Of Mica, Sally, and G'lendal

The days that followed dragged by interminably, although the nights were all too brief, for at night G'lendal would call on me, ostensibly to ask more questions, to continue her "interrogation," although on her second visit things began to get more interesting. Before that night was out, I found myself in bed with lovely, delightful G'lendal, and *those* details are none of your business.

During the day Mica, Scoti, and two or three others would visit me at intervals, mostly to answer questions, make suggestions and point out avenues of thought I hadn't yet followed.

During my captivity in Staunton, I gradually pieced together the whole story of the Paratimers or at least that part of it made available for my consumption. In another nutshell, it was something like this:

In the Romano-Albigensian Lines from which Mica, Scoti, and about a third of the Paratimers in Staunton had come the European Renaissance that followed the fall of the original Roman Empire and the so-called Dark Ages had reached a full and early flower in early-thirteenth-century France under the religious heretics called the Albigensians, Arian Christians who denied the oneness of Jesus the Christ—the Messiah—and God the Father. After successfully resisting the persecutions of the Roman Church and finally raising an army of their own, the Albigensians established their independence from both the emerging French nation and the orthodox church—and set about revolutionizing the world.

Despite the decades of religious war that finally led to the philosophical sundering of the Christian world, the Albigensians embarked on a serious program of learning. Their newly discovered and rediscovered knowledge spread like wildfire across Europe centuries earlier than it had in the world in which I now dwelt. The American continents were discovered in a steam-driven ship and fully colonized by Europeans within a century; a technological civilization evolved while Sally's people were still wondering what electricity was; world wars were fought; and finally, as the atomic age exploded across half the world and the first tentative steps to the stars were begun, the cultural descendants of the heretic Albigensians established a world at peace with itself.

Nearly a century ago, already with colonies on the Moon and on Mars, with a starship abuilding in orbit around Earth, they discovered the parallel universes and set out on a cautious voyage of exploration. Then, less than thirty years ago, Martin Latham found them.

Under Latham's direction the Romano-Albigensian Paratimers explored eastward into Paratime, found that what he had said was true and set about undoing the work that the Kriths were doing.

By the time I was captured by them the Paratimers consisted of quite a large number of individuals from various Lines to the Temporal West, and all were devoted to the total and final destruction of the Kriths and all those who worked with them.

There must have been a great deal of truth in these things, I told myself, as there is much truth in every great lie, no matter how well hidden and distorted it might be. I didn't doubt that in essence what I was told was true, for the most part, at least as far as it concerned the humans from the West, though I could not be so sure of their altruistic motives, as they denied the same motives on the part of the alien Kriths. And, of course, I was not ready to accept any of the things they said about the Kriths—though there were enough doubts in my mind by now so that I had some questions I was certainly going to ask Kar-hinter about when I saw him again—*if* I ever saw him again.

As far as Kar-hinter and the rest of the world outside Staunton were concerned, I was kept in total ignorance. What was happening in the war in Europe was unknown to me, though I could not force myself to feel very concerned. That had been a job when I was involved in it, but now I was no longer directly involved, and it didn't seem to matter too much. There were bigger things on my mind and, anyway, things would probably turn out pretty much as Kar-hinter had planned, though now he would have to do it without Count von Heinen and his American wife.

I wondered what kind of conclusions Kar-hinter had reached about my disappearance. He had known that I was waiting for him with the two captives, and he knew that we—Tracy, Kearns, and myself—had fought two short battles with men in an alien skudder. So, with very simple arithmetic, he would arrive at the conclusion that the men in the strange skudder had rescued the captives and had either killed me or taken me prisoner. I suspected that at that moment Kar-hinter was doing his damnedest to find out for sure. If I could only get a message to him.

Okay, then, I had decided early in my stay in the plush cell under the American earth, that was my sole objective: to get my hands on a radio and broadcast a message to Kar-hinter. But just how was I going to do that? Simple, convince the Paratimers that they had converted me, worm my way into their confidence, learn where there was a radio—and then do everything in my power to get a message out.

Simple. In a pig's eye!

When two weeks had passed—I assumed that it was about two weeks; I counted days in terms of G'lendal's violent, sensual lovemaking—I decided that I was ready to play the part of a convert.

Mica came in for his brief daily visit.

"How are you this morning, Captain Mathers?" he asked, seating himself on the sofa, glancing through one of the books I had deliberately left there, several key passages underlined on the open pages.

"Well enough, I guess," I said.

"What's this?" he asked, noticing a passage I had underscored.

"What?" I asked in all innocence.

"This that you have marked," he said. Then he read aloud: " 'Despite their alien form, the Kriths have done surprisingly well in their efforts to win the confidence of humans. Their shrewd understanding of human psychology has enabled them to do this, playing on human vanity, while at the same time projecting a powerful father/hero image that even the strongest and most self-reliant men seem to find attractive. However, most humans cannot help feeling a basic animal revulsion to these creatures who, at best, can only be described as parodies of men.'"

Beside the passage I had put two or three exclamation points.

Mica smiled. "Is there a special significance to this, Mathers?"

"There is to me."

"And what is that?"

"I'm not really sure," I said. "It's just something that, well, puts into words what I've felt about the Kriths, I suppose."

"Few men *like* Kriths."

"I never said I liked them as individuals."

"But you admired them. Am I correct in using the past tense?"

"Hell, I don't know," I said. "You people have me so damned confused."

"Observe what you just said, Mathers, and keep it in mind. 'You people. . . .' We are people, human beings like you."

"That's hardly proof that you're telling the truth."

"We have been through all of this before."

"Yes, I know.'" I paused, wondered if I were going to be able to convince him. Maybe. I was about halfway ready to believe it myself. "Look, Mica, let me put it to you straight."

"I wish you would."

"Some of what you've been telling me is bound to be true, and maybe all of it is. I don't know how much to believe of it yet, but give me time. I'll sort it all out eventually."

"What are you getting at?" Mica asked, the ghost of a smile flickering around the corners of his mouth as if all this were something he had heard before. Maybe so.

"I'm not sure. Except this. You damned people have put some pretty big doubts in my mind about the Kriths. Some damned big doubts. You've just about knocked the props out from under my world."

Mica smiled broadly at this. "Glendal told me this two or three days ago, Eric," he said, using my first name, rare for him. "I have just been waiting for you to say it."

So I'd fooled G'lendal already. That was something.

"Damn it, Mica," I said, hoping this would convince him of my sincerity, "I'm not saying that I really believe you or that I'm ready to join you. All I said was that you've made me doubt."

"That is the first big step, Eric. The rest is downhill." He paused for a moment. "The world will never look the same to you again."

I'll be damned, I was thinking. He really does believe me.

"If I offered you transportation back to the place where Scoti picked you up, would you accept it?" he asked slowly.

"You mean set me free?" I asked, almost but not quite startled, then realized that it was an obvious trap that I wasn't going to let myself fall into. "I don't know. I mean, I'm not being treated badly here at all, but I would like my freedom. But as for going back with the Kriths right now, well, I don't think so. Not right now, anyway. I'd want to think about it and about what I'd do and about how I'd resolve these questions before I do anything."

"An appropriate answer," he said. "But do not worry. That is the last place you will be going, even if you were given your freedom. Excuse me for a moment."

He rose, crossed to the intercom on the wall, and spoke a few alien, French-sounding words into it. A voice that I tentatively tagged as Sally's answered back. Mica smiled.

When he turned back to me, he said, "This button will ring Sally's quarters."

"Okay."

"I just told her that you are to be given limited freedom in her custody. She requested that she be your 'guardian,' as it were, should you be put on probation. She will accompany you wherever you go outside your room, tell you about our little world here, and help you reach some further conclusions. I hope that is agreeable with you."

I smiled back at him. "Yes, quite agreeable."

"Now listen carefully, Captain Mathers," he said, his face suddenly becoming hard and cold. "You must remember that you are on a very limited probation. Sally has explicit orders what to do if you step out of line. I would hate for her to have to shoot you because of a stupid mistake. Ask her before you do *anything*."

I nodded understanding.

"Very well," he said. "She will be down before dinner to give you a Cook's tour, as they say, of Staunton. I probably will not see you again today." Then he smiled a halfway convincing smile. "Welcome to the human race, Eric."

When Sally arrived a couple of hours later, she was wearing tight shorts and an equally tight halter that matched the golden color of her hair and failed to cover her body very effectively. Though she wasn't the stunning beauty that G'lendal was, she was still a very attractive young woman and a person whose presence I enjoyed.

Yes, I told myself, I even *liked* Sally better than G'lendal. Sally was a fairly simple person. By this I don't mean stupid. She certainly wasn't that. But rather she was what she seemed to be, said what she felt, did what she believed to be the right thing to do. I could understand Sally and perhaps that was because I understood the culture in which she lived and where she had been formed. And she still reminded me of Kristin.

As for G'lendal—I understood absolutely nothing about her or about the world from which she had come. It really didn't exist for me. It was as unreal to me as the beautiful Cross-Line Civilization that the Kriths had told me about—and which, I suppose, I had even then begun to doubt.

But, back to Sally.

"Mica tells me that you're willing to listen to us," she said as the door closed behind her.

"Yes, I guess you could say that," I said, noticing the small bulge on her right hip under the shorts that obviously wasn't a part of Sally's anatomy—the bulge that could only be the shape of a very small handgun which I assumed was quite deadly.

"Would you like me to show you around?"

"Yes, I suppose so."

"Let's go then."

Staunton, I learned that afternoon, consisted of two major sections of underground burrows in addition to a dozen or so other tunnels separated from the two main ones. To my surprise I had been kept in the smaller one.

The Americans, the natives of this Line, dwelt and worked in the larger section that was, in reality, a small city built under the earth with a population nearing ten thousand. Here there were stores and shops and theaters and meeting halls and factories and machine shops and printing plants and weapons stores. And here the leaders of the American rebels directed the operations of their guerrilla war against the British overlords. This was, simply, the nerve center and store house of the American rebellion, A.D. 1971.

And I thought that Mica must have been pretty well convinced of my sincerity to allow me to see even that much—or pretty well convinced that I would never escape to tell anyone else what I had seen.

The other section, the smaller one where my cell was located, was devoted to the Paratimers' quarters and their Outtime devices. Most of this area was secret, and apparently even Sally didn't know all of what went on there, though she did show me what she was permitted to.

Unlike the American burrow city, that of the Paratimers consisted of little more than sleeping quarters, machine shops, laboratories, storerooms, one large cafeteria, and, of course, a few detention cells. For personal shopping and amusements the Paratimers visited the American section.

The Paratimers, as I said before, consisted of individuals from at least a dozen different Lines, and this was evidenced by the bizarre decorations and unusual costumes, or lack of costume, worn by the people in the Paratimer quarters. I learned later, however, that when visiting the American section they did their best to hide their differences. When in Rome. . . .

Sally officially lived in the American section, of

course, but I somehow got the impression that she spent very little time there. This, added to the fact that I had already suspected that there was some kind of relationship between her and Mica, aroused an uncomfortable feeling of jealousy in me. But what reason did I have for feeling that? Sally certainly owed me nothing —and what did I owe her?

Other than my life, perhaps. . . .

No one, either in the American or Paratimer sections, showed us any special attention, though I got the impression that everyone knew Sally and they all were very glad to have her back with them and not across the sea in the Holy Roman Empire where she had spent the previous year as the wife—in name, at least—of Count Albert von Heinen.

The tour ended in the cafeteria in the Paratimer quarters, where we joined perhaps half a thousand people having their dinner.

When we had finished eating Sally told me that she would have to take me back to my quarters now. She had things she had to do that evening. She did not say that she was going to be doing those things with Mica, but I certainly got that impression.

I guess I got more impressions that day than outright information.

We went back to my quarters, and Sally locked me in.

For a while I paced the floor and wondered just where any radio equipment was located and glanced anxiously at my watch—which had been returned to me at last. having been found harmless—wondering whether G'lendal was going to come as she had come every night since I had been there.

Back to the radio question. I had not thought it wise to come right out and ask Sally about it, though I was sure that somewhere the Paratimers had radio gear, even though they must have used it sparingly to avoid detection by the Kriths and my own Timeliners. Well, I had to somehow find out where it was and learn to operate gear that I was sure would not be of any make I'd ever seen before and would probably not even be labeled in any language that I could read.

Okay, I comforted myself, you're a damned sight closer to it than you were. Just be patient and take it easy and you'll find out.

Then I lit a cigarette and paced the floor some more and waited for G'lendal's knock on the door.

16
Of Democracy, Sautierboats, and Guns

The next four weeks went quickly, though my anxiety grew greater as I was continually frustrated in my efforts to discover radio equipment. I knew that there had to be some means of contacting the outside world, but I was unable to find it.

My days were full and interesting as I learned more and more about the world in which I found myself, as I learned more about the Paratimers who were beginning their secret war against the Kriths and Timeliners. And the nights . . . well, they were interesting too. Mica did not see fit to let me sleep alone a single night or even sleep very much. There was Jonna, of course, and even G'lendal, who came back to me a few times, and Deean and Suski and two or three others, all lovely and willing and fully experienced in bedtime pleasures.

I will not attempt to detail those four weeks, much of it would be repetitive and most of the details are, from my present viewpoint, unimportant, though I will hit on a few of the high points.

The American rebels of Saunton were self-governing and made a very big thing out of getting everyone involved in the democratic machinery that elected the governing council. The actual process—party meetings, speeches, nominations, campaigns, elections, and so on —was not unlike some other democratic processes that I had seen before. The outstanding thing was the fervor and dedication of these Americans. They not only believed in democracy—they loved it.

Every two years the five-man governing council of Staunton was elected and it so happened that the late spring of 1971 was the time of that election. Sally, who was an official of the Jeffersonian Party, invited me to attend the nominating convention of that party, which occurred one weekend, beginning on Friday evening and lasting through Sunday evening. As much as the rebels loved their democracy, they could not afford to allow it to interfere with their ordinary workweek.

Sally came for me after dinner on that Friday evening clad in a very conservative dress adorned with a large metal pin printed with a stylized picture of one of the rebels' heroes, the American patriot named Thomas Jefferson who was said to have been largely responsible for the writing of the American Declaration of Independence nearly two hundred years before and who had been brutally executed by the British after the collapse of the first rebellion.

"We'd better hurry," she told me. "It will begin soon."

We hurried.

One of the main features of the underground burrows of the American section of Staunton was a huge amphitheater cut from the stone and earth. My guess was that it would hold, when packed full, something on the order of four or five thousand people. And on this particular night, it was packed. There was hardly standing room for all the people who were attending, or rather attempting to attend, though Sally as a party official was able not only to get in, but to get us seats fairly near the front where we could see as well as hear the speakers on the stage. I wondered if the people in the rear of the theater could even hear despite the elaborate sound system of the theater—a Paratimer installation.

We had hardly got into our seats when music began to play, recorded, I supposed, since there was no visible band. At once Sally tugged on my arm, so I rose with her and followed her example of placing my right hand over my heart. I didn't recognize the music, but it was heroic and stirring, and I realized how much it must affect the people who knew it and the principles it represented to them.

Anyway I've always been a sucker for that sort of thing.

"Remain standing until I sit down," Sally whispered to me.

I nodded.

A group of men dressed in antique costumes that must

have represented the period of the first American rebellion paraded onto the stage. Three of them led the procession—one played a horn or whistle of some kind that I didn't recognize, one played a drum, and the man between the two carried a flag that I believe was one of the original flags of the rebellion. They were followed by ten more men dressed as farmers, clergymen, clerks, backwoods trappers, soldiers, and the like of that period. When the procession reached the center of the stage, it stopped, turned to face the audience, waited until the end of the music, and then the flag was carefully placed in a socket in the floor of the stage.

Two or three patriotic songs followed, one of them called "Yankee Doodle" or something like that. For some reason another of them stuck in my mind, and later I wrote the words down with some help from Sally. It was about the man called Mad Anthony Wayne, one of their principal heroes, and the words went something like this:

> Bang! Bang! the rifles go; down falls the startled
> foe.
> Aim! Fire! exclaim his eyes; bang! bang! each
> gun replies.
> Ran-tan! the bugles sound; our force has still the
> ground.
> Tramp! Tramp! away they go; now retreats the
> beaten foe.
> Many a red coat, the Continental scorning,
> Shall never meet the blaze of the broad sunlight
> that shines on the morrow morning.

> His sword blade gleams and his eyelight beams,
> And never glanced either in vain;
> Like the ocean tide, at our head he rides,
> The fearless mad Anthony Wayne.

> [This is followed by the Chorus:]
> Bang! Bang! the rifles go; down falls the startled
> foe;
> Many a redcoat, the Continental scorning,
> Shall never meet the blaze of the broad sunlight
> that shines on the morrow morning.

Was e'er a chief of his speech so brief,
Who utters his wishes so plain?
E'er he utters a word, his orders are heard,
From the eyes of Mad Anthony Wayne.

Chorus

It is best to fall at our country's call,
If we must leave this lifetime of pain;
And who would shrink from the perilous brink
When led by Mad Anthony Wayne?

Chorus

Let them form their ranks in firm phalanx;
They will melt in our rifle ball rain;
Every shot must tell on a redcoat well,
Or we anger Mad Anthony Wayne.

Chorus

Then they repeated the whole introductory chorus again before ending the song.

I'm not sure why that particular song impressed me so. It may have been that its jingoistic fervor showed more than any other the dedicated militancy of the American rebels which I was coming to understand. I'm not sure. But the song did stick with me.

When the song was finished, the costumed retinue retired, and two men carried a microphoned rostrum to the center of the stage. Moments later a clergyman carrying a huge black Bible under his arm came out, placed the Bible on the rostrum, opened it and began reading something from Moses that I can't seem to recall at the moment.

He then asked the Christian God for His blessing on this assembly and on the proceedings and asked His guidance in making the right choice of nominees for the council. During his prayer he alluded to men and events I was unfamiliar with, but which must have had some meaning to the native Americans. Then he retired from the stage, and the convention got down to business.

I won't try to relate the convention at all. There was too much of it, too many things happening at once, and

I was never quite sure just what was really going on. In a way it reminded me of the way some elections are held back in my own Homeline—since we Greeks invented the idea, anyway—but there were a lot of differences too.

One thing I do remember, though, was when a man I didn't know got up and nominated Sally for a position on the city's governing council. Sally immediately rose, told them that she couldn't accept; she had been gone too long and was out of touch with things in Staunton, but she certainly did appreciate the gesture. She received a standing ovation.

Then there were other nominations and secondings and acceptance speeches, and sometime long after midnight on Saturday, when my eyelids weighed a ton each, the voting got started in earnest, with more yelling and cheering and calls to order and just about everything else you can think of.

I managed to slip away while Sally was making some parliamentary point and at last got some of the sleep I so badly needed—and I was grateful that Mica didn't send someone to keep me company that night. I wouldn't have been up to it.

"I don't think anyone before us really understood the principles behind the sautierboat, or skudder, as you call it," the gray-clad technician told me, pointing toward the huge craft that now occupied fully half of the hangar. "I mean, the Kriths could skud, but they never really knew how they did it. It was just something they did. I mean, men have been able to think for thousands of years, but we're only now really learning *how* we think."

I nodded.

Sally had brought me to the hangar, introduced me to the technician, and then gone on her way, saying she'd be back later to get me. In the meantime, he was trying to help me understand how their Transtemporal sautierboats worked.

"Well," the technician said, "when the Kriths had human beings start building skudders for them, they did it pretty much on an empirical basis. The human engineers learned the mechanics behind Krithian skudding and reproduced them in a machine without really learning the fundamental laws that govern this sort of thing. They didn't have to since all they had to do was reproduce a mechanical model of the skudding mechanism inside the Kriths. Follow me?"

"Yes, I believe so."

"I don't pretend to understand it all myself," the technician said, gesturing toward a shelf of technical manuals and reference books above his elaborate workbench. "I just know enough to repair these things when something goes wrong, but despite that I think I know a hell of a lot more about it than any of *your* people." The way he put an emphasis on "your" gave me the impression that he, for one, didn't really trust me, but he was going to give me a rundown of their sautierboats as Sally had requested and Mica had approved.

"I wouldn't doubt it," I said, hoping that would put him more at ease. "I've seen your boats do things I thought were impossible."

"That's exactly what I mean," the technician said. "How about a cup of coffee?"

"Okay. I could stand one."

While he dropped coins into the vending machine and waited for the hot coffee to come gurgling out, he went on talking. "The engineers say that you can't really talk about sautiering in words; they say you need a special set of mathematics for it. And I guess that it's true, but I'm doing well just to follow the math when it's on paper and explained for me. I can't tell you much about it."

"That's okay," I said. "I probably wouldn't understand any of it anyway. Cigarette?"

"Thanks," he said, taking my offered pack and knocking a cigarette into his hand.

I got the two cups of coffee from the machine, handed him one of them.

"Go on," I said. "Explain to me what you can."

"All right," he said, taking a light from my lighter. "It all has to do with what they call probability potentials and probability indices. It's as if nothing *really* is; everything is just *might be*. Like, ah, the universe can't make up its mind. Follow me?"

"Not really."

"That's okay. I don't think anyone does really. Well, they say that back when the universe first started there was just one Paratime, one Line, the Original Line, and it had a probability of 1.0000 forever. It was *real*. Then the first uncertainty happened. I mean, something came up that could have gone one way or the other. And the universe couldn't decide which. So both happened. Each new Paratime had a probability of 0.5000.

"Okay, so far?" he asked.

I nodded, sipped my coffee, puffed my cigarette.

"Well, when it all started, the Original Paratime had a probability index of 1.0000, like I said. When there were two Paratimes, one had a probability of -0.5000 and the other had a probability of $+0.5000$. The *plus* and *minus* represent what you call T-West and T-East. Well, let's say that the *plus* Line came to a fork and two new Paratimes were formed, each with a probability index of 0.2500. One was a $++0.2500$ and the other was a $-+0.2500$. Still with me?"

"I guess so."

"Okay. The *double plus* Line hit another fork, and the result was now a $+++0.1250$ and a $-++0.1250$. And this would go on and on and on toward infinity, with each new fork lowering the probability and increasing the number of signs. They figure that the probability of any given Line is now somewhere on the order of 10^{-85}."

I tried to visualize the number, but all I got was a string of zeros running across a sheet of paper and dribbling off the side. I couldn't comprehend it.

"That's an oversimplification, way over. The way I understand it," the technician was saying, "is that the probabilities don't break apart even. I mean, it isn't *always* a fifty-fifty chance. You might come to a fork with, say, a thirty percent probability one way and a seventy percent probability the other, but that only confuses the probability values that much more. But you get the basic picture, don't you?"

"I think so," I said. None of this was very new to me. The Kriths had been able to tell me this much a long time ago.

"Okay, then, every Paratime had its own particular

value in *pluses* and *minuses* and its own numerical index. It's kind of like a fingerprint; there's no two alike."

"I understand that."

"Well, that's how we travel across the Paratimes," the technicial said smugly. "The sautier generator, well, creates its own probability potential. We adjust it to—well, to whatever we want to adjust it to and then the boat and everything within the field of the generator sort of seeks its own level."

"I'm with you."

"I guess that's the best I can do to explain it."

"That's good enough," I said, "but I still don't understand how you can move about in space. The Kriths can't do that."

"Okay. As I said before, you and the Kriths don't really understand what it's all about," he said. "Oh, they're right about the relationship of probability generators and most other types of machinery. You can't fly a sautier-boat with a jet engine, but we've found out how to turn that into a positive advantage.

"Now, the Kriths have a vague idea that there are two, well, dimensions to sautiering, skudding, I mean plus and minus, but what they don't understand is that there are three more. I mean, as well as having Transtemporal plus and minus probability, there are three spatial coordinates involved in probability. That is, even within a given Paratime the probability of one thing or place varies from all the others."

"You've lost me," I said. This was something new to me. The Kriths had never talked about anything like this.

"Me too," the technician said, smiling. "Look, you're familiar with the mass displacement phenomenon, aren't you?"

"Yes."

"Okay, the Kriths know that an object entering a Paratime from Outtime cannot occupy the same place as an object already in existence in a Paratime. The newcomer, since it has a much lower probability within the Paratine, must give way to the one that's already there. Its mass is displaced in space a sufficient distance to avoid coming in physical contact with the thing that's already there. Right?"

"Right," I said. I guess if that weren't so, skudding would have been next to impossible.

"Well, whereas your people and the Kriths seem to accept this and go on, our people wanted to find out why, and when they did, they learned about probability interactions. The best I can tell you is that there are some kinds of interactions between the separate Paratimes. Some things are, well, more probable than others even in the same Paratimes. Take Here and Now for example. Going *plus* and *minus* across the Paratimes, we'd find a number of worlds almost identical to this one, but each slightly different in some respects. Even though this hangar isn't native to these Paratimes and doesn't exist on any other, let's pretend that it does, okay?"

"I guess."

"Well then, if we were to take the nearest five Paratimes in either direction and built a composite picture of the hangar, we'd find some things identical in some, but different in others.

"All right, they all add together in a sense. Let's say, in the totality, that this building has the highest order of probability, then the tools on the bench, then me, then you with the lowest. Okay, then each item in this room has an order of probability in relation to each other item as a part of the total probability index of this Paratime because of the, well, interaction of the other ten Paratimes. Still with me?"

"I think so."

"Okay. Suppose the index of this Paratine is $5+^{25} \times 10-^{25}$. Now everything in this Paratine has varying potentials. If we assign 1.000 to the most likely thing, the hangar itself, the sautierboat might be, say, 0.7500 and the tools on the bench 0.5000 and me 0.2500 and you, say, 0.1250. Now each of these things here has a value, call it a field, that centers on the object itself, but extends outward, diminishing in force, still with a probability focal point."

"I'm getting a headache."

The technician smiled. "I'll cut it short. Take this sautierboat. We can adjust the generator to take us to a given Paratime. Right?"

"Granted."

"Now within that Paratime we can subtly vary the sautier field, alter the probability potential just a little. Well, if we can move from Paratime to Paratime by seeking the level of the generator, it follows that within a given Paratime we can move from place to place by varying the field within that Paratime. Got me?"

I nodded. "That sounds awkward, though. How do you know which way you're going to go when you vary the field? And how can you be sure that you're not going to jump right out of this Line into another?"

"As I said, all this is oversimplification," he said. "We've got instruments that can detect the variations of probability within a Paratime. And these instruments feed into the boat's computer. I guess you know that most electronic devices, like most living organisms, don't seem to be bothered by probability fields. Don't ask me why. I don't know." He paused. "Anyhow, a human being never has to worry about any of these things anyway. All he does is set the controls to take him to a certain spot. The instruments gauge the probability potentials around the boat, find the levels that will take the boat where the pilot wants to go, and the computer varies the generator's potential accordingly."

"I see," I said, "and that would also prevent the boat from slipping into another Line by accident, I guess."

"Right," the technician said. "Say, if you can get permission from Mica, I'll take you for a ride sometime and show you how it works.

"I'd like that," I said, thinking that I had overcome the technician's initial distrust of me—and also thinking that his sautierboat would be sure to have a radio in it.

But I was sure that it would take some time before I could persuade Mica to allow me to take the offered ride, and I just might not have that time.

The arsenal of the Paratimers under the West Florida earth contained weapons of every imaginable type from crossbows to thermonuclear bombs big enough to sterilize half the planet. And I wondered why they had weapons that big and if they would really use them if it appeared that the Kriths were winning on this Line.

"Now this is one of my favorites," Scoti said to me, taking a well-oiled handgun down from its wall cradle. It was a big, heavy six-shot revolver that reminded me a little of the Harling that Scoti had taken from me. I wondered where it was now.

"This is from a fairly nearby Paratime," Scoti was saying. "And it's one of the most efficient pistols I've ever seen. It's called a .44 Magnum, and it packs one hell of a punch."

"Single-action, isn't it?" I asked to keep up my end of the conversation.

"Yes," Scoti agreed, "but I'm partial to them."

"They're dependable."

"This one sure is. Notice the construction of the cylinder." He snapped the weapon open. "Rugged as hell. There's virtually no way in the world to foul it up. And the hammer spring, well, it just won't wear out. That's the beauty of it—simple, efficient, and it's one of the most accurate big-bore pistols you'll ever find."

For an instant I wished that there were shells in the cylinder. Given half a chance, even now, I might be tempted to try to shoot my way out of here. Then I smiled and handed it back to him.

"If you can get Mica's permission," Scoti said, "I'll see if you can try it out on the range."

"That might be fun," I said, though again I doubted that Mica trusted me that much—enough to let me have a loaded weapon in my hands even on a target range surrounded by guards.

I just smiled again, and Scoti put the pistol back and started to show me another of his favorite weapons, an R-4 power pistol from his own Line.

It was two or three days later that Mica dropped his bomb.

We were sitting in his office one morning having coffee, discussing some of the Paratimes we had been in, when he almost casually mentioned his Homeline.

"It must be very interesting there," I said.

"Yes, I suppose it is," Mica replied. "You'll have a chance to see for yourself soon."

"How's that?"

"Next week Trebum and I will be going home to make

a progress report to our governing council. We will be taking you along."

"Oh?" I said, unable to think of anything any more intelligent at the moment.

"Yes," Mica replied slowly. "The council would like to speak with you also. It isn't often that we get a Time-liner convert."

"How long will I be there?"

"I'm afraid that I cannot say. It will be up to the council. However, I doubt that you will ever be returning *here*."

I started to ask why, but decided against it. I knew why. They just didn't trust me that much, not enough to leave me here this close to my "friends," though they trusted me enough not to kill me.

"I trust that you do not find that an unpleasant prospect," he said, a statement rather than a question.

"No, of course not," I told him. "It should be very interesting."

But I had already made up my mind about what I was going to do.

17
"Red Mobile to Red Leader"

Mica told me that we were going to his Homeline on Friday. I acted on the Monday before that.

The Monday morning after a solitary breakfast I buzzed Sally's quarters on the intercom, hoping that I'd catch her before she left. I was lucky. She was still there.

"Yes, Eric," she said over the intercom.

"Are you busy?"

She paused for a moment before answering. "Well, no. Not really. I have a few things to do, but nothing urgent. Why?"

"Oh, no reason, really," I said. "I've just got a touch of claustrophobia. I'd like a chance to get outside for a breath of fresh air."

"We could have gone to the surface yesterday," she said. "There was a picnic, you know."

"I know, but I didn't feel like it then. How about it? Can you take me up for a few minutes, just to look around?"

"Okay," she answered at last. "Give me a few minutes. Then I'll come for you."

"Good. I'll be waiting."

Of course I'd be waiting. I still couldn't even open the door by myself.

It was nearly half an hour later when Sally showed up wearing bright yellow shorts, halter, and sandals. I was pleased to note the bulge of the small handgun that was still on her hip under the shorts. I had been fearful that their trust of me was enough for Sally to have come without the gun now. It wasn't. Good. I needed that gun.

"Ready to go?" she asked.

"Ready," I answered

We followed the corridors to the stairs and took the stairs up to the surface, out into the bright springtime morning light. It was almost summer then all across the Lines.

When the door closed behind us, I took a deep breath of fresh air, looked up at the cloudless blue sky through the dark pine trees above, and then looked around and located the hangar off through the trees. That was my ultimate destination.

"Is there any place in particular you want to go?" Sally asked.

"No," I replied, "let's just walk."

So we walked away from the hangar across the flat countryside through the pine trees toward a small stream that cut through the forest, making its way toward the Gulf of Mexico less than fifty miles to the south.

"I'm going to be leaving soon," I said as I fished into my pocket for a cigarette.

"I know," Sally replied. "Mica told me."

"In a way I'll hate to leave here. I sort of like it."

"I envy you," she said.

"Envy me. Why?"

"You're getting to visit Mica's Paratime. I've never had a chance. It must be a wonderful place."

"Oh? You mean you've never been to where they come from?"

"No, very few of us have."

I wondered why, then dismissed the thought. It *might* have some kind of significance, but I doubted it. And it didn't matter. Not at the moment. I had no intention of going there with Mica.

"I guess it will be interesting," I said, "but I'd rather stay here."

"What difference does it make to you? This isn't your Homeline. I thought that one Paratime was as good as another to you."

"Some are better than others. I've come to like it here."

"As a prisoner?"

"I've had freedom that's been a lot worse than this prison, and, hell, I've got such nice guards."

"You mean like G'lendal and Jonna?" Sally asked, a smile flickering across her face.

"Yes, like them and you."

"Me? What am I to you, Eric?"

"I don't know, Sally. I just like you."

"Guilt feelings?"

"Guilt? Oh, for kidnapping you and all? No, not really. Back then you weren't a person to me. Just a job. I don't have any reason for guilt, do I?"

"I'm not a person to you now either, Eric. I'm just a turnkey."

"No, more than that."

"I'm just your guard, Eric," she said, an edge to her voice. She had come to a stop near the base of a huge old pine. "I could never be anything else."

I turned to look at her, my hands going to her shoulders, memories of Kristin coming to me, beginning to hate myself for what I was about to do. "You could be a lot more than that, Sally."

"No, never, Eric."

"Why? Because you're married to Von Heinen? What's he to you?"

"Not Albert," she said, a strange mixture of emotions on her face. "You know—you must realize by now that I'm Mica's mistress. I'm. . . ."

That's when I acted.

I had never seen Sally draw her hip pistol while wearing those shorts. She must have had some easy access to it, though I didn't know how and didn't have time to investigate. I just grabbed the shorts at the waist, jerked down and forward and hoped that the fabric or the stitches that held it together would tear. Something gave way.

Sally was as well trained in hand-to-hand combat as any woman I'd ever met, but fighting was my business, and I was bigger and stronger than she was. She fought back as I tore off her shorts, grabbed at the small holster strapped across her now-naked hips, wrapped my fingers around the weapon's butt and pulled it free. Then I shoved her away, jumped back and leveled the pistol at her, snapping the safety off. It was a small automatic of a make I didn't recognize, .22 caliber.

"Hold it, Sally," I grasped.

"Goddamn you!" she cried, on her knees and starting to rise, but then looking at the weapon aimed at her. "You lying, sneaking bastard. I trusted you. I . . ."

"I'm sorry, Sally," I said as calmly as I could. "I hate to do this, but I've still got a job to do."

"You still believe them," she said, her eyes filling with fire and hatred, and tears. "You still believe those monsters are telling the truth. You traitor, you filthy. . . ."

"That's enough," I said sharply. "I'm doing what I have to do."

"Don't hand me that shit."

"That's not very ladylike."

"Don't mock me, you. . . ." What she said next was even less ladylike.

"Get up," I said. "We're going to the hangar."

"You're not stupid enough to think you can steal a boat, are you? You don't even know how to operate one of ours."

"I don't need to. Now get up and do as I say."

Sally came to her feet, clutching her torn shorts around her waist as well as she could with one hand, turned in the direction I pointed with the pistol, started walking.

Well, I thought, I'm into it now. If I don't make it . . . Well, it's a bullet in the head for old Thimbron Parnassos if I don't pull it off this time. There'll never be another chance.

Sally did not speak again as we made our way back along the trail toward the hangar in which the Paratimers kept their sautierboats there on the surface, hidden from British airships by a thick cover of trees.

In a few minutes we were within sight of the hangar. Exactly as I had hoped, the big hangar doors were open, and I could see inside. Two of the alien skudders sat there, the big one and the smaller one, and inside the hangar, dark against the bright light outside, I could see two men, gray-clad technicians doing whatever technicians do when they don't have anything else to do.

"Don't make a sound, Sally," I whispered, knowing that we were still outside their range of hearing. "If you do. . . ." I let my voice trail off.

She turned to look at me, hatred still in her eyes, and for an instant I—well, damn it, I loved her. I guess that's what it was. And damned if I knew why. And when that instant was gone, I knew that I couldn't trust her. She might—probably would—yell a warning to the technicians inside the hangar as soon as we got close enough. And I didn't think I would be able to kill her if she did.

I'm sorry, Sally, I said to myself, dropping the pistol, balling my fist and snapping my knuckles across her jaw in a single motion.

She looked startled for a moment, then collapsed quietly onto the soft, pine-needled floor of the forest.

I took off her halter, feeling guilty as I undressed her, and used it to tie her arms crudely to the trunk of a small tree. With my handkerchief and a strip of her torn shorts I formed a gag and hoped that she would be found soon. I didn't want her to strangle.

Looking regretfully at her for one last time, wondering whether I'd ever see her again, I left the now-nude girl behind me and began slipping through the thinning forest, around the hangar so that I could come up from the other side.

Standing only inches from the two huge open doors at the hangar's front, I could hear the two technicians talking, though I couldn't understand them. They were speaking that French-like language that was common to the Paratimers.

After a while I decided that I was gaining nothing by delaying. I might as well go on and do it before I was discovered. So I waited only until I thought I could pinpoint their locations from their voices, both together, standing not far from me near the hangar's doors.

Leaping out into the open, turning, and aiming the pistol, I said loudly, "Hold it! Don't move!"

The two technicians turned to face me, startled expressions on their faces, words cut off in mid-sentence.

One grabbed at the tool belt he wore, grasping at something that vaguely resembled a flashlight, but might well have been some sort of laser device that could be used as a weapon. I pulled the triggr.

The technician staggered backward, grasping his shoulder, blood spurting between his fingers.

"Don't move again, either of you," I said, wondering if

the report of the tiny pistol was really as loud as it had sounded to me in the stillness of the surface forest.

"Tie him up," I told the uninjured technician, the one that had explained to me the workings of their sautier-boats a few days before. "And hurry. I don't have much time."

The startled technician seemed disinclined to argue with the tiny but effective weapon I held. Without speaking he bound his companion hand and foot and gagged him with black electrical tape under my supervision.

"Okay. Now drag him over there out of the way," I said. "And don't make a move toward any of those tools."

When he was finished, he looked back at me fearfully, or rather at the pistol. He could not seem to take his eyes off it even as he spoke.

"He'll bleed to death," he managed to say. "You hit an artery."

"Do both those boats have radios?" I asked. Right then I couldn't afford to care if the other technician did bleed to death. I was more concerned with my own life.

He was nodding.

"Which is the most powerful?"

"N-neither. Both are same kind."

"Okay. The big one." I gestured toward the larger of the two craft. The technician didn't ask any questions. He just started across the hangar.

I wasn't foolish enough to believe that I could steal one of their sautierboats. I had no idea how to operate the controls, and I could not trust the technician to do anything that complex. The best I could hope for was one of the radios—if I could just get a message on the air and if Kar-hinter still had people monitoring and if I happened to find the right frequency and if. . . .

The technician opened the hatch of the large craft, stood for a moment waiting for me to tell him what to do.

"Get in," I said.

For an instant I had the same feeling I had had back in the stables of the villa near Beaugency, back when I was fleeing from the Paratimers in an Imperial motorcar with Sally and Von Heinen as captives, so long ago and half a world away. There was the sensation of another presence in the hangar, and out of the corner of my eye I caught the impression of a figure standing back deep in the shadows at the far end of the hangar.

I spun toward the image, leveling the small pistol, but when my eyes focused in the shadows, there was nothing there. Had there ever been?

I went on into the boat, feeling a strange chill on my back. Ghosts?

Inside the boat I recognized the controls as being basically similar to those of the craft that had brought me to Staunton, what I had seen of its control panel. The radio transceiver was easy enough to locate, though the lettering on the controls was foreign to me.

"Okay," I said, "tell me what does what."

The technician looked at me for a moment, perhaps wondering what he could get away with, then, gazing at the pistol, seemed to decide that he'd better play it straight and nodded. "This—this is the on-off switch. The receiver and the transmitter operate on the same frequency. That's controlled by this knob."

"What does that dial indicate?"

"Megahertz. Vernier control here and these—these buttons will select preselected channels."

"Go on."

"Yeah. This—this is your power amplifier tuning. The meter should register fifty percent when you're ready to transmit. This is. . . ."

In five minutes I thought I could operate it. Maybe the technician had given me the wrong information about the radio set, but I doubted it. He was too scared—and one VHF transceiver is pretty much like another when you get the basic idea of what it is supposed to do.

My worry was about the type of modulation this set was using, FM. And the Kriths mostly used AM in the VHF ranges. Why, I don't know, but they did. And if I transmitted an FM signal into an AM receiver, even if I were exactly on frequency—well, they wouldn't get much out of it on the receiving end. I just hoped that the Kriths had planned for an eventuality like this and would be able to demodulate my FM signal.

"Sit down over there and stay quiet," I told the technician and began flipping switches.

Less than a minute later lights and meters said that I was ready to transmit. And if I were correct in remembering the Krithian emergency frequency and if the set were really transmitting and if . . . Hell, worrying isn't going to do any good. Just try.

"Red mobile to red leader," I said into the microphone in Shangalis. "Red mobile to red leader. Do you hear me, Kar-hinter?" Then I realized how foolish all that was and decided to give it to them straight. "If anybody's listening, this is Eric Mathers, Timeliner, under Kar-hinter's supervision. I have been captured by invaders from another Timeline. I am held prisoner in a place called Staunton somewhere in West Florida. Lock in on my signal and triangulate. Inform Kar-hinter at once and tell him to get here fast. I've come across the biggest thing we've ever seen. . . ."

That was the gist of my message. I repeated it three times, then switched to another frequency and did it again.

I was on my fourth frequency when I heard the banging on the hatch.

"Who's in there?" a muffled voice called from outside. "What's going on?"

The technician looked at me for an instant, then back at the hatch.

"Stay still," I told him—but that didn't do any good. He was a brave man, that technician, to be as scared as he was and still do what he did.

Still looking directly into the barrel of my pistol, he jumped at me, a yell of pure hatred on his lips. I fired. There wasn't much else I could do. And then his face wasn't much of a face anymore.

The technician lay at my feet, his blood splattered over me and the deck, and he was very still, and I hated very much that I had had to kill him.

The banging on the hatch had stopped, but a voice called, a different voice that I thought I recognized as Scoti's: "Mathers, we know you're in there. Come out and . . ."

"Come get me," I yelled back, switched to another frequency, and delivered one last frantic message into the microphone.

Outside, through the transparent dome, I could see a cluster of men in the hangar's open doors. Scoti came out from under the bulk of the craft, running and gesturing for the other men to clear out of the hangar. I only caught a brief glimpse of the weapon he held in his hand. But that was enough. He had showed it to me once before and told me a little about it. An R-4 power pistol. If I had been a praying man, I would have delivered my most heartfelt prayer at that moment. But all I could do was wait. There wasn't a damned thing else I could do.

Now the space in front of the hangar was vacant except for Scoti, who knelt with left elbow on left knee, left hand around right wrist, sighting across the barrel of the weapon he carried. I saw the muzzle flash. . . .

And I saw the universe explode. And I felt heat and flame and blinding light so bright that I could not see it. And that was all for a long, long time.

18
Voices

The world is a very unpleasant place to be in when your face is a mass of raw flesh and your eyes won't open because they're sealed shut with blood and both your legs are broken and you've got internal injuries that are leaking blood into places where there shouldn't be blood and you're lying on a bed of broken glass and twisted metal and some damned fool is shaking the universe like a baby crib.

I couldn't see, but I could hear, and I really didn't want to do that, but I didn't have the strength to fight it.

"Is he dead?" a voice asked.

"No, but he ought to be," answered another voice, maybe Scoti's. "Don't worry. He won't last long."

"What about Joal?" That voice might have been Mica's. I'm not sure.

"He's dead. Mathers shot him in the face."

"Bastard. Kick him once for me."

He did. In the ribs. I passed out again.

The next time I heard voices the universe was holding a little more steady and the bed was just lumpy rocks rather than broken glass, but it would be hard for me to say that I was more comfortable. Maybe a little less painful.

"He needs a doctor," someone said from above.

"Screw the doctor," Scoti spat. "Let the bastard bleed to death."

"Okay."

"Have they found Sally yet?"

"I don't know."

"If he killed her. . . . If he killed her . . ." Then Scoti's voice came close, right up to what used to be my ear. "Mathers, can you hear me?"

There wasn't much I could do to let him know. I couldn't even groan.

"Listen to me, bastard," Scoti said. "If you hurt Sally,

I'll see that you live. You'll live so that I can slowly take
you apart piece by piece. I mean slow, damn it!"

I think he kicked me again, but I couldn't really be sure.

I was somewhere between life and death, consciousness
and unconsciousness when I heard a voice yelling, "Scoti,
look up there!"

"What is it?" Scoti yelled back, his voice dwindling as he
moved away from me.

"Airships," the other voice, or one of the other voices,
said. "British airships."

"Call Mica! Full alert!"

I heard running feet and yelling voices, but everyone
seemed to have forgotten about me, and that was okay. I
just wanted to be left alone to die in peace.

There was a strange chill in the air, an alienness, an unknown quanity that I couldn't identify but knew was more
than the feel of shock and pain, and all around me was the
stillness you only find in a nightmare. I thought maybe I
was dead and had gone to hell.

A voice was speaking to me, and the voice was that out
of a nightmare, a masculine voice with a familiar ring to it,
but my mind could not place the voice. It was saying,
"Stay alive, Eric. For God's sake, man, hang on just a little
while longer. They're coming to help you. The pain won't
last long. You can stand it, Eric. *I did.*"

And then the voice was gone, and I floated down into a
painful darkness, but I knew that I would try to hang on.
Help was coming, the voice had said.

Later, how much later I don't know, but later I heard
the whine of airship motors and another, different whine
that ceased abruptly with a clap of air and it might have
been the probability generator of a skudder—sautierboat—
the other Paratime craft that had been in the hangar, because it was gone later. Then I heard small-arms fire from
outside the hangar and a voice that yelled, "Fall back into the. . . ." And the chatter of a machine gun that cut off
the voice and the sudden rasp of an energy pistol that had
not been made on this world and a voice yelling in Shangalis, and I went black again.

* * *

Someone was bending over me, holding my head up, putting something to my mouth that was cold and wet and very welcome. I think I also got an injection of something, but I didn't feel the prick of the needle.

"Eric, Eric, can you hear me?"

It was a voice that I ought to remember. I thought I knew who it was. Sally? No, it wasn't Sally. She had a soft contralto voice. And this voice wasn't soft. It was harsh and rasping, and there was a British accent to it that was too pronounced to be real.

."Eric, for God's sake, old man," the voice said. "What is this?"

"Get Sally," I somehow managed to say to that voice that I ought to recognize, but didn't yet.

"Who?"

"Sally. Back in the woods. Save Sally. Don't let them get her."

"Don't let who get her?"

"*Them, them.* Don't let *them* get her.

But who *they* were I wasn't sure, and I'm not sure to this day.

This time when I awoke the bed was softer still, but it was moving, upward, lurching, and I wanted to vomit all over the place because I didn't want to be moving. Not now. Not ever.

"Get us some altitude," the strange/familiar voice said.

"I'm doing the best I can," another voice answered, another one that had something to do with me, my past, that I ought to know. "This damned thing's no fusion rocket, you know."

"I know, but get us out of here. They're going to bring up their big guns soon."

"I know. We'll make it. How's Mathers?"

"Pretty bad. He must have been in that skudder we found."

"How in God's name did he live through that?"

"He's too mean to die."

"What about the girl?"

"I gave her a shot. She's still out."

"She ought to have some clothes on."

"I didn't bring a change. How was I to know?"

"Well, cover her up with something."

"Does that bother you, her being naked?"

"Yeah."

"I enjoy looking at her."

The other voice grunted and then said, "Man, is Karhinter going to be glad to get these two back."

"I am too."

"I know."

"Eric and I have been together for a long time."

"Tracy! Look down there!"

"What is—"

It was just one of those days when the universe wouldn't behave itself.

A great fist came up from below, aimed directly at the bunk on which I was lying, thumping it with such force that I was thrown into the air, out of the bunk, and onto the hard floor beside it. And then the BOOM! so loud and so terrifying that I thought it would shatter whatever was left of the world.

"They blew it up," one of the voices said incredulously. "They blew up the whole damned place."

Then I went down into the darkness.

19
Recovery

It was a long, long while later before I had truly lucid moments. I think I remember a long sequence of nightmares, most of them false, some of them real. I remember strangely gentle hands carrying me out of a British airship on a stretcher and across a landing field to a horse-drawn ambulance and an unbelievably bumpy ride across an infinite, pitted earth. And I remember a fifty-foot-tall Mica, with skin as white as a parson's blessing, but with eyes that were as dark and empty as interstellar space, and he had an enormous knife that he used to probe my liver and said over and over and over "What did you do with Sally?" And I remember the bright overhead lights of an operating room and a doctor who said, "Easy, Captain Mathers. Rest easy. You'll be asleep soon," in a voice of the archangels, and then he started putting me back together again. And a bomb that kept exploding across the Timelines, wiping out world after world, destroying the whole complex of continua. And somebody swabbing my hot forehead with cotton dipped in alcohol and asking me to sip some kind of liquid and crushed ice through a straw. And then G'lendal, naked and beautiful, her big breasts pointed at me like twin cannon, standing before me and slowly, gradually changing into a naked and hideous Krith with a wide, sneering grin and a hungry look on its face. And a universe that consisted of paper cutouts and a voice that I ought to know telling me that this was reality, all the reality I would ever find.

Then, after a while, I woke up, and the nightmares were over, most of them.

At first I couldn't have said for sure where I was. Oh, it was a hospital room, of course: pale-green walls and a stark white bed and all the other paraphernalia that goes with a hospital, all with the overtones of a second- or third-level technology, just like the world in which I had been and where I still might be.

Above my head and to the right was a cord that I assumed rang for the nurse. I pulled on it, or rather tried to pull on it, and as I fought to wrap my weak fingers around it, I noticed the glucose drip that was plugged into my left arm, the bottle half-full of colorless sugar. Finally my hand closed around the cord, and I tugged and thought that off in the distance I heard a bell ring, and then let my arm fall back to the bed and waited to see what would happen.

Five hundred years later, more or less, the door directly opposite my bed opened and a tall, thin man wearing a white smock and rimless glasses came in. I started to try to speak, realized that I wasn't sure what language to use, and waited for him say the first words.

"Oh, you've come around, Mathers," the white-clad man said in Shangalis. He was a Timeliner.

"Yeah," I managed to say.

"You've had Kar-hinter worried," he said.

"I've had me kind of worried, too," I said in short gasps.

"Rest easy now," the man said, coming to the side of the bed, taking my right wrist in his left hand, feeling the pulse while he looked at his wrist watch, saying, "I'm Dr. Conners."

"Where am I?"

"Bakersville, South Africa," Connors answered when he had finished counting the beats of my heart. "You're still on the same Line, though, if that's what you mean. This is a hospital that the British have turned over to us. We're all Liners here."

"What happened?"

"I'm afraid I couldn't tell you," the doctor replied. "But Kar-hinter and two of your friends are outside if you feel up to talking with them."

"Yes, please," I said, then lay back on the bed and closed my eyes and rested and tried to gather what strength was left in my body. But before the doctor left the room, I was forced to ask, "Just how bad am I?"

"You'll be fine. Nothing's missing," Conners said, and for a moment I thought that was all he was going to say. "You had both legs broken and several ribs as well. We also had to replace your liver. Your face was pretty badly cut up, but plastiskin is going to cover the scars. You'll never know the difference. And, well, you ought to be up and walking around within forty-eight hours."

Thank God for the medical science we've picked up across the Lines! I wouldn't have lived if I'd had to depend on the local skills.

"While you were here," Conners went on, "we also replaced your augmentation control center. Apparently it was deactivated."

I nodded.

"And we replaced your missing fingers," he completed.

I looked down at my left hand and saw that I had a full set of fingers on it. The grafting scars were either already healed or very skillfully hidden by plastiskin.

"I'll send your friends in now," the doctor said.

"Thanks."

So I just lay there waiting for Kar-hinter and whoever else was with him to come in and thought and wondered: How was Sally? And, in fact, where was she? Had they really found her and taken her with me? And what had happened to Staunton? Had it really blown up? Or was that just a part of my nightmares? And. . . .

The door opened, and Kar-hinter, Tracy, and Kearns came into the room. The alien was naked, of course, and the two men were dressed in British uniforms.

"I told you that he was too mean to kill," Tracy said, smiling. "How are you, old man?"

"Bloody damned poorly," I said, trying to answer Tracy's smile.

"Hello, Eric," Kar-hinter said in his precise English that somehow reminded me of Mica's. "Feeling better, I trust."

"Damned if I know," I said. "I don't feel much of anything right now."

"You must have given them hell, Mathers," Kearns said, a strangely misplaced smile on his face.

"Not as much as they gave me," I told him.

"I don't know," Kearns said. "Tracy and I found at least two bodies that you must have killed."

"That was my limit for the season," I said, wishing they'd get over the small talk and that somebody'd answer some questions for me.

Kar-hinter must have sensed my feelings, for he said,

"We have many questions to ask you, Eric, but first we will answer yours."

"Okay," I said weakly. "What about Sally?"

"Count von Heinen's wife?" Kar-hinter asked, something that might have been puzzlement in his voice. I wasn't sure. You can never be sure about a Krith. "She is well. Hillary and Ronald found her when they rescued you. She is now at an interrogation station on an adjacent Line."

Thank God for that, I said to myself. "What happened? From the beginning."

Kar-hinter gave me what passed for a smile, said, "As you know, Hillary and Ronald crossed the Imperial lines to safety on the morning of the raid on the villa. We then established contact with you. When your signal ceased abruptly, we investigated as quickly as possible, found that you and your captives were gone. We assumed that you had been taken by the people in the strange skudder you had fought earlier. We could do nothing but wait until you tried to contact us, though we were following up clues."

"You know who those people are, don't you?" I asked.

"We know now," Kar-hinter replied. "Countess von Heinen gave us that information under the first mind probe."

"Had you suspected?"

Kar-hinter smiled. "Suspected, but nothing more. But, to go on, we had nearly given you up for dead when your message was received at the Butt of Lewis."

"Then you did get my signal?"

Kar-hinter nodded in a very human fashion. "Yes, we have had continous monitors on all frequencies with recording equipment attached. Computers determined that you were using FM and demodulated accordingly. We came as soon as we could get a fix on your signal."

"How did you get there so fast?" I asked Tracy.

He smiled back at me and said, "Kearns and I were working out of Victoria, Virginia. Kar-hinter sent us there with a couple of platoons of men to investigate a resurgence of Staunton-rumors. He thought that they might somehow be connected with the—er—Paratimers who captured you. We didn't know who they were then, of course."

"What about Staunton?" I asked. "Did you get inside?"

Tracy shook his head. "We only got as far as the hangar where we found you. And we were damned lucky to get away from there. We lost most of our men. They blew up the place, y'know."

"I thought they did," I said. "I thought I remembered it," I paused, took a deep breath, then asked, "Was it with atomic weapons? They had quite a stockpile of thermonukes."

"No," Kar-hinter said. "The explosives they used were chemical. Their nuclear weapons did not go off, fortunately for this world. We are in the process of recovering them now. They will be shipped Outtime at once."

I nodded, looked back at Tracy. "How many sautier-boats—skudders were in the hangar?"

"Just the one," Tracy said. "The ruined one you must have been in. Were there others?"

"One," I said. "Some of them must have gotten away in it."

"It would appear so," Kar-hinter said.

"Were there any captives?" I asked.

"A few," Kar-hinter answered. "But they were only locals and most of them knew less than the countess. By the time we were able to get another force in there most of the survivors had fled and gotten into hiding."

"Well, what about the Imperial Baltic plant?" I asked. "We didn't get the count for you."

"An alternate plan was used," Kar-hinter said, though he did not tell me what the plan was. "When we raided the plant, we discovered evidence of Outtime activities."

"But you've shut down the plant?" I asked.

"Quite completely," Kar-hinter said. "One of their experimental weapons went off 'accidentally' and totally destroyed the installation."

Before I could ask anything more, Dr. Conners stuck his head in the door. "Gentlemen, Kar-hinter, I suggest that you let Captain Mathers sleep now. He needs the rest."

"Of course," Kar-hinter said, rising. "I will be seeing you again tomorrow, Eric."

And in a moment they were gone, and I drifted off into a long drugged sleep punctuated with hellish dreams of monster Kriths and equally monstrous Micas and Scotis, and I wondered if those two had escaped the destruction of Staunton.

When Kar-hinter came back the next day, accompanied by the tall, swarthy, black-uniformed Pall, his bodyguard, I was more nearly able to carry on a decent conversation, though now it was his turn to do most of the talking. Pall, as was his custom, said nothing at all.

Mind probes had been used on Sally, Kar-hinter told me, and her every memory was now recorded in tiny molly cubes that were being scanned by computer, extracting important data about the Paratimers and their operations. Already Kar-hinter knew more about them than I did, though he did ask me a few questions to confirm certain things that Sally had believed to be true.

"You have done us a great service, Eric," Kar-hinter said at length, "a truly great service to both mankind and Krith. We now know who our true enemies in this Timeline are."

I just nodded.

"Tell me, Eric," Kar-hinter said slowly, peering into my eyes, "you were there six weeks, under their eyes, constantly bombarded with their propaganda. What has that done to you?"

I had the sudden feeling of fear, as if Kar-hinter were about to uncover some deep, hidden guilt.

"What do you mean?" I asked.

"Sally von Heinen deeply believes that we Kriths are monsters involved in some great, elaborate plot to conquer and enslave mankind on all the Timelines. Has any of that belief rubbed off onto you, Eric? What has the experience done to you? Do you doubt us?"

"For God's sake, Kar-hinter," I said, trying to convince myself as much as him, "I sent those messages, didn't I? I called you there."

"I know that," Kar-hinter said, "but that is not the answer I want. Are there any doubts about us in your mind?"

"Run a mind probe on me," I said defensively. "Then you can tell if I'm lying."

"Eric," Kar-hinter said slowly, "you know that we cannot run a mind probe on you. You are a Timeliner. You are conditioned. A mind probe would kill you."

"Oh," I said weakly, foolishly. "That's right, isn't it?"

"It is, Eric. I will have to trust you. I will have to believe what you tell me."

Pall's dark eyes gazed at me with a cold look that seemed to cut through my skin. I didn't feel that *he* would trust me no matter what I said or did.

I looked back at Kar-hinter. "Then it's this," I said slowly and knew that I was lying even as I said it, but there wasn't anything else I could say, "I'm the same man I was six weeks ago. Nothing has changed. I still believe in what we're doing, we, all of us, Kriths and Timeliners. Those people—the Paratimers—have made some kind of terrible mistake. They're the ones who are wrong."

"I believe you, Eric, and I am glad of it. You are too valuable a man to lose." He paused. "Now tell me, what is this Von Heinen woman to you? We must assume that she is a widow now, if that helps you any."

"I don't know what she is to me, Kar-hinter," I said, and this time I was speaking the truth. "I really don't know. Maybe she just reminds me too much of someone I knew a long time ago." I shook my head. "But I can assume that she hates my guts now."

"For betraying Staunton?"

I nodded. "She trusted me. She thought I had been converted to their side."

Kar-hinter was silent for a few moments. "We are finished with her," he said. "We have gained all the knowledge we can from her. You may have her if you wish. I am sure that our technicians could see to it that she, ah, felt differently about you."

"No!" I said vehemently. "Don't tamper with her mind."

"As you wish," Kar-hinter said, rising, his short tail lashing the air behind him. Pall rose with him. "You may decide whether you want her and, ah, as she is. Tomorrow or the next day you will be debriefed at length concerning your stay in Staunton. Routine formality, you understand. But when that is over and Dr. Conners releases you from the hospital, you may take a rest. I am sure that you have earned it."

"Thanks," I said.

"I thought that you might like a cabin in one of the Eden Lines," Kar-hinter said. "You and Sally."

"I'll think about it."

"Please do, Eric. A long rest is prescribed for you."

And I did think about it for the next few days.

20
With Sally in Eden

I didn't really know exactly where the Eden Lines were located. Somewhere to the far T-West of RTGB-307, beyond the Carolingian Lines. Why the worlds there were uninhabited I'm not sure either. Chemical warfare seems to be the most likely thing since the Earth there shows no signs of thermonuclear craters, nor does its air carry any deadly bacteria. So, I guess, on those worlds men had developed deadly gases which they had used to destroy themselves. In a way I was glad of that since that left maybe half a dozen Lines that the Kriths had taken over and cleaned up, using automated equipment to transform them into virtual earthly paradises. They were rest and recuperation stations for weary human Timeliners of rather high status. I was honored in being offered a cabin in one of them.

Sally didn't feel quite so honored, though she accepted her fate with stoic calm. She hardly spoke to me from the time we boarded the airship in Bakersville, South Africa, to when we stepped out of the skudder somewhere in North America in one of the Eden Lines.

"Here you are, Captain Mathers," said the tall, dark-skinned skudder pilot who reminded me a little of Pall. "Eden. You know the rules. You're not allowed to bring in any Outtime artifacts. Everything you will need is provided by the cabin."

"I know," I said.

"Then, ah, would you both please undress and give me your clothing." He smiled awkwardly. "This *is* Eden, you know."

I remembered the Judeo-Christian myth that had given the Eden Lines their name.

"Yeah," I answered and began stripping.

Sally stood silently staring at us both, hate and defiance

in her eyes: So must Kristin have stood when the governor's men approached her.

When I had removed my clothing and handed it to the pilot, I turned to her.

"Come on, Sally," I said. "You've got to play it by the rules."

"I'm your prisoner," she said. "I'll do as you say. I have no choice."

"I wish you wouldn't take that attitude," I said, trying not to look at the skudder pilot.

"Well, it's the truth, isn't it?"

"Only partly. Oh, damn it, get undressed."

Sally did, without expression, quickly and efficiently. In a moment her blouse and shorts and panties were a bundle wrapped around her shoes, and she handed the bundle to the skudder pilot.

It's funny. I don't think I've ever really described Sally to you. I suppose it's about time.

I had really only seen her naked once before, back when I was trying to get to the radio transceiver in the sautier-boat in Staunton and then I didn't have time to appreciate the view. Now I did—not that I hadn't appreciated how she looked from the moment I saw her. But that's all beside the point, isn't it? I was going to tell you how she looked.

Sally appeared younger than her twenty-six years, fresh and almost innocent. She had blond hair and a funny color of green to her eyes; she was five feet five inches tall, and her measurements were something like 37-22-36. So much for statistics. What can they really tell you?

Maybe she didn't have the *tremendous* proportions of G'lendal, but what she did have was perfect. Like her breasts, for example: high, round, firm, tipped with small, round nipples, and if she had ever worn a bra in her life I couldn't imagine why. Her waist was slender, flaring out to perfectly rounded hips and the neatest set of buttocks I've ever seen. The clump of hair between her thighs was so pale and blond as to be almost invisible.

Her face was midway between being oval and triangular, and her eyes seemed almost too large for her face, but that wasn't bad at all. Her lips, even when she was 'angry, seemed to have a tendency to want to smile, and when she really did smile, she showed teeth that could hardly have been better formed. Her face was surrounded by the blond hair that was very long, though she usually kept it piled high atop her head, with bangs curling down across her forehead almost to her eyebrows, while another bunch of hair cascaded down her back to her shoulder blades.

If there were anything wrong with the appearance of Sally Beall von Heinen, I don't know what it was, unless you'd be foolish enough to say that she wasn't *quite* as beautiful as G'lendal. But then maybe G'lendal was a little bit too perfect.

And, as I said before, I thought there was more to my feeling for Sally than just the hot urges I felt below my waist.

"Thanks," the skudder pilot was saying as she handed him the bundle of clothing, and he looked at her with something in his eyes that wasn't hard to read. He'd like to have been in my place.

"I'll be back for you in a month," he went on. "You two have a nice time." He paused, then said, "Oh, by the way, Kar-hinter said to tell you that he'd probably drop in on you in the next few days, if that's okay with you."

"Yes, I suppose. Thanks," I said.

Moments later the pilot closed the skudder's hatch, waved to us through the bubble. Then a time-wrenching buzz filled the air. The skudder vanished.

"Let's go take a look at the cabin," I said to Sally.

"Let's get something straight right now," she said, holding still. "I know exactly what my status is here. I'm your prisoner, and you can make me do whatever you want. Because I know that, I'm not going to put up a fight every time you tell me to do something. I don't have that kind of fatal pride. I'll do what you say." She paused for breath. "But get this straight, Eric Mathers or whatever your name is, and get it straight right now. I'll only be doing what I do because I have no choice, because you and your goddamned Kriths can make me do it—and not because I want to. Do you understand me?"

There was no point in arguing at this stage of the

game, so I simply said. "Yes, I understand. Now let's go look at that cabin."

I took her by the hand and led her.

The field in which the cabin sat consisted of perhaps half a dozen acres of cleared land, green and gently rolling, each rise topped with fruit trees of different kinds, apples, cherries, peaches, oranges. you name it. Bushes grew in profusion, many of them flowering and all of them carefully trimmed. Paths ran between the trees and bushes, rock-bordered and lined with other types of flowering plants. The grass was a bright, rich green, closely cropped and soft as an expensive carpet under our naked feet.

The cabin itself sat just to the left of the center of the carefully tended clearing and reminded me of a brick and glass model of the planet Saturn, cut in half, or maybe half-buried in the earth. The ring was a low wall that circled the house and the planet was the brick and glass dome of the structure, a hemisphere sheltered by the wall that circled it and the trees that rose above it, shadowing the cabin under their leaves.

Inside was a single room, divided by low partitions into four roughly equal sections. One was the sleeping area, containing two big double beds, the second the autokitchen and indoor dining area, the third was a living area with library access console, video tape player, multichannel music gear and miscellaneous games and things. The final section of the house was a huge sunken bathtub and a toilet cubicle. It was done in soft pleasant earth colors, and sometimes it was hard to tell where the walls ended and the broad expanse of windows looking out into the gardens began. It was a nice place to be marooned with a beautiful woman, even one who wanted to see me dead.

"Sit down," I told Sally, gesturing toward the comfortable-looking furniture in the living area. "I'll see if I can get us something to eat."

"I'm not hungry," Sally replied, sitting, but refusing to look at me.

"Okay, then, I'm ordering you to eat."

She didn't protest, at least not out loud, so I went into the kitchen and studied the menu. The autokitchen had been programmed to suit the culinary tastes of men from hundreds of different cultures, everything from the obscure and involved vegetarianism of some of the Indus Lines to the cannibalism of the Dramalians, though in this case the "long pig" was synthesized. The Aegean squid appealed to me since it was one of my favorites and a delicacy I hadn't tasted in years, but I gave way to my concern for Sally and punched out something that her Anglo-Saxon upbringing would have found more tasteful: roast beef, baked potatoes, etc.

A few minutes later the plates popped out of the oven, and I wheeled the trays into the living room, where Sally sat in the same position, apparently having moved nothing but her eyes during my absence.

"Now here it is," I said. "I won't try to force you to eat, but you won't be hurting anyone but yourself if you don't."

I sat down across from her and began devouring my meal. After a while Sally began to eat as well, but without any great gusto.

"Pretty good, isn't it?" I asked between mouthfuls. Sally nodded morosely.

After a while, having eaten perhaps half of her serving, Sally put down her fork, looked up at me, and said slowly, "Why did you bring me here?"

I looked back at her for a long while before I answered. "You know, I'm not really sure. Kar-hinter suggested it, more or less, and it seemed like a good idea."

"Kar-hinter?" she asked. "The Krith?" The way she said it made it sound like a dirty word.

"Yes."

"Hasn't he done enough to me?"

"Did he harm you?"

"You wouldn't understand," she snapped.

"Maybe I would. Try me."

"What does a man like you know about honor?"

"More than you might think," I said. When she didn't speak again, I went on. "I suppose you're referring to the mind probe he had used on you?"

"Of course."

"Okay, so he forced your mind to divulge everything you know about the Paratimers. You had nothing to do with it really. I mean, it's not as if you betrayed them voluntarily. Kar-hinter just. . . ."

"He invaded my soul!" Sally said angrily. "He raped my mind!"

"Now wait a minute. All he did was. . . ."

"I know what he did and you can't explain it away. He made me betray everyone and everything I love." She paused for a moment, fought with her emotions. "Why did you let him do it, Eric? I . . . I thought we could trust you. Mica did too. We all did. We . . ."

"I'm sorry about that, Sally, but I did what I had to do."

"What you had to do! *Why?* I can understand your working for *them* before, when you didn't know any better. But . . . but how could you after you *knew,* after we told you what *they* are?"

"Just calm down for a minute and listen to me."

Sally crossed her arms below her naked breasts, her fingernails digging into her upper arms, her face a complex of unreadable expressions.

"All I had was the word of the Paratimers as opposed to the word of the Kriths. Mica was never able to offer me any real proof of his claims. I know that *you* believe what he told you, and I think he believed it too. But belief isn't proof, no matter how strongly the belief is held and no matter by how many people. It's just a belief unless there's objective proof—and I never saw any really objective proof that couldn't have been faked."

"Are you saying that Staunton and Mica and Scoti and all the others and the books and tapes and all that are, well, built on lies? Can you believe that's true?"

"Aren't you and Mica trying to tell me that everything I've seen in my own Lines is based on a Lie?"

"Yes, of course. . . . Oh."

"You see? It was easier for me to accept Mica and his world as a lie than it was for me to accept the experiences of my whole life as a lie."

For a moment I almost thought I had got through and that she was going to be able to see it from my point of view, but then she said, "How can you be so blind?"

"I could ask you the same thing. Just look around you. Does this look like the work of man-hating monsters?"

"It's just a part of their scheme to lull you into trusting them."

"Here we go again," I said, rising and looking out the vast expanse of window. "Our arguing won't convince either of us that the other is right. I spent six weeks in your world. Now you spend a month in one of mine. Maybe you'll see why I couldn't accept what I was told."

"No," Sally said. "You won't be able to brainwash me that easily. I know better. I know what the Kriths are, and I won't believe their Lie."

I suddenly wished that I knew what the Kriths were and what they wanted, what they really wanted from us. And I realized then, maybe for the first time, that Sally and Mica and Scoti and the others in Staunton had planted some serious doubts in my mind, doubts that I would, sooner or later, be forced to resolve.

In the garden behind the cabin was an enormous swimming pool, a great free-form thing some hundred yards long and maybe fifty yards wide at its widest point. One end was no more than a few inches deep, but the other, where the diving boards were, was at least fifteen yards to the bottom. And the water was a clear crystal, pure, reflecting the cloudless blue sky above.

Along the sides of the pool ran a wide strip of soft, spongy green material, a vast mattress for sunbathing. Here and there were reclining chairs and two extensions of the autokitchen for dialing meals and drinks.

We had been there for three days by then, and Sally had begun to relax some, at times even seeming to forget where she was and why and that she was, by her own definition, my prisoner. We had been swimming in the pool, diving and splashing and even occasionally laughing at our own foolishness. Finally, exhausted, we had climbed out of the pool onto the sun-deck and lay dripping with water. I dialed us drinks and lay back looking up at the clear blue sky of this Earth, a world uncluttered by the more obvious works of civilization.

"Eric," Sally said suddenly, a sharp edge of seriousness to her voice, "we can't go on like this."

How many times across the Lines have women said that and for how many different reasons?

"Why?" I asked in all seriousness.

"I'm beginning to like you too well," she said. "I really believe you're sincere about what you say." She paused. "Sometimes I even forget and just, well, enjoy myself and then I remember and. . . . Well, when I remember what I am and what you are and what this place is and why we're here, when I remember these things I hate myself for enjoying it and I hate you for making me enjoy it. And I think that sooner or later I will come to hate you enough to kill you."

"I wouldn't want you to do that," I said, jealously thinking about her relationship with Mica. Back in Staunton she had told me that she was his mistress. I somehow just couldn't bring myself to imagine her in bed with that cold fish, and I wondered just what it was that she felt for him. I couldn't believe it was love or even real sexual attraction to him.

Why then, I asked myself, had Sally been his mistress? Well, maybe you could attribute it to hero worship, gratitude for what she believed he and his Paratimers were doing for her and her people. If she could marry Count Albert von Heinen to advance the American rebel cause, couldn't she be bedding with Mica for just about the same reason? It seemed sort of likely to me—especially when she had never shown any real affection toward the Paratimer leader—and it did help my ego a lot to thiink it was so, as if I didn't have to compete with the man if I could show him up for what he was—whatever he was.

Then she brought me out of my thoughts.

"Listen to me," she said, sitting up. "One of us is right and the other is wrong. Do you agree?"

"Well, yes. There must be objective proof somewhere."

"Then if we learn what's true, can't we both accept it?"

"Yes, I'll accept it if we can find real proof."

"Can you call your Kar-hinter some way?"

"No, but the skudder pilot said that he'd be coming here to see us in a few days. Why?"

"Ask him about this Cross-Line Civilibation you talk about. Ask him to take us there and show us that it really exists and that it's as wonderful as they claim it is. And then, if he does, I'll believe that the Kriths are really what you think they are and that the Paratimers are as mistaken as you believe."

Perhaps Sally and her friends had made me doubt the Kriths, I thought, but it also looked as if I had somehow made Sally begin to doubt what she had been told. We were both doubting the verities by which we had lived—but they could be proved, one way or the other. Kar-hinter could take us to the Cross-Line Civilization, show us how men and Kriths worked together to build a perfect world—and that would solve our problems, destroy my own growing doubts, and show Sally that everything I had told her was true. It was so simple. Why hadn't I thought of it before?

"Okay," I said. "We'll do that. We'll get Kar-hinter to take us there.

Four more days went by before Kar-hinter arrived.

It was night. The yard-tending robots had completed their work and the carefully controlled nightly rain had begun to fall. Sally and I were inside the cabin watching a videotape of the classic *Pirates of Avalon*, with English dubbed, when I heard a rapping at the door.

"What's that?" Sally gasped, almost leaping to her feet.

"I'll see," I said, rising and crossing to the door.

When I told the door to open and the cabin's light spilled through it out into the darkness, I saw the tall, naked form of a Krith.

"Kar-hinter?" I asked, not sure that I recognized him in the poor light. And all Kriths do look pretty much alike to a human.

"Hello, Eric," Kar-hinter replied, water running down his face from the steady rain, dripping from his chin, trickling down his nearly olive-colored, hairless body. "May I come in?"

"Of course," I said. "We've been expecting you."

As Kar-hinter came into the room, shook water from his body like a dog, and found himself a chair, I cut off the video player and turned up the lights.

"Hello, Sally," he said. "I hope that you are finding Eden to be a pleasant place of captivity."

"There are worse prisons," Sally said, forcing herself to smile just a little despite the revulsion she must have felt. She moved back in her chair, trying to cover herself with her arms and legs as if there were some reason she should not let the alien see her naked, though I have never known a Krith to find any human being sexually attractive. I have the impression that their ideas of sex bear little resemblance to ours, but I don't know anything about them.

"I am glad you have accepted it," Kar-hinter said. "Eric is not an unpleasant jailer, I trust."

Sally looked at me, but did not reply.

"At least there is no open enmity," Kar-hinter said. "I had even hoped that pehaps you were lovers by now. Eh, Eric?"

"We get along," I said.

"Ah, but you sleep in separate beds, I think," the Krith said.

"Does it matter to you?" I asked, knowing that there was an angry, resentful edge to my voice. What business *was* it of his?

"I only want you to be satisfied, Eric," the alien said. "And you, Sally, do you still consider me a monster and Eric a traitor to mankind?"

"I've seen nothing yet to change my opinion of either of you," she said coldly. I wondered how much of it she really meant.

"You are doing a poor job of converting her, Eric."

"Is that my job?"

"No," Kar-hinter said. "Her conversion is of no importance to me. She can believe what she wishes. I only want to see you happy, Eric, rewarded, so to speak, for what you have done for us."

"Us?" Sally asked.

"Ah, yes, must I explain every plural pronoun I use?"

He was as close to being angry as I had ever seen him—him or any other Krith.

"By *us*," Kar-hinter was saying, "Sally, I mean allied mankind and Krith. We are partners in our own salvation."

"I wish I could believe that," Sally said.

"Do you really?" Kar-hinter asked. "That would be a beginning, at least."

"Kar-hinter," I said "let's cut out this verbal fencing for a minute."

"Of course, Eric."

"I want to make a request."

"Anything that is within my power to grant is yours," the Krith said.

"I want you to take Sally and me to the Cross-Line Civilization."

"Why, Eric?" He didn't seem surprised at my request, but then did anything ever seem to surprise him?

"Well, that's one of the cornerstones of the Paratimers' arguments against the Kriths," I said. "They say that the Cross-Line Civilization is one of the Great Lies, the other one being the Contratime signals. Well, if we could show Sally that the Cross-Line Civilization does exist, she would accept that *she* is the one who has been lied to."

"But, frankly, Eric, it is of no importance to me what *she* thinks is true or false."

"It's important to me."

"I see." Kar-hinter paused for a moment. "And you, Eric, why do *you* want to see the Cross-Line Civilization?"

"I just told you."

"Did you? Or, Eric, might it be that you too have begun to believe her and her Paratimers? Is *she* converting *you*, Eric?"

"Does it matter?" I asked. "If we can visit the Cross-Line worlds, neither of us would have any reason to doubt."

"But it does matter, my dear Eric," Kar-hinter said slowly, spreading his manlike hands. "You know as well as I that skudders are scarce this far West and must be used only for work of vital importance to the master plans. We just cannot call up a skudder every time we want to take a pleasure trip, especially one so long as the one you propose."

"Surely you could arrange it if you tried," I insisted.

"I could, Eric, I believe, but only if I were convinced

it would be worth the while. I am not, not for *her*. She does not matter to me or to the plan."

"Do I?" I asked slowly, playing what I supposed was my trump card.

"Of couse you do, Eric. You are becoming one of our most valuable operatives."

"Then would you arrange such a trip to convince me?"

"Are you that near to defection?"

"I don't know," I said slowly, being more honest with him than I had been before and on purpose. "I don't want to know." I paused, then said to him: "I admit that I've been pretty shaken by some of what has happened. The Paratimers were awfully convincing. And I do have some doubts, not many, but some, and I don't like them. I want absolute certainty that I'm doing the right thing, that I'm fighting on the right side. And you can give me that certainty if you'll just take us to the Cross-Line worlds. If you don't. . . . Well, I don't mean to be threateneing, Kar-hinter, but if you don't, I'll wonder why. And I'll suspect that maybe you didn't take us there because you couldn't, because there's really no such place."

"Quite a speech, Eric," Kar-hinter replied at last. "I did not know that it had gone this far with you."

For the first time I felt fear of Kar-hinter and the whole Krithian machine. What if Sally were right? What if Kar-hinter were really the monster she believed he was? It would be the easiest thing in the world for him to bring in a squad of men and wipe us out here and now. No one would ever know, and my doubts would never have an opportunity to spread if he killed us both now. I wonder if my fear showed.

"So you might turn against us," Kar-hinter was saying slowly, but without antagonism. "I would not want that to happen, Eric. Perhaps I should not have given you this woman."

"She has nothing to do with my doubts at this point," I said. "Can you convince me that what I am doing is right?"

"As I said, Eric, skudders are hardly available for pleasure cruises, but perhaps this is important enough. I will see what I can do. I will return tomorrow and tell you." He rose from the chair where he had sat. "I will leave now. Good night, Eric, Sally."

The not-quite-human smile on Kar-hinter's face faded into a look of intense concentration, and then he flickered out of existence, and Sally and I sat there quietly, looking at the place where he had been and wondering what he would do tomorrow when he returned.

21
Across the Lines

Kar-hinter appeared simultaneously with the skudder, both arriving in the middle of the garden before the cabin just a short while after noon on the day following his visit. The Krith waved for the skudder pilot and the black-uniformed Pall to remain in their seats and walked quickly up the path toward the cabin, smiling broadly in an almost human fashion and waving to Sally and me. We had just come out after hearing the unmistakable whine of the skudder's probability generators.

"Eric," he called, "I have been able to arrange the transportation for the two of you. We shall leave at once for the East. Are both of you ready?"

I looked at Sally.

"I didn't bring anything here with me," she said, "and there's nothing I want to take." She paused. "But, well, I would like to comb my hair and put on some makeup."

Since she had resigned herself to being nude while in Eden, Sally had taken to using body makeup from one of the Europo-Minoan Lines that was supplied by the cabin. Not that I thought she really needed it; her face and body looked fine without it.

"Very well," Kar-hinter said, still smiling as broadly. "There is clothing for you both in the skudder. I do hope that you have eaten."

"Yes," I said. "We just finished lunch."

"Good," the Krith said. "It is a long trip."

"So we've been told," Sally said, her voice suddenly doubtful, as if she were feeling the same sort of fear that I had felt the night before, as if she suspected that Kar-hinter was now arranging to have us both killed before we could express our doubts to anyone else.

"Hurry, then," the Krith said to Sally. "Fix yourself and we shall go."

She went back into the cabin, almost seeming fearful of leaving me alone with Kar-hinter.

* * *

It wasn't long before we entered the skudder and began the trip across the Lines.

The small skudder was crowded with the five of us in it, though neither the pilot nor Pall spoke, and Pall hardly even moved. Pall, if you weren't looking at him, was easy to ignore.

After a while you can almost become adjusted to just about anything, even the mind-wrenching, stomach-twisting sensation of skudding across the near infinity of parallel universes. Flicker. Flicker. Flicker. At least I seemed to become more adjusted than usual as the trip lengthened from minutes to hours and still we moved.

Sally, Kar-hinter and I talked very little after the first few minutes. Despite the adjustment, talking in a skudding craft seemed to be more trouble than it was worth.

There were two bundles of clothing for us, brightly colored, nearly transparent, form-fitting sleeveless shirts and knee-length pants, pointed shoes, and peaked caps. Kar-hinter assured us that these were the height of sartorial splendor in the first of the Cross-Line worlds that we were about to visit.

To pass the time, Kar-hinter had provided us with a stack of magazines from Sally's native Line, some of which I suppose she found interesting. I was left to boredom. A large thermal bottle of coffee sat on the floor between us and after our stomachs had more or less adjusted to the flickering, we each, Sally and I, had a cup.

What happened after my first cup of coffee seemed unimportant at the time, but in retrospect it loomed much larger, and I later thought it might be the key to the whole sequence of events.

When I finished my cup of coffee, I set the cup carefully on the floor beside me, picked up one of the magazines, a cheap colonial picture magazine devoted mostly to news, gossip, and rumor about the British nobility, pictures of castles and of peers of the realm, subtle hints of what lord was sleeping with whose wife in articles written for a child's mentality. My eyelids began to grow heavy in the middle of a story about a party held by the Earl of Something and attended only by the Duchess of Whatsit (she was the complete guest list) and how neighbors and servants later claimed that they saw them dancing in the nude in the earl's garden to the music of the fifty-piece orchestra the earl had hired. I never did find out what happened after the nude dance, but I have a good imagination. I put the magazine down and saw that Sally was nodding too. This didn't strike me as unusual: the skudder trip had now become dull and uninteresting, and sleep would be the best thing for us both until we got to our destination. I shifted into a more comfortable position, closed my eyes and thought about as little as I could until a warm, comfortable drowsiness slowly settled over me.

My next memory was that of Kar-hinter shaking my shoulder, saying, "Eric, wake up. We are nearly there."

I shook myself, forced my eyes to open, and felt for an instant a great sense of impending doom that I was now sure was unjustified.

Can I say that things looked any different when I awoke? No. The skudder was exactly the same. My empty coffee cup still sat on the floor where I had put it. The magazine, its pages open, was exactly where I had laid it. Sally sat in the seat across from me, leaning against the wall, sleeping. Kar-hinter, the skudder pilot and Pall were as they had been, looked the same in every detail. Nothing had changed. Or had it? I felt that something had, but I could not say what and chalked it up to my imagination.

"I must have fallen asleep," I said, rubbing my face, feeling my hands on my cheeks, knowing that I was doing exactly what I was doing, but still somehow unsure of it.

Actually, even now, I'm not sure how much of this sensation of unreality I felt at the time and how much of it has entered my memories since the events—which I have gone over in my mind so many times that I have probably lost the original memory under layers of, well, remembering the memories.

"Awaken Sally," Kar-hinter said. "We will be there in less than five minutes."

"Okay," I said, fully awake now.

I shook Sally's shoulder. Her eyes blinked open; she looked up at me, shook her head, yawned, and nearly smiled.

"We're almost there," I said.

"Oh, good," she said. "I was having the most pleasant dream."

"Momentarily you shall have a most pleasant reality," Kar-hinter said.

I became aware of the flickering of the skudder's probability field as it slowed and then stopped, and bright late-afternoon sunlight flooded the interior of the craft through the transparent dome.

"Everybody out," the skudder's pilot said, rising from his seat, then pushing a button that caused the craft's hatch to open.

"I hope that your sleep has been sufficient," Kar-hinter said as he rose. "We will be here several hours, and you will have little opportunity to rest before we leave."

"We're fine," I said.

"Good," Kar-hinter replied. "Come. We are expected."

The place where the skudder had come to rest was a shallow circular depression in a wide field composed of what I thought to be concrete, though the substance was blue-green in color and I discovered upon disembarking from the craft that it was soft under my feet. The field extended perhaps a hundred yards in all directions, pitted every few dozen feet with other depressions and in perhaps a third of them sat skudders like our own, though some were brightly decorated with designs that I didn't recognize.

On our left the field terminated in a broad green meadow which was apparently a landing field for another type of craft: fragile-looking teardrops of metal and glass that I tentatively identified as some type of antigrav aircraft. To our right the field gave way to a gray concrete slab upon which rested a slim golden tower that reached into the sky perhaps a hundred feet. On the top of the tower sat a transparent globe maybe ten feet in diameter or a little larger. I don't know what it was. Beyond the tower was another grassy field across which a number of people were strolling and playing a game that looked similar to the golf of Sally's Line. Beyond the field was the city.

It was a fairyland of towers and turrets and minarets and bright flags and streamers waving in the breeze, bridges and catwalks of spun glass connecting the towers, sparkling in the sunlight. Here and there in the air above them were the teardrop aircraft.

Two men and two women waited outside the craft, smiling, but not speaking until we had climbed down to the blue-green field and had taken in our surroundings. Then Kar-hinter said, "Eric Mathers, Sally von Heinen, please allow me to introduce our guides. Dylla, Jocasta, Dicton, and Hallacy."

The first two were women and the other two men, all with the rich earthy features of south Europe, the kind of Latin beauty you can find in some of the Roman statues that still exist in Sally's Line. There was a similarity about them, as if they were all of a single family, brothers and sisters, though I never really knew for sure. They all smiled in reply, offered their hands and welcomed us to Calethon I in flawless, idiomatic English of Sally's Line.

Just a few words about these people and their clothing. Like Sally and me, they were dressed in sleeveless shirts and knee-length pants made of an almost transparent material, transparent enough so that their excellent bodies were quite visible. And every square inch of their skin was artificially pigmented in bright, yet pleasant colors.

Dylla, the larger and more sensual of the girls, was sky-blue: her face, her arms, her legs, her torso, even her hair were blue, but of a darker shade, and her thin clothing was blue as well. She had an almost round, though not moonlike, face, with deep, dark eyes and full lips. Her breasts were large and it seemed as if they were about to tear through the thin fabric of her blouse. My eyes were drawn on down her slender waist to the triangle of dark-blue hair that grew between her thighs. I tore my eyes away to look at the others.

Jocasta and her clothing were a canary-yellow. She was a shorter girl than Dylla by several inches, and the proportions of her body were a little less impressive, though not bad at all. She made up for this lack—if it can be said to be a lack—with one of the prettiest faces I've ever seen and a smile that was simple, friendly, ingenuous. She was like somebody's kid sister who had suddenly become a woman, but still had the innocent openness of a child. I liked her instantly.

Dicton was the largest of the four, a red man well over six feet tall and with the features and physique of an Adonis. He spoke rarely and then only in short sentences, and I didn't know whether that was because he wasn't too bright or because he was very bright and didn't want to waste time with useless conversation.

Hallacy was shorter, stockier, more bullishly masculine in all respects than Dicton—an orange Hercules to his red Adonis—and a loquacious fellow with a keen sense of humor once he got started. He was a likable person, but I suspected that he could be a hard man to deal with if you ever got his temper up.

These were our guides.

Calethon I, they explained, once the formalities of introduction were out of the way, was the most westward of all the Lines that made up the Cross-Line Civilization. To the East forty-nine more Lines extended, all interlinked and mutually interdependent, all differing phases, as it were, of the same "world." There were a dozen Calethon Lines, then five Matthen Lines, the sixteen Manshien Lines, and so on. Calethon I was, they told us, the Westward Terminal Line for the Cross-Line worlds, a transfer and processing world, in essence, though there was some light industry and a number of Transtemporal research centers and universities specializing in Timeline studies, history divergence and things of that sort.

"What will be first?" orange Hallacy asked. "A tour of Bershaw?"

"No, I think not," Kar-hinter said. "Let us save that until last. First I would like to prove to our friends that what we are saying is all true. Take us to the terminal head, please."

"Certainly," said Dylla, the girl of the big blue breasts. "We can take our aircar into Bershaw and leave it there." Turning to me and smiling a very warm—and was it inviting?—smile, she said, "That's the largest terminal head in this hemisphere, you know."

I certainly didn't know. I didn't even know what a
terminal head was. But I smiled back, and then Sally
and I followed the smiling foursome and Kar-hinter
across the field to one of the teardrop aircraft. Pall, silent
and enigmatic, brought up the rear, perhaps standing
guard over us.

The crystal fairyland that I had noticed on arrival was
the city of Bershaw, or as near to a city as these people
of Calethon I had. It was a vast, intertwined complex of
shops and open-air markets and government offices and
amusement centers, though it was not a city in the sense
of being a dwelling place for people. The natives of
Calethon I lived in isolated houses scattered across the
world, never in tight clusters like most of the Lines I
knew. Someone, probably Hallacy, told me that the per-
manent population of Calethon I was somewhere in the
neighborhood of eight hundred million, and there was
plenty of room for everyone to have privacy. There were
certainly no population problems here.

Jocasta, the little canary girl who piloted the aircar,
set us down in another green field in the very center of
the city, directly in front of a long, colorful building of
glass and metal and stone that must have covered an
area equal to a dozen city blocks in Sally's world. The
front of the building showed a long series of doors
through which a constant stream of people moved, in and
out, many of them in costumes differing wildly from those
worn by ourselves and our guides or in no costumes at
all. It reminded me a little of the mixture of cultures I
had seen in Staunton and seemed to remind Sally of the
same. At least her face clouded, though she did not
speak.

From the rear of the building or perhaps from a landing deck on its top rose dozens of large aircars, or perhaps airlorries would be a better term since they
appeared to be cargo-carrying vehicles. An equal number
came dropping out of the sky to replace those that rose,
all moving easily, silently, even gracefully.

We all climbed out of the aircar, crossed the grassy
field, and stepped onto a moving sidewalk that carried us
effortlessly toward the gaping doors of what our guides
had called a terminal head.

"Just exactly what is this place?" I asked Hallacy, who was standing at my side.

Before the orange man could answer, Kar-hinter interrupted, saying, "Wait a moment, Eric, and we shall show you. That would be more effective than telling you. Would it not?" he asked of Hallacy.

The orange Hercules nodded, and I said, "Okay."

"Where shall we go?" the lovely blue Dylla asked.

"You make the choice," Kar-hinter answered. "Merely make it interesting for our guests."

"Very well."

With Dylla leading us with her swinging buttocks, we stepped off the moving sidewalk just outside the building, stepped onto another, and were carried into the terminal head.

The building was interesting in the way that many public buildings are interesting, decorated with vast, colorful murals and exotic statuary, but all in all it wasn't too unlike many other buildings that I had seen before. Except, that is, for the *conveyors*.

The far wall of the enormous room consisted of rows of booths that extended dozens of yards in both directions, small rooms that reminded me more of elevators than anything else, and my first impression was that that was exactly what they were. People in the line ahead of us stepped into the booths, punched a series of buttons, and the doors closed. Moments later the doors opened and the booths were empty.

I noticed that just the opposite seemed to be happening at the booths at the far end of the row. People got out, but no one got in.

"What is this?" Sally asked, perhaps with a touch of fear in her voice.

And then we were entering a booth ourselves, all eight of us, and the doors were closing behind us as Dylla punched on the button panel. I had an instant of fear myself, the thought that perhaps Kar-hinter had taken us all this way to. . . . *Don't be foolish*, I said to myself. *He's only doing what you requested.*

"Calethon IV, I think, would be a good place," the blue girl was saying.

Then flicker. Flicker. Flicker.

Exactly like being in a skudder, I thought. Then, by God, that's what it is. A skudder!

The doors opened and we were back in the terminal head. Or, rather, *a* terminal head. One very similar to the one we had just left, but differing in some respects, minor things that were hard to pin down. Except for the people. Most of them were lighter-skinned than those we had encountered before, and their clothing was of a different cut, more elaborate and decorative, though there was a liberal sprinkling of other costumes, not a few clothed as we were and with brightly pigmented skin like that of our guides. I still had not seen a single Krith besides Kar-hinter in the Cross-Line worlds.

"This is Calethon IV," Dylla said, "one of our heavy industry Lines. Let's go outside for a moment; then we'll go on to Matthen II."

Following the blue girl's swaying butt and then stepping onto a sliding sidewalk, we moved out of the terminal head and out into a city that looked more like what I thought a city should look like: regular streets, buildings of steel and stone and glass, moving vehicles that stayed on or near the surface. Beyond the city, from an observation deck located on top of the terminal head, we saw the dark structures of factories stretching toward the horizon, belching thin, filtered smoke into a sky that was still very blue. Somehow the factories had an esthetic charm of their own, but I would find it hard to describe. It wasn't at all unpleasant.

"There are more skudders produced here in a day than on all the other Lines combined," red Dicton said proudly.

Then, a little while later, after stopping for drinks in a luxurious lounge in the terminal head building, we reentered one of the conveyor booths and flickered again.

Matthen II was the spaceport Line of the Cross-Line worlds where huge, silvery, needle-thin spaceships rose silently into the sky, bound for the Moon and Mars and Venus and the asteroids, there to discharge passengers and cargo and reload with raw materials and a few finished products from the extraterrestrial colonies and return them to Earth. Space travel was comparatively rare across the Timelines; it was generally far more expensive than skudding, but even here in the Cross-Lines there were a few products that were cheaper to get from the Solar planets than to try to collect across the Lines.

Hallacy told me that a fantastically huge spaceship with a faster-than-light drive was being built in orbit around Earth. Soon it would carry a load of colonists across the light-years to a very Earth-like world that scouts had recently discovered some three hundred light-years away. And he said that he was sorry that we could not wait around an hour or so until it got dark and then have a chance to see the ship. Even though it orbited rather far out, it was large enough to be easily seen from Earth after dark.

I was impressed.

After that, just before we returned to the terminal head, Dylla whispered something to me about Manshein IX which I didn't fully understand, but left me with a pleasant, excited feeling of anticipation.

Our next stop was Matthen V, the "Sea World," they called it, where most of mankind had moved into the oceans, leaving the land little more than a carefully landscaped playground, a world where men talked with dolphins, had learned to live in their aquatic environment, breathing through surgically implanted gills. Together, men and dolphins, they were building a culture unlike any on any other Timeline known to the Kriths.

Manshein III was a Timeline devoted entirely to the arts. Here there were settlements of writers where the greatest literature of all the Lines was slowly coming into being, we were told: artists' colonies where painting and sculpture were reaching unparalleled heights; groups of musicians who were evolving new and exciting forms of musical expression; photographers and holographers, engravers and printers and lithographers and dancers. You name it. We had no more than a few minutes to glimpse something of each, though even then our senses were overwhelmed with the sound and color and beauty of it all.

I hated to leave there, and that may sound odd coming from a professional killer like me, but it was true.

Manshein IX—the one blue Dylla had hinted about—was a Line devoted to nothing less than pure sexual hedonism, a world of constant Saturnalia, a place to which people came from the other Lines to spend a few days—or perhaps years—in erotic escape.

It was here, in the city that occupied Bershaw's place on this world, as darkness was beginning to fall, that our party became divided. And I was sure that it was by intent, though who engineered it I didn't know, nor did I really care.

Dylla and I found ourselves alone, wandering down a wide avenue filled with people and one or two Kriths. The humans wore the most exotic and erotic dress I have ever seen, and the evening air was filled with pleasant, sensual odors and sounds and sights.

"We have a few moments together," Dylla said, looking at me with an inviting smile in her eyes. "Shall we spend them in pleasure?"

I looked back at her, my eyes following the full length of her blue-dyed body, nodded, felt a familiar urge rising in me.

"Come then," she said, leading me across the wide street and down a narrower one into a great green park that consisted of labyrinthine hedges and soft, yielding grass and the odor of flowering plants. Around us were the soft, rustling sounds of body against body and subdued cries and moans of pleasure and excitement, though the producers of those sounds were hidden from us by the growth of hedges and flowers.

"Here," Dylla said after a while, leading me into a hedge-surrounded recess as large as a medium-size bedroom and covered by soft grass.

"Now, dear Eric, do you want me?"

I didn't speak, and there was no need to. Dylla quickly undressed us both and then lay back on the grass and opened herself to me. I moved above her and entered her easily, finding her warm and moist and passionately ready for me.

It just didn't last long enough—but then does it ever?
The universe shattered with our orgasms.

Then, after a while, we rose, dressed, and returned to
find our companions near where we had last seen them.

Into the terminal head and then back out again—into
Manshein XIV, the university world, an earth given over
to study, research, contemplation, to vast library computers that cataloged and refined all the knowledge of the
other Lines, where men sought the ultimate answers to
the ultimate questions about the nature of time and space
and man and Krith and the "what" and "why" of the
universe—but for some reason I didn't think that even
here they had found the answers to those questions, not
really.

Manshein XV—again a Timeline where men sought
ultimates, but here in dark robes and the quietness of
cloisters, in meditation or the mind-expanding sensation
of half a hundred kinds of drugs, a half million religious
orders sought whatever it is that men call God in their
own diverse ways—and I wondered if any of them had
made it.

"Time is running short," Kar-hinter said at last. "Take
us back to Calethon I. We shall eat and see the sights of
Bershaw before we must leave."

Following the undulations of Dylla's blue hips we
walked back to the terminal head and flickered across
the Lines back to Calethon I and the city of Bershaw.

Bershaw—a city out of the *Arabian Nights,* though
lacking the barbarism and cruelty of ancient Arabia. A
pageant of light and color and sound, an orgy of food
and wine and music under the stars and crystal towers, a
symphony of beauty, a collection of all that is lovely from
uncounted worlds.

Bershaw—the gateway to the Cross-Line Civilization.

Six hours or a little more had gone by when Sally,
Kar-hinter, Pall, and I returned to our waiting skudder,
Sally and I at least still stunned by what we had seen and

experienced. We said good-bye to beautiful blue Dylla, to yellow Jocasta, to red Dicton, to the Herculean-orange Hallacy, and began our trip back to—well, back to an Eden Line that would seem more dull than it had before.

Flicker. And the Cross-Line worlds were behind us.

"Are you satisfied now?" Kar-hinter asked as we settled down for the trip back.

"They lied to me," Sally said, pain in her voice. "It was all a lie. They said that the Cross-Line Civilization did not exist. But it does."

"Yes, it does," Kar-hinter said seriously. "It is exactly as we have told it. Is that not so, Eric?" I nodded. "And the contratime communication is a fact as well, though I cannot prove it so easily."

"I don't think you need to, Kar-hinter," Sally said, apology in her voice. "We can accept that, too. Can't we, Eric?"

"Yes, of course," I said. "You've shown us more than enough, Kar-hinter. Please let me apologize for ever having doubted it."

"Don't concern yourself," the Krith said. "I am merely pleased that your questions have been resolved. Now we can go about our proper business of preparing for the future. Now, sit back, relax, for the trip ahead of us is long."

And I did, sitting back in the seat, letting drowsiness take me, feeling again that odd sense of unreality, that nothing was quite what it seemed to be, and somehow knowing that I was still lying to Kar-hinter, knowing that despite everything we had seen and experienced, I was still not really convinced.

Something was wrong, but damned if I knew what.

22
Dreams and Nondreams

Kar-hinter awoke us as the skudder came to rest in the Eden Line from which we had started.

"Give me your cothing," he said. "You still have over two weeks of your stay left. Enjoy it."

So we gave him our clothing, climbed out of the skudder, and in the darkness watched it flicker out of existence. Then we went into the cabin.

During the days that followed Sally gradually began to adjust to the idea that her life had been compounded of lies and dreams, that what the Paratimers told her was false. One doesn't change a lifetime of belief overnight, but her strange, almost ambivalent feelings toward Mica slowly solidified into resentment, and he became the focal point of her growing anger; *in absentia* he bore the brunt of her disgust. And I, whom she had always wanted to like, became the pole to which she was attracted. She used me, I know, as a solace for her growing disillusionment with Mica and all that he represented, but I did not mind that use and still hoped that eventually her feelings for me would mature into something deeper. But even without this I had no cause for complaint.

On the night of our visit to the Cross-Line worlds we each slept alone. On the next night we went to our separate beds, though I had tried at least to persuade her to come to mine. She had resisted, though I thought I could feel that her resistance was weakening.

That second night I lay there in my bed, listening to the nightly rain as it began to fall, turning things over in my mind, things about Sally and Staunton and Kar-hinter and Calethon I and Dylla and other things that I couldn't quite put tags on—though in time I would come to, I knew. After a while, a long while, listening to the rain and Sally's distant breathing, I fell into a shallow sleep and was per-

haps on the verge of dreaming when I felt a soft warm-
ness coming up against me, a hand placed on my naked
chest, a mouth suddenly pressed against mine.

"Sally," I murmured against her lips.

"Yes, Eric," she answered, moving her body closer still
and then up over mine. She was nude, of course, and her
soft breasts were crushing against me.

I pulled her mouth to mine again, and her answer was
savage, demanding. I was almost gasping for breath when
she pulled her lips away.

"Yes, Eric," she said again, still lying atop me.

"I want you, Sally," I said. "I've wanted you from the
first time I saw you."

"I know," she whispered.

I did not speak again, but pulled her mouth back to
mine and kissed her as savagely as she had kissed me. And
as we kissed, her hips began writhing against mine, pushing herself down on me, demanding, almost begging.

Then suddenly she broke her lips away from mine and
cried, "Now, Eric. I want it now."

Later our lovemaking settled into a comfortable pattern
and we learned the intimacies of each other, the little ways
of giving greater pleasure to each other, the sharing of our
pleasure, and it was even better.

Eden was beginning to live up to its name.

But there were other things.

While the visit to the Cross-Line worlds appeared to
have solved all the problems for Sally, it hadn't for me. The
feeling of unreality had not left me but rather grew as the
days went by. I could not have said why, but there was the
feeling, the vague, deep idea, that what we had experienced had not been real.

Sally could accept it easily enough. She had not seen
the work that the Kriths could do, how they could implant
memories into the minds of men that were more real then
the actual experiences; she did not know how the Kriths
could alter men's personalities. I did. And I wasn't convinced.

Then there was the dream. I suppose that's what did it
for me.

It was more than a week after our visit to the Cross-Line worlds. I had found it difficult to go to sleep that night. Sally had sensed something in me, had sensed that something still bothered me, though she had not asked me outright to tell her about it. She believed, I think, that I would tell her when I was ready.

So I lay there in bed beside her, waiting for sleep to come, and when it finally did come, it was a very disturbing sleep. The dream was like this:

We were in the skudder, Sally and Kar-hinter and the pilot and Pall and me. Sally and I were dressed in the costumes that we had worn in the Cross-Line worlds, and we had drunk our coffee and had fallen asleep.

Then the skudder stopped suddenly. My eyes half opened, then closed, and I could not force them open again, though I could hear the voices of Kar-hinter and the skudder pilot speaking in Shangalis.

"We're here," the pilot said.

"Good," Kar-hinter replied. Then I heard him move to a place beside me, felt him place his hand on my forehead, pull back an eyelid and peer into my eye. I could see his nonhuman face, though it was blurred and I could not focus on it.

Moments later the skudder's hatch opened, and other voices spoke, voices that I thought were those of Kriths.

"You have them?" one of the voices asked.

"Yes," Kar-hinter replied. "They are quite unconscious."

"Very well," replied one of the unnamed Kriths. "We will help you carry them out."

Arms came under my shouders and knees. I was lifted, carried, handed down, carried again, then placed on some type of wheeled conveyance, and rolled for a long distance.

"The tapes are ready, I asssume?" Kar-hinter's voice asked.

"Yes."

"Both identical?" Kar-hinter asked.

"Yes," the other voice signed. "Except for viewpoint. They are self-programming, self-adjusting interacting."

"Very good."

The other Krith gave a very human snort. "It is quite

complex, you know, the sort of interacting pseudo-memories you require for these two."

"I know," Kar-hinter's voice said. "But they must be convinced."

"They will be convinced. Of that I am absolutely sure. We worked all night on them. Six hours of tapes each, covering every human sense. There will be no reason for either of them to doubt their experiences."

"Are you sure?"

"Of course I am sure."

"Eric has a strong will. The Paratimers even tried telepathy on him, but it did not work."

"Yes, I know that, but when we are through, even he will be satisfied."

"I hope you are correct. You do not know this man as I do."

"I am correct."

There was a long silence, marked only by the faint squeak of the wheels of the thing on which I lay as it rolled along.

"Is this man really important?" the other voice asked.

"I believe he is," Kar-hinter said, "and the *Tromas* agree with me, though they seem to see even more in him than I do." He paused for a while before he went on. "He has been of great value to us in the past. I believe that he will be of even greater value to us in the future, once his loyalty is established beyond question."

"In six hours it will be."

Then I heard doors open, close behind me, and moments later the motion stopped.

"I will return in six hours," Kar-hinter said.

"They will be ready then."

My eyelids were peeled back, then held back by tape. Two small, cold glass objects were placed against my naked eyes. At the same time I was stripped of my clothing and felt cold metallic objects touching my skin in different places.

"Is the woman ready?" one of the Krithian voices asked after a while.

"Yes, sir," a human voice replied.

"Very well, begin the tapes."

Suddenly I could see again, into the skudder, and a

voice was saying into my ear, "Eric, wake up. We are nearly there." It was Kar-hinter's voice.

And then I relived the whole visit to the Cross-Line worlds!

The dream was just a dream, wasn't it? Or was it a real memory that had been suppressed by drugs?

But was that possible? I had been told that the Kriths were not able to tamper with a mind that had been conditioned as mine had. But, then, had they actually tampered with my mind? No, in the dream they had merely drugged me, and then, while I was drugged, they had fed me false sensory data. They had not tried directly to manipulate my mind or to alter anything that was already in it. Yes, I supposed that it was possible.

Okay, I thought, suddenly convinced, this whole damned thing was faked. As I sat up on the side of the bed, my thoughts went on: I was never in the Cross-Line worlds. Kar-hinter took us a few Lines away, drugged us, and then planted the false memories. Why?

Well, that was pretty simple. There was no Cross-Line Civilization after all. Mica had been telling the truth about it. It was all an enormous plot.

I lit a ciagrette, looked down at Sally, who still slept soundly.

What the hell was I going to do about it?

"Sally," I said shaking her shoulder. "Wake up."

Her eyes opened. She looked up at me with a startled expression on her face, recognizing the urgency in my voice.

"What is it?"

"I've got to talk to you."

"Okay," she said, sitting up and accepting the cigarette I offered her.

I dialed for coffee on the autokitchen extension, lit myself another cigarette.

"What's bothering you, Eric?" she asked as the coffee arrived.

"Listen to me carefully, Sally," I said.

"I will. Tell me."

"It's all a lie just like Mica said it was. There is no Cross-Line Civilization."

"But, Eric, we were there. We saw it."

"We only thought we did. It was all faked. False memories."

"How do you know?" Sally asked, something on her face saying that she almost doubted my sanity.

I told her about my dream, about how I thought I remembered all the preparations for implanting the false memories.

"But maybe it was just a dream," she said.

"No."

"How do you know? How can you be sure?"

"I don't know, but I'm sure. You don't know the Kriths the way I do, Sally. They can do things like this. I've seen it done before."

"But would they do it to you, Eric, knowing that you know they can do it?"

"They did it," I said. "They must have a lot of faith in it."

"But it's fantastic."

"Hell, it's all fantastic. That's as easy to believe as any of the rest of it."

"I don't know, Eric. I mean . . . I don't know what to believe now."

"There's truth somewhere," I said. "And we've got to find it. And I know that we won't find it with Kar-hinter's help."

"Then how will we find it?" she asked.

"We'll go find Mica and ask him."

Sally looked at me, and by this time she was firmly convinced that I was insane. Maybe she had a right to be.

23
The Western Timelines

By the time the skudder came to take us back to Sally's world I had her sufficiently convinced of the truth of my beliefs so that she at least agreed to go along with me.

When the Krithian skudder materialized in the garden before the cabin, Sally was half way ready to accept once more the belief that Mica and his kind were the saviors of mankind. I wasn't, not quite, but least I was willing to accept them over the Kriths, whom I now knew to be liars on a scale I had never before imagined possible.

Well, as I said, the skudder materialized in the garden. The pilot stepped out, waved to us with a big grin.

"You people ready to go back?" he called as we walked down the path toward him.

"Try to smile," I whispered to Sally. Then louder, "No, not really, but I guess we have to. Everything in the cabin's on standby. I guess we can leave now."

"Good," the pilot said. "Kar-hinter said to get you back to him as quickly as possible. He has some news for you."

"What kind of news?" I asked, now within handshaking distance of the pilot.

"Didn't say. He just said that it was something that both of you would find very interesting."

"I guess we'll find out soon," I replied.

The pilot now opened the hatch, gestured for Sally to climb in, offered her his hand. "I've got clothes in here for you."

"Good," I said, keeping a false smile on my face.

"Must be nice here," he said as Sally placed one foot on the lip of the hatch, hoisted herself in with both hands.

For a moment the pilot's eyes strayed from Sally's bare buttocks to the cabin and the blissful, idyllic panorama that surrounded it. And that was exactly what I wanted.

I could see Sally in the hatchway out of the corner of my eye as she pulled herself erect, then slowly, carefully turned so that she was facing outward, then lashed out with her foot to the back of the unconcerned pilot's head.

I switched into combat augmentation and was satisfied that everything worked perfectly. The world slowed to my senses; sounds grew deeper and shifted toward the bass; light shifted toward the red.

"Aaaaacccchhh," the pilot groaned slowly, floating forward from the impact of Sally's foot. I grabbed him by the shoulder, spun him around to face me, threw my right fist into a face that had not yet registered the shock of the violent action. I put my left fist into his stomach, my right into his face again as he folded. Then he was unconscious on the soft green ground before he realized that he was being attacked. I cut out the augmentation.

"He's out," I said, bending over him, quickly running my hands over his body to see if he carried a weapon, which I doubted. "Nothing," I told Sally, then dragged him a few feet away from the craft and made him as comfortable as possible. They'd come after him soon, very soon, I feared.

When I got into the skudder Sally had already found the clothing that he had brought for us, standard civilian-type clothing from Sally's Line or one very near it. It didn't matter much to me how we were dressed since I had no idea what kind of costumes we'd find at our destination.

While I was dressing, Sally said, "Oh, Eric, I hope that we're doing the right thing."

"No more than I do."

"Are you sure you can find Mica's Paratime?"

"Sure?" I asked as I buttoned up the shirt brought for me. "No, I'm not sure, but I've got a fair idea; at least I do if Latham's book was true."

"What exactly do you mean?" she asked. "You never have really explained it to me."

"Okay, just a minute," I said, sitting down in the pilot's seat, feeling back under the control panel to where the energy pistol was supposed to be within reach of every skudder pilot. You never know what you might run into when you flicker across the Lines.

I found the cold metal butt, the stud that released the weapon. Click! The pistol snapped into my hand. I drew it out, looked at it for a moment. Standard-issue energy pistol. Full charge. You could do a hell of a lot of damage with that baby if you wanted to. I might want to. I slipped it into my belt, feeling more like a man than I had for a good long while and feeling a hell of a lot more confident of our ability to get away with our scheme. It's funny what a weapon can do to a man.

"Sit down there," I gestured toward the seat beside me, studying the familiar skudder controls. "Keep a watch on our friend out there. If he wakes up, we'll get out of here in a hurry."

"Okay, but tell me what you're going to do."

"Well, you've read Martin Latham's book, haven't you?"

"*The Greatest Lie?* Of course."

"You remember how he found the Albigensians?"

"Yes, he left his own Paratime and went West as far as he could."

"Okay, that's the key. I've read that part three or four times," I said, "and I remember it pretty well. Latham had a standard four-man skudder just like this one. He got it out of the skudder pool, so I'm pretty sure that when he did, the power cells were at full charge. They always are. He removed the governor and deactivated the telltale, but other than that, the skudder he used was exactly like this one."

"Uh-huh," Sally grunted.

I reached under the control panel again, fumbled, then found what I wanted and pulled at two wires. They broke free from their connections.

"Our telltale's off," I said. "They can't trace us by it now. It's just a safety device, so it's not hidden." I smiled to myself. "I'm not going to bother the governor. That's a job for a licensed mechanic—or an engineer like Latham. But we don't need to remove it anyway. We don't have nearly as far to go as Latham did, and we don't need top speed—I hope."

"Oh?" Sally said.

"Well, to get back to what I was saying: A skudder of given mass with a probability generator of a given maxmum potential can only go so far on a set of full power cells, governor or no."

"Oh, I see," Sally said, beginning to follow me. "You can tell how far Latham went from the amount of power he used. All you have to do is find his starting point, right?"

"Right," I said. "Now I don't know exactly where Latham started. He didn't give the Paratemporal coordinates, but I've got a pretty good idea, to within a few dozen Lines, anyway."

"What do we do then?" Sally asked.

In answer to Sally's question I flipped back the covering panel of the skudder's miniature computer and began tapping on the exposed keys.

A four-man skudder's computer is a simple-minded beast, not much more than an electronic slide rule, really, but given the right data, it can give you fairly quick and accurate answers. I just hoped that I was giving it the right data.

The Line where Latham had been working was a long way East, much farther East than the Eden Line where we were now—on the other side of my Homeline, I believed. The place where he had finally come to rest was a very long way West. We were now somewhere in between, though exactly where, I didn't know for sure yet. The computer would give me that too in a few moments, based on the skudder's power consumption since leaving the only Line whose coordinates I was sure of, the Line from which Sally and I had originally come, RTGB-307.

A few minutes later I was satisfied with the approximate number of Lines that Latham had crossed before he ran out of power. Yes, it was a hell of a long way West.

Now, assuming that this skudder had come from Sally's Homeline, from our base at the Butt of Lewis in the Outer Hebrides which was still Kar-hinter's base of operations, and assuming that it had started out with full power cells—which I was sure it had, regulations required it—it had come exactly X number of Lines. X from Y, being Kar-hinter's base of operations, left Z number of Lines and our present location. Our location then, after a little more figuring using the computer, was A number of Lines to the Temporal West of the Line from which Latham had supposedly started his trip, plus or minus a dozen Lines to allow for my own errors. All this meant that we had about *B* number of Lines to cross to reach the place where Latham had run out of power—Mica's Homeline.

Okay, then, if my memory and assumptions were valid, and I hoped to all the gods that I knew that they were, we had enough power in the cells to make a round trip, plus. Very good, I thought, since we'd probably have to do a lot of maneuvering to find the exact Line we were looking for.

I sat back at last, dug a pack of cigarettes out of the skudder's supply compartment, and smiled a big smile at Sally.

"Are we ready?" she asked.

"We are now if we'll ever be." I glanced out through the skudder's dome. "Our friend's still out."

"You hit him pretty hard."

"Yeah. Okay, brace yourself. I'm not the world's best pilot, but I can manage."

My hands slowly went to the controls. I cut on the probability generator, watched dials show the gradual rise of power, heard the hum that filled the air grow in intensity, become a whine, an almost physical sensation. While the probability potential grew, I adjusted other controls. Initially I set the controls just a little short of where I expected Mica's Homeline to be, planning to stop and recon the Lines before plunging all the way in. I still wasn't sure enough of what we were getting ourselves into to jump all the way in at once. "Caution preventeth a fall . . ." or something like that.

"Ready?" I asked.

"I guess."

"Here goes."

I hit the activating switch.

"We're on our way," I said.

Flicker.

Fortunately we had both eaten before the skudder came, but even at that we began to feel hunger before the trip was into its second half. We'd just have to wait it out. There wasn't much in the skudder to eat besides emergency rations, which I didn't want to break open short of an emergency, and we didn't dare stop anywhere. Not for a long while yet.

More than once I had a strong desire to bring the skudder out of probability into, well, "reality" to see what kinds of worlds we were passing through now. By the middle of the trip we had gone beyond the Lines known to the Kriths, and we were now in largely unexplored Lines, unexplored by the Kriths and Timeliners, at least, though I assumed that Mica's people had been there, were probably there in force, though keeping themselves hidden from most of the locals as they were on Sally's world. But, well, I didn't want to cause an incident by coming out in some place where our kind was unknown, where we might be taken as alien invaders or something, maybe smeared with thermonukes or shot with arrows or whatever kinds of weapons they might have.

So we waited and watched the dials indicate the passage of time and Paratime as the master destination dial said we were slowly nearing the place where I had determined that we would come out for the first time.

We didn't speak much, Sally and I. There wasn't too much left to say now. We just waited and held hands and felt scared and hoped that Mica or somebody would be waiting for us with open arms.

The automatic destination settings terminated. The final cross-Line jump flickered. I held the energy pistol in my hand, safety off, held my breath and. . . .

We came out.

I don't know what we expected, but what we found wasn't it. It was like nothing we had hoped or expected to see here, in a part of the Lines where we had expected to encounter a high and complex civilization of cross-Line travelers.

Oh, there had been a high degree of technology here once, but now. . . .

The transparent dome of the skudder gave us a 360 degree view of the countryside surrounding us, if it could be called by so generous a term as "countryside." The sky above us was blue-black, sprinkled with a smattering of the brighter stars, and in that sky hung an enormous, bloated sun whose corona beamed brightly around it. It was broad daylight, yet the sky was more than halfway dark, and I knew that this Earth had very little left of its atmosphere, more than the Moon, but not enough to support human life or much of any other kind of life as we know it.

Before us a rocky, gray-brown plain stretched toward the horizon, then abruptly ended two or three miles away in a huge pile of rocks, a chunk of the Earth lifted up and tilted skyward, revealing a thousand centuries of geological evolution, though at the moment that didn't interest me very much.

In the other directions the view was essentially the same: gray-brown stone and earth, waterless, airless, lifeless rock, a world that was totally dead, that might have always been dead, that might have never known life and men, though I doubted it. I had seen worlds like this before, though I don't believe I had ever seen one so totally devastated.

A skudder's hull, the result of millions of man-hours of research and labor, is impervious to most forms of radiation except visible light which is allowed to pass through the dome. So I wasn't too worried when the counters on the outer hull went wild, measuring a nuclear radiation level a million times or more higher than it should have been.

"God, haven't they had a war here!" I said.

"What is this place, Eric?" Sally gasped, her voice filled with fear.

"The *where* is exactly the place where we started," I said slowly. "It's the Parawhen that matters." I paused. "There's been a war here, Sally. One hell of a war. This planet's good and dead. Let's get the hell out of here. We've still got a way to go."

The probability generator was standing by. All I had to do was spin the destination dial for a few Lines ahead, hit the actuating switch and flicker.

Flicker. Flicker. Flicker.

"I . . . I've never seen anything so horrible. How did it happen, a war like that, I mean?"

"I don't know," I said. "I don't even want to know. Don't worry. We'll find Mica's Line."

Flicker. Flicker. Flicker.

We came out in a world that was different, but not very much. The sky was more like a sky, bluer but not as blue as it should have been. The Earth was desolate, the same dead gray-brown, and the radiation level was almost as high, and we were just a few hundred yards from the edge of an enormous crater that still glowed in its depths, down in the hot shadows.

"Not again," Sally gasped.

"Parallel war," I said. "Maybe not as bad as the other, but just as total as far as human life is concerned."

"What is this, Eric? Could we possibly be near Mica's Paratime? He never told me about anything like this."

"Maybe he was ashamed of what his relatives had done," I said, feeling a growing apprehension. "We'll go on."

But as I glanced at the controls and the dials and the computer read-out, I saw that we were very nearly smack on top of where I thought Mica's Homeline should be. Well, I thought, maybe his Line is an island in all this destruction. That's possible. It's happened before. But we'd better go a little slower.

Flicker.

The next Line was almost identical, except that the nearest crater was a mile away and the radiation level in the vicinity of the skudder was a few roentgens lower.

Flicker.

It was as if we were back in the first Line we had seen. The atmosphere was blasted away, and a naked sun blistered the naked rock of a dead, naked Earth. The radiation was high enough to scare me even inside the skudder.

Flicker.

The sky was almost blue. The earth was brown and barren, though here and there I saw the stark skeletons of what had once been trees, and a brown ash covered the earth that might have once been grass long ago. The radiation level was still far too high to allow any kind of life that I knew.

Flicker.

Blue sky, brown earth, radiation levels that perhaps men could survive if they were buried deep under the ground.

My heart was sinking, and there was a lump where my throat should have been. I was beginning to believe that my assumptions were pretty far wrong. Maybe Latham. . . .

"There just could be someone alive here," I said. "Mica's people could even have an outpost here."

I flicked on the skudder's radio, scanned the frequencies from the lowest up to the edges of microwave. Nothing. If there were anyone alive here, he wasn't using radio. I can't say that I was too surprised.

"We'll go on," I said.

Flicker.

Things were about the same on the next Line. The radiation level was a little lower, a few notches; men would have had a better chance of surviving here than on the last Line; Mica's people would be more likely to have an outpost, if we were anywhere near their Lines, which I had begun to seriously doubt now, though, according to my figures, we ought to be right about there.

The radio was dead. The air was silent. No one answered my transmissions.

We went on.

Flicker.

In the next Line the sky looked normal enough, though no clouds were visible. The earth, as far as we could see, was brown and gray, scorched grasses and burned trees and nothing much else. The radiation level was lower still, but high enough to kill an unprotected man almost instantly.

Out of a hope that I knew now to be foolish I cut the radio's receiver on again, slowly scanned the frequencies —and nearly fainted when I picked up a carrier at 104 MHz.

"What is it?" Sally gasped when she saw the expression on my face, realized that the buzz from the receiver meant something.

"There's somebody here," I said.

"Paratimers?"

"I don't know. It could be locals who survived the war,

or it could be Paratimers. No Krith or Timeliner has ever come this far to my knowledge."

"Talk to them."

"I'll try." Then I realized something and said, "I don't know the language. Albigensian, I mean. You talk."

"Okay, what do I say?"

"Just tell them who we are and why we're here."

"Okay. Show me what to do."

"Well, you just. . . ."

Ahead of us and to the right, maybe a hundred and fifty feet or a little more, the air shimmered and flickered for a moment, then a solid object materialized out of the nothingness, a squashed sphere that was unmistakable: a Krithian skudder.

I did not doubt for a moment who it was. I merely wondered how he had followed me so easily. What had I overlooked?"

"Eric!" Sally cried.

"Easy."

"Who is it?"

"I can make a guess. The skudder pilot said that Kar-hinter had something to tell us. I guess he's come to tell us what it is."

"Oh, God, Eric, and we were so close."

"Don't worry."

"But they'll have guns."

"I've got one, too," I said. "There are no guns mounted on their hull. There's never been a reason for it before now."

"What are we going to do?"

"Well, as I see it, we've got three choices. We can try to call for help, but I don't know how much good that'll do or how soon. I'd hate to have to count on it. Two, we can run, but I don't know how much good that'll do either. If Kar-hinter could follow us this far, I suppose he could keep on following us until he caught us. Or, three, we can talk to Kar-hinter and see what he wants with us."

"What good will *that* do?"

"Damned if I know, but it can't hurt."

My hands fell to the radio controls and I switched to the Krithian/Timeliner emergency broadcast frequency, thinking that was probably what Kar-hinter would be using. It was.

". . . Eric. Please respond if you are receiving me."

"I hear you," I said into the microphone, satisfied that the voice on the other end was that of Kar-hinter.

"Eric," the Krith answered at once. "Please do not be a fool. You do not know what you are getting into."

"I have a fair idea," I said. "Listen, Kar-hinter, your false memories didn't take. I saw through them. We know now that there's no Cross-Line Civilization, and we can assume that all the rest of it is lies, too."

"You listen to me, Eric," Kar-hinter snapped back, anger in his voice, a very human-sounding anger. "We have already sent patrols into the worlds where the Paratimers claim to live, their world of origin and all."

"And where's that?" I demanded.

"Here, Eric. Here and there is no human life here, not for a hundred Lines in either direction."

"Another lie," I said flatly. "There's someone on this Line using radio, Kar-hinter. I just picked up their carrier."

"I said *human*, Eric. The Paratimers are not human."

24
Kar-hinter, Kearns, Tracy, and Death

Eric, this is Tracy," said another voice from the radio's loudspeaker, a voice which I recognized. "What Kar-hinter is saying is true, old boy. I've seen them the way they *really* are and they aren't human beings."

"You're crazy," I said because I couldn't think of anything else to say.

"No, it's true," Tracy's voice said. "We've been making recons into these Lines ever since we picked up you and Sally from Staunton, and we've found out the truth about the Paratimers. *They* have a base somewhere on this Line—and, for God's sake, Eric, they aren't people."

"Eric," Kar-hinter's voice said, "you know that there is someone using radio here. They will probably pick up our signals if we continue to talk by radio. We do not have sufficient force to defend ourselves from an attack on their own ground. I suggest, then, that we cease using radio and meet outside the skudders to discuss this further."

"How can I believe anything you say?" I asked.

"You can believe me, can't you, Eric?" Tracy's voice asked.

"I don't know what to believe anymore," I replied.

"We are going to turn off our radio equipment," Kar-hinter said. "We will dress in survival suits and leave our skudder. We will wait for you midway between our craft and yours. We will be unarmed. Please, Eric, give us—and yourself—a chance."

There was a click and the carrier of their transmitter died away.

For a long while I sat there silently before the transceiver, gazing blankly at its controls. *What the hell am I going to do now?* I kept asking myself, and I really didn't have any answers.

226

"It's a trap, isn't it, Eric?" Sally asked at last.

"Probably," I said, "but Tracy. . . ."

"Who's Tracy?"

"A friend of mine. I've known him for a long time. He was with us the night we kidnapped you."

"Oh, yes," she said, "the one who was wounded in the leg."

I nodded. "I don't think he'd lie to me," I said. "At least not intentionally."

"Do you think they're forcing him?"

"Maybe. No, I don't think so." Tracy wasn't the sort of man who was easily *forced* to do anything. "I don't know. Damn it, I just don't know!"

We were silent for a while longer.

The hatch of the other skudder opened, and three of its four occupants, clad in emergency survival suits, stepped out onto the barren, radioactive earth of this world. Two of the figures were probably human from their size and proportions. The third was tall, built like a Krith, built like Kar-hinter. The three slowly advanced across the scorched ground and finally stopped about halfway to our skudder. There they stood and waited. Assuming that one of the men was Tracy, who was the other? Pall? If so, who was still inside the skudder? Maybe my old buddy Kearns. Or maybe it was the other way around. Did it matter? I'd learn soon.

"What are you going to do?" Sally asked.

"I'm going out there," I answered, finally making up my mind.

"But. . . ."

"I have to go," I said, cutting her off. "There's too much that we don't know. None of this makes any sense at all, and I've got to find out why."

I got up and walked back to the rear of the skudder, to where the locker containing the survival suits was kept.

"You stay in the skudder," I told Sally. "I'll leave the probability generator on, and I'll set the destination controls for your own Line. If anything happens, well, all you'll have to do is press one switch and the skudder'll take you home. I think we've still got the power to do that."

"Please don't go, Eric," Sally said as I opened the locker and pulled out one of the four survival suits.

"I've got to go," I said. "If what Mica and his people said is true, we ought to be in one of their Lines now. I really don't think that my figures were that far off."

"But you *could* be wrong."

"I could be, yes, but for some reason I'm convinced that I'm not. There's something going on here that they haven't told us about. Maybe what Tracy said is true. Maybe the Paratimers aren't human."

"That's not true, Eric," Sally said slowly. "Mica's as human as you are. I *know*."

I slowly turned to look at her. *That's right,* I told myself, visualizinig Mica, naked and pale white, lying atop my Sally. Human or not, I hated him for a moment.

Still if anyone knew, she would. She had been Mica's mistress; she had lived with him; if he weren't human, she would know it.

But what's human? I asked myself. And if Mica were, suppose, just suppose for a minute, some kind of alien being disguised as a man, well, what outside of moral scruples would prevent him from making love to a human woman if he wanted to and had the proper equipment? I mean, in situations where women—or other men —weren't available, men have been known to have sexual relations with creatures that certainly aren't human or even sentient. Everyone's heard stories of farmboys and their cows and chickens and sheep. I felt a little sick. Okay, maybe. . . .

"I have to go out there, Sally," I said slowly. "You can't talk me out of it. Please, just do as I say."

I pulled the survival suit over my clothing, jerking the straps tight. After tucking the helmet under my arm, I went back to the front of the skudder's cabin, adjusted the controls to return Sally to her own Timeline if anything happened to me.

"Just push that button," I told her, then led her back to the rear of the craft again.

"Be careful, Eric," she said as I helped her into a similar survival suit. When the skudder's hatch was opened, the interior would be liberally dosed with deadly radiation. In fact, the skudder would probably not be safe for an unprotected human being without some serious de-contamination once the hatch had been opened in this world.

"I'll be careful," I said, slipping the energy pistol into one of the suit's capacious pockets. "I'm taking this pistol along just in case."

"Come back, Eric," Sally said. "I won't know what to do if you don't."

"If I don't, then get the hell out of here. Do what you can to. . . . Well, just get home and hide."

I kissed her and then clamped the helmet down over my head, sealed it, and then turned toward the hatch.

"Good luck," Sally's voice said through the muffled speaker of her own helmet as she sealed it.

"Thanks, sweetheart."

The hatch opened before me, and I leaped down to the dry, burned, barren soil of this Earth. The hatch closed behind me. I walked toward the place where Kar-hinter, Tracy, and the other man waited for me.

I don't suppose that I thought about very much while I crossed those seventy-five feet of space between us. There wasn't much that my mind could do, except wonder. But the time for asking idle questions was over. I wanted some hard answers.

"I am glad you came to us, Eric," Kar-hinter said when I was within range of his voice as it came from the speakers of his survival helmet.

"I want the truth now," I said in reply. "I know that you've been lying to me."

"I will admit that there is no Cross-Line Civilization, as such, Eric," Kar-hinter said slowly. "It was a lie, but one that we told because we had to."

"And the Contratime communications business?" I asked.

"That also is untrue," Kar-hinter said just as slowly. "The truth is much more fantastic."

I ignored his last statement for the moment and looked at the two men with the Krith. One of them was Tracy. And the other was our old companion, Kearns, the same inexplicable expression on his warrior's face. Then was the fourth one, the one in the skudder, Pall?

"They both know," Kar-hinter was saying.

"I won't ask you why you lied," I said. "I don't want to hear it now."

"But you must hear it, Eric," Kar-hinter said. "It is. . . ."

"It's another lie!" I yelled. "And I don't want to hear any more lies from you! Tracy, who are the Paratimers?"

"I don't really know," Tracy replied. "They're from the West, a hell of a damned long way to the West. They do have a base here, but it looks like it's just one of many they have in these Lines. There are more of them farther West, but we don't know much about them yet."

"You said they aren't human," I said. "How do you know?"

"We raided one of their bases about a week ago. We captured some of them alive."

"Then what are they if they aren't human?" I asked.

Tracy spread his hands to show his ignorance.

"They are as different from you as we are, perhaps more so, considering," Kar-hinter said. "The ones you have seen have been surgically modified to look like men."

"Then what do they really look like?" I asked, still looking at Tracy.

"Well, they look something like us," he replied. "At least they're humanoid, except, well, they're almost hairless and their skin had a kind of almost bluish tint to it, and they have six fingers on each hand, and their eyes have pupils like a cat's. But, well, they're mammals. We caught one of their women, and there's no doubt about that. They're more—more like us in looks than the Kriths are, but, well, Eric, they don't think the same way. I can't explain it. They're *alien*, Eric, I mean real damned alien and I think they hate us more than we could ever understand. I—I can't really explain it. You've got to be with one of them, the way they really are and not pretending to be people, to know what kind of *things* they are." Then he seemed to run out of words to say the things he wanted to say.

"I find all this pretty hard to believe, Tracy," I said.

"I do too, Eric, but, well, it's true. I'm not lying to you."

"Do you think that one of them could make love to a human woman?" I asked.

"Yes, I suppose it's possible," Tracy said after a moment of thought. "I mean, they're physically capable of it. They're built a lot like us."

"That much?"

Tracy nodded.

"What do they want here?"

"I don't know. I wish I did."

"Listen, Eric," Kar-hinter said. "We are now in the Albigensian Lines. Much of what the one who called himself Mica told you is true. The Albigensians *were* a highly developed people. They may have developed skudder travel independently. But they encountered these *others*. What do you think caused all this destruction?" His hand gestured sweepingly around.

"War," I said bitterly.

"Damned right it was war," Kearns said. "War with the bluies. The Albigensians fought back, but they were wiped out. The war destroyed dozens of Lines before it was over and those blue bastards had won. Damn it, Mathers, you've got to make a choice. Now! Maybe you don't trust Kar-hinter. I don't know whether I do. But for God's sake, man, the Kriths never did anything like *this*."

"Eric," Kar-hinter said when I turned back to look at him, "given time, I could perhaps explain *our* motives to you, but now we do not have the time and you have stated an unwillingness to listen. But we, both mankind *and* Krith, are on the verge of war with these aliens. You must decide which side you are on. That of mankind or that of the blue-skinned aliens."

"He's right," Tracy said. "Eric, whatever else the Kriths are, and I think I know now, they aren't half as bad as—as these others."

"I don't know that."

"Damn it, man, look at this world!" Kearns said.

"I have only your word," I said, "and I'm sick and tired of taking other people's word for things. I'm going to find out for myself."

"You'll get yourself killed in the process," Kearns said.

"It's my life."

"Your life belongs to the Timeliners," Kar-hinter said, a sharp coldness to his voice that I had never heard before.

"The hell you say!" I yelled. Then, more calmly, "I'm sorry, but I can't take your word for anything any longer. I'm leaving." I started to turn away.

"Stay, Eric, we are not finished yet," Kar-hinter said in that same tone.

"Hold still, Mathers," Kearns snapped and when I turned back I saw that he held an energy pistol in his hand.

"I thought you were supposed to be unarmed," I said.

"Don't be a fool," Kearns said in disgust.

The look on Tracy's face inside the helmet was blank astonishment. He had not known that Kearns was bringing a gun. "Wait," he finally managed to say. "We told him. . . ."

"To hell with what we told him," Kearns said. The pistol in his hand slowly came up, then leveled at my stomach. "You've talked yourself into this, Mathers, you damned, bloody, human fool."

Three things happened at once. I threw myself to the earth, rolling, grabbing toward the energy pistol in the pocket of my survival suit. Kearns' energy pistol rasped, sending a jet of hell through the radioactive air where I had been standing. Tracy threw himself against Kearns, knocking him off his feet. They both went down together.

As I rolled, I tugged the pistol out of my suit, but before I could aim and fire, the air was lighted by another energy blast, this one from a pistol in the hand of Kar-hinter. That was the first time in my life that I had ever seen a Krith hold a weapon—that I knew of.

Tracy's survival suit blackened, burst into flames, for it was he that Kar-hinter was aiming for. Tracy's screams were loud in the near silence of this dead world, but he died quickly.

Yet even before Hillary Tracy died, Kar-hinter joined him. My pistol fired, poorly aimed, but aimed well enough, and the clothing covering Kar-hinter's chest flamed and disintegrated, as did the living flesh under it.

Even while all this was happening, I was able to see out of the corner of my eye the fourth figure emerging from the skudder. Whether it was man or Krith I couldn't tell. I was rolling to my knees, swinging the pistol around at Kearns, who was coming up, throwing Tracy's body aside. I fired. My beam seared off the top of Kearns' helmet, and the top of his head and bone and blackened brain burst out.

Kearns should have died instantly. Any *normal man* would have, but he didn't. His body kept moving, rising upward, coming awkwardly to its feet, the energy pistol still in its hand and firing wildly. I blasted again, and Kearns' half-headless corpse, now missing an arm, nothing left but a cauterized stump, staggered backward and fell to the earth, its legs still kicking.

I only know of one kind of higher creature that can live with its head blown away and that only because it has three brains and can go on living for a while without its head-brain. And I realized that there was a lot that I had never suspected about the Kriths—and I realized that the blue-skinned Paratimers weren't the only ones who could make use of plastic surgery. Kearns had no more been a human being than Kar-hinter. He had just looked more like one.

At the time I wasn't thinking about these things very much, though. I was thinking about the fourth figure who was running across the barren soil toward me, a seven-foot figure of a man with an energy pistol in his hand, aiming at me.

Perhaps I had the advantage of anger and adrenalin over Pall—for that is who it must have been. Perhaps he hadn't had the time to take it all in, time to prepare himself to kill. I had. And the weapon in my hand was surprisingly steady as it came up and fired, almost on its own, into the middle of the man's torso.

Pall stopped, then staggered backward, his chest and abdomen flaming, and finally fell forward on his face, still thirty feet from me. I didn't know whether he was dead or not, but it he weren't, he wouldn't last long in this environment.

I gasped for breath, felt myself shaking in reaction to the violence that had just taken place, and looked at the three bodies close to me. Only Tracy's body was human, some part of my mind thought, and he had trusted the

Kriths. It had cost him his life. I knew that I could never trust them again. Never. Nor ever believe anything that they said.

I shook my head sadly, bitterly, returned the energy pistol to the pocket of my survival suit and turned back toward the skudder where Sally waited—and had crossed no more than half that distance when I saw the other skudder, no, sautierboat, come sailing across the hills, its externally mounted machine guns firing—at me.

25
"They Are Almost Human"

There was very little protection out there. The nearest was thirty or forty feet away—the skudder—and I ran toward it. The aim of the machine gunner in the boat was fortunately lousy and I crossed the distance without getting myself killed.

Sally started to open the hatch for me, but I waved to her to keep it closed. I wanted to meet the men in that sautier-boat, but I wanted to be alive when I did it.

I walked a few steps away from the skudder, waved my hands above my head, gesturing that I surrendered.

The gunner in the boat must have got my message, for the firing ceased and the craft came to earth a few yards from my skudder. I stood silently waiting, hoping that whoever came out looked like me and not like the things Tracy had described.

While the sautierboat settled and its hatch began to open, I let one of my hands slip back toward the pocket that held the energy pistol. I wasn't that confident yet. Maybe. . . .

The hatch was fully open now, and a figure clad in something that was probably a radiation protection suit climbed out, a long, ugly-looking weapon in his hands. Two more followed him, both as well armed.

The helmets that covered their heads and faces protected them from my view pretty well while they were in the shadow of the boat, but when they walked forward, speaking in some language that I had never heard before and knew wasn't Albigensian, and the late afternoon sunlight shone directly on and through their transparent helmets, I could see their faces—and I knew that at least Tracy hadn't been lying to me.

The faces, well, they were almost human, but *almost* wasn't good enough. Their eyes were too big and their noses too flat and somehow their mouths weren't in the right place and their jaws were hinged wrongly and there was an unmistakable tinge of blue to their skins. And there was something menacing about them that was more than just their appearance.

Sally must have seen them too, for she screamed, but she still had the presence of mind to open the hatch and yell, "Get in!"

All at once my energy pistol was out and firing, so close to my body that I felt the terrible backwash of its heat even through the insulation of the survival suit. And three submachine pistols were screaming and chattering in the space between the two craft, and the whole universe tried to come apart at the seams.

Something smashed through the fabric of my survival suit below my left thigh, and my leg suddenly became a column of mush that didn't want to hold me up and I felt the salty taste of blood in my mouth as I bit through my lower lip. But my energy pistol kept firing, and light and heat and flame filled the air, and the three alien figures before me, scant feet away, stopped coming forward, stopped firing at me, and fell apart screaming.

Then a woman's arms, impossibly strong, were pulling me backward, upward into the skudder's open hatch, and I tried to help, pulling with my arms and somehow together, Sally and I, we got my uncooperative body into the skudder as the machine gun on the sautierboat turned around and began to blast into the skudder's open hatch.

"Hit the switch!" I screamed, and Sally must have understood me. She stumbled across the skudder's deck under a hail of bullets and hit the activating switch on the skudder's control panel.

WHAM!

I aimed the energy pistol through the open hatch, held the firing stud depressed, searing at the metal hull of the sautierboat, until. . . .

Flicker!

"Get the hatch closed," I gasped.

Flicker.

"Are you hurt badly?" Sally cried.

Flicker.

"My left leg," I said, but all I remember after that is. . . .

Flicker. Flicker. Flicker.

26
Out of Probability

The machine-gun bullets from the sautierboat must have penetrated the skudder's hull, must have damaged the craft, for within a few minutes red warning lights began to flicker on in the craft's control panel. I don't remember it. Sally told me about it later.

She cut away enough of the survival suit to get to my leg, shattered by a bullet, and she was at least able to stop the bleeding, though she was afraid to try to do anything more with the radiation level within the craft still dangerously high.

When I finally came out of the grayness, hours later, I saw the danger lights, and I struggled to sit up.

"Eric," Sally asked, "what do those lights mean?"

"The probablity generator," I said. "It's. . . ." Another light flickered on, and a dial swung into a red danger area.

"Open the hatch!" I cried.

"What?"

"Open the hatch. Now!"

Sally did, and I pulled myself across the deck, trying to ignore the pain that told me that I ought to lie down and die.

"What are we going to do?"

"This damned thing's going to blow up. Help me to the hatch. We're going to jump."

She didn't ask any more questions. She just helped me. "Get me to my feet."

Painfully, more painfully than I like to remember, I came up, standing on one leg. Sally supported me on the other side. We stood in the hatch for a moment.

"I'm going to count," I said. "When I get to five, jump. Exactly on five and together, or we won't even end up in the same Line."

"Okay," Sally managed to say.

"One."
Flicker.
"Two."
Flicker.
"Three,"
Flicker.
"Four."
Flicker.
"Five. Jump!"
We jumped.

Don't ask me to try to tell you what it was like—
leaping out of a probability field into "reality." It didn't
kill us. And that in itself is something of a minor miracle.
We both were battered, and Sally's right arm was broken
were she fell on it, and a couple of my ribs were cracked,
but we lived through it, and that's about all that matters
now. We lived.

27
"Something's Got to Be Done"

The rest isn't too important.

We found ourselves in a wood, but one that showed the works of man, tree stumps cut by power tools and footpaths, and off in the distance we could hear the sounds of surface vehicles on a paved road.

We took off our survival suits, and Sally, little more than half-conscious, made her way to the road and stopped one of the vehicles and asked for help in English and was more than surprised when the vehicle's driver answered in the same language. She told him, convincingly, I suppose, and with great presence of mind, that we were the survivors of the crash of an aircraft—she didn't say "airplane," though that is the word Here and Now—and that we had made our way through the woods this far.

The vehicle's driver, a kind, generous man, took us to a hospital where we spent the next few days, groggy and only halfway aware of our surroundings.

After a while, though, I learned that we had made it back to a Line that didn't seem to be too far from Sally's own world, but in this one the American rebels had won their war for independence nearly two hundred years ago.

The fact that our crashed aircraft has not been found has led to some questions from the American authorities, but we both claim to be British subjects—which is almost true—but that has created other problems that we haven't solved yet.

Now, well, now we are in a hospital in a world that doesn't suspect the existence of the parallel worlds and the almost unbelievable menace of two equally alien and non-human forces approaching each other across those Timelines, nearing the inevitable clash that might well mean the end of human life on all the Lines.

We're here, stranded, and there's no one to listen to us.

But it can't end this way. By all that's holy, it can't! Something's got to be done. Someone's got to be told. Someone, somehow, must stop this hell before it destroys billions upon billions of human beings across the Lines and all the magnificent civilizations we've built.

And if nobody else will do it, I guess it'll be up to Sally and me.

But damned if I know how.

BOOK TWO
NO BROTHER, NO FRIEND

This book is dedicated to the memory of Jefferson Conan Meredith, May 1966–July 1975. One couldn't have asked for a better son. . . .

9
The People of Tapferkeitenhaven

The place of rendezvous was a small fortress, a miniature marble castle out of medieval Germany, though built less than a century and a half ago by a Sclavanian nobleman to defend the ill-defined border between Sclavania and New East Anglia as much as it had been to guard against attack from the Skralangs, who at the time weren't at all amicable toward the Imperial colonists. Neither were they at present.

We arrived there as dawn brought the sky from black to gray. The thick overhang of cloud and the rain that had begun to fall from it gave the world below a pale, washed-out, shadowless appearance and effectively hid our party as we reached the "castle."

There had been little difficulty getting from the barbed-wire border crossing to the fortress, which I later learned was called Tapferkeitenhaven, except that for the first mile or so I required assistance in walking. Wexstan and the priest, Faeder Baldwin, took turns half-supporting me, allowing me to lean on their shoulders as I recovered from the shock of being too long under augmentation, as I adjusted to the pain from the flesh wound in my right thigh. Finally enough strength came back to me to allow me to walk alone, unassisted, and still keep up with the rest of the company, though I knew it would take several good meals and some long hours of sleep before my metabolism fully recovered. That's the price you have to pay for such advantages as augmentation.

The wound in my thigh had bled copiously, but wasn't serious.

During the final two hours of the march Freya was never far from me, again taking on her role of nurse and remaining solicitous of my health.

So with dawn a grayness streaking the cloudy sky and

the long expected rain a drizzling reality, we came out of the forest at Tapferkeitenhaven and were met by two men in civilian clothing who carried military rifles and spoke Anglisch with accents that made it almost impossible for me to understand them. Von Heinen and Aelfric spoke with them, apparently established the identity of the party, for the guards finally indicated that we were to go on toward the fortress.

I believe I saw glimpses of a dozen or so more men hidden in the trees and brush on the edge of the forest, steel eyes watching our movements closely.

With Aelfric in the lead, we walked single file down the path the guards had indicated and reached a set of massive wooden gates in the castle's stone wall. The spiked porticus was raised and the gates were opened for us and inside we were greeted by more armed men who didn't wear military uniforms, though several of them wore a distinctive, medieval-looking livery of black and orange.

After a few minutes of milling around in the courtyard, we were taken into a large room within the fortress' main keep where there was a roaring fire in a huge fireplace and a large oaken table covered with platters of cold cuts and pitchers of beer. The man who appeared to be the senior of the castle's liveried guards told Aelfric that we should eat and dry ourselves before the fire. Soon the *Herr* would be about and would meet with Aelfric and the other officers.

Freya requested fresh, dry bandages for my wound, which were delivered at once. She and Faeder Baldwin saw to the injury, cleaned it, rebandaged it. When they finished it seemed to hardly bother me. We addressed ourselves to other matters.

To me, and obviously to the others, the cold cuts, black bread, and thick, tangy beer were more than welcome. I devoured three sandwiches as quickly as I could, washing them down with the lukewarm beer. I must have looked half-savage, wolfing down my food, and Faeder Baldwin did comment on my haste in eating, but when I was finished and sat by the fire with my fourth mug of strong beer, I felt that I just might survive the ordeal. The only thing I needed now was ten or twelve hours of sleep, but I rather doubted they were likely to come any time soon. I was right.

When most of us had finished eating and sat in a half-circle around the fireplace drying ourselves, Faeder Baldwin announced he would hold a "short mass" in one corner of the large room for those who felt a need to thank God for our safe passage.

About half of the Anglianers expressed a desire for the holy sevice. Faeder Baldwin converted a table into an altar by the use of draperies, candles, and other para-phernalia he'd brought with him, but had said hardly more than *"Credo in unum Deum,"* when a man entered the room and told Aelfric, in thick accents, that the "Herr" was ready to see him, Von Heinen, and the other officers.

Aelfric nodded, directed that Von Heinen, Freya, Wexstan, Harold Winfredson, and I accompany him. I was only half-surprised that I was asked to go along to the meeting; Von Heinen's plans for me, I strongly sus-pected, had just begun.

Although there had been electric lights in the hall where we had eaten our cold-cut breakfast, there were none in the long hallway down which we walked af-ter leaving the room. The hall was dim and sooty, lighted by torches spaced some distance apart. There was a chill in the air, a dampness, and a patina of mois-ture on the walls. This place was an excellent reproduc-tion of a medieval castle, I thought, right down to the inconveniences. I wondered if it had indoor plumbing, and thought I'd probably find out sooner than I wanted to.

When the hallway ended we mounted a flight of stairs that led up one floor and down another torch-lit hall-way to a pair oaken doors bracketed by two guards in black and orange livery, carrying automatic rifles. The guards didn't speak as the multi-clad man who led us opened the doors and admitted us to another large room.

This room didn't have the austerity of the one we'd left behind. It was lighted by a brace of elaborate electric chandeliers that depended from the high ceil-ing and cast their light over the room's rich furnishings and luxurious appointments. It had more the appearance of the parlor of a sixteenth-century French king than that of a sixth-century border lord.

There were six people waiting there for us, six people whose names and positions I soon learned, and who were to play important parts in the events of the days to come.

They were:

Herr Jurgen Matthausen, a Sclavanian and the lord of Tapferkeitenhaven. He was a large bear of a man with heavy Teutonic features, hair more gray than blond. There was a ragged scar on the right side of his face, running from temple to jawbone, and there was a slowness to the movements of his left hand that indicated some sort of impairment. What had caused these I never learned, though I didn't believe they'd come from war. More likely from a hunting accident; Herr Jurgen was a great one for the hunt as the trophies on his wall indicated. As he greeted us in almost flawless if slightly condescending Anglisch, he was dressed in an elaborate smoking jacket of blue trimmed in gold, with silvery brightwork, and was smoking a large cigar that could have only come from Cuba, or whatever it was called in this Line. On the table beside the chair in which he'd been sitting was a brandy snifter, all but empty.

Herr Jurgen had once been a loyal Sclavanian and subject of his Imperial Majesty Conrad VIII, but events during the past few years had turned him against both the Emperor in Wursburg and the Colonial government in Neu Fulda, a city on the coast of an area known as Florida on some Lines. What was most important to Herr Jurgen, besides the Emperor's alliance with the "damned Franks" and some of the political machinations of the Emperor and his cronies, was the recognition by the Empire of the "Godless and unholy Antipope," Benedict XIV, who was now in sanctuary in one of the Emperor's palaces in Wursburg, surrounded by his "renegade bishops and false cardinals." Herr Jurgen was loyal to the "true heir of St. Peter," Pope Gregory XVII.

Although Herr Jurgen may have dominated the room, his powerful presence wasn't enough to totally distract from the others, the most striking of whom was a short, dark-haired woman in her twenties, now dressed in tan

layed so long, postponed by the European Settlement of 1942, was at hand.

But it wasn't my world, and its problems weren't mine or Sally's.

"Should we stay here?" Sally asked. "We might stand a better chance of catching a ride if we went down into the town."

"I'm not sure I could walk that far," I said, unwilling to admit it, but even more unwilling to try to make that long trip on foot, three or four miles.

"I'm sorry," Sally said quickly. "I didn't think."

"That's okay."

A huge, diesel-powered truck, laden with coal, was making its way up the slow incline of the road from the valley to the mountain's crest, its headlights weak and feeble far below us, smoke rising from its stack to mingle with that which lay so thickly in the valley. It was too far away for us to see the name emblazoned on the side of its cab, but we'd already seen many like it that day, rumbling across the face of the coal-mining land. The lettering would say: UNITED STATES NATIONAL COAL COMPANY. And in smaller lettering: Property of the People and the State, U.S.A. And more likely than not it would have also, upon the door of its cab, a small decal of the American flag, red and white stripes on two thirds of the flag, the upper left section a blue field containing a great eagle bearing a cluster of arrows.

The headlights proceeded slowly up the hill and I wondered what chance we might have of hitching a ride in a coal truck of the national mines. Regulations would forbid it, of course, but the real decision would be the driver's. If he got a good look at Sally, he might pick us up. Sally's looks had gotten us several rides so far. But then if he got a good look at me, he might not. My looks had cost us several rides.

"Which way do you think we should go, Eric?" Sally asked, her eyes also on the approaching truck.

I shrugged. "South or east, I suppose. I am not sure it matters."

There were other questions I'm certain she wanted to ask, but didn't. I was glad she didn't. I didn't have any answers, and I knew the questions as well as she did.

And I was tired. Tired mostly of running, for since slipping from that hospital somewhere in Missouri—as that area of North America is called here—we'd been running and hiding, fleeing from the authorities and their questions, and from something else that this world didn't have a name for, had never imagined.

East we had fled, through cities and towns, past vast military reservations and past equally vast "Black Detention Camps," past convoys of military vehicles and past convoys of trucks with such names on their sides as "National-Standard Oil" and "RCA General," these labeled with inscriptions stating: PRIVATE PROPERTY, PROTECTED BY NATIONAL LAW.

We'd fled east, "from" and not "toward," for we had no real destination, except that we get as far away as possible from those who followed us, who had come to whisper among themselves that we might be "enemies of the people and the state," those white-coated doctors and nurses and interns and orderlies who stood in obvious fear of the national police, of some half-secret organization known as the FBI and its auxiliary arm, quasi-official, the KKK. We had fled and still we fled.

The diesel truck chugged on closer in the falling darkness, now finally making the crest of the hill, roaring as if rejoicing its victory over gravity. Sally and I, our suitcases on the ground beside us, struck the classic pose of hitchhikers, right arm crooked, thumb extended in direction of travel.

The yellow-seeming headlights bore down on us and I thought that the driver was going to ignore us, sweep past us, and throw dust in our faces in his wake. But then as the F-O-R-D emblazoned on its hood was about to go beyond us, air brakes squealed and puffed and the ponderous vehicle began to slow. It came to a stop some two dozen yards beyond where we stood. We grabbed our suitcases and ran, Sally faster than I. My limping slowed me badly.

The door of the truck's cab opened, some feet above the ground, and an ugly, friendly face. showed itself. "Where y'headed?" the truck driver asked.

"Where're you going?" Sally asked.

1
The Daleville Diner

I didn't pay any particular attention to the green, four-door 1970 Packard sedan as it pulled into the station, except maybe to note that its left rear tire was a little low and could use some air. And I suppose I thought that I should mention it to the driver, tell him that I'd check all his tires if he liked. Sometimes it was worth a little tip, but not very often.

The Packard, occupied by four men, pulled into the station, up next to the "ethyl" pump and I heard the powerful sound of its twelve cylinders roar more loudly just before the driver switched off the ignition and the engine died. I wiped my hands on a rag only a little less dirty than my hands, hanging out of my hip pocket like a cow's limp tail, and went across the gravel toward the car.

There was nothing special about that morning, but looking back on it I think I felt some apprehension even then, some premonition of what was going to happen. During the past weeks, months, I'd been expecting something to happen, maybe almost hoping that it would. It was like sitting on top of a bomb that might, or might not, be a dud, and wondering whether you'd ever know whether it was, even if it went off. I wanted to know.

I stepped up to the driver's side as the window was being rolled down and asked, "What'll it be, sir? Fill 'er up?" I'd learned to talk like that pretty quickly under Jock's expert tutelage.

Even then the driver of the car was just another customer to me, despite the vague apprehension I felt. I hadn't yet looked at the swarthy face under the shade of the hat's brim; I hadn't yet noticed how terribly tall he was.

13

"No, thank you," the driver said, his voice oddly accented. "We have sufficient gasoline.".

Then his right hand came up out of the shadows of the car's interior and I saw the big, black, ugly energy pistol in it, a weapon that had no proper place in this world.

The Kriths had found us after all.

I knew it was the Kriths and not the Paratimers who had found us, for I recognized the man as he tilted his face up and I could see it clearly.

"I thought you were dead, Pall," I said, letting my humble, stupid service-station-attendant role fall from me like last year's fig leaf.

"Please step back," Pall replied slowly, quietly. "Three or four paces should be sufficient." He paused. "And, Mathers, please do nothing foolish that would force me to kill you. As much as I would like to do that, it is desired that you be brought back alive."

With the metal-and-ceramic tip of the energy pistol pointed directly at my chest, there wasn't a thing I could do except exactly what Pall ordered me to do. I stepped back his three or four paces, cursing him silently.

Pall opened the door of the big green Packard, still holding the ugly gun pointed at my chest, unfolded his seven-foot frame from the car. Pall was a *big* man; maybe it wouldn't have been improper to call him a "giant," and every inch of him was lightning-quick muscle.

Still he seemed to be moving more slowly now than he had the last time I'd seen him, and maybe some of his movements were still painful to him. But then the last time I'd seen him I thought that I'd killed him with an energy pistol blast that had hit him right where his pistol was aimed at me now.

He obviously wasn't very dead.

"Keep still now, Mathers," he said once he had gotten out of what must have been cramped confines and stood fully erect. Now, even without his midnight black uniform, high boots and shaven head, Pall was an impressive figure of a man, and I didn't think I wanted him any more angry at me than he already was—at least not until I was armed as well.

The other man in the front seat of the car—I was certain that he was a *man*, though I wasn't quite as certain about the two over-coated figures in the back seat—moved over into the driver's position and turned the key in the ignition. The Packard's big V-12 growled to life. A cloud of exhaust smoke drifted up from behind it, gray in the bright autumn sun.

"To the back," Pall told the new driver after he had looked around, up and down the highway and across the lot of the National-Standard service station and the diner, the only buildings along this stretch of highway. Pall and his buddies had picked a good time; Monday morning just after 10 A.M. The truck drivers wouldn't start pulling in for lunch for nearly two hours. There was nobody there but me and Sally and old Jock Kouzenzas who owned the diner and the service station.

The Packard pulled away, slowly crunching gravel under its sixteen-inch tires, and the driver took it around to the back of the little diner where Jock kept his Hudson parked.

"Let's go inside now, Mathers," Pall said softly, his voice still laden with the accent of a place and a people I knew almost nothing about. He gestured not so gracefully with the energy pistol. "I do hope that the Countess von Heinen is here as well."

I didn't answer. He'd know soon enough that she was.

I'd like to be able to say that my mind was racing, roaring into high gear and developing plans for outwitting Pall and his companions as he marched me across the gravel lot toward the diner's neon sign which read, "Daleville Diner, Jock Kouzenzas, Prop." and the double doors below it which led inside, but I wasn't. My mind was numbed, stunned. Oh, all along I'd had the fear, the premonition that sooner or later the Kriths would find us, but now that they *had* found us, I couldn't figure out how they'd done it. What bit of superscience that I didn't know about had enabled them to track us across the nearly infinite Timelines and find us in this particular and rather obscure one? The power of the Krithian machine frightened me again, and that wasn't the first time, nor would it be the last.

I opened the diner's doors and stepped through. Pall followed me with the energy pistol leveled. My skin felt raw and itching low in my back, waiting for the searing blast that didn't come, afraid that Pall would find his orders a little too much to take and go ahead and do what he really wanted to do to me.

"Eric?" Sally's voice called from the back. "Is that you?"

"Out here, Sally," I called back. There didn't seem to be anything else I could say.

"Is something wrong?" she asked, sensing something out of tune in my voice, and then stepped through the swinging, jalousie half-doors that led from the kitchen. As she came up to the counter her eyes saw beyond me, saw the huge, powerfully built man in the business suit and wide-brimmed hat, and she saw the Outtime energy pistol in his hand. She froze.

A half-dozen mingled expressions went across Sally's lovely features and her hands automatically, involuntarily clutched between her breasts, pushing the white starchiness of her apron into the cavity between them. Her green eyes were open wide with fear.

"Countess von Heinen," Pall said in a low voice, nodding. That was all he said to her and it didn't sound much like a greeting. "Is there anyone else here?" he asked me.

"Where's Jock?" I asked Sally. I knew that Pall and his friends would find him if they tried, and figured it might be better if we admitted from the beginning that he was here. I didn't want anyone to get hurt—at least not until I might be in a position to direct the hurting.

"In the back. Taking a nap," she answered, awkwardly regaining control of her voice.

"He's just an old man," I told Pall. "He's not involved. He doesn't know anything."

Then, through the doorway left of the kitchen, a wooden door marked EMPLOYEES ONLY, came the three others who had been in the car. That door stood at the end of a hallway that ran from the rear of the building. They had come in without passing through either of the apartments that formed the rear half of the building: the one apartment, to the left facing the rear, where Jock lived; the other, to the right, that Sally and I shared. They hadn't yet awakened Jock. I hoped they wouldn't. I knew they would.

The first of the unsavory trio was a man who could have been Pall's brother, except that I was inclined to believe that Pall had never been born from womb, but was spawned by a pool of stagnant water that had mated with dog's excrement. This one was tall, a full seven feet, built like a wrestler, but with no fat, and he carried an energy pistol exactly like Pall's—big, black, and ugly as patricide and incest.

The second man was a human being too, I thought, though I had my doubts. He was as dark as Pall and the other, but not nearly as tall, about my height, I guessed, slender, wiry, yet something about him, his feline movements, his strangely masculine grace, suggested strength that perhaps would be a match for that of Pall or his look-alike.

For an instant I thought this was a second case of return from the dead; I had the fleeting idea that he was a person—a *being*—whom I'd known before in another time, another place, but I *knew* that the one I'd known before was dead. I'd killed him myself.

But like the dead one, worlds away in space and time and paratime, whose brother he could have been, this one's face had a somehow alien, not-quite-human cast to it. It was a face made of sharp angles, craggy planes, lined with tiny white scars that could have been caused by his once having put his head through a plate-glass window.

This one didn't carry a pistol openly, although there was a suspiciously large bulge under his left arm, ample enough to have been a standard-issue Timeliner energy pistol.

He didn't speak, but held the door open for the final member of the party, one about whom there was no question of whether or not to apply the label "human."

This one was a Krith.

Somewhere between the green Packard and the diner's main dining room the Krith had doffed the heavy overcoat and the shadowing hat that he had worn in the automobile and was now naked, without ornaments of any sort, as was customary with Kriths.

And there was something on the alien face that I believed to be the equivalent of a human smile, not one of friendliness, but of triumph.

"Eric Mathers," the Krith said in perfect local English.

I nodded.

"And this I believe is the Countess von Heinen, nee

Sally Beall," he said—gesturing in Sally's direction and then giving her a formal semibow, a courtly gesture wildly in variance with his naked, alien appearance.

Sally now broke from her frozen posture, began to move toward me, her actions jerky like those of an inexpertly handled marionette. Her face wore an expression of shocked fear.

"Stay where you are!" Pall barked.

Sally froze again, though now she gave me a look that appealed for my help. I wished that there were some way that I could give it to her.

"I am known as Tar-hortha," the Krith said, looking at me with eyes that were enormous, brown and liquid. Light coming in through the diner's windows glistened wetly on the moist spheres, the highlight suggesting a pupil in reverse. "I am," he continued, "what you might call, well, a 'special investigator.' "

Why he was speaking local English rather than Shangalis I didn't know, except that it might have been for Sally's benefit.

"It has been my duty," the Krith was saying, "to locate the two of you."

I didn't ask why, I thought I knew some of the reasons.

"Tar-hortha," Pall said in a respectful tone, one that indicated his position inferior to the naked, alien Krith, "there is another person present in this building."

The Krith nodded. "A local?"

"Apparently," Pall ansered.

"Another Outtimer is quite unlikely," Tar-hortha said. "Countess von Heinen, my dear, would you please be so kind as to show Marth the location of this other person?" As he spoke to Sally he gestured toward Pall's look-alike, who then took several steps in Sally's direction. I read them as menacing steps and Sally must have too, for a greater level of fear showed through the shock on her face. "I would prefer that this other person not be harmed," the Krith added, "at least if it is not necessary."

"Go on, Sally," I said at last, feeling the way Benedict Arnold might have felt in conscience-stricken moments. "Get Jock. I don't think they'll hurt him. There's no reason for them to." Who was I lying to?

Sally gave me another look that appealed for my help,

but I was still as helpless as ever, feeling more so all the time.

"Go on," I said again, Judas in my voice.

Reluctantly Sally stepped from behind the counter and led the dark giant, whom Tar-hortha had called Marth, back toward the apartments in the rear, toward the room where Jock slept soundlessly, not dreaming that there were creatures anywhere such as these that were in his diner now.

As they went back, Pall crossed over to the front doors of the dining room, clicked the night latch into position after worrying with it for a moment and then pulled the blinds down over the glass windows, blinds upon which were stenciled in fading red paint the word CLOSED.

"You are acquainted with Pall, I believe," Tar-hortha was saying now. "And this is my companion, Mager." He was now referring to the dark, slender man with the craggy face and the bulging coat. "The other is Marth, a Turothian as well, who is currently serving as what you might call my bodyguard. Pall is with me on special assignment.

"I can suspect why," I said.

The Krith gave me his smile-equivalent. "He does have a special interest in you, Eric."

There was silence for a moment, the four of us now in a rigid tableau: Tar-hortha's tail being the only part of his body that moved, save for the row of tiny openings below his eyes that dilated with heartbeat regularity; the giant Pall stood like a stone tomb guard from some ancient, lost, and fabulous empire; the not-quite-human-looking Mager peered at me as if he were examining the entrails below my clothing and my flesh; and myself, in too great a state of confusion to know what movement to make.

Finally I spoke.

"How did you find us?" I asked the Krith.

And while I waited for his slow-coming answer, I wondered how it was that I'd ever trusted his kind, how I'd ever felt them to be the friends of mankind.

"Finding you was not as difficult as you might expect, Eric," he said slowly, his thick, heavy lips moving across the rows of sharp, almost fanglike teeth. "You see, the late Kar-hinter never did fully trust you, you know, at least not after your encounter with the so-called Paratimers." He nodded his large head, shaped rather like a slightly distorted and somewhat lumpy egg. "He had suspected, even from the time that you were brought from Staunton in RTGB-307, more dead than alive, that upon your recovery you *might* consider turning your coat on us, so to speak. The Paratimers were persuasive with you, I understand, so while you were in the Bakersville hospital he took the liberty of having planted a small transmitter with a very distinctive signal on your body."

I felt as if somebody had just struck me on the back of the head with an oversize baseball bat. Of course! God, how could I have been such a stupid ass? I should have known that he'd have done something like that! Dammit, I should have known *that* when he found Sally and me in the Albigensian Lines after our flight from Eden—how else could he have followed us there as easily as he had, across that many Timelines, even though he must have suspected our destination from the beginning? I was more glad than ever that I'd killed Kar-hinter, but that small satisfaction would do nothing to help us now.

"Oh, it was tedious, I will admit that, Eric," Tar-hortha said, the rows of feathery membranes that ran from about where a man would have temples to the middle point of his jaws twitching in the air like the nose of a curious rabbit, "checking individually Line by Line until we found the only one where the telltale signal was being transmitted, a long way from your last known *geographical* location. You know how long it has taken us, but I doubt that you appreciate the Krith-, man- and computer-hours that have been packed into that time. But . . ." He paused as if ruminating thoughtfully, the short, prehensile tail that grew from the twin mounds of his humanlike buttocks twitching aimlessly in the air as if swatting flies. "But now I have you and I suppose that it has been worth the effort." I don't think he was certain of it. He had his own orders from his own superiors, I suppose.

I'd known that the Kriths considered me to be dangerous, but up until then I hadn't suspected just how dangerous they considered me. To have spent all the time and manpower it must have taken to check *all* the Lines that

Sally and I had crossed in fleeing from the Albigensian Lines . . . Somebody wanted me pretty badly.

"The Tromas do consider you important, Eric," Tar-hortha was saying, "even if I am personally uncertain of the value they place on you. Surely they know better than I." That was as near to heresy as I'd ever heard a Krith speak, suggesting that it might be possible to doubt the mysterious and sacrosanct Tromas of the Krithian Homeline.

"Thanks for the compliment, I guess," I said. "At least the one from the Tromas."

Before more could be said the EMPLOYEES ONLY door opened and Sally and Jock Kouzenzas, followed by the giant Marth and his energy pistol, came into the dining room. Poor old Jock, his thin white hair amuss, his slender, lined face still slack from sleep, was confused, dazed, frightened as he tried to rub the sleep from his eyes. I'd never planned on getting the old man involved in this mess, but I should have known better from the beginning, when I let him take us under his wing.

"Eric," Jock said, seeming to see me before he had taken in the others who were in the room, his voice not quite his own, "what the hell's goin'—"

Then he saw Tar-hortha, came to a stop in midstride. His mouth dropped opened and his eyes seemed to bug from his head like a comic-strip character as he looked at the sable-brown, satin-skinned, prehensile-tailed, and totally naked alien.

"My God!" he gasped.

"Easy, Jock," I said, my voice sounding foolish even in my own ears.

"Holy God in heaven," Jock said, making the sign of the cross in the air before him. The blood drained from his face. A pallor like death came over him and for a moment I was afraid that he was going to have another heart attack. It's a wonder he didn't. Sally grabbed his arm and helped to steady him.

"It's not really the Devil, Jock," I said, though now as I looked at the Krith through Jock's eyes, I could see how he might mistake Tar-hortha for Satan. "But as close as we're ever likely to see on this earth," I added, looking into the Krith's deep, brown, pupilless eyes.

Sally helped Jock to a chair at one of the dining tables. The old man, seeming to have added another decade to his years in seconds, looked up at Sally beseechingly, and said in a faint voice, "What is all this, Sally? Can you tell me what this is?"

"There's no need to bring him into this," I told the Krith angrily, angry at myself for not having said so before. "He didn't know anything about this before now."

Tar-hortha looked at him for a moment, but didn't speak, one of his hands casually resting on his flat, well-muscled stomach. After a while he turned to face the one he called Marth, still not speaking, but asking questions with his eyes, the lines around his huge, wide mouth.

"He is probably telling the truth," Marth said, his voice accented much like Pall's, in the fashion of the Turothian people. "I do not think that they have told the old man anything about Outtime worlds."

"How unfortunate is his innocence," was all that Tar-hortha said, but those sinister words were enough, coming slowly from the alien's mouth as he stood casually scratching himself.

Standing there in that room, the dining tables, the chairs, the jukebox filled with country and western records against one wall, the red-topped counter with its cash register and a transparent case displaying slices of cake and pie and doughnuts, the soft drink and coffee and milk dispensers behind the counter, frosty with cold, the checkered red-and-white curtains across the windows, the yellow, fading walls on which hung reproductions of paintings of pastoral scenes, and a large picture calendar from one of Jock's suppliers which showed a litter of three- or four-week-old kittens and which said September 1971, but which should have been changed several days before, all so commonplace and prosaic in the world of Jock Kouzenzas, yet all in its own way exotic to one from some other Line, some other world—standing in that room, the air filled with a tension that I could almost reach out and touch with the tips of my fingers, I wondered why the Krith and his human and maybe not-so-human companions didn't get on with their business. They'd put a lot of effort and expense into it and the thing was about ready to culminate and although I didn't know exactly what that business might be, I was certain that I wasn't going to find it pleasant.

Better to get it over with, maybe. . . .

Tar-hortha's double-lidded eyes had surveyed his surroundings, the people in the room. "It all seems satisfactory," he said precisely after a few moments of silence. "Please be good enough to hold them here for a while, Pall. I will consider you the responsible agent here."

A strange expression flickered across the thin, craggy face of the one called Mager, though whether that expression was wry amusement or annoyance or something else entirely I couldn't tell.

"I will be back shortly," Tar-hortha said.

Pall nodded, but didn't speak.

An expression that might have been that of intense concentration came over Tar-hortha's sable-brown face; his double eyelids blinked in rapid succession several times; the nipples of his mammalian, almost feminine breasts hardened; his tail twitched, as did the feathery membranes along the sides of his face; his hands tightened into fists; and his hairless body tensed as if it were in expectation of *something*.. . . .

Then, like the Cheshire Cat from *Alice in Wonderland*, Tar-hortha began to fade from our view, to vanish, as they say, into thin air.

In less time than it takes to tell it, he was gone, and there was only a small clap of air left behind to tell us that he had ever really been in our presence.

Jock Kouzenzas crossed himself again and groaned and whispered something that might have been *Ave Maria* in a strained and guttural Latin.

He was now convinced, if he hadn't been before, that Tar-hortha was the true and living Prince of the Power of the Air, Beelzebub, the Devil himself.

But then maybe old Jock was right.

2
A Killing

The six of us left in the diner didn't speak for some time. There seemed to be little to say, and I doubted that Pall or Marth or Mager would be very willing to answer the questions I had to ask them. And I hardly need to observe that the energy pistols in the hands of the two large men put something of a damper on the festivities.

Pall hardly moved at all, and Marth, standing near the table at which Jock and Sally sat, was no more active, although the wiry, craggy-faced Mager now seemed nervous, filled with a pent-up energy he had not shown in Tar-hortha's presence, and began pacing the floor in silence.

While I dared not approach Jock and Sally, I did take the liberty of pulling a chair out from a table and sat down. The solidness of the chair under my buttocks felt good and I realized how suddenly tired I felt, how drained of energy, and how weak my legs had become. It was almost as if I had just gone through a period of great physical exertion—although I felt certain that such exertion was yet to come. I would *have* to do something sooner or later, but right then I didn't have the slightest idea what.

I'd been sitting in the chair for less than a minute when I found myself speaking almost without realizing it, almost without wanting to. "I never expected to see you again, Pall," is what I was saying.

The giant of a man looked at me for a few moments, an amused expression on his ugly face, a face usually so devoid of emotion, usually as cold and expressionless as that of a corpse. Then the amusement turned to bitterness to remembered anger. "Yes, I suppose it was something of a surprise to you, was it not, Mathers? You assumed me dead, no?"

"I did."

"That is obviously not the case, you see," he said, some portion of his amusement returning. "I was fortunate. When you so treacherously shot us down in that so-called Albigensian Line, the survival suit I was wearing deflected most of the energy of your weapon, as you should have suspected that it would. And furthermore, your aim may not have been as good as you thought—those were awkward circumstances, no? I was able to get myself back into my skudder once you and the woman"—there was something nasty about the way he said that last word—"you and the woman had fled from those who *attacked you.* Alone, I crossed-Lines to a place where I could receive medical aid from fellow Timeliners. Then, of course, I set out to locate you." There was finality, bitterness in those last words.

"Of course," I said.

"And now I have found you," he added, the amusement fully back now and something more—triumph, probably.

"Now that you have, Pall, what are you going to do about it?"

"Unfortunately that decision is not mine to make," Pall said slowly, the bitterness returning; maybe that's where a lot of it had come from in the first place, the realization that, captive though I was, I wasn't mouse to his cat. "Tar-hortha and *his* superiors will determine your final disposition."

"I see," I said.

"Whatever it is," Pall said, half-turning as if gazing out through the curtained windows, "I am rather certain that your murder of Kar-hinter will not go unavenged."

"Will you tell me where you're going to take us?"

And as I expected, Pall's only answer was, "You will see, Mathers. In time you will see."

All this time Sally had been watching the two of us, her face a mask of consternation and fear, her wide green eyes asking me to do something, anything.

I wished I knew what to do, but still I didn't.

Jock mumbled to himself old, childhood prayers and seemed fearful of looking directly at our captors.

There was silence again in the room while we waited for Tar-hortha's return. I didn't expect the Krith to be gone long. I suspected that he had done no more than self-skud across to an adjacent Line, uninhabited and/or controlled by Kriths, where a skudder stood ready to come pick us up once he and his companions had captured us, as now they had.

My guess, it turned out, wasn't far wrong.

Very little time had gone by when suddenly, in the air before us, coming first as a vague smear of haziness, the ugly, naked figure of Tar-hortha rematerialized, seemingly more quickly than he had gone. There was something that I read as satisfaction on his flat, noseless face.

"It is set," he said without preamble. "Marth, go start the car at once."

The swarthy giant, Tar-hortha's bodyguard, nodded, turned, and went out through the doorway and down the hallway to the big Packard parked in the rear.

"We have a short trip to make," the Krith said, directing his words at me and Sally. "I hope that it will not be too inconvenient for the two of you to leave this world now."

"As if we had any choice," I said.

Tar-hortha smiled as the V-12 engine of the Packard out back roared to life. He said nothing more.

"What about this one, Tar-hortha?" the craggy-faced Mager asked, gesturing toward Jock who still sat at the table, dazed and in fear.

"Actually he is of no use to us," the Krith said. "If we were to take him with us, he would be, what you might call, so much excess baggage. We had best leave him here."

"Alive, Tar-hortha?" Mager asked coldly.

Kriths are not really very much like us. You can never tell what might be going on inside those large, lumpy heads of theirs, but I'd never known a Krith to be unnecessarily cruel, nor particularly kind either. That wasn't their way. So I hadn't expected Tar-hortha to go out of his way to treat Jock gently, but neither had I expected him to be totally uncaring of him. Kriths can be aware of the existence of other creatures, if not particularly concerned.

"We have not the time to wash his memory of these

events," Tar-hortha said without emotion, human or Krithian, in his voice.

"He can't possibly harm you," I said.

"Nobody would believe his story even if he told it," Sally said urgently. "And even if anybody did believe him, what could that—"

"The Tromas have been explicit on that point, my dear," Tar-hortha interrupted. "Some things must never be revealed to those who are not, shall we say, 'initiates.' "

"But—" I protested.

"Enough!" Tar-hortha snapped, silencing me with a wave of his very manlike hand, a snap of his simian tail. "Do take them out, Pall," he went on, pointing to me and Sally.

Pall gestured with his energy pistol.

I stood there for a moment without moving. Old Jock was a nice fellow. He'd been good to Sally and me. After we'd fled from the hospital where we were on the verge of becoming prisoners of the national police after we'd hitchhiked a third of the way across the North American continent, after we'd been treated as hobos and criminals, Jock had taken us in. He hadn't known a damned thing about us except what we told him, and even though what we'd said was a pack of lies, he believed us or at least pretended to believe us. He'd given us work and a place to stay and three meals a day and he didn't ask us any questions that we didn't want to answer.

I don't know what Jock had really believed us to be, and I really don't know why he'd been so kind to us. Maybe he realized that we weren't actually criminals, Sally and myself, though we'd committed our share of petty thefts to stay alive until we found Jock and he took us in. We'd been strangers in a strange land if ever there were, and maybe he dimly realized that, maybe he was vaguely aware that we were fugitives from something far more evil than our petty crimes had made us. He never said so, but maybe he believed that we were really fugitives from the Fourth Reich of Chancellor Heinrich Goertz: we didn't speak exactly the same dialects of English as did Jock and the people of this part of the United States of America, and we were obviously ignorant of native customs. We must have seemed an odd pair to old Jock.

I don't know why he took us in.

But I do know that Jock had been good to us, had given us a chance to catch our breath and look around ourselves and think about what we were going to do next while we hid behind the disguises of waitress in a second-class hash house and a rather inexperienced grease monkey.

And I liked the old man.

I wasn't about to let them . . .

"Go out to the automobile," Pall said in a soft tone that was filled with all the ice of a Pleistocene glacier.

At that moment I had risen from my chair and was standing somewhere between Pall and Mager, both of whom were about the same distance from me, Mager nearer to the table where Sally and Jock still sat. Tar-hortha was a little farther from me.

"Okay," I grunted to Pall and started slowly toward the rear door. Sally and Jock were still seated at the table, Sally trying to comfort the old man; they and Mager were between me and the door.

"Let's go, Sally," I said.

She looked up at me, her face incredulous.

My back was now to Pall and the Krith; I could see neither of them. I could see Mager and the expression on his face, the energy pistol that he'd now decided to draw from the shoulder holster inside his coat. As I walked toward him I gauged my distance, the force I would need, what actions I would have to make, and how I would have to make them. I had little room for error.

And, gingerly with certain sensory channels, I checked out my long unused combat augmentation. The "augie" circuitry and components were all in working order, so I was told by returning sensory impressions from inside my body. I hoped it was so. I put them on standby, ready for activation at an instant's notice.

Tar-hortha knew I was an Augie, of course, but was he really taking that into consideration now . . .?

I moved forward as if I were obeying Pall's command and . . .

Good old Sally! I said to myself. Now the incredulity

was gone from her face, replaced by hints of understanding. She must have realized what I had in mind, what I was about to do. She rose to her feet as if obeying *me*.

"Stay where you are, old man!" It was Pall's voice. He was speaking to Jock who seemed to think that he should rise and go with Sally. He was still too shocked, too stunned to fully take in what was happening, to realize what they intended for him. *That's okay*, I told myself, *better for him now*.

"W-what are you—" Jock started to ask in a broken and stammering voice.

"Get down, Jock!" I yelled, willed my combat augmentation to click all its components into operation, leaped.

The world around me started to run down, to become slower and slower, until everything but myself was moving at only one fifth of its normal pace. Lights seemed to shift to the red—although this may have been more imagination than fact—and sounds dopplered toward the bass.

Sally, in seeming slow motion, shoved Jock aside, grabbed the back of the chair she'd risen from, lifted it off the floor, swung it toward Mager's midsection as I moved across the last paces toward him, my augmentation coming up to full speed. The chair connected with the craggy-faced man's abdomen before he could react, before he could switch on his own augie circuits—human or something else; he was a Timeliner too and was certain to be augmented. He stumbled backward, cursing, gasping for breath.

Pall too yelled and cursed, his voice sounding slow and hollow, meaningless rumblings, and as my hands grabbed Mager, snatching him upward and grabbing at the energy pistol in her nearly lax hand, I heard from behind me the rasp of an energy pistol, distinctive, even slowed as it was, and felt the heat of its beam pass near me—the speed of light doesn't seem to slow up a bit, even at X5. I don't suppose it does.

Sally was screaming now and Tar-hortha yelled, his words dragged out in so long a rumble that I thought he might never finish what he was saying, and though I couldn't understand a word of it, I felt that he was yelling to Pall: "Don't kill him, you fool! The Tromas ordered that we bring him back alive."

The chair in the gut had only stunned Mager for a moment. His eyes began to clear and he switched in his own combat augmentation even before I could get the pistol from him. He was quick! And he was even quicker as his actions and reactions came up to five times as fast as they had been before. He straightened, his arm flung out to knock me aside.

The barrel of his pistol came across my right cheek, slashing skin to the bone and spraying the air with lazy droplets of my blood. My head was knocked back so rapidly that had my vertebrae not been suitably strengthened, I'm sure my neck would have been broken. My body was carried along with the blow, staggering backward, fighting to hold my balance. Inside my head lightning flashed and stars novaed.

I caught myself in my backward stagger, lurched forward again, and then leaped toward Mager before he could bring the pistol back into firing position.

This one called Mager was really no bigger than I am, but there was a fierce, wiry strength about him that would have made him a good match for Pall or Merth, and he was augmented and as well trained in hand-to-hand combat as I was. Still I'd like to think that maybe I could have handled him if it had been a fair fight, dazed as I was.

But it wasn't a fair fight.

I'd never expected it to be.

I'm not that big of a fool.

Pall must have gone into augmentation about the same time as Mager, for suddenly there he was with us, coming up behind me with his energy pistol reversed in his hand, grasping it by its hot barrel, maybe even crisping the tough skin of his palm. I hope so.

I didn't see any of this at the time, of course. I just figured out later that this is what must have happened.

As Mager and I struggled in a reddened world filled with bass booming sounds, other noises that maybe only dogs normally hear, Pall reached us, swung the pistol, connected with the side of my head just under and behind my right ear.

Now whole galaxies, not just single stars exploded inside my head and I felt my legs going out from under me. The floor came up toward me slowly at first, and then more quickly as my augmentation automatically cut itself out.

I slipped into grayness, once, then several times, the world coming into ragged focus and then going out again, and I lay there on the floor, unable and unwilling to move. The blow had been an awkward one and hadn't connected as squarely with my skull as Pall might have liked. That is, he hadn't broken my head. But it did rather incapacitate me for a while.

Pall and Mager took their time in switching off their augmentation. I suppose they wanted to make certain that I wasn't coming up for another round, but at least when they spoke again their voices were normal.

"It is time we left this place," the accentless voice of the Krith said from somewhere a long way off.

Sally sobbed, said something I couldn't understand.

"He is not badly hurt," Tar-hortha said, "though I must say that his being injured has not been unpleasant for me to witness."

"*You* go on," I heard Mager say, his voice coming with a ragged breath; he must have been talking to Sally.

"Let's get *him* out of here," Pall's voice said from somewhere above me during a gray spell.

Then rough hands grabbed me under the armpits, hoisted me up as if I were a rather large sack of corn meal. My legs were rubbery under me, but I thought they would hold me up if I wanted them to badly enough. Did I?

"It will be easier for you if you make an effort at walking, Mathers," Mager's rough voice said in my ear. "I hope you follow my thoughts."

"Yeah," I groaned. I tested my legs, half stumbled against a table, supported myself with it while my head swam a long distance up the river and then floated back down it with the current. Maybe I could walk.

Dimly, through eyes that I found hard to focus, I saw Marth come back into the diner. He came up to Mager, they exchanged words, and between the two of them, with what little assistance I was able and willing to give them, they hauled me down the hallway toward the green Packard sedan sitting in the rear, its motor still going with a loud kitty-cat *purrr*.

Dammit! I still wanted to struggle, to fight them, to kick in their ribs and gouge out their eyes, to kill them before they could kill old Jock, but . . . Dammit!

I stumbled down the three steps at the rear of the building, leaned for a moment against the fender of Jock's red 1968 Hudson Hornet and then, after Mager had opened one of the Packard's rear doors, Marth dumped me inside the vehicle. I think that I went under again for a moment or two. I'm not certain. Everything was one shade of gray or another anyway.

Then Sally was starting to get into the car with me, but Marth said, "No, you are going to ride in the front seat, Countess." His voice was not as polite as the words might sound.

"He needs help," she said in protest. I thought that she was probably talking about me. I wasn't sure. I couldn't get my eyes open to see.

"Do not worry about him, Countess," the Outtime giant said. "He is not badly hurt."

I wanted to tell him differently, but I couldn't.

"But . . ." Sally protested. It didn't do any good. Marth wasn't a man to listen to a lady's plea. He probably tied tin cans to stray cats' tails too.

Marth had opened one of the car's front doors and was gesturing for Sally to get in when I was able to pry my eyelids open. She quit protesting and did as he said. Maybe the energy pistol he jabbed in her ribs had something to do with it.

Both Pall and Marth got into the car then, but Tarhortha and Mager weren't there. They were back inside the diner.

I thought I knew why.

Then, through the fog and pain that were inside my head, I heard an energy pistol rasping again from inside the building.

I did know why.

And I hated the Kriths and their Timeliners and everything they stood for even more than I had before, more than I thought I could have ever come to hate anything in all the universes, and it was a hate compounded out of fourteen years of experience as a Timeliner, a mercenary soldier fighting the Kriths' wars for them, out of times and places and experiences far away in space and time and paratime; it was a hate built on their lies and their deceptions and their broken trust, a hate built on the blood and pain and terror and death of uncounted millions; it was a hate that came up out of the bowels of the earth like molten stone and down out of the heavens like a vile and seething rain. . . .

One day I'd get even with them for killing that old man, for that and for so damned much else.

One day . . .

But right then all I did was pass out again.

3
A Drive in the Country

The automobile trip wasn't the most pleasant experience that I can recall, but then it could have been a lot worse. I wasn't conscious through a lot of it.

How far we traveled I'm not certain, but it was probably about twenty or twenty-five miles up U.S. Highway 441 out of Daleville. When I finally did get my eyes fully open I vaguely recognized the country. I'd been that way a couple of times before with Jock on errands connected with the service station and the diner.

Once we passed a tavern called The Snake Pit, gaudily decorated with a great red and green cobra with hood expanded, covering half of the front of the building. From its half-open doors, as early in the day as it was, came a loud, whining voice singing of an unfaithful woman and nights spent drinking to forget her, the voice accompanied by a twanging, off-key guitar. Though I'd never been inside the place, I knew where it was located: ten or twelve miles south of Milledgeville. I had my position in space fixed in my mind, though what good that knowledge might do me I didn't know.

After a while I was able to sit up straight in the seat, cramped as it was with Mager close on one side of me and sable-skinned Tar-hortha on the other. In ' the front seat Sally sat between Marth, who was driving now, and Pall. Every now and then Sally looked back at me, trying not very successfully to smile.

"Eric," Tar-hortha said as I moved against the pain, felt the gash on my right cheek which was almost closed now, covered with caked blood and dirt, as I gingerly rubbed the side of my head where there was a great lump and more dried blood, "are you feeling any better now?"

"Go to hell," I told him in as friendly a manner as I could muster, which brought no response from Tar-hortha but an immediate one from Mager. He poked me in my left ribs with the barrel of his energy pistol and said in guttural tones, "It would be wise for you to watch your language, Mathers." He was speaking in Shangalis now, not in English. *"He* is not someone to whom you speak in that manner."

I looked into those strange brown eyes set into an ugly, scarred face and wondered if Mager were a human being or something that was just made up to look like one. "Yeah," I muttered and started to add some additional wisecrack, but thought better of it and kept my mouth shut.

"Forgive me, Eric," the Krith said in his usually emotionless voice. "My intentions for you do not require either pain or humiliation. At least, not for the moment. These you have brought upon yourself."

"Just what are your plans for me, Tar-hortha?" I asked, still trying to get my eyes to focus. Right at the moment they'd slipped totally out of control and I was seeing two Tar-horthas, one situated to the left of and just above the other; the world behind him had the same disturbing quality.

"As you have been told before, Eric," Tar-hortha said in the tone you'd use to scold a small child for raiding the refrigerator for the last slice of cake you'd been saving for yourself, "you will be made aware of them in due time. As for the present, your best course of action is to give us as little difficulty as possible."

"I think I understand." I wondered how it was possible for me to be sitting there so calmly between Tar-hortha and Mager when back at the diner Jock's body lay on the floor, cut down by an energy blast that the Krith had ordered and that Mager had executed. I should have been in a blind, killing rage and trying to take them both with my bare hands.

But then maybe I wasn't that stupid. I wasn't going to avenge Jock and protect Sally by getting myself killed out of hand; and I still suspected, orders or no, that Tar-hortha and/or Pall would gladly kill me if I were to force the issue.

And, well, a throbbing head, a nauseated gut, and knees made of half-set gelatin aren't exactly conducive to sudden and violent action.

I sat in the rear seat of the automobile as it bounded down the highway, sixty or seventy miles an hour, and tried to get both my eyes to look in the same direction at once.

On the road a cream and black car of the national police, red light mounted atop its roof, machine gun hidden under its hood, roared up behind us, honked twice, and then gunned its motor and sped around us. Two hard-faced nat-cops sat in the front seat, black uniformed and (I suppose) jackbooted. One was driving, the other gazing off into space, a huge, black cigar between his teeth. Then the Plymouth was dwindling out of sight, turning a curve and vanishing.

I wondered what the two nat-cops, so despised by Jock and his neighbors, would have thought if they'd known that Sally and I, people they'd seemed suspicious of anyway, were being kidnaped by two giants, a craggy-faced non-man and a monster who, literally, looked like the Devil.

Had the circumstances been a little different, I might have laughed out loud.

"I do hope that you understand *now*," the Krith said just after I lost sight of the national police car.

"Eric," Sally said cautiously from the front seat, "are you really okay?"

"I'm okay," I said, hoping it was true. "They didn't hurt me."

It appeared that she wanted to say a great deal more, but decided that she shouldn't. Not now at least.

I turned back to Tar-hortha. "You really didn't need to kill him, you know." I don't think any emotion showed in my voice. I hope not.

"Perhaps, perhaps not," the Krith said, only barely looking in my direction. "Yet what is done is done, is it not, Eric?"

"You're very philosophical."

"Hardly," he replied sarcastically. "But what happens on this Timeline is of little concern to you now."

"Then you are taking us Outtime?"

"Of course."

Then, as if to reinforce what he'd just said, Tar-hortha

told Pall and Marth to be on the alert for the turnoff, it should be coming up soon. Pall grunted an affirmative; Marth nodded.

If I hadn't spent so much of my time during the past fourteen years skipping from one Timeline to another, I might have found the situation odd. It was a warm day in early October. The sun was shining brightly through a nearly cloudless sky; only near the horizon was there a cluster of white, puffy, cauliflowerlike cumulus clouds, and they certainly weren't indicative of bad weather. Birds were singing in the brush and the trees that lined the highway in this isolated section of central Georgia, trees beginning to show autumnal colors. The chill of fall was still a long way off, it seemed, despite earlier indications to the contrary, and the grass and the shrubs and brush seemed mostly to be as bright and green as they had in early summer when Sally and I had first arrived in this world, quite by accident in this particular one.

It was, all in all, a lovely, rather pleasant place, this world in which we'd found ourselves, or rather this portion of this world, for outside, away from the seclusion of Jock's diner, this world had its full measure of trouble: the "Black Detention Camps" recently formed by the Washington government; the summary executions of "security risks" and "communist sympathizers" and anyone else too vocally opposing the Wallis administration; the specter of war that loomed on the horizon, a war that would surely engulf the whole of the civilized planet and include the use of nuclear weapons; so much else I didn't have time to catalog.

Yet still, somehow, I thought it was a nice world, or could have been a nice world if more people in it were like Jock Kouzenzas and were certain changes made in the manner of men who governed it. . . .

I said that the situation would have seemed odd had I not experienced so many different paraworlds in my life, and maybe it did despite that, for there had been moments during the past few weeks, since Sally and I had come to work for Jock and live with him, that I'd begun to believe that this world, with all its faults and short-

comings, was really mine, the one in which I would spend
the rest of my life, the one in which the children that
Sally and I would have would be born and raised.

Oh, maybe I'd never really believed that. Maybe it
was just fantasy, wishful thinking, for often there were
times when I wished that I'd never heard of the multitude
of worlds that exist side by side in time.

But I did know of them, that there were many universes beyond this one, universes I'd seen, experienced,
and beyond that was our knowledge, mine and Sally's,
that there were forces active across those universes that
were not working for the benefit of human kind, two
great alien forces moving from both ends of the transtemporal spectrum that would one day meet, strike head on,
and what came out of that would probably be war,
perhaps was already war that would soon sweep across
all the Timelines, blasting, burning, destroying world
after world after world . . . until, maybe, at last there
wouldn't be anything left at all. Nothing. Nobody.

I know, Sally knows, and maybe no one else does, I
thought. Maybe no one else knows in all the damned
universes that lie side by side like the pages of a book
with more pages than a human being could hope to count
in a lifetime, and each of these pages is a whole world,
a complete human world with men and women and children and hopes and loves and fears and desires and
ideals, with plans for making the world a better place,
with schemes of enslavement and destruction, with glory
and suffering and . . .

Dammit! Dammit! Dammit!

What could I do?

How was I going to save the world?

Hell, how was I going to save Sally and myself?

The big autombile slowed as Marth applied his foot to
the brake pedal. At first I couldn't tell why. The highway
before us seemed to stretch almost to the horizon and
there wasn't the first sign of an intersection. I figured that
we were still at least three or four miles from Milledgeville, maybe farther.

Then I saw the dirt road off to the left, just beyond
the shield-shaped sign that read "U.S. 441 North," a dirt

road that cut through the pines and brush, it unmarked, undistingushed in any way. But then that figured.

Marth braked the car almost to a complete halt on the deserted highway and cut the wheels so sharply that the power-assisted steering mechanism let out a great, unhappy whine. Then he hit the accelerator again and the car bolted forward down the bumpy dirt road, my teeth chattering against one another and my head hurting worse than it had before.

Marth's driving was apparently too much even for Tar-hortha, who said, in a tone of great but restrained annoyance, "Please do slow down a bit, Marth. Actually we are not in that great a rush, you know." This in Shangalis, not English.

The swarthy giant behind the steering wheel didn't reply in so many words, though he let his foot slide back from the accelerator and the car slowed.

I started to say something, to pose a speculation to the Krith who was my captor, but suddenly words became superfluous. We rounded a bend in the dirt road and I saw what our destination was.

From its appearance the clearing in the woods hadn't been there long, days at the most, perhaps only hours. Trees and brush had been hastily chopped away and pulled to one side, portions of the piles still green and fresh. In places it looked as if the vegetation had been bulldozed to the bare earth. It was a scene of quick and merciless rape of the forest, but that wasn't what really caught my eyes.

What I did see were the two huge, squashed spheres that sat in the middle of the clearing, two very familiar glasslike bubbles mounted on small, dark bases, vehicles never designed to move in space, only across the Lines of Time. Two skudders.

Neither Tar-hortha nor the others offered explanation then. They merely waited until the automobile came to a full stop, opened doors, and told Sally and me to stay put until we were ordered to move.

And they didn't tell us to move until the two humans, Pall and Marth, Mager (human or not) and Tar-hortha had climbed out, the men drawing their pistols and aiming them at us. During this time the two men who had been in each skudder climbed from their vehicles, bringing their own energy pistols with them. Seven guns faced us.

"Now you may get out," Tar-hortha said in local English.

"I don't believe we're trusted," I said lamely, trying to keep up a good front, more for Sally than anything else. Nothing I could say or do now could conceivably intimidate the Krith or his companions.

Tar-hortha Krith-smiled again, saying, "I would advise you not to use your augmentation *here*, Eric. Human reflexes, even without augmentation, are sufficient to cut you down. And all these men *are* augmented, by the way."

"I'm sure," I said.

"Now I will tell you this much," the Krith said, standing quietly in the early October sun near the edge of the clearing torn from the forest, the ring of armed men around me and Sally, all their energy pistols ready to burn us to smoldering, unrecognizable crisps should their alien superior deem it necessary. "We are going to board those skudders and we are going to take a very long trip across the Lines. We are going to a place that even you, Eric Mathers, have never visited. I hope that will satisfy your curiosity for the time being."

All this in English for Sally's benefit.

And that was all he would say on the matter, though I wondered if our destination were the legendary Krithian Homeline or somewhere near it. Maybe so. There had once been a time when I had wanted very much to visit there. Now I didn't exactly feel that way about it.

"Pall," he said, turning his attention away from us," "would you please take the Countess into that skudder." He gestured to the one on the left. "Tomaz and Robart will accompany you. You have your orders and you know our destination."

Pall, his face of carven stone, yet looking as if he would prefer to stay where he could better guard *me*, nodded without speaking.

"You, Eric," the Krith said, facing me again, his face now even more unreadable than a Krith's usually is, "will accompany Marth, Mager, and myself in the other skudder."

So they were separating us, I thought. Did they consider us so dangerous that they were afraid to have us together in the same skudder? Maybe that was a compliment. Wasn't it?

"Proceed, Pall," Tar-hortha.

With a caustic look in my direction, the big, swarthy man reached out to grab Sally by the waist. She tried to pull away from him, fear and anger on her face, but he was too quick for her. She said nothing as his huge hand closed viselike around her wrist, but from the look that now suddenly came to her face, I could tell that he was hurting her. But then maybe just being touched by him would have been painful to her. I could understand why.

"Sally," I cried, now unable to hold the words back, "I'm sorry."

"No, Eric," she cried.

I made a tensed motion toward her, but the barrels of the six remaining energy pistols leveled at us both held me back.

Oh, dammit! Again. My head was still throbbing from my last attempt to do something about the situation, and now and again blood still came from the gash on my cheek. And what had I accomplished the last time? Jock was dead. That's all.

I felt gorge and fury rising inside me. I wanted to strike out again, to do something, *anything*, just to show them that I wasn't going to be led quietly like a steer to the slaughter. I wouldn't let them hit me in the head with a hammer and then cut my throat . . . but I knew how hopeless it was, my trying to do anything now.

And—maybe this was the only thing that kept me from doing something stupid then—I knew that they had no intention of killing Sally. If they had, they would have already done it. Sally was valuable to them, just as I was. She'd been with me into the desolated Albigensian Lines. She'd seen what was there. And, furthermore, Sally knew the so-called Albigensians, the Paratimers, far better than I did. Hadn't she been the mistress of one of *them?*

Still, knowing, believing that they really wouldn't harm her, not yet at least, I didn't want her parted from me. I wanted . . .

What difference did it make what *I* wanted? I couldn't do a damned thing about it. Not yet.

"I believe they're taking us to the same place, Sally," I said, weakly, maybe foolishly. "They won't keep us apart for long." I wanted to look at Tar-hortha, to ask him to confirm what I was saying. I didn't. I was afraid to.

For a moment she seemed weak and frail, like a frightened child, but then the Sally I knew reasserted herself. She drew herself erect, threw back her shoulders, and even managed to give me a smile as Pall led her away toward the skudder.

If I'd known then how long it was to be before I saw her again, I might have fought despite the guns and the odds against me.

"Now you, Eric," Tar-hortha said, switching back to Shangalis again.

"Do I have a choice?" I spoke the same language as the Krith.

"No more than did the Countess," he said. "This way, please."

The two men who had originally been in the second skudder preceded us. Tar-hortha walked at my side, unarmed in the Krithian fashion, and Marth and Mager followed, their energy pistols pointed at the back of my head and the small of my back respectively. It may not have been a guard of honor, but it was nonetheless a guard.

The first two climbed into the craft, stooped within the hatch and waited until the Krith gestured for me to climb in ahead of him.

There seemed little point in argument. I did as I was told.

And as I climbed into the skudder I felt a jet of wetness enter my skin from a strange-looking gunlike thing that had seemingly materialized in the hand of one of the men inside the craft, a jet that cut through the cloth of my shirt as if it weren't there, but which caused me no pain.

"I regret that this is necessary, Eric," Tar-hortha said from behind me as I stared in a mixture of anger and humilation, becoming aware of what they were doing to me. "A simple precaution, you know."

"Drugs?" I asked, holding my voice and my fists under tight rein.

"I am afraid so. Nothing dangerous, mind you. You may even find the effect pleasant. Some people use this drug for the simple pleasure of it."

"Thanks."

I continued my movements into the skudder, even as I did beginning to feel something of the drug coming over me, dizziness, disorientation, perhaps even hints of hallucination.

At least it made my head stop hurting.

For a while.

4
Skudding

Kriths aren't stupid, are rarely careless, so what happened was mostly dumb luck.

Or maybe I did have fate on my side, as I sometimes felt that Tar-hortha believed.

Anyway . . .

The drug they'd given me was some sort of hallucinogenic, I believe, though maybe it did some other things too, and was slow to reach its full effect, though I did begin to feel it almost at once after the injection. As I settled myself into the seat as directed by Tar-hortha, Marth beside me, the Krith, Mager, and a young guard named Sulla across from me, the skudder pilot cramped into his own seat, I felt dizziness, the disorientation, the beginnings of something like hallucination, at least some distortions of time and space—but I don't believe that yet my mind was very dulled. I thought I was thinking clearly, as one does after two or three drinks, not yet in a state that could be called drunken.

The skudder pilot, a man with the reddish skin and the aquiline nose of an American Indian, flipped switches across the control panel. A buzzing began as the craft's probability generator came to life, an electrical sound that was accompanied by the smell of ozone, less real than imagined. "Everybody ready?" the pilot asked in Shangalis.

"Ready," Tar-hortha replied with unusual terseness. He may have been nervous, if a Krith is ever in such a state.

The pilot waited until the generator rose to full potential. From where I was sitting I could see across his shoulder, saw the familiar indicator lights come on as circuits reached operative levels.

"The Paratimers are one up on this, you know," I said, waiting for the final signal lights to come on, my

45

tongue becoming thick and fuzzy in my mouth, yet still able to function without impairment.

"What do you mean?" Tar-hortha asked.

"Their sautierboats," I said, glad to have some needle to prick him with, small as it might be, "their version of the skudder. It doesn't have to be wheeled around from place to place, you know. It can move through space just like an aircraft."

"Yes, we are aware of that," Tar-hortha said coldly. My needle had pricked him! "It may be of interest to you," he went on defensively, "that we have captured several of these so-called sautierboats. They have been taken to Indus 29 Prime where they have been studied thoroughly for some time." A few months at best, I told myself. "We are already adding modifications to our skudders to give them the same capabilities."

"Good for you," I said.

Marth gave me a dirty look, but at least he had put his energy pistol away. So had Mager. But the guard whose name was Sulla, the one who had given me the drug injection, hadn't. It was in his lap, sitting across from me. Almost within my reach if I were to move fast enough . . .

"Potential achieved," the red-skinned skudder pilot said, the final green light flickering on. "Stand by."

That was all the warning we got. He hit the single activating switch.

Flicker!

The world outside the skudder ceased to be for a moment, and then was there again, but different. The raped area was gone. Trees and brush, loblolly pines and magnolias, mimosa with feathery autumnal leaves under a cloudless sun grew right up to where the skudder sat, seemed almost to be growing right inside it. A jay was frozen in flight by the stroboscopic effect of our quickness and I caught a glimpse of a big diamondback rattler sunning himself on the ground below the skudder, not yet ready for winter's hibernation.

The other skudder, the one Sally was in, was no longer visible. We had moved Outtime first. It was "following," maybe at this instant in the meaningless limbo between worlds. I didn't expect us to be sufficiently in phase to see it again until we reached our destination, if then. . . .

Flicker! Flicker! Flicker!

We were moving across the Timelines, accelerating until the passage of universe after universe was no more than a flash of light and then a flash of grayness that represented Nothing with a capital "N."

My stomach jerked each time a world flickered by us and I wanted to vomit, but didn't. It was as though a huge, savage hand had gotten inside my guts and was trying to pull me apart from the inside. Skudding had always affected me that way. It does most *people*.

Of the occupants of the skudder only Tar-hortha now seemed at ease. It wasn't bothering him. But then he was built for skudding. He had evolved that way. Or so I believed at the time.

Mager was grimacing with each flicker, but I somehow had the feeling that his discomfort was phony, that he was just putting on a show for ignorant slobs like me. Why? What *was* he, anyway?

"Relax, Eric," Tar-hortha said in a soothing voice, perhaps to annoy me, to demonstrate his own lack of a discomfort that must have been obvious on my face. "The drug you were given *can* be pleasant to experience, I am told, even within a moving skudder. Allow it to give you that pleasure."

And I began to realize what he meant. As I started to adjust to the flickering of the skudder, I found myself beginning to lose all sensations of discomfort. A pleasant sort of euphoria came over me, and I found the sights and sounds and even the odors around me growing more intense, more interesting, more pleasant. I found myself noticing subtleties of the skin color of the Krith that I had never noticed before, slight variations here and there across his flesh, spots of olive and green amid the brown, a greenness that grew like living plants in the springtime of the world, lush and lovely and clustered with bright flowers and singing birds, and gurgling fountains around which beautiful, naked nymphs played as they . . .

Stop it! I yelled at myself inside my head. The drug was beginning to do to me exactly what the Krith wanted to do, to make me docile, quiet, co-operative, tied up in a subjective existence that I found more agreeable than the world outside—and damned if I was going to let him get away with it!

I fought against the pleasurable sensations of the drug and called up half-forgotten rigors of my early Timeliner training and did battle with the pleasure of the drug, and as I fought I asked myself what I was going to do about all this. Sally was in that other skudder and there was no way for the two of us to get together again before we reached our destination, whatever that might be, and I didn't want to be separated from Sally any longer than necessary. I didn't want to admit to myself, even then, that what I felt for her was something frequently called "love," but I suppose it was, or something so like it that I couldn't distinguish between them.

Yet, I thought, if I waited to try to do anything until we did get to wherever we were going, then it would probably be too late to do anything at all, and Sally and I would be at the mercy of whatever it was that Tarhortha's superiors intended for us. But if I were to get away somehow, maybe I could later get to Sally, unencumbered with gun-carrying guards and a not-so-friendly Krithian "special investigator." Maybe my only hope of ever finding her again was to let her go now.

Did any of this make sense?

Maybe I was already too far gone under the drug.

Flicker! Flicker! Flicker!

An hour or so may have gone by—time distortion seemed to be one of the drug's first effects—while I sat in the skudder's seat, pretending to be under the influence of the drug. Sometimes I wasn't pretending.

All this time the guard named Sulla had been sitting quietly across from me, his head nodding every now and then as if he were about to go to sleep despite the stomach-wrenching sensations of the skudder's movement across the Lines. The energy pistol still lay in his lap, and his right hand rested on it, but lightly.

Finally, when I believed them all to have been lulled into a sense of security by the steady, now almost hypnotic flickering of the skudder, I decided to act. I hoped that the drug had had no effect on my augmentation circuitry, though I feared that it might have. I'd just have to try it and see.

And what I was going to do after that no sane man would have, except me, I guess, assuming that I'm sane. But then I'd been through it once before and I knew it *could* be done, though it wasn't a pleasant thing to consider. Yet, what else could I do? I couldn't hope to take command of the skudder—so my only choice was to get out.

Carefully, hoping that the slight tensing of my body wouldn't be noticed, I willed certain little-used muscles to move, and in their movement did the equivalent of flipping switches in a tiny control until buried between my shoulder blades.

For a moment I thought that something was wrong, that it wasn't going to work after all, that the drug had had a direct effect on my electrobiological augmentation systems.

Then the world slowed. The "flicker" became a "fliiickeer" and the buzzing of the probability generator became a rumble. I was ready.

Something swept across me; a rapid succession of images confused me. The hallucinations came on quickly, struck me hard, then departed, leaving behind a tangled, faded web of colors and sounds, odors and tactile sensations that hardly related to any world I knew. A fraction of a second and my mind was as clear as ever, I thought. I hoped.

There may have been the dawning of comprehension in Tar-hortha's large, brown eyes. He may have noticed the increased rate of my breathing, the batting of my eyelids, something. But it was only a dawning when I moved.

My hand was darting across the space between me and Sulla, brushing away his limp hand. My fingers curled around the butt of the energy pistol, snatched it away.

As I stood up, the weapon in my hand, both Marth and Mager seemed to show awareness too, perhaps began to prepare to activate their own circuitry. They couldn't do it before I pulled back on the energy pistol's trigger and sent a beam of pure hell down between my feet, a tight, narrow beam into and through the floor-board and into the delicate maze below that was the heart and brain of the skudder.

Marth came into augmentation amid a blaze of red-dish light and slowly billowing smoke. His scream of pure anger started slowly, but came on more quickly as he moved toward the full speed of his augmentation.

I leaped back, swinging the energy pistol in a wide swath that did little real damage, ionizing air and singe-ing surfaces, hair, clothing. Marth fumbled for his weapon in the awkward clothing he wore, and so did Mager, also coming into augmentation. They were both too slow, too late.

Mager, who was more nearly behind me than across from me now, managed to free his pistol from his shoul-der holster—but I shot him in the face while I straight-armed Marth out of the way.

In the blaze of light and coherent energy from the pistol in my hand, Mager's head became a ghastly, cauterized lump of burned meat and blackened bone, but he kept on moving, kept on struggling to aim his pistol —as I'd been afraid he'd do. I shot him again, in the chest where I suspected his secondary brain to be, and then turned to burn away Marth's right hand, which then held his energy pistol.

The pistol in what was left of the giant's hand did exactly what I feared it would do—and wanted it to do.

Covering my face with my left arm, I threw myself toward the seared and smoldering plates of the skud-der's floorboard, while the energy pistol in my right hand continued to fire.

I hadn't quite reached the floorboard when the cramped interior of the skudder filled with light and bass-dopplered sounds and slowly flying bits of metal. Marth was screaming and so was Tar-hortha, and maybe I was too. I don't know. I don't really remember.

For only a moment did I attempt to lie still, feeling, more than hearing, the Flicker! Flicker! Flicker! of the skudder slipping from one universe to another, though now it seemed to do so less smoothly, more erratically.

Then I rose again, partly blinded, burned and cut in more places than I wanted to become aware of.

Mager was quiet now, maybe dead at last, two of his brains burned away in the energy blasts—did he have still another? Marth was writhing in pain, screaming in incoherent agony. Tar-hortha was bleeding from at least a dozen minor wounds and seemed too concerned over his own injuries to care what I did. And the guard named Sulla had taken a piece of gun fragment in his right eye; he wasn't ever going to move again. Only the skudder pilot seemed unhurt, and he was too busy fighting the dying controls of the damaged vehicle to try to stop me— and what I was going to do was suicide anyway, according to all the rules.

Stumbling over broken flesh and writhing bodies, I reached the skudder's hatch, undogged it and jerked it open, and was hit by something like a wind that was blowing out of the inner regions of a frozen hell.

"You did it before," I said to myself aloud, "and it didn't kill you. Dammit, man, you can do it again."

But another part of me, the one that once in a while makes very good sense, said, ."The hell you can! One time you were lucky. Now you're pushing it too far."

And behind me Tar-hortha was coming out of his initial shock, growing angry as only Kriths can grow angry, for the race of Kriths is very, very sensitive about personal injury. Indeed!

I tried to steel myself for the jump, but felt a cold fear wash over me and that voice was telling me again that what I was about to do was almost certain death, when a sable-brown hand closed around my left ankle and tried to jerk me back. The sounds that were coming from Tar-hortha's full-lipped mouth were not English, weren't Shangalis, weren't even coherent, and one glance back at him showed me his mouth, opened in savage rage, rows of sharp teeth like a great cat's coming to tear at my flesh.

And behind Tar-hortha, amid the smoke and carnage that filled the skudder, stood a shadowy, almost formless figure with the vague outlines of a standing man, an alien presence that I might have somehow found comforting if there'd been time to think.

Then I jerked my ankle out of Tar-hortha's grasp, and

in the process threw myself out of the skudder and into nothingness right in the middle of a Flicker!

There's no point in trying to describe the sensations I felt before I lost consciousness. But unconsciousness was a welcome, blessed thing when it did come.

5
"And the Sky Broke"

The universe moved aside, shattered by strokes of violent
violet lightning that walked across the sky like God and
yelled a meaningless thunder in His voice.

Sky grew up from craggy plains, umber and ocher
and sienna, the plains, boulders, and weathered fragments
of rock, fractured and shattered; sedimentary rocks like
sandstone and shale and limestone were absent, but in
ample quantity were broken slabs of slate and marble,
hornfels, and quartzites, glistening phyllites and crystalline shists, of quartz and mica and chlorite, gneisses
of moscovite and hornblende, and too were fragments
of obsidian and black basalt, pumice and andesite and
rhyolite as if the earth had fractured again and spilled
extrusive stone, hot volcanic lava across the ancient
and broken slates and marbles. Here were ragged crests
and harsh shadows in the flickering light of thunder-
bolts that came from somewhere above, sky abuilding.

And all the while the sky grew up, piece by piece like
a mosaic, building itself into a faceted dome of vari-
egated colors and textures, though blue was the dominant color and smooth the dominant texture.

At last the sky was complete, a dome over the plain
that was the world and for a few eternal moments
held itself in place by the power of its will, fast and rigid,
unyielding to the spheres passing through it, singing their
songs as they would.

And then, from the invisible edge of the world, beyond
the crags and peaks and strewn boulders and fragmented
slabs, across the broken and littered earth, came the
voices as if out of the wind, as if they were the wind
in and of themselves, these voices unearthly in beauty,
and terrible.

And with the voices, as the voices sang and their
sounds echoed from the dome that was the sky, faceted

dome of blue, dome of glass and gems and minerals dome of azurite and galena, of calsite and gypsum, of talc and blue quartz, of amethyst and onyx, of aquamarine and dematoid, of tourmaline and emerald, of blood-stone and jade, of lapis lazuli and hematite, of zircon and sapphire . . .

And the universe quaked, shuddered as if in mortal fear.

The sky broke, came tumbling down in a thousand bright fragments, pieces sharp as ice, cold as glass, and below them on the ragged plain was I, and the pieces of falling sky struck me, cut me, killed me, and as I died I saw that which was beyond the sky.

It was nothing.

Nothing at all . . .

When an Augie loses consciousness, his circuitry automatically cuts off. That's a characteristic that can save him. Augmentation running too long can easily burn the life out of a man. That would have happened to me when I fell out of probability, had it not been for that built-in safety factor. I can thank the Kriths for something.

Even as it was, I don't suppose I missed death by much, and it still frightenens me to think about it. But what was worse at the time was what the drug Tar-hortha's men had given me did to me while under augmentation and what followed.

With my metabolism running at its normal pace the effects of the drug had been rather mild, sufficiently mild for me to have planned and executed my escape. But when augmented . . .

Well, while under augmentation I hadn't really noticed; the time had been so brief and so much had happened so quickly; but when I came out of it, stunned and battered by leaping out of the skudder's probability field and coming harshly to earth in some unknown Timeline, well, the effects were multiplied by five, maybe more.

For a while it was hell. . . .

There were moments of rationality, moments when I opened my eyes and realized that wherever I was it was night and it was raining. I was lying on the sodden ground, rain pelting across my tattered clothing and my battered body. I was cold and shivering and aching in my head and in other places and I was afraid that maybe my left leg, in which I'd taken a bullet not too many months before, was broken again.

But then the hallucinations and the dreams and the fantasies and mingled memories would come over me again and for a while, maybe seconds, maybe minutes, maybe hours, I would be lost in them again.

The rain came down harder, and off in the distance there was true, not illusionary, lightning breaking from the sky and for a few moments illuminating the sodden earth.

I rose to my hands and knees and tried to focus my eyes and see what was around me, but all I could see was trees, pines and oaks I thought they were, and brush and brambles and tangles.

When I tried to get to my feet there was another great flash of lightning as if the whole sky were breaking apart as in my fantasies. Then my legs gave away and I fell. I remember my face splashing into mud and water, but that's all I remember for a while.

Now I was in the motionless sautierboat with the technician and was trying radio frequency after frequency, but didn't know whether I'd make contact with Kar-hinter's base in the Outer Hebrides. Then there was a banging on the hatch.

"Who's in there?" a muffled voice called. "What's going on?"

The captured technician looked at me for an instant, then back at the hatch.

"Stay still," I told him, but that didn't do any good. Still looking directly into my pistol's barrel, he jumped at me, a yell of pure hatred on his lips. I fired, and then his face wasn't much of a face.

The technician lay at my feet and I hated very much that I'd had to kill him.

The banging on the hatch had stopped, but a voice called, that of one of the Paratimer leaders, Scoti, and was saying, "Mathers, we know you're in there. Come out and . . ."

"Come get me," I yelled back and delivered one last, frantic message into the microphone.

Through the transparent dome I could see men cluster in the hangar's open door. Scoti came out from under the craft, running and gesturing for the others to clear out. I caught a brief glimpse of the weapon he held. But that was enough. An R-4 power pistol.

Now the space in front of the hangar was vacant except for Scoti who knelt with his left elbow on right knee, left hand around right wrist, sighting across the weapon's barrel. I saw the flash. . . .

And I saw the universe explode. And I felt heat and flame and blinding light so bright I couldn't see it. And that was all. . . .

The rain let up and I thought I saw a glimmering of dawn along the horizon, but I may have been mistaken. Or perhaps I saw the flashes of artillery, though I never did hear that there'd been any sizable cannon used in the area where I lay for so long. Perhaps it was only hallucination.

I wanted to stand up and try to walk away to a drier place, but I was too weak and too scared to make the effort. It was easier to lie there and let the rain fall on me.

And maybe it didn't matter anyway. I wasn't going to be alive much longer and then it wouldn't matter whether I was wet or dry.

Then there was a strange chill in the air, something out of my memories from just after the explosion of Staunton, an alienness, an unknown quality that I couldn't identify but knew was more than shock and pain, and around me was the stillness you find only in nightmares.

A voice was speaking, a voice out of a nightmare, yet with a familiar ring to it, though I couldn't place it. It was saying: "Stay alive, Eric. For God's sake, man hang on just a little while longer. They're coming to help you. The pain won't last long. You can stand it, Eric. *I did.*"

And then the voice was gone and I was lying on the rain-sodden ground and wondered if it had been a memory of something that may have happened——or had someone, something just been there with me.

I didn't know.

I began to float away into illusion again, but I knew I'd try to hang on. The voice had said help was coming, hadn't it?

And I remembered that message that was supposed to have been projected backward in time to a receiver on the desolate surface of the Moon:

FROM THE YEAR 7093 (which is about 4000 A.D.), GREETINGS. WE HAVE WAITED UNTIL THE LAST POSSIBLE MOMENT TO SEND THIS BACK TO YOU. BUT WE KNOW THAT WE CAN WAIT NO LONGER. WE ARE ALL DOOMED. WHILE THERE IS STILL TIME LET US TELL YOU WHAT HAS HAPPENED TO US ALL.

THERE IS A CIVILIZATION OF BEINGS ON THE FAR SIDE OF THE GALAXY. THEY ARE TOTALLY ALIEN, INIMICAL TO ALL THAT IS HUMAN AND KRITH. THEY HAVE BEEN BIDING THEIR TIME, AWARE OF US, BUILDING A GREAT ARMADA OF INTERSTELLAR WARSHIPS TO COME AND DESTROY US ALL.

WHY THEY HATE US SO WE DO NOT KNOW. NOR DO WE KNOW HOW TO FIGHT THEM.

HUMANITY AND KRITH STAND ALONE AGAINST THE ALIEN HORDES COMING TO DESTROY US. AND WE ARE ALL BUT DEFENSELESS AGAINST THEIR WEAPONS.

ALL THE WORKS OF OUR GREAT MUTUAL CIVILIZATION SHALL PERISH UNLESS . . .

It was cold and dark and raining and around me were the dark silhouettes of loblolly pines and live oaks and the call of a night bird off in the distance, but as I struggled to my knees and tried to focus my eyes the scene changed. The pines and oaks soared, towered into the sky and then were not trees, but buildings. The grass and vines and brush gave way to streets and parks and the darkness gave way to globes of light that floated in the air.

I could see the city but dimly and with double vision, poorly and out of focus and half-hidden by rain and mist, but what I saw told me that it was no city I'd ever seen before. Something about it told me that it was no city ever built by humankind.

Despite the floating light globes much of the alien city

lay in darkness and shadow, and after a while I saw movement in those shadows, furtive movement, stealthy and quiet, a figure here, another there, wrapped in dark clothing, but now and again betrayed by a glint of light from metal. All the moving figures in the quiet city carried weapons.

One of the dark-clad figures stepped briefly into light and for a moment I saw him clearly: a man in his thirties, tall, scarred from battle, tanned, blond with a short beard; he carried a Paratimer R-4 power pistol in his right hand, a knife in his left. This man whom I shockingly recognized instantly turned as if facing me, as if peering into *my* eyes, and on his lips was a twisted, bitter smile of anger and hatred, of satisfaction and revenge. Then he turned away and vanished into shadows.

In another place another figure revealed itself momentarily and it was a tall, scarred, blond and bearded man in his thirties, though he carried a large, heavy energy rifle in both hands.

And in still another place, stepping out of the shadows for a moment to make his way forward, was the same man.

An army of men in the night, all identical, all perhaps cloned from a single person.

The army of raiders slipped silently through the night, all headed for a single destination wherein lay something they/he wished to destroy.

There was a chill in me such as I'd never felt before.

Time had gone by now, how much of it I don't know, and they had almost reached their goal when, in the sky above the non-human city, a great light burst, white and brilliant, destroying the shadows and revealing those who had been hidden in them.

For a moment the raiders stopped in their tracks, startled by the light, then, as if guided by a single mind, darted forward, running through the streets, across the parklike areas toward the largest building of the city.

From that building gunfire opened, sending shot and flame down into the streets and parks, and from the portals of the building issued an army of men, they too all identical or nearly so, and all of them looked very much like a man—a being—whom I'd known as Mager.

The Mager force rushed into the streets, automatic slug-throwers in their hands, spitting leaden death into the attackers.

The leading element of the raiding force was within range and one of the blond men took a bullet in the chest. . . .

I staggered back from the impact of the slug as it ripped through my right chest, just below the nipple, I thought, shattering ribs, puncturing a lung, exiting through my back, tearing away great globs of flesh. I staggered backward more shocked than pained, stunned, dazed, knowing as the pain began that the wound was mortal and I was going to die.

I tried to raise the captured R-4 power pistol, to take at least one of the Magers with me, but I didn't have the strength; the pistol was too heavy, slipped from my weakened grip, fell to the earth, and in moments I followed it, darkness, pain, and death coming over me as I fell.

The first of me died, but more of me came on, a dozen, two dozen, and here and there, as the collective-I rushed forward, the individual-I took more wounds. One of me was hit in the head, my skull shattered. I died instantly.

But I'd also taken a gut wound, a me some yards away, and lay in agony as blood seeped onto the ground.

And I ran forward, a different me, a stream of bullets ripping away my left arm, but somehow I still fired with my right until I collapsed in agony.

Yet still, dying here and there, others of me wounded terribly, I came on against the Magers and still they killed me, though I wouldn't stop until they'd killed me all. . . .

And maybe they never would.

The hands that touched me were probably very gentle, but at the moment they seemed rough and savage, like angry men pawing over my corpse to see if there were anything of value on it.

Dimly I could see their dark faces in the early light and vaguely I could hear their voices, but I couldn't understand a word they were saying. They seemed to be speaking a language I'd never heard.

I had the impression that the rough hands and gruff voices were trying to help me, that they were those whom a vision had promised, but right then I was unable to respond to them. I let them do as they wanted with me, confident only in the feeling that they knew I was alive, if barely.

Then my mind drifted off again. . . .

Sally and I were in a stolen skudder, flickering across the Lines of Time. I held an energy pistol in my hand, safety off, held my breath and . . .

We came out of probability.

I don't know exactly what we expected to find, but what we did find wasn't it, was like nothing we'd hoped to see here in a part of the Lines where we'd expected to encounter a high and complex civilization of cross-Line travelers. .

Oh, there'd been a high degree of technology here once, but now . . .

The transparent dome of the skudder gave us a. 360° view of the countryside. The sky was blue-black, sprinkled with a smattering of the brighter stars, and in that sky hung an enormous, bloated sun whose corona beamed brightly around it. It was broad daylight, yet the sky was halfway dark and I knew that this earth had little left of its atmosphere, more than the moon, but not enough to support human life.

Before us a rocky, gray-brown plain stretched toward the horizon, then abruptly ended two or three miles away in a huge pile of rocks, a chunk of earth lifted up and tilted skyward, revealing centuries of geological evolution, now all but ended.

In the other directions it was the same: gray-brown stone and earth, waterless, airless, lifeless rock, a world totally dead, that might have always been dead, that might have never known life and man. I'd never seen a world so totally devastated.

A skudder's hull is impervious to most forms of radiation, so I wasn't too worried when the counters on the hull went wild, measuring a nuclear radiation level a thousand times higher than it should have been.

"What is this place, Eric?" Sally gasped, her voice filled with fear.

"The *where* is exactly the place where we started," I

said slowly. "It's the parawhen that matters." I paused. "There's been a war here, Sally, one hell of a war. This planet's good and dead. We've still got a long way to go."

The probability generator was standing by. All I had to do was spin the destination dial for a few Lines ahead, hit the actuating switch and Flicker! Flicker! Flicker!

We came out in a world that wasn't very different, just a bit less totally destroyed.

"Not again," Sally gasped.

"Parallel war. Maybe not as bad as the other, but just as total as far as human life is concerned."

"Could we possibly be near Mica's Line? He never told me about anything like this."

"Maybe he was ashamed of what his relatives had done," I said, feeling a growing apprehension. "We'll go on."

But as I glanced at the controls and computer readouts I saw that we were nearly on top of where I thought Mica's Homeline to be. Maybe his Line's an island in all this destruction.

Flicker!

The next Line was almost identical, except that the nearest crater was a mile away and the radiation was a few roentgens lower.

Flicker!

It was as if we were back in the first Line. The atmosphere, what of it mattered, was blasted away and a naked sun blistered the naked rock of a dead, naked Earth.

Flicker!

The sky was almost blue. The earth was brown and barren, though here and there were stark skeletons of what had once been trees and a brown ash that might have been grass long ago covered the earth. The radiation level was still far too high.

Flicker!

Blue sky, brown earth, radiation levels that perhaps men could survive if buried deep under ground.

"There could be someone alive here," I said. "Mica's people could have an outpost."

I tried the radio, but there were no transmissions.

"We'll go on."

Flicker!

Things were about the same on the next Line. The radio was dead. The air silent. No one answered the signals I sent.

We went on.

Flicker!

The next Line had a blue sky that looked normal enough, though no clouds were visible. The earth, as far as we could see, was brown and gray, scorched grasses and burned trees and nothing much else. The radiation was lower here, but still high enough to kill an unprotected person almost instantly.

Out of a hope I now knew to be foolish I cut in the radio's receiver, slowly scanned the frequencies—and picked up a carrier on 104 Mhz.

"What is it?" Sally gasped.

"There's somebody here," I said.

"Paratimers?"

"I don't know. It could be locals who survived the war or it could be Paratimers."

"Talk to them."

"I'll try," I began to say, "but . . ."

Ahead of us and to the right, maybe a hundred and fifty feet, the air shimmered for a moment, then a solid object materialized out of the nothingness, a squashed sphere that was unmistakable.

"Eric!" Sally cried.

"Easy."

"Who is it?"

"I can make a guess," I said and told her that I believed it to be my former Krithian boss, Kar-hinter.

"What are you going to do?"

I weighed the possibilities in my mind, said, "We can talk to Kar-hinter and see what he wants."

"What good will *that* do?"

"Damned if I know, but it can't hurt."

My hands fell to the radio controls and I switched to the Krithian/Timeliner emergency frequency.

". . . Eric. Please respond if you are receiving me."

"I hear you," I said into the microphone, satisfied

that the voice on the other end was that of Kar-hinter.

"Eric," the Krith answered at once, "please do not be foolish. You do not know what you are getting into."

"I have a fair idea," I said. "Listen, Kar-hinter, you know that what you've been giving us is nothing but a pack of lies."

"You listen to me, Eric," Kar-hinter snapped back, a very human sounding anger in his voice. "We have already sent patrols into the world where the Paratimers claim to live, their world of origin and all."

"And where's that?" I demanded.

"Here, Eric, here and there is no human life for a hundred Lines in either direction."

"Another lie," I said flatly. "There's someone on this Line using radio, Kar-hinter. I just picked up their carrier."

"I said *human* life, Eric. The Paratimers aren't human."

I tossed and turned upon what I later perceived to be a small army-type cot, fought with delusion and hallucination and madness and fought with a fever that came from some illness I'd caught lying on the wet earth in a chill October rain while my mind wandered across the universes.

Someone fed me warm soup and cleaned me up when I fouled my bed and shaved the stubble from my face.

For four days I was totally out of touch with the world except for the briefest flashes of rationality, and I wasn't certain that *they* were anything but more illusion.

One of those brief flashes, though, seemed harder, more real than the others, as if it were fact and not something conjured up by fever and drugs, and it was one in which I opened my eyes and saw a dark-haired, hard-eyed man standing above me who was very familar, a man whom I'd once shot and kidnaped while in the service of the Kriths, a man who had once come very close to death because of me, a man whose wife had gone running across the Timelines with me in search of answers we never found. . . .

This man, if he were real and not some fantasy, stood

above my cot dressed in clothing that might have been called combat fatigues, olive drab and loose fitting, an ammunition belt across his chest and a big pistol on his hip. He wore no emblems of rank on his uniform, yet there was about him an air of command. He looked down at me with a strange expression on his face.

I tried to speak, but my tongue was still too thick in my mouth and nothing came out but a gagged mumble.

"Mathers," he said slowly, speaking the brand of English used in the Line where his wife, Sally, had come from, the Line where I'd first met him and her, "I don't know whether to kill you and feed your corpse to the Skralangs' dogs, or whether to welcome you as a comrade." He paused, his face twisting into an odd grimace. "I don't suppose I need to decide just what to do with you yet. I can let you live for a few more days and then decide."

He was still standing there looking down at me when I slipped back into unconsciousness.

My last thought was to wonder whether I'd ever wake up again. A shooting, a kidnaping, the stealing of his wife—though she'd been wife in name only, not in point of fact. Graf Albert von Heinen had reason to hate me.

6
Niew Est Anglia

Freya Athelson could have been the daughter of a Viking chieftain, blond, statuesque, in her twenties, her hair fixed in two long pigtails. Her eyes were blue, her nose straight, her lips full and red against her fair skin. The Viking illusion, though, was broken by the fact that she was clad neither in the linens and silks of the hearth and boudoir, nor in the leather and chain mail of the battlefield. No Valkyrie she, though soldierlike she dressed in a blouse and slacks of olive drab, heavy leather boots, a web pistol belt from which depended a holster loaded with a big, military-issue revolver, and simple gold squares on the lapels of her blouse. There was a silver ring through the lobe of her left ear and on the middle finger of her right hand a silver ring in the likeness of a serpent eating its own tail.

Freya was my nurse and jailer. She was the one who'd been feeding me and bathing me and washing away from my body the excrement I hadn't been able to control during my delirium.

Of course I didn't know about all this until I was able to sit up by myself and hobble to the toilet and back to bed, when I could hold a spoon in still-quivering fingers and transfer the meat-and-potato soup from a bowl to the vicinity of my mouth without spilling more than half of it.

Then I was given clothing not unlike that worn by Freya and the others of this place, but for a while I was told nothing about where I was or who they were or why they'd saved my life, these bearded soldiers and fair-skinned women. They might have wanted to tell me, but they couldn't. The language they spoke was unknown to me, and I could offer them none they could understand.

And it wasn't for several days that I found out whether

I'd actually seen Albert von Heinen or whether it had just been another feverish fantasy.

By observing, though, I was able to learn a few things about the world into which I'd been plunged when I'd leaped out of Tar-hortha's moving skudder.

Obviously the people who'd rescued me were soldiers. There was no doubt that theirs were military uniforms, nor that their weapons had been issued from a single armory, nor any doubt that the one whom I believe to be called "Ufan" Aelfric Dagrefson was an officer, the one in charge, nor that "Leufan" Wexstan Wilhelmson and "Leufan" Halga Hrothgrason were his junior officers and part of his staff; Freya also carried the title "Leufan," I learned later.

Each of them wore in his or her left earlobe a silver ring, as did a sizable percentage of the enlisted personnel. A badge of some kind of distinction.

The stone and timber building in which they lived might have once been a farmhouse, I thought, for it consisted of:

A large, old-fashioned kitchen dominated by two huge, intricately decorated wood-burning stoves which still served their original purposes, tables and chairs, cabinets and cupboards;

What might have once been a living room or parlor now converted into an office containing Aelfric's large, oaken desk, strewn with papers and maps, and including the equally paper-strewn desks of the three eufans of the company;

Bedrooms which had been converted into barracklike sleeping quarters by the addition of an odd assortment of bunk beds and cots and partitions;

And the room in which I was finally kept, one not much larger than a healthy broom closet where I was continually under the watchful eyes of Freya or one of the enlisted men.

The house lacked indoor plumbing and at first I wasn't allowed to go to the outhouses in the rear yard. I had a chamber pot.

When I was strong enough I was allowed to walk around a bit, to peek into the other rooms, to even eat at the officers' table in the large kitchen where the officers were served separately, but I was allowed this privilege only as long as Freya was at my side and I didn't get in anyone's way.

Outside the farmhouse was a wide, grassless area of clay and sand in which were parked several vehicles developed by a technology I would have guessed to be slightly prenuclear, powered by internal combustion engines, heavily armored with thick steel plates, painted a motley green and brown and ocher, sporting deadly-looking cannon and large caliber machine guns, equipped with tanklike treads in the rear, wheels in the front— in another world they might have been called "half-tracks."

The symbol emblazoned on the side of each was a stylized red dragon, European type, not Chinese, and the lettering under the dragon was in characters that re-sembled N E A in some outlandish variation of the Roman alphabet. Other characters, that might have been derived from Arabic numerals, were painted below.

Beyond the vehicles were the other buildings you'd normally associate with a farm: a barn, now converted into a combined barrack and garage; a silo, empty save for a few wooden crates that seemed to contain am-munition and other military supplies; several sheds con-verted into workshops, excepting one under which sat a vehicle that looked very much like a farm tractor, but which appeared to be damaged and badly rusted; and a structure that might have been quarters for hired hands and/or servants, now converted into what might best be called a "beer garden," a place to which the enlisted per-sonnel flocked at night after the day's duties were done.

There was always activity out there in the yard, olive-clad men and women, the men all bearded if old enough to grow them, the women all with pigtails, going about one sort of business or another, or drilling in classic military formation to the barking of non-commissioned officers.

There were no signs of the animals usually seen around a place like this had once been, except for several large dogs of indeterminate breed. I supposed that all the chickens and pigs and cows had long since been butch-ered and eaten. Such fresh meat wasn't in *my* diet.

And now and again an individual of strikingly different appearance would stride through the area, getting respectful, even fearful glances from the others.

He was shorter than most of the whites, this man whose skin appeared to be copper in certain light, who wore his black hair done up in pigtails not unlike those of the women. He wore a handful of feathers in the band of his wide-brimmed hat and a brightly colored poncho. His trousers and shoes were of soft brown leather. His chest was crossed with bullet-laden bandoleers. Upon his right hip he carried a pistol like that worn by the officers and upon his left a long knife of stainless steel. And from what I could make of Freya's words when she spoke of him, this one's name was An Mona Steorra and he was a "Skralang."

Sometimes, especially at night after the beer garden had closed and the farmhouse was quiet save for sentries walking their rounds outside and occasional sounds from the improvised workshops where a job hadn't been completed during the day, I would hear a remote booming, a series of rumbling sounds very much like distant thunder, but equally like the roar of heavy artillery beyond the horizon. We apparently weren't too far from an actual combat zone, though whether it was moving closer, drawing away, or remaining in the same place, I couldn't tell.

And try as I might, when with the lovely Viking Freya or with the young officer who could have been Freya's brother, Leufan Halga Hrothgrason, or with one of the enlisted men who sometimes guarded me, I couldn't pick up more than a few isolated words of their language, though I was soon certain that I knew something of its origins, and believed that they called themselves Anglianers, or, when speaking more formally, Niew Est Anglianers. I believed their language to be called Anglisch. And if that were so, then the language should be quite easy to learn once I'd grasped its basics. I set out to do that.

7
Count Albert von Heinen's Return

On the morning of the fourth day after my "recovery" I was again allowed to breakfast with the officers, and after the meal we sat at the table, drinking from dragon-symboled procelain cups a strange brew that was more like tea than coffee, though from what plant it came I wouldn't venture to guess. Sufficiently sweetened it wasn't bad.

Aelfric, Freya, Wexstan, and Halga were involved in some discussion I couldn't follow, though I thought I recognized certain landmarks on the rough map Aelfric drew on the tablecloth with a stick of charcoal; the geography of this place, of course, was identical to that of the Georgia I'd left behind in Tar-hortha's skudder. Aelfric was indicating something apparently some miles to the south and talked about it in angry tones, making motions of destruction with his hands.

His words were interrupted when a young enlisted man came up to the table and, in an apologetic tone, spoke to him. All I caught was the name "An Mona Steorra" and the phrase *"an Sclavanianer."*

A smile suddenly came across Aelfric's face and he spoke a few words to the others. Freya looked at me and then back at him as if asking a question. Aelfric pondered for a moment, twisting the end of his ash-blond mustache between the thumb and forefinger of his left hand, then shook his head, said, *"Nan."*

The others rose, though Freya gestured for me to return to my broom closet of a room.

It wasn't until later that I learned that the Skralang had brought back an enemy soldier from a brief raid across the border. The captive, it turned out, was tortured for information he didn't possess. An Mona Steorra's delight at the sadism he inflicted on the captive, Freya told me later when I could understand her, was not a pleasant thing to behold. I suppose it's just as well I was denied permission to witness it.

For some time I sat alone, smoking vile-tasting cigarettes from a pack given me by Freya—it seemed that in this world tobacco hadn't been given the care and concern it should have—leafing through a magazine entitled *Foegift*, trying to decipher some meaning from it. The pictures were clear enough, scenes · of people and places in a world in the middle stages of heavy industrialization, a Victorian, puritanical world dominated by the Church and the Aristocracy, a world perhaps ready for a sudden, chaotic leap into post-industrial civilization.

I recognized the relationship between some of the words printed on the magazine's pages and some of those in the version of English I'd learned from my Timeliner assignment in RTGB-307, Sally's Line. And I was still convinced that I was about to stumble on to the keys to the language and a lot of it would then fall into place.

Then, as I was crushing out a cigarette in the tin-can ashtray provided me and wishing that I had some of the beer ration that would be served with the evening meal, there was a knock on the door and Freya, without waiting for an answer, came in, excitement on her face, speaking words I found impossible to comprehend.

At last, through a few simple words—*cuman* and the like—and some equally simple hand gestures, I did understand that she wanted me to go some place with her.

With Freya leading and the two of us following several other clusters of the olive-clad company, I went outside of the farmhouse-cum-headquarters for the first time since my unconscious arrival.

And outside I saw the reason for all the excitement.

Two more of the armored, tracked vehicles were there now, even at that moment rumbling to a halt in the grassless area before the whitewashed farmhouse. Both had obviously been in recent combat; both showed scars of bright metal and areas of blackened, blistered paint, and the engine of one was clattering so loudly that it was hard to hear the welcoming voices above its noise; the threads of the other looked so damaged that I doubted that it would have been able to travel much farther, and I wondered how far they'd come; how distant was the place where they'd been fighting?

The engines of the two vehicles roared more loudly for a few moments. Then their ignition switches were cut off and they grumbled to silence.

The men who climbed out were as battered as their vehicles, their clothing tattered, their wounds bandaged with dirty rags, their eyes red and weary. Yet they were smiling and I knew they hadn't come back in dishonor and defeat.

The officers of this group, beneath their tattered and soiled clothing, wore what appeared to be a kind of body armor akin to the chain mail worn in an earlier era, and carried upon their hips, in addition to firearms, short swords that reminded me of those of the soldiers of Imperial Rome, when there had been an Imperial Rome. And a few of them wore steel helmets decorated with dark, curving horns that could have come only from American Bison. An odd admixture of military accouterments from different eras, it seemed to me, but then I was standing on the outside looking in, not judging this culture from within its own context. I didn't know enough about it yet to accept it on its own terms. But then maybe I wouldn't be there long enough to do that.

I stood beside Freya as the men clambered from the war machines and felt her mounting excitement. There was something, to her at least, very special about one of these returning soldiers—and in a few moments I began to realize why. And who.

Had I not been thinking of him, had I not thought I'd seen him not long before, I wouldn't have recognized the third man to climb from the first vehicle and plant his jackbooted feet on the dry, dusty soil.

But I *was* looking for him and when I saw him, despite the bandage wrapped around his forehead, despite the grime and beard upon his face, I recognized those features of Teutonic nobility. . . .

Feldmarschall Graf Albert Frederick Maximillian Joseph von Heinen, late of the Armies of His Imperial Majesty, Franz VI, by the Grace of God, Emperor of the Romans . . . but then that was in another world.

Von Heinen spoke a few words with Ufan Aelfric

Dagrefson, closely and confidentially, and then turned to face me—or rather face Freya first. He only seemed to notice me after he had reached her, took her hands in his soiled ones, kissed her soundly on the lips and let her bury her head for a moment against the dirty uniform blouse that covered his chest, the words she tried to speak broken by sobs of what I took to be happiness.

His reunion with Freya finished, or at least the first, public stages of it, he turned to face me and said in *his* Outtime version of the Enlish language. "So you lived after all, Mathers. I had my doubts. I heard Kar-hinter was no easy one."

"I lived."

"But then you're a tough bastard yourself, for what I've been told."

"You don't appear to be any too soft, Graf," I told the man who not so long before had been one of the highest ranking officers in the Army of the Holy Roman Empire, circa A.D. 1971, Timeline RTGB-307.

"You expected me to be a cripple?" Von Heinen asked, his voice touched with bitterness. "Your aim wasn't all that good, Mathers."

"It was dark," I said, "but I'm glad to see that you recovered." Then I added: "I think." Despite the glibness with which these words came to my lips, despite my gratefulness at finding someone who could speak a language I knew, I was still disturbed and even a bit frightened at finding him *here,* in this where-and-when. Coincidence I can accept, but this seemed a bit too much for coincidence—but then, I asked myself, what else could it have been?

"I believe we have a great deal to discuss, you and I," Von Heinen said, "but that will have to wait. I have some, well, what you might call 'debriefing to go through. We've just returned from a rather important mission, and a somewhat successful one, I might add, and I *am* expected to report to Ufan Dagrefson, though not as an underling. And you might be interested in hearing about what we've done. Later."

"I might be," I said, "if I knew who the hell was fighting whom, and why."

"Of course," Von Heinen said with a laugh, "you *don't*

know, do you? We're 'Anglianers,' at least that's what
the others are. Anyway, the Independent Constitutional
Thanedom of New East Anglia, headed by Thane Leo
IV and Mootan First Speaker Hama Halgason, a loose
member of the Anglish Commonweal"—now his tone
was pedantic, like an old German schoolmaster he might
have learned under his youth—"is fighting to preserve
its territorial integrity against a limited invasion by the
Franks of Neustria from the north and their allies, the
armies of the Imperial Colony of Sclavania to the south.
They are trying to crush 'us' between them and divide
Niew Est Anglia among themselves. We're trying to stop
them"—his voice was shifting to a more conversational
tone—"and it's beginning to look as if we just may
succeed."

"And who else is involved?" I asked.

Freya, standing at Von Heinen's side, looked anxious
and confused. Aelfric, a few feet away, looked anxious
and annoyed. That neither of them spoke I considered
to be a compliment to Von Heinen or an admission of
some authority he held.

"Who else?" There was now a teasing sound to his
words. "Well, on this continent the Saxonites from the
far north and the Skralang Nations to our west are allied
with New East Anglia, as, of course, are the member
countries of the Anglisch Commonweal—it's not an empire here, you know—but then the Dual Allies, as Neustria
and Sclavania call themselves, have assistance from Europe as well. The Empire and Franklande are on their
side." He paused, maybe to catch his breath. "But that
isn't really what you're asking, is it?"

"No, not really."

"The Timeliners and the Paratimers are both involved
too, of course."

"Of course," I said and nodded, not surprised. How
else could Von Heinen have gotten here had there not
been Outtimers involved as well? But exactly why was
he here? I wondered. "And which side are you on?" I
asked pointedly.

"Which side, Mathers?" he said, repeating the question,
then answered cryptically, "My own, of course. I really
must get on with Ufan Dagrefson. He has his own su-

periors to report to. We'll talk later at greater length, Mathers, if you behave yourself."

After a quick kiss of Freya's cheek and muted words to her in Anglisch, he joined the other officers with whom he'd been in combat, none of whom wore the silver earrings I'd seen so frequently at the farmhouse, and with Aelfric they went inside and closeted themselves in Aelfric's office for several hours.

Freya's eyes followed him worshipfully.

So, I told myself, maybe I didn't know a great deal more than I'd known before, but perhaps I knew some of the questions now.

There were some things I had to do and just maybe Feldmarschall Count von Heinen could help me do them.

He'd come from Outtime, but unlike myself he'd come to this Line willingly. He'd known how to leave it. He'd know the location of a skudder, a sautierboat, a transtemporal device.

At least I was counting on his knowing.

"It's hard to remember the exact date now, the days had all begun to run together, but it must have been the first part of November when Von Heinen and I finally had our talk.

It was late one evening and I was fumbling my way through a rather simple child's history text under a bare light bulb behind the heavily shuttered windows of my broom closet. Nursing the last of my warm evening beer, I was having trouble concentrating.

I'd been disturbed on Jock's world when I'd thought about things, even though I'd had Sally to keep me company and some feeling of security.

There was none of that here. Sally was gone—Tar-hortha had her now. Somewhere. Somewhen. And my sitting here wasn't going to do her, or me, one bit of good. So much for the noble ideas I'd had when I decided to escape from a moving skudder. Sally must assume me dead by now.

And I was convinced that my ugly acquaintance, Tar-hortha, not really hurt in the scramble in the skudder, wasn't sitting on his tailed rear end. My hidden transmitter was still lodged somewhere inside me and still beeping out its telltale signals, and I was certain that the Kriths and the Timeliners were searching up and down the Lines for it again—and they probably had a fair idea of where to look.

How much time did I have?

And, well, there were things I had to do, and before I finished them a lot of time might pass, time whose seconds could be as precious as rare jewels—or drops of human blood.

I'd been doing a lot of thinking during those long, lonely nights in bed by myself in that farmhouse, and I'd made up my mind that I wasn't going to sit back much longer and let things *happen* to me. There were still a lot of questions I wanted to ask, and about the only ones who could give me the answers were the Kriths. And they weren't likely to give them willingly.

If I were ever going to know just what was going on across the Timelines, if I were ever going to know what the Kriths were up to and what the Paratimers were up to and exactly why the two were at war—and if I were ever going to do anything about it all—then by God, I was going to have to get moving.

Maybe old Albert von Heinen could help me do that.

I put the book down, finished my warm beer, lighted a cigarette, coughed and sputtered a couple of times—and told myself again that the local cigarettes must have been made of grass, burlap sacks, and horse manure. Maybe they really were.

Just as I'd buttoned my shirt, brushed back my hair, combed my three-week beard with my fingers and re-hearsed the words I'd say to the guard who stood just outside the door, somebody knocked.

"Yes, who is it?" I asked in my best local Anglisch, which wasn't yet worth a damn.

A voice answered in a version of English I could more easily understand: "It's Von Heinen. I want to talk to you, Mathers."

"How's that for perfect timing?" I said, twisted the knob and opened the door.

Count Albert Frederick Maximillian Joseph von Heinen was dressed in three-day-old fatigues with all the starch gone out of them. His hair and beard looked as though a family of rats had moved in for the winter though there was a big gun on his hip and strength in his eyes above the bags of weariness. "How's that?" he asked, his English only slightly flavored by an aristocratic Imperial High German accent.

"Nothing. Strictly rhetorical. Come on in."

"Would you like for us to have our talk now?" he asked politely, maybe meaning it seriously.

I laughed, sat down on the edge of the bed, offering my visitor the room's only chair.

"I do think it's time we talked, Mather," Von Heinen said, drawing a large cigar from his breast pocket and then lighting it.

"I've been waiting."

"And I've been busy. I'd meant to talk with you before, but there just hasn't been the time."

"Decent of you to think of me."

"Don't get smart, Mathers! I could still shoot you out of hand or turn you over to One Moon Star." He paused. "And I might yet."

It didn't seem polite to make a wise answer to that. I let him have the floor.

"Well, what do you think of Scragheafod?"

"What?"

"Scragheafod," he repeated. "That's what old Gawolf, the fellow who ran the Marauders before Aelfric, called it. This place here."

"I'm withholding judgment until I know more."

"I'll do what I can to fill you in, but there are some things I want to know first."

"Like what?"

He didn't answer immediately, but sat in the chair looking worn and tired, rubbing his chin through his dark beard. Finally he spoke, "Your being here is one of the strangest things I've ever encountered. I can't believe it's just coincidence, but I can't figure out what else it might be. I know you're no Krithian agent and you said enough in your delirium for me to have a pretty good idea of what happened to you, but I'd like to hear it in a little more coherent form, if you don't mind."

I attributed his abrupt reversals of mood and attitude

to his fatigue, and to the fact that he was trying to convince me that he was my friend, or least ally, but still held the power of life and death over me.

"Okay," I said after too long a pause, figuring that if I gave him information he'd reciprocate. "Where do you want me to start?"

"Well," he said, pondering for a moment, "I know about your stay in Staunton, of course, and your escape. I know that the Kriths gave you my wife as a reward for your services to them." I'm not sure how much bitterness there was in his voice, after all Sally had been his wife in name only, a political alliance, not one of love or sex. "And I know that finally you became disillusioned with them, though I don't know the full story of that. I'm not certain any of the Paratimers do."

Does that mean that old Albert now considers himself a Paratimer? I wondered.

"It appears," he went on, "that you and Sally tried to get to the Albigensian Lines to confront the Paratimers on their own ground and ask them why the Kriths were telling their 'Great Lie' about the alien invasion in the future. Right so far?"

"Essentially."

"The Krith named Kar-hinter and some of his cronies caught up with you before you got there—I didn't correct him—"and there was apparently something of a fight. You and Sally and the Krith's bodyguard were apparently the only survivors, and you and Sally dropped out of sight for months. Then suddenly you turn up here, of all places." He puffed on his cigar, went on. "Some of the Skralangs found you and, seeing your blond hair, thought you were an Anglianer and brought you here to Scragheafod. Aelfric was ready to throw you to the wolves—literally!—when I thought I recognized you. You know the rest." He paused again. "How I'd like for you to tell me what actually happened to you between the time you had the gunfight with Kar-hinter's gang and when you got here."

"That's really not too much of a story," I began.

I didn't know how much I ought to tell him. I knew he wasn't on the side of the Kriths, but if he were working with the Paratimers now, would he believe me if I told him that theirs was no more a *human* organization than was that of the Kriths? I decided to play it slow and easy and wait to see just what he was going to tell me. So I told him the bare bones of what had happened since the shootout in the Albigensian Lines, though I didn't mention that half of that shoot-out was between me and some blue-skinned characters who didn't look much like my kind of people, but then maybe he already knew that.

There was a twisted smile on his face when I finished.

"So here I am," I said, "lost on some Godforsaken Saxon-British Line and the Kriths have whisked Sally off for interrogation somewhere way in the T-East maybe all the way to their Homeline."

"So what are your plans?"

"I'm not in a position to make many plans right now."

He smiled again. "No, I suppose you aren't."

"But maybe I could if I knew what you're doing here and just where you stand."

Once more he smiled that twisted, weary smile. "It may be that you're not the only renegade along the Lines, Mathers. Have you ever considered that?"

"Well, I never did think myself to be what you'd call unique," I said, feeling a glimmering of hope. Could Von Heinen . . . ?

"I'll indulge you," he said, knocking a long, gray ash from his cigar into the tin-can ashtray on the table beside the bed. Then a thought seemed to cross his mind; his weary eyes brightened. "Mather, would you care for some schnapps?"

"Would I?"

He rose, stuck his head out the door and barked an order in Anglisch. In a few moments an orderly came darting into the room with a bottle of what appeared to be some Outtime bonded bourbon, two glasses, and a bucket of ice.

"We can at least be civilized about this, can't we?" Von Heinen said as he poured himself a drink. "Over ice?"

"Is that really what it looks like?"

"Exactly."

"On the rocks, please."

With a bit of warmth inside us now, he began to talk again. "I said I'd indulge you. As you may recall, I wasn't in very good shape when the Paratimers took me to Staunton."

"I recall," I said, remembering how I'd put a big .62-caliber slug in his stomach one night, but that was in another world, in more ways than one.

"They kept me there for a while, a couple of weeks, and then transported me to a Line where I could be given better medical treatment. That's how I happened to be absent when you made your dramatic exit from Staunton."

"I can't say that I was in very good shape when I left there myself."

"So I understand," he said, sipped at his whiskey. "After the blow up of Staunton the Paratimers decided that I'd served my usefulness on that Line and proposed that I go to work for them Outtime."

He sipped whiskey again. "The Paratimers seemed to consider me a potentially valuable agent for them, and contact with them had made me anxious to see some of the other worlds for myself," he said. "I accepted their offer. Anyway, things didn't look at all good for the Holy Roman Empire with the Paratimers pulling out and the Kriths still backing the British. If I'd gone back home to the Empire, I'd probably have gotten myself killed in combat or been tried for war crimes when the British finally won—as I suppose it's certain they will, there." He wasn't happy with that idea, but he'd accepted it.

"With the Kriths' help," I said, and then asked, hoping he'd give me a negative answer, "So you're a Paratimer now?"

"In a manner of speaking."

"Will you explain that?" I asked when he didn't speak again for what seemed like a long while.

"Well, I was sent here by an old acquaintence of yours," he answered at last, "an Albigensian named Mica. I'm certain you remember him."

"I do. He's still alive?"

Von Heinen nodded above the rim of his glass. "More of the Paratimers escaped from Staunton than you might think. But, as I was saying, Mica sent me here as an 'adviser' to the New East Anglianers. The Paratimers are backing them on this Line. The Kriths are aligned with the Imperials, or more particularly the Colonial Sclavanians down in the area known as Florida back in my Homeline."

"Just like RTGB-307," I said, thinking that there must now be a number of worlds on which very similar situations existed. "Hidden Kriths waging war with hidden Paratimers and most of the dying being done by ignorant locals."

"Yes, and also like on my Homeline, we don't think that the Kriths and their Timeliners are aware of the presence of the Paratimers. It seems that only a few Anglianers and Sclavanians are aware that Outtimers are assisting them. I don't think even King Edmund IV of the Anglisch Commonweal nor Emperor Conrad VIII know about the aid they're getting, only a few of the highest political and military leaders in Nordniwerda —North America—and a few lower-ranking people in very 'need to know' positions, like your friend and mine, Ufan Aelfric Dagrefson." The final words were spoken with sarcasm.

I nodded and let him continue.

"The Outtime forces here are struggling for control of the Line and New East Anglia has become the place of their contention for it. It does have considerable importance, on this world, at least."

"New East Anglia? How's that?" I asked.

"Let me explain: If you were to take a map of North America here and now and draw a line from the western end of Lake Erie down to Mobile Bay, you'd have to the east of that the area that has been settled by Europeans." There was a touch of the German schoolmaster in his voice again. "To the west are the Skralang Nations. Now, if you'd draw a line west from the bottom of Chesapeake Bay you'd have New East Anglia and then Sclavania below it and Frankish Neustria and then the Northern Alliance above it. With me so far?"

"I think so." I did wish we had a map so that I could see what he was describing a little better, but I had an idea of how this North America was laid out politically, though I wondered who ran the Far West. Skralangs? Chinese? But I didn't ask.

"As I told you, Neustria and Sclavania want to divide New East Anglia between them, but because of a number of conditions imposed on them from the outside, Imperial considerations, and the opinions of both the Popes—the one recognized by the Empire and Frank-lande and the one recognized by the Anglisch Common-weal and some other nations—all out war on the North American continent is unthinkable. So far the extent of the war has been some rather intense border clashes, very concentrated firepower in very limited areas, in terms of the local military technology."

"Okay," I said, as he refilled my glass.

"Mainly the hope on the part of Neustria and Sclavania is to wear down New East Anglian resistance, get some territorial concessions from the Mootan— the New East Anglian parliament—and then, when the matter of Papal succession is settled in Europe, hope-fully for them with Benedict XIV being recognized as the Pope by all the churches, they'll continue to carve New East Anglia into smaller and smaller pieces until it really no longer exists."

He refilled his glass, took a long sip before he contin-ued.

"Well, it's a long-term thing, maybe twenty years, but if the Kriths can eventually whittle New East Anglia into nothingness, Neustria and Sclavania will effec-tively have a common frontier, a common border. From what we've been able to learn, the Kriths believe that in such a situation trade and cultural exchange between the two powers would greatly increase and some time in the future, maybe within the next century, they would form a confederation, push westward and eventually come to dominate Nordniwerda and become a major power in their own right—*its* own right, whatever this combined nation might be called."

"Then the Kriths would use this New World continental power to help direct history toward their own ultimate goals?" I asked.

"Yes, that and more. We believe they'd then bring in a lot of Outtime technology and make this Line one of their staging points for the invasion of other 'nearby' Lines. This would become a Krithian Prime Line and from here they'd seek to dominate a whole series of related world sectors."

"I see." I saw. I felt a chill.

"On the other hand the Paratimers want to prevent the establishment of a Prime Line. They believe that the best hope for ultimate freedom and strength for this world"—I wondered if the Paratimers cared any more about human freedom than did the Kriths, but I didn't say so—"is a balance of powers in the New World, small, independent nations biding their time while the European powers, already decadent, crumble and collapse under their own dead weight. They feel that within a century to a century and a half there'll come a renaissance in the small nations of the New World."

"And what would this 'renaissance' bring?" I asked.

"A world of truth, justice, light, and peace," Von Heinen said, sarcasm suddenly thick in his words.

"Then you don't believe it?"

"Should I?"

"Then why fight for them?"

"Whoever said I was fighting for *them?*"

"I see."

"I'm doing a job, that's all," he said, though there was little sincerity in these words either.

Again I said, "I see."

He took a cigarette from the pack I had on the table to replace the soggy, burned-out butt of his cigar, lighted it, inhaled deeply.

"Gawolf's Marauders—the commando group that Aelfric now heads—have been given a special assignment," he went on slowly. "I'm to advise them and help lead them as one of three elements which will attempt to take command of the Krithian headquarters for this Line, which is believed to lie only a hundred or so miles south of here, just across the Sclavanian border. I think we can do it, and if we do, I think we can just about put the Kriths out of business on this Timeline, as well as capture a lot of valuable equipment, if our timing is right."

"If you make it, then it'll be a Line won for the Paratimers," I said.

"Rather to offset the loss of the Line you call RTGB-307, you might say."

"Okay, then explain yourself," I said, deciding it was time we put some of our cards on the table. "Just why are you telling me all this? You know I'm no friend of the Paratimers."

"You're no friend of the Kriths either," he said.

"Maybe I'm nobody's friend."

He smiled his twisted smile again. "Maybe you're mine, Mathers. Or could be." He sipped at his whiskey. "I said that I'm a Paratimer in a manner of speaking. True, I'm here on an assignment from Mica, and true I'm carrying out the ostensible purpose of that assignment. I want to see that Krith HQ knocked out."

He took a long pause, finished what was left in his glass, poured another. I dropped new ice into my own empty glass and let him refill it once more.

"I've seen some things that bother me, Mathers. Some things that scare hell out of me."

There was another long pause as he turned things over in his mind, and for the first time since I'd known him I could almost tell what he was thinking. Almost.

"Mathers," he began slowly, carefully, "we both know that the Paratimers the *real* Paratimers, are no more human than the Kriths. The real Paratimers, the ones who call themselves Albigensians, are just made up to look like people."

I lighted a cigarette of my own and as I did I remembered the ones I'd seen, vaguely and indistinctly, on a ruined world where the true Albigensians had once lived.

"Then what are they?" I asked Albert Von Heinen. Maybe he *did* know.

"I don't know how to put it," he said. "They're alien, I guess you'd say, but they're Earthlings too, just like the Kriths claim to be, evolved on a world a long, long way across the Lines."

I nodded.

"I saw some of them once," he said slowly, as if in fear and awe. "I wasn't supposed to and they didn't know

I saw them. It was when I was in a hospital on some
Julian-Roman Line where they'd transferred me from
Staunton, just before they asked me to join them."

I nodded, listening to him, drawing on my cigarette
and then sipping at my whiskey.

"They came into the room where I was," he went on
as slowly as before, "and they thought I was alseep. They
just stopped for a minute to look at me and then went
on. They didn't say a word among themselves."

He looked at me, something close to a plea in his eyes,
a very strange thing for *this* man. "They were about the
height of a normal person and they had two arms and
two legs and all, but . . ." His voice broke and he came
to a stop and I remembered how it had been when
Hillary Tracy had tried to describe them to me just before the Kriths killed him.

"I don't really know what they are," Von Heinen
went on after a long silence. "But from bits and pieces
I've gathered that they'd contacted humans before they
ever left their own world. This is crazy, but I've got
well—the idea that they were—dammit!—artificial!"

"What do you mean by that?" I asked, puzzled.

Von Heinen was obviously badly agitated, even frightened, and he hated for me to know it, but now he
wanted to talk. I wasn't going to let him stop.

"Androids, maybe," he said. "Is that the word?"
Some self-control seemed to come back to him. "I've
got the idea that originally they were the result of some
experimentation on a very high-tech world a long way to
the T-West. They, or rather their ancestors, were created as slaves or domestics or something on that order to
do the work that the people of that civilization felt
themselves above doing. A race of flesh-and-blood robots created in laboratories, but fully alive, self-
reproducing, and all that." The words began to pour out
of him in a torrent, tumbling over each other.

"Well, Mathers, if I'm reading things right, if I understand any of it, the slaves soon began to outnumber their
human masters, developed self-awareness, consciousness,
and even the ability to genetically increase the abilities of
their offspring. After a time they just took control of *that*

Earth and killed their masters, the humans who'd made them."

He paused and gasped for air like a landed fish. "Does any of this make any sense?" he asked.

"I don't know," I told him. "It's crazy, like you said, but then so's everything else in this damned universe. Go on."

"Remember, I don't know any of this for a fact," he said, speaking slowly once more, "but I think there's a lot of truth in it."

"Okay."

"Well, after the androids had complete control of their world, they stumbled across the 'facts of Paratime,' as they call it—or maybe someone from another Line with cross-Lining facilities found them. I don't know, but they got their hands on skudders—sautierboats—and set out across the Lines themselves."

"With what in mind?"

"Damned if I know. Maybe nothing. Maybe they just decided they'd see how many worlds they could take over. Their hatred of humans was pretty intense by then, I suspect."

"Then they discovered the Kriths?"

He nodded. "But before that they ran into the real Albigensians. They had a vey high-tech culture themselves, maybe one of the highest in all the human Lines. And there was a war."

"I saw the results."

Von Heinen nodded again. "I figured you'd actually gotten all the way to the Albigensian Lines. Pretty bad, wasn't it?"

"It was."

"It was right after their war with the Albigensians that they found out about the Kriths. That's when they started disguising themselves as humans—no mean trick!—and infiltrating worlds in the same manner as the Kriths. They want the same thing as the Kriths. I guess, total domination of all the human Lines."

"You think so?" I asked.

"Of course. Don't you?"

I shrugged. I didn't know, but somehow I didn't think it was all that simple.

A new sternness, or a return to his older sternness,

came over Von Heinen, and perhaps something of shame in his having let me see the fear he felt at the beings who called themselves Paratimers.

He looked at me almost coldly, sipped at his whiskey, then got another cigarette from my pack.

"Enough of this kind of speculation. Current reality is what matters now. I want you to help me knock over the Krith HQ I told you about. But certainly not for the Paratimers. I want some of the equipment for myself."

I sipped again at my own drink, thinking. . . . So Von Heinen was, or claimed to be, a renegade just like me, an enemy of both Outtimer groups, though nobody knew about him yet. No public enemy he. Not yet. Though he wanted one to join him.

And then what?

We had the rest of the night to talk about that.

And before the night was over I intended to get a few more hard answers.

Von Heinen raised his glass in toast and said, "Hail, brother."

8
The Night March

On the third night of the march south the smell of rain to come was heavy in the air, though now and then the clouds would break for a moment or two and through the break I could see the stars. The ground under our feet was rough, uneven, a crude path beaten into the earth by the passing of animals and men, hardly a superhighway, but then we'd left our vehicles far behind us. There were great masses of dark trees, huge pines, towering oaks to our left, and to the right smaller vegetation, less massive, but just as forbidding.

Up ahead Von Heinen spoke with Aelfric, Wexstan, and another officer named Harold Winfredson, one who didn't wear the silver ring of the Marauders in his left earlobe, though all wore the anachronistic body armor under their fatigues and carried swords they never used. The three of them, and An Mona Steorra who was farther ahead then they, led the party of nearly two score men and pigtailed women, all in the uniform of the Army of Niew Est Anglia, toward a destination somewhere south of us. Beside me Freya was silent, as were most of the others who followed, excepting Faeder Baldwin Edgarson, the Gregorian Catholic priest of the commando force, who was giving a worried soldier a late-night blessing, speaking softly in a strangely accented Latin.

As we made our way during the long night march there was a November feel to the air, to the countryside, for it must have been November by then—the name the locals gave this month sounded something like "November", though I'm not not certain how closely the local calendar agreed with any I was familiar with. There was a feel of winter in the air, a cold, chill winter, and one that I thought would be unpleasant in more ways than one.

Von Heinen must have come to trust me by then, for this was more than just a minor patrol—this was the begin-

ning of the "big one"—and he had given me weapons.
Now I carried on my hip a big revolver, a heavy, ugly
weapon called a Slean that reminded me of the Harling I'd
once carried and wished I still had. But this pistol would
probably do; I liked the feel of it. And slung across my
left shoulder was a smaller caliber but quicker firing semiautomatic Fiurer carbine which I'd never had a chance to
really practice with, but that seemed like a simple and efficient weapon. I figured I could do some damage with it at
close range.

After a while the path we followed took a sharp turn to
the south and plunged into deeper and darker woods. The
trees bridged above us and hid the cloudy skies, and the
smell in the air was that of moist earth, rotting and disturbed vegetation. The sounds of nighttime insects filled
the air and now and again came the cry of an owl. Noc-
turnal beasts roaming the forest fled at the sound of our
approach.

The party grouped tighter as it followed the dark path
and Freya walked closer at my side, our arms brushing
through the heavy clothing we wore. I could sense the
tension in her—and I shared it.

As I was about to speak to her, to say something to
lessen the tautness of the night, the blackness ahead shifted
and something loomed in front of me.

Von Heinen had stopped and was waiting until we
caught up with him.

"Mathers," he whispered, "I want you to take the point
with me."

I followed him as he set a pace that soon put us out in
front of the others. We slowed again, alone in the lead except for An Mona Steorra who was some distance ahead of
us, invisible in the night.

"We're nearing the Sclavanian border," the German
whispered to me in Outtime English. "It'll be another fifteen or twenty minutes before we get close enough to run
into any scouts or border patrols, probably, but I don't
want to take any chances. And you're our chief weapon,
you know."

"How's that?" I whispered back, trying to see his face in
the darkness. All I saw was a black oval with two little
glints where his eyes were.

"You're the only Augie we've got."

"Oh." I should have known.

"Just keep your eyes and ears open, and be ready to go into augmentation at the first sign of real trouble. I hope there isn't any. I hope we can get there without having to fight. But be ready."

"I understand."

Our destination was somewhere on the other side of the Sclavanian border, outside of the New East Anglian constitutional thanedom of Beo IV. We were now some distance south and to the west of where the fighting was taking place, concentrated in border clashes as the rules of this war demanded, and we didn't expect to find ourselves in a real combat situation, although neither did we expect to be able to just walk across the Sclavanian border without opposition.

On the other side of the border that separated New East Anglia from the Imperial Colony of Sclavania, south and west of us, was a military installation that the Anglianer high command was convinced was the Krithian headquarters in the Timeline, the place from which they initiated their efforts to aid the Sclavanians and their Neustrian allies in their war against New East Anglia. Our present destination was a rendezvous for the personnel who would comprise one of the three elements of the force that would attempt to capture that headquarters. The attack itself, or more properly raid, was to be a sudden, swift surprise effort by small, highly mobile units rather than a massive frontal attack and was planned for three nights hence.

Even then I had no real plans of my own. For the time being I was going along with Von Heinen. Right then his plans suited me. He wanted to get his hands on Krithian transtemporal equipment, not for the benefit of his Paratimer employers, but for his own purposes. I suspected that he had in mind doing a little theivery here and there once he had the equipment for flickering from Line to Line, stealing wealth and materiel, and then finally settling down in some backwater Timeline where he could be cock of the roost with Outtime wealth and technology to help establish and maintain whatever kind of empire he wanted. He wouldn't be the first to try that. The idea even appealed to me. Maybe I was a fool for not doing it.

But then I had other plans, vague as they were, and maybe they were even more grandiose than Von Heinen's, but going along with him just might enable me to get my hands on a skudder. That's what I wanted. And preferably one of the newer ones outfitted for spatial locomotion like the 'sautierboats" of the Paratimers—Von Heinen had informed me that he'd already seen one such Timeliner craft in operation.

Some time had gone by when Von Heinen signaled for us to slow. I didn't know how he knew it in the darkness, but the Sclavanian border was now only some few hundreds yards ahead of us, beyond a rise in the land that swelled and crested like an ocean wave.

We came forward to a clearing in the forest and then he commanded the group to stop, giving the order as if he were the chief Anglianer officer.

During the three nights of the march Ufan Aelfric Dagrefson had shown deference to Von Heinen, though grudgingly. Apparently someone farther up in the chain of command had given him orders to let the Outtimer run this particular show—orders that must have been inspired by the Anglianers' Paratimer allies.

When the march halted Von Heinen took the officers and myself to one side.

"Mathers, Ufan Dagrefson, and I will go ahead and scout things out," he told us in a whisper. "We'll see just what the border's like here and what it'll take to get us across. The border's bound to be guarded, but I doubt heavily. The Sclavanians haven't the manpower to guard every mile of it and most of their men should be farther east since that's where the fighting is. Acceptable, Ufan Dagrefson?"

"Acceptable," Aelfric muttered. He didn't seem to be taking his inferior position to Von Heinen with very good grace.

"I didn't know for a fact where An Mona Steorra was at that moment, but I assumed that Aelfric, to whom alone he seemed loyal, had sent him ahead scouting.

"Let's go then," Von Heinen said, rose from his crouching position and turned toward the rise that separated us from the border.

The clouds were darker and heavier now and the stars

were gone, though there was a moonglow creeping up from the horizon through the overcast. There was a heaviness and an invisible gloom in the air, growing stronger, and I was certain it would begin to rain before another hour had gone by. Maybe some rain would be in our favor. Anything that would help conceal us would help.

We reached the crest's top, crossed it, and then as we slowly crept down the southward side of the slope, aware that the trees and brush, all the larger stands of vegetation had been cleared, we saw headlights approaching from the west, bouncing up and down as the vehicle on which they were mounted rumbled across the rough terrain.

"Motorized patrol," Von Heinen whispered.

As the headlights grew nearer they revealed a strip of land maybe a hundred and fifty to two hundred yards wide that had been cleared; we were on the northern edge. Down its middle was a twisted, tangled mass of coiled barbed wire, ugly and glittering in the headlights, freshly galvanized metal, the wire newly laid down. They'd learned the barbed wire trick here too and had put it to good use.

As the vehicle grew closer—though at its closest it was still on the other side of the wire, some distance away —I could make out some of the details in the light reflected back from the ground. It was a terribly ordinary-type military vehicle, a common design on a lot of worlds at this technological level: rectangular of shape, boxy and unesthetic, with four wheels, two seats in front and two in back, two headlights with yellowish auxiliary lights below them, a spare tire and a spare petrol tank mounted on the vehicle's rear, a heavy weapon that looked like a machine gun, and three occupants—the driver, the gunner, and a man with a rifle in the back seat. He was probably the officer in charge.

The vehicle—I want to call it a "jeep"—was doing something like twenty miles an hour, and that was probably fast enough considering the ground. The headlights were covering a large area, throwing eveything into sharp relief, though in this case "everything" consisted of nothing more than the rough ground and the barbed wire. I noticed that there was a spotlight mounted near where the officer sat, but he wasn't using it.

We hugged the ground as the car came as close to us as it would and then roared on, though we were far outside the range of its lights.

"About what I expected," Von Heinen said softly as the car swept away, its headlights dwindling. "They're not too concerned with this area and haven't the manpower to patrol it well. They don't figure we'll try anything here."

"I wonder how often it comes by," Aelfric pondered aloud.

"Hard to say," Von Heinen replied. "It must be pretty often or it'd have no effectiveness at all."

"Then we can assume the car doesn't have a large area to cover," Aelfric said.

"I think that's right," the German Outtimer said. "A ten-mile stretch, not much more than that. Of course, that would make it a twenty-mile round trip."

"Then it could take as much as an hour to make that round trip," Aelfric said in a whisper.

"It *could* take that long, but it might not," Von Heinen replied.

"I'll get the others," the Anglianer officer said. "Time *is* of the essence." And without another word he slipped off into the darkness, hardly making a sound.

"If we were all augmented like you, I wouldn't worry," Von Heinen whispered in Outtime English. "We could just go augie and cut through the wire and slip across in no time."

"It's not really that simple."

"I know." But he didn't explain what he meant by that remark.

Very little time had gone by when Aelfric and the others returned. The party was together again—except for An Mona Steorra who hadn't rejoined us. And right then I wished the Skralang was with us. I didn't like him, but I thought it would be good to have him on your side in a situation like this. If I'd judged right.

"We're going to have to move fast," Von Heinen said after Aelfric told two troopers to get their wire cutters out. "We can't be certain how long it'll be before the patrol comes back, but we'd better be across before it does."

Nods and grunts of affirmation.

"Then let's get moving," Aelfric said quickly as if to get it out before Von Heinen did.

As we moved down the slope I became more aware of the faint moonlight that seeped through the clouds, the nakedness of the slope, and I felt terribly exposed. It would have taken very little light to reveal us there.

The two enlisted men with wire cutters had started ahead of us, acompanied by Wexstan and a non-commissioned officer named Efor, both of whom now carried hand torches they covered with their palms until they reached the tangle of wire. The rest of us stopped a few paces from the barbed coils, knelt on the cold ground, peered off into the darkness and hoped that there'd be no sign of headlights until we'd all gotten through the wire.

For a while the only sounds were those of the cutters' snick! as they cut through the thick, twisted strands of galvanized metal. Gloved hands, those of Wexstan and Efor, pulled away the severed sections and the two men with cutters inched forward again. It was slow going; the wire was terribly thick and tangled, rising half again as high as a standing man, and if that machine-gun carrying car came back before we got through, our damage to the barbed coils would be obvious. We'd be the proverbial sitting ducks for the Sclavanians' spotlights and bullets if we weren't able to get out of there in time. I didn't like it, but then nobody'd asked my opinion.

The feel of the rain had grown stronger and a chill had entered the air, a breeze carrying more dampness, and after a while Von Heinen came creeping back through the darkness to where I knelt.

"Mathers?" he whispered loudly.

"Here," I answered in the same sort of voice.

At a crouch, as if ducking under low-hanging branches or to avoid gunfire, he came to where I was, stopped, peered at his luminous wrist watch dial. "They're better than halfway through, but it's been almost fifteen minutes since they started. I'm worried about the time."

I grunted an affirmation, anticipating his next words.

"I want you to finish the cutting."

I nodded to myself. "In augmentation," I said aloud. It wasn't a question.

"In augmentation," he echoed. "I think I've got an idea of how that drains a man, but even that's better than being dead."

"There've been times when I've wondered."

"Come on." He made a motion to rise.

With a sigh I didn't have the will to resist, I slung my carbine back across my shoulder and rose to follow him.

When we got to the maze of wire Wexstan called for those with the cutters to pull back. One of them gave me his gloves and his heavy wire cutters and I handed my carbine to the German; it would only get in my way as I crawled through the wire, but I'd still have that big revolver. I hoped I wouldn't need it on that particular night. Another time perhaps.

True to what the Count had said, Wexstan's men had cut something slightly better than halfway through the wire, but that had also taken them something close to seventeen minutes. Von Heinen was expecting me to better than double their combined rate. At X5 augmentation I thought I could do it, though I didn't like the idea of staying under that long. However, Von Heinen was right. *I* didn't want to be there when that "jeep" came back.

I crawled and willed the electrobiological controls into operation. There was a momentary sense of disorientation as the world around me slowed, but not as much as usual since there wasn't a great deal of sensory data coming to me right then anyway.

I glanced down at the dial of the watch given me before leaving Scragheafod and saw the terribly slow creep of its second hand, moving more like a minute hand now.

I started cutting.

Snick! Snick! Snick!

Three minutes times five is the equivalent of fifteen minutes and that's about how long I'd been at it when I thought I caught a glimpse of light. When I turned to look there was nothing there and I supposed that I'd just imagined it or that it'd been some random "noise" of retinal nerves giving my brain the impression of light.

But then I saw it again, bouncing above the earth, oddly slow, and saw that it was a pair of ल : ghts, a long way off, coming toward me at one fifth of its twenty miles per hour.

I hadn't many more strands of wire to cut and figured *I* could make it before the "jeep" reached me, but I doubted that any of the others could. Without cutting out my augmentation, I made an effort to speak as slowly as possible, calling back to the others. "Cooomeee oon." I kept on cutting.

They must have understood me, for a few moments later I heard a series of bass rumblings that I took to be Von Heinen and/or Aelfric yelling orders. Some people claim to be able to understand spoken words in X5, but I don't see how. It all sounds like a Greek chorus of sick frogs.

I "snicked" on at the wire and in a few more moments had cut through the last `strands. Dropping my cutters, I forced an opening as wide. as I could and pulled myself through. Now I wished I hadn't left that carbine behind, as awkward as it might have been getting it through. But I had the heavy revolver, .441 caliber and carrying the equivalent of 240 grains, and maybe it would be sufficient. Maybe it would have to be.

As far as I could see the first members of the party were about to enter the tunnel through the wire, but there was a long line behind them and the progress through the tunnel would be slow. There were nearly forty of them and by the time the car got to where its occupants could see us, very few of them would have gotten through.

"Hurry up," I yelled, knowing full well they could no more understand me than I could them. I pulled the revolver out of its flapped holster, worked the mechanaism. The six slugs in its cylinder would have to be put to very good use soon if . . .

I came fully erect and held the gun before me, left hand steadying right wrist, right aim only slightly crooked. The "jeep" was coming on with agonizing slowness, but the people behind me were moving even more slowly.

I waited. The car drew nearer.

I held my breath, tensed my body into stillness, felt a tremor of nervousness, tasted flat, dry metal in my mouth. It was always like that just before it started.

Then the time was up.

The report of the big pistol going off in my hand really didn't seem much deeper than usual, but it must have been, and I thought I could see the bullet as it moved toward the car, reflecting the light of its right headlight—until it met the headlight and shattered it.

I fired again as quickly as the mechanism of the single-action Slean would allow and was again amazingly lucky —the other headlight went out. I jumped to one side.

The car wasn't that near, but the slugs bursting from the machine gun slung over its hood were. The fellow manning that gun hadn't been asleep and he had damned good reflexes. I know he couldn't have seen me yet, but he nearly pegged me.

I rolled, came to my knees, aimed.

The officer in the back seat was awake too. He had the sense to flip on his spotlight as the headlights went out and began to sweep with it as the driver tried to brake the vehicle to a halt.

I fired . . .

. . . and hit the officer without hitting the spotlight, though the slumping of his body must have hit the handle, for it flipped skyward, beaming upward at the clouds like a glowing eye. I didn't waste any more bullets on him.

The flash of my weapon must have given me away to the machine gunner. His chattering weapon began sweeping in my direction again, vomiting light and smoke and bullets. I dived toward the earth again even though his sweep seemed slow, and I fired an awkward shot toward the vehicle. I didn't think I'd hit anything.

Coming to my knees, no more than a few yards from the slowing car, I could have seen both living men had there been decent light. There wasn't, so I put my next shot through the door of the car where I thought the driver might be. I didn't know whether I'd hit him. I didn't have time to check.

The machine gunner was fast; I'll give him credit for that. But he wasn't as fast as a man in X5. He continued to swing his gun toward me, my location again revealed by the Slean's muzzle-flash, but, coming to my feet and breaking into another run, I outdistanced the sweep of his gun, came up on the other side of the "jeep," and put a bullet in the back of his head before he knew I was anywhere close to him.

I was about to turn my attention to the vehicle's driver, but discovered it wasn't necessary. Out of the darkness came an indistinct figure I was certain was clad in poncho and leather pants, moving with the quick, graceful quiet of a cat; I could doubly appreciate An Mona Steorra's movements in my augmentation.

The Skralang had leaped into the vehicle's front seat, landed at a couch beside the driver who fought to bring up a pistol, and deftly slid a knife into his left breast.

Cutting out the augmentation, I felt a wave of fatigue sweep over me and a sharp pain in my right thigh. I'd been in augmentation in excess of eight minutes, I thought. It had taken a lot out of me, how much I wasn't yet sure.

I noticed that it had started to rain.

An Mona Steorra climbed out of the car, said something to me that I couldn't understand. I grunted back to him as pleasantly as I could and leaned against the side of the car, and waited for Von Heinen and the others.

The Skralang signaled to them with the vehicle's spotlight.

It was while we waited that An Mona Steorra and I simultaneously noticed the box slung under the vehicle's dashboard to the right of the dead driver, a box with a glowing pilot light and a grille from which came words in a guttural language I didn't recognize—which wasn't at all unusual of late. But then this was a military patrol car of the Imperial Colony of Sclavania.

What the words meant I didn't know, but their tone was urgent and I suspected that they were directed at the car's deceased occupants. Someone on the other end of the live radio may have known about my attack, must have heard the sounds of shooting and death.

We hadn't time to waste now. Whoever was on the other end would probably very shortly send somebody

to find out what was going on, a number of some-
bodies, armed.

While An Mona Steorra deliberately drew his side
arm and put a bullet through the radio's pilot light,
chuckling as he did, I called to Von Heinen, "We'd better get out of here while we can. This car's equipped
with—"

Then a wave of grayness came over me. I staggered,
wavered, realized blood was running down my right leg,
then gave up the fight.

of the parlor of a sixteenth-century French king than that of a sixth-century border lord.

There were six people waiting there for us, six people whose names and positions I soon learned, and who were to play important parts in the events of the days to come.

They were:

Herr Jurgen Matthausen, a Sclavanian and the lord of Tapferkeitenhaven. He was a large bear of a man with heavy Teutonic features, hair more gray than blond. There was a ragged scar on the right side of his face, running from temple to jawbone, and there was a slowness to the movements of his left hand that indicated some sort of impairment. What had caused these I never learned, though I didn't believe they'd come from war. More likely from a hunting accident; Herr Jurgen was a great one for the hunt as the trophies on his wall indicated. As he greeted us in almost flawless if slightly condescending Anglisch, he was dressed in an elaborate smoking jacket of blue trimmed in gold, with silvery brightwork, and was smoking a large cigar that could have only come from Cuba, or whatever it was called in this Line. On the table beside the chair in which he'd been sitting was a brandy snifter, all but empty.

Herr Jurgen had once been a loyal Sclavanian and subject of his Imperial Majesty Conrad VIII, but events during the past few years had turned him against both the Emperor in Wursburg and the Colonial government in Neu Fulda, a city on the coast of an area known as Florida on some Lines. What was most important to Herr Jurgen, besides the Emperor's alliance with the "damned Franks" and some of the political machinations of the Emperor and his cronies, was the recognition by the Empire of the "Godless and unholy Antipope," Benedict XIV, who was now in sanctuary in one of the Emperor's palaces in Wursburg, surrounded by his "renegade bishops and false cardinals." Herr Jurgen was loyal to the "true heir of St. Peter," Pope Gregory XVII.

Although Herr Jurgen may have dominated the room, his powerful presence wasn't enough to totally distract from the others, the most striking of whom was a short, dark-haired woman in her twenties, now dressed in tan

9
The People of Tapferkeitenhaven

The place of rendezvous was a small fortress, a miniature marble castle out of medieval Germany, though built less than a century and a half ago by a Sclavanian nobleman to defend the ill-defined border between Sclavania and New East Anglia as much as it had been to guard against attack from the Skralangs, who at the time weren't at all amicable toward the Imperial colonists. Neither were they at present.

We arrived there as dawn brought the sky from black to gray. The thick overhang of cloud and the rain that had begun to fall from it gave the world below a pale, washed-out, shadowless appearance and effectively hid our party as we reached the "castle."

There had been little difficulty getting from the barbed-wire border crossing to the fortress, which I later learned was called Tapferkeitenhaven, except that for the first mile or so I required assistance in walking. Wexstan and the priest, Faeder Baldwin, took turns half-supporting me, allowing me to lean on their shoulders as I recovered from the shock of being too long under augmentation, as I adjusted to the pain from the flesh wound in my right thigh. Finally enough strength came back to me to allow me to walk alone, unassisted, and still keep up with the rest of the company, though I knew it would take several good meals and some long hours of sleep before my metabolism fully recovered. That's the price you have to pay for such advantages as augmentation.

The wound in my thigh had bled copiously, but wasn't serious.

During the final two hours of the march Freya was never far from me, again taking on her role of nurse and remaining solicitous of my health.

So with dawn a grayness streaking the cloudy sky and

the long expected rain a drizzling reality, we came out of the forest at Tapferkeitenhaven and were met by two men in civilian clothing who carried military rifles and spoke Anglisch with accents that made it almost impossible for me to understand them. Von Heinen and Aelfric spoke with them, apparently established the identity of the party, for the guards finally indicated that we were to go on toward the fortress.

I believe I saw glimpses of a dozen or so more men hidden in the trees and brush on the edge of the forest, steel eyes watching our movements closely.

With Aelfric in the lead, we walked single file down the path the guards had indicated and reached a set of massive wooden gates in the castle's stone wall. The spiked porticus was raised and the gates were opened for us and inside we were greeted by more armed men who didn't wear military uniforms, though several of them wore a distinctive, medieval-looking livery of black and orange.

After a few minutes of milling around in the courtyard, we were taken into a large room within the fortress' main keep where there was a roaring fire in a huge fireplace and a large oaken table covered with platters of cold cuts and pitchers of beer. The man who appeared to be the senior of the castle's liveried guards told Aelfric that we should eat and dry ourselves before the fire. Soon the *Herr* would be about and would meet with Aelfric and the other officers.

Freya requested fresh, dry bandages for my wound, which were delivered at once. She and Faeder Baldwin saw to the injury, cleaned it, rebandaged it. When they finished it seemed to hardly bother me. We addressed ourselves to other matters.

To me, and obviously to the others, the cold cuts, black bread, and thick, tangy beer were more than welcome. I devoured three sandwiches as quickly as I could, washing them down with the lukewarm beer. I must have looked half-savage, wolfing down my food, and Faeder Baldwin did comment on my haste in eating, but when I was finished and sat by the fire with my fourth mug of strong beer, I felt that I just might survive the ordeal. The only thing I needed now was ten or twelve

hours of sleep, but I rather doubted they were likely to come any time soon. I was right.

When most of us had finished eating and sat in a half-circle around the fireplace drying ourselves, Faeder Baldwin announced he would hold a "short mass" in one corner of the large room for those who felt a need to thank God for our safe passage.

About half of the Anglianers expressed a desire for the holy sevice. Faeder Baldwin converted a table into an altar by the use of draperies, candles, and other paraphernalia he'd brought with him, but had said hardly more than *"Credo in unum Deum,"* when a man entered the room and told Aelfric, in thick accents, that the "Herr" was ready to see him, Von Heinen, and the other officers.

Aelfric nodded, directed that Von Heinen, Freya, Wexstan, Harold Winfredson, and I accompany him. I was only half-surprised that I was asked to go along to the meeting; Von Heinen's plans for me, I strongly suspected, had just begun.

Although there had been electric lights in the hall where we had eaten our cold-cut breakfast, there were none in the long hallway down which we walked after leaving the room. The hall was dim and sooty, lighted by torches spaced some distance apart. There was a chill in the air, a dampness, and a patina of moisture on the walls. This place was an excellent reproduction of a medieval castle, I thought, right down to the inconveniences. I wondered if it had indoor plumbing, and thought I'd probably find out sooner than I wanted to.

When the hallway ended we mounted a flight of stairs that led up one floor and down another torch-lit hallway to a pair oaken doors bracketed by two guards in black and orange livery, carrying automatic rifles. The guards didn't speak as the multi-clad man who led us opened the doors and admitted us to another large room.

This room didn't have the austerity of the one we'd left behind. It was lighted by a brace of elaborate electric chandeliers that depended from the high ceiling and cast their light over the room's rich furnishings and luxurious appointments. It had more the appearance

CONTENTS

PROLOGUE
North America, Line RTBA-79A, Summer

There was a touch of early fall across the land that year, a chill to the air that was autumnal, as we fled from nameless, unidentified terrors, dark-uniformed and jack-booted national police, as we sought sanctuary that we knew no place in this universe, perhaps in all the universes, could provide us.

The driver of the pickup truck, a man whose name we never learned, had taken us some two-hundred-odd miles to the east, across states with unfamiliar names, and had finally deposited us, as evening fell, on the crest of a hill overlooking a mining town in the valley below, a dark, sooty, unpleasant-looking place, half-hidden by the rising smoke, the stale air.

The red taillights of the pickup vanished as it turned down a dirt road that led back into the hills and to the nameless man's Appalachian home. Then we stood alone on the road, Sally and I, and wondered how long it would take us to get another ride, and where it would take us, and whether it was really worth it, all the trouble we were going to.

"How do you feel, Eric?" Sally asked me, her green eyes not smiling now. They hadn't smiled in a long time. I couldn't remember how long.

"I'm okay," I said, sitting the battered suitcase on the road's dirt shoulder, easing some of the weight off my left leg. It still hurt me very much then. "How about you?"

"I'm okay too," she said. She'd never complained about her own pain, her own injuries, though I knew they had troubled her. And I knew that she was hungry then, as hungry as I was. We hadn't eaten since the day before. I told myself that I'd find a way to get us food soon, and I too would ignore the pain that throbbed up from my leg. It would pass.

9

We waited on the side of the road for another car or truck to come our way so that we might try to hitch another ride, so that we might be carried farther from the hospital in a place called Jefferson City and from people in places of authority in this world who had begun to ask questions that we couldn't answer. Or if we had answered, they would have thought us insane and locked us away.

The sky above us deepened to a redness streaked with crimson clouds, great bloody stripes across the evening sky, and against the red sky were silhouetted the hills and mountains, purplish and gray, their outlines ragged with uneven tops of trees, forests slashed away here and there to make way for the great open sores of strip mines. In this country coal was king and all else made way for his coming.

Lights had come on in the sooty darkness of the valley town, yellowish, most of them, but brightened here and there with other points of color—reds and blues and greens of neon signs of taverns and restaurants and pool halls and a theater and stores of one sort or another. The headlights of cars and trucks and a bus or two moved along the town's streets, weaving paths like glowing worms.

The river which ran through the center of the valley, a narrow thing with an awkward Indian name, had been a silvery serpent catching the last light from the darkening sky when we climbed from the truck that had carried us out of Ohio. Now it was dark, almost invisible as the valley's shadows deepened, darkened.

And there were lights on the opposite hillside, the stationary and the moving lights, all yellowish, of the incessant mining operations that went on day and night, continually, for this was a nation that couldn't live without a constantly replenished supply of coal, this was a nation on the verge of war with a "yellow-skinned, slant-eyed" neighbor across the sea, and all things had to be in readiness when the day came when the two great rivals for domination of the Pacific Ocean decided it was time to try their cases before the world in combat. Trial by arms had not yet passed from this world.

It was August 1971, and the Second World War, de-

quasi-military slacks and blouse, an outfit that one might wear on an African safari on some other world than this.

Gwendalfa Halgason, as I soon learned her name to be, was a very attractive woman, in her own distinctive way as lovely as Freya, though there was a hardness and a bitterness around her brown eyes and an angry quickness to her movements. Now, as she sat in Herr Jurgen's luxurious parlor dressed in masculine clothing, her long, dark hair tied up in a bun on top of her head in a manner as harsh and masculine as her clothing, her femininity was betrayed by the curves of her body beneath the clothing she wore.

And although she was unarmed now, she wore a web belt in addition to the leather belt of her trousers, a belt obviously designed to carry a holster and ammunition.

Gwendalfa, I also learned not too much later, was the niece of Hama Halgason, then First Speaker of the New East Anglian Mootan, daughter of the late Halga Halgason, formerly First Speaker, assassinated by a Neustrian agent some months before, and sister of the late Maufan Anslem Halgason, an Anglianer officer who'd died in a very brutal way at the hands of one of the Emperor's most expert torturers. She *was* a bitter young woman and had come into Sclavania as an agent for Anglian military intelligence in order to satisfy some of that bitterness.

The third person in the room was a middle-aged, potbellied, red-faced man who looked as if he should be a journeyman carpenter or an innkeeper, but he was actually another Anglianer agent carrying the rank of maufan—major or its rough equivalent. Artos Alaricson, bearded and jovial, though a shrewd military officer, had been working behind Sclavanian lines for some three years now and spoke the language perfectly.

It was only later that I learned that his "cover" actually was that of an innkeeper in Trier, the city nearest the military installation believed to be the Krithian headquarters for this Line.

Geoffry Dunstanson, a handsome, beardless young man also in mufti, carried the rank of ufan and was, like Aelfric, the leader of a company of commandos working across the Sclavanian border. He'd brought with him a party similar to ours, though smaller, which was now quartered in Tapferkeitenhaven. They'd arrived the night before last, having a shorter distance to come than we. They were to supplement our force when the raid took place on the base near Trier.

And the other two—I should have been expecting men like them. . . .

One was named Devoto Baugh. He was a quiet, aloof man, small of stature, swarthy of skin, unhandsome in the manner of a rodent, though, as I was to learn later, tough and quick-witted. Like myself and Albert von Heinen, he wasn't a native of this Line—he was Paratimer, though he didn't claim to be an Albigensian. He was the co-ordinator of our phase of the raid on the Trier installation, Fort Lothairin.

Kjemi Stov looked like an Irishman, but wasn't. Just below middle height and stocky, a man of apparently great physical strength, with blue eyes and hair almost impossibly red, he was Devoto Baugh's lieutenant and was later identified as being from a "Norse-American" Line not greatly distant from the Saxon-British Line we were presently on.

I'll admit that when I discoverd that there were two other Outtimers, two *Paratimers,* in the room, I was startled, shaken. Right then I had no desire to be "discovered" by the Paratimers. They had no more love for me than I had for them—but Von Heinen had prepared for this, though he hadn't told me so. His idea of a joke?

"This is Franz Anselem, of whom I told you," Von Heinen said as he introduced me to the Paratimers— and so I was to be, a Frisian Saxonite from the Northern Alliance, an area that extended from where upper New York is on some Lines to the location of Quebec. This accounted for my accent and ignorance of local customs. The members of Aelfric's commando squad had apparently been briefed, for they showed no surprise. And I wondered why Von Heinen hadn't warned me—maybe he enjoyed the joke he played on me. That wouldn't have been out of character.

Once the introductions were over, Herr Jurgen offered

us chairs through the person of an elderly servant, and
brandy with his own voice. Aelfric, speaking as the officer
in charge of the Scragheafod group, declined politely.
Both Von Heinen and I might have accepted, but neither
of us did, for differing reasons.

"Welcome to Tapferkeitenhaven," Herr Jurgen said
again when we were all more or less comfortable. "I may
say that I'm delighted that our Saxonite allies have seen
fit to be represented in this endeavor." He was referring
to me. "The ultimate result of our activities will benefit
all honest and God-fearing men the world around. These
heathen monsters—your Krithian *things*"—he spoke these
words to the Outtimers—"must be banished from our
world. It's God's will, so I'm certain, that we work our
destinies out in this world, and not have them imposed
on us by outsiders *who aren't even human beings.*" The
emphasis placed on these last words suggested to me
that Herr Jurgen, good Catholic by local standards as he
was, might well consider the Kriths to be agents of His
Satanic Majesty, as an old man in another Line must
have done before he was murdered by them.

"But enough of this talk," Herr Jurgen said, having
sipped away the last of his brandy and nodding to the old
servant for a refill. "I'm merely acting as what you might
call an innkeeper for more active and daring men than
myself. I'm merely providing a place from which to begin
your efforts to rid our world of this menace." This self-
deprecation was totally false and obvious to everyone.
"Therefore it would be best if I were to turn this meeting over to Master Devoto Baugh and let him outline
your plans. Master Baugh?"

Devoto Baugh wasted no time on preambles, but unfolded a map which he spread out on a table provided by
Jurgen's elderly servant. It was a map of the lower
portions of North America as politically arranged on this
Line, New East Anglia to the North and the Imperial
Colony of Sclavania to the south, stretching to and then
swinging southwest like a crescent around the Gulf of
Mexico, taking in the peninsula of Florida as well as the
southern portions of what were Alabama and Georgia
in Jock's world.

As we clustered around the table I saw that several

places had been circled in red and labeled in a neat handwriting, among which were Scragheafod, from which we'd come in the north, Tapferkeitenhaven, our present location, and to the southwest the city of Trier and the nearby installation, Fort Lothairin. There were other red circles, both above and below the border west of Trier; he didn't identify these at once.

"We are presently here," Devoto Baugh said in a voice pitched lower than one might have expected from a man of his small stature, tapping the red circle that represented Tapferkeitenhaven with the eraser end of a pencil. "Our objective is here." The eraser tapped Fort Lothairin. "On the third night from tonight we shall make our raid, which will be co-ordinated with simultaneous raids by anti-Krith forces"—he was careful not to say "anti-Sclavanian" or "anti-Imperial" forces, for Herr Jurgen didn't consider himself a traitor to either; perhaps more of a true patriot—"operating from here and here." He tapped two more of the red circles on the map, one almost directly west and another more northwesterly of Fort Lothairin.

"The raiding forces will consist of three elements which will originate from these points, headed by Paratimer officers working in close conjunction with local officers. Each element will consist of three units, about which I shall tell you more later." He paused, surveyed the group, continued. "I shall be the superior Paratimer officer of this element, designated number one, with Kjemi Stov and Count Albert von Heinen as my executive officers. We will work through Ufan Dagrefson and Ufan Dunstanson who will be in charge of their respective Anglianer groups. Is that understood?"

Von Heinen, Stov, Aelfric, and Geoffry Dunstanson nodded their understanding.

"Herr Jurgen has kindly offered us his services as Quartermaster and Chief of Logistics for element one.

"Now each element of the strike force," Devoto Baugh went on, tapping his pencil against the hard oaken table, "will have a specific goal, or to be more precise, several specific goals, each of which will be essential to the success of the mission." He paused as if pondering for a moment, then continued. "It would be well to make clear now that our objective is the *capture*, not *destruction*, of the Krithian installation at Fort Lothairin. Destruction will be a last alternative if capture proves impossible. This responsibility, should its need arise, will be in the hands of another element.

"*Our* goals, ladies and gentlemen, are twofold.

"Firstly, the temporary disruption of service from the main power plant which supplies electricity to Fort Lothairin. It is a steam-powered generating plant located on the reservation and no great distance from the Krithian skudder shelters and communications center. I have maps of the area and some photographs taken from reconnaissance balloons which you will be required to study prior to our departure.

"Our second goal, due to our proximity to them, will be the capture of both the Krithian skudder shelters and their skudders, should any be present, and the capture, if possible, of their communications center. The highest priority lies in the capture of the skudders, which we understand are of the newer type provided with locomotion facilities—putting them nearly on a par with our sautierboats. The communications center is of lesser importance and may be destroyed if capture presents significant problems."

He paused again, looked at the faces around him, particularly at those of Von Heinen, Stov, the two ranking Anglianer officers and me.

The look that Devoto Baugh gave me, as might be expected, was one that asked for agreement with the plan he'd outlined, the supposition being I was a Saxonite ally. But mixed with that was an inquisitive look that I wasn't supposed to see, a look that made me wonder if he'd wholly swallowed Von Heinen's story that I was from the Northern Alliance, a local comrade in arms.

"I am certain that you all have a number of questions at this stage," Devoto Baugh said momentarily, sitting back down in the chair he'd occupied earlier. "If Herr Jurgen would be so kind as to provide us with coffee and his inestimable cigars, should the ladies have no objection, I would be glad to answer them wherever possible."

Herr Jurgen "harrumphed" at the elderly servant who scuttled from the room and then suggested we make ourselves comfortable. Cigars and coffee would be coming soon.

I tried to do as the Sclavanian border lord suggested, then and during the several hours that followed while more details of the planned attack on Fort Lothairin were divulged, though what I wanted most desperately was sleep, good, sound sleep to allow my body to recover from the stresses through which it had gone.

Eventually I got that sleep, in a small, comfortable sleeping room which Von Heinen and I were to share during our stay at Tapferkeitenhaven, but not before I had some further words with the German count.

"Well, what do you think, Mathers?" Von Heinen asked as each of us sat on our beds, unlacing our black combat boots. "Can we pull it off?"

"If this Devoto Baugh of yours is right," I replied, dropping the butt of one of Herr Jurgen's cigars into a large ceramic ashtray, "and if the Kriths have no idea that there are Paratimers on this Line, and if they believe that the location of their headquarters *is* secret, it *might* work. Surprise should be in our favor if they're really not expecting to be attacked."

"You don't sound as if you're altogether sure."

"I think it'd be dangerous and stupid to underestimate the Kriths at this stage of the game," I said. Since entering the privacy of the sleeping room we'd been speaking the English native to Von Heinen's Line. It was easier for both of us than local Anglisch.

"You think they might be aware of the Paratimers here?"

"They could be."

"What do you consider our chances, yours and mine," he asked, "of stealing a skudder and getting the hell off this Line?"

I thought carefully for a moment before answering. "Well, if everything goes okay, there should be no great problem." We'd hardly discussed our plans after getting into the Krithian skudder pool, but I believed we'd been thinking along the same lines. "I'll be in augmentation and I doubt there'll be many Augies besides me around. There'll be plenty of confusion, as there always is, and *we* should have the element of surprise on *our* side. It should work, if everything else does." I paused, then posed him a question: "Where do we go once we leave this Line?"

"I haven't really decided my destination yet," he answered slowly. "You can probably offer me suggestions. We can work that out when the time comes. Agreeable to you?"

"I guess it would be best not to count too many chickens yet," I said. "We can work out something when we need to."

"Very good."

There was something else in the back of my mind that I'd considered telling him: the transmitter Kar-hinter's physicians had placed in my body was still functioning as far as I knew, broadcasting a signal that even now Tar-hortha's crew was probably trying to track down. And that transmitter put me in danger; Von Heinen as well. Maybe I should tell him of the disadvantages of having me around, as well as of the advantages.

But what good would that do? I wondered. The medical science of this Line wasn't such that I'd want their doctors probing around inside me trying to find a device that was probably no larger than a pea. They just might kill me before they found it, or take out half my augmentation by mistake.

And when I thought of being killed, I considered that it might not be by accident. Von Heinen might decide that I was more of a liability than an asset with that thing on me. Cremation wasn't an unusual funeral practice on this Line, and an excellent means of certifying that the transmitter stopped broadcasting my location.

No, I thought as I drifted off toward sleep, I'd just keep that bit of information to myself. Things were bad enough without bringing that up.

The much-needed sleep into which I drifted was one disturbed by dreams of Sally and Tar-hortha and of the things the Kriths might be doing to her in order to extract information from her, information she might well not have.

My sleep was not as sound as I would have liked, nor as long.

10
Dinners, Lessons, and Agents

We were awakened an hour or so after dark by one of Herr Jurgen's multitudinous servants, this one a young blond girl named Fredericka, dimpled, full-busted, long-legged, who didn't look to be over sixteen, but whose beauty must have made her the goal of every male under thirty in the neighborhood, and a good number over that age. Would her parents demand a high bride-price!

Mein Herr Jurgen, we were informed in halting if correct Anglisch, was expecting us for dinner, which was at eight of the clock sharp. The attire would be formal. She pointed out for us clothing that had been brought in while we slept.

When the girl departed I found, after a short search, that Tapferkeitenhaven, despite its antique appearance, was equipped with such amenities as indoor plumbing. After using the chrome and tile facilities, I returned to the sleeping room to find Von Heinen talking with a portly, middle-aged man in the black and orange livery of Herr Jurgen, who was to serve as our valet while we dressed in the proper clothing in the proper manner—which seemed like an odd occupation for a man with his flintlike eyes. And I wondered how it was possible for Herr Jurgen to keep any secrets with this number of people running loose. I figured that either they were awfully loyal or half of northern Sclavania would know of our presence by then.

While we dressed, the valet, whose name turned out to be Otto, kept up a running conversation, or more correctly monologue, since Von Heinen and I were hardly given a chance to speak during the time he was with us. He informed us, among other things, that Herr Jurgen *always* expected his dinner guests to be in proper attire. Rebel though he might be against some of the practices and religious positions of Emperor Conrad and his nobles, Herr Jurgen believed in keeping up the traditional standards.

111

Too many of the nobility, Herr Jurgen believed, had tended to "go native" after settling in the New World, a fate that would never come to the House of Matthausen.

As the last touches were put on our clothing, elaborate blouses, coats, and trousers of bright-colored silks and linens, Otto informed us that a person whose presence had been wished at this dinner had been unable to attend, that worthy being one Mistress Chlodwilda Johannes, a young lady of a wealthy loyal family who'd recently become betrothed to Herr Jurgen, whose first wife had died some two years previously. Her absence was regretted, Otto said. She was a bright and cheerful young person who added sparkle to any gathering. ·

I thought this gathering would need all the "sparkle" it could get.

Unfortunately I was correct. The meal, though of excellent quality, if not cooked to my taste, was dull and uninteresting, everyone save Herr Jurgen seemingly too inhibited or too concerned with the future to talk freely. While the lord of the castle drank wine with his meal, the rest of us, at Devoto Baugh's "suggestion," had only water. It seemed that there was work for us to do later and we didn't need wine "dulling our wits."

When the table had been cleared of the last course, when the coffee had been drunk and the cigars smoked, Devoto Baugh asked Herr Jurgen to excuse us and we went to that work, which consisted of three full hours of careful study of aerial photographs and maps of the Sclavanian military installation and the suspected layout of the Krithian HQ.

Exactly where the Paratimers had gotten their information about the Krithian base Devoto Baugh didn't say, though from his admitted uncertainty about some areas I suspected that it hadn't come directly from spies in the pay of the Paratimers or the Anglianers. Rumors, gossip, and hearsay may have been the only basis for the data, though as things turned out it was largely correct. I learned more of one of those sources later.

The studies of the photos and maps took place in a large room below the gound floor of Jurgen's castle, something that could have once been a small gymnasium—or a dungeon. In it now were only the tables and chairs we used, a stand on which a large pot of coffee gurgled as it percolated, a large map of Sclavania on one wall and an equally large blackboard on another. Devoto Baugh, assisted by Von Heinen and Stov, led us, pointing out certain things on the large map and sketching out quick, draftsmanlike diagrams on the blackboard.

We'd been divided into five teams of two each, each team at a separate table with its own set of lithographed maps and photos. My luck, good for the first time in longer than I cared to remember, was to have me paired with the lovely, if dangerous-looking lady called Gwendalfa Halgason.

We listened as Baugh told us how unit one, the largest, led by himself and Stov, would attack the power plant. Immediately prior to this one of the other elements, from a site directly west of the fort, a force consisting of New East Anglianers, Skralangs, and Paratimers, would create a diversion which should attract attention away from our targets.

When the power plant was reached by unit one, units two and three would move in. Unit two, led by Von Heinen, had as its goal the capture of the Krithian skudders. Unit three's goal was the communications center, which was to be hit the moment the power died. It was led by Aelfric and would consist solely of his own people.

When the power plant was under control and had been temporarily shut down, Devoto Baugh would leave a skeleton force to guard it and come to the assistance of units two and three, should they need it.

"Well, what do you think of the plans?" I asked Gwendalfa when Baugh, at Von Heinen's suggestion, allowed us a short break for coffee and cigarettes.

She smiled back at me with her lips, though not with her eyes, and said across the rim of her coffee cup, "I believe it will be successful. Don't you?"

Speaking slowly and choosing my words carefully from my still limited lexicon, I said, "I have every reason to believe it will. It seems to have been some time in the planning."

"It has," she said, her words chopped short as she turned to gaze—or more nearly glare—at Devoto Baugh. When she turned back to me a few moments later, she said, "Many good men gave up their lives to make this possible. It had better be successful." Then suddenly she drew one of the maps near her and pointed with a long-nailed finger. "What exactly is this? Do you know?"

"It's one of the transformers fed by the . . ."

As I gave her what information I had about the type of power-generation systems used at this Line's level of technology, in this case a steam-driven turbine, I wondered if all the hatred in her were directed at only Devoto Baugh and his Paratimers, or did he and his kind share it with the Dual Allies and the European powers supporting them?

I'd learned that her brother had been an agent of New East Anglian military intelligence somewhere in this area when he was uncovered and taken, ultimately to be tortured to death by the Imperial Sclavanians. Did she feel that Devoto Baugh was responsible for her brother's death?

All I could do then was speculate, for she wouldn't speak further on the subject.

It was nearly midnight when Devoto Baugh finally rapped on the table at the head of the room and said, "This should suffice for tonight. I suggest that all of you get to bed at once and get what sleep you can. The day will begin early tomorrow. There is much to be done." He rose and added, as if as an afterthought, "Good night."

Over what I thought to be the final cigarette of the night, I asked Von Heinen about Gwendalfa.

"It's true that she has little love for Baugh," he admitted, "and not much more for me or Stov. She doesn't like Paratimers and their sort mucking around with her world, if you follow me."

"I'm not certain I do," I told him.

"I think you understand enough of it," he said, and that was all, virtually ordering me to turn out the light.

I didn't reply. I turned out the light.

Though I'm certain that I was as tired as Von Heinen, perhaps more so, I couldn't sleep. Too many thoughts were churning in my mind, too many questions unanswered.

As I lay back on the soft bed, staring at the white ceiling, my eyes becoming adjusted to the darkness, I wondered how many plots were going on in this vast castlelike home of Herr Jurgen's, how many different webs were being spun and broken, how many . . .

Then, almost imperceptibly, I seemed to become aware of another presence in the room, someone other than Von Heinen and myself, yet I could see nothing and I'd heard no sounds of entry.

It was a sensation I'd felt before, when I'd seen, or thought I'd seen, the shadowy, insubstantial form that I'd called "the shadowy man," a thing I thought had come to warn me or advise me several times during the past months, something that had almost made me doubt my sanity. And it was there again, though not a word was spoken, a sound made.

A greater tension filled me as I heard the sounds of movement just outside the door, one voice speaking to another in tones too low for words to be distinguishable.

Had I been warned again? I wondered.

Slowly, carefully I turned my head on the pillow and saw the rectangle of light that seeped around the edges of the door. At the bottom the strip of yellowish light was broken in four places. Two pairs of feet. Standing just outside.

Between the beds that Von Heinen and I occupied was a small, two-drawer night stand and in the second of those drawers I'd placed my personal belongings, which now included a .441-caliber Slean revolver. Instinct told me I should get it, while good sense told me I couldn't be in danger here. Instinct won.

Without giving it much thought, save to know I might regret it later, I alerted my control circuits to prepare for augmentation, and then began a stealthy movement off the bed, my hand fumbling in the semidarkness for the drawer.

Then my knees were on the floor, the bed not having made a sound as I slipped from it. The drawer was open and my fingers were closing around the pistol's butt. Von Heinen was breathing deeply, slowly, regularly, with just a hint of a snore. I feared he might awaken rather abruptly soon.

I heard one of the voices, male, speaking distinctly now;

the words were: *"N'rachateur pa'thieral, natle. M'relim ad haang."*

The language was Shangalis.

Two Timeliners were about to come through to kill me.

A second voice spoke, one fainter and more highly pitched, the voice of a woman, and she was saying that she wasn't certain of the wisdom of their decision, that they should contact "headquarters" before they did such a thing; what real proof did they have that these men were Outtimers?

The male voice—which sounded very familiar—replied as softly, saying he was certain that he'd seen "him" or "his" picture, and it wasn't on *this* Line. Kill them first, he said. Investigations could come later when they'd notified headquarters of their coup, which was certain to get them both a promotion.

The female voice sighed, agreed, and the masculine one said, *"Mashalla na! Ba'tora Devoto Baugh han, Kjemi Stov han."*

When they'd finished with me and Von Heinen, they'd seek out and kill the Paratimer leader, Devoto Baugh, and his assistant, Kjemi Stov.

I went into augmentation, came to my feet as the door opened.

The world slowed, reddened around me.

Then the portly valet named Otto and a sweet-looking girl who appeared to be no more than sixteen stood framed in the yellow torchlight from the hall. Both had Timeliner energy pistols in their hands. Neither had apparently considered the personal danger sufficient to require augmentation.

They didn't until it was too late.

The big Slean exploded in my hand as I pulled the trigger, throwing a heavy leaden slug into the face of the valet. As his skull slowly dissolved under the impact of the spreading lead, I cocked the single-action pistol, pulled the trigger again and put the second slug into the full left breast under the white, starched blouse of the pretty little blonde. Fredericka staggered backward, living seconds longer than Otto, long enough to pull the trigger of her own weapon and send a burst of furious coherent energy coruscating across the room, above, my left shoulder.

I was temporarily blinded as I fired the third slug. Later I found that it had hit the girl just above the navel, exiting through a shattered spine.

As my eyes regained their sight and I came out of augmentation, shifting back to the world's normal perspective, Von Heinen was coming up from the floor to which he'd rolled during the shooting, crying in his native German, "What the hell's going on?"

In the English of RTGB-307 I said quickly, "Timeliners. They tried to kill us." I shoved the smoking pistol into his hand. "Tell them you did it."

"Why?" he demanded as feet came thudding down the hall toward us, voices yelling in the night.

"I'll explain later," I said. "Take the credit now."

Two liveried servants, closely followed by Geoffry Dunstanson appeared in the doorway, shocked and stunned. One of the servants had the presence of mind to snap on the room's lights; then they could clearly see the two broken bodies, and they could see Von Heinen and the gun he held.

"Enemy agents," Von Heinen stammered.

Then Baugh arrived, followed by Herr Jurgen, Kjemi Stov, and a handful of others.

"What is this?" Baugh demanded. He was dressed and in his hand was a weapon never manufactured in this world. Had the two taken us, they might not have been able to take him.

"They're agents," Von Heinen said, giving me a glance meant to be surreptitious. "I was forced to kill them."

The scarred frame of the window in the far wall, the scorched wall and the smoldering curtains were evidence of an Outtime energy blast fired into the room.

"So it would appear," Baugh said, stepping closer to the two corpses and bending to examine them. "But your aim was too killing. I would have liked to question them."

"I—I didn't have time to think about that," Von Heinen said.

"I see," the Paratimer leader replied, then turned to a breathless and pale-faced Herr Jurgen. "I hope you will excuse this, sir," he said. "A regrettable incident of war."

Herr Jurgen's mouth moved, but no words came out.

To Stov, Devoto Baugh said, "See about cleaning this

up," and to Von Heinen he said, "Come to my room. I want a full report now."

Von Heinen didn't look at me, nor speak, as he placed the pistol in the night stand's open drawer and followed the Paratimer out.

Halfway down the hallway, the Paratimer stopped once, turned back to the scene of the shooting and gave me a look that chilled.

How much *did* he know?

11
Lessons, Paratimers, and Blessings

It was nearly an hour, several cigarettes, and two brandies from a bottle donated by Herr Jurgen later when Von Heinen returned to the room we shared. In the meantime, under Kjemi Stov's direction, servants had removed the bodies, swabbed up the blood, and replaced the scorched curtains. The odors of burnt cloth, blistered paint, and cordite still seemed strong in the air.

The German Count came into the room slowly, closed the door behind him, and sat down on the edge of the bed across from me. his face expressionless.

"Well?" I asked in Outtime English.

"He believed me."

"Are you certain?"

Von Heinen shrugged. "I hope so. I mean, he knows there's something not right about you, but he's taking my word you're okay."

"Does he believe you killed them?"

He shrugged again. "He doesn't know how I could have reacted so fast, but I don't think he suspects you're an Augie."

"I see." I lighted another cigarette and poured two tumblers of brandy.

"He and Stov examined the bodies," he went on after taking a long drink of brandy. "They were both augmented, by the way. Timeliners without a doubt."

"The girl seemed awfully young."

"The girl was older than she appeared. You could tell that with her clothes off, though she wasn't so pretty with those holes in her." He took another drink of brandy and got himself a cigarette from my pack.

"What about Baugh's plans?" I asked.

"The raid? He's not surprised at agents being around. Sclavania's crawling with Timeliners, but he doesn't think

119

the raid's been compromised. He believes they really didn't know who we were or they'd have had a bigger force to deal with us."

"He's right. They were acting without orders or the knowledge of their superiors."

"You heard them talking?"

"That's how I knew what they were."

Von Heinen nodded. "Well, the raid's still on as far as Baugh's concerned, though he's going to check with his superiors before anything else develops."

"Who *are* his superiors?" I asked.

"Paratimers higher up in the chain of command. I don't know their names."

"Are you sure?"

"What do you mean?" he demanded.

I sat forward on the edge of the bed, giving him as hard a look as I could, but said nothing.

Shrugging away my gaze, and after sipping brandy again, Von Heinen said, "I've already told you what I know about the Paratimers. Now what can you tell me about the Kriths . . . ?"

It was nearly dawn before fatigue forced us both to sleep, brief though it was. And I still hadn't gotten around to asking Von Heinen why he'd really gotten himself mixed up with inhuman monsters like those so-called androids who only wanted to enslave and/or destroy mankind.

I did dream about it during what little sleep I got.

It could have been no more than an hour after we fell to sleep that servants rushed us both out of bed and hurried us down to the large room we'd first entered upon arriving at the castle. It was barely light outside.

No word was said about the agents who'd been killed during the night, but there was a tension in the air, about the people, and a sense that the security of Tapferkeitenhaven had undergone a stringent change during the past few hours.

An ample breakfast was spread across the tables, with officers, enlisted men and women, and outsiders like An Mona Steolla and myself sitting side by side eating as quickly as possible, Devoto Baugh, looking rested and eager, urging us on.

The Paratimers hurried us out of the room at quick-step and we stayed busy until dark and well past it.

Outside the castle keep in a large, paved courtyard, an area sufficiently large for the parking of a number of motor vehicles, though none were in evidence, some-one had marked upon the pavement with chalk a series of squares, with arrows leading from one to the other, each carefully labeled in Anglisch.

"This is not to scale," Devoto Baugh said as we be-gan to inspect the markings on the pavement. "Sufficient room for that is not available, but this should give you some idea of the area we will have to cover and the time we will have to do it in."

The markings on the pavement represented the area of the Sclavanian fort we were to penetrate, the roads, walkways, buildings, steam-turbine power plant, skud-der pool, and all. We were to walk through the operation.

Devoto Baugh and Kjemi Stov divided us into our three units: Baugh's which would take the power plant; Von Heinen's which would take the skudder pool; Aelfric's which would take the communications center. It was then that I learned that unit two was to be com-posed of Von Heinen, Gwendalfa, Freya, Harold Win-fredson, Faeder Baldwin, the non-com Efor, several others, and myself.

With Devoto Baugh's surprisingly deep voice barking orders, we went through our paces, each of us trying to pretend as best he could that the chalk marks were ac-tually structures.

We continued at this until shortly after noon, most of our movements at a dead run, the slowest at a trot. That he hadn't loaded us down with field packs must have been an oversight on Baugh's part, I thought at the time.

During the morning I'd noticed the Paratimer's eyes on me a number of times, though all he ever said to me concerning the event of the night before was: "Fortunate for you that Albert is such a light sleeper. Had those enemy agents been successful, they might have killed you as well, Franz Anselem."

Had there been sarcasm in his voice? I wondered.

The midday meal, which I managed to share with Gwendalfa, consisted of hot sandwiches and coffee in the courtyard where we'd been running through Devoto Baugh's script, and we were all grateful for the opportunity to sit down, grateful for the food and coffee.

"Well, what do *you* think of it *now?*" Gwendalfa asked me when we were halfway through our sandwiches.

"What do I think?" I said. "Oh, about the same as last night, I suppose. If we have the element of surprise in our favor, it ought to come off well enough, though I expect higher casualties than Devoto Baugh seems to expect, and I'm not as certain as he seems that New East Anglian forces can come in to relieve us after we've taken Fort Lothairin."

"Do you doubt the fighting abilities of New East Anglianers?" she asked.

"Not that at all," I said. "It's just that the logistics of the situation aren't right. And from what I hear, New East Anglia hasn't really a great number of troops it can spare from the fighting along the Neustrian border."

"You seem to know a great deal about this sort of thing," she said, a bare hint of something to her words I couldn't quite decipher.

"I've been in my share of combat situations," I said.

"I'm sure you have, though that's unusual for a Saxonite, wouldn't you say?"

All I could think of saying was, "Not necessarily," but she didn't seem to expect any answer anyway.

For a few moments of silence Gwendalfa sipped at her coffee, nibbled halfheartedly at her sandwich. "What do you think are our chances if they're expecting us?" she asked at last.

"Very poor," I told her. "It seems the only things we have in our favor are surprise and mobility. They're ahead of us in numbers, weapons, and position. If they know we're coming, they'll probably let us walk into a trap and then spring it."

"Do you think they know?"

"I have no reason to suspect they do, but it's stupid to ever underestimate your enemy. And sometimes fatal."

She nodded slowly, bitterly. After the passage of a few more minutes during which I finished my sandwiches and coffee and refilled both our cups, she said. "I'm sorry if I seemed cold toward you last night. I was upset."

"I think I understand."

"You know about my brother? Everyone does."

"I know he was captured by the Sclavanians and turned over to the Imperials. He died at their hands."

"Did you also know he was working on an assignment directly under Devoto Baugh at the time, something related to this mission?"

"I suspected. And you blame Baugh for his death?"

She nodded sharply, the bitterness tight around her eyes again. "I wish I could tell you the whole story, but I can't," she said. "And maybe they're right and I shouldn't feel as I do, but I can't help it. I hate the man and that's the way it is."

I nodded; there seemed no correct words to use.

"I'm sorry, Franz," she said suddenly, trying to smile. "I'm getting into one of my moods again."

"I understand."

"Do you?"

"I do."

As the afternoon wore on, each unit went through the movements it would follow after element three had created the diversion and we had breeched the fences of Fort Lothairin. And this time Baugh did see fit to load us down with equipment, weapons, and the packs we'd be carrying when we made our raid.

He and Stov ran us through our paces until we were ready to drop, and then allowed us to rest while the other units went through theirs—resting to the extent that we were off our feet, though he insisted that we spend our time memorizing every square foot of Fort Lothairin so that we could make our way through it blindfolded if necessary—it was possible that we might have to do the real thing under circumstances as bad.

* * *

The evening meal was pleasant enough, more relaxed than had been the one of the evening before, despite or perhaps because of the killing of the Timeliner agents for which Von Heinen seemed to be held in high honor. I didn't mind. Better the eyes on him than me. And during the meal Devoto Baugh didn't deny us wine when Herr Jurgen offered it, though he cautioned us to be moderate.

After two glasses of the heady wine I actually found myself enjoying the Imperial Sclavanian style of cooking.

When the meal was finished and Herr Jurgen's numerous servants had cleared the table, brandy snifters were placed before each of us and we were all but ordered by the nobleman to join him in a series of toasts that followed, toasts to, first of all, "the noble men from out of Time who have come into our world to aid us in our time of peril," to "our gallant neighbors to the north, the New East Anglianers who, like ourselves, recognize God's true Vicar on Earth," and to "our allies of the more distant north, the Saxonites and New Frisians of the Northern Alliance." He'd been looking at me when he said the last, he at least still firmly believing me to be what Von Heinen had claimed.

The toasts relaxed us all a bit more, excepting Devoto Baugh, who'd grown more tense and silent as the evening wore on, though he did have the presence of mind to offer a toast to "our noble host and ally, Herr Jurgen of Tapferkeitenhaven."

At last, more snifters of brandy later, as Herr Jurgen was in the middle of suggesting that we retire to the sitting room for coffee and cigars, Baugh came to his feet suddenly, half-spilling the brandy that sat at his right hand. Had he not had so little wine during the meal, so little brandy afterward, I would have thought him drunk. Perhaps he was anyway.

"I hate to put a damper on these festivities," he said slowly as if picking his words with great care, "but we must keep in mind that our raid on Fort Lothairin is tomorrow night. We must all be in the very best possible condition. Therefore I suggest that we decline Herr Jurgen's generous offer and retire to our respective apartments to rest. We must rise before dawn tomorrow."

There was no audible grumbling from anyone, but neither were there any sighs of pleasure. I wasn't unhappy with his suggestion; I'd hardly slept the night before and was feeling it.

"I am sorry this must be so," Herr Jurgen said, his florid face more flushed than usual, "but if it is necessary, so be it. I wish you all a good, good night, though first—Faeder Baldwin?" He addressed the diminutive priest who sat across the table from me.

"Yes, Herr Jurgen."

"As a priest of the True God and His True Pope, His Holiness, Gregory XVII, I would like for you to give this final meeting of ours the Lord's blessing."

"I would be most happy, m'lord," Faeder Baldwin replied. "First let us pray," he requested, half bowing his head, clasping his hands together and waiting for the rest of us to do the same. *"Orate, fratres. Dirigator, Domine, oratio mea. . . ."*

When the "Amen" was said and the prayer finished, Faeder Baldwin spread his arms as if attempting to embrace the entire table and said a few additional Latin words: *"Deo gratias. Pax Domini sit semper. . . ."*

"Thank you, Faeder," the Lord of the castle said when the priest resumed his seat. "Now I wish you that good night, and God's speed on your venture tomorrow. I have no doubt that the Lord, His Holy Saints and His Blessed Angels will be on your side."

Trier and the Sign of the Purple Cow

The Sclavanian city of Trier was located some forty miles southwest of Tapferkeitenhaven and less than twenty miles south of the Sclavanian-New East Anglian border, had a population of sixty thousand, sat at an altitude of 212 feet above sea level, and was located on the Graystone River.

The Anglisch-language pamphlets Baugh handed out to us said that it was the business center for an agricultural area devoted to diversified farming, most importantly, cotton. The raising of livestock and the packing of meat were also important means of livelihood for the local population. Industry consisted of textile mills, thread finishing, cottonseed oil and fertilizer works, as well as a small-armaments plant producing handguns, and facilities producing trade goods for the Skralang market. Trier was also noted for the large quantity of excellent-quality Skralang-made products, brought from the Skralang Nations to the west.

Historically the city had first been an Anglianer possession, though at the time no more than a trading post deep in teritories controlled by Skralangs. In the early 1800s Imperial colonists had displaced the Anglianers and the city of Trier was founded and given Imperial charter in 1836. In 1842 it was the site of the signing of the Treaty of Die Rasiermeisse which established the border between the Imperial Colony and the Skralang Nations, which still stood.

It was also noted as being the birthplace of the famed colonial artist Adolph Gottfried in 1873 and of the statesman Ernst Hugoner in 1902.

The city, composed roughly of the Old Town and the New Town, was an interesting specimen of the mixture of Old Imperial architecture and of the newer styles of the twentieth century, we were told. More important was the fact that Trier lay under martial law and was filled with both Colonial Sclavanian and Imperial troops. Martial law had been imposed some six months before when segments of the population of Old Town, fanatically loyal to Pope Gregory, had revolted when Benedictine priests had taken over the city's churches. Martial law had remained partly because of the nearness of Fort Lothairin and the belief that sooner or later the border war would shift in that direction. It was felt necessary that our element pass through Trier on its way to Fort Lothairin, and while there we were to conduct ourselves with the utmost discretion. Still, we weren't expected to be in Trier long.

After breakfast and the briefing we were told to take hot baths and prepare ourselves for the attentions of Herr Jurgen's barbers, who would shave off the beards of the men and shorten their hair, and would help the ladies rearrange their hair more in the Sclavanian style. There were some objections to this, but we realized the necessity of it, and I especially welcomed the prospect of being without a beard again; mine had gotten rather itchy. Finally we were given clothing and identification papers that Herr Jurgen had obtained for us.

In the end we hardly recognized one another and didn't think that Sclavanians would take us for Anglianers from appearance alone.

We were to leave Tapferkeitenhaven prior to noon in several groups and proceed to Trier by dfferent means. One party, dressed in Herr Jurgen's black and orange livery and accompanied by the lord himself and Devoto Baugh, were to travel in the Herr's personal vehicle into the city. Preparations for Jurgen's journey had been made days in advance; he was expected in the city, one of the more notable of the local gentry, visiting his bride-to-be, Mistress Chlodwilda Johannes.

Another group disguised as a miscellanea of local types was to take a railroad train from the nearby village of Conradin into the city.

And still another party, dressed as a surveying team and a road construction crew, was to proceed to the city in vehicles that looked remarkably like official Colonial Sclavanian Road Ministry steam trucks. It was in this latter group that I was placed, along with Gwendalfa, Freya, Wexstan, Harold, Faeder Baldwin, "Apel" Efor Columson, and, of course, Von Heinen himself, who would pose as the chief surveyor. The Paratimers had given him a good command of the local language, Alaman, as well as Anglisch.

When all was ready, Herr Jurgen asked Faeder Baldwin and his own personal priest, a tall, thin man named Faeder Johan, a "Gregorian Catholic" as well, to each bless our ventures and invoke God's assistance. Herr Jurgen saw what we were about to do as an attack not so much on the Imperials and the Kriths as upon the antipope who called himself Benedict XIV. That was okay by me. A holy war is a good an excuse for killing your fellow man as any, I suppose.

"Pax Domini, sit semper vobiscum . . . sed libera nos a malo."

The blessings given and God, the Saints, and the Angels securely on the side of truth, light, and justice, we began to leave the fortress in our separate ways.

Since the means of locomotion of Von Heinen's party was expected to be the slowest, we were the first to leave. Outside in the large, paved courtyard now sat three gray steamers, great trucklike affairs with canvas-covered trailers attached to the steam tractors which had metal-covered cabs perched atop their boilers. Those boilers were already hot and steam was hissing from valves in an almost musical fashion.

Locals, men loyal to the Gregorian faction of the Church and recruited by Herr Jurgen, dressed as employees of the Imperial Road Ministry, sat in the cabs of the vehicles. After instructing Gwendalfa, Freya, Harold, Faeder Baldwin—now wearing no visible signs of his profession—Efor and myself to climb into the back of the leading vehicle, Von Heinen entered the cab. The rest of the party mounted the remaining two vehicles.

After a few moments of waiting, listening to the "chug-chug-chug" of the steamers' engines, the order was given, the driver engaged whatever transmission system the vehicles used and it began to rumble forward. Looking out the back I saw great puffs of steam emitted by the other two steam trucks as they too began to roll.

Gates ahead of us opened; orange-clad servants of the Herr waved us "good-by" and we slowly left the grounds of Tapferkeitenhaven—forever, it was to turn out. For me at least. Some of the others may have returned, but I'll never know whether they did.

The steamers of this Line must have had some things to their advantage, inexpensive fuel, low maintenance costs, something, but whatever advantages they had, speed certainly wasn't one of them. During the trip to Trier the highest speed we reached couldn't have been much over fifteen miles an hour and frequently it was less than that. It was afternoon before we reached our destination, but I don't suppose we were in any great hurry. Not yet.

— Faeder Baldwin, who at times seemed quite a resourceful man, produced a pack of cigarettes of a type I hadn't seen before—on the pack was a picture of a barebreasted, brown-skinned girl wearing a big smile and a colorful sarong, behind her palm trees, and superimposed over the trees the name in Anglisch, *Happy Times*. When the priest passed them around I found them to be much better than I'd smoked before on this Line. Faeder Baldwin informed me that they were manufactured in one of the few remaining Anglisch colonies in Midniwerda—Central America—and were very difficult to come by.

While Gwendalfa, Faeder Baldwin, Efor, and I puffed on the surprising cigarettes, I asked the niece of the First Speaker of the New East Anglian Mootan how familiar she was with Fort Lothairin.

"I've never been on the reservation," she answered, "But I think I know it just about as well as any of us. I've heard enough descriptions of it."

She looked significantly at the maps Leufan Harold Winfredson had spread out on the floorboards of the steamer's trailer.

"You've spent some time in Trier, I take it."

"I've lived there for the past eighteen months."

I knew she'd said words to that effect before, though I had never heard her say what she'd been doing there during that time.

"I take it then that you're one of those who helped prepare the maps?"

Faeder Baldwin gave me a look that was sharp, piercing, but I couldn't imagine what he meant by it.

"I am," she said, though there seemed little pride in her words. "Artos and I and some others supplied most of the information."

"And none of you have been inside?" I asked.

"None who lived to tell about it," she said slowly, bitterly. "Since the Kriths' arrival the security around Fort Lothairin has been of the very highest. I'll give the Imperials that credit."

"Well," I began to ask, Faeder Baldwin giving me another look and a slight shaking of his head. I thought of cutting my questions short, though I couldn't understand why he felt I shouldn't ask them.

"Who'd we get the information from?" Gwendalfa said. "Was that your next question?"

I nodded.

"From our customers. Artos runs a tavern, you'll recall."

I nodded again.

"I have my own business," Gwendalfa said, a heavy bitterness in her voice.

Faeder Baldwin bowed his head. Freya and Harold suddenly seemed very interested in the maps. Efor looked as puzzled as I felt.

"A one-woman business," Gwendalfa continued, almost defiantly, "which deals exclusively with male military personnel." She paused, then said, "Do you think a lonely soldier would be willing to spend a few *tollier* for a night with me?" Her eyes challenged mine.

I started to say something like, "I'm sorry. I didn't mean to pry." But I didn't.

"I'm a common prostitute, Franz Anselem, if that's really your name," Gwendalfa said without allowing any of the bitterness to leave her voice, "though I believe I ply my trade more for the benefit of New East Anglia than for monetary gain."

I shrugged. "Women have been doing it for centuries, and not always for such motives."

"Oh, my dear Franz, my motives may not be as pure as you think."

I shrugged again. "I suppose that's your business."

"It certainly is!"

Faeder Baldwin crushed out the butt of his cigarette. Freya and Harold ventured to raise their heads from the maps. Efor continued to inspect his fingernails.

Gwendalfa, still with all that bitterness, said to them, "The ostriches can pull their heads up out of the sand now."

"I'm sorry," Faeder Baldwin said. "This is no business of ours."

"Isn't it?" Gwendalfa said enigmatically. Then she turned to peer into my eyes again, her brown ones bright even in the shadows of the steamer's trailer. "And what about you, *Franz Anselem?* Now you know what I am. What are you?"

The others, who knew me to be an Outtimer, shot me a startled set of looks.

"It's an open secret," I said, "except to Devoto Baugh. I hope it's closed to him."

"Then you're no Saxonite?" Gwendalfa asked. "I never thought you were."

I shook my head.

"You're a Paratimer like Devoto Baugh?" she asked.

"I'm neither a Paratimer nor like Devoto Baugh," I told her. "But I'm not from this world."

"And Baugh thinks you're a—a native?" she asked.

I nodded.

"Why?"

"Why is he kept in the dark?" I asked.

It was Gwendalfa's turn to nod.

The four others in the rear of the steamer became even more attentive. They apparently didn't know why the ruse was being pulled either. I wondered how much of it should be told.

"I suppose you could say I'm a friend of Albert von Heinen," I told them. "At least we met in another Timeline. Now it suits my purposes to work with him and it suits his purposes to keep my identity from his superiors."

"And what are those purposes?" Gwendalfa asked.

"I can't tell you," I said slowly, "though I assure you

that our interests don't run counter to those of New East
Anglia. Neither of us have any love for the Kriths *or*
their allies."

"I see," Gwendalfa said. "I think."

"I'm sorry, but it's best that I don't tell you any more
than that," I said.

"Very well."

Faeder Baldwin passed around his cigarettes again and
each of us took one this time, Freya and Harold included, and each of us accepted a drink of sherry when
the priest passed a bottle of that around as well.

Then we relaxed as the steamer made its slow and
ponderous way across the Sclavanian countryside under
an autumn sun, chugged and puffed toward Trier, Fort
Lothairin, and the darkness of the coming night.

In many respects Trier was an odd mixture of the
medieval and the modern—modern by local standards.
Although the city was only something over a hundred
and fifty years old, much of its construction was of a
style some centuries old even then: massive stone structures sat alongside buildings that were little more than
barely habitable hovels; narrow, winding streets with
hardly the width to pass a single vehicle the size of our
steamers; business houses juxtaposed with private dwell-
ings; lack of proper sewage and sanitation; Gothic and
forbidding, the Old Town, it was called. The center
of downtown Trier wasn't at all an attractive place.

Outside the heart of the city, however, concessions had
been made to a more advanced technology. The streets
were wider, most of them sufficient to allow two-way
traffic and some of them even as wide as four lanes. Buildings were taller and composed of more modern materials:
brick, concrete, steel, and glass combined in different
and sometimes bizarre fashions as if the architects who
designed the newer quarters of the city have been al-
allowed to give their imagination free reign. Shopping
areas, broad and well-lighted, were separated from office
buildings; tall apartment houses helped relieve the over-
crowded conditions so manifest in the center of the city;
government buildings numerous, large, ornate, and con-

spicuous, as were the churches and a handful of cathedrals.

Conspicuous too was the city's larger number of both Sclavanian and Imperial soldiers. These were easily distinguished from the local citizenry who for the most part were dressed in rather simple clothing of dull colors, save for a few of the gentry who affected more striking clothing in what I was informed was the Continental Imperial style. Almost all the men were clean shaven.

That the city was under martial law had been told to us before leaving Tapferkeitenhaven, but if we hadn't been told we would have learned it when our three-steamer convoy reached the outskirts of the city and was stopped by a roadblock where Sclavanian soldiers forced us all to climb out and present our papers. We and our papers passed their inspection without difficulty—Herr Jurgen had seen that we were provided with good forgeries, may his God bless him.

Then we traveled into the city proper, through the outer, newer portions, and then into Old Town, hovels, stone, and stink. West of what Gwendalfa told us to be the very center of Old Town, the steamers pulled into a large government parking area, where Von Heinen, in his role as the government official in charge of the convoy, presented our papers again. He was told, so Gwendalfa translated for us, that we would be permitted to take on water and fuel and to park our steamers there for a while, but that they would have to be moved before the vehicles that normally used the parking facilities returned for the evening. He came back and told us we could climb out of the steamers' trailers.

In order to avoid being conspicuous and to avoid any possibility of our getting into trouble with the local authorities through ignorance of language, customs, and law, the majority of the party was ordered by Von Heinen to go a block or so down the street to a large cinema. They were to go in groups of two or three or singly and were told to leave the cinema over a period of fifteen to twenty minutes some three hours later. We would all meet back at the steamer park, eat a meal we would procure then, and leave the city, heading west toward our final rendezvous. He placed Harold Winfredson in charge of this operation, and told Gwendalfa and myself to remain with him.

When the others had started on their way to the cinema, the three of us stood in the shadow of the first steamer while its valves hissed faintly under falling pressure, our jackets pulled tightly around our bodies, for a cold wind was blowing through the city now despite the sunshine that created sharp, deep shadows. The clouds of the previous day were gone from the skies now, if not from our minds.

"Gwendalfa," Von Heinen said in Anglisch, "you're familiar with Artos' inn, aren't you?"

Her smile was a strange one, but the words were even, undistinguished. "Yes, I'm familiar with it."

"Would you take us there, please?" he asked.

"Are you certain you want to be seen with me?" she asked, perhaps a little bitterness in her voice now, though she managed to keep her smile.

"I have no objection," he said. "Eric?"

"So that's your name," Gwendalfa said to me.

"A lot of people know me by that one," I told her, "and I have no objection to being seen anywhere with a woman as attractive as you."

She smiled again, but there was no humor in it. "Even if she's one of the most notorious whores in the city?"

"Even then," I said.

"Would you show us the way?" Von Heinen asked.

Without speaking, Gwendalfa headed left down the street, in the direction away from the cinema.

The area we were in now separated—or joined, if you want to look at it that way—the city's two divisions, the older inner circle, the newer outer circle. It was a mixture of the two. Some of the buildings were of the older, medieval style, and others were of a more modern design. The cinema was a combination of the two: an older, blocky, rough-hewn building on to which had been placed a contemporary façade, glass and shiny metal over the worn stone.

There was a red-and-blue-clad policeman on every corner and two soldiers for every policeman and there was about the city an air of repression and something bordering on hostility, even some distance as we were

from the heart of the rebellious Gregorian quarter. The
people we met on the streets were mostly of a Nordic,
Teutonic racial type, blond or brown hair, fair of skin,
though there was a smattering of darker, southern Europeans and more than just a few who could have only
been of Skralang blood, pure and half-breed. Most of
them, clad in their drab and all-but-colorless clothing,
looked at us suspiciously, save for a few of the better,
more stylishly dressed types, Teutonics all, who chose to
ignore us—excepting one or two who recognized
Gwendalfa and had the boldness to raise a hand or yell
a greeting to her.

Gwendalfa led us some three blocks in one direction,
then angled off down a side street and led us another
three dark blocks in toward the heart of the old city,
where darker skins were more prevalent, and to a small
building nestled between two larger ones and before
which hung a sign painted with the image of a large-
uddered cow, purple in color, and obscure lettering I
couldn't read. Gwendalfa told us—or rather me, since I
assumed Von Heinen could read the sign—that this
place was called "The Sign of the Purple Cow" and it
was the inn of Artos Alaricson, or Rudolph Genseric,
the name he used here.

"Gentlemen," she said, pausing before the door.

Since I was closer I opened the door, and she preceded us into the inn.

It was dark and smoky, a place of candles and torches
and open beams above and plastered walls around, concrete and sawdust below, a place of the odors of beer
and wine and roasted meat and hot bread and human
sweat, a place of men clad in an assortment of clothing
from the rags of a beggar who knelt just inside the door
and held out a metal cup to the colorful lace and frills
of a drunken dandy who pounded on his table with a
metal tankard and demanded another jug of "Rudolph's"
best wine, a place where a half-clad girl whose parentage
might have been partly Skralang danced on a low stage
under two incandescent spotlights while a young, fair-
skinned man played on a guitar in a style that could
have been called "flamenco," a place where another
woman, twice the age of Gwendalfa, with painted face

and tight clothing, plied her trade in the semidarkness, hoping to find a night's trick among the more drunken.

As the doors closed behind us and our eyes began to adjust to the large room's dimness, half a dozen male voices called "Gwendalfa" or merely "Gwen."

Gwendalfa yelled back to them, her face broken by a wide, wild smile, a grin of flashing teeth, her long, dark hair swirling behind her turning head, while with one arm she clung to Von Heinen and with the other to me.

Carefully steering us with her arms, she led us across the room to the far end of the bar where there were fewer people, pounded on the bar with open hand and called, "Rudolph, Rudolph . . ."

A few moments later a heavy-set, bearded man in a stained leather apron came bustling out of the back of the tavern.

It took me a few long moments to believe that *he* was someone I knew, had met at Tapferkeitenhaven. It was more than merely a change of clothing, more like a total change of personality, that made the difference between the Anglianer officer Artos Alaricson and the tavern-keeper Rudolph Genseric.

"Ah, Gwennie," he cried, rushing up to her and kissing her across the bar as if it had been weeks, not hours, since he'd seen her last. He spoke a few words to her, she to him, and then she introduced us, Ferdinand Gottfried and Conrad Albertric, as I heard the names. I was Conrad, I think.

A few moments of unintelligible pleasantries went by and then "Rudolph" sat a tankard of ale before each of us, urging us to drink, drink, drink. At least I think that's what he was saying.

Then, while we were doing as he requested, he whispered to us in Anglisch, "Third room on the left, top of the stairs." This said, he took away our now empty tankards, refilled them to overflowing, made another, more open gesture toward the stairs at the end of the room and went to see about another customer who'd begun to pound on his table.

"We'd better do as he says," Gwendalfa whispered, took a deep drink of the dark, pungent ale and broke away from us, leading the way up the dark stairs, and

an equally dark hallway to the third door on the left.
She paused, knocked twice rapidly. We waited.

After a long pause we heard the shuffling of feet on
the other side of the door, again a silence, then a voice
speaking a single word of query, *"Voe?"*

"Glitterstraggin," Gwendalfa answered.

The door clicked from the inside, opened inward. The
light of incandescent bulbs spilled out, bright and yellow
in the darkness of the hall.

"Come in," Devoto Baugh said in Anglisch.

Inside, awaiting our arrival, were the Paratimer leader,
Kjemi Stov, Geoffry Dunstanson, Wexstan, Herr Jurgen,
and the Skralang, An Mona Steorra, dressed in the garb
common to the lower classes of Sclavania.

"So we were assembled," the Paratimer leader said as
he closed the door behind him.

"So we are," Von Heinen agreed. "I'm surprised you
got here this far ahead of us."

"Those steamers of yours are hardly the fastest means
of transportation available," Baugh replied, "even on *this*
Line."

The manner in which he said those last four words
did nothing to endear him to the others present in the
room. The locals seemed to take an unvoiced offense
at them, though I don't believe they'd had any particular
love for the Paratimer even prior to this.

"No problems?" he asked Von Heinen.

"None."

"Very good. We seem to have gotten this far without
difficulty. I hope we can do as well with the next stage."

Von Heinen nodded.

"And exactly what is your next stage, if I may ask?"
Herr Jurgen, apparently ill at ease in the presence of the
Skralang, asked.

"A resumption of our journey west," Devoto Baugh
said. "As soon as there is cover of darkness we shall
continue on, planning to be in place outside Fort Lothairin
by the last hour before midnight."

"What about the other elements?" Von Heinen asked.

"They are proceeding with relative smoothness," Baugh
said, "although element number three has had some de-
lay. Nothing serious."

We were element one, by Devoto Baugh's designation. The element proceeding from the west of Fort Lothairin was two and the one from the northwest was element three. It was three that was to create the diversion that would give elements one and two the opportunity to stage their attacks at separate points along the fort's perimeter. We needed number three very badly. Even I knew that.

"Then it would appear that my services are no longer needed," Herr Jurgen said, shifting nervously in his chair.

"For a while longer, sir," Baugh said. "At least I would like you to remain available in the city until we are all outside its limits. Then you may consider yourself free of any further obligation. I would suggest that you return to Tapferkeitenhaven at once."

"That is exactly my intention," the Sclavanian nobleman said. "Anyone caught outside his home this night will be under the gravest suspicion."

"Of that I have no doubt," the Paratimer said.

"And your means of escape?" Herr Jurgen asked.

"If we need them, these are provided for," Devoto Baugh said.

Early in our stay at Tapferkeitenhaven the Paratimer leader had told us that once Fort Lothairin was in our hands, New East Anglian forces poised only a few miles beyond the border that separated the two nations would sweep across the less-than-forty miles and complete seizure of the fort. I didn't believe it. I'd said as much to Gwendalfa earlier. From what little I knew of the situation I didn't believe New East Anglia to be in a position to do even that, nor did I believe that the Mootan or General Breccason or the Anglianer chiefs of staffs would be willing to commit so great a breach of the rules by which this border war had thus far been fought, not at this stage of the game, anyway. I believed the Anglianers involved in this mission to be sacrificial lambs to be yielded to the Sclavanians and the Imperials once the primary Paratimer goal had been achieved: the destruction of the Krithian HQ and the capture of its skudders and other Outtime equipment, and its Outtime personnel, if possible. Devoto Baugh and Kjemi Stov didn't really give a damn about what happened to Aelfric and

Freya and Gwendalfa and Artos and all the others once they'd gotten their hands on what they wanted.

But was I in any position to be critical of them?

Did I have any more noble intents in mind?

I didn't, though I thought that I could justify my means—weren't my ends worth it?

But surely they each, Baugh and Stov and Von Heinen, in each of their separate ways, must have felt the same way.

God, how relative is morality!

During the hour or so that followed, in the small room above The Sign of the Purple Cow, Devoto Baugh once more went over our plans. From time to time Artos would drop in on us and during one of his visits he brought us a huge platter of sandwiches, went back down and returned with two gigantic pitchers of ale. We ate well, we for whom this might be a last meal. Artos had also arranged for several street urchins whom he trusted to deliver hampers of sandwiches to the steamers prior to our departure from the steamer park later in the day.

Finally, satisfied with our food, though apprehensive of the next few hours, Devoto Baugh dismissed us, though only after a quiet, private talk with Von Heinen in a corner. I could hear nothing of what was said, though I noticed the senior Paratimer's eyes on me more than should have been usual and a very frequent shaking of Von Heinen's head. When the *tête-à-tête* was over, Baugh nodded as if grudgingly; Von Heinen smiled and patted him on the back. I was allowed to leave the room alive. Von Heinen must have talked well in my favor.

It was later than midafternoon when our steamers chugged to life, raised a head of steam, and slowly rolled out of the park and back onto the streets of Trier. We headed west out of the city.

Fort Lothairin lay some ten miles or so southwest of Trier, but we covered only about half that distance by steam-driven vehicle. Five miles beyond the last military check point the steamer's driver turned off onto a dirt road that led back into nearly virgin forest—lumbering hadn't yet hit hard on this side of the city, as it had to the north and east.

A mile or so south on the dirt road the steamers took another turn, this time into even denser forests, down a road that became a trail that became a path that vanished. The steamers ground to a halt; the engines were allowed to bleed their steam into the air while the petro-fueled boilers cooled. The vehicles would be left there to cool, to rust, for none of us ever expected to come back for them. They'd served their purpose.

"This area has been thoroughly mapped and scouted," Von Heinen told us as we knelt in the small clearing where the steamers had come to a halt. "We should encounter no obstacles for the next four miles. After that it's possible we'll run into one of the infrequent patrols sent outside the fort's fences. But if we stay away from the roads we should have no trouble avoiding them. And we need to cover most of that four miles before dark. There'll be few enough paths for us."

He looked at each of us as if asking for final questions or comments before moving on: Gwendalfa, Freya, Faeder Baldwin, Harold, Efor, the others who'd been in the other two steamers. No one said a word. Words enough had already been said.

Once guns and equipment had been distributed, Von Heinen checked his watch, ordered each of us to synchronize his own watch with his, and then ordered us to move out. Gwendalfa and I were to take the point at the beginning. He and Harold Winfredson would bring up the rear. Later he would trade places with Gwendalfa.

As before, Von Heinen wanted me with my augmentation in the lead, though I hoped that this time I wouldn't need it—not until we were inside the fences of Fort Lothairin.

And I didn't relish having to use it then, but I knew I would, to suit my own purposes if nothing else.

I had a long way to go before the sun rose, on this Earth or on any other across the Lines.

13
"Alarums in the Night"

The sky was clean and clear and the stars seemed impossibly bright, a painted sky or a piece of some black material pierced with holes through which lights from some grander world than ours shown, or like jewels embedded in black velvet. There was no moon. It had set early.

There was a display of meteors, bright pinpoints of light flashing out of the sky, seeming to come from the constellation Leo like a fleet of attacking starships or a sign from pagan gods of approaching disaster.

We sat on the cold ground, wrapped in warm clothing, though shivering from the cold and from something more. We glanced at our watches and then up at the sky and then ahead through the forest where we could see the lights of Fort Lothairin beyond the electrified barbed-wire fences. And we waited.

My arms were folded across my chest, my gloved hands tucked under my arms. A woolen cap was pulled down over my ears. My carbine was in my lap, my .441 Slean on my hip, six hand grenades dangled from my belt. I carried no additional equipment.

Gwendalfa sat beside me on my left and Faeder Baldwin on my right. We'd just sipped away the last of his sherry and wished for more.

The little priest had given us one last blessing as we'd neared this place and then requested that Von Heinen give him a weapon. This was his war too, for this *was* a war against the antipope who called himself Benedict XIV and it was his duty, as a Soldier of God, to wage His war on Earth however he could.

Von Heinen asked him whether he knew how to use a gun. When the priest displayed half a dozen marksmanship medals, Von Heinen ordered that he be given one of the extra carbines and an ammunition belt. The priest thanked him, loaded and cocked the weapon after dry-firing it several times, then slung it across his shoulder as the last stretch of the march toward Fort Lothairin continued.

Now we were there, the last hour before midnight less than sixty minutes away.

And we waited.

"Eric," Gwendalfa whispered. "That is your name, isn't it?"

"Yes," I said, not wanting to waste time explaining my "names."

"Forgive me for being such a bitch. You've done nothing to cause me to take my bitterness out on you."

"That's okay."

"No, it isn't," she said, "but I don't guess there's much we can do about it now."

"I appreciate that, Gwendalfa."

"There'll be other—" she started to say, then bit off the words. "Who am I kidding? There may never be another chance. . . ."

We both looked at our watches in the starlight. Their luminous dials told us we had forty-three minutes before the diversion began.

"We have time enough," she said slowly, softly. "Come with me." She began to rise.

I thought I should protest, but . . . As she said, there was time.

Von Heinen looked at us as we started back into the forest, away from the line we had formed facing the fence.

"Thirty minutes," I whispered to him.

He nodded in reply, a ghost of a smile on his lips.

Faeder Baldwin said something in Latin, a blessing, I think.

A hundred yards, no more than that, Gwendalfa led me back into the forest, not far, but far enough.

"I wish we had more time, Eric," she said, stepping away from me and dropping her carbine to the leaves and pine needles that formed the forest's floor. "We'll use what time we have."

She didn't speak, nor did I, as she unclipped her web belt, dropped it, removed her jacket. I started to protest

when she removed her blouse, to tell her it was too cold
for that, but held my tongue. If this was the way she
wanted it, then this was the way it would be. Her boots
and then her trousers followed her blouse and she stood
in the cold night air in only her undergarments.

"You know I'm a whore," she said as she unsnapped
her bra. "I've done this with hundreds of men." ___

"I know."

"But this—well, it's different, Eric." She slipped her
panties down her hips, her legs, kicked them aside.

"I know that too," I said, looking at her for long moments before I began to undress.

There was a strangeness in the air, something more
than the chill of the night and the cold light of the
stars, something beyond the rustling of the night wind
in the upper limbs of the pines and the sounds that came,
faint with distance, from the fort, something I couldn't
identify, but would remember. A sense, perhaps, of en-
chantment.

In the darkness and starlight, Gwendalfa stood naked
and beautiful waiting for me, her body a lighter shape
against the trees and brush behind her, the darkness of
her hair as it stirred in the cold breeze, soft curves of
light across her breasts and waist and hips and thighs,
shadows under those breasts, rounding into her stomach, the blackness of the triangle between her thighs,
her eyes bright as if they too were stars. She was half
human, half a strange forest nymph come to make love
to me for some purpose unknowable to mortals. I
shivered as I dropped my jacket to the earth, but from
something more than the cold.

As my clothing joined the dark pile of hers, I felt
the cold raise bumps along my arms and legs. Then I
stepped toward her and forgot about the cold, as I think
she had forgotten about it.

We stood together for a long while, our bodies pressing
together, blending, melting, merging as were our lips,
and then Gwendalfa slowly slipped from my grasp and
lowered herself to the leaves of the forest floor.

"The time, Eric," she whispered.

"I know," I said. "I know."

* * *

We waited until the last possible moment and then dressed quickly, terribly aware of both the shortness of time and the cold breeze against our skin.

"I'm glad," she said to me, looking up at me, her eyes still as bright as they'd been before.

"So am I."

We slung our carbines across our shoulders, exchanged one last kiss, and headed back the hundred yards to Von Heinen's line.

We were halfway there when . . .

The quiet and darkness of the night were torn to shreds.

From somewhere some distance away, far beyond the nearer buildings we could see through the fence, came a great flash of light followed by a tremendous roar and a shaking of the earth. For a moment or two I thought I was going to be both blinded and deafened by it. I hurried forward.

"That's some diversion," I said, but I doubted Gwendalfa understood me.

Von Heinen was on his feet when I reached him and was yelling something. I could tell he was yelling because his mouth was open, but I could hardly hear what he was saying. I didn't really need to know. None of us did. We acted.

So did the others of our unit and the other two units of our element.

Several hundred feet to our right in the forest lay Devoto Baugh, Kjemi Stov, Geoffry Dunstanson, Artos Alaricson, and the other members of the largest unit, number one, whose goal was the power plant. Some distance to our left was Aelfric's unit three, the one designated to take the communications center.

Unit one moved out first, hit the fence in three places simultaneously with thermal grenades that burned and melted their way through the metal strands, creating a great deal of light and arcing of electricity, but little noise, but it would have taken a very great deal of noise to be heard over the sounds coming now from the far side of the fort: smaller explosions, the roar of a great fire coming into being, the burp! and chatter! of handguns, machine guns, the crump! of a mortar, the boom! of a hand grenade and even the yells and screams of men and women.

There was no question that element three had arrived on time and was doing its best—and a bit more!—to create the diversion required by our element and the other, some distance away, bent on some other errand.

A large selection of the electrified fence had fallen before the onslaught of unit one, collapsing into smoldering, sizzling piles of metal, some little more than slag. The men of unit one, led by Devoto Baugh, a submachine gun in his hand chattering, swarmed across the broken fence, headed toward the power plant and toward a guard post that sat beside the large, unlighted warehouse across a wide firebreak from the power plant.

The sentries had come staggering out of their hut, half-asleep during the dull duty near the fort's perimeter, raising their weapons and yelling incoherent words. Geoffry Dunstanson's submachine gun chattered as had Baugh's and the stunned guards staggered back in bloody surprise, some falling, grasping wounds, screaming. Other weapons joined Geoffry's and the perimeter guards died before having the opportunity of taking down even one of the Anglianer attackers.

Then Geoffry was joining the rest of his unit as they stormed the power plant, Devoto Baugh in the lead, screaming like a madman and cutting down anyone in his way with his blazing submachine gun. Hardly the quiet man we'd known at Tapferkeitenhaven, but I wasn't surprised.

Those of us in unit two stood on the edge of the forest, yards from the broken fence, waiting for the time to come when we'd move out. It wasn't long now. My palms had gone dry and my mouth felt as if it were filled with cotton. There was an angriness in my stomach that wasn't butterflies, though I couldn't have described what it was. I knew that in a very few minutes it would all be gone. When I began moving I'd forget it all, concentrate only on what had to be done, what I had to do to achieve my goals and to stay alive.

Gwendalfa stood beside me, a quietness in her now, her face bathed in the red and orange light of the distant fire. She was an avenging angel, a dark-haired

Valkyrie satisfied in seeing something done at last to destroy her enemies.

She watched the men who ran across the clear area toward the great doors of the power plant, then batter them down, watched the tan-and-olive-clad soldiers coming to protect the plant, dashing into the light to be cut down by the New East Anglianer marksmen Devoto Baugh had stationed just beside the fence, watched her friend Artos Alaricson take a Sclavanian bullet in his chest, spin on his feet, cursing and then falling, perhaps dying. She sobbed loudly when this happened. I put my arm around her shoulder. That was all I could do.

In moments, in hardly more time than it takes to tell it, Devoto Baugh's unit one was inside the power plant and from there we could now hear the chattering of submachine guns, the less rapid firing of semiautomatic carbines and pistols, then the roar of a well-placed grenade or explosive charge. A dynamo let out a great metallic scream of agony that rose above all the other cacophony that filled the night. Lights across the area flickered, dimmed, but didn't go out. Moments later the metallic screams had died away and the standing lights along the firebreak were again as bright as ever.

"Let's go!" Von Heinen yelled and from some distance away, to the left, I heard another voice that was probably Aelfric's yelling a similar thing.

We headed forward at a trot through the verge of the forest, to the fence, through it and onto the reservation.

Not far behind us, I could see as I glanced over my shoulder, was unit three, Aelfric, Wexstan, An Mona Steorra dressed now in his usual poncho and leather trousers, a carbine in one hand, a bright-bladed knife in the other. Some Sclavanians wouldn't die easily this night. The rest of unit three was on his heels.

The area of our concern consisted of nine buildings and the guard hut. To the left of the firebreak stood the guard post nestled under the bulk of a warehouse equally as large as the power plant opposite it. Beyond that warehouse was the skudder pool, surrounded by a high fence, though this one wasn't believed to be electrified. The skudder pool consisted of several closed

sheds, the roofs of which joined to make them effectively a single, partitioned structure. Beyond the skudder
pool was another warehouse.

To the right of the firebreak was the power plant
which was already being taken by Devoto Baugh's unit.
Beyond that were four smaller structures set two by two.
The nearer right, hidden behind the bulk of the power
plant, was an electronics repair shop; the near left was
a supply room. The far-right building of the four, also
hidden from our view, was a small electronics warehouse. The building to the far left was the critical one
of the cluster—it was believed to be the Krithian communications center for all Timeliner operations on this
Line. That was Aelfric's goal. Beyond the cluster of
buildings was another large building and an even larger
parking area filled with various types of military vehicles.
A motor pool. Our only concern with it was to see that
the vehicles weren't used against us. A few of Aelfric's
men would fill that place with explosive charges.

The layout of this area of Fort Lothairin was fresh
in my mind from the maps and aerial photographs I'd
seen so frequently during the last few days, and now
were fleshed out into three dimensions as I saw the
structures themselves, lighted by the mounted lamps
that lined the firebreak and by the garish light of the
blazing fire that now towered over the buildings it consumed.

My carbine was in my hand, safety off, cocked, when
I caught up with Von Heinen who'd taken the lead. Now
we were into the firebreak. There was hardly any opposition before us, only a few scattered Sclavanians and
Imperials not taken by Devoto Baugh's men—Was it
too easy? I was asking myself. Were they letting us
in . . . ?

"When are you augmenting?" the German asked in
gasps as we ran, pausing briefly to cut down a foolhardy
Sclavanian who showed himself, both our weapons firing
at once.

"Not until I have to."

Now, more quickly than we'd expected, we were
within hand grenade range of the fence that surrounded
the skudder pool, the locked gates, and of the men who'd

come running out of the sheds, armed and ready to defend the Outtime vehicles in their care. I wondered how many of these men were locals, Sclavanians and Imperials, and how many of them were really Timeliners brought in by the Kriths, men whom I might know, might have worked with in the past. Then I had no more time to think of that.

In the hellscape of red-orange, flickering firelight, long and strangely illuminated shadows, of exploding bombs and firing handguns, the smell of burning oil and wood and plastic and flesh thick in the air, a cacaphony of noise composed of booms! and cracks! and sizzles! and screaming of wounded, dying men, Von Heinen and I both knelt, dropped our weapons and pulled grenades from our belts. Small-arms fire popped! into the dirt around us. Other weapons from behind covered our movements, defended us. As if from long practice, together we pulled the grenades' pins, drew back our arms, pitched the bombs into the air—and threw ourselves onto the earth of the firebreak.

The grenades went off almost simultaneously, two or three yards apart, caught in the mesh of the wire fence, ripping, tearing, bringing down a section of the fence wide enough for three or four men to enter abreast.

Then we were on our feet again, spitting dust and tasting oily sand, our weapons in our hands and firing again. The rest of unit one, Harold, Gwendalfa, Freya, Faeder Baldwin, Efor, and the others were on our heels as we leaped across the broken fence and stormed the skudder pool, all but stumbling and falling across the dead and dying bodies of men we'd killed to make our entry.

By the time we were inside the multistructure of the sheds our number had been reduced by a third, the mangled, broken, bloody bodies of Anglianers fallen across those of Sclavanians, Imperials, Timeliners.

Faeder Baldwin lay dying behind us, a ragged string of holes across his chest and abdomen. Harold limped and almost collapsed from a jagged wound in his left thigh. Von Heinen's right arm ran with blood, though the index finger of that hand kept pulling back the trigger of his submachine gun. There was a redness of her own blood in Freya's blond hair, a fragmentation wound across her scalp that hadn't slowed her.

Yet still I felt, *It shouldn't be this easy.*

I stood for a moment gasping for breath, Gwendalfa half a pace behind me, her carbine still firing through the wooden doorway before us. The Fiurer carbine in my hand had roared until its firing pin had clicked on an empty chamber and as I paused I threw in a fresh clip, while Von Heinen kicked open the last door, sprayed the interior of the shed with bullets. Gwendalfa did the same. Then she and I followed Von Heinen in.

And there in the shed, under the row of naked incandescent bulbs that ran in a line slung just below the ceiling, reflecting their light, was a huge, glasslike bubble mounted on a small, dark base, a squashed spheroid with a hatch and leatherlike seats inside and a control panel for the pilot—and a series of projections upon the base I'd never seen before, bright and shiny metal as if but recently installed.

We'd found the skudders.

We'd also found one of the Krithian masters, standing only inches from the device, shock and fear on his olive noseless face, his great pupilless eyes wide. His naked body shown under the lights like metal, the sweat of fear. He was unarmed and seemed too frightened to think of self-skudding, though that was a natural protective action of his race. Wasn't it?

I shot him three times, slowly, carefully, precisely. Once in the face, once in the middle of the left breast and once in the abdomen, just above the navel. He moaned once as he fell to the floor. Then he died.

I hadn't fully realized until that moment how much I'd come to hate his kind, an insane, irrational hatred that only later would I come to despise in myself, justified as I might think my hatred to be.

The others of our unit poured into the shed, stopped and gaped in awe of the dead being and of the machine.

It wasn't that the skudder was all that large or imposing, but it was obviously the work of a technology far in advance of that of this world, and the Anglianers could see that instantly. And they had some idea of the capabilities of the vehicle, of its ability to pass from this world into others, Earths different from this one, parallel worlds split off from the main branch of Time by *either/or.*

And if they'd doubted the Paratimers' stories of a race of non-humans behind the Timeliners and the war that now erupted across the borders of their nation, they could no longer doubt. The creature who lay dead on the floor before them had never been born from a woman's womb, had never come to life on *this* Earth.

"Mathers," Von Heinen said, speaking only my name and giving me a significant look. I knew what he meant. This one was *our* skudder.

"Okay, spread out," he yelled. "Let's find the others."

Just as the party was about to do 'as he orderd, the ground shook under our feet again, the air roared with sounds an order of magnitude louder than before, and the shed was plunged into darkness as the incandescent bulbs faded to a dim yellow and then out.

"They got the power plant, and damned good," someone said unnecessarily.

Then there was a brief respite from the sounds of war from outside, a moment of shocked silence as all of Fort Lothairin was plunged into the same darkness, a darkness unevenly lighted by the great fires outside.

"There are auxiliaries," Von Heinen said.

"Probably," I agreed, fingering the hot barrel of my carbine, wondering when I should go into augmentation. I'd held off for a long time. "And they should come on automatically."

With the power plant knocked out, though probably not seriously damaged, Baugh would have accomplished his primary goal. The time between the planting of the last bomb and his arrival where we stood could only be a matter of brief minutes. I'd hoped to be góne before he came.

In the darkness I took a few steps in the direction of the skudder. The time had almost come.

Then came sounds of more people entering the skudder pool's shelters, the yelling of voices in Anglisch, the cry of our code word *leoghin.* I recognized none of the voices.

"Leoghin," Von Heinen yelled back, something strange

in his voice. "Mathers," he called to me in Outtime English, "watch yourself."

"What do you mean?" I asked in the same language. I brought my carbine once more into firing position, took a few more steps toward the skudder, readying my augmentation.

Von Heinen didn't answer.

Since it was one of the models equipped for it, I shifted the Fiurer carbine from semiautomatic to full automatic. It held a nearly full magazine of ammunition. I had the sensation I was going to need every bit of it.

Somewhere not too far away an auxiliary generator, its system triggered by the power failure, came into operation with a loud coughing of a petro-powered engine and an unpleasant, grumbling electrical hum. The row of bulbs inside the shed flickered to glowing, though dim and yellow.

But that was light enough.

The interior of the shed was a tableau: I was nearest the skudder; Von Heinen only a few feet from me; Gwendalfa, Harold, Freya, half a dozen other Anglianers between Von Heinen and the shed's door. We'd all turned to see who it was entering, who yelled *"Leoghin"* again in an outlandish accent as bad as mine.

"Mathers!"

The word was a scream, a yell, a curse.

"Mathers!" it came again.

Two men stood in the doorway and neither of them had been born in this Timeline—and maybe neither of them were *men.*

One was Devoto Baugh, his clothing tattered and stained, his face blackened with soot and ash and spotted with tiny burns. But it wasn't him I saw.

The other, who also held an automatic pistol in his hand, was tall, thin, his skin a cadaverous white even under the yellow light in the shed. He'd never really looked quite human to me before. Now I was certain he wasn't.

I'd hoped that Mica was dead.

I could tell he wasn't.

"Good-by, Gwen," I yelled and would have liked to have said a great deal more, but there wasn't time. I cut in my augmentation and squeezed the carbine's trigger simultaneously. A stream of bullets burst from its muzzle, headed for Mica and Devoto Baugh.

They leaped out of the way, both of them going into augmentation only instants after I did.

Von Heinen must have expected this, or at least feared it. He must have known that Mica would be among the Paratimers involved in this venture; I should have guessed it days before. He'd really have been Von Heinen's superior. He'd have been on this Line.

And the German nobleman hadn't seen fit to tell me that. There was probably a hell of a lot more he hadn't seen fit to tell me, despite the confessions he'd made. And if I felt any loyalty, any obligation toward him that wasn't yet fulfilled, now I had ample excuse to forget it —as I'd planned to do anyway.

Von Heinen could worry about his own neck now.

My own was concern enough for me.

I ducked in the yellowish light that seemed to have gone reddish in X5 and heard the long, low sounds of augmentation as the pistols in each of the Paratimers' hands fired. I squeezed off a second automatic burst from the Fiurer, hoping to hit the Paratimers but miss the Anglianers who stood between us, who were now slowly throwing themselves to the floor, realizing something of what was happening. I only chipped paint from the wall and the doorway.

Firing again, I danced backward toward the skudder, hoping to pin the Paratimers against the wall until I could reach my destination. I wasn't very successful.

With a yelled word from Mica, the two Paratimers leaped toward me, both pistols firing. I felt a searing pain across my ribs, felt a fist knock me backward, but as I staggerd I let off still another carbine burst that cut across Devoto Baugh's upper chest, neck, and face. His head seemed to explode like a rotten melon.

Mica kept firing at me as I regained my balance, fell back against the glasslike dome of the skudder. Holding the carbine in my right hand, I fired two short bursts that narrowly missed him, but shook him so that his aim was bad. My left hand fumbled for the skudder's hatch.

I hadn't been watching Von Heinen. I'd hardly con-

sidered a non-augmented man a danger even though he
was certain to understand now that I was betraying him.
I was foolish. Even as slow as he was relative to my
augmented speed, he could still bring his submachine gun
up, aim it, pull the trigger.

I saw the bullets coming, cursed him, ducked, jumped
aside, knew he was trying to kill me. I didn't want to
kill him, but . . .

My carbine slugs cut his legs out from under him and
he fell slowly, heavily to the floor.

At this moment Kjemi Stov stumbled into the open
doorway with the slow movements of an unaugmented
man, a smoking gun in his hands, incomprehension in his
eyes.

Now the skudder's hatch yielded to my hand, popped
open. I fired one final burst at Mica, hoping that this
one found its target, but not taking time to see, turned
and leaped through the open hatch as quickly as I could
with the pain I had in my side.

Two slugs roared through the hatch before I was able
to get it closed.

Mica was moving more slowly when I saw him next,
and redness was beginning to blossom across the front
of his New East Anglian army blouse, but he hadn't
stopped. Stepping across the prone Von Heinen, he
grabbed up the German's submachine gun and aimed it
at the skudder's most vulnerable part—its base.

Freya, dazed, confused, bloodied, moved slowly in the
smoke and dim light, crawled across the floor toward the
bleeding form of Count Albert von Heinen. She'd left
her weapon behind, but she didn't seem to care about
anything but getting to her man. No one else seemed to
notice her. I wondered why I did.

My hands danced across the skudder's controls, bringing
the probability generator to slow life. Some of the contols
were new, unfamiliar to me, but I'd worry about that later.
Right now all I wanted was to get off this Line—
and quickly.

The weapon Mica held now had begun to fire, waving
back and forth across the base of the skudder, slugs
ricocheting away, though I knew that before long one
of them would find a seam in the black material that

composed the base, make its savage way in, shattering delicate circuits, fragile components. I had to get out before that happened.

I wondered what would happen to the skudder—and to me—if I were to hit the actuating switch before full potential was reached. I didn't know. I didn't really want to find out.

Mica's submachine gun continued to fire, though there was total silence inside the skudder's dome.

The Paratimer would probably have been able to stop me, destroy my skudder, had he not made the same mistake I had—ignoring people without augmentation. They might be slow, but they weren't *that* slow.

Gwendalfa apparently comprehended what was going on, apparently knew that the blur of motion she saw as Mica was trying to kill me—and for some reason she didn't want that to happen.

While the indicators made their slow way to full power, while Mica sprayed the skudder with leaden shot, Gwendalfa, with what appeared to me to be agonizing slowness, raised her pistol, aimed at Mica, pulled back on the trigger—and sent a .441 slug into his back.

The Paratimer fell forward, a final burst of slugs slapping against the skudder's base. One of them penetrated. . . . The skudder screamed. . . .

The next events took place too quickly for me to fully comprehend them, even in X5, though I had some awareness, some shock, some horror. . . .

The skudder pool's lights surged back to full brilliance, illuminating the broken, bloody tableau. Kjemi Stov, now in augmentation, came from his frozen state, charged toward the skudder, a cry of half-insane rage on his lips, though the words he yelled could have only been a Timeliner's Shangalis!

And into the bright and bloody skudder pool charged the troop which had waited until this moment to spring their trap, a troop of blue-clad Timeliners with energy weapons, olive-clad Sclavanians firing slug-throwers, all led by a sable-skinned Krith with a look of fury and of triumph on his flat features, Tar-hortha!

He too was in X5 and he yelled above the roar and the screams in Shangalis, and I thought I could hear him even through the skudder's dome: "You have lost, Eric. You have lost again."

Still moving as only a man in augmentation can, though wounded twice, Mica turned as he fell, and fired his submachine gun once more before he hit the floor, not into the Anglianers so much as through them toward the Krith and his augmented Timeliners. Energy weapons replied to his slug-thrower—and Mica's mutilated body seemed to explode in their blaze.

Caught in the sudden and swiftly ending cross fire, Gwendalfa had taken two of Mica's slugs. She pitched backward as if struck a giant's blow, two bloody holes between her breasts. On her face was a shocked expression, then it went blank and her eyes stared emptily at the ceiling. I knew she was dead.

The other Anglianers had no more chance than she. The Timeliners' weapons caught them in blazes of coruscating energy. I watched my friends die so quickly that few of them even knew what was happening, dying as their bodies were torn apart by energy weapons.

Kjemi Stov, untouched by the lead and coherent energy that swept the shed, had almost reached the skudder. Now Tar-hortha was close behind him.

And as I screamed out my fury at Mica's dying retaliation, something happened in the circuits, the wiring, the generators of the skudder under me. A scream to match my own, a yell, a roar of mechanical pain came from it. Lights flickered erratically across the panel. My hands fell to the controls, but I didn't know what to do. Something was wrong, but . . .

Ignoring Kjemi Stov, Tar-hortha had come to a stop only a short distance from the skudder, looked at me through the glasslike dome, a strange expression on his alien features, a look of concentration and of something else, something more. For an instant a smoky, inhuman, unholy figure seemed to fill the space between us, a thing that brought to mind a mythological being I'd once heard of that would come back into the world only at the very end of Time itself, and then to announce the End of the World.

Then the world outside the skudder grayed again. It didn't exactly flicker, but it was gone, and for a few moments there was nothing, nothing at all but grayness.

I was moving across the Lines, but . . .

Then there was a true flicker, a ragged, uneven one, a sick and screaming one, but it was a flicker and then a world appeared outside and then it was gone, a world of darkness and distant lights, here no Krithian base at Fort Lothairin, yet there was something: not far from the skudder, silhouetted against the distant lights, barely illuminated by light that now spilled from automatic illumination that had come on inside the skudder, was the six-foot-plus, sable-skinned, naked figure of a Krith, and though I couldn't see it, I knew that there was a look of triumph upon Tar-hortha's face. I couldn't escape *him* by skudding.

The skudder's generators screamed again as it flickered, as lights died across the control panel, as smoke came from unseen places into the interior, as the smell of ozone and burning insulation grew stronger.

Grayness.

Then darkness and the dim figure outside, unmoving in relation to the skudder.

Then grayness again, a faltering flicker.

Darkness once more and the final agonized scream of mechanical pain as the skudder, damaged too much to go on, died and with it the power that moved it across the Lines.

Outside Tar-hortha yelled: "Give it up, Eric. I told you that you had lost again."

14
... and in Another Place

I came out of augmentation and for a few long moments
sat unmoving in the dead skudder, nausea and pain filling
me, blood trickling down my side from the wound I'd
received.

Lost. It's all lost, I thought. Everything. The Anglianers
had fallen into the Kriths' trap. The Paratimers had failed
in their attempt to take the Krithian headquarters in
Sclavania and were dead. And so were Gwendalfa and
Freya and Faeder Baldwin and so many others. So was
Von Heinen. So was . . .

I alone had escaped, if but momentarily. Outside was
the Krith who'd sprung the trap. I'd lost just as had
the Anglianers and the Paratimers. Now Tar-hortha
would . . .

As a sense of utter futility filled me, and a depression
and a self-disgust threatened to carry me to inaction, I
remembered the side arm I still carried, the .441 Slean
revolver in its holster on my hip. If Tar-hortha wanted
me, he'd still have to fight me.

Painfully I rose from the control seat, moved to the
skudder's hatch, manually opened it since it was no
longer powered. Outside, in a dim shadowiness, the Krith
awaited me.

"Come on out, Eric," he said as I stood in the open
hatch, my eyes slowly adjusting to a faint illumination
that came from unseen sources. "I wish you no physical
harm."

I kept my hand away from the pistol. Maybe he hadn't
noticed it, hadn't thought about my still being armed.

"Come down, Eric," he said slowly. "We still have a
long way to go, you know."

"I know," I said, meaning things I didn't yet fully
comprehend, as I leaped from the lip of the hatch to

the hard pavement, the shock of my heels hitting it flashing up my weary legs.

Pavement! I thought suddenly, for the first time becoming aware of my surroundings.

We weren't in an open field as I'd thought, as I'd seen outside the skudder during the previous flicker. Oh, we were outside. I could see the sky above, hard pinpoints of lights, stars almost untwinkling. But the area in which we stood was enclosed on three sides by the high walls of buildings, hard, unyielding walls of buildings that might have been made of concrete, but which might have been of some substance unknown to the world of the Anglianers. And there was about them a strangeness of design, an alienness, perhaps, that brought into my mind remembrances of remote dreams, nightmares of other worlds, of death and destruction in unknown places.

Enclosed on three sides, the fourth side was open. Away stretched the pavement as if to the horizon, where the blackness of Earth met the lesser blackness of the nighttime sky. Perhaps there were tall, cylindrical shapes outlined distantly against that sky, but I wasn't certain.

And it was quiet, terribly quiet.

There seemed no sounds save my own labored breathing and creaking and popping that came from the damaged skudder as overheated components cooled.

"Come, Eric," Tar-hortha spoke softly, his voice sounding terribly loud in the silence. "We still have a long way to go," he repeated. "I will find you conveyance. We must go to where Sally is."

I turned to face the Krith again and let my right hand drop to the holster that carried the heavy revolver. "I'm not going anywhere with you, Tar-hortha," I said.

"But you must."

"I'll find my own way to Sally."

"I doubt that you can do that."

"I've already done a lot of things you didn't expect," I told him.

"Not as many as you might think, Eric."

"What do you mean by that?"

He laughed softly in the night, but only said, turning has back on me, "Come this way, if you please."

"It doesn't please me, Tar-hortha," I said and pulled the weapon from its holster.

The Krith paused in midstep as I cocked the pistol, slowly turned as he heard the click of its chamber turning into position, aligning a bullet with the barrel, with the firing pin.

He laughed again. "Please do not be foolish. Can you not realize that you have lost?"

"Maybe I haven't yet," I said, leveling the pistol at his chest, "but I'll follow you. Just remember I have a gun on you."

"I will remember," he said. "Now please come with me."

I knew that he was leading me into another trap, but I also figured that somewhere inside that trap would be another skudder. If he wanted to take me anywhere, to any other Line, he'd have to have a skudder. And I *did* have a gun on him. Maybe that would be enough to get me out of the trap. I hoped. . . .

The sable-skinned alien led me across the pavement at a slow walk, away from the openness that seemed to stretch to the horizon and toward the most remote of the three gray walls.

"Where are we?" I asked after we'd walked in silence a distance that must have been a hundred yards or better.

"Oh, you might call this a marshaling yard, Eric," he said without looking back at me, seemingly uncaring of the weapon only inches from his naked back, "or a material depot. No doubt you saw places like it during your service with the Timeliners."

"I'm not sure," I said. I'd seen places *something* like this before, of course, vast storage places of the Timeliners on uninhabited or sparsely inhabited worlds where supplies and equipment were kept for their endeavors across the Lines. Yet there was a silence and an alienness about this place that was like nothing I'd ever seen before. Whatever else they might be, Timeliners are human . . . and this wasn't a human place. What it was I didn't know.

We walked on.

"You are puzzled, Eric?" Tar-hortha asked. The wall was nearer now. We must have crossed half the distance to it. "This does not quite seem like a Timeliner depot to you, is that so?"

"That's so," I admitted.

"About that, you are correct. This is not a place built or manned by Timeliners. This is strictly *ours*."

I didn't speak. I thought I knew what he meant by that.

"As you already suspect, there is a great deal about my race that you people do not know. There are a number of things we have chosen not to reveal. One of these things is the fact that we have a few selected Lines set aside for our own use. This is one of them, but newly established. You might say that the paint is hardly dry."

Was this an uninhabited Line? I wondered. One so near that of the Anglianers? If uninhabited, how had it become that way? Or if inhabited, what had the Kriths done with the inhabitants? I didn't think any of the answers would be very pleasant. I didn't have a very high opinion of the Kriths' tactics then.

We were quite near the wall now and Tar-hortha spoke a single, alien syllable. The wall before us broke open, a portion of it sliding away to reveal a long, brightly lighted corridor leading into the structure.

"If you will continue to follow me, I will lead you to the place where skudders are kept," the Krith said with a pause in his stride. "You will need one to continue to our destination."

"What makes you think I'll go wherever it is you want me to go?" I asked as we stepped across the threshold into the building, into the bright white light of the corridor.

"You have questions you want answered, do you not?" Tar-hortha asked, his simian tail swishing in the air behind him. "The only way you will find these answers— and the only way you will find your Sally—is to do as I say."

"I don't understand you, Tar-hortha," I said.

"I would be rather surprised if you did," the Krith replied, glancing over his shoulder and giving me a strange, though rather human smile.

Some feet into the corridor a panel slid open in one of the walls and a device of gray-metal, about four feet tall, not anthropoid but a machine with arms and hands and glittering lenses for eyes, rolled out into the passageway. Tar-hortha spoke to it in a language I'd never heard before. It fell in beside him rolling silently on hidden wheels, or perhaps on a cushion of air, two or three feet to his left.

"A mechanical companion," he said.

"A bodyguard?" I asked.

The Krith shrugged.

The corridor seemed endless, leading farther and farther into the building. There were a million questions I wanted to ask, but right then none of them seemed worth asking. The answers I really wanted wouldn't come easily.

There was a growing nervousness within me, a fear, a realization that I was doing exactly what the Krith wanted me to do, that somehow he'd planned for me to come to this Line in that damaged skudder,' or had at least *known* I'd come there, and a realization that if this were a trap, I was doing absolutely nothing to avoid it.

Yet there was also within me a sensation of—what?— inevitability? Predestination? That what I was doing I had to do, I'd already done, and there was nothing I could do to alter the events that were to take place, that had already been charted in a past/future that was as fixed as the events of recorded history. If I were to fall into Tar-hortha's trap, that was because I *had* to, and if I were to avoid falling into his trap, that also was because I *had* to. It wasn't just fatalism, depression, fatigue, but something more, something deeper, something far more awesome and frightening, as if both the Krith and I were caught up in the workings of forces far greater than either of us, forces perhaps greater than even those of the vast Krithian machine that sprawled across the Timelines.

I shuddered with a chill though it was quite warm within the strange building, within the bright corridor.

More panels of the corridor's walls slid open as we passed, more machines of gray metal came out to join us, silent, anonymous, identical, all gliding silently beside us. At last there were six of them, one before Tar-hortha, one on each side of him, one on each side of me, and one behind. My revolver was still pointed at his back.

"We are almost there, Eric," the Krith said, speaking after a long silence.

By then I felt so weak I could hardly speak, the wound in my side, the period of augmentation during the battle at Fort Lothairin, the long, long hours without sleep had all combined their weight upon my shoulders, yet I knew that rest, the kind of rest I really wanted, wouldn't come for a long while. I spoke to the Krith, "Almost where?"

"To where the skudders are kept."

To my surprise the corridor before us branched and without being told the leading robot turned and headed down the leftward one. The Krith, the remaining robots, and I followed.

Some hundred feet more and the corridor ended before two large metal doors marked with characters as alien to me as were the robots. Whatever language was used in this place, it wasn't Shangalis.

The first machine paused for a moment before the doors which quietly opened, sliding away to the right and left. The robot moved forward. We followed.

Beyond the door was a huge chamber, high and wide and as brightly lighted as the corridor, and in it sat some half-dozen skudders, large ones, elongated ovals of metal and paraglas capable of carrying a dozen or more people and tons of equipment, and I noticed that they were equipped with the projections I'd seen on the skudder in the Sclavanian pool, part of the system that allowed them spatial movement as well as transtemporal.

"We are here now, Eric," Tar-hortha said, stopping and gesturing toward the skudders. "I suggest that you allow me to set the controls of one of them for you. It will carry you to our destination."

"I'll do my own control setting," I told him, stepping forward and pressing the pistol into his back. "I'll—"

"Eric, please do not be foolish," the Krith said calmly. "It would be very unwise for you to do anything other than what I suggest."

"Your robots?" I asked.

"They will see that no harm comes to me."

"Are you sure?"

"I am sure."

Three of the devices moved closer to me, raising their

metal arms in a manner that wasn't menacing, but could
have been.

"Put the foolish pistol away and come with me," Tar-
hortha said.

The robots moved closer.

"I'm going to have some answers," I said.

"Of course you are, but killing me will not give them to
you."

"And if I do as you say . . . ?"

"You will be my prisoner, of course."

"I won't put myself in that position again, Tar-hortha."

"I believe you already have."

A metal hand shot out from one of the faceless machines, clamped down suddenly on my right wrist.

I tried to jerk away, to pull myself out of its grasp, but
the second of the machines came up behind me, grasped
both my arms above the elbows, pulled me backward.

"Tar-hortha!" I screamed in anger.

The thing that held on to my right wrist must have
weighed a ton or better, but as I unconsciously switched
into augmentation, as the world slowed, as electrobiological circuitry came into operation once more, I felt that I
could move it, or at least the pseudohand that held my
wrist, if only an inch or two.

Pain reddened my vision as I fought against the two
machines that held me, as I willed my right hand to move
against that pain, as I swung the pistol's barrel a few
inches to the left, as I pulled back on the trigger. . . .

The roar of the pistol was sudden and loud in the
room's near silence, unexpected and terrible.

I felt a bone snap in my wrist and I saw my fingers release their hold on the pistol; I saw it drop slowly toward
the gray floor, but, dammit! I'd done something, I
thought, as I came out of augmentation.

Tar-hortha was screaming shrilly, staggering away,
clutching at a wounded arm, broken between the wrist
and elbow, red, manlike blood gushing from an open
wound. He slowly dropped to his knees and there was no
anger in his eyes, no look of triumph now, only fear and
horror, for he'd been hurt, hurt by a human being, and
that was something that never, never happened to a Krith.

"You will die, Eric," he cried, resting now on his knees, blood pooling below him. "You will die!"

And with the words the four gray robots moved toward me to aid the two that held me, one by my upper arms, one by my broken wrist.

The pain was coming to me stronger now, and along with it vertigo and nausea. So now I'd never know. Now I'd . . ."

A grayness came over the room that I thought for a moment was caused by the pain, by a coming loss of consciousness. I thought I was going to go under and would probably never wake up again. Yet . . .

The Greeks had a phrase for it: *deus ex machina*.

Only this "god" wasn't from a machine, at least no metal and ceramic, silicon and germanium machine I knew about. This "god" was a hazy fog in a shape something like that of a man, though vaguely.

"This isn't the way it should be done, Eric," a strangely familiar voice said from nowhere and from everywhere, "but there's no other way now."

I wanted to ask what was happening, but the words wouldn't form in my mouth.

The robotic hands that held me relaxed their grip; the machines glided back a few paces.

"Quickly now," the voice said out of the air. "I can hold them only for moments. Act, dammit!"

Somehow I managed to get to my feet, looked at the limpness of my right hand dangling from a broken wrist, looked at the Krith who knelt in a pool of his own blood.

He had a way out, didn't he? Yet I knew that a Krith *couldn't* self-skud while in pain or fear, and Tar-hortha was feeling both now, yet . . . Yet if that were a natural action of self-protection as I'd been told, wouldn't evolutionary processes have made such moments as those of pain and fear the very ones during which self-skudding could be achieved? Why was it that . . . How rational was *I* then?

"The gun, Eric!" the shadowy voice out of the air said.

I remembered the pistol, bent to grasp it in my left hand, looked at the now immobile robots.

"Hurry!" the voice said. "We haven't long."

I stood up, holding the pistol awkwardly. "Into the

skudder," I told the Krith, shaking my head to clear it, moving toward him.

He shook his head too in a very human fashion.

I pointed the .441 revolver at his face, only inches away. He sighed deeply through wide, wet lips, his great, pupilless eyes wider than ever, but then slowly came to his feet, moaned, staggered before me toward the nearest of the transtemporal machines.

How long the robots would remain immobile I didn't know, but the voice had said not long. I didn't want to have to fight them again. I knew who'd win.

Prodding the wounded Krith on, we soon reached the skudder's hatch. It popped open at the touch of my pistol's barrel and we tumbled in.

I reversed the pistol in my hand and swung it toward the Krith's skull, hopefully not hard enough to crush it, but hard enough. Tar-hortha seemed more shocked than stunned, his great eyes accusing me as they opened wider, then closed as he fell forward to the deck, into the silence of unconsciousness.

Pulling the hatch closed behind me and dogging it, I turned toward the pilot's compartment at the forward end of the roughly egg-shaped craft, half transparent, half opaque, about the size of a Greyhound bus of Sally's native Line. The control panel I found was twice the size of that I was more familiar with, and filled with controls I didn't recognize, though there were enough I did to satisfy me. I could at least get it going, out of *this* Line. Later I'd worry about the strange knobs and dials and meters.

It all seemed familiar now, hitting the switches, adjusting the levers and dials that would bring up the probability potential, while outside robots of gray metal came out of their mechanical lethargy and glided across the large room's floor toward the shudder, their arms reaching out as if to grab my vehicle and keep it from slipping into Probability.

Oh, so damned familiar.

Green lights clicked on across the panel and I prayed to twice a dozen different gods that I could get away from this Line before the robots found some way to damage the skudder—I didn't want to have to start all over again. I didn't think I could have.

More green lights clicked on. Meters showed rising potentials.

Outside the gray machines came closer, their extended appendages all but reaching the skudder's metal base.

Inside, inside me was a great weakness, a dizziness, a desire to forget it all and lie down and sleep and never, never . . .

"Probability Potential Achieved," a green light told me, a meter repeated.

With my left hand I moved the destinatrol for several dozen Lines to the East, then shifted that hand toward the main actuating switch as metal clashed against metal, as the robots reached the skudder, struck it, rammed it, fought to hold it in. . . .

Flicker!

And the cavernous room was gone. I was in darkness, in a Line where there was no building, no lights, nothing at all that I could see outside the skudder.

Flicker! again.

And I thought I was going to pass out.

I held myself up in the seat and tried not to think about the throbbing in my broken wrist, my lacerated side.

Flicker! Flicker! Flicker!

Maybe I'd make it after all.

15
Tar-hortha's Answers

I had to reset the destination controls twice more, moving much farther to the T-East than I'd intended before I found a world sufficiently ruined.

Outside was a desolate, moonlike Earth similar to those Sally and I had seen in the far T-West in the so-called Albigensian Lines, a world without life or atmosphere and high in nuclear radiation. Here technology had advanced a little more quickly than it had on the world of the Anglianers and the Sclavanians, perhaps, and conflicts had arisen that hadn't been settled at negotiation tables or in brushfire guerrilla war. Here nuclear warfare had swept the world and its inhabitants had blasted themselves to radioactive ash. It was sad, but I didn't take time to ponder over it, nor to concern myself with the radiation. Inside the skudder I was safe, and I didn't intend to go outside. Not on this world.

After resting for a few moments in the pilot's seat, I took pills from the first-aid kit to help ease the pain, then crudely splinted my broken wrist and bandaged my other injuries, had a long, sweet drink of a high-energy liquid from a long, red bulb, took the .441 Slean into my left hand, rose, and went back to see about Tar-hortha.

The Krith had regained consciousness, was holding his wounded, shattered left arm in his right hand. There was great pain etched in the lines of his alien face, but a kind of bitter satisfaction as well.

"You are a fool, Eric Mathers," he said in a cold, crisp voice that betrayed none of his pain, "a damned fool. You have ruined everything now. You have lost again and in a way you cannot understand. Your beloved Anglianers are all dead now and you are . . ."

I stood above the alien, my hatred for him and his kind and all they had ever done rushing up at me in a maniacal rage. I could see Sally their captive and

Gwendalfa and Freya and Faeder Baldwin and all the others dead behind me; I could see world after world after world in ruin, desolation, submission. . . .

He laughed at me.

I shot him.

Later I realized what a stupid, savage, insane thing I'd done, firing that pistol at Tar-hortha then. But I don't believe that at that moment I was quite sane. I'm not certain that anyone could have expected me to be.

But I won't try to justify my actions. I did what I did, and whatever the guilt or blame might be, I will accept it, for that and for so much more.

Tar-hortha didn't die at once, though I'm sure a man would have with that kind of a hole in his chest oozing blood and body fluids. He was in terrible pain at first and I did what I could to stanch the flow of blood and ease the pain with drugs—the Krithian metabolism is surprisingly like ours. I didn't tell him I was sorry.

When he was able to talk, weakly, feebly, not altogether coherently, he said, "I fear that yours is something of a Pyrrhic victory, Eric. I take that as a comfort."

"I don't understand," I said, standing above him, holding myself erect by sheer will, looking down at the dying Krith.

"You are alone, Eric," Tar-hortha said. "Whatever you might be, whatever powers might sometimes be behind you, you are now very much alone. There is no one to aid you, to assist you in this thing you are setting out to do, this thing the real nature of which you do not yet know."

"Then tell me, dammit!"

"I will not. The power behind you has not told you, perhaps cannot tell you. You must learn for yourself if you are able. So the Tromas have said, even as they said you would come to me in the skudder pool, that we would travel to . . ." He smiled a weak and humorless though almost human smile. "They did not predict *this*, however."

"I still don't understand."

"I regret to say that I have no sympathy for you, Eric. You would destroy my people as I have destroyed your

Anglianers. I have no love for you. No desire that the power behind you—whatever it is"—there was true anguish in his voice—"destroy my people."

Puzzled, more confused than ever, I asked, "But will you answer me three questions?"

"Why should I?"

"I can make you suffer more," I said, though inside me was a sickness and I don't believe that even then I could have brought myself to torture him. I was sick of it, so damned sick of the pain and the killing and . . .

"I could hardly suffer more," the Krith said, bitter satisfaction again. "But what are your questions?"

"One, where's Sally? Two, what are the co-ordinates of your Homeline? Three, just what the hell *are you*, you and the whole damned Krithian race?"

Tar-hortha chose his words carefully, hoarding what little strength was left to him. "I will answer one of your questions," he said. "That may bring you to the answers to the others." He paused and breathed deeply, painfully. "You will find, among the references in the pilot's compartment, a book which lists the co-ordinates of the major Lines, among them you will find listed KHL-ooo."

"That's the Krithian Homeline?" I asked.

Tar-hortha didn't answer. He closed his eyes and willed himself to die.

So I'd avenged Jock Kouzenzas. Somehow it didn't seem to mean so much now.

As Tar-hortha had said, there was a book in the pilot's compartment that listed the probability indices of several hundred major Lines, each followed by a brief description. And I wondered why I'd never seen such a book before. Was it something new, recently introduced? Or, more likely, was it something reserved only for certain skudders stationed on Prime Lines? Or . . . The speculation was pointless. I opened the book. The first entry was:

"KHL-ooo, the Krithian Homeline . . ." It gave the probability index values, co-ordinates in paratime. "This is the home and major headquarters of the Krithian race. This is the Line upon which they evolved and from which they began their exploration of the Timelines." The book was lying, of course. "It is a sacred world to the Kriths and may be entered only with express authorization from the highest authority. WARNING: UNAUTHORIZED ENTRY OF KHL-OOO WILL NOT BE TOLERATED. UNAUTHORIZED SKUDDERS WILL BE DESTROYED ON SIGHT."

I looked at the probability indices again. It *was* a long way in the T-East. A hell of a long way.

But that's where I was going, to Sally perhaps, maybe to some answers, probably to my death.

But that's where I was going.

16
To Line KHL-ooo

It was winter across the Lines, January, maybe, but more likely February—I'd lost track of days and weeks—and the broadleaf trees of the forests of the North Temperate Zone had long since lost their leaves. There was a chill across the Earths, across so many of them, as if this winter were to be an unusually long and cold one. I felt it in the marrow of my bones, this long, cold winter, yet with it was a satisfaction, and a sadness.

Before this winter was out I would know something. Or I would be dead.

My stolen skudder was moving smoothly and silently across the Lines of Time, flickering from grayness to grayness as world after world, universe after universe fell behind me.

My injuries were healed—thanks to the skudder's automedic—and I'd made some modifications of the skudder's controls and some of its systems. I added missile bays and launching tubes that could project small, nuclear-tipped rockets. I'd added defensive force-field projectors and I'd found a means of coupling additional modules into the skudder's computer, increasing its capacity several fold. I thought these things might improve my chances of staying alive. Might.

I thought I was as nearly ready to meet the Kriths on their own ground as I would ever be, though exactly what I was going to do when I got there, when I got to KHL-ooo, I didn't really know. Chances were I'd be putting myself exactly where the Kriths had wanted me for so long.

But, dammit, I was coming in under my own power. I was coming in armed to the teeth. I was coming in with a skudder that could move through space as well as though paratime. Maybe I would have *some* bargaining power.

And maybe I just didn't care any longer.

I wanted some answers.

And I was going to get them if it cost me my life.

But they'd know I'd been there.

Damn the torpedoes and full speed ahead!

The counters clicked down the number of Lines. I'd checked and rechecked the co-ordinates of the Krithian Homeline against known locations in paratime, and each time I'd seen that the settings had been right.

I'd cleaned my personal weapons, rifle and pistol. I'd dressed in a survival suit, complete with battle armor, body shield, and life-support systems.

Now, with the last few Lines flickering by, ready for just about anything the Kriths might throw at me, I sat down in the pilot's seat, popped open my helmet, smoked a final cigarette, looked out at the black-white-black-white of the worlds snapping past.

Many thoughts went through my mind then, a chaotic jumble of thoughts, feelings, memories, impressions, hopes, dreams, people, places, things. . . .

Maybe it was all going to end there, a few Lines away. Maybe I'd have the answers and maybe I wouldn't. Maybe . . .

Maybe that's what Tar-hortha had meant by a Pyrrhic victory.

Maybe.

The last flicker was coming up.

I crushed the cigarette beneath my heel, said aloud to myself, "This is it," took a deep breath, prepared my augmentation circuits should I need them, prayed, waited. . . .

Flicker!

The probability generator went to stand-by. Some systems temporarily closed down. Others opened up. The skudder had ceased its flickering.

I looked out.

I had only moments.

And what I saw in that brief span wasn't all that impressive, not the sort of thing I'd imagined of KHL-ooo during those long, sleepless nights of preparation and waiting.

What was outside the skudder, a place that in another

space/time was an area of northern Georgia, was a
scene bucolic, pastoral, a long vista of undulating landscape, carefully cropped grass, groves of fruit trees scattered here and there, a remote building that might have
been a farmhouse or might have been the temple of
some rustic god, two or three bipedal figures that at that
distance could have been humans or Kriths; nearer the
skudder, beside a stream that had, somehow, an artificial,
not-quite-natural look about it, were half a dozen white,
fluffy animals that could have been nothing but sheep,
but were something else, guarded by a big, shaggy, bright-
eyed dog upon whose back perched a winged creature
that was not a bird, something like a giant butterfly with
a body more mammalian than insect. Had I been able to
hear sounds from outside the skudder, had I thought to
turn on the external microphones, I felt that I would have
heard the sounds of real birds singing and bees buzzing.

But all that lasted for only a moment, seconds or less
than seconds.

A speaker in the panel before me, despite the fact that
my communications systems were on stand-by and not
fully activated, came to life and a harsh masculine voice
—whether human or Krithian I couldn't tell—said in
Shangalis:

"You are in violation of prime ordinances. Express
your authorization to enter KHL-ooo at once, or you will
be destroyed."

Outside the skudder there was no sign of the point of
origin of the signal, no skudder nor aircraft nor ground
car, only the sheep-things and their dog and the remoter
bipedal figures whom I thought had now turned to look
in my direction.

Without thinking it out, my hands fell to the controls
of the radio-video transmitter, and I found myself speaking as lights across the panels told me they had come to
life: "I am here under no authorization but my own," I
said. "My name is Eric Mathers, né Thimbron Parnassos,
former Timeliner agent, and I have come to ask some
questions of the Tromas. I request permission to remain
in KHL-ooo until I have accomplished that purpose."

I don't know what I was thinking at that moment, that
long awaited moment when I was finally, at last, within

the Krithian Homeline, but my hands were doing some of my thinking for me. Even as I spoke those hands were activating the firing systems of the missile launchers I'd mounted on the external hull.

"Permission denied," the voice said harshly. "You have five seconds to depart this Line."

I had no intention of leaving. My self-directed hands were now moving to the spatial positioning controls, the locomotive facilities of the skudder I'd learned to operate during the weeks since leaving the dead Tar-hortha on some unnamed, atom-blasted world in the T-West.

"You have three seconds to depart this Line," the voice said ·as the skudder, moving more quickly than conventionally propelled craft, rose vertically into the air, a quick, lurching sensation that should have left my stomach sitting on the ground below me, but didn't. Some sort of inertial compensating device?

The skudder rose several thousand yards straight up and I was preparing to move off in a horizontal direction —but which way? I had no idea of how this world was constituted politically, where might lie the centers of power, where I might find the mysterious authority that the Kriths called the Tromas.

I elected to head east, toward the coast; there, along the seaboard, in most worlds, would be the centers of population—and power.

Another set of controls was activated and the skudder leaped forward, eastward toward the coast, accelerating up to hundreds of miles an hour faster than I can tell it —but it was still too slow.

"You are judged to be in violation of prime directives and are hereby ordered destroyed," the harsh voice stabbed from the loudspeaker. . . .

. . . and from out of the sun, somehow undetected by the skudder's automatic sensing gear, came three swept-wing, teardrop-shaped craft, plummeting toward me at supersonic velocities, weapons already beginning to blaze.

What happened next was too rapid for human senses to deal with, to react to even in the X5 augmentation into which I had gone. I let this skudder's computer take over —and was damned glad it was a sophisticated one with some fine offense/defense programs.

The skudder began evasive action, darting in an arc toward the trees and the earth below, bringing from stand-by to full operational modes a set of inhibitor and deflector fields around the craft. The world outside took on a yellow-greenish hue as the fields broke apart the white sunlight, then turned the red-orange of flame as a laser beam from one of the attacking craft splattered against the fields.

Helpless and horrified, I sat and watched as the skudder leaped skyward again, its fields opening for split fractions of seconds so that the missile launchers on the outer hull could throw needles of steel and nuclear fire back at my attackers.

The skudder lurched again, an oncoming missile exploding only yards outside my paraglas dome, half-blinding me despite the defenses of the fields. I felt the heat and the shock wave, but not the awful acceleration as the skudder leaped and lunged again, spitting out more needles of death. Had it not been for the skudder's inertial compensation, I would have by then been nothing more than a red jelly spread across the inside of the pilot's compartment.

But one of my missiles had found its target, broken through the defensive fields of one of the delta-winged craft. For instants there was a new sun in the sky, only thousands of feet from the earth, yellow-white and blinding in intensity. Then it faded and became a climbing, boiling ball of superheated gas.

I had no more time for observation. The two remaining craft now began to co-ordinate their actions, directed themselves in a graceful dance across the sky until they were in a position to make simultaneous attacks upon me from widely separated directions. Their lasers blazed and they spit out their missiles as they converged on the skudder that could no longer outmaneuver them—but then no skudder had ever been designed for this sort of thing.

I gave the computer a brief command—my own defenses dropped for a moment and every missile I had left was launched as quickly as possible, two clouds composed of three-foot-long lances, propelled by small but powerful cores of solid fuel, carrying tiny, sophisticated thermonuclear warheads. I couldn't beat them, but I'd damned well . . .

Then the two aircraft bent from their trajectories toward me, swung in sharp arcs. And my computer was trying to tell me why. I saw why.

Help had arrived.

But not for me.

A behemoth skudder had appeared in the sky a few hundred feet above my own skudder, an egg-shaped monster the size of an ocean liner or a starship.

. . . and the power that drove my skudder through space and through paratime died within the bowels of the craft. Suddenly the machine was nothing more than a lifeless, powerless collection of metal and paraglas and ceramics, a heavy jumble of plates and panels and solid state circuits which happened to surround a very fragile organic creature—name of Eric Mathers.

The dead skudder began to describe a trajectory that would bring it to earth some few miles ahead, somewhere in the middle of a forest that had suddenly leaped across the horizon, accelerating as I fell at 32fps².

Again the communications loudspeaker came to life; some few, select circuits returned to power for a moment, and a new voice said, "Repeat your true name and give your former Timeliner identification number."

My voice worked, though I didn't expect it to, and I said, "Eric Mathers, born Thimbron Parnassos, former Timeliner identification number . . ."

Somewhere along in there, just as I was concluding rattling off that series of numbers that had been indelibly etched into my brain, I must have begun to black out. The ground was rushing up to meet me, the vague formlessness of the remote forest beginning to define itself into separate trees as the trajectory brought me ever nearer them, when a grayness began to creep over my vision, a remote kind of buzzing enter my ears.

But there was no time to think about that. I was going to be dead in seconds. There was only time to curse my foolishness at not having made some kind of preparations against this, some means of protecting my power sources and circuits—but then I'd had no way of knowing they could do something like this, no way of knowing how they were accomplishing it.

Dammit! My first step into the Krithian Homeline, and without batting an eye they'd canceled me out. They'd gotten me where they wanted me and now they were finishing me off.

Tar-hortha had been right. I hadn't known what the hell I was getting into.

Then the trees, turning gray in my vision, resolved themselves into leaves and branches and the egg shape of the skudder was crashing into them. . . .

I thought I was dying, and I was furious.

Mager was dead, and so was his look-alike, a fellow who'd called himself Kearns, but for a moment, as I opened my eyes and blinked them into focus, I could have sworn that they'd both been resurrected and sent to haunt me.

The two of them stood beside the bed upon which I lay, dressed in simple white clothing of an unusual cut and design. Their hair was short and they were beardless. They carried no weapons and something about them— maybe it was the way they smelled—suggested the medical profession.

They looked enough alike to be twins: slender, wiry, with sharp, angular faces lined with tiny white wrinkles that could have been scars. And neither one of them was a human being, not the way I would have then defined the term.

Once I'd gotten over the shock of seeing them, and after I realized that they weren't the ghosts of Kearns and Mager, only peas out of a very similar pod, I raised my head up enough to look around the room I was in, surprised to find that my injuries consisted of nothing more than a few bruises and abrasions.

The room was clean and antiseptic, walls and ceiling and floor of a pale green, with only a functional white cabinet and the bed on which I lay for furniture, with only one door leading out, and no windows. In addition to the antiseptic smell in the air, there was a faint, remote humming sound, like that of a distant generator, or maybe a giant air-conditioning unit.

My two companions didn't move, didn't speak, waiting for me to finish my inspection.

"Well, you didn't kill me," I said when I looked back at them.

"No, we did not," said Thing One. "I am not certain why."

We were speaking in Shangalis, of course. It came to me more naturally than the language I'd learned as a child.

"We have been instructed to keep you well," said Thing Two.

I looked at them questioningly, but didn't speak. What was there to say?

"You wonder why?" asked Thing One; Shangalis didn't come as easily to him as it did to me.

"Yeah," I said, raising myself on my elbows and feeling a surge of dizziness go through my head, but passing quickly. "But maybe I wouldn't like it if I knew."

A wooden smile came across Thing One's craggy face. "The orders are from the Tromas, Mathers," he said. "From the Tromas themselves."

"Oh, how nice," I said in as acid a tone as I could. "I'm very flattered that the Tromas show so much interest in me."

"I do not think I would feel that way if I were you," said Thing Two.

What could I say in reply to such sparkling wit? I gave him a dirty look.

I lay back on the bed, feeling more naked than dressed in the thin smock that was now my only garment, and wondered just what the hell was going to happen next.

At least I was still alive, and I hadn't much expected to be. Not that there was very much I could do right at the moment. Even if I hadn't felt as weak as a kitten, I didn't think I could accomplish very much against the two of them unarmed, not if they had the other characteristics of Mager and Kearns, and I was certain they did, augmentation and all.

And even if I could jump out of bed and overpower the two of them, where the hell could I go? Outside, no doubt, was a whole world filled with their kind and with Kriths.

I figured I'd better wait a bit and see what developed. As it turned out I didn't have to wait too long.

The two Mager types retreated to opposite walls and stood silently like turned-off machines, their hands behind their backs and their backs against the walls, both pairs of eyes remaining fixed on me.

Maybe thirty minutes went by—though at the time it seemed like hours—before the room's single door opened and in walked two individuals. I say "individuals," not people. One was a Krith, big, naked, hairless, and olive-green, and another Mager type, dressed in white and carrying a bundle under his right arm.

The Krith, a specimen even larger and uglier than the late Tar-hortha, raised a hand in greeting, smiled a toothy, wolfish smile, approached to within a few feet of my bed and stopped.

"So you are Eric Mathers," he said simply, in perfect Shangalis, yet with a kind of precision artificial even for Kriths, and I was certain for the first time in my life that Shangalis wasn't their native language, at least it wasn't his.

I raised myself on my elbows again—it's awkward as hell greeting someone from flat on your back, especially if you're not sick. "I am," I said.

"I am Cal-sarlin, a Minister to the Tromas," he said, bowing slightly, a gesture I still find ridiculous when performed by a naked monster. He glanced at the two characters who'd been keeping me company. "You may go now," he said. "He is in my charge."

The two Magers bowed in return, departed.

"Rise, Eric," Cal-sarlin said when the door had closed again. "The effects of your, shall we say, recent debacle should have worn off by now. You can rise, can you not?"

"I can."

As I slowly sat up on the bed the Mager type who'd come in with him stepped forward, presented his bundle to me. As he did I noticed a bulge under his left armpit that didn't look like a part of his anatomy. The butt of a pistol in a shoulder holster, no doubt.

"Clothing for you," Cal-sarlin explained as I sat the bundle in my lap. "I would like for you to dress."

"Why wasn't I killed?" I asked, looking up into those

deep brown eyes. "I thought unauthorized entry into KHL-ooo was supposed to bring about immediate destruction."

"It almost did for you," Cal-sarlin said, smiling a carnivorous smile again. "You were saved only in the last moments, and only because the Tromas have a special interest in you."

"How flattering," I said. "It's nice to know you're loved."

"I said 'interest,' Eric, not affection," the Krith said, still smiling the same smile. "It may be that you will find what awaits you to be less desirable than the death you might have had."

"Your words reassure me to no end."

The smile went away in annoyance. "Your flippancy will gain you nothing, Eric. I suggest you offer full and complete co-operation. Only in that way might you hope to gain anything at all."

"And what might 'anything' be?" I asked.

"Would you be so good as to dress?"

I got dressed. And what I got dressed in wasn't the antiseptic white garments I'd almost anticipated, but rather a double-breasted shirt of a design and colors you'd expect to see at a Hawaiian luau, trousers as gaudily decorated and that came to just below my knees, soft leather ankle-high boots, and a hat, the kind you're supposed to wear in the Tyrolean Alps. When I had them all on I wasn't certain I was any better dressed than I had been in the white smock, and wondered if maybe, among other things, I was the butt of a not-very-funny practical joke. Did people around here really wear this sort of thing?

Cal-sarlin didn't seem to think it was funny, but then maybe he had no sense of humor. Kriths usually don't.

"Let me advise you of this again, Eric," the Krith said. "The only thing you can possibly do to improve your fortune in any respect is to co-operate fully with the Tromas and their ministers during the forthcoming interview. Lack of co-operation will be punished. Cooperation will be rewarded, in so far as it is possible to reward one under a sentence such as yours."

I wanted to give him another wise answer, something

to show him that I wasn't afraid of his threats, but somehow I'd run out of them at the moment.

All I said was, "Okay. I'm ready."

He nodded toward his white-clad companion who opened the door for us and held it open as Cal-sarlin led the way out of the room.

17
The Tromas

I had little opportunity to observe my surroundings, to determine whether I had been held in a hospital or a prison or something entirely different from either, for Cal-sarlin led me from the room where I'd awakened down a short, empty hallway directly to a closed conveyance that somewhat resembled an elevator: a cubicle some eight feet or so on a side that began to move as soon as the doors closed behind us. The initial sensation was that of vertical movement; later there was movement in a more lateral direction, through some underground tunnel, I thought at the time.

At the end of the trip that may have been forty-five minutes long, the "elevator" made a final upward lunge and came to a stop in a low building of unusual architectural design, little more than an earth-covered mound surmounted with a high peaked roof. It served as nothing more than a terminus for the cubicle.

The Krith led me out into a parklike area between clusters of buildings, no two of which seemed to have been designed by people of the same era, or even of the same Timeline; all in all a strange conglomeration of contrasting and often conflicting architecture, as if a miniature Taj Mahal had been placed beside an Inca temple, across a grassy avenue from Saint Sophia, a few hundred yards from a pagoda on the north and a Swiss chalet on the south. Equally odd was the admixture of trees and shrubs that dotted the park area: a cluster of half a dozen carefully tended poplars separated from another cluster of date palms by trellises and arbors covered with something that might have been related to grape vines; tropical plants grew alongside vegetation from far northern regions, and interspersed were plants of types I was certain I had never seen before, plants that might not have been native to *any* Earth.

Within the parklike area, which must have covered several acres, there were, walking in twos and threes, Kriths, unclothed as Kriths always are, and men in costumes of various places and times, costumes, for the most part, brightly colored and lavishly decorated, costumes Burmese and Peruvian, Elizabethan and Malayan, Tahitian and Roman.

I say "men" though I'm not at all certain that some other word from some other language might have been more appropriate; they were persons of the Mager type as I'd begun calling them in my mind, all of them slender and wiry, with lined angular faces, with expressions on their faces, looks in their eyes that I was certain I would never be able to read. Oddly enough, it seemed to me at the time in this bucolic, almost pastoral setting, a number of them appeared to be armed, for here and there under their clothing were bulges that had distinctive, gunlike shapes.

Few of them seemed to be aware of us as Cal-sarlin led me through the park and down a path, dark and shadowy under towering oaks, that led out of the park and toward a low, rambling white building that stood alone some distance away.

Finally Cal-sarlin volunteered some information: the place we were approaching, he told me in Shangalis, was something that could be roughly translated into English as "the palace of the Tromas," or could be translated as "the place wherein dwell the all-wise Mothers." This was the first time I'd heard the word "mother" used in connection with the Tromas, and I wondered exactly what that meant. I didn't ask Cal-sarlin. I didn't figure he'd answer.

As we crossed the last few hundred feet to the entrance of "the palace of the Tromas" and the armed, uniformed Mager guards who stood silently on either side of it, a flight of dartlike aircraft swept across the sky, half a dozen silvery shapes that had a very military look about them, revealing no sign of whatever propulsion systems they used. I was becoming convinced that KHL-ooo was not quite the idyllic place it might look upon first glance.

Then we were at the doors and Cal-sarlin was speaking to the guards in a language I didn't understand. The guards saluted with their weapons, doors opened and we entered.

Inside, "the palace of the Tromas" was plain and quite the sort of thing you might expect of those who supposedly are the wise and ancient givers of guidance to a race whose power spans uncounted hundreds of Earths. It wasn't the sort of thing I'd expected, anyway, though I'm not really certain of what sort of ostentatious show of power and wealth I'd expected. I don't suppose I'd given it much thought.

Cal-sarlin led me across a broad, empty entrance hall, undecorated save for a wall-size inscription in a language I couldn't read, and then down a long corridor to where we were met by two other Kriths, these two wearing what I at first thought to be some sort of jewelry: silvery disks maybe four inches in diameter and half an inch thick suspended around their necks by fine silvery chains. Later I found out what they were, after Cal-sardin had donned his and I had been given one to wear.

The Krith who brought me there bowed slightly toward the two, who bowed in return, and then introduced me to them: one was named Vor-kawin and the other Ces-karlet. They were also "Ministers to the Tromas."

Vor-kawin now seemed to become the spokesman for the Krithian trio, telling me that, "This is a very great honor for you, Eric Mathers, though I am not altogether certain why the Tromas have summoned you. I have some inkling, perhaps.

"Nevertheless, remember your place. The number of other humans"—there seemed to be a bad taste in his mouth when he said that last word—"who have been given audience with the Tromas could be counted on the fingers of one hand. It is an experience you will never forget."

He paused, seemed to ruminate for a moment, scratched himself as Kriths often do, then continued. "I doubt that there is very much I can say to prepare you for your first meeting with the Tromas. I could try to explain to you who and what the Tromas are, but then you will learn that for yourself very shortly. I could try to answer for you some of the questions your *people* have been asking about us for many decades, but again those answers will soon be obvious to you. I would warn you of the power and the wisdom and the insight possessed by the Tromas, but once again this will all soon be made known to you by the power of experience, which is far greater than mere words.

"So I will say only this to you, Eric Mathers: be fully aware now and henceforth, you are about to enter the presence of the most powerful and most wise beings in all the Timelines, the rulers of the Krithian race, the framers and the guardians of all the plans and hopes and dreams and aspirations of our people. Remember at all times that a single word from the Tromas is enough to bring about the destruction of an entire world.

"You will be expected to behave with the proper respect." There was a long pause which could only be described as pregnant. "Failure on your part to do so will bring about the most dire results. Do you understand?"

As much as I hate to admit it now, Vor-kawin had put into me exactly the fear and awe he'd hoped to. I nodded, said, "Yeah, I understand."

"Let us proceed," Vor-kawin said and led the way, with Cal-sarlin and Ces-karlet walking on either side of me. I wouldn't have been surprised if there'd been a pair of Mager types with big, heavy guns bringing up the rear, but there seemed to be none of *them* inside the building.

The plain, functional hallway down which we walked made two sharp turns, one right and the other left, and finally brought us up to a pair of doors, decorated with obscure carvings resembling the inscription I'd seen in the entrance hallway, and bracketed by two more Kriths wearing silvery medallions. They were not introduced, did not speak; they merely opened the doors and let us enter into the presence of the Tromas.

Whatever I'd expected, whatever I might have imagined the almost mythical Tromas to be, I wasn't prepared for what I saw when Vor-kawin led me through those doors and into their presence.

There were about a dozen of them; I never did count the exact number. But that number seemed to fill the large room they occupied, seemed to fill it both physically and in some other way, some psychological fashion, and though my initial sensation was one of revulsion, I was never totally unaware of that second kind of presence, that almost overpowering psychological aura, that sense of power that filled the air, and even though the Tromas themselves didn't always seem to be its source, I'm certain they were.

I'll try to give a physical description, though I feel a terrible inadequacy of words. Oh, but could I trade a thousand of them for just one photograph!

Imagine, if you will, a Krith: a naked male mammal, erect and biped, standing in excess of six feet tall, coloring ranging from sable-brown to olive, a big, egg-shaped head, enormous eyes like brown marbles, below the eyes a nostril row and below that a large, toothy mouth, along the sides of the head feathery membranes something like the gills of a fish, almost no neck, broad shoulders leading down humanlike arms to five-fingered hands, broad chest, flat stomach, manlike genitals, short legs, webbed feet, humanlike buttocks sprouting a prehensile tail like that of a monkey.

That's the sort of Krith I'd always known before, a male Krith.

Now I learned that there were females to the race, a few at least.

Now, with that Krithian image in your mind, remove the male sex organs, add vagina and breasts, keep it still naked, still hairless.

Now add five hundred pounds of flesh and a hundred years of age.

Got that in your mind? A gross, deformed series of mounds of flesh, wrinkled in places, but mostly bulging blubber, so heavy that it is unable to get around under its own power, but must be carried from place to place on wheeled, electrical carts; sable or olive sheen blotched here and there with liver spots; face almost obscured by folds of fat, holding in deep sockets eyes still bright and brown.

I couldn't help my feelings of revulsion; I don't think anyone could have. But I also felt a kind of unwilling respect; I still felt that aura in the air, that sense of power. I was awed, in several ways.

Foremost of the Tromas—the word is the same singular and plural—was the most ancient-looking one of all, one whose once-olive coloring had gone to gray and purple splotches. This one spoke in a high, twittering, almost girl-like voice, and in a language I'd heard only once before.

The medallion hanging from a chain around my neck began to speak as well, in Shangalis—some sort of translation device, probably hooked through a radio linkage to a computer which did all the work. Neat.

What the medallion said was this: "So you are Eric Mathers."

I nodded, bowed, said, "Yes, that was the name I used on my last Timeliner assignment. I've grown rather accustomed to it." As I spoke I heard alien words from the Tromas' own medallion in a voice that resembled my own.

"Then that is the name by which we shall call you." A pause, a wave of a gross hand. "Vor-kawin," the Tromas said, "you and your companions may depart. We wish to speak with this one alone."

"Is that wise?" he asked, and added some word that the translator was unable to convert into Shangalis, a word that carried respect and sounded something like *"Kiotogivan,"* yet rolling and twittering. "You know this man's history. He is dangerous and is not to be trusted." Vor-kawin paused, then added the clencher, "And he has been responsible for *killing two of our people* and others of the *Kanombajil.*"

"We are aware of that, Vor-kawin." The translated voice sounded a bit peeved. "But we do not foresee danger at his hands. We are safe. Leave us."

"Yes, Kiotogivan," Vor-kawin said, bowed, and with Cal-sarlin and Ces-karlet, left the large room.

"You know who we are?" the old Tromas asked when the doors had closed and I was alone with the dozen or so *female* Kriths.

"I think so," I said. "You are females of the race."

"The females of the race," the Tromas said. "The only living females of our race."

I was stunned at that moment, shocked, but after another moment I found that I wasn't all that surprised. I was beginning to understand why I'd never seen a female Krith before, or ever met anyone who had.

"You find that surprising, do you not?" the translator on my chest asked.

"I do."

"We are all pregnant. We each give birth at least once a year. Yet still we are few, terribly few to maintain a race as widely spread as ours, is that your thought?"

"It is."

"There are other means of maintaining our race, of propagating our species, not always satisfactory, but available and used. It was not always so. Once our chances of survival were minimal. You might find it a wonder that there are Kriths in this universe at all."

"Other means?" I asked.

The ancient-looking female Krith nodded her great head, smiled through her folds of fat, seemed again to be speaking not only for herself but for the silent, motionless others in the room: "Laboratory methods, you might say. But all that is unimportant in our present conversation, Eric. There are other things of much greater significance."

"Yes, there are," I said quickly when she paused, wishing I could sit down, but I hadn't been offered a chair and was forced to remain standing. "I came here to ask some questions, to KHL-ooo, that is, and I would appreciate very much the opportunity of asking them." Politeness to the Tromas seemed to be in order; I'd been warned that I'd better be polite.

"We will answer some of those questions without your asking them, Eric," the speaker for the Tromas said, "and the others we will, perhaps, allow you to ask later, but there are some things we would like to know about you."

"About me?"

The gross head nodded again. "We have many questions about you, Eric Mathers. Many questions."

"I'll answer them if I can."

"Very well." There was a long, thoughtful pause. "Perhaps you are aware of the reputation we have among our own people of being able to see into the future. Is this so?"

"I've heard Kriths say things about the Tromas that sounded as if there were precognitive abilities involved."

"Carefully put! You tread this ground with caution."

She smiled. "And it is true that we do have certain, as you say, 'precognitive abilities,' among other, er, 'gifts.' In some place/times we might be called 'clairvoyant,' though that is an awkward and sloppy term, as are most others connected with psionic abilities. You humans know little about such things, but—alas!—*we* know but little more, though we sense the gifts when they are bestowed upon us, and use them."

There followed another long, thoughtful pause. Since I didn't know in which direction the Tromas was heading, I didn't speak, but waited.

"Our psionic abilities, it would seem," she went on at last, "are something to help offset other handicaps, some of which are now obvious to you, I am certain. We of the Tromas and our ancestors of the Tromas before us have made every effort to put these abilities to use for the benefit of our race. It has been said that these abilities have enabled our race to survive and to achieve the place in the Timelines it holds today. That may be an overstatement, but I feel that there is some truth in it. We are proud of what we have done for our people, and hope to continue to assist our race in the achievement of its goals."

In the pause that followed, I threw in one of the things I wanted to ask: "And just exactly what are the goals of your race?" Maybe my voice was a little harsher than I'd intended.

The Tromas smiled again. "In time, Eric. First, our questions. We know much about you: your birth name and the place of your birth, the history of your younger years before entering the service of the Timeliners, your training there, your operations as an agent of the Timeliners, and your final defection. Up until the time of your defection, up until the time of your captivity in that place called Staunton by the Paratimers, your record was a good one; you showed devotion and ability. You were an *almost* exemplary example of your profession. Then all that changed.

"We are not asking you to tell us why you defected, if 'defected' is the correct word. We know of your flirtation with the Paratimers, and of your subsequent disillusionment with them as well. We know *why* you have done many of the things you have done in the months since your rescue from Staunton, but we are not certain *how* you have done them."

"How?" I asked. "What do you mean?"

"You are not gifted with psionic powers yourself. We are certain of that. If you were, this would have been detected years ago, and if not then, we would have known it when you came into our presence just now. You are not psionic, yet sometimes you behave as if you were."

I started to ask what she meant by that, then began to have some inkling of what she was getting at, things about me—or things that happened to me—that had disturbed other Kriths. I let her go on.

"There are times when there is another force about you, something that connects itself with you and helps you alter the normal course of events." A pause. "You should have died in Staunton, you know. In reviewing the events, in immersing ourselves in the progression of time in that time/place, all things point to your death then and there. But you did not die. Why?"

Without giving me a chance to answer, she went on in a sterner, more anxious voice. "You should have believed the things Kar-hinter told you about the Cross-Line Worlds, you should have accepted the mental programming given you. But you did not. Why?

"Again you should have died in the so-called Albigensian Lines. You did not. Why?

"Closer in time: How is it, against all odds, when you escaped from Tar-hortha's moving skudder, you found yourself in a Line where there was another Outtimer known to you, who befriended you—when he should have been your enemy—and enabled you to gain access to another skudder? What got you *there*, Eric Mathers?

"Even among the Anglianers, there were times when you *should have died*, but you did not. Why?

"We want to know why!"

The eyes that looked at me now were not soft and warm, brown and friendly but cold and hard, a bitter, frozen fire.

"The Shadowy Man," I said, not knowing exactly what I meant or what I was trying to explain.

"The Shadowy Man!" the Tromas said. "What is the Shadowy Man?"

"I don't know," I said simply, honestly.

"You do not," the Tromas agreed. "We are aware of that. Yet you must have feelings about this thing, some theories, perhaps."

"Feelings, yes," I said. "But I don't have any theories. I don't know what he is or why he has—well—befriended me."

"Tell us about your feelings then."

"Well, my initial sensations, I suppose, were fear. It was like seeing a ghost or something. Yet, there was something familiar about it—him, I began calling it in my mind, for the Shadowy Man is male and more or less human."

"Familiar?" the Tromas asked. "In what way?"

"I don't know. There was just a sense of familiarity, friendliness, as if he were someone I'd known once, or—or might know in the future."

"Ah!" the Tromas cried. "'. . . in the future.' You had a sense of futurity about him then?"

I nodded. "Each time I encountered him I got a greater sense of, well, 'time,' as if time, the future and the past, were all wrapped up in him."

"Is there anything more?"

"Nothing I can put into words."

"Yet you have this feeling of *time*."

"I do."

"There is another falsehood that you and countless others have come to accept, a falsehood which has been 'proved' mathematically to a vast number of scientists."

"And what's that?" I asked.

"That travel through time is impossible, travel from one point in time to an earlier point in time."

I looked at her.

"Time travel *is* possible, Eric, travel from one location in *linear* time to another location, future and/or past. It is something we do not wish to become common knowledge. It is a secret we must keep at the peril of our racial lives."

I'm not certain that I believed her then, but I said, "Why tell me?"

"We do not believe that you will be in a position to reveal this to others."

"Oh," I said. The sword was still dangling precariously over my head.

"And the Shadowy Man, whatever he or *it* is, is aware of the possibility of time travel—is, in fact, a time traveler or something somehow akin to that. That is one of the reasons we fear him—and you."

For a moment I thought I had misunderstood her. They were afraid of me? The Kriths with all their power, all those vast worlds under their domination, were afraid of *me?* It was almost laughable. Almost.

"We can tell you that, Eric. We fear you—you and your Shadowy Man because you are a factor in muddying the waters of the future. Events that involve *you* and this—this Shadowy Man do not turn out as they should." Perhaps a bit petulantly: "What good is it to be precognitive if the futures you see do not work out as they are seen?"

What could I say to that?

"Eric Mathers, you are a danger to us." The words were spoken in a voice strong and harsh, a voice accustomed to exercising power and demanding respect. "You make it difficult for us to perceive the events that are to come, and that is one of our foremost functions. Yet"—the voice softened just a bit, a note of sadness entered, maybe—"we can still recognize some things about the future, some things involving you and this Shadowy Man that, shall we say, manipulates you?"

"I don't like that term, 'manipulates.' "

"Yet you are being manipulated by him."

"Okay, maybe I am, but that's not half so bad as being manipulated by Kriths."

"Are you certain?"

I didn't answer that one.

"What we see is some great power behind this Shadowy Man, some great power that may not yet have even come into existence, that is reaching back through time to alter events—perhaps it is altering events in order to bring itself into existence."

"What?" I asked involuntarily.

"This is a universe of probabilities, Eric, *Probabilities.*

Higher orders and lower orders of probability. It is a universe in which the *future* can reach back into the past in order to increase its *probability*. Lower orders of probability. That is so! Kriths know that.

"This power," she went on after a short pause to allow me to digest what she had just said, "is reaching back in time, we believe, in order to manipulate you and those you come in contact with toward some dark future end that is involved with, in some way we do not yet fathom, the *possible* destruction of the entire Krithian race!

"Your Shadowy Man is trying to kill us, Eric."

"That's what Tar-hortha said," I muttered almost to myself, the words of the dying Krith coming back to me.

The Tromas nodded. "Exactly how this Shadowy Man intends to accomplish this goal, if in fact this is his goal, we do not know. We are merely aware, in a vague and often insubstantial way, that this is so."

"And you blame me?" I asked.

She nodded, but with no great zest. "We know your feelings toward us, Eric Mathers. We know you have no love for us, that you would prefer that we did not 'meddle' in human affairs. You do not know our goals, but you suspect them to be sinister and you believe that we do not have the best interests of the human race in mind. Is this not so?"

"It's so."

"You believe we have lied to you and to thousands of others. You believe the future danger to mankind and Krith to be a falsehood. You believe we have told the 'Greatest Lie' and many, many lesser ones."

"That's also so."

"In some respects, you are correct. In some you are not." There was a long pause, and during it I felt something in the air, an electrical charge, perhaps, and yet not that. What it was I couldn't be certain, but I had the feeling that, below or beyond my senses of perception, a complex conversation—and a judgment—was going on between the members of the Tromas, the gross and ugly female members of the race of Kriths.

Finally their speaker addressed me again: "Well, Eric, we will tell you some things few humans have ever been privileged to know."

The way she said it had the sound of another nail being driven into my coffin.

"We will tell you a tale," she began. "There is a certain human Timeline, the designation and co-ordinates of which I will not tell you; that is very carefully guarded by the Kriths and their Companions. Even the highest ranking Timeliners are unaware of it. It is one world that we will allow no tampering with, no inrush of Outtimers, no alterations. The natives of that Line are unaware of alternative Earths and shall be kept that way for some time into the future—until *we* are ready. It is a very important world to us—exactly how important I will explain to you.

"This particular world is more technologically advanced than are most of the Lines. Though its inhabitants are unaware of other worlds in paratime, they are well aware of other worlds in space. They are already, in this year, planting colonies on the Moon and Mars and soon will go on to the stars. Within a few decades they will invent a means of circumventing the speed of light and the stellar universe will be open to them. They will, in a little over a hundred years, begin to establish colonies on worlds outside the Solar System.

"They will encounter many obstacles among the stars. There are few worlds as hospitable to humankind as is this Earth. Most of the planets they will find will be forever beyond the reach of human colonization, and many of the others will not be suitable, for one reason or another, for settlement by human stock of the kind evolved so tediously over the ages.

"Yet the technologies of these people are not limited to those of space flight alone. They have also made great advances in the life sciences. They are—or will be—masters of biology, of genetics. Genetic engineering—the manipulation of the chromosomes of newly fertilized human ova —will be one of their accomplishments. With radiation and with microscopic instruments, with transplantation of DNA, it will be possible for them to vastly alter the genetic patterns of the unborn, to create from offsprings of humankind other sentient beings who may not always look as you think humans should look, descendants of humankind adapted to environments far colder or far hotter, far dryer or far wetter than any in which *you* and people like you could survive.

"They will seed the star-worlds with *people* of this kind."

. Nothing of what she was saying was new to me. I'd seen or heard of all these things before on other Lines, but there was something about the way she was stringing them together that made a chill run up and down my spine, that brought a flat, dry nervousness into my mouth. I had some idea of what she was getting at.

"You are familiar with the Breston Star Catalog?" she asked.

I nodded. "It's in use on a number of the more advanced worlds," I said, "though few of those people are aware of the Breston Survey, at least by that name."

"Just so," the Tromas said. "There is a K0 star some twelve light-years from Earth, a star orange in color, with an absolute magnitude of +0.8. A pleasant enough star. It is listed in the Breston Catalog as UR-427-51. On some Lines it is listed as Beta in the constellation of Gemini, the zodiacal sign of the Twins. It is the companion star of Castor and is often called Pollux. You may be familiar with that star, if you have ever been given to stargazing.

"Its fourth planet is of greater size than Earth and is largely covered by water. It is a very cloudy world, given to vast and terrible electrical storms. It would not be a pleasant place for the likes of you.

"Yet, it is a world rich in resources, rich in life, mostly aquatic—multitudes of swimming creatures abound in its vast seas. It is a world that some found—will find, I should say—most interesting, and one suitable for habitation by properly adapted, genetically modified colonists.

"Someday in the future the people of the Line we told you of will find it desirable, for reasons that are of no great interest to you or to us now, to plant a colony of properly modified human stock on that world.

"They will do so. It will have fateful consequences for the future, I assure you."

She paused for a long while as if thinking carefully over what she would say next.

"Eric, I will tell you another story before I conclude

this one, for the two stories must come together in the
end, or we fear their meanings will not be cicar to you.

"This universe, this universe of universes, of parallel
worlds, of alternative Timelines is a more fragile thing
than you might think, far more fragile than wɛ have ever
revealed. It appears that this universe of universes of ours
is not as utterly vast as we might like to think, not as
limitless in its resources. There is, in a way that you might
have never imagined, a very real Law of Conservation of
Matter/Energy. The universe is limited in its resources.
That is, it cannot go on forever spawning Timeline after
Timeline after Timeline. There are limits! And once
those limits are past, there will be disaster."

I was trying not to form judgments, not to come to conclusions. On the one hand there was a sense of sincerity,
of total and complete honesty exuded by the o.d female
Krith, yet, on the other hand, over the years the Kriths
had told so many lies, so many lies that had seemed to be
totally convincing, I found it hard to credit truth to anything a Krith said without hard objective proof to back it
up. And yet . . . this wasn't an ordinary Krith; this being
before me represented the masters of wisdom of their
race, the fountainhead of their plans, the guardians of
their knowledge and maybe also their most accomplished
liars?

I wasn't believing or disbelieving yet. I wasn't even certain I fully understood what I was being told.

"Try to imagine this, Eric," the speaker for the Tromas
was going on. "In the beginning, when the universe first
came into being, when there was only one master Timeline and it existed in and of itself, it contained in itself all
the chronal or parachronal energy, all the temporal potential that would ever exist. Then as the Lines began
branching, as the various alternative worlds came into being, that temporal potential began being divided among
them."

"I understand that much," I said in the pause that followed. "The various probability potentials, East, West, positive, negative, are what make passage from Timeline to
Timeline possible."

"That is correct," the Tromas said. "But have you ever
considered that each succeeding Timeline, as history

progresses, is lower in potential than those which had existed earlier?"

"Of course," I said, not yet realizing the full implications.

"And that the universe *is* limited?"

"Yes," I said. "We know that the universe isn't really infinite, but—"

"Something is either infinite or it is finite, Eric," the Tromas said with a voice like steel. "If something is infinite there is no end, *ever*. If it is finite there is a limit that, sooner or later, must be reached.

"The probability energy, one might say, of the universe is large, large beyond imagining, yet it is not infinite, and for billions of years it has been spreading itself thinner and thinner as more and more Timelines come into being to further subdivide that potential. The introduction of sentient life into the universe some tens of thousands of years ago greatly accelerated that process, a process that continues to accelerate as intelligent life spawns more and more alternatives, more and more probabilities."

It began to dawn on me what she—they?—were getting at. "You're trying to tell me that sooner or later the universe is going to—what?—run out of probability potential or something?"

"Not exactly that, Eric. There was so much parachronal energy available at the beginning of the universe and there is just as much available now—the laws of entropy, of increasing disorder, as they are normally understood, do not have full application regarding parachronal energy, since forces can, in a sense, reverse or reduce the amount of *parachronal entropy* in the universe. What I mean is that there is now no more nor no less probability potential available than there was, it is just spread more thinly."

"Are you saying then that there will come a time when that potential is spread between too many Timelines?"

"Exactly, Eric, and when that time comes, the laws of conservation of energy—or something very like them—will come into play to rearrange the probability indices of the Timelines."

"What?" I asked, getting lost with that one.

"In order to maintain itself—though not exactly in the

forms to which we have become accustomed—the universe will have to make major readjustments within itself.

"Timelines vary in their probability, Eric. Some are *more likely* than others, more *probable*, and possess, even now, greater values of parachronal energy than do Lines of lesser likelihood."

"I think I follow that," I said, finding that, despite myself, I *was* believing her.

"Those with lesser likelihood, with lower orders of probability will *cease to exist* and their parachronal energy will be redistributed among the Lines of higher orders of probability. That is to say that a vast number of Timelines will cease to exist in order that a smaller number, with greater likelihoods, will be able to continue to exist."

"I see," I said, not altogether certain that I saw it at all.

"All that I had been saying is a great simplification, Eric. Let me qualify it by saying this: there are *indications* that the universe has reached this sort of situation a number of times in the past, the *remote* past as humans and Kriths measure the passage of time, and has, in each case, reordered itself, achieving greater simplification and less entropy, reduced the number of existing Timelines, and increased their individual parachronal potentials."

"And this has something to do with the Kriths' master plan?" I asked.

"This has *everything* to do with our 'master plan,' Eric," the Tromas said. "Let me return to my original 'fable,' if I may."

I nodded. There didn't seem much to say at this point.

"Someday in the not-too-distant future, the inhabitants of a certain Line will establish a colony on the fourth planet of UR-427-51, a large, aquatic world given to vast electrical storms. Those who make up this colony will be of modified human stock, adapted to a very wet climate, a thick atmosphere, a higher gravitational field than Earth's and to a constant barrage of atmospherical electrical energy.

"Even for them, those genetically modified colonists, it will not be a pleasant world, and they will often dream of the Earth they left behind, the Earth to which they will never be allowed to return—even though, with minor adaptations, they could thrive in Earth's more benign climate. They are exiles, never really at home on the world they have been· given, compelled to drag out their lives amid swamps, rain, and lightning in order to provide those on Earth with luxuries and delicacies they could well do without."

At this point her tense shifted from the future to the past. I didn't comment. I thought I understood.

"In a few more decades other things became apparent to these colonists, other even more unpleasant things. The genetic engineers on Earth had not done their job as well as they might have. There was a flaw, several flaws in the genetic patterns of the colonists. One was a sex-linked defect, carried by the males, but passed on to the females, one that caused a terribly high infant-mortality rate among the females of this new subspecies, and that left those who survived with glandular problems even the most sophisticated endocrinologists could not have remedied."

Of course I'd suspected who these modified-human colonists were. Now it was confirmed.

"Other genetic flaws showed up with the passage of time, even some th·t were. in the long run, beneficial. The females that survived the traumas of birth, that survived the effects of glands run wild, seemed to possess certain abilities not yet fully understood back on Earth, psionic abilities, limited powers of telepathy among themselves, the power to gain glimpses of the future—and to see that there was not a single, simple future, but a multitude of them, all existing simultaneously, real and valid.

"The colonists, in their rain-drenched huts in the swamps of UR-427-51-IV saw stretching to the parachronal East and West of them a multitude of alternative worlds, and dreamed of them, dreamed of escape, of flight to other Lines of Time where they were the masters and not the slaves of the *normal people* back on Earth.

"And they began questing about for a means of achieving those desires.

"You are following us, Eric?"

"I'm following you, but I'm wondering where you're going."

"You shall see.

"Decades went by, desolate, unhappy decades, until the colonists discovered that they had the power they sought right within themselves—the power to escape the world-frame that held them.

"You might consider this a coincidence too great to be countenanced, a wildly improbable coincidence not worth crediting if you did not have the living evidence before you of its truth.

"Yet, Eric, it is a coincidence only in one way of looking at it. There were a number of Timelines on which UR-427-51-IV was colonized in this fashion—Timelines branching from the very fact it was colonized—and on most of those Lines, on all of them but one, the colonists were doomed to a servile existence until Earth tired of them and forgot to send them essential supplies and the colonies died out.

"On one of these possible worlds, on one out of many, the right combination of factors existed, the right genetic *flaws* came together to produce what might be called a 'benign mutation' had normal evolutionary processes been in operation. In one of the UR-427-51-IV's these genetic flaws within the neural organs originally engineered to help the colonists cope with the vast electrical potentials within the atmosphere of the planet provided the means of escape—the ability to *skud* across the Timelines which the deformed, but psionic females had discovered.

"The Kriths were born."

The Tromas fell silent. I looked into her great brown eyes and, despite myself, I found myself believing every word she'd said. Somehow, despite all reason, everything she'd said made sense.

"We will try to keep the rest as brief as possible. Time is running short.

"In a nutshell, Eric: with this newly found ability, these abilities, our ancestors were able to psionically commandeer a supply ship from Earth and in it returned to their home planet. When there, as a collective group numbering only some several hundred, they began to skud across the Lines of Time in search of a suitable Timeline to call home.

"After some searching, this Line, this very world upon

which we are presently living, was found, far to the T-East and here, for a time, we settled. All would have been well for the descendants of those original Kriths, save for the precognitive abilities we females possess.

"In the long years that followed we peered into the future, we studied and researched our powers, and looked farther and farther into time to come, and at last we saw that, at some point in the future, exactly when is unknown, more than a few hundred, but less than a few thousand, years from now, the universe will be forced to 'reorder' itself along lines of fewer alternative worlds.

"*And* we saw that the Timeline that had given birth to the Kriths would be among those worlds, those Lines with too low a probability to remain in existence after the reordering. Timelines would wink out of existence as if they had never been, our Line of origin with them—and we ourselves as well.

"The race of Kriths had too low an order of probability to exist *after* the reordering."

"My God!" I said despite myself. Now I understood. If she wasn't lying. And I didn't believe she was.

"Perhaps you see now, Eric, why we have been doing what we have been doing. It is not so much to enslave mankind, as to save ourselves, to reorder as many of the Timelines as possible along lines that would not have existed without Kriths, to weave the Krithian race as firmly as possible into as many worlds as we can—in short, to create the highest possible probability for the Krithian race."

"This almost makes sense," I said, more to myself than to the Tromas.

"How it was we discovered the one Timeline that had achieved true time travel I will not go into, nor how it was that we, our entire race, migrated back in time hundreds of years in order to begin our 'remodeling' as early as possible. You must merely accept these things as so, as you have seen for yourself."

"But . . ." I stammered, a thousand other questions bursting into my mind.

"The time allowed for our interview grows short, Eric. Ask only your most important questions."

I fought to bring my jumbled thoughts into some sort of

order. There seemed no time to ask detailed questions, nor to form moral judgments. Later—if I had a later—I would take time to do that. Now . . .

"The Paratimers?" I asked. "What are they and—"

"We can tell you almost nothing about them, Eric. Our knowledge is nearly as limited as yours. Even our psionic abilities cannot reach far enough across the Lines of Time to locate their place/time of origin or to determine their real motives. We only know these things: they *are not* human nor are they likely to be of human stock; they are the sworn enemies of the Kriths and their plans, and perhaps of all mankind as well; and if they were to have their way and restructure the Lines to suit *their* purposes, *we* would lose much of the probability we have worked for so long to create. We cannot allow that to happen. We *will* find means of stopping the Paratimers."

There was finality in her voice, both in regard to the Paratimers and in regard to my questions about them, I thought.

"I came to KHL-ooo," I began in the silence she left me, "for two reasons. One was to ask—"

"We know the reasons, Eric," the Tromas said. "We have answered all the questions we may. When you leave here, you will be taken to the place where Sally Beall von Heinen awaits you."

"And then?" I asked, hoping for one more answer, hoping . . .

"We have not taken this time to speak to a man who will soon be dead, Eric Mathers. It is not *our* intention to have you taken from this place and be put to death."

"What is your intention?"

She smiled a long, languid smile that was somehow very out of place on that gross face, and I wondered what a female Krith would look like without those "genetic flaws" she'd spoken of.

"There are things about you *we* want to know, things you yourself cannot answer for us—and we want to meet this Shadowy Man of yours. We would like to talk with him —or it—or *them*. It may be that our goals are not as mutually irreconcilable as might first appear. There are perhaps mutual goals to which we can all aspire."

"Then I am to be kept as a prisoner?"

"A prisoner, yes. But we will make your captivity as pleasant as possible—and as pleasant as you will allow."

"I seemed to have heard that somewhere before."

"Among the Paratimers in Staunton?"

I nodded.

"Then there is nothing more we can say," the Tromas, in a collective voice, said.

The doors behind me opened and three Kriths, Calsarlin, Vor-kawin, and Ces-karlet entered.

"Come with us, Eric," Vor-kawin said.

I did.

What else could I do?

And hadn't the Tromas said that Sally was waiting?

18
Sally Again!

Cal-sarkin led me from the Palace of the Tromas. Vorkawin and Ces-karlet, quiet and perhaps even respectful toward me after my interview with the Tromas—an interview during which they seemed to have expected me to be struck dead or something—gave us a terse good-by, remaining behind to minister to the Tromas, or whatever it was they did for a living.

"We have been informed that your execution has been stayed," Cal-sarlin told me as we walked down a long, narrow path through towering arbors that bore flowering plants that resembled roses, a little, leaving the palace on the side opposite the one we entered, "postponed indefinitely. The Tromas appear to have plans for you."

"So it would appear," I said, my voice as noncommittal as I could make it.

"Do you know what these plans are, Eric?"

Was he asking just to see if I knew? Or did he want to know himself?

"Well," I began, "it seems that the Tromas want me to help them get in touch with a friend of mine."

"And you are going to do it?"

I shrugged. "It would seem I have little choice but to co-operate but, to tell you the truth, I don't know how to get in touch with him any more than they do."

"A friend, you say?"

"In a manner of speaking."

The pseudoroses gave way to a large, circular grassy area dotted here and there with exotic, fragrant shrubs. The path led across the circle, through a cluster of willow-like trees to what at first appeared to be nothing more than a low mound of earth covered with grass and flowering plants. But it had a door in it.

In the sky above us birdlike creatures sang, and beyond

them, farther away, a delta-winged craft flashed in the sunlight, went on toward a distant horizon.

"Would this be the one called 'the Shadowy Man'?" my Krithian companion asked.

"It would."

Since leaving the presence of the Tromas I had been trying to avoid looking at the Krith, at any Krith. I didn't want to look at them, to see them in the new light cast by the revelations of "the guardians of Krithian wisdom."

But I couldn't help myself.

I *knew* the Tromas hadn't been lying, not this time.

The Kriths *were* human beings, or their ancestors had been. They were the descendants of *my kind,* modified almost beyond recognition by genetic manipulation. A new and different species, in some ways superior to *us,* in some ways with abilities far beyond those of mankind, yet in other ways so terribly handicapped I found it hard to believe they'd survived at all.

And when my eyes, despite themselves, strayed to the naked form of the Krith who walked beside me, I saw the resemblances, the evidence of their kinship to my people that had been there all along, which I had ignored all these years, which so many people had ignored.

They are bigger than us, and colored differently, with features and anatomical characteristics that varied from ours, yet on a moonlit night, from a distance of only a few yards, it would have been difficult to distinguish a large naked man from a large naked Krith, if you didn't happen to see the Krith's prehensile tail or his absence of ears or one of the other minor characteristics that would show up in silhouette.

Yet physically—and, I realized, maybe psychologically too—they had more in common with us than they didn't have.

Dammit! I should have known all along.

All the facts had been there. Except for this theory of "Universal Timeline Probability Potential Reordering" or whatever the hell you wanted to call it, everything the Tromas had told me had been out in plain sight for years. I'd known about Timelines that had starflight. I'd known Timelines that had mastered genetic engineering. I'd known about human adaptations to hostile environments. I'd known about . . . All of it!

Yet I'd never put all the separate pieces together to come up with the Kriths.

I wondered if anyone else had.

And if they had, what had become of them?

Squelched by the Kriths?

"This woman, this Sally," Cal-sarlin was asking me as these things were running through my mind, "is she really worth the danger you have put yourself in?"

"I think she is," I said, though Sally was but one of the two big reasons I'd come to KHL-ooo.

"I am no judge of your women, of course," the Krith said. I wondered what he meant by that.

We were nearing the mound at the end of the path. The one with the door in it.

"I am taking you to her now," he said. "That was my instruction."

"I was given to understand that," I said.

The mound's door opened automatically and we stepped into another of those elevatorlike cubicles. The door closed behind us and Cal-sarlin spoke a command in his alien language. The cubicle moved downward and then horizontally under the earth.

"I gather that you maintain that this Shadowy Man is as much a mystery to you as to us, is that so?" the Krith asked.

"That's so."

"Yet, this power has befriended you in the past?"

"That's so too."

"You are alive only through the agency of this Shadowy Man?"

I nodded. I didn't want to say "That's so" again.

"Yet you have no idea who or what he is?"

"I have ideas. Hundreds of them. But none that makes sense."

"And the Tromas expect the Shadowy Man to appear to you again, and they will then interrogate him?"

"Something like that, I suppose."

"You will go along with this?"

"Have I any choice?"

Maybe I should have been frightened. I'd been given a

sentence of death, and it hadn't yet been countermanded, just postponed, it appeared. And, probably, when the Tromas found out whatever they wanted to find out about the Shadowy Man, that death sentence would be reinstated and Eric Mathers would go to the block or the gas chamber or the firing squad.

But I wasn't frightened. Maybe I was numb. Or just stupid. Or maybe some part of my mind expected the Shadowy Man to come riding in like the U. S. Cavalry to rescue Sally and me just in the nick of time.

Or maybe I wasn't frightened because I was too excited about seeing Sally again.

The cubicle made a lurch and headed in an upward direction. In seconds it came to a stop and the door slid open.

"She is being kept here," Cal-sarlin said as he led me out and pointed toward a towering needle of a building that looked something like an Egyptian obelisk magnified a hundred times or more, set in the middle of a wide, grassy plain on the edge of which some bovine animals placidly grazed.

"A jail?" I asked.

The Krith smiled. "We do not call it that."

"What do you call it?"

"Oh, you might translate the term as 'restricted apartment complex' or even as 'minimal security detention facilities,' whichever is more pleasing to you."

"How about 'jail'?"

"If you insist." He was still smiling.

A flagstone path led from the cubicle's mound to the large glass door that led into the lobby of the "minimal security detention facilities" and a brace of Mager types with ugly automatic weapons that reminded me of characters I'd seen in a dream a long time ago. It had been a dream, hadn't it?

Cal-sarlin spoke briefly, in unintelligible terms, with one of them, who then turned and spoke into a communications device mounted in the wall. When equally unintelligible words came back in reply, we were allowed to proceed, entering another cubicle that was a real elevator that whisked us upward toward the top of the spire.

"You will be allowed to spend the night with this

woman," Cal-sarlin told me as the elevator climbed. I didn't care much for the way he pronounced the word "woman," but then Kriths are that way. "Tomorrow you are to be interviewed by certain members of the, er, government."

"Government?" I asked.

"Ruling council, chamber of elders, parliament, there is no exact term in Shangalis for their function."

"Okay."

"You did not think the Tromas exercised complete civil authority, did you?"

"I suppose I assumed it."

"An erroneous assumption, Eric. Their work is far too important for them to concern themselves with the day-to-day functioning of society. Such mundane work is in the hands of others."

"I see," I said, but wondered if I did, and wondered what kind of complexities there were in Krithian society. Were there in it, as in most human socieities, rival factions, contending bodies, divided opinions; was it possible that the great Krithian machine was not nearly so monolithic as it appeared from the outside? Maybe I'd never know, but it made interesting speculation.

Then we were there, somewhere high in the building. The elevator came to a stop, doors opened, and Cal-sarlin preceded me out of it into a short corridor that made a sharp "L" turn and led to two more Mager types, armed like the ones below, standing before a door marked with runic characters I couldn't read.

Cal-sarlin spoke to them, they replied, stepped aside and let the Krith knock on the door.

From a hidden loudspeaker—or something that served a similar function—a word I didn't understand was spoken by a voice I knew.

The door opened.

The Krith led me in.

Sally let out a gasp of surprise, astonishment.

She hadn't changed.

Sally Beall, once the wife of Albert von Heinen, once the mistress of Mica: blond hair, greenish eyes, five-five in unshod feet, built like a beautiful woman ought to be built.

Sally whom I loved. . . .

She was dressed in a short blue garment that had something of the look of Classical Greece to it, and her hair was done up in a kind of bun on the top of her head. There was a slender book in her hand. . . .

And in her eyes a look of surprised delight mixed with apprehension.

"Eric," she said slowly, mastering her astonishment.

I brushed around the Krith's big form, took her in my arms.

"Eric, what are you doing here?"

"I came to find you," I said, and then smothered her words with my mouth. I didn't give a damn if the Krith *was* watching. What did he know about such things?

Finally Cal-sarlin's voice interrupted us: "I will leave you to your pleasures."

I broke from Sally and turned to face him.

"Sally can explain the rules to you," he said. "There are but few of them. You will not find your confinement a hardship, I assure you, unless you are terribly foolish."

I nodded, grunted that I understood.

"Do not forget," he went on. "Tomorrow morning, as soon as you have completed breakfast, I will return for you."

"To see your government?" I asked.

The Krith nodded. "Until then, adieu." He actually said the word, "adieu." I wonder where in hell he picked that up. Then he was gone and Sally and I were alone. At last!

"You shouldn't have come here, Eric," Sally said when I turned away from the door that had closed behind the Krith. "You've done exactly what they wanted you to do."

"I know."

"Why did you do it?"

"Just don't have good sense, I suppose." But as I looked at her, I saw that I did have a very good reason for having come to KHL-ooo. Sally alone was reason enough. And I wondered how it was that I, that hard-bitten, free-booting old lecher, had ever gotten myself in this kind of an emotional relationship with a woman. Not *a* woman. With Sally. She was the reason. I actually did love her. . . .

"How have they treated you?"

"Not badly, actually," she said and made a sweeping

movement with her hands that took in the room we were in and the rest of the apartment I hadn't yet seen.

"They've questioned you?" I asked.

"Oh, yes. Under hypnosis and with drugs and once or twice I think they used telepathy on me. It was never actually painful. They haven't *really* hurt me, but I don't think I was able to keep anything from them as if I knew anything they didn't already know." There was a long pause. "But I was lonely, Eric. I missed you."

"I know. I came as soon as I could."

"You shouldn't have. They may kill you."

"I know," I repeated. "But I had to find you. And I had to ask the Kriths some questions. I just came from the Tromas."

"The Tromas!"

Briefly I told her of my interview with the females of the Krithian race and what they had told me about themselves, about their plans and goals, and about the future of the universe itself.

"And you really believe them now?" she asked when I'd concluded.

"I do. Damn me, but I believe that this time they're really telling the truth. I'm not sure why, but I do believe them."

"What kind of proof have they offered?"

"None. Maybe that's one of the reasons I believe. I mean, always before the Kriths have bent over backward to show proof of their tales, which turn out to be lies. Now they don't seem to care whether I believe them or not. I think that's the way they'd act if they were telling the truth."

"I'm not sure I understand."

"I'm not sure I do either."

"Are you hungry?"

"Famished. I can't remember the last time I ate."

"Let me get you something. And a drink."

"A drink. Yes. I can use one."

Thirty minutes later, sandwiches and the warmth of liquor inside me, my boots off and my shirt unbuttoned, more comfortable than I could recall having been since the days in Jock's diner near Daleville, Georgia, I sat back in a huge overstuffed chair in the living room of Sally's apartment/jail cell, my feet propped up and Sally sitting beside me on the arm of the chair.

"What are we going to do now, Eric?" Sally asked.

We were both drinking a delightful white wine and I was smoking a huge, mellow cigar she'd conjured up from somewhere. "Right now I don't plan on doing a damned thing."

"You know what I mean."

"I know. And I don't know what we're going to do." I looked around the room. "I suppose this place is bugged?"

"I suppose it is. I haven't tried to find out."

"With the technology they've got to call on, you'd never find evidence of it. But I'd be very surprised if they aren't watching every move we make, recording every word."

"I'm sure you're right."

I waved at invisible cameras, said "Hi!" to unseen eavesdroppers.

"Not that I've got any great big secret plans I don't want them to hear, I just like privacy when I'm with my woman." Unfortunately, I was telling the truth. I didn't have any plans. The plans I'd formulated had never gone beyond getting to the Krithian Homeline, finding Sally and some answers. What was going to happen after that I'd never worked out. Now that I was really there—had my Sally and some of my answers—maybe I'd better try to figure out what was next.

"We could turn out the lights," Sally said softly, her hand brushing my cheek.

"I doubt that would do much good. I'm sure they've got ways of seeing in the dark."

"I'd feel better if it were dark." The brush became a caress. She slid from the arm of the chair into my lap. My arms went around her, pulled her closer.

"God, I've missed you, Eric," she whispered.

"And I've missed you," I whispered back and drew her face to mine and kissed her longer and better than before.

"Let me show you where the bedroom is," she said softly when the kiss was over. "I think you'll like it."

"I know I'll like it."

I wanted to see my Sally again, see her body under the

gown she was wearing, see the curves and mounds of her as my hands touched and caressed and fondled, but she insisted on darkness, fooling herself that the Krithian spy devices couldn't see what we were doing in the darkness. I was sure they could, but . . .

So in the darkness, on a great bed that had been designed to hold more than one, I felt the warmth of her, the curves of soft flesh that my hands had felt so often before, and then the secret places of her that awaited me.

"I've missed you so much," she whispered to me in the darkness, yielding, opening to me. "I've wanted you so badly, but for your sake I'd hoped you'd never come."

"I had to," I whispered back.

The bed rocked under us, slowly at first, then with increasing tempo.

"I'm glad."

"So am I."

A gasp, a deeply drawn breath, a sigh. "Now, Eric. I can't wait any longer."

Now, I agreed silently. For neither could I wait longer. Oh, my Sally! My Sally. My Sally. . . .

19
The Shadowy Man

"What do you think they're going to do to you?"

Outside the world was in darkness, creeping toward a dawn but a few hours away. We'd slept and then awakened, like newlyweds on honeymoon, to make love again, and now we lay side by side on the bed, a dim lamp our only illumination, looking up at a mosaic ceiling, a half-smoked cigarette between my fingers.

"I don't know," I told her. "I suppose it'll depend on what happens."

"The Shadowy Man?"

"Uh-huh," I grunted.

"Do you think he'll come?"

"I don't know. I never know."

"What is he, Eric?"

"I wish I knew."

I snuffed out my cigarette and rolled over to kiss her again.

"Already?" she asked.

"Not yet." I said, smiling down at her. "But I wish . . ."

She smiled back, didn't speak.

Another kiss and I rolled onto my back again, looking up at the dim and distant ceiling.

"If there were any way I could contact him—if I knew how—I'd tell him not to come here."

"Do you think they could capture a ghost?"

"I don't know. But he's been my friend and I wouldn't want to put him in that danger."

"Are you certain he's your friend?"

"He's helped me. He's kept me alive."

"I wonder . . ." she began, then let her voice trail off as she became aware of something that was also coming to my attention. There was in the air of the room something akin to a chill, a tension that also reminded me of the feel

217

of the atmosphere before the beginning of an electrical storm, and I thought I could almost smell ozone.

"What is it, Eric?" Sally whispered, sitting up in the bed, clutching the sheet at her breast and throat.

"Wait," I whispered back.

The sense of tension grew. I half-expected to see St. Elmo's fire dancing across the furniture, to see a bolt of lightning leap from the ceiling's light fixture to one of the bedposts.

Then there was a *presence* in the room, a vagueness with a manlike shape in the darkness of the far corner, a thing only half-visible in the gloom, yet there was in me no doubt that the room was occupied by *something* in addition to Sally and myself.

The Shadowy Man spoke: "It was very difficult this time," the strangely familiar voice said, "getting here. I didn't think it would be this hard."

"Eric!" Sally cried, dropped the sheet, drew herself against me.

"It's okay," I said. "I know who it is."

"That's your voice, Eric," Sally stammered out in a whispering voice.

"There is little time," the Shadowy Man said, now as solid and concrete as I'd ever seen the form, still little more than a column of smoke with a manlike shape standing in the gloom. "And the forces involved in this are beyond your present comprehension. In moments, if not already, the Tromas will know I'm here and then—Well, you've got to get out of here, the two of you."

"Out of here?" I asked stupidly.

"That's why I came, dammit!, to rescue you two." Somehow the voice, the words it spoke weren't as vague and alien as the shape that spoke them, but solid and real, the kind of words a human being would have spoken, that I would have spoken.

"There's a way to escape," the Shadowy Man said, "and if you'll listen to me I'll tell you how to do it."

"We're listening," I said.

"Very well," the Shadowy Man said, and in a terse, strained voice he told us how to get from Sally's apartment to the roof of the towering spire of a building, a half-secret stairway that would take us up to where there would be "a means of escape" waiting us. There would be guards and obstacles before us, though the Shadowy Man would do everything he could to help pave the way for us.

"And then what?" I asked, my voice coming out around an awkward lumpiness in my throat.

"You escape," the substantial voice from the insubstantial form said. "What you do after that is up to you, Eric, and you, Sally. I can't tell you what to do once you escape this Line. I've already done far more than I should. I'm not yet certain just where in the orders of probability —or improbability"—there was a half-chuckle in the voice—"all this lies anyway. We may one day find out that none of it has happened anyway."

"What do you mean?" I asked.

"Nothing," answered the Shadowy Man.

I thought I detected a second form of tension in the air, again something like the rapid approach of a thunderstorm, an electrical charge growing in the air, yet somehow different from what had gone before, in a way alien and full of menace, and in a fashion that brought into my mind the image of a gross form that could have been feminine in some other context.

"Now you must work out some simple ruse to distract the guards outside the doors of the apartment," the ghostly figure said. "Sally, you can help in this. Draw them into the room. Get their attention. Then perhaps Eric can do something. And remember, they have no women of their own. They're drawn to human women, some of them."

Sally might have asked him to explain that, but she too seemed to be growing aware of the new element of tension in the air, seemed to be caught and held by it like a fly in amber.

"They know!" the Shadowy Man said suddenly, his voice grown thin.

I knew exactly what he meant. For the briefest of instants I seemed to occupy the same place and time as the Shadowy Man, and if I did not see through his eyes and feel through his senses, I was aware of the same things as he, shared his memories and sensations, saw the danger that lay some miles away in space, yet which was exerting some powerful and rapidly growing

force against him, a psionic force that in moments could
sweep over him and destroy him.

I gasped aloud in shared pain.

"Eric!" Sally cried.

Another universe of memories, thoughts, feelings, impressions swept over me, shared with me in that fraction
of a second by the being I'd been calling the Shadowy
Man.

"You're me," I said aloud in a strangled voice.

"In a sense," he answered. "You might be me. You
might become me, given time."

And I knew that the Tromas hadn't been lying to me.
What they had said was true. But—but it wasn't the
whole story. Not all of it. And there was much yet to
be done. Oh, so damned much!

And the odds against my living were enormous.

Yet here was some future version of myself, some
projection of a future version(s), somehow come back
in time to aid me—the temporal paradoxes of it all were
almost overwhelming.

. The universe was a can of worms, and each worm
was bending back upon itself to eat its own tail. . . .

Lightning flashed in the apartment's bedroom, leaping
from some point near the ceiling toward the form of the
Shadowy Man. And this time it wasn't imaginary lightning.

The Shadowy Man blazed with a halo of light.

"I will fight them as long as I can, but I don't know
how long that will be. I'm a long way from home. . . ."
Lightning crackled again, briefly illuminating the room,
filling the air with the scent of ozone. "Hurry!" he cried.

By now I'd gotten myself out of bed and was drawing
Sally with me. Among the things half-registered in my
mind was the awareness that the Shadowy Man was
fighting an unequal battle, was pitting *his* already strained
psionic powers against those of the Tromas, fresh and
strong and close. How far from us the Shadowy Man
really was I had only the vaguest of concepts.

"Come on," I said to Sally and half-dragged her, the
both of us naked, from the bedroom and toward the
luxurious apartment's living room and entrance hallway.
Behind us lightning, and other forces less apparent to the

eye, flickered and flashed through the bedroom. It was a wonder that everything there wasn't already ablaze.

"What're we going to do?" Sally asked as we neared the door that led into the apartment—and out of it.

"Start screaming," I said, coming to a stop. "Just stand there and scream your head off."

"What're . . ."

"Just do it."

"Now?"

"When I say so. Stand right there."

At the end of the short entrance hallway Sally stood, naked and lovely. At the other end was the doorway beyond which stood the two Mager types who guarded us. At least I thought there were two and assumed they were still there.

I threw myself flat against the wall at the end of the hallway, around the corner, just out of eyeshot of someone entering the door. I triggered the preparatory circuits of my augmentation, those that I hadn't already triggered unconsciously.

"Now," I said.

Sally looked at me for a moment, a puzzled, frightened expression on her face. In the now-distant bedroom a caged beast growled savagely. Sally screamed. I don't think she had to fake it.

I shifted into augmentation and felt the world slow around me, heard the sounds of Sally's scream slide from shrill to a bassness like some terribly low, sad brass instrument, saw a redness enter the world that hadn't been there before.

An eternity slowly dragged itself along, limping like the world was whimpering to an end.

I heard a rumbling from the far end of the short hallway. The door was opening.

Then deep thuds, slow and menacing, and a booming bass drum of a voice asking Sally questions I probably couldn't have understood even if I hadn't been in augmentation.

Sally just kept screaming.

"Come on, come on, come on," I said to myself.

Thud. Thud. Thud.

With a slowness I didn't think I could endure much

longer, one of the Mager guards advanced into the room. His buddy must still be waiting outside, probably with one of those ugly automatic weapons aimed down the hallway. So be it.

Then he came into sight, the tall, slender form in an outlandish uniform, weapon in hand, yet with a puzzled bemused expression on the rugged planes of his face. What was it the Shadowy Man had said about their having no women of their own?

For a moment my attention was drawn away from the approaching guard, for from out of the bedroom behind us came a figure even more startling in its appearance, startling even to me who had seen him but moments before.

The Shadowy Man came into the apartment's living room, his smoky, ghostly form now clothed in glimmering lightnings and halos of incandescence; sheets of auroral flame surrounded him, flickering in neon colors across the spectrum from the edges of infrared to the margins of ultraviolet. The air around him was ionizing; carpeting and woodwork smoldered as he brushed across them, moving even more slowly and ponderously than could be accounted for by my augmentation.

For instants I was again a part of the Shadowy Man and "saw" what he "saw," "felt" what he "felt," fought with him against the Tromas who had wished him to come and now that he was here wished only to destroy him forever, him and all the menace he had brought to the Kriths and their plans to alter the altering of the universe.

The Shadowy Man was locked in combat—mortal or perhaps immortal combat—with the minds that guided the destiny of the Krithian race. Blindly he—and I with him—stumbled forward, hardly aware of the shadowy form that was all he had of a body in this space/time. His mind—his ultramind, his supermind, his composite mind—ranged beyond the spatial locus where plays of light and shadow, focuses of scattered matter and energy formed the figure which I had seen, the voice which had spoken to us.

And then, as quickly, I was myself again, and was

aware of the Mager type advancing slowly toward Sally.

Then I leaped.

Maybe the guard was ready to go Augie himself. He should have been. But I never gave him a chance. I was on him before he had an opportunity to wonder where I was, on him and carrying him down to the floor, one hand around his throat, the other doubled into a fist and battering at the cartilage of his nose, one knee in his groin. "Get down!" I yelled to Sally, knowing she couldn't understand me.

Then we were on the floor, the Mager type and I, his eyes bulging out, his tongue swelling, his face turning red around a shattered nose.

Sally was throwing herself down, and out of the way, a graceful slow-motion dance of escape as a splatter of bullets burst from an automatic weapon at the far end of the hall. The other guard was going into augmentation, but there was nothing I could do about that now.

It couldn't have been more than seconds, but it seemed like ages, that we rolled across the floor, bullets cutting the air around us, gouging through the carpeting into the floor—the second guard didn't seem to care whether he killed his companion, as long as he got me. But I killed his buddy first—I think—I felt the cartilage of his windpipe crush beneath my savage fingers; he gagged, spit blood, then his eyes rolled back and I tore his weapon from his weakening fingers, pushing him away from me.

If I hadn't been certain of killing him—for Magers, like Kriths, are unusually hard to kill—that doubt was settled for me when a random spray of bullets, meant for me, ruptured through his body, stitching a line down his side and hips. Nothing inside him could have withstood that!

But that second guard—Augie that he was—didn't give himself a fair chance. He was standing right there in the open doorway, light from the outside corridor behind him. He couldn't have set himself up any better if he'd been doing it at my suggestion. He was cut almost in half when he went down and I released my grip on the automatic's trigger. I was certain I'd gotten both the primary and the secondary brain.

I let my augmentation run down. As much as I wanted

to keep it on, I knew Sally couldn't keep up with me if I did, and I couldn't very well talk with her either.

"Let's go," I cried as the world came back into focus. "We need clothing and . . ."

I was coming to my feet, the blood of the dead man—or whatever he was—who lay on the floor splattered on my shoulders, face, chest.

"No time," I said, grabbed Sally's wrist and propelled her toward the door.

I grabbed the second Mager's automatic and threw it to Sally. It *might* help if we were both armed.

Waving good-by to the Shadowy Man, who I'm certain didn't see *me*, I said to Sally, "That way," and pointed in the direction where the Shadowy Man had said lay the half-hidden stairway that would take us up to the roof and our "means of escape."

And as we moved away from the apartment, I could feel, could sense the awful battle that was being waged there, the terrible energies that were flashing, flickering back and forth across time and space and coming together in that luxurious living room. The Tromas, ancient and wise in the use of their abilities, were bending all their available energies on the crushing of the insubstantial form I called the Shadowy Man. And I didn't think it would be long before they did. Maybe we could get away in time. Maybe.

But that was a chancy thing.

Though I couldn't hear it as Sally and I ran down the hallway and found the door that led to a small and dimly lit stairwell, I could feel the alarm that was already screaming through the building, an alarm that would have raised my hackles if I'd known what they were, and that sent a note of distress through the both of us. They knew —the Mager types and the Kriths—that Sally and I were trying to escape and they didn't plan on letting us do that.

We didn't take breath to talk, though we did clasp hands, and together leaped every other step on our way up. And now, when a spasm of weakness and vertigo went through me, the aftermath of augmentation, it was Sally's strength that carried us on.

How far? I wondered. Our shadowy friend—even now

that I had some inkling of what *he* was, I still thought of him much as I had before—the Shadowy Man hadn't told us how far it was to the roof.

From below, from far away, but soon growing nearer, were the sounds of our pursuit.

Half a dozen more flights of stairs, I thought, my breath coming raggedly and burning in my throat, and they'll catch us.

We went on. Step after step after step.

Hoarse voices called in an alien tongue. Other voices answered. Doors slammed. Feet sounded on the steps below. Dim lights flickered far below us. Then a gun fired. The bullet lodged in a wall or a step somewhere behind, below.

How much farther?

The alarm siren throbbed through me. A psychological thing? I wondered. Something to throw fear into the quarry?

Guns fired again. Nearer. But the maze of alternating staircases was too complex for a simple-minded bullet to find its way through unless aimed more expertly than those had been.

Is there anyone waiting for us above? I asked myself, a lance jabbing into my side every time I lifted my right leg, several times a second. Maybe not . . . Was that too much to hope for?

"Eric!" Sally gasped, loosed my hand, pointed ahead.

Above a dim red light blinked on and off, after one more turn, one more flight of stairs. The exit?

As we darted across the small landing and mounted still another flight of steps, I suddenly became aware of something else. For a moment I didn't know what it was, this loss, this absence. Something had been there, in my mind, only moments before and now it was gone. A tooth that I'd taken for granted had suddenly been removed and my tongue sought for it, found an empty socket—that's what it was like.

"He's gone!" I cried, almost coming to a stop. "They've beaten him."

Sally grabbed my hand, pulled me on. "Hurry," she said. "We're almost there."

The Shadowy Man was gone. I knew that. In the room far below, in the bedroom Sally and I occupied, where we'd made love, and in the living room where I'd eaten and sat and talked with her before going into the bedroom, there was no longer that vague shape of smoke with a manlike form. It was as if I could see those rooms: bedroom walls, floor, ceiling scorched and smoldering, bed turned on one side, sheets torn and flickering with dying embers, a mirror in a thousand bright fragments across the tattered carpeting; in the living room much the same scene of ruined furniture and pieces of art that had decorated the brightly colored walls, smoke and flickering tongues of flame, fragments of wood and plastic and pottery, a vase of flowers turned brown by the brief passage of intense heat. And all of it empty of life save for a gloating *presence* that had won, that had cast the Shadowy Man out of its world, that had broken him and the power that had propelled him across time and space to that strange battlefield.

We were alone again, Sally and I. . . .

She dragged me up the last few steps, to the door above which the red light flashed on and off, on and off. She dropped her weapon and with both hands jerked open the manual door and revealed to us a flat, moonlit pavement, dark like tarmac and as empty and desolate as the surface of the Moon.

My heart sank again. I'd expected a skudder waiting for us there, a skudder or *something*, but what I saw now was nothing, the empty pavement. Had the passing of the Shadowy Man left us without our means of escape? God . . .

Guns fired behind us. Close. Too damned close.

I broke out of the trance I was in, turned, fired back down the stairs toward our pursuers. Then we turned and ran on across the pavement toward—what?

There was a spot ahead of us, in about the middle of the paved rooftop, where the moonlight did not dimly illuminate the dark, flat surface. It was as if there were a spot there that drank the moonlight, greedily swallowed it, and left an area in space darker than the rest of the night.

"There's *something* there, Eric," Sally said between gasps for air.

"I hope so."

I let her run on ahead of me so that I could cover her lovely rear, then stopped for a moment and fired into the doorway we'd just left.

We must have been halfway to the inky blackness when it hit me.

It had all the strength of a physical blow, a poleax to the head couldn't have dropped me any quicker. Waves of pain shot from some point deep in my brain. My vision faded and most of my other senses failed me. My body went limp and I hardly felt it when the pavement came up and slapped me in the face, a sharp blow that opened my cheek to the bone.

"Eric!" I heard Sally's voice cry from a long way off, and then felt her hands touching a body that seemed only halfway mine. "Eric, what is it?"

Someone else, a wrecking crew, was inside my head, slashing out with sharp, heavy instruments, tearing through the fragile stuff of my consciousness, ripping to shreds my sanity. There was a force in my mind that wasn't a part of me, an angry, alien force that now desired only to see me dead. No words, no thoughts, no visual images came to me, no attempt at communication, only the awareness that something that now hated me was trying to destroy my mind and was doing it in the quickest, most brutal way it knew how.

"Eric, get up," Sally's remote voice yelled at me, angry now. "They'll catch us."

And then I thought I heard the rattle of distant guns, and moments later, closer at hand, louder and more savage still, Sally's gun replied.

"Dammit! Get up!" she yelled, and in my nose I could smell the sharp fumes of cordite or whatever they used here for gunpowder.

Sally's hands went under my armpits and she was dragging me across the pavement, not gently; my buttocks, thighs, calves, heels scraped across the rough surface. A still rational part of my mind realized she couldn't drag me all the way there—wherever *there* was.

But only a part of my mind was rational, only a small part. The rest of it was being battered to pieces by pain, by fire, by mental blows for which there are no words in any language I know.

I forced my mouth open, took deep breaths, willed augmentation circuitry into operation. Maybe it would only make it worse, but . . .

The pain seemed to become only more intense as the world wound down to one fifth its normal speed, as sounds dopplered toward the lower registers, and the moon and stars in the sky above took on a more reddish hue.

The blows came less frequently, came with a slower impact that I could more nearly deal with, could mentally duck away from, could hide from back in the deep recesses of the bony cavern of my skull. Maybe I could get far enough away from them, something in my mind said, maybe I could creep back down deep enough that they couldn't get to me. There was some remote recess in the more primitive parts of my brain stem that the Tromas couldn't reach. Maybe there I'd be safe.

Maybe that's exactly what they wanted me to do: give up the fight and hide away in some catatonic refuge.

Sally released me, let my head and shoulders fall to the pavement. I forced my eyes open and looked up to see her drawing her semirifle up again, level it and fire. I thought I could see the slugs as they erupted in flame from the weapon's barrel.

Now there were pauses between the psionic blows hammered at me by the Tromas and during the next pause I summoned together all the strength left in my body, drew it into my arms and legs, rolled over onto my stomach and forced myself to my hands and knees. Then I was standing erect, staggering forward in a half run.

Sally must have had some understanding of what was happening to me, had sense enough to take up the defense of our escape, and did her best to cover me as I stumbled toward the remote spot of total lightlessness that was our destination, fire her gun until its magazine was empty, and then grab up the one I'd dropped and fire again.

A few feet forward I'd staggered when the next blow came. I put my legs on automatic pilot and withdrew into what sanctuary there was for me, feeling the psionic blows smashing outward from some central point in my brain that the Krithian females had selected as their attack point. For a few moments there was painful darkness, filled with flickering reds and yellows and oranges like some great, world-consuming fire. Then I think I blacked out.

When consciousness came to me again I was on the pavement once more, another gash in my face, more blood on my shoulders and chest. Sally was beside me, speaking words I couldn't understand in their bassness, but felt she was telling me to get up again and go on, we weren't as far as we had been. I did like I thought she was telling me.

How many times I rose and stumbled forward and then fell when the war-ax blows split my skull open, only to rise again during the interval before the next blow, I could never say. Far too many times.

But I did keep getting up again, and I did keep stumbling forward a few feet, a few yards. And Sally kept firing, holding back the ones who'd come up the stairwell to capture us, to kill us.

I don't suppose there was time for them to get air support in. If there had been they'd have wiped us out with no great bother. One missile. One fire bomb. One strafing run. That's all it would have taken. I guess we were lucky.

Or did luck have any part in it at all?

Fire licked at what remained of my consciousness, my sanity. My body was a mass of bruises and cuts. Sally's gun, the one that had been mine, must have been nearly empty.

"We're almost there, Eric," Sally was crying—or at least I thought that's what she was crying—and through eyes that would only halfway focus, I could see before me a spheroid of total blackness, seeming to hang a few inches from the pavement like some ancient star collapsed down to a black hole whose gravitation was so great that not even light could escape.

Whatever it was and I couldn't even guess then—it was our escape route, and this was no time to question it. The Shadowy Man *must* have known what he was doing.

I grabbed Sally by the arm and threw the both of us into ...

20
Vestiges of Time

I came out of unconsciousness, and out of augmentation, lying flat on my back on dry, dusty soil under a bright yellow-white sun that had the look of midmorning about it. The sky that contained the sun was a rich, pale, clean-washed blue with a few wisps of cloud near the horizon. The air was warm and dry, stirred by a breeze I probably would have found pleasant under other circumstances.

After a few moments of deep breathing I forced myself up on my elbows so that I could look around. A few feet from me, covered with dust and sweat, showing a few bruises and minor cuts, standing naked beside something that looked strangely like an overgrown mushroom, semirifle still in her hands, was Sally. Her back was to me, but she must have heard my movements, for she turned to face me, yet with a wariness that made my eyes search farther to where I saw the three dead Mager types a few yards beyond her, their uniforms ripped and bloody where the slugs from Sally's gun had torn into them.

Her smile was weak and sad. "I guess we made it," she said in a trembling voice.

"Yeah, I guess we did," I said.

Then she dropped her weapon, fell to her knees beside me, wrapped her arms around me, and said between sobs, "God, Eric, is it over now?"

Later when a little strength had come back to me and my hands had stopped their palsied shaking, when Sally had found water in a stream that flowed through a grove of willowlike trees not far from where she found the skudder that waited for us, when I felt not only that I would live, but that I wanted to live as well, she told me what had happened.

"When we leaped into that 'black hole,'" she said, sitting beside me in the shade of the giant mushroom, "some sort of, well, 'force' took hold of us, something that seemed to sort of turn us inside out and that carried us across space and time and—I guess—paratime. I guess this is another *Line*, isn't it?

"It was as if we were 'flickering' in a skudder, and yet not exactly that. I felt I could see, or sense in some fashion that wasn't quite seeing, each world click by, one after the other.

"I had a sensation of 'timelessness,' I guess I'd say, as if the universe had stopped in its tracks and then, maybe, began moving in the opposite temporal direction. It's hard to explain. It's something you're just as well without, Eric. I wouldn't have minded being unconscious then.

"Anyway, and I can't say how long—I have no idea of elapsed time, or even whether time can be measured in that context—I felt that we were falling. Then there was suddenly bright sunlight and we both plunged a few feet more until we hit the ground here.

"The first thing I did was check your pulse and after I found it and it seemed normal, I went to see if I could find the gun I'd had when we entered the 'hole.' I was afraid I might need it."

"And you found it," I said.

She nodded, said, "And I needed it. It couldn't have been more than a minute or two after we got here that *those three*, looking like they'd already been through a battle, fell out of the air. I mean that literally! Right out of the air! Well, I—I shot them. I didn't have any choice."

"I know."

"So then I just waited."

"And . . . ?"

"Nothing," she said, shrugged. "I just waited for you to wake up. There wasn't much else I could do."

No more Mager types came.

None ever came.

Sally told me that she'd seen the skudder even before I'd awakened, but she didn't want to leave me. So she waited until I woke up, until she'd gotten me water in her cupped hands.

"You feel like walking now?" she asked.

"I guess." I hurt inside and out, but figured I could walk as far as that skudder. I wanted to see it. "Help me up."

She did, and with a painful limp, I walked with her across the dry soil, through clustering clumps of grass, past "groves" of ten-foot-tall mushrooms toward the small stream and the skudder that lay beyond it. Among the bending branches of the willowlike trees, birds—or something very like birds—sang. From farther away, nibbling at grasses that grew within a great circle formed by gigantic red puffballs, the wary eyes of a four-hoofed, single-horned animal followed us. It could have been a unicorn had it not been so much overweight.

As we waded in the cool water of the stream I saw that the skudder was a beautiful one, of a design I'd never seen before, looking to be just off the assembly line, bright and untarnished, and ready to move as far across the Lines of Time as anyone might wish to go. I wondered whether it was armed.

Sally looked at the machine as we came out of the water, apprehension written on her face, then turned to me and said, "What do you think?"

"Another present from the Shadowy Man," I said, a sensation of sadness coming to me. Was he dead? Or . . .

"You're sure?"

"What else could it be?"

With slow, aching movements, I opened the skudder's hatch and looked inside. It was as beautiful inside as out, brightly decorated and luxuriously appointed. And there was a note taped to the main control panel, written in a handwriting that was painfully, shockingly familiar.

"That's your handwriting, Eric," Sally said, confirming what I already knew.

"But I never wrote it. I guess I will, one day."

I climbed inside and got the note, climbed back out as quickly as I could I wasn't ready yet for *that* skudder. It was haunted. By my own ghost?

I held the note so that we could both read it.

"Dear Eric and Sally," it began.

"If you read this note you will have escaped from the Tromas and have found the refuge I selected for you. You're safe here as long as you wish to stay.

"I know you're curious about your means of transportation from KHL-ooo to here and I would explain it to you if I could, but none of us has the proper mathematical background to really understand it. I could tell you it's a 'parachronal convolution,' but what would that explain? Labeling something doesn't necessarily define it.

"This skudder, from some decades into the future, as you two have been reckoning time, is yours. It's fully provisioned and ready to take you wherever you might wish to go, spatially or paratemporally. You may use it when you will.

"Some miles to the west of here you will find a village. It is an outpost of a kingdom barely out of the Bronze Age, though its inhabitants are friendly and pleasant people. You will find yourselves welcome there, though don't be too surprised if you're treated as something a bit more special than a pair of naked wanderers. They're expecting a couple of exiled godlings. Try to act the part.

"In time you're a few weeks 'downtime' from our conflict with the Tromas. In the past as you see it.

"In space you're still in North America, the Florida peninsula.

"In paratime, well, you're one hell of a long way to the T-East, far beyond the Lines the Kriths call KHL-ooo. It's as safe a place as any you could hope for, but try not to be disturbed by the oddness of some of the things you find here. There are some aspects of the evolutionary process that have worked out differently here."

When I read this line I looked up and saw the clusters of gigantic mushroom-things growing not far away and the brown, one-horned beast that grazed among them. Yes, the course that evolution had taken on this world so far distant across the Lines of Time was somehow slightly different from that on the Lines to the T-West of us, the Lines of Man. Were the *people* here the same as *us?* I wondered.

"The Kriths and their Companions can't find you here, except by hunting down that transmitter that's still buried deep in your flesh, Eric. But you *can* do something about that, if you must. You can find a Line not too far away where a good surgeon can go in and get it out and do away with it. That's really no problem.

"As for advice, I can give you none, as much as I would like to.

"The future is yours to do with as you wish.

"I think.

"Yours, Eric Mathers."

I read the note over again and then handed it to Sally. She carefully folded it up and put it inside the skudder's open hatch. I closed the hatch and then we bathed in the stream.

"Feel like taking a walk?" I asked Sally after we'd bathed and rested and eaten a meal from provisions we'd found near the haunted skudder.

"If you do."

"Which way's west?"

The world out there is pleasant enough. It's a world a long way from any I've known before, but somehow familiar. It's kind of like ancient Greece was supposed to have been, the Classical world. A world of small city-states, island kingdoms here and there, a few larger kingdoms, and maybe an empire or two on the continental mainlands. Maybe someone had discovered how to work iron, but nobody locally knows yet.

Oh, there are bad things about this world. Ignorance and cruelty, slavery and superstition. They're all here in more than ample measure—Sally and I *are* given a reverence beyond that deserved by mere mortals. But the bad things weren't as pronounced as on some Lines I've seen.

Sally and I are learning the language and I don't think it will take us long to establish ourselves rather comfortably, as if we weren't comfortable now, by local standards.

And the people—well, as far as I can tell they're humans exactly like us. If there are differences, I haven't found them yet, though Sally had put a limit to my, well, "anatomical studies."

Our skudder is still hidden away, sheltered in a remote spot where no one's likely to find it. It's safe until we want it. And I'm sure we will.

I've got Sally now and a lot of the answers I wanted, but . . .

There's still a lot left unanswered.

And a lot left undone.

I don't exactly see myself in the role that's been cast for me, but on the other hand I'm not certain that I can avoid the role even if I try.

I wouldn't be alive today, nor would Sally, if the Shadowy Man hadn't come *back through time* to help us, whatever his is/was/will be; however it is, I'm part of him and he a part of me.

So, there are things I have to do, things I don't suppose I can avoid doing.

Soon I'll have to leave here. I want Sally to stay until I can come back for her. I don't know whether she will, but I don't want her risking her life again.

Maybe one of these dark nights, when I'm certain that her place has been firmly established in this world and she won't suffer any want if I leave, I just may creep away and go to the skudder and quietly slip away across the Lines in search of the Shadowy Man. . . .

Anybody know where I can pick up a good time machine cheap?

BOOK THREE
VESTIGES OF TIME

CONTENTS

1

The Slums of VarKhohs

The late afternoon sun should have been brighter and warmer than it was, for it had been a late summer day in the city of VarKhohs. But now the light seemed dim and cold, as if from an aged, weakened sun, as it fell into the dark and narrow streets through which I slowly followed a man I knew by the name RyoNa. Although he was still several blocks ahead of me, I could easily make him out, a large, heavy man in a rich, dark robe, one decorated with the symbols of his rank and caste, a man seemingly very out of place in the slums into which he had led me.

I tried to throw off the gloom that settled over me as I followed him farther into the decaying slums, past the ramshackle buildings that filled the quarter of the city nearest the river. I pulled my own robe more tightly around me against the imaginary chill, a robe not so dark or so regal as that of RyoNa; but then I wasn't trying to appear to be a member of one of the ruling castes of NakrehVatee, the nation and society that dominated North America in the summer of A.D. 1972 on this *particular* Earth. I was just trying to get by until I could get my hands on what I had come so far across the Lines of Time to find. And I thought RyoNa could help me find what I wanted: a "time machine." In a sense, it turned out that he was helping me do that, although he didn't know it at the time, and I couldn't have guessed just what that "time machine" was to be.

RyoNa turned a corner ahead of me, passing in front of a temple dedicated to one of the Dark Lords of

7

Death, the god Themfo-Okketho, by name, and for a moment he was lost from my view. I hurried forward a little more quickly, as quickly as the folds of the robe around me would allow, and placed a hand on the comforting bulge of an energy pistol under my left armpit. I wouldn't have felt very comfortable in *that* section of the city without a weapon. I hadn't been in VarKhohs long, but I'd been there long enough to have heard tales of what took place in those slums after dark, of what happened to well-dressed men and women foolish enough to be down there after daylight had gone and there was no longer even a pretense of police protection.

Finally I reached the corner where I'd seen RyoNa turn, and as I rounded the corner myself, passing through the shadow cast by the statue of the hideous deathgod, I saw RyoNa's bulky figure, not as far away as it had been. Apparently he had slowed to make certain he didn't lose me. He knew I was following him, of course. Only I wasn't certain whether he knew that I knew of his awareness. Our understanding was a rather tacit one, if it could be called an understanding at all.

A small, ragged child, who had been standing in the open doorway of one of the crumbling buildings of gray stone and cracked brick, made a motion as if to accost me, perhaps to ask for a handout, or, equally likely, pimping for his mother or sister, but I held him off with a curt shake of my head, a hard look from my eyes. I'd never been what you'd call handsome, and the events of the past year or so had done nothing to improve my looks: I have an especially unpleasant-looking scar on my right cheek where it once was opened to the bone by a pistol barrel. I guess my face was enough for the poor urchin. He went back into his doorway. Silently I wished him well, knowing how unlikely his well-being in this world was.

There were a few others in the streets of the slums

of VarKhohs, other tatter-clad children like the boy in the doorway, male and female alike dressed in the sexless rags of poverty, and there were adults as well, weary, disillusioned—if they'd ever had illusions—old before their time, too far down the ladder of this world's society to concern themselves with the badges of their caste. When you're that far down, it doesn't much matter, except perhaps in the ingrown subcultures and the jealously guarded pecking orders that must exist even for the lowest.

The poverty wasn't all that new to me. I'd experienced conditions as bad, and even worse, in dozens of other cities of the parallel worlds of time. I didn't like it, but I'd grown accustomed to it. Yet . . . what did disturb me about the poverty of the people of the slums of VarKhohs was its total lack of reason. The poverty wasn't necessary!

Only a few miles from the streets through which I followed RyoNa stood the wealthy center of one of the most highly developed civilizations I'd ever seen. It was a culture based on the technologies of nuclear fusion and plasma physics, a civilization with the wealth to send fleets of starships to Alpha Centauri and Tau Ceti, where human colonies flourished, with the wealth to build the shining, shimmering towers in which the upper castes of VarKhohs dwelt, soaring penthouses that seemed to reach the clouds and from the windows of which one could look out across the ocean and see the sleek yachts moving between the luxurious artificial islands that floated a few miles offshore, with the wealth to construct tombs in the southwestern deserts for its rulers that made the most lavish of those of ancient Egypt look cheap and mean by comparison. This civilization had the affluence to allow a select few of its members to live—and die!—in luxury such as human beings had seldom known before but didn't have the wealth—or rather the desire—to give a decent meal to those who stooped at the bottom of the social pyramid under the crushing weight of all those who stood above.

Eric Mathers, I suddenly found myself asking silently, where in Hades did you ever develop a social conscience? And I didn't have an answer for that one, nor really the time to speculate about it. I had something to do that I felt was even more important than concern over the lower classes of VarKhohs. I had to find the Shadowy Man. And that probably would require a time machine.

The man I knew as RyoNa had slowed a little more, allowing me to come nearer to him, and then turned down a still darker, narrower street, no more than an alley. I moved after him and reached the entrance of the alley in time to see him entering a large, open doorway and pause in the deeper shadows there as if to make certain I was still with him.

I entered the alley, glanced back down the street from which I had come, and saw the statue of Themfo-Okketho, the deathgod, silhouetted against the deepening afternoon sky. For some reason it sent a chill through me and brought to mind an old phrase about someone stepping on my grave. I tried to ignore it and went on into the alley.

Now there seemed to be no one else around. Just RyoNa and me. So maybe it was time I caught up with him and finally spoke to him. We'd played this silly game long enough. Now I'd like to hear him say in no uncertain terms that he could get me one of the so-called chronal-displacement devices—a machine that allegedly could travel not horizontally across the Lines of Time from parallel Earth to parallel Earth, as does a skudder, but forward and backward in time, into the future and into the past—in short, a "time machine," as one writer had long ago dubbed such a machine, but on an Earth very different from this one.

And maybe, I thought, RyoNa had decided on the

same thing, for he still seemed to be waiting for me just inside the large doorway.

As I reached the doorway, RyoNa took a few steps backward into the darker interior and then spoke a word that I couldn't make out, for it was hardly more than a whisper and, as it turned out, not directed toward me at all.

I could hardly make them out at first, those who came from even farther back in the darkness, several of them, men as big as RyoNa or even bigger, and more given to muscle than the plump, well-groomed man I'd been following. And I knew they weren't jumping out to bid me good evening and welcome to their humble abode.

As I stepped backward, trying to gain the advantage of what little light there was in the alley, I did two things: externally, my right hand made its way through the folds of the robe I wore and found the butt of the energy pistol I'd been carrying in case something like this did happen; internally, I switched my body into combat augmentation. The world around me seemed to slow down; sounds dopplered toward the bass registers; what light I could see seemed to shift toward the red end of the spectrum; and certain rods and cones of my eyes allowed me to perceive more of what was taking place in the shadows of the alley as they electronically shifted into lower-light modes.

The pistol was now free of the robe, and I brought it up, clicking off the safety, trying to get it up in time to fire, though even with augmentation coming into operation I wasn't fast enough for that.

In the moments I had left, I could see that there were six of them, as big as I'd thought, all clad in black, and with furious determination written on their faces. What kind of men were these that RyoNa had sent at me? And why had he done it? Then there was no more time for speculation. . . .

An expertly swung, heavily booted foot came up

and knocked the energy pistol from my hand, for an instant stunning my right arm, but by that time I'd come up to full X5 and was able to lash back at the man before his foot was on the ground again. My half-numbed, half-stinging hand was balled into a fist that must have loosened a few teeth and may have broken a nose as it skidded across his face. I didn't have time to check. The rest of them were on me.

I think I gave a pretty good account of myself, all things considered, but there were six of them—now five, then four—but even with the advantages of augmentation, I'm no superman. While I was tangling with three of them, one having somehow latched on to my left arm with a grip I couldn't break, the fourth got behind me and did his damnedest to break open my skull with something very heavy and very blunt. He came too close to succeeding for my comfort.

I was only half-aware of the sensation that knocked my head forward, brought a flash of lightning to my eyes, and robbed me of all ability to direct the actions of my hands and feet. I went limp and felt my augmentation automatically cutting itself out. I held on to consciousness for only a few seconds longer, just long enough to hear the voice of RyoNa, who came closer to me now, speaking EKhona, the language of this part of the local world. "I didn't expect you to put up such a great fight, Harkos. I am astonished at your prowess. You *are* the man we're looking for, I'm certain. Welcome, friend, to the BrathelLanza."

I didn't know what he was talking about, or much care right at the moment, and let whatever consciousness I had left slip away from me.

2

A Visiting Shadow

I have only vague recollections of the next half hour or so, though I dimly recall being half dragged, half carried into the building to which RyoNa had led me, and down a long, dimly lighted corridor to the doors of what must have been a huge cargo elevator—at the time I could only vaguely wonder at the presence of the elevator in a decaying building in the city's worst slums. The elevator doors closed behind us, I seem to remember, and then there was the sensation of dropping, going down, down, down. And that's all I can remember for a while.

When I opened my eyes next I was lying on a cot in a small room illuminated by a single strip of light that ran across the ceiling, a dim light that revealed damp walls of concrete or stone. To my nostrils came the odors of stagnation and decay, as if this room had been long unused, and when it was used it wasn't for the most pleasant of purposes.

RyoNa stood not far from the cot on which I lay, a vague smile on his face. Behind him stood two of the black-clad apes, one on each side of the doorway, and they looked at me without kindness or sympathy. I thought that the big red bruise on the cheek of one of them might have something to do with their lack of friendliness.

At last RyoNa spoke, and the tone of his voice was more friendly than the looks I was getting from his companions. "It's unfortunate that it had to be this way, Harkos." HarkosNor was the name by which RyoNa knew me. "But I could hardly be certain of

your cooperation once—well, once you found out that
I really have no connections with the chronal-displacement project at all."

I suppose I should have been surprised, and if my
head hadn't hurt so much I might have been, but right
then I was only disappointed. He'd lied to me, strung
me along—not that such a thing seemed greatly out of
character for him—but to what end I couldn't then
guess. As I was about to open my mouth and try to
get my voice working so that I could ask him, he
spoke again.

"Others will be coming soon to speak with you,
some very important people, and they will answer
your questions for you, so don't even ask them of me.
I was instructed to say that you are valued highly and
that they would prefer that you suffer no more hurt."

"I'd prefer it that way myself," I finally managed to
say.

"I'm sure," RyoNa said, then took a hesitant step
forward and fished something out of the folds of his
dark robe. "This may be of some help to you." He
bent forward, still more than an arm's reach from the
cot where I lay, and placed a small bottle on the
floor. "Drink that. It won't hurt you and may help
to relieve the pain in your head."

I looked at the bottle with suspicion and then back
at RyoNa with the same feeling.

"If we wanted you dead, you would already be
dead," he said, with the hint of a smile on his lips.
"And why should we waste time with poison?"

Maybe he had a point there.

Then he backed to the doorway and allowed one
of the black-clad characters to open the door for
him. As he disappeared between them, he said, "Please
wait as patiently as you can, Harkos. The others should
be here soon."

The two men in black, still looking uglily at me,
moved through the doorway and closed the door be-

hind them. I heard the distinct sound of a heavy bolt
sliding home. *Clack!* Sure, I'd wait. What else could
I do?

I lay still for a while before I carefully lifted myself
from the cot and went to get the little bottle of colorless liquid that RyoNa had left for me. Maybe it was
something to help my head; with the passage of time
the pain in it had not lessened much. It could have
been something other than what he'd claimed, but,
on the probability that it was a painkiller, I decided
to take it. What did I have to lose now anyway?

The simple movement from the cot to the bottle
and back again was enough to double the pounding
in my head and make me wonder if the blow had
caused a concussion, or worse. I drank the liquid—
right then I might have taken it even if I'd strongly
suspected it to be something worse than it actually was.

There was an oily, fruity taste to it and the tang
of alcohol, and it burned my throat as it went down,
but almost instantly I began to feel better, or thought
I did.

In a few minutes I could sit up on the side of the
cot, feeling something not greatly worse than a moderate hangover, and that too seemed to be passing. I
silently thanked RyoNa for the medicine, if for nothing
else.

With the passing of the pain I was able to examine
my new surroundings a little more closely, though I
found them of little interest. The cot was the room's
only article of furniture. Three of the walls were flat,
damp concrete, I saw now, with a slightly slimy feel
when I touched them with my fingertips. The fourth
wall was different only in that a door had been cut
in it, a heavy door that seemed to have been made
from a single piece of wood, which I knew to be
bolted from the outside. The floor was made of the
same concrete as the walls, and so was the ceiling,
which was distinguished only by the dimly glowing

strip that ran from one of the side walls to the other. From inside the room there appeared no means either of turning off the light or of controlling its intensity. And exactly how the strip, which appeared to be made of translucent plastic maybe a quarter of an inch thick and three inches wide, produced its light, I didn't know, nor did I concern myself greatly with it.

Having examined the room and discovered nothing that would help me out of my predicament, I went back to the cot, sat down, and was about to begin what I hoped to be a dispassionate analysis of my situation, when I became aware of something else in the room, something that had not been there a moment before.

In one of the two corners most remote from the door, in the shadows where the glowing strip illuminated to an even lesser extent, there seemed to be the beginning of the formation of a cloud of smoke, hazy wisps turning slowly in the air, extending from the floor nearly to the ceiling. There was also, in the atmosphere, even less tangible but nonetheless real, a sensation that had become an almost familiar one to me: a sense of electrical tension, a feeling such as one sometimes has at the approach of a thunderstorm, the sense of power that you can't see or hear or touch or smell but that you know is there.

The smokiness in the corner grew thicker, more intense, more opaque, and now had begun to take on the shape I'd come to expect—from top to bottom the hazy form was about the height of a man, and, like a man, it had the outlines of two legs, a torso, two arms, a head set above shadowy shoulders, though within the head there could be discerned no facial features whatsoever. Now the shadow, the haze, had solidified as far as I thought it would, had become as substantial as it could.

I waited for the Shadowy Man to speak, as I knew he would.

"Well, Eric," the voice said out of the haze, a voice uncertain at first, then more positive, a voice that I knew to sound exactly like my own, "I hope you're not feeling too badly now."

I shook my head. "I'm okay." Then I said to him, "I was afraid the Tromas had destroyed you back in KHL-000." He knew what I was talking about.

A chuckle came out of the shadowy haze. "Damn," my voice said from the corner, "this could get confusing."

"What do you mean?" I asked.

"What you're talking about is in your past, you see," the Shadowy Man said, "but it's in *my* future. It hasn't happened to *me* yet, so I don't know the outcome of our fight with the Krithian ladies any more than you do."

"I see," I said, though I wasn't certain that I did.

"I hope you do, though I'm not positive I do. As I said, it *could* get confusing."

"Yeah," I said, and grunted, and then waited for him to tell me whatever it was he had to tell me. He'd come for a reason, I was certain of that.

"Your head's not hurting now, and don't worry, you don't have a concussion. That lump will go away in a few days."

"That's comforting," I said, despite myself feeling awe in *his* presence, and still wondering just what our relationship was/would be, for somehow in the confusion of time future and time past, the Shadowy Man and I were very closely linked, terribly closely.

"And I suggest that the best thing for you will be to cooperate with the members of the BrathelLanza when they come to visit you."

"The what?" That word again!

"The BrathelLanza," he repeated. "You'll find out what it is in due time. For now, cooperate with them as fully as possible, for from cooperating with them will come answers to the questions you want to ask of me, and a means of action."

"A means of action?" I asked stupidly.

"Yes, a means of action, the action that will bring . . . well, you'll see," he said, and chuckled as if he were playing a very funny joke on me.

"What in—" I started to ask, but it was already too late. The haziness in the corner was beginning to lose its manlike form, to become vague, mixing fogs that dissipated even more quickly than they had formed. The electrical tension was gone from the air.

"Damn!" I said aloud, and got up from the cot and walked to the corner. There was nothing there, of course. Nothing at all.

"Why do you have to be so damned mysterious?" I asked the empty air, and if I did hear a chuckle for answer, I was probably imagining it. Wasn't I?

I sat back down on the cot, cursed the Shadowy Man—whoever, whatever, he was—wished for a cigarette, of which I had none, or a cup of coffee, of which I had as little, and wondered just exactly what it was this "BrathelLanza" had in store for me. Probably not a time machine—not if RyoNa had finally been telling me the truth. Then what? Answers? "A means of action." Now what did that mean?

Damn, damn, damn, I said to myself, and sat on the edge of the cot and waited for the arrival of those "very important people" that RyoNa had promised were coming.

3

From the Far World to VarKhohs

While I waited in that dim, dank cell somewhere
under the city of VarKhohs on a Timeline that the
beings I called Kriths had been very secretive about—
though not secretive enough, it seemed at the time—I
found that despite myself I was reviewing the events
of the past year or so, the sequence of events that
had led me from what had been a rather comfortable
if sometimes dangerous condition to one far less comfortable and perhaps even more dangerous, and I
wondered about the wisdom of some of the decisions
I'd made; even up until three or four months ago I
could have stayed out of it—I think—and lived not
a bad life with Sally way off there on a world of the
far Temporal-East. But my curiosity, and maybe a
taste for vengeance, wouldn't let me . . . and here I
was.

Thanks to the help of this mysterious Shadowy Man
—whoever, whatever he is—Sally and I had escaped
from the Tromas on KHL-000, had escaped to a place
the Shadowy Man had picked out for us, a pleasant
enough world a long way to the T-East where we
probably could have spent the rest of our lives in
comfort, if I hadn't been so damned stubborn, so
damned curious, so damned determined to see if I
could get in a lick against the Kriths.

The Shadowy Man had provided us with a skudder
and I couldn't resist, sooner or later, using it. Somewhere, somewhen in time, I was to be mixed up with
the Shadowy Man again, was somehow to become a
part of him, it seemed, and to do that I was going to

have to be able to move about in time itself, future time and past time. I had to have a time machine. So I thought.

Once I was certain that Sally would have no problems if I were gone, would live like a queen or a demigoddess in the semibarbaric kingdoms of the world we'd found, I went back to the skudder in the woods, leaving her a note that told her what I was doing and why. I hoped she'd understand. And I was going to miss her like crazy, but I couldn't let her risk her life again by going along with my insane ideas. *Maybe I'd* be able to come back to her.

So, like that thief in the night, I took the skudder the Shadowy Man had provided for us, and set off across the Lines to see what I could find.

Specifically what I was looking for was the one known world that had developed/would develop a device capable of moving about in time. I was relatively certain that such a world did exist, although finding it wasn't easy.

Like the spectrum of a beam of sunlight shown on paper through a prism, there is no sharp distinction from world to world, but only very subtle changes that over a vast number of parallel worlds can lead to surprising differences. World B might differ from world A only in something so minor as the first name of a head of state in a rather unimportant nation. In world C that same head of state might have a different last name, and in world D he might have a somewhat different personality that would give his nation a chance for success in a minor war that it wouldn't have had in worlds A and B. By the time you get to world J, that nation might not be so minor and on world Z it might dominate the planet. Or destroy it.

So I had to search large areas of paratime, moving carefully from world to world, searching for clues that would tell me I was at least heading in the right direction.

And on one world where I spent more than a few days, a world with a more highly developed medical science than most, I found a not-too-scrupulous surgeon who removed the transmitter the Kriths had buried in my body long before. I gave the surgeon a large amount of gold and he gave me a local anesthetic, and while I watched, my hand resting on the butt of my energy pistol, he removed and destroyed the telltale. I thanked him and went on my way, hopeful that Kriths wouldn't find me as easily as they had before, if they were still looking for me. And I suspected they were.

At last, by following leads and hints and rumors too obscure to go into now, I found the world for which I had been searching, or at least I thought I had found it. I hoped I had.

I skudded into that particular world when it was late at night in eastern North America and hid my skudder near a small town not too distant from what appeared to be the major city of the continent, Var-Khohs, capital of NakrehVatee. The language here, called EKhona, was a remote kin of one I'd learned on another Line when in the service of the Kriths, so fortunately it didn't take me too long to master the local speech. It took me a little longer to get the hang of local customs, but I managed to stay out of jail and trade some of the large quantity of finely worked gold I'd brought along for local currency. With that I was able to buy myself a computer identity that would account for my light skin, my accent, and my relative ignorance of the ways of the world: I was a mercenary soldier named HarkosNor from the Central European country of SteeMehseeh, who had bought his way out of indenture with loot gained in a brushfire war in the Far East and who had applied for a visa to enter NakrehVatee, where he would seek permission to join the nation's "foreign legion" and serve again as a mercenary. The man who sold me the

identity, a shady type who I hoped was more trustworthy than he looked, assured me that HarkosNor
was a real person, though dead now, and that my identity would hold up under the closest scrutiny. I hoped
he wasn't lying.

So there I was, officially, if illegally, a member of
the local culture. I was as ready as I'd ever be to go
into the city of VarKhohs to try to find myself a
time machine.

Finding what I was searching for was just about as
difficult as finding this world in the first place, but
there are always people around who are ready to offer
information about supposedly secret things if you
cross their palms in the proper fashion. Thus it was
that after several weeks in VarKhohs I began spending
a great deal of time in a place with an unpronounce-
able name that was a combination restaurant, lounge,
massage parlor, steam bath, and brothel, frequented by
members of a moderately-high caste and their hangers-
on—the caste given over to electronic engineering and
other technologies. And it was there that I made the
acquaintance of a certain RyoNa, not a technician
himself, but a member of one of the administrative
castes and supposedly a friend of the engineers and
technicians.

It would have been difficult to say exactly what time
it was, getting on toward the wee hours, and both my
new friend RyoNa and I were close to exhaustion.
We'd eaten and drunk our fill in the lower levels of
the elaborate and luxurious pleasure-house and then
had moved upward to the levels devoted to the games
and the girls. We'd gambled for a while, losing more
than we won, and had picked up a brace of twins,
girls even darker of skin than most of the locals, with
long black hair and flashing black eyes, dressed in
styles that revealed not only their profession but the
lovely tools of their trade. As they led us off to their

bedroom apartments in the towering building, I felt
a pang of guilt at betraying Sally, again, and wondered
if she was being as faithful to me as I was to her.
I hoped not!

We parted company, RyoNa and his girl, I and
mine, and indulged ourselves in the wicked pleasures
of the flesh—and I discovered that the dark-skinned
girl, whose name I'd already forgotten, was a past
mistress of the arts of sexual pleasure. When I'd finally told her good-bye, with a kiss and a handful of bank
notes, I was totally exhausted and felt the beginnings
of a hangover.

Downstairs, in one of the lounges, I found my buddy
RyoNa exactly where he'd said he would be, drinking
a dark, heavy liquid from a tall tumbler. A similar
tumbler, this one full, was on the opposite side of
the table.

"Sit down, Harkos," RyoNa said, seemingly still
amused by the outlandishness of my name. "I've already ordered for you."

"I see. What is it?" I asked as I sat down.

"Try it."

I did, and found it to be a very pleasant fruit mixture that probably would have been rated ninety proof
or better on a world that rated alcoholic content in
that fashion.

"Is it good?" RyoNa asked.

I grunted, nodded.

"And was she good?"

I grunted, nodded again.

"I told you she would be. Those EstarSimirian girls
are just about the best around. Raised from childhood
to master the arts of bed pleasure, you know."

"I certainly wasn't disappointed," I told him with
a weary sigh.

"And what did she think of you?"

"Me?"

RyoNa nodded, and smiled with a wicked gleam

in his eyes. "It is very rare for a fair-skinned barbarian to bed with the girls of a VarKhohs pleasure-house."

"Oh, yeah." I sighed, and sipped my drink again.

Though I hadn't yet really begun to sort out the history of this world and its many cultures, I had some idea of what he was referring to. The fair-skinned people of northern Europe, on this Line, were not the first ones to develop a technological civilization. That fell to the darker people of the eastern Mediterranean, western Asia, and northern Africa. It was they who first sailed the "Inland Sea" and learned to tack against the wind and who finally set out into the great oceans of the West and of the Southeast, who circumnavigated the globe for the first time and then began to colonize the New World, who built steam engines and invented things like the telegraph and telephone and the airplane, and who ignited the first atomic bomb somewhere in Africa and burned away the better part of a great city.

The blue-eyed blonds, of which I am one even though as a child I spoke a version of Greek, had been to the Asians as the American Indians had been to the Europeans who colonized North America in Sally's world: savages to be dispossessed of their land for the benefit of the "more civilized" people from the South and the East. Long years of warfare followed, during which most of the natives of northern Europe were exterminated, though when the wars came to an end, the surviving Europeans, by then hardened by decades of combat, came to be a warrior caste among the spreading colonists, a people apart, to be used to wage their wars.

Such a one to them I seemed, accepted now as nearly an equal by the "enlightened moderns," but still—was I feared, or respected, or looked upon with a kind of awe by people to whom active participation in warfare was a thing of the past?

"I don't suppose I greatly disappointed her," I said at last, finishing my drink.

"Another," RyoNa said, a statement, not a question, and punched out another set of drinks on the table's ordering keys. "I doubt you did disappoint her. By Themfo-Okketho, what a pair you two must have been! I wish I could have watched."

"I'm exhausted," I said.

"No doubt the girl is too."

"She may be."

"Oh, when I go to my tomb and journey to the Dark Lands, I'd like to take an EstarSimirian whore with me, the Dark Lords willing."

When the drinks came, delivered by a waitress of low caste, clad as revealingly as the dark girls had been, RyoNa was silent for a while, then cast his eyes about the darkened room in a conspiratorial manner.

"I will name no names, friend Harkos," he said, "nor state any facts. But I believe I know where to find the man you seek."

"The man I seek? What do you mean?"

"No names. No facts. But you have let slip to me that there is a certain *thing* you would like to have access to. Is this not so?"

"Yes, there is a thing I need."

"A thing the very existence of which is supposed to be known to only a few, is this not so?"

I nodded. We were talking about a prototype of one of the chronal-displacement devices, and we both knew it. My hints in the past had been sufficient to establish that.

"It is one of the earlier models, you know," he said softly. "Not as refined as the ones now being tested, but it seems to do the job for which it was designed."

"Where is it?"

"Ah." He sighed. "That I cannot say. But let me say this: it is not where it is supposed to be. It was to be sent to one of the nations allied to NakrehVatee, a nation whose name I cannot speak. It was shipped, but it never arrived at its destination. A—shall we say, a friend of mine knows its present location."

"Can you take me to this friend?" I asked.

"It may be possible. I must visit him myself and discuss with him the arrangements. It will be very costly."

"I had anticipated that."

"*Very* costly."

"How much?"

He stated a figure that would be meaningless without a knowledge of the local currency, but it was a high one, one that I thought I could just barely meet. I'd brought a lot of gold with me.

"Very well," RyoNa said, once I'd nodded in agreement. "When I go to visit my friend I will need a token of your good faith."

"How much?"

"Ten per cent should suffice."

"When?"

"The day after tomorrow, mid-afternoon. Meet me here. It must be in hard currency. No paper."

"It will be."

"Very good."

We finished our drinks in silence and then departed the pleasure-house.

At the appointed time I sat in the pleasure-house lounge with a sack that held the hard currency, small, flat bars of platinum embossed with the symbols of the highest castes of VarKhohs. I had just finished my drink when RyoNa entered, took a seat across from me, and waited while I ordered drinks for us.

"You have it?"

I passed the leather sack to him under the table. I felt like a fool. What did I know of this RyoNa? How far could I trust him?

"Good," he said. "I will drink my drink and then

I must go. Wait here for me. I should be back shortly before dark. I will then have the arrangements."

"Okay." I sighed, and sipped my fresh drink, while he swallowed his in a single gulp and then rose and left the lounge.

After a short wait I rose to follow him. He probably expected me to.

Damned right he'd expected me to!

That's how I'd ended up in a cell, remembering all this while I waited for his "very important people" to visit me.

4

Into the Underground

It wouldn't be correct to say that the time was interminable, but it was much longer than I would have liked, alone in the cramped room under the earth, but at last RyoNa did return and with him were three others, as well as the two black-clad guards, who may have been outside the room the whole time.

The guards entered the room first, looked me over carefully as if there were some means by which I could have gained weapons in their absence—fat chance!—and then stood on either side of the open door. RyoNa entered next and suggested I get up off the cot and remain standing. Remembering what the Shadowy Man had said, I stood up.

AkweNema, so the first man was introduced, a name that had an almost familiar ring to it, though I couldn't recall where I'd heard it. He was a big man, larger and heavier even than RyoNa, more given to fat, with long hair of an unexpected, astonishing red and a florid cast to his swarthy complexion. This North America too was a melting pot of racial types, it seemed. His robes were rich and dazzling, of a dark red material with silvery piping that reflected the room's dim light, and he wore the symbols of an elevated caste and of the medical profession on his chest and sparkling rings on his fingers.

AkweNema bowed slightly when introduced, a gesture he expected me to reproduce, which I did, and then he looked me over with an intelligent if somewhat piercing gaze, and with a bit of the clinical about it.

I later learned that he was, in fact, a medical doctor, among other things.

Then he nodded to RyoNa and gave him a pleasant, you-have-done-well sort of smile. RyoNa was pleased and I felt like a side of beef that he had just procured for AkweNema's pantry.

The second man was smaller than either AkweNema or RyoNa, a slender, almost wizened man of indeterminate age, with bright eyes set deep in their sockets under heavy eyebrows. He could have been fifty years old or he could have been seventy. He too was dressed in the luxurious robes of one of the higher castes, a technologically oriented one, I suspected from the decoration of his robe, and if I read the symbols rightly, he practiced his profession in the academic manner of a university instructor. His name was Kaph-No and he carried an honorific that could just barely be translated as "professor."

The third man was the youngest, in his late twenties, I suspected, although his full beard initially gave the impression of someone older, as did his eyes and the premature streak of gray in his long, carefully coiffured hair. Though his robes were less lavish than those of the first two, the symbols on his chest were those of one of the highest castes of all. Lord Dessa-Tyso, as he was named, stood closer to the peak of the social pyramid than did the others, although I soon began to suspect that he was in a lesser position to exercise actual power than were his two older companions. He affected a bored, supercilious expression and I thought that he had probably been very spoiled as a child.

That he was still spoiled, I learned later.

When the introductions were completed and the three men had finished their inspections of me, Akwe-Nema, the headman and ringleader, spoke again. "We have no desire to constrain you against your will, Master HarkosNor"—he addressed me as a gentleman of his own social rank: odd—"though we will do so if necessary. We would prefer your cooperation, and I suspect that once you know who we are and what we are doing, and once you have seen the rewards we have to offer you"—he paused in mid-sentence and smiled—"and once you have forgiven us for the deception we played on you, we think you will be very willing to cooperate."

I was already, I thought, but I'd want to know more very soon. Addressing him as an equal, I said, "Master AkweNema, this hasn't been a very pleasant welcome you've given me, and I'd like to know what you're up to. Right now all I can feel is cheated and used."

"Very shortly we will explain it all to you, I promise," AkweNema replied in a conciliatory tone. "If you will give us your word, for the time being, that you will attempt neither to escape nor to use violence against any of us, we will allow you a certain limited freedom under your own recognizance."

"For how long?" I asked.

"Until you have let us speak our piece and we have made you an offer," the big, red-haired man said.

"And if I refuse your offer?"

"I doubt that you will," he said.

"We shall speak of that later, Master HarkosNor," said the lord DessaTyso, using the condescending address of a superior to his social inferior.

"Come," AkweNema said in a jovial tone of voice, "I am certain that this place is as unpleasant to you as it is to us. Let us go to a place where we can relax and have a cup of wine."

I shrugged.

"Then you will give us your word?" the lord DessaTyso asked.

"Yeah," I said, and grunted, giving his rank no recognition. "What have I got to lose?"

Lord DessaTyso gave me a crooked smile but didn't speak.

"RyoNa, you may go," AkweNema said. "We will contact you when we need you."

"Very good, sir," RyoNa said, using the address one would use to a social superior, though not quite as honorable an address as the one he might have used toward the lord DessaTyso. Then he turned to face me. "You'll think better of me when these gentlemen have had their say, Harkos."

I just looked at him without speaking.

With a shrug toward me and a bow toward the others, he turned and left, and as he did I thought I could hear the jingle of platinum bars in a leather sack he carried under his robe. A good day's pay for services rendered.

"You are excused as well," AkweNema said to the guards at the door, who gave me unfriendly looks as they left the room. They seemed not to think as highly of me as AkweNema did. "And now, gentlemen and sire, to my suite, if you will."

AkweNema led us from the room, with Professor KaphNo directly behind him. Lord DessaTyso was careful to stay at my side. I wondered if he was armed. I suspected so.

The first part of the journey was through what must have been some very old underground service tunnels, no longer in use, saved from total decay by the efforts of AkweNema's people. The tunnels had been cleaned up and buttressed to prevent their collapse and had been provided with illumination strips sufficient for safe passage through the tunnels. But this wasn't where the bulk of their efforts had been exerted.

We had gone perhaps half a mile through the underground passages when we came to a metal wall that blocked the tunnel from floor to ceiling, and through which passed a pair of heavy metal doors, which were guarded by two burly, black-clad men carrying automatic pistols and with what might have been gas grenades clipped to their belts.

AkweNema spoke a greeting to them, to which they responded by opening the doors, allowing us to pass into another section of the Underground. The guards eyed me with suspicion, but, unlike their fellows, not with open hatred. They hadn't been among the bunch on the surface.

Once we were through the metal doorway I saw that here a great deal more than simple cleaning and bracing of the tunnel walls had been done. Bright parallel strips of illumination, like glowing railroad tracks, dwindled in the distance of the long, long corridors. The walls had been smoothed and painted or paneled and were decorated with bright photographs of outdoor scenes of the world above and with vividly graphic posters that said such things as THE WORLD IS AWAITING OUR COMING and THE FUTURE RESTS IN THE HANDS OF THE BRATHELLANZA and THE CHILDREN OF TOMORROW WILL BE OURS. Carpeting had been laid across the floor, soft and cushiony. Doors led off from the tunnel into other chambers cut into the earth and stone. Far ahead I could hear voices and the movement of men and machinery.

Just inside the metal doorway an attractive young woman in a bright blue gown sat behind a desk, and to each of us she handed a yellow disk, which we fixed to the fronts of our robes. AkweNema, making no introductions, asked her, "Is my suite ready?"

The girl smiled, nodded, and said, "Yes, sir, it is."

"Please have food and drink delivered there. We are not to be disturbed until you are notified."

"Yes, sir," the girl said again. "But, ah, sir, the lady OrDjina has been asking about his lordship."

DessaTyso shot a quick glance at AkweNema, who nodded in return. "I don't suppose her being there would create any problem." To the girl: "Inform Lady OrDjina that she is more than welcome."

"Very good, sir."

And with that AkweNema led us on again, a hundred yards or so down the brightly lighted tunnel, to a large wooden door before which stood an elderly man in a simple blue uniform. Without speaking, the man bowed and opened the door for AkweNema.

"Food is coming," AkweNema said to the blue-clad servant. "Please see to it."

"Very good, sire." The servant used a higher form of address than had the girl at the desk; he hung from lower rungs of the social ladder.

The lord DessaTyso and I followed AkweNema and KaphNo through the doorway.

A series of lavish rooms lay beyond the wooden door, though at first I saw only one of them, the first and largest, something that could almost have been out of *The Arabian Nights:* plush carpets and great down-filled cushions in place of chairs; tables on which sat beautifully detailed vases and tall, elaborate lamps; wall hangings and tapestries of the richest materials, the most complex of designs (made by hand or by computer-directed looms? I wondered); in the middle of the room stood a marble sculpture of a mermaid rising from the sea; in the background, a beautiful if esoteric music played.

"Sit down, gentlemen and my lord. Refreshments should be arriving soon," AkweNema said. "I trust that you could do with food and drink, Master Harkos-Nor."

"I could," I admitted.

As we sat down on the cushions, again DessaTyso looked me over carefully, coldly, as if inspecting a horse someone had offered to sell him—or a slave. I didn't care much for his appraisal and I tried to tell him so with a cold, hard look of my own. He must have caught my meaning, for he smiled crookedly and looked away without speaking.

"We must wait a bit more, HarkosNor," AkweNema said. "It would be inhospitable on my part to begin our talk without offering you refreshment."

I nodded and continued to look around the room, trying to estimate, in terms of some monetary system, the cost of the items that filled the apartment. A fortune, easily, but exactly how great a fortune I couldn't guess.

The lord DessaTyso appeared to be on the verge of speaking when there came a rap on the door, gentle, servile, but clearly audible, and then the door opened to allow the blue-clad steward to enter, pushing a great wheeled cart that looked too big for him, and which was laden with bottles and goblets and dishes and covered bowls. As he entered and was about to close the door behind him, another person appeared and was framed for a moment in the open doorway.

"OrDjina," DessaTyso called out, half rising to his feet and gesturing for the newcomer to enter. "Please come in."

"Yes, please do, my lady," AkweNema said, also rising halfway and getting off an awkward little bow.

I figured I might as well rise too, as the others had done.

Old KaphNo, silent and perhaps brooding, made no effort to rise.

The woman, who brushed around the steward and came into the room, was almost enough to make me catch my breath in my throat. To say that she was beautiful is hardly adequate.

Perhaps in her early thirties, mature and fully in possession of herself, she was tall, nearly six feet I would have guessed, and beautifully proportioned. She wore a dark, clinging gown that molded itself to the contours of her body, revealing and yet hiding each line and curve of her torso and legs; her arms were bare except for silvery bracelets on her forearms and dazzling rings on her fingers.

She had dark, dusky skin the color of an old and highly polished piece of prized oak, and long black hair that trailed down her back to below her shoulder blades; tiny gems, like stars, twinkled in her hair. Her eyes were large, black, bright, intelligent; her lips, very full, covered perfect, bright white teeth that showed as she now smiled at us, as she entered the room and closed the door behind her.

It was only later that I realized that there were no badges of rank and caste on her breast, and wondered why.

"Thank you, AkweNema," she said, equal-to-equal, briefly offering the man her hand. Her voice was melodious and rich, a slightly husky alto. She could have had a great career as a singer or an actress, I thought.

She nodded to KaphNo and spoke his name, but she seemed to expect no reply other than the upward glance that came from under his bushy eyebrows. Then her gaze came to me.

"And you must be the barbarian warrior Harkos-Nor," she said, offering her hand, which I briefly clasped as AkweNema had done. I could detect no condescension in her voice.

"I am HarkosNor," I replied.

When she had retrieved her hand, perhaps pleased that all the fingers were still there, she went on past me to where the lord DessaTyso again sat on the cushioned floor, there to sit down beside him and take one of his hands fondly between both of hers.

Yes, I told myself, the lord DessaTyso is still very much the spoiled princeling.

By this time the steward thought it safe to move again, and rolled the food-and-wine-laden cart into the middle of the room, up next to the mermaid sculpture.

"Shall I serve you now, sire?" he asked of Akwe-Nema in a servile tone of voice.

"No, no," AkweNema said, dismissing him with a wave of his fat hand. "We can serve ourselves. You may go."

"Thank you, sire." The blue-clad man then quietly vanished.

"Then let us eat," AkweNema said, rising again and crossing to the cart the steward had brought in. "Then we may talk."

While we ate, and while I glanced in OrDjina's direction whenever the conversation would decently allow—a conversation of small talk that I could barely follow, talk of palace intrigues among the higher castes of VarKhohs, of hinted scandals, of corrupted bureaucracy burdened almost to the point of self-destruction by its own complexities—I wondered just what it was that AkweNema and his friends would have to say when the time for serious talk finally arrived.

And I remembered again the Shadowy Man's most recent advice. His advice had served me well in the past, though some of the things he had led me into hadn't always been of the most pleasant nature.

How would this one turn out? I wondered.

5

The BrathelLanza's Proposal

"Master HarkosNor," AkweNema began over tall goblets of white wine after the meal was finished, a "snack," he had said, which had consisted of several courses of fish and fowl and flesh, "we know that you are a stranger in our land and have been among our people for only a short while, and we know that you have come here in the hope of gaining for yourself one of the so-called time machines that our technicians supposedly have built and are testing."

"Chronal-displacement devices," KaphNo threw in, his voice a bitter grumbling. I think it was the first time he'd spoken since we'd arrived in AkweNema's suite.

"I stand corrected," AkweNema said, smiling. "Chronal-displacement devices." The smile went away. "And for what purpose you wish one we do not know. It is no concern of ours." His face said differently; and I wondered what he thought a barbarian warrior like HarkosNor wanted with a time machine—to go back into time to save his people from the humiliation of subjugation, or merely to get away to a simpler world where a warrior stood in higher honor? "But we may be able to help you get one, since that is your wish," he was saying.

"I thought that was what RyoNa was in the process of doing earlier today," I said, letting my voice sound as bitter and angry as I dared.

"I can understand your feelings," AkweNema said, "and I understand your anger at us. Your anger may seem justified to you now, but please hold it in abeyance for a while." He paused, sighed, then continued: "I am afraid that RyoNa lied to you in several respects. There is no time—no chronal-displacement device in all of NakrehVatee, nor in all the world, that is not under the heaviest of guard. There are, in fact, only four of them in existence, and they do not work nearly as well as the popular imagination would lead you to believe, and may never—and, in addition, it would be impossible for you to gain one of them, imperfect as they are, without the aid of an army, or without the aid of a new government in power in NakrehVatee.".

I gave him back stare for stare but didn't speak.

"Which brings me to my point," he said. "With *your* aid, we can provide you with both—an army *and* a new government.

"As a newcomer to our land, you may be ignorant of the many injustices that now exist in our nation. We may be the greatest power on Earth today, but as things stand now our society is rotten to the core. Over the years the caste system, which has many good and truly admirable points, has been abused by certain groups in positions of power. The castes themselves have multiplied and subdivided to such an extent that the whole system has become unwieldy and at times even self-destructive.

"New castes have been formed as offshoots of older castes to serve new functions as society has developed, which is well and good; but older castes whose functions have ceased to be of value continue to exist, and those born into them, some of the lower ones, have no way out of them, save through death and hopefully a better change during their next reincarnation, if they as individuals have earned the karma for another chance at life."

The eyes of the others in the room were more on me than on AkweNema. I hoped my face looked as noncommittal as I was trying to make it look.

"We have, on the one extreme," AkweNema was saying, "castes in positions of power and wealth that have no useful function and are only parasitic to society, consuming vast quantities of goods and services, yet contributing nothing. And on the other extreme are castes which have fallen far down the scale of society and now exist to no good purpose, consuming little, but with their members doomed to live in poverty and hunger, with no hope of ever finding gainful employment in their present lives. They are sustained only by thoughts of the Dark Lords and passage beyond the lands over which they rule, for what need is there for a caste of chimney sweeps when there are no chimneys left to sweep? Castes such as those are also parasitic to society, though I'm certain that the people who are members of them do not wish to be.

"Let me say here, Master HarkosNor, that we of the BrathelLanza—the Brotherhood of Life—are not anarchists or wild-eyed radicals out to destroy the caste system entirely. Not at all. We merely wish to purify it, to restore it to the state of cleanliness that made NakrehVatee the great nation it once was not so many years ago."

KaphNo looked up briefly, a crooked, unpleasant smile on his face as if he had just bitten into a lemon and didn't want to admit how sour it was.

"Our goal," AkweNema said, "is to return a better life to the castes, to the people, of our nation."

As he talked further of the evils he saw in the present society of NakrehVatee, as he further enumerated the wrongs that must be put right and how the BrathelLanza would go about doing it, his words came more quickly, more harshly, and there came into his eyes a gleam I didn't like, a glow perhaps of fanaticism, or of madness.

And when I glanced at the other faces, I saw reflected in their eyes that gleam I'd seen in AkweNema's.

I'd gotten myself mixed up with a bunch of fanatical revolutionaries, by God!

But the Shadowy Man had said . . .

It may have been thirty minutes later when Akwe-Nema finally came to find a specific direction in his harangue.

"So we have banded together in the BrathelLanza," he said, "the Brotherhood of Life that will set things right in NakrehVatee, Lord DessaTyso and Professor KaphNo and myself, Ladies OrDjina and EnDera, Drs. ThefeRa and SkorTho, psychologist GrelLo, and the many others whom you will meet in the coming days, if you agree to join us in our sacred cause.

"We have formed cadres all over the nation, and the people who believe as we do, who believe that the time has come to cleanse the nation, have come to us, have joined us. We are training them and arming them so that when the day comes we can rise as one force, solidified in our resolve and our commitment, and put down those in positions of ill-gained power."

He paused, licked his dry lips. I wondered how much of his speech had been memorized and how much of it had come to him as he spoke.

"We have already formed the nucleus of the new government," AkweNema continued, his voice calmer now. "Lord DessaTyso will be our chief of state, for such has been his training from birth and such is the right his lordship has inherited from his magnificent ancestors, the founders of our state." Lord DessaTyso smiled broadly and basked in OrDjina's obvious admiration. "With humility, KaphNo and I will do our best to serve as his ministers Sinister and Dexter. The cabinet largely has been appointed and will join us here when the time comes. The people will supply the new parliament when the castes have been purged."

"And when will all this take place?" I asked when he paused again.

"We will rise a year from now, perhaps," Akwe-
Nema said. "I hope no longer in time than that. You,
Master HarkosNor, can be a factor in helping us deter-
mine the date."

"Okay," I said. "So you've got a place somewhere
for me in all this. But where it is I can't imagine."

"We need a fighting man to lead our troops," Akwe-
Nema said, "and we need the nucleus of a fighting
force that we hope to make superior to anything the
government presently has in the field."

"And I can do that?" I asked incredulously.

"We believe you can," he replied. "We have studied
you from the day you first approached our agent
RyoNa," he admitted. "For example, the girls you have
slept with—they are all our people, and they have
studied you well."

"Oh?" I said.

He nodded. "We have also checked your background, and we find it of the sort we need. Your experience in combat is greater than that of any other
man your age in all of VarKhohs, perhaps all of
NakrehVatee," AkweNema told me.

And I thought: The guy who sold me my computer
identity said it would be everything I'd ever need. I
guess he was right. It had cost enough.

"We are satisfied with you, HarkosNor," DessaTyso
said. "You are the sort of man we need."

"Then will you join us?" AkweNema asked.

"What exactly do you want of me?" I asked in reply.

"You shall be our general in the field. You and your
private army"—he smiled as he said these words—
"will spearhead the takeover of the central government
buildings of VarKhohs."

Old KaphNo looked up from under his eyebrows.
"You are familiar with the concept of cloning, are you
not, Master HarkosNor?"

"Of course," I said, wondering why he asked.

And as if I hadn't answered, he continued: "Every

cell of the human body—save only the sex cells designed for diversity in the next generation and a few very specialized cells like those of the blood—holds a complete genetic blueprint of the parent body. That is, every bit of genetic information that existed at the time of your conception, in the combined sperm and egg of your parents that grew to be you in your mother's womb, is repeated in exact replication in the cells of, say, the skin of your left index finger, or in the cells of your intestinal lining."

I nodded, beginning to suspect. Sometimes I may be slow, but I'm not *that* dense.

"From any one of those cells," old KaphNo went on, "under the proper conditions, there can be grown an exact duplicate of you, HarkosNor, down to the last detail." He paused, then added: "Except, of course, for the effects that environment has had on you. A clone grown from the cells of HarkosNor would have neither the scars you carry on your body nor the memories you carry in your head."

I nodded, then said, "I know."

"We propose, then," AkweNema picked up after KaphNo grew silent, "to take sample cells from your body—a simple and painless operation, I assure you—and from them *grow* an army of your physical duplicates, an army which you will train and which you will command."

"There is a phenomenon called 'resonance,' " KaphNo said. "Through it, so it appears, the senior member of a replicated partnership or group—in this case, yourself—is able to exercise a significant degree of, shall we say, telepathic control over the junior members. It is not yet well understood, although the same or a similar phenomenon—'sympathetic awareness,' it is often called —was long ago first observed in identical twins, which have many similarities to multiple replicates.

"Furthermore, resonance is even more pronounced when the senior of a replicated unit is an adult at the time of replication. During the later stages of maturation, so it seems, the senior may totally dominate the 'offspring' replicates: that is, by moving in before the brains of the replicates have been exposed to any significant number of external stimuli—we'll go into more detail regarding all this later—and by establishing a resonance pattern before these external stimuli have 'awakened' the brain and allowed it to begin to develop a distinct personality of its own, the senior may exercise *complete* mental, psychological control over the junior replicates, even when separated from them by great distances."

"An army of flesh-and-blood robots controlled by telepathy," the lord DessaTyso said. "Something the fools in power today have feared to create. Fear of the anger of the gods. Ha! More likely fear of creating a power greater than themselves."

Ignoring his lordship, AkweNema said, "Such an army we propose to give to you,. Master HarkosNor."

I remembered a dream I'd once had—it now seemed like a long, long time ago—a nightmare in which I was an army of duplicate people going up against a similar army that was even greater than mine. I shuddered in remembrance of that dream, tried to push it from my mind.

"And in return for your services, HarkosNor," Akwe-Nema was saying, "we offer you a 'time machine,' if you still want it when the victory is ours. We offer you a place in the ruling cabinet of the new NakrehVatee. We offer you wealth and power such as you might never have dreamed of before."

"You have my word on this, Master HarkosNor," the lord DessaTyso said, beaming in his magnanimity.

"And ours as well," AkweNema said.

In the pause that followed, I refilled my wineglass and drank it empty again.

"We shall not demand that you answer at once," AkweNema said. "We will give you time to think, to decide. We will not rush you, but we hope that you can see fit to join us—and soon."

"We need your help, barbarian," the dark woman OrDjina said, speaking to me as an equal, despite the title she'd just given me.

"We do indeed," her lord agreed.

I nodded, grunted, and finally spoke. "It's a tall order."

"It is late now, gentlemen, my lord, my lady," AkweNema said, "and I am certain that Master Harkos-Nor is tired." Looking at me, he said, "A suite has been made ready for you."

"And to show you that we mean you well," the lord DessaTyso said, "the first of your rewards will be waiting for you there. Is that not so, OrDjina?"

"EnDera is there, my lord, awaiting the barbarian," OrDjina said, and gave me a wicked smile, the meaning of which wasn't exactly unclear to me.

AkweNema rose to his feet, offered me his hand, and said, "Come with me, then. I will show you the way."

And as I followed AkweNema out of the luxurious suite and down the brightly lighted corridor, I hoped by all the gods of all the Earths across the Lines, including the dark ones of VarKhohs, that the Shadowy Man was really on my side this time. But hadn't he always been?

6

EnDera

The suite to which AkweNema led me was not as large
as his or quite as luxuriously appointed, but there had
been no stinting in it either—nor was there stinting in
the first of the "rewards" offered me by the Brathel-
Lanza for my future services.

The girl named EnDera was in her early twenties,
with a distinctly Oriental look about her, an almost
yellowishness to her skin, and epicanthic folds that
gave her eyes a slightly slanted appearance. My first
thought was that she might have been Japanese, but
I was mistaken about that.

Her almond eyes were bright and sensual; her lips
were curled in a smile; her hair was as long and as
black as that of OrDjina, though it fell without curls
down her back; her body was as rounded and as
mature as that of the older woman, and the sight of it
under the sheer, light blue gown she wore, a filmy thing
more transparent than opaque, created for me nothing
less than seduction. Between her breasts, visible through
the fabric of her gown, dangling on a golden chain,
was a looped cross of beaten gold, an ankh, an ancient
symbol of life.

Had I not just met the beautiful lady OrDjina, I
would have said that EnDera was easily the most beautiful woman in all VarKhohs. She was the second
most beautiful, then. Who was I to complain?

AkweNema quickly made the introductions and as
quickly left us, saying only that come morning we
would talk again about the matter of my service to the

BrathelLanza. I agreed, but I was in no hurry for morning to come—and in no hurry to feel the pangs of guilt I would feel when I thought of Sally, so far away. . . .

"So you're the barbarian?" EnDera said in a lilting voice that carried just a trace of an accent as she sat down on the floor cushions and gestured for me to do the same. Before her sat a tall bottle of wine and two glasses.

I sat down as she poured the wine, and said, "I wish people would quit calling me that."

"Barbarian?" She handed me one of the glasses. "Well, you do speak like one. Your accent is worse than mine."

"Well, I'm sorry about that, but that doesn't make me the next best thing to a trained ape. I am house-broken, you know, and I rarely chew up people's slippers."

"I'm sorry," she said. "I didn't mean to offend you."

"You didn't really," I said. "But I'd prefer you called me Harkos." I'd really have preferred that she call me Eric, but I knew that was out of the question, and before she could say what I knew was coming next, I added, "I know that's a barbaric name too, but that's the name I've got." You pays your money and you gets potluck.

She smiled again and daintily sipped her wine.

"You're a NakrehVatea?" I asked, to break the silence that followed.

She nodded. "I was born in the West, near MaKohl. But my parents were immigrants from PalaBarhah." That was the name, Here and Now, for southern China. "We moved to VarKhohs when I was very young. I consider it my home."

"And you're a member of the BrathelLanza?" I asked, hoping I was pronouncing it correctly.

"Of course," she said, seeming surprised that I

should even ask. "And what of you, Harkos? What have you told them?"

I shrugged. "Nothing yet. They've given me time to think it over and make up my mind."

"I hope that you will agree to join us," she said earnestly, looking at me with a frank, open expression. "Such a man as you is needed. NakrehVatee isn't famous for its soldiers."

"Yeah, so I've gathered."

"And you would be doing the people a great service," she said just as earnestly, though not so fanatically as AkweNema might have said it. "There is much that AkweNema and KaphNo and the lord DessaTyso would do to make things better for the people, but they need help."

"Is it necessarily *my* help?"

"It could be your help. And the rewards will be great, although the knowledge that one has done the right thing should be enough." There was a gentle chiding in her voice, I thought.

"But NakrehVatee isn't my country," I told her, "and its problems aren't mine."

"Are you so much of a barbarian that you owe no debt to your fellow man?"

"I have some pressing things to attend to, EnDéra. I'm not sure I can spare a year or two to assist your people."

She looked doubtfully at me. "That pressing?"

I nodded, though I wondered where I'd ever have another chance to get my hands on a time—correction, on a chronal-displacement device. I just might have to give them a year or two to get it. And maybe that's what the Shadowy Man had been hinting at.

Another thought that had been nagging just below my level of awareness surfaced now, and I put the question to her as she refilled our now-empty wineglasses.

"Look, maybe you can answer something for me."

"I'll try."

"Well, for the sake of argument, suppose I do agree to go along and give up a couple of years of my life to help the BrathelLanza. Okay, we're speaking of maybe a year to complete the training and the preparation of the revolutionaries and then some months of fighting until the BrathelLanza has crushed all government resistance, right?"

EnDera nodded. "That's about right."

"Okay, then, how can this army of clones—replicates, whatever—that they're talking about 'growing' from cells of my body possibly be ready in time to do any good? It takes almost two decades for a human being to become anything like mature. Are they planning on sending year-old babies out to fight a war?"

She laughed, but gently. "KaphNo is getting old, Harkos. He didn't mention the GATs—growth-acceleration techniques—they've been using on animal and on some human replicates?"

"GATs?—no, I don't think so."

"He will. But it's true that the BrathelLanza now has techniques that the government's scientists and medical people know nothing about which can greatly hasten the acceleration of maturation."

"Hasten it enough to 'grow' an adult army in a year?"

"In less than a year."

"Okay," I said grudgingly.

"I'm certain that KaphNo will tell you all about it. You'll see."

I shrugged. There was a hell of a lot I had yet to learn about this world—for it was a complete world with centuries of history behind it about which I knew next to nothing, with patterns of culture I'd had only glimpses of, with technology and techniques I had encountered nowhere else across the Lines of Time. It would take a very long time for me to feel at home in it, if I ever did, and I knew I couldn't wait *that long* to make up my mind. I had to come to a decision on the basis of very scanty data and to act on that decision—and I had begun to doubt very seriously that with a negative decision on my part I would ever be allowed to leave the Underground alive. But I wasn't telling anyone anything yet.

"We want your stay here to be as pleasant as it can be," EnDera said into my silent thoughts.

"And that's why you're here, isn't it?"

She nodded. "You were told to expect a reward, weren't you?"

"I was. And you're it?"

"I'm it. Or rather the first one. There will be many more rewards, of various types, to follow, if you decide to join us."

"I'm beginning to wonder if I'm really going to be allowed any choice in the matter."

EnDera refilled both our wineglasses, took them in her hands, and rose slowly, gracefully from the floor.

"Let me show you the rest of the suite," she said as she turned her back on me, and I let my eyes follow the sweep of her dark hair down the curves of her back and hips to her ankles and feet. "It was carefully prepared for you. We hope you will find it comfortable."

She led me down a short hallway that branched off to two rooms, the one on the right a dining-room-cum-kitchen with what appeared to be automated food-preparation equipment, which she offered to show me how to operate—later. The room to the left was a study complete with a small library of books, a library of disks and tapes and playing machines for them, and one wall that was some sort of holographic-projection unit that could re-create life-size three-dimensional dramas, comedies, concerts, and readings. Again she offered to show me how to operate the equipment—but later.

The doors at the rear of these rooms led to hallways that joined and then in turn branched again and led to two more rooms, one a toilet with an enormous sunken bathtub, more nearly a pool; the other was a recreation room, in all appearances, fully outfitted with games, exercise equipment, and even a rifle range.

The rear doors of these rooms led to a common hallway that finally ended in a huge bedroom—literally a *bed*room, for its entire floor was a single great mattress that reached from wall to wall. A mahogany-paneled console stood in the middle of the room under a circular illumination disk surrounded by mirrors that covered the remainder of the ceiling. EnDera didn't have to tell me what the mirrors were for, but she did tell me that the console was a combination wet bar, entertainment center with holotank, and clothes closet. She opened one panel of the console to show me the costumes it held for me, an assortment of outfits that included, among other things, a harshly cut uniform that had a very, very military look about it. They were prepared, I could say that about them, these people of the BrathelLanza.

And so was EnDera.

"Now," she said, lowering herself to the mattress-floor, having kicked off her shoes as we entered the room, as I had done also, "I will try to convince you of the wisdom of joining us."

"Okay," I said, a huskiness suddenly coming to my throat.

She handed me one of the glasses filled with wine. Despite all I'd already drunk that evening, I felt I needed that one too.

"Come join *me,* Master HarkosNor," EnDera said softly, one hand holding the wineglass, the other going to the fasteners that held her gown together in the back. "I think I can at least persuade you to do *that.*"

The gown fell away from her breasts and crumpled around her hips. She began to work herself out of it.

"Yes, you can do that," I said, and lowered myself beside her.

She did persuade me.

7

Of Replication

When I awoke the next morning, my mouth filled with the unpleasant aftertaste and thickness of too much wine consumed the night before, and an incipient headache, I found that EnDera was way ahead of me. She had already been up for a while and there was a hot breakfast awaiting me, complete with a steaming cup of coffee—the most inviting thing I saw at the breakfast table, except for EnDera herself, who now wore only a lacy apron that was hardly a covering and couldn't have been much protection against anything, and a bright flower with yellow petals in the darkness of her long hair. Her welcoming smile was as bright as the flower she wore.

"Did you sleep well, my lord Harkos?"

"The sleep of the just and guilt-free," I said with a touch of sarcasm I don't think I really meant—at least I didn't mean for the sarcasm to be aimed at EnDera.

"What?"

"Nothing, nothing," I said, and sat down at the table, now realizing how hungry I was.

"The lord DessaTyso, AkweNema, and KaphNo will be coming to see you soon," she said as we ate. "Akwe punched up before you awoke to check on you."

I nodded, with a mouthful of food, but made no effort to speak.

"Akwe was hoping that you'd come to a decision and would speak with them of it this morning."

I nodded again, and sipped the hot coffee.

"Well, have you?"

After swallowing the coffee and gesturing for En-

Dera to refill the cup, I said: "Last night I said I didn't think I was really being given much choice in the matter."

"That's what you said."

"Well, I'm not. Am I?"

"Certainly you are. Nobody's forcing you to do anything." Was there a mocking smile barely hidden by her composed features?

"Tell me, frankly, what would happen to me if I refused."

She looked at me with a blank expression for long seconds.

I sipped hot coffee again. "Come on, tell me."

"Honestly, Harkos, I don't know, but . . ."

"Ah!" I wagged a finger at her. "If the BrathelLanza is a secret revolutionary organization, as it obviously is, and if the existing government is out to crush all such revolutionary movements, as it obviously must if it is to remain in power, then is AkweNema—the brains behind this revolution, as he seems to be—is he going to turn me, a potential government informer, loose to tell all I know to the government in possible exchange for 'rewards' from *them?*" That was some mouthful to speak that early in the morning, especially since I'd just scalded my tongue with coffee.

EnDera shook her head. "I don't know exactly what they would do in that case." Her eyes seemed to say otherwise.

"I don't know *exactly,* either, but if I were in Akwe- Nema's shoes, I could think of several things—but none of them would be very pleasant for Master HarkosNor, soldier at arms and intrepid hero."

"I see what you're saying."

"It's got to be the old carrot-and-stick game, En- Dera." I paused, gave her a long, hard, questioning look that somehow evolved into a leer. "And to tell you the truth, my dear, I much prefer the carrot to the stick, one particular carrot indeed."

At this she broke into a reluctant smile. "Then you're going to accept?"

"Like I said, do I have any choice?"

When AkweNema and KaphNo led me deeper into the underground complex of the BrathelLanza and began showing me the various parts of it, I was reminded of another underground complex on another Earth, distant across the Lines from this one, and of the people there who had also been plotting a revolution, colonial North America scheming to rise against Mother England. But that place no longer existed; destroyed by its builders to prevent its capture by the people who came to rescue me from them. And now Sally was waiting for me Somewhere Else. And I missed her and wondered when I would ever see her again.

Portions of the Underground here were devoted to offices and to sleeping quarters for both the permanently subterranean personnel and those who worked and partially lived in the world above and came into the Underground only on occasion, such as AkweNema and the lord DessaTyso, who still had active parts to play in the society of the surface. Farther back, the offices and quarters gave way to supply dumps, to equipment and matériel they were slowly collecting, building, enlarging, in preparation for the day when the BrathelLanza and its allies would come out of their hidden places and attack the power structure that ruled NakrehVatee.

Still farther on were large, brightly lighted exercise areas and drill fields carved out of the earth and stone, in which was completed the training of the cadres that would soon issue forth to begin the training of others around the nation. The uniforms they wore, the men and women who were presently the crack forces of the BrathelLanza, were not greatly unlike those worn by the armies of many another world: blouses and slacks of tan—khaki, the word was in some places—metal helmets, heavy boots; and the weapons with which they exercised were bright and sparkling, highly sophisticated automatic rifles and pistols capable of throwing leaden slugs or explosive shells great distances with a high degree of accuracy, compact particle-beam weapons and hand-held lasers capable of projecting fragments of shattered atoms, electrons, protons, beams of coherent light and heat. Unfortunately, however, the soldiers were not as sophisticated as their weapons. But then, I suppose, that's why they wanted someone like me.

And beyond the training areas lay the biological laboratories. This was where I would be occupied initially. Only later would I be spending the bulk of my time in the training areas, drilling *my* troops and advising the training of others.

We entered the bright, antiseptic labs, smelled the clean, almost sterile air, watched the efficient movements of the physicians and scientists and technicians as they went about their esoteric business—esoteric to me; but now I could see that old KaphNo was finally in his element. He seemed a different man, alive, excited, animated by his love for the laboratories and what was taking place in them.

"Everything is ready for you, Master HarkosNor—or should I say 'General' HarkosNor?" KaphNo said, beaming at me. "We could even begin today if you wish." He paused for a moment, ruminated. "We have several human replicates, which you will see later, in various stages of maturation, developing with no indication of trouble.

"In fact," he said, speaking more slowly, more emphatically, "we even have several fully matured replicates living in the Underground now. You would not be able to distinguish them from other people—in fact, I'll see that you meet one of them soon, and you can see for yourself what I mean.

"Yes, all in all, everything is proceeding even better than we had expected. We anticipate no problems in cloning several hundred replicates from the cells of your tissues."

"That's very good," AkweNema said, a strange, uneasy expression passing across his face. "Perhaps ThefeRa could give the general a tour of the replication facilities."

"Of course," KaphNo said, and gestured toward two white-clad men who stood discussing something at a table not far away.

The two men joined us and were introduced. The elder, a tall, thin, almost cadaverous man with a great shock of white hair, was named ThefeRa and was both a physician and a microbiologist specializing in replication processes: in short, a "genetic engineer." He was, under KaphNo, the project's head.

The other, a shorter, heavier, young man, with unusually handsome features, was named SkorTho. He also was a microbiologist and served as ThefeRa's second in command.

When the introductions were completed, ThefeRa led us into the section of the laboratories that was to be of particular interest to me.

"This is our operating room," the white-haired physician said, gesturing with his left hand toward a large set of white doors. He glanced at AkweNema and KaphNo, then back at me, and said: "When you are ready, General, it is here that we will take the sample tissues from which your replicates will be grown."

"A painless operation, I assure you," AkweNema put in, sounding like the physician he was. "A simple biopsy, a few thousand cells you'll never miss. That's all."

I shrugged.

Farther on: ThefeRa gesturing, speaking. "In these rooms the cells we will have taken from your body will be placed in special media which will provide them with ample nutrition and in which they will be encouraged to grow, to reproduce. At this stage, all we want is to establish that the cells will breed true—that is, skin cells produce more skin cells, muscle cells more muscle cells, whatever."

"In essence," KaphNo interjected, "the sample cells from your body will be encouraged to reproduce themselves a number of times over, so that when we are finished here we will have a much larger amount of tissue with which to work."

It all sounded rather grotesque to me, and I wasn't certain that I wanted to see that actual process. I mean, that would be *my* tissue, all raw and naked, growing like the still-beating heart of some long-dead chicken. Ugh!

"Not so long ago," KaphNo was saying into my gruesome thoughts, "the process of developing a viable replicate was a much more complex and less trustworthy operation. We have refined and simplified the process greatly here in recent years, thanks largely to the efforts of ThefeRa and SkorTho."

The two genetic engineers somehow managed to look both humble and proud at the same time.

"Not so long ago," KaphNo continued, "we could reproduce only viable female replicates by a rather messy and involved process which involved the transplantation of a cell nucleus from the body of a donor into a fertilized egg cell from which the nucleus had been removed, and then this egg had to be implanted into the womb of a surrogate mother."

Looking proud of himself and his co-workers, the old scientist said, "Well, now we have been able to bypass the egg-cell implant stage and the surrogate mother altogether. We can persuade an even rather specialized cell to develop embryonically. The womb of the surrogate mother has been replaced by something that I can only call a marvel of engineering. You will see what I'm referring to shortly."

"The next step," ThefeRa said into the silence following the end of KaphNo's speech, gesturing toward another pair of white doors, "once we have what we feel to be a sufficient culture to work with, will be the separation of individual cells from the clone mass. That's where the word 'clone' comes from, you know, a Greek word meaning 'throng.' We apply it to a heterogeneous mass of genetically identical cells."

"I know," I said, not mentioning that a version of the Greek language had been my native tongue. They didn't need to know *that*.

"And that is why," KaphNo said, "we prefer the word 'replicate' to 'clone' when speaking of the *individual* produced by this process."

I nodded, understanding.

"Once replication has sucessfully begun," the physician ThefeRa continued, "the embryos—for at this stage they can be considered embryos, having no zygotic stage in the true sense of the term—are transferred to another room. For the first few days the embryonic replicates are kept under constant surveillance. At this stage we lose about one out of every three embryos."

"Lose?" I asked, unable to constrain myself. I was getting curious about this whole thing; after all, weren't they going to grow some new *me*s here?

KaphNo answered: "This science is still in its infancy, General. And it is here in this room that we must catch the bulk of our mistakes. Faulty stimulation of genetic patterns. Failure of replication processes. Mutations—even underground here there's more radiation than we would like. Other genetic defects caused by the very methods we are using. One third of the embryos we bring into this room are not suitable for further cultivation. By the time the embryos leave this room, we will have lost seven out of every eight of the cells we started with. That is why we need a relatively large number of cells initially."

Again I felt that tug of revulsion. Maybe I didn't have as strong a stomach as I'd thought.

"At the end of this stage, however," ThefeRa picked up the narrative, "we can be certain of the survival of a large percentage of the embryos. From here they will be transferred to the room ahead and on our right, where we can begin to apply certain growth-acceleration techniques we have developed that will . . ."

On and on we went, from room to room, lab to lab, ThefeRa and KaphNo leading, AkweNema and I behind, the microbiologist SkorTho silently bringing up the rear. And as we went I was shown the various stages of growth through which the replicates would pass, was shown various human replicates in the actual process of growth and development, spanning years of maturation in days.

"We have three types of vessels for the postnatal replicates," said ThefeRa at one point. "We have coined the word 'encanter' for the replication vessels, which you are about to see. The smallest of these are for replicates with a chronological maturity from 'birth' up to six years."

An encanter, it turned out, was something like a cross between a Skinner box and an overgrown test tube and looked something like a deranged chemist's idea of a tropical-fish aquarium.

ThefeRa led us into a long, low room, the walls of which were lined with glass cylinders each about four feet tall and two feet in diameter. Beside each cylinder was a large electronic console more complex than the controls of a good-size cargo skudder, with banks of dials, gauges, meters, buttons, switches, and CRTs. The cylinders themselves were topped by large metal rings from which tubes or pipes ran back into boxes and junctions in the wall. From the bases of the cylinders similar tubes ran into similar boxes and junctions at the bases of the consoles. In all there appeared to be several hundred of these cylinder-console combinations. The cost must have been enormous.

Then ThefeRa led us down the row of cylinders until he reached one that stood a hundred feet or so from the door through which we'd entered.

"This should prove interesting to you," he said, gesturing for me to come nearer.

Before I even reached ThefeRa, several things about this particular setup became obvious to me. Initially: the console that stood beside and was connected to the cylinder was not dark and quiet as had been the others —its panels were lighted, tiny indicator lights flickered on and off, meters showed various readings, and the console itself hummed with electrical life. Next: the cylinder beside the console was less transparent than the others, filled with a thick, murky fluid that seemed to be in constant motion.

"See him?" ThefeRa asked.

I bent slightly, peered into the cylinder. I saw him.

The form of a naked boy of about five years old hung/swam suspended in the liquid, long, dark hair swaying in the gentle motion of the cylinder's fluid contents. His eyes were closed, and my first impression was that he was dead—a grotesque display of child murder committed by some maddened scientist of the underground laboratories. Then I saw that his chest rose and fell with a slow but unmistakable rhythm.

"The liquid in which he floats contains oxygen which the lungs are capable of extracting," ThefeRa said, seeing the look in my eyes. "He is alive and well, developing physiologically normally in almost every way."

"Except for the rate of growth," KaphNo said, coming up behind me. "We began the replication process eight weeks ago, and now he shows a maturation of about five and a third years."

"How—how long," I stammered, "how long until he's, ah, mature?"

"We will able to carry him to a maturation level of eighteen years over a period of just less than ten months. But don't try to work out the direct chronological equivalents in normal maturity. There is not a one-to-one congruity. Some stages we can accelerate more, some less."

I nodded, too flooded with information to speak at that moment, and in my silence the scientists led me on down the row of encanters and showed me the two "brothers" of the boy—two more replicates genetically identical with the first, triplets growing in the laboratories of the BrathelLanza deep beneath the surface of the Earth.

I was not told their names—if they yet had names —or who had donated the cells from which they were growing. Perhaps it wasn't important.

· Then we went on to the next set of encanters, larger than the first, designed to hold replicates from maturation levels of about six years to about twelve years. In one of these I was shown what ThefeRa called "one of our happier replications"—a naked, black-haired girl who somehow looked astonishingly familiar, floating, sleeping in the murky liquid.

"Don't you recognize her?" ThefeRa asked.

"Yes . . . yes, I think so."

"Little OrDjina," KaphNo said with a laugh, "that's what we call her. And as you can easily see, she is a replication of our lord DessaTyso's mistress. A beautiful child, isn't she?"

I nodded but couldn't find words to speak.

"On the day of her final decantation, a little over four months from now," ThefeRa was saying, "a celebration is planned. That should be interesting— two Ladies OrDjina in our Underground."

I wondered exactly what he meant by that, but I didn't ask.

Finally we followed ThefeRa to the last of the encanter chambers, a room which held the largest cylinders of all, those built to hold replicates at maturation levels from twelve years to maturity. Only one of these encanters was occupied; it held the form of a lovely young girl of about fifteen, her hair a startling shade of red.

AkweNema, without speaking, brushed around the rest of us and took a place directly in front of the large glass cylinder. For a long while he gazed silently into the murky fluid. There appeared to be moisture in the corners of his eyes. No one spoke.

Finally he turned awkwardly from the encanter, and faced us, his eyes seeking mine. He spoke: "My daughter." Then he left the encanter room alone and went back toward the other sections of the Underground, muttering something to himself that may have been "May the Dark Lords have mercy on us all."

ThefeRa was the first to speak. "His true daughter is dead. A tragic skimmer accident a few months ago. She was almost sixteen years old, just a bit more mature than her replicate here. We were able to retrieve some still-living cells and are growing this replicate for Akwe. She will reach maturation in about two months if we continue the process."

"But that's not enough," KaphNo said, an unexpected softness in his voice, an affection for the red-haired man and his dead daughter. "If only we had complete cerebral recordings of her! With those we could give him back his daughter just as she was."

Huh? I asked, but silently, to myself.

Old KaphNo turned, wiped incipient tears from his eyes, grasped my upper arm with a surprisingly strong hand, and led me out of the encanter chamber.

"Cerebral recordings, General. I haven't spoken of them, have I?" he asked when we were again in the corridor.

"No, you haven't."

"Well then, it's time I told you about them. They

play a very important part in our plan. Now, I am certain that you are familiar with the fact that the human brain constantly gives off certain forms of electromagnetic emissions, brain waves, the so-called alpha waves and so forth; that is to say . . ."

8

Of the Underground

That night I lay·in the room-filling bed beside EnDera,
both of us warm and satiated, drifting toward a welcome sleep—or at least EnDera seemed to be. I wanted
to sleep but found it impossible. There was too much
in my head. Clones and replication processes. Brain
waves and cerebral-recording techniques. Replicates of
the lord DessaTyso's beautiful mistress and of AkweNema's dead daughter floating in tanks of life-sup-
porting fluids. The identical boys in similar encanters.
Wars and rumors of wars in a world the complexities
of which I could not yet begin to understand. The vast
underground city of the BrathelLanza—for it was almost a city in size and complexity, similar in some
respects to the underground city-fortress of the Paratimers and the American Republican Army on another
Earth.

And that similarity with the place called Staunton disturbed me. Not similarity in detail, for there was little
or none of that. But in scope and concept, in size and
complexity, and especially in purpose. Staunton and
this Underground, so similar in many general ways,
had both been built for the purpose of overthrowing
the existing power structure and replacing it with another.

The Paratimers—whatever the hell they *were*, and I
didn't know—had financed and helped build the underground city of Staunton.

What of the underground city of the Brathel-
Lanza? . . .

I supposed that EnDera needed the sleep—she had

earned it well during our romp on the great mattress, earned it every bit as well as the EstarSimirian prostitutes earned theirs in the pleasure-house in VarKhohs —but I had to talk with someone, and she was the most available. I rolled over, touched her cheek with my fingertips, and whispered into her ear, "EnDera, EnDera."

"What is it?" she asked sleepily.

"Would you mind staying awake just a little while longer? I'd like to talk."

A frown crossed her lovely face in the room's dim light. "Is something bothering you?"

"This place, this Underground, I can't figure it out."

"What do you mean?"

"Well, I mean I'm impressed and all. I've never seen anything like it." Which wasn't exactly the truth, but close enough to it. "It's hard to imagine how something like this could have been built, and all this equipment and all these people brought in, without anyone knowing about it."

"Oh, lots of people know about it."

"That's not what I mean. The government. How is it that they didn't learn about it long ago?"

"Oh, I'm sure a number of people in the government have known about it. Never the top people, of course, but a lot of people lower down the line. It's been seen to that they never pass their information on to the top."

"What do you mean 'seen to'?"

"Oh, a few bribes strategically placed, maybe a little extortion, maybe a little blackmail, maybe an 'unfortunate accident' here and there."

"I see." Maybe the BrathelLanza wasn't just *playing* at revolution after all. Maybe they were deadly serious. Assassination. That's deadly serious.

"I can't say that we're entirely safe here," EnDera went on. "Sooner or later some overly zealous agent is going to put two and two together and come up with the right answer and we won't be able to stop him from alerting the ones on the top, but we hope that day can be put off long enough for us to finish our work here."

I nodded, understanding.

"Really, Harkos, we don't have too many illusions down here. We know we're under sentences of immediate execution on the spot, or prolonged torture in some of the lords' dungeons, if we're ever caught. We just hope we can put off being caught for a few more months."

There was a coldness in her eyes and in her words that showed me a new side of EnDera and maybe a new side of this whole underground setup.

"That's one of the reasons we were in such a rush to get your cooperation," she went on, her fingers unconsciously touching the looped cross of life she wore. "Don't flatter yourself by thinking you're the only man in the world we could use. There are lots of others. We even have some people in our organization now who could serve in your place in a pinch. But you're the most available of the best suited, if you follow me."

"And this business this morning when I asked you what they would do if I refused?"

"I know. I guess I was playing with you. But I didn't want you to agree unless you wanted to cooperate. I didn't want to scare you into it. But . . . but you're right. If you hadn't agreed this morning, you would probably be dead by now. I'm glad you agreed."

"I am too."

A long, quiet pause followed while I framed questions in my mind, working out a means of getting from her the kinds of answers I wanted.

"This place must have cost a fortune to build, several fortunes. Who's paying for it?"

"A lot of people, an awful lot of people, Harkos. The lord DessaTyso and his family, for example. They've come close to destituting themselves to aid us. He's the most wealthy of us, of course, but a lot of other people in the higher castes—people as fed up with things as we are—have helped us, have given us every bit of aid they could.

"And it's not just rich people, either. Poor- and middle-caste people all over the nation have chipped in what they could to help us—and in a lot of cases, maybe in most of them, they didn't even know what they were giving their money to, but they were told that they were working for the good of all the people. And that was the truth."

She wasn't as fanatic as AkweNema, maybe, but there was a dedication in her that burned like a bright fire.

"We have other friends too."

My heart skipped a beat. *Other friends?*

"People and organizations outside NakrehVatee," she said, answering my unvoiced question. "Other governments. Private organizations. Wealthy individuals. A lot of people think the world would be better off if there were a different kind of government here in VarKhohs.

"And maybe some of them aren't so friendly. Maybe they'd like nothing better than to see internal turmoil paralyze NakrehVatee so they could go about their business without the interference of our government. Okay, we'll take their money and their aid. But we're not committing ourselves to anything or anyone outside the BrathelLanza." Where had I heard similar sentiments expressed before? "We're not going to stage our revolution so that some other nation can jump into an international power vacuum and start dominating the small nations in our sphere of influence. That's one thing we're not going to do. We'll keep up our nation's strength against foreign powers."

I wasn't certain that I followed her line of reasoning, but that's not what was coming to concern me right at that moment. "Other friends," she had said, and those two words led me to think about the world in which I had found myself, how I had come there, why I had come there; to think of the Kriths and the Tromas who directed them and what they had said that had led me to the world of the BrathelLanza and NakrehVatee. "Other friends" seemed to abound.

And I was remembering some words spoken to me some months before by a gross and alien female Krith. The words came clearly into my mind as if I were listening to a recording of that conversation:

"There is another falsehood," the speaker for the Tromas had said to me, "that you and countless others have come to accept, a falsehood which has been 'proved' mathematically to a vast number of scientists."

"And what's that?" I'd asked.

"That travel through time is impossible, travel from one point in time to an earlier point in time."

I had just looked at the female Krith.

"Time travel *is* possible, Eric, travel from one location in *linear* time to another location, future and/or past. It is something we do not wish to become common knowledge. It is a secret *we* must keep, at the peril of our racial lives."

And later on in that same, long conversation:

"How it was we discovered the one Timeline that had achieved true time travel," she had said, "I will not go into, nor how it was that we, our entire race, migrated back in time hundreds of years in order to begin our 'remodeling' as early as possible. You must merely accept these things as so, as you have seen for yourself."

All this was clear in my mind, and the realization that the operative sentence was: *It is a secret we must keep, at the peril of our racial lives.*

This was that world, the one with true time travel, I was almost certain, and if that were so, then there could be no chance of the Kriths having allowed Paratimers *or anyone else* to have infiltrated this world, to

have financed and assisted with the planning of a
revolution that would probably drastically alter the
government of this Earth's most powerful nation. Nor
would the Kriths or the Timeliners meddle with this
world, but merely stand outside it and make certain
no one else did.

(How, then, did you get into this world so easily?
a portion of my mind asked. They should have been
watching for exactly the thing you did—a stranger
coming skudding in to make use of this Line's "time
machines." They should have caught you. If this *is*
the right world . . .)

And again: If this is the right world, if I haven't
made a terrible blunder, then would the Kriths allow
even the natives of this world, the BrathelLanza and
people like them, to make drastic alterations in its historical processes?

(And another part of my mind: But the Shadowy
Man wouldn't have advised you to cooperate with the
BrathelLanza, to allow them to clone your cells and
to have you lead an army of replicates so that when the
revolution is all over you can get your hands on a
chronal-displacement device, if this is the wrong world.
The Shadowy Man is on your side. Isn't he?)

And again: But if the revolution is staged and
executed solely by natives without any Outtime activities involved at all, would not that revolution be a
part of that world's natural historical process, something that must have happened here if the future is to
turn out as the Kriths see it?

(But there is an Outtime influence! You!)

But the Kriths don't know it, do they?

(They should.

(If you're on the right world.

(If you haven't made the worst blunder of your life.

(If the Shadowy Man isn't playing you for a fool.

(If . . .)

EnDera was looking at me strangely but didn't speak. She had had her say.

So I just kissed her, and she returned the kiss, and I pulled her naked body closer to mine and kissed her again and for a while I forgot about all those things running through my head. For a while . . .

9

A Conversation with KaphNo

Although AkweNema, KaphNo, ThefeRa, and a score
of others had insisted that the taking of the tissue
sample from my body would be absolutely painless,
I discovered that they had stretched the point just a
bit. Oh, the taking of the sample itself was painless
enough, I admit. I was given a local anesthetic in my
left hip, placed on something that looked like a hybrid
of a conventional operating table and a dentist's chair,
had a strap placed across my chest, and ThefeRa himself—I should consider this an honor, I was told—
placed a device against the outside of my left thigh,
which sent a small, circular blade about an inch into
my flesh, taking out a core a few millimeters in diameter of skin and flesh and muscle tissue. During the
taking of the biopsy, KaphNo, who stood at my left
hand, told me the approximate number of cells that
would be removed, but I've forgotten how many he
said. Sufficiently large for their purposes, with a good
loss factor figured in.

The biopsy was over in a matter of minutes and the
small wound in my thigh was closed and sealed with
something I would have called "plastiskin." They
wouldn't let me try to walk until the anesthetic had
worn off, but when it had I didn't much want to walk
anyway. That's what they hadn't told me about: once
the anesthetic wore off, it did hurt terribly for a while.
You know how puncture wounds are. But I didn't complain to anyone. Generals don't cry, do they?

I spent the rest of that day, my second full day in
the Underground of the BrathelLanza, resting in the

"study" of my suite, using the equipment that EnDera had finally shown me how to work, sipping cold beer —they brewed some fine beer Here and Now—smoking cigarettes, which I'd finally been able to obtain— the use of tobacco being almost unknown in Nakreh-Vatee—and skimming through the spools of an encyclopedia, familiarizing myself with the more salient facts about the city of VarKhohs, the nation of Nak-rehVatee, and the world of which they were a part.

This world, I determined, was one of a series of related Timelines that the Kriths collectively called Neo-Carthaginian. Carthage. In the Phoenician, *Kart Hadasht*. In the Greek of my ancestors, *Karchedon*. The Jewel of North Africa. The Mother of Kings—in this world at least.

In the history of these so-called Neo-Carthaginian worlds, the tactics of the great general Hannibal had been more successful than on many another Line. Iberia had remained in the hands of Carthage during the Second Punic War. Hannibal crossed the Alps and fell on Rome with all his fury. And it had been the Romans, in the year B.C. 200, who had gone down in flames, not the descendants of the Phoenicians.

Rome was leveled and her colonies taken over by the Carthaginians. Though later rebuilt as a satellite of Carthage and renamed, the city of Rome never gained great importance outside the Italian peninsula. The centers of power remained in the Near East and the Far East, moving to Europe only centuries later when it too was colonized and dominated by Asiatic and African peoples who had risen to power following the fall of the Cartho-Byzantine Empire.

All this, in much more detail, I learned as I read books and scanned tapes that day, relaxing and attempting to enjoy myself.

Late that evening, after sharing a large meal with EnDera, which she'd prepared with aid from the autokitchen, I was paid a visit by Professor KaphNo, who now seemed to be a rather happy, animated old man.

"Well, Master Harkos, we have begun," he said, sitting on a cushion across from me, gazing into the foam in his mug of beer, which EnDera had also provided.

"The replication?" I asked.

"Not the replication exactly, but the first stages of cloning that will lead to replication. Your cells have been placed in the growth media and are already beginning to respond. We should have an ample quantity of cells to begin the actual replication processes by the end of the week, I would say."

"And then?"

The bright eyes in the deep sockets sparkled. "Then . . . well, in about ten months, General, you should have your army."

"The replicates will be mature then?"

He nodded. "There are some other things you should keep in mind, however."

"Okay."

"When the replicates reach a maturation level equivalent to eighteen years of age—ML-18Y, that's the way we say it in the labs—they will be ready to be decanted. However, you cannot expect them to be able to immediately function as would a normal human being. Their muscles will have a lot of developing yet to do. Although they will have been fed certain data during the last weeks of their development—data concerning the use of their muscles—much of this data cannot be fully integrated by them until after decanting. What I am saying, Harkos, is that it will take the replicates several weeks to *learn to use* their bodies, to be anything more than helpless babies."

I nodded over the top of my own beer mug.

"Also, during the last few weeks of their development prior to decanting, they will have been carefully fed certain portions of your cerebral recordings. That is, with your assistance, during the recording, the editing, and the playback, we will want to feed your replicates that data from your memories which is felt to be of value to them.".

"I think I follow you," I said, "but I'm not altogether certain. Now I'm supposed to have this, well, telepathic control over—"

KaphNo raised a hand to interrupt. "We prefer the term 'resonance.' In your case, resonance control. 'Telepathy' is such a sloppy term."

I recalled another being in another place who had said how sloppy were human terms for psionic effects. I guess she was right.

"You will be expected to exercise resonance control over the replicates. They, in turn, will follow your commands in terms of resonance *response.*"

"Okay," I agreed. "This resonance control I'll have over them—won't that make it possible for them to do anything I tell them without their having, well, personalities of their own?"

"That would hardly be practical, Harkos," KaphNo said flatly, perhaps doubting my understanding of any of it. "We are talking about *several hundred* replicates. Of course, you could personally direct one or even two to a very large degree, but to control even two well, or three or four in any fashion at all, would be a fulltime job. You would have to be placed in a sensory-deprived situation and then spend all your waking hours flitting from one subject to another, directing its every task.

"No, Harkos," he said loudly, "you are to be the *general* of hundreds, not the *puppet master* of a handful. Your replicates will have, to a limited degree, of course, distinct memory patterns, distinct experience programs, distinct behavior patterns—in short, for want of a better term, personalities. Your control over them will be of a more general, over-all fashion.

"Here's the way you'll do it: 'Harkos R52, take six men and try to knock out that guard post on the next street. Harkos R87's platoon will converge with your detail and together you will go to the assistance of Harkos R210 two blocks to the north.' That, Harkos, is the way you will direct your troops."

I leaned back, smiled, sipped my beer to the bottom of the mug, then called EnDera and asked her to please get us both a refill.

"Do you understand the distinctions now?" KaphNo asked, sitting down.

"I think I'm beginning to, but tell me, just how does this resonance business work—no, how will it *seem to me?* I guess is what I'm asking."

"I don't think I can give you a definitive answer to that as yet. Oh, thank you." EnDera had brought us the beer. "Never before has anyone attempted resonance control with so many replicates. Experience in the past has dealt with no more than two or three replicates and their senior. But we know there are three levels of integration with your replicates.

"RCL One—RCL stands for resonance-control level —RCL One would probably very closely coincide with your normal, waking, conscious operation. You will be very much 'in your own head,' as it were, and your directing of the replicates would be very analogous with the way a conventional commander in the field directs his troops: he uses radio and/or video; whereas you will be, well, directing by means of your thoughts, so to speak, your 'sympathetic awareness.' We doubt that this will be greatly taxing, and you should be able to master it quite easily, almost instinctively, one might say.

"RCL Two we consider an intermediate stage. In it, which would require slightly greater mental concentration, you would be directing your attention to one or a few replicates, more fully aware of their thoughts and activities, of their sensory input, but hardly fully integrated with them.

"RCL Three will probably be the most difficult to

adjust to, for in it you would be allowing your response patterns—your *self,* your *soul,* if you feel poetically inclined—to fully mesh with that of a single replicate." He spread the fingers of his thin hands and then brought them together so that the fingers of one hand entwined with those of the other, mating with one another like the teeth of cog wheels. "At RCL Three you would be able to see through the replicate's eyes, hear with his ears, taste with his tongue, even speak with his vocal cords—and, of course, experience his pain. In essence, you and he would be a single person inhabiting two bodies.

"We do not believe that it will be necessary for you to use RCL Three to any great extent. In fact, we advise against it."

"I see."

"The training, as you can see," he went on after a moment, "will not be all on the part of the replicates. You yourself will have a great deal to learn in the process."

I nodded dismally. Maybe it wasn't going to be the sinecure I had thought it would be.

"But I am certain you will find it interesting and rewarding," KaphNo said, as if to cheer me up.

"Tell me about this cerebral-recording business," I said, my mouth damp with beer and foam. "You explained to me about the so-called brain waves and all that, and I think I've got some idea of what you're doing when you're making these recordings—"

"Essentially similar to the recording of any electromagnetic phenomenon," KaphNo interjected, "but the modulation end of it is a lot more sophisticated."

"So you told me. But what am I going to be doing while all this is going on?"

KaphNo smiled one of those rare smiles of his, stretched, drank beer, relaxed, and said, "We are getting a little out of my field. This is more in psychologist GrelLo's domain, but I'll tell you what I can.

"The recordings will be accomplished through several phases, as I think I mentioned to you earlier. First of all, before any actual recordings are made, you will make up what we call a 'mnemonic autobiograph,' with GrelLo's help, of course. Your life experiences will then be broken down into a number of clearly defined categories—any of which you consider of a highly personal or private nature and/or nonrelevant to our training purposes will be struck from the initial records. Prying into your personal life will be avoided as far as possible. She and her technicians will go after the specific memory types desired."

After calling to EnDera for still another refill of our beer mugs, I asked, "How is this done?"

"During the recording sessions, which GrelLo will supervise, you will be given drugs to help you relax and to facilitate memory retrieval. Half a dozen or so electrodes will be placed at various spots on your scalp and the back of your neck. That's all. Very much like an EEG, if you've ever had one. The machines and the computers do the rest."

"And after the memories are recorded?"

"They will be played back to you in a shorthand fashion and you will be given the opportunity to edit them before GrelLo and her staff further edit them. After that, the tapes will be ready to be played to your replicates."

"Well, it doesn't sound like there's anything to be afraid of there," I said, wondering if that was true. How great a chance was there that I might give myself away as not being what I claimed to be? I'd have to play that carefully indeed.

KaphNo was giving me another of his smiles. "As if there were much you have ever feared, my general."

"Don't overrate me, KaphNo. I'm no superhuman warrior out of some Norse saga. Just a simple soldier."

"No longer that. Not when you have an army that will literally obey your slightest whim."

"That does scare me a little."

"It shouldn't. You have the capacity to handle it."

"I hope you're right."

"This isn't something we've undertaken lightly. We know what kind of man you are, HarkosNor, otherwise we wouldn't have chosen you."

Do you really? I asked myself. And was hit by a sudden feeling of chill: What if they *did know?* What if they knew who and what I really was?

(Maybe they do know, said that cantankerous part of my mind. Maybe they've known all along.)

And thoughts like that could have led me down the dark paths I'd followed the night before, down into plots within plots within plots, and I wasn't ready for all that again.

"Are you feeling well?" KaphNo asked.

"I'm okay. I think I ate too much for supper. A touch of indigestion."

"Should I call EnDera? She could get you something."

"No, I'm fine now. Would you like another beer?"

We each had another, and then another, and before the evening was over KaphNo was weeping like a baby, telling me about a sweetheart he'd once had, long ago, the most beautiful girl he'd ever seen, and how he'd lost her to another.

EnDera was already asleep when I groggily crawled into the room that was a bed. I didn't bother to wake her. We both needed the sleep.

10

Of EnDera and KaphNo

Within the crystalline vessels called encanters, the
manipulated and irradiated cells whose DNA carried
data identical to that within my body began to grow
and divide, and grow and divide again, in a fashion
very similar to that which takes place within a mother's
womb. Cells that had originally been unspecialized
began to differentiate and develop particular characteristics the parent cells had not had. Still hardly more
than microscopic, within the embryos, the rudiments
of organs—heart, liver, brain, lungs, digestive tract—
began to take shape. In the murky fluid of the encanters
the masses of cells curved, fattened, backbones began
to grow, and the buds that would later be arms and
legs began to sprout. Not yet did they look even
vaguely human, but the indications were there if you
knew how to look for them. With the passage of days,
of weeks, the cells continued to grow, to change, to
become. . . .

As the embryos within the replication encanters in
the laboratories of the Underground evolved through
recapitulation toward "birth," which for them would
consist of no more than being placed in larger encanters
where most of the organs and much of the tissue of
their bodies would begin to function in more nearly
normal fashion, I was going through some processes
myself.

With a voice recorder, a note pad, and a pencil, with
the help of psychologist GrelLo—a rather mature
woman, attractive, and not unpleasant to work with—
I was putting together what they called a mnemonic

autobiograph, but which was more nearly a quickly sketched outline of the principal memories of my life and the structure of my life as I saw it in retrospect— which was one hell of a thing to do, since I had to make up a lot of it as I went along.

As far as possible I used real events from my past, modifying the suitable ones to fit into the patterns of this world as I knew them. Claiming to be a foreigner, born and raised in the Central European country of SteeMehseeh, helped in covering some of my fabrications—but not much.

However, GrelLo didn't seem to be as much interested in my life itself as she was interested in categories of memories, my "epistemological mnemology," she called it: the taxonomy of my mind. She wanted to know how I classified my thoughts and memories, to determine what categories were relevant to the clones —excuse me, the replicates—and to determine how best to call up those specific memories for recording.

For example, she didn't much care when or where or how I'd learned to operate and maintain an automatic slug-throwing rifle, but she did want to know and to record everything I had ever known about the subject itself. My personal feelings about slug throwers and the experiences I'd had with them were irrelevant, or at best secondary, unless they told how to use and maintain a slug thrower in the field, how to load and fire with accuracy under real combat conditions. This saved me a lot of embarrassment, and from their discovery of my falsified past. Or so it seemed at the time . . .

By the time the replicates could justifiably be called "babies" and had been placed in the "newborn" encanters, GrelLo and her assistants and technicians had already begun to record my memories.

When I wasn't in session with GrelLo and her people, or in conference with ThefeRa and his people—

for I had a lot to learn before I could ever hope to begin training the replicates—or in conference with AkweNema and the lord DessaTyso—learning the ins and outs of the BrathelLanza, the breadth and depth of the organization, their plans, their goals, the structure of their organization and the structure of the organization to which they were opposed, and, of course, the tactical and strategic goals of the revolution in military terms—when I wasn't involved in these things, all of which consumed large chunks of time, I furthered my own education with the tapes and disks and books in the suite they'd given me, and called upon the Underground's central library computer, and, on occasion, I spent a little time with EnDera, for she would live in my suite for as long as I wished, and with KaphNo, who was becoming almost a friend.

Of the two, I'm not certain which was the less complex person. Perhaps it was EnDera. A beautiful, intelligent girl she certainly was, and one whose parents, foreigners themselves, had tried to raise as a normal citizen of NakrehVatee. They had come from southern China, immigrants to North America who, because of their background in their native land, were allowed to enter one of the higher middle castes devoted to artistic endeavors. EnDera had done much the same things as other girls of her caste and social status, gone through the same sort of training and education, the same introductions to their segment of society, to their prescribed version of life and love and sexual experience, for within certain caste-limited bounds, the society of NakrehVatee was rather permissive sexually. But there had always been a difference for EnDera: she wasn't quite like her peers, her skin wasn't the same darkish color, nor her hair the same texture, nor were her eyelids shaped the same. And for those reasons, and for some others, neither did she think in the same ways.

After completing her education in the arts, hoping

that her parentage and her Oriental ancestry would give her the mastery of brush and pen for which "China" had long been famous in this world, she found that this did not satisfy her, and ultimately, after some initial successes, she largely gave up her painting and began to devote herself to revolutionary activities— for which she was eventually jailed and given psychiatric treatment. The treatment failed to change her views, although she simulated recantation sufficiently to be released. Upon her release she immediately sought out the strongest revolutionary movement of them all, the almost legendary BrathelLanza. In the Brotherhood she found the acceptance that had so long been denied her. Now she lived full time in the Underground, going to the surface only on occasion, working again as an artist and designer—not such a strange occupation for a revolutionary, if you think about it. Part of her artistic efforts were devoted to the design and execution of posters thought up by the BrathelLanza's propaganda department—the leaders of the Brotherhood knew the necessity of getting their message across to the masses. The rest of her efforts were spent on more innocuous types of art, these to be sold through the art galleries of VarKhohs and the profits channeled into the treasury of the BrathelLanza. The mysterious artist who signed her delicate, almost esoteric works merely "ED" had become something of a rage among certain castes of the city who took seriously the collecting of art. EnDera also worked in other capacities for the Brotherhood, one of which was as companion and mistress to a newly appointed general, a barbarian with the outlandish name of HarkosNor.

"And you're happy living like this?" I asked her once as she sat before her easel, a watercolor landscape ablaze with bright flowers evolving under the deft strokes of her brush.

"Happy?" she said, pausing to dip her brush in clear water. "I don't usually think of myself in those terms,

but—well, I suppose I am, as happy as I can be in the
world the way it is. Someday, perhaps . . ."

"Someday?" I repeated, making the word a question.

"Someday the world will be different and I will be
free and happy in it. When that day comes, everyone
in NakrehVatee will be happy." Her brush moved
toward the ceramic palette and a pool of brilliant yellow color.

"Everyone but the ones we"—I now used the first-
person plural when speaking of the BrathelLanza—
"throw out of their positions of wealth and power, is
that right?"

"Well, of course *they* won't be happy. But they've
had their day. Like the dinosaurs. And they'll be ex-
tinct too."

A yellow flower blossomed on the rough texture of
the watercolor paper.

"But everyone else will be happy?" I asked.

"I certainly hope so."

"And what about you?"

"Isn't that what I said?" She rinsed the brush in
clean water. "I'll be happy then. I'll have done my
job." There was an angry, disturbed look in her eyes
as she dipped the brush into a green pool and then
began to paint a stem and leaves for the still-wet yellow
flower.

I said no more. Maybe I'd already said too much.

But I wondered.

What does a born revolutionary do when all the
revolutions are over?

Well, there's always another government to overthrow somewhere else, I suppose.

As for old KaphNo, except for bits and pieces I'd
gathered here and there, mostly when he was rather
deep in his cups, his life was a closed book. What had
changed him from a satisfied member of one of the
higher and more affluent castes to an almost fanatical

revolutionary bent on destroying the society in which he'd lived the first fifty or so years of his life, I never learned, though I did learn that he was just as I have described him: whereas AkweNema and the lord DessaTyso and the bulk of the members of the Brathel-Lanza desired only to simplify and reorder the caste system of NakrehVatee, to introduce into it more elements of justice and mobility between the castes, Kaph-No would have been truly satisfied with nothing less than the total abolition of the caste system itself. That was his desire. But he was an intelligent and realistic enough man to know that that was something he'd never see in his lifetime. He would have to settle for half of that loaf: the accomplishment of the stated goals of the BrathelLanza. But it galled him.

And, as a rule, he was a shy, reserved man, little given to talking in the presence of strangers, or even in the presence of close acquaintances unless it was concerning one of the many subjects of which he had mastery.

A high-level technologist by birth and training, KaphNo had never stopped his education, and could, at the drop of a suitable hat, argue medicine with Ak-weNema and ThefeRa, microbiology with SkorTho, psychology with GrelLo, or aesthetics with EnDera. And as often as not he would win those arguments.

Why he seemed to like me so well I had no idea—it was certainly not because I was his intellectual peer! —but I found myself flattered that he did. In turn, when I learned to take his frequently taciturn behavior with a grain of salt, I got to like him as well. Of all those in the Underground, he was the only man I really did like without reservation.

And I wasn't certain whether I really liked EnDera all that well. I felt a strong physical attraction for her, of course, and there were many things I did like about her personality, her mind, and I could understand her problems and even sympathize with them, but I'm not certain that I sympathized with her revolutionary ardor, though I'm sure her hatred of the system against which she fought was very similar to the hatred of the Kriths and all they stood for that had grown in me.

Yet—and this is the strange part—neither did I sympathize with KaphNo's even greater revolutionary ardor, and I called him friend.

"All the world's a bit queer, but for thee and me," said the old Pennsylvania Dutchman, "and sometimes I wonder about thee."

You know, there are times when I wonder a little even about myself. . . .

11

Of a Dream, and of Identities

When I had been in the Underground only a little over a month, my replicates had reached ML-2Y and looked very much as I must have looked as a two-year-old. Their lives differed in that they were never really conscious, and were taken from their encanters every other day for brief periods during which their muscles were exercised—cerebral programming had given them only the vaguest hint of what walking was all about. Then the replicates looked like 342 identical little brothers, normal and happy, if always "asleep."

In many ways it seemed much longer than a month to me, though I was certain that by now it must be about the first of October, as time was measured by the calendars of a world a long way from this Here and Now.

Two weeks later AkweNema's "daughter" was decanted for the last time and gradually awakened to the world outside the glass cylinders in which she'd grown from the cells taken from a dying girl's body. Education, in addition to the cerebral data fed to her before decanting, was begun, and every effort was made by the psychology team to re-create in the replicate a personality as similar as possible to that of the real daughter. AkweNema's reaction to the seeming resurrection was hard to gauge, but I got the impression that it alternated between delight and horror, and filled him with an almost morbid fascination he could not effectively fight. And there were times when KaphNo seemed to regret the growing of the replicate; things might have been easier for AkweNema had his daughter died once and for all.

At the same time as the replicate girl's decanting, my own replicates had reached the stage of three-year-olds and looked like a band of miniature HarkosNors—or Eric Matherses, the name to which I was more accustomed—or even Thimbron Parnassoses, as I had been called when I was their age, or rather at their "maturation level."

Like AkweNema, I didn't know whether I was fascinated and awed by the replication process or disgusted and frightened by it. Maybe it was a mixture of both, with a touch of narcissism thrown in for flavoring.

And as the time passed in the Underground, the dream I'd had a year before kept coming back to me:

A city of towering buildings and streets and parks illuminated in the night by floating globes of light, a city that I could see in my dreams but dimly and with double vision, poorly and out of focus and half hidden by rain and mist, but what I saw told me that it was no city I had ever seen before, no city ever built by humankind.

Despite the floating light globes, much of the alien city lay in darkness and shadow, and after a while, as my vision cleared, I saw movement in those shadows, furtive movement, stealthy and quiet, a figure here, another there, wrapped in dark clothing, but now and again betrayed by a glint of light from metal. All the moving figures in the quiet city carried weapons.

One of the dark-clad figures stepped briefly into light and for a moment I saw him clearly: a man in his thirties, tall and scarred from many battles, tanned, blond, wearing a short beard; he carried a Paratimer R-4 power pistol in his right hand, a knife in his left. This man, whom I shockingly recognized, turned as if facing me, as if peering into *my* eyes, and on his lips was a twisted, bitter smile of anger and hatred, of satisfaction and revenge. Then he turned away and vanished into shadows.

In another place another figure revealed itself momentarily. This too was a tall, scarred, blond, bearded man in his thirties, and he carried a large, heavy energy rifle in both hands.

And in still another place, stepping out of the shadows for a moment to make his way forward, was the same man. An army of men in the night, all identical, all perhaps cloned from a single person—so went my dream.

The army of raiders slipped silently through the night, all headed for a single destination wherein lay something they/he wished to destroy. In my dream there was a chill in me such as I'd never known before.

Time had gone by now, how much of it I didn't know, and they had almost reached their goal when, in the sky above the nonhuman city, a great light burst, white and brilliant, destroying the shadows and revealing those who had hidden in them. For a moment the raiders stopped in their tracks, startled by the light; then, as if guided by a single mind, they darted forward, running through the streets and across the parklike areas toward the largest building of the city.

From the building gunfire opened, sending shot and flame into the streets and the parks, and from the portals of the building issued an army of men—they, too, all identical, or nearly so—and all of them looked very much like a man—no, a *being* whom I'd known as Mager, a being who was slender and wiry and had a face made of craggy planes and tiny white lines like scars, who had neural organs complex enough to be called "brains" in addition to the one he had in his head. His type was very hard to kill. . . .

The Mager-force rushed into the streets, automatic slug throwers in their hands, spitting leaden death into the attackers, whose leading element was within range of the defenders' weapons. One of the blond men took a bullet in the chest. . . .

I staggered backward from the impact of the slug as it ripped through the right side of my chest just below the nipple, shattering ribs, puncturing a lung, exiting through my back, and tearing away great globs of flesh. I staggered backward more shocked than pained, stunned, dazed, knowing as the pain began that the wound was mortal and I was going to die.

I tried to raise my stolen R-4 power pistol, to take at least one of the Magers with me, but I didn't have the strength; the pistol was too heavy, slipped from my weakened grip, fell to the earth, and in moments I followed it, darkness, pain, and death coming over me as I fell.

The first of *me* died, but more of *me* came on, a dozen, two dozen; and here and there, as the collective *I* rushed forward, the individual *I* took more wounds. One of me was hit in the head, my skull shattered. I died instantly.

But I'd also taken a gut wound, a *me* some yards away, and I lay in agony as blood seeped onto the ground.

And I ran forward, a different *me,* a stream of bullets ripping away my left arm, but somehow I still fired with my right until I collapsed in unbearable pain.

Yet still, dying here and there, others of *me* terribly wounded, *I* came on against the Magers and still they killed me, though I wouldn't stop until they'd killed *me* all. . . .

And maybe they never would.

There my dream ended; it always ended there every time. And I wondered about it.

Oh, the Tromas in their wisdom had assured me that I had no psionic abilities, none at all, so I couldn't possibly be precognitive, could I? The dream couldn't possibly be some dim vision of the future, seen through a glass darkly, could it? Well, could it?

Religion didn't play a major role in the lives of the common people of NakrehVatee. It was there and was given lip service. The Bright Lords of Life and, more importantly, the Dark Lords of Death were given their due, but no more than that. Only among those of the higher castes, those who truly believed that through the cycles of reincarnation they had at last reached the point where they could hope to abandon the Wheel and look forward to an eternity in the land of the Blessed beyond the darkling waters of the Mountains of the West, was a great deal of thought given to the preparation and maintenance of the tombs in which their physical bodies would be preserved. Rather than a way of life, to most NakrehVatea religion was a mood, a coloring that seeped down to them from the higher reaches of the social pyramid, and really not much else.

And if most of the people of NakrehVatee had little regard for religion in their day-to-day lives, then the members of the BrathelLanza had even less. The revolutionary movement did not embrace atheism, didn't exactly reject the idea of godhood itself, but it did at least reject the polytheism tacitly accepted by the bulk of the nation's population. Monotheism was the order of the day among the avant-garde of the BrathelLanza and, like so many other people who have traveled the long road from pan- to poly- to monotheism, they looked toward the sun as the physical manifestation of their concept of the deity—a la the golden sun disk of Aton introduced to the world by Ikhnaton some thirty-three centuries ago.

For this reason the BrathelLanza, along with the rest of the NakrehVatea on the surface world above, did celebrate at least one religious holiday each year, that of the Return of the Sun King from the Dark Regions of Cold, the Deliverance of Helios from the Lords of Death, the winter solstice.

It was also an opportunity to throw one hell of a party.

So on the evening of the day that would be called December 20 on some calendars, all work in the city of VarKhohs and in the underground chambers of the BrathelLanza came to a halt; shops and offices above, labs and training areas below were all closed, and the membership of the Brotherhood of Life congregated in the Underground's largest room, that which contained the drill field, a great, brightly lighted cavern cut out of the living stone.

I won't go into what was eaten and drunk that night, or what followed in the darkened corridors and shadowy rooms. I'll only say that when the morning came there was many an aching head and many a guilty conscience.

To soothe those consciences, and in an effort to overcome those aching heads, most of those who were able to drag themselves out of bed went to a morning service that was a mixture of religious teachings, astrological mumbo-jumbo, ancestor worship and moral indoctrination.

Although I was one of those able, if barely, to drag myself out of bed, wondering where EnDera had spent the night, for it certainly hadn't been with me—those hours for me had gone by in the company of a dark young lady whom I later learned had not been born from a mother's womb but from an encanter flask, but she was warm flesh and blood for all that—I wasn't one of those who went to the services.

Rather, after a breakfast of coffee, raw eggs in milk and a brace of pills I hoped would make me feel halfway human again, I cleaned myself up, dressed in the military-type garments I'd begun to wear and went for a walk through the subterranean chambers.

My wandering footsteps unconsciously but purpose-

fully took me through the strangely quiet and empty
tunnels and passageways to the laboratories and finally
into the large chamber where the 340 surviving replications of myself were still sleeping peacefully, totally
unaware of the frenzy and gluttony that had passed
through the chambers the night before.

For a long while I stood there looking at them, the
replicates, the clones, the miniatures of me.

About two weeks before they had been transferred
from the first of the maturation encanters to the second,
where they would remain until they reached a maturation level of twelve years, which was still some two
and a half months away. Now they were at ML-7Y,
looking for all the world like sleeping little boys of
seven years of age who would soon wake up and want
to go outside and play ball or something.

And that mixture of awe and revulsion passed
through me again, and once more I wondered about
the wisdom—and the morality!—of this thing I'd gotten
myself involved in.

So deep was I in these thoughts and feelings that I
didn't hear the footsteps behind me until they had nearly
reached me. When I did hear them I turned.

"Good morning, General," said OrDjina, the lovely
mistress of the lord DessaTyso, with perhaps a slightly
mocking tone in her voice as she spoke the last word,
my title.

"Oh, good morning," I replied, wondering what had
brought her here. To view her own replicate? I wondered, but remembered that the more mature clone of
the cells of this woman was in another chamber, having
some weeks before been encantered in a cylinder large
enough for the final stages of her growth to maturity.
So . . . ?

"You are not a religious man, I take it, General,"
she said, again with a mocking sound to the final word.

I shook my head and I looked her up and down
in a fashion that I was sure was obvious to her, though

she made no attempt to shrink from my gaze, to show a modesty I knew she didn't possess. More an exhibitionist than a shrinking violet, she.

Her clothing this morning was a tan outfit consisting of a thin, loose-fitting blouse with lace sleeves that ended at her elbows, the neckline of which plunged almost to her waist and under which she wore nothing, her full breasts straining to escape the capturing fabric. She wore equally loose-fitting trousers, which were cut with checkerboard squares down the outsides of her hips and legs and through which her dark skin showed from thigh to ankle, warm skin, inviting skin. The color of the clothing was slightly lighter than that skin, a shade that looked well with it.

Her black hair, brushed and gleaming, sparkling with a cluster of jewels above each temple, swept loosely across her shoulders and down her back. In her eyes was a sparkle that might have been mischievous had she had a greater air of innocence about her. But then, like modesty, innocence was a quality Lady OrDjina lacked. And she did not seem to regret that lack.

"And what about yourself?" I asked. "You don't feel a need for the sacred services?"

She laughed, flashing bright teeth. "I rather doubt it would do me any good. I am far beyond that point. Like yourself."

She turned to look into one of the glass cylinders that contained what appeared to be a naked seven-year-old boy. "You were a handsome child, General."

"I like to think so myself."

"And one who showed great promise for the man he would become," she said, and almost leered as she gestured toward the child's genitals. "And I rather imagine you were a nasty little boy as well."

"What do you mean by that?" I wasn't offended by either comment, only curious about the second.

"All little boys are nasty, you know. Some are just a bit more wicked than others."

"Do you really think so?"

"Of course."

"Well, maybe I was. At least my parents seemed to think so. I got more spankings than any other boy I knew."

She laughed. "You must have been a terror to the little girls when you grew a bit older."

I shrugged again.

Then she asked, something flintlike coming to her dark eyes, "And who were those parents you just spoke of, General?"

I turned to look her fully in the face. "Why do you ask that?"

"Curiosity. I would like to know a number of things about you."

"Such as?" What was she getting at?

"Oh, such as, where did you *really* grow up and what was your name then? Such as, what kind of a city or town did you live in and what was the language you spoke then?"

"You want to know a lot, don't you. Why?"

"Curiosity, as I told you." There was a pause, and the wicked gleam in her eyes sparkled brightly. "Because, General HarkosNor, I don't think there's a single word of truth in all those things you told psychologist GrelLo."

"Everything I told her was supposed to be kept confidential."

"Oh, General, it is being kept confidential, I can assure you. I haven't told a soul a thing I know about you—which, in truth, is absolutely nothing."

"But GrelLo let you go through my tapes and notes, is that it?" I should have been angry, but at the moment I was only worried. What was it that OrDjina suspected about me? The truth? Hardly that, I thought. I hoped.

"Honestly, General, do you think GrelLo could have prevented me even if she'd wanted to and tried?

I am the lady of his lordship, you know, and with his permission I can do just about anything I want."

"Just about?"

She sighed, placed a hand between her breasts, fingers touching the column of her neck. "I must admit that even his lordship finds it wise to defer to Akwe-Nema at times. For now," she added with an ominous weight.

"I see."

"Are you certain even of that, General?"

"Right now I'm not certain of much of anything."

" 'A wise man is one who admits his ignorance.' That's an old saying of my people. My people have a great number of old sayings." She paused long enough to look me up and down as I had looked her up and down a short while before. Then she spoke again: "I have been around a bit, General. NakrehVatee is not my home, as I'm certain you've surmised. My experiences have been, shall we say, a bit more cosmopolitan than those of most of the others here. And I know that you are not what you claim to be. General, your accent isn't even that of a SteeMehseeha, you know."

She raised a hand toward my face to keep me from speaking until she had finished. "I've been looking into your computer identity records, General, and I must say they are excellent forgeries. It would take an expert to find fault with them. But they're all lies, aren't they?"

"Does it make any difference what I say?"

"None whatsoever. Unless you wish to tell me the truth. But somehow I doubt that you'll do that."

"You're right there at least."

"Then should I go to AkweNema and KaphNo and tell them what I know? Should I ask them to do a little checking about you, more than they've already done?" She laughed a strange, almost bitter laugh. "Oh, those poor fools! You could be a government agent for all they know, come to infiltrate the BrathelLanza and bring all the power of the state down to crush them."

"I'm not that."

"I know."

"You're certain?"

"I'm certain of several things that you aren't, General. One of the things you aren't is a government agent. Another is a barbarian mercenary come across the sea to sell your fighting skill to the highest bidder. What I don't know is what you *are*."

"Then why don't you do like you said, tell Akwe-Nema and KaphNo and Lord DessaTyso what you know? Why didn't you do that before you even spoke to me?"

"Honestly, General, I have no desire to do that. I suspect certain things about you, things that I'm not even sure I can put into words. But I also suspect that you find it to your advantage to do exactly what the BrathelLanza expects of you. Whatever else you are, I don't think that you're about to betray them."

"You're right in that too."

"So I will not tell them."

"I'm still not certain I understand why."

"Your understanding is not necessary, General, only your knowledge that it is so."

"Okay. I guess."

She smiled that wicked smile again. "Just continue to do as they wish you to do, General. You and I are on the same side, you know, and it is to the advantage of us both to see that the BrathelLanza is successful. Isn't it?"

With that she turned, gazed briefly once more into the cylinder, at the naked little boy inside, then turned back to me again, a frank look coming to her eyes. "Wicked little boys can be a lot of fun."

Did I comprehend her meaning? I wasn't certain until her hands went to the clasps of her thin blouse, released them, and her breasts broke free of the fabric.

"We are quite alone," she said as she shrugged out of

the blouse. "I took the precaution of locking the doors when I entered."

"But . . ." I began to say, then thought better of it.

"You are interested? You would like to make love with me?" she asked as the blouse fluttered to the floor and her hands went to the belt of her trousers.

"I would be a liar if I said no."

"Then do not lie to me about that, General." She released the belt and then the clasps that held the trousers at her waist and allowed them to drop to the floor.

"Am I not as beautiful as you imagined?" she asked, smiling wickedly.

"More so," I said, feeling the stiffening within my own trousers, forgetting any fears I might have had of being discovered by the henchmen of the lord Dessa-Tyso. To hell with him.

"And let us see if you have fulfilled the promise the boys within the encanters show," she said, stepping toward me, reaching to loosen the clothing I wore.

"Oh, yes, General, you have fulfilled that promise," she said, flowing into my arms, her breasts crushing against my chest, her hands going to the throbbing point of passion I presented her.

"The floor here is not soft," she whispered as she went to her knees before me, "but it will do when the time comes for that. But first . . ."

Later, when she was gone and I was alone in the encanter chamber, silent except for the soft sounds of the machinery that supported the lives of the 340 replicates of myself, I wondered just what was the meaning of all the words she had spoken to me before the passionate, almost savage bout of sexual delight had begun.

My speculations could be endless and would probably be equally fruitless. How could I begin to understand a woman like her?

I shrugged and dressed and started back toward my suite, thinking that now my stomach might be able to take some solid food. With the lady OrDjina I had worked up quite an appetite, another appetite having been quite thoroughly satisfied.

12
Of OrDjina

In early January, as I logged the days in a private journal, OrDjina's replicate, finally given the name QueZina, was decanted and gradually brought to consciousness, as had the replicate of AkweNema's daughter before her. QueZina, looking like an unusually beautiful eighteen-year-old, was not to be given extracts of her senior's memory, but was to be allowed to develop her own personality through educational experiences not greatly unlike those of a normal human child, though starting from a psychological maturity much greater than that of a newborn and proceeding at a much more rapid pace. It was more on the order of an experiment than anything else, and one to which OrDjina and the lord DessaTyso had given their blessing.

I saw little of AkweNema's "daughter," who had been named AkweIetana. AkweNema spent more of his time on the surface than he did in the Underground, while the replicated girl remained below, usually in his suite, with nurses and teachers when she wasn't being given mnemonic instruction by GrelLo's people. The few times I did see her, during rare visits to AkweNema's suite, left me with the impression of a very shy little girl inhabiting a big girl's body and totally uncertain of what to do with it. And each time I saw her, or OrDjina's replicate, QueZina, or one of the other half dozen or so adult replicates that lived in the BrathelLanza's Underground, I again felt those perplexing mixtures of feeling I had experienced before and that grew stronger with the passage of time. My attitudes toward replicates, even my own, never really did become clear to me.

In the early part of February, if my record keeping and calculations are at all accurate, my own replicates were placed in the last of the series of developmental encanters, the ones in which they would grow to maturity and from which they would go into a more or less normal kind of existence.

The boys, the 337 duplicates of myself at twelve years of age—another three had died; however, I was told, this was a surprisingly low rate of attrition—all had long blond hair upon their heads, silken like that of girls, and pubic hair, still little more than pale fuzz, had begun to grow around their genitals. Puberty was coming to them, and I wasn't at all certain that I was ready for that yet. Another 337 of *me* out running loose and leching after women. Mother, bar the door! Could the universe really stand that?

Meanwhile, the recording of my memories was progressing well, though it was a time-consuming operation, as KaphNo had warned me. In another month or six weeks, psychologist GrelLo assured me, the work would be all but completed and be ready for my editing, which should be accomplished rather quickly.

My training and education in other areas had been nearly completed by then, and I found myself with more free time than I'd had before, free time that I thought I should guard jealously, since once the replicates were finally decanted, I wasn't likely to have any time of my own. Day and night I would be preparing *them* for the target day of the revolution, which I figured to be about 1 September 1973.

The lady OrDjina hadn't spoken with me or approached me again, though I'd noticed her observing me at odd and unexpected times, and wondered just what in blazes she was up to. But then, could anyone answer that question for me?

As we looked through the index of tapes before the wall-filling holotank, EnDera asked, sounding as innocent as she could, "Is the lady OrDjina following you around?"

I looked up from the index display and said, trying to sound innocent too, "What do you mean?"

"Oh, nothing." Still little-girl innocent. "It's just that she keeps turning up at the oddest places, but only when you're there too."

"So you've noticed it."

"Uh-huh. Well, is she?"

"Following me? It looks that way."

"Why?"

I shrugged. "Damned if I know."

"I don't like it." Jealousy in her voice?

"It is a little disturbing sometimes."

"She must have a reason."

"Maybe she just likes me."

Jealousy in her face now. "She'd better keep her distance."

"Oh?"

She nodded. "If she's trying anything with you . . . well, if I don't get her, the lord DessaTyso will."

"The jealous type, is he?"

"Uh-huh. And he knows how to use that little gun he carries."

"Does he really go around armed?"

"Uh-huh. He's got a flat little pistol under his armpit. Nasty thing."

I just nodded. I wasn't surprised. And I thought I'd better watch myself if the lady OrDjina wanted to roll in the hay another time. Not that she wasn't a very delightful partner, but I didn't like the idea of being shot at by a jealous lover.

"And I'm the jealous type too, Harkos," EnDera was saying, as if perhaps she'd caught a glimpse of the memories of OrDjina that were passing through my mind.

"Yeah, I'm beginning to realize that." And maybe EnDera's relationship with me was now more than just an assignment from her superiors in the BrathelLanza. But then I'd suspected that for some time. "She's a strange one," I said aloud.

EnDera grunted affirmatively.

"She's not a NakrehVatea, is she?"

"No, she isn't. If I understood correctly, she's from somewhere in EkhoVro." That was the political entity that governed a portion of southern Europe and areas of northern Africa in this Here and Now. "I don't even think she's ever become a citizen." A smugness, a superiority in EnDera's voice? I wasn't certain.

"Then what's she doing in the BrathelLanza?" I asked. "I thought only native-born NakrehVatea were allowed into the inner circle—except for me, of course."

"She's here because of DessaTyso." She didn't give him his honorific, I noticed. Maybe she wasn't any too fond of his lordship. "She has been his mistress for some time now, I understand, but his family doesn't approve of her. They think he ought to have only native-born girls of his own caste sharing his bed. So there was something of a family brouhaha over her— and it wasn't even kept in the family: the Blues got wind of what was going on and let it leak to the public, mention was even made of it at the Council of Forty, which got DessaTyso's father, Lord DessaAnjoh, into hot water. The Reds supported DessaAnjoh in a vote of confidence in the council, but it put him in a bad spot for a while. The families of the members of the Council of Forty are supposed to be above reproach. Anyway, to smooth things over, DessaTyso let it be known that he was parting company with Lady OrDjina and pretended to send her away. Actually what he did was get AkweNema to consent to let her live down here, with a suite and all, and even a personal servant for her. He claimed she was always one of us in spirit anyway. And she seems satisfied enough—or so I thought. And I don't doubt that DessaTyso is."

"Must be a nice arrangement for him. This way he

can mix business and pleasure whenever he comes down."

EnDera nodded.

"What do you know about her background before she was his mistress?"

"Not too much. Mostly gossip, rumors, you know. The story is that she was some sort of *entertainer* in EkhoVro. Now, I wouldn't say exactly *what kind* of entertainer. Some say she was a singer or actress or something, but there are others who claim she did most of her work from flat on her back, and if she used her mouth it wasn't to sing or talk."

How right you are, I said to myself, but to EnDera I said, "I follow you. The same way she earns her keep now?"

"Exactly, only now it's with just one man and not a parade of them. Anyway, it seems that there was this government minister in EkhoVro she got mixed up with; they had a very wild, flashy affair or something. He left his wife and family and moved in with OrDjina in a pleasure-house where she was performing as a nude dancer and maybe staging some private sex shows with male dancers—and even a baboon, so one story said. Anyway, when word of this got out, there was a major scandal and a shake-up in the government. The minister was relieved of his position and OrDjina found it wiser to leave the country the first chance she got.

"And exactly how a person with her reputation ever got a visa to enter NakrehVatee, I'm not certain, but it may be that the lord DessaTyso"—when she pronounced his honorific this time it was with a touch of sarcasm—"already knew her then and pulled some strings to get her admitted. Anyway, that's what the Blue Chairman said, and that's why DessaTyso's father got in trouble. You just don't mess with immigration rules, you know."

"Still, it seems odd," I said. "I mean, allowing an

alien like her into the very heart of something that's supposed to be as secret as the BrathelLanza."

"You're an alien too, Harkos, at least technically."

"Well, I've got something the BrathelLanza needs— my skills."

"OrDjina's got something DessaTyso needs too—and it's right between her thighs."

"Okay. Okay."

"Not that I'm saying I approve," EnDera added quickly. "I can't say that I like her or trust her, and neither does Akwe. One of the rules he set up and made DessaTyso agree to was that she wouldn't be allowed to leave the Underground or communicate with another outsider prior to the revolution."

"That sounds wise."

"But I'm not certain Akwe can enforce it."

"Why's that?"

"If DessaTyso wants to smuggle her out some night when Akwe's not around, who's to stop him? KaphNo doesn't have the authority, and I think he's about the only one who'd even have the guts to try to stop him."

"I see what you mean." I paused, then asked: "Do you think there's any chance that she's an agent of some foreign power? EkhoVro or some other country?"

"The thought has crossed my mind. Why do you ask?"

"I don't know. There's just something, well, strange about her."

"That's what I've been trying to tell you, Harkos."

"So we're in agreement."

"As long as you don't try to get firsthand information about her background *or* her professional skills."

"Don't worry. I'd just as soon go to bed with a she-tiger."

"That would be just about as safe as touching her, I promise you."

"I accept the warning, and give you my promise that I'll stay clear of her." And maybe I really meant it.

EnDera laughed. "I wasn't really worried."

I glanced at the illuminated tape index and then back at EnDera. "Do you really want to look at a tape? I can think of a better way to pass the evening."

"Yes, I believe I can too," she said, a smile flickering across her lips as she began to open the loose gown she wore.

"Right here?" I asked as I reached for her, one hand entering the open gown and cupping a full breast.

"Right here would be fine," EnDera replied in hardly more than a whisper, her hands beginning to tug at my clothing. "Right here would be delightful."

13

The End of the BrathelLanza

On the morning of 4 March—of that date I am as certain as I am of any in my life: 4 March 1973—KaphNo joined me for breakfast. EnDera wasn't there. The day before, she had gone up to the surface to transact some business concerning the sale of her paintings and to collect some sums of money due her, and although she had been expected to return by the evening of that day, she still wasn't back the next morning.

I really wasn't too worried about her: EnDera was a grown woman, and she could take care of herself in the streets of VarKhohs perhaps better than I could have myself; but I was a little on edge because of her absence, and even more so when KaphNo, over coffee and rolls, told me that EnDera wasn't the only one who had failed to return from the upperworld during the past two days.

"Are you certain?" I asked him.

KaphNo nodded as he nibbled on a sweet roll, then said, "Day before yesterday two of my technicians went up to see about procuring some equipment for one of the labs—rheostats and such for electrical control units. They should have had no trouble obtaining them."

"But they didn't come back?"

KaphNo grunted. "I sent another technician up yesterday to find out what happened to them—they were young fellows, you know, and might have stopped for a drink and had a few too many. You know how it is. I wasn't worried. *Then* I wasn't worried."

"You are now?"

He grunted again, munched his roll, and swallowed

106

with the aid of coffee. "The one I sent up to check on them didn't come back either."

I shook my head. "Any idea what's going on?"

He shook his head in return. "None, but I did give Akwe a call last night, and he said he'd see that it was checked out from his end. I haven't heard from him yet. Maybe he'll call soon. I hope he does."

"And now EnDera," I said, mostly to myself.

"If I don't hear from Akwe soon, I'll punch him up again and have him get someone to check on her. Will that make you feel better?"

"I'll feel better when I know she's okay. Has anything like this ever happened before?"

KaphNo shook his head again, opened his mouth, popped in the remnants of the roll, and washed it down with more coffee. "Don't get too worried yet, Harkos. It may be nothing at all."

"And it may be something."

"Let's hope not," he said, and I remembered EnDera's words: "Really, Harkos, we don't have too many illusions down here. We know we're under sentences of immediate execution on the spot, or prolonged torture in some of the lords' dungeons, if we're ever caught. We just hope we can put off being caught for a few more months."

"Cheer up, boy," KaphNo said as he refilled his coffee cup and reached across the table for another roll. "Your memory-recording sessions are just about over, aren't they?"

"Another two or three days. Then we'll start editing them."

"GrelLo and her people are going to have to start pushing their end of it. ThefeRa and SkorTho are anxious to start giving the replicates some preliminary tapes."

"It's a little early for that, isn't it?"

"Not for the most basic kinds of stuff, mainly muscular control, dexterity, that sort of thing. The boys are at ML-14Y, you know." There was in his voice a genuine affection for my replicates. "We could use some of the tapes we already have on this sort of thing, but we'd prefer to use yours from the start. It could save a lot of retraining later."

"So I've been told."

"And how are the other things going?"

"Well enough. I think I pretty well know my job now, and who the bad guys are."

KaphNo smiled. "And who the good guys are too?"

"They're the ones I wonder about sometimes."

"Anyone in particular?"

"Yes. The lord DessaTyso's playmate, the lady Or-Djina."

KaphNo gave me a serious look and nodded. "I know exactly what you mean. If it had been up to me, she would never have come down here in the first place."

"Do you think she could be a danger to us?"

KaphNo tilted his head to one side, pursed his lips. "I don't know," he said seriously. "I can't say that I entirely trust her, but she's never given me any reason to think that she might be, well, a danger to us. I mean, I've no reason to think she's a spy or a government agent or anything of that sort."

I could have said that maybe I did, but I didn't say that. If I were to tell him that much, then I'd have to tell him a lot of other things I didn't want him to know, like who and what I really was and why I was there.

"I guess I'm just worrying too much," I said finally.

"In a place and a situation like this one, we all worry too much, Harkos. And it's bad for the digestion." Then he sighed and forced a smile onto his face. "But it won't be much longer now. Two months or so more for the replicates to complete their maturation, and another two months or so to train them. In four months, five at the most, you'll be ready, your 'army' will be ready, we all will be ready. Then we'll show some people what a revolution is all about." The thought of coming violence, though it might not reach quite to the ends he desired, seemed to animate the old man, to quicken the blood in his tired veins and bring a fresh light to his deep-set eyes.

"I'm getting sort of anxious myself," I said.

KaphNo started to say something more, but was interrupted by the chiming of the kitchen communicator. Since he was closer to it, he reached up and punched the holotank to life, which quickly displayed the image of a young man whose name I didn't know, one of the security guards who, in AkweNema's absence, answered to KaphNo.

"Yes, what is it?" KaphNo asked.

"Master KaphNo, sire," the young guard began in an uncertain voice, "please excuse me for calling you at this hour, but, sire, I thought I'd better report it to you."

"Report what?" KaphNo asked, an edge of annoyance to his voice; he wasn't any too fond of his responsibility for security matters. "Spit it out, boy."

"The lady OrDjina, sire," the guard continued with the same hesitancy in his voice. "She is not in her quarters. Her servant says she has not been there since sometime yesterday."

"Are you certain?"

"Yes, sire. We are now in the process of searching the Underground—at the captain's orders, sire—but she does not appear to be anywhere about."

"Damn!" KaphNo muttered. "Well, continue the search, and inform your captain that I'll meet him in his office at once."

"Yes, sire. Very good, sire."

KaphNo turned off the communicator with an angry gesture, a frown wrinkling his face.

"What does that mean?" I asked.

"Damned if I know, Harkos," KaphNo said, suddenly looking very old again. "But, on top of everything else, I don't like the sound of it at all."

"Well, I . . ." I began, but was interrupted when the communicator buzzed again.

With another savage gesture KaphNo flipped the device back into operation. The image of GrelLo, the psychologist, developed in the tank this time.

"What is it, GrelLo?" KaphNo snapped.

"Is the general there?" she asked.

"I'm here."

"Oh, General," her voice said from the speaker, "have you forgotten? My technician is standing by for your recordings this morning."

"Oh, damn," I muttered. "I forgot the time." I glanced at KaphNo.

"Go on to the session," he replied. "Our security people can handle the other matter." He turned back to the holotank. "He'll be right there, GrelLo."

He switched off the device and turned to me: "Go on and get to the studio, Harkos. Those recordings are important too."

"Okay, but keep me posted, will you?"

"Yes, I'll certainly do that. As soon as I know what's going on."

KaphNo left the suite while I was dressing to go to the mnemonic-recording session. I never saw him again. I didn't know it then, of course, but I had already seen most of the members of the BrathelLanza for the last time.

Fifteen minutes later I was sitting in a large, comfortable chair with padded back and seat and supports for arms, legs, and head, while GrelLo's technician, a slender young man named MaLarba, was affixing electrodes to my scalp.

"Comfortable, General?" he asked. "You should be feeling the effects of the drugs soon."

Even as he spoke I could feel my body relaxing, seeming to begin to drift away from me, while at the same time my mind seemed to become sharper, clearer, more finely tuned, and the sensory data that came to me seemed more intense and more detailed, though soon I would lose consciousness of most of my senses, except for sight and hearing. I didn't particularly enjoy taking drugs that totally incapacitated me, that made me as limp and helpless as a newborn kitten, and then, on top of that, having myself strapped into a chair. I felt so vulnerable then. But that was one of the necessities of mnemonic recording, so I was told, and I went along with it. Two or three more sessions of it were all I would have to endure. I could stand that, couldn't I?

"That's the last of them," MaLarba said as he stepped away from the back of my head and came into my line of vision. "Now, if you'll allow me to strap you in." Not that there was much I could have done to stop him; I was now hardly aware of having arms and legs.

The technician passed the straps across my torso, arms, chest, hips, and legs, then tightened them down. I'd been told that the straps were purely for my own protection. I supposed it was so.

"All in place now, General. Let me know when you're ready to start."

My signal for that was a rapid batting of my eyelids; about the only things I had left that I could control volitionally were my eyelids and my eyes themselves.

Now I felt as if I were floating freely, a disembodied personality, only remotely connected to the outside world by eyes and ears.

I batted my eyelids.

"Very good, General," MaLarba said. He keyed the memory recorder; its buzzing indicated that the tapes were turning slowly above and behind me. "Now, yesterday, at the close of our session, General, we were . . ."

The passage of time while drugged was a very difficult thing to determine. I would drift off into memories and follow them through torturous paths and only after some time would I break out of my reverie long enough even to look out through my eyes. If I wished, there was a large chronometer on the far wall that I could see if I moved my eyes to the limit of their leftward motion. This time I didn't do that. Not yet.

I did open my eyes, however, and slipped back into a state of consciousness sufficient to comprehend what my eyes were seeing, my ears hearing.

Now MaLarba wasn't alone in the small recording room. A young female technician whose name I didn't know was standing facing him, twisting her hands together, a worried, even frightened expression on her face.

"I'm scared, really scared, MaLarba," she was saying.

"Maybe it's nothing. I'll go with you and we'll have a look."

"It might be better if we stayed here," the girl said.

"Now, GweZa, you're being silly. It can't be anything that bad. We'll go see."

The girl finally nodded agreement, but reluctantly.

MaLarba turned to glance at me, saw that my eyes were open, and stepped closer to speak to me. "General, there seems to be some kind of disturbance up front. I don't know what it is, but I'd better have a look. You'll be okay. We'll be right back."

I batted my eyelids in acknowledgment.

"Be right back, General," he said again, and went from the room with the girl.

With a mild but growing anxiety, I found that I couldn't go back inside and pick up my train of thought.

MaLarba would have to help me do that. When he came back . . .

A sudden fear struck me.

If he came back.

KaphNo's technicians hadn't come back, not the first two or the one he'd sent after them. And EnDera hadn't come back. And OrDjina was no longer in the Underground.

But, I told myself quickly, MaLarba isn't going to the surface, isn't leaving the Underground. He's just going a few yards up the tunnels.

It didn't help a bit. Something was wrong, I felt certain. And maybe getting a lot worse.

I turned my eyes as far to the left as they would go. The chronometer read 11:24:06. The digits that counted the seconds turned exceedingly slowly. At 11:24:57 I heard sounds, faint and remote, and at first I couldn't determine what was making them, chatterings that came and went like . . .

The sounds were louder, coming closer, and now I knew exactly what they were: automatic slug throwers, rifles and pistols both, chattering as conical slugs of metal erupted from their barrels. And I knew why EnDera and the three technicians hadn't come back from the surface. Why AkweNema had never returned KaphNo's call. They'd been arrested, maybe drugged, probably tortured, but definitely arrested. The day that EnDera and the others had dreaded, had hoped would never come, now had come.

The government finally was acting. The Brathel-Lanza was dying.

But what of OrDjina? How did her absence figure into this? . . . unless she had known, had perhaps even assisted the government. But I didn't think so. Then what? No answers. No more time to ask the questions.

Running feet outside the door. Hoarse calls and cries. A gagged scream. The sound of something heavy striking the floor. The terribly loud sounds of automatic weapons coming still closer.

More feet in the hallway outside the room, stumbling. A thud that rattled the wall beside the door, then a scratching on the door itself. The door opening slowly as if pushed by a small, curious but timid child. Someone entering, someone whom at first I didn't recognize; his face was a bloody wreck, part of his cheek blown away, white bone and shattered teeth exposed. Two ragged holes in the starched, white blouse of a technician, holes surrounded by a red wetness that spread even as he staggered toward me, then turned back, stumbled to the door, shut it, latched it, locked it. Then again toward me.

A distorted voice that bubbled with blood: "Police. General. Police. Come. To. Kill. Us. Kill. Us. All . . ."

What was left of MaLarba staggered forward another step or two, tried to get something else out, but the blood was too thick in his throat and he could not speak. He almost fell, then caught himself and grabbed the arm of my chair, wiping blood across it and across my hand. He bent, tried to reach for the buckles of the straps that held me in the chair, and touched one of them but was unable to loosen it.

Try, dammit, try! I yelled silently within my head.

He tried, yes, dammit, he tried to get me loose, but it was too late, he was already too nearly dead.

His knees gave way under him and he dropped to the floor, turning and rolling over as he did so that finally he lay halfway crumpled on his back. He turned his ruined face toward me, trying to say something with his eyes, but couldn't. He gagged on the blood, coughed, died. I hoped the Dark Lords beyond the Mountains of the West would receive him kindly.

I sat in the chair, unable to make the slightest move, filled with horror and fear. My friends, my allies, were out there dying, and their warrior, their battle leader, was helpless and was likely to die very soon himself.

Shadowy Man, I screamed inside my head, goddamn you, Shadowy Man, what have you done to me now?

There was no answer. I had expected none.

Outside the room, automatic weapons chattered still, though more randomly; hoarse calls still filled the air, orders, commands, a scream of pain, a cry for help, more explosive chattering.

My eyes went leftward. The digits of the chronometer said it was 11:29:44. Only five minutes?

More feet, more orders, more chattering of weapons, which had now almost come to a stop.

It was 11:32:07. Two pairs of feet outside the doorway. One stopping. Then the other, stopping, returning.

"What's this?" a voice asked,

"Probably just a storeroom or something. Let's go. We're just about finished."

"Sure about that?"

The thud of a booted foot kicking the door.

Now they'd find me. I was dead. Damn you, Shadowy Man!

"I said leave it," an authoritative voice said. "We got our orders. We got all the live ones and now we go back to the surface. Then we seal the place off and turn it over to the inspectors."

"It won't be very nice for them when they get around to it, if they're as slow as they usually are."

"That ain't our worry. Let them wait a couple of weeks if they want to. That's their tough luck if this places stinks like a slaughterhouse when they get here. Come on. Let's go. We'd better give NaTyso a hand with those prisoners."

"Yeah. Will do." A pause. "But, you know, it beats me why we couldn't have used gas down here. Would have been a whole lot easier and not nearly so messy."

"Hell, man, you know as well as I do that there's two ways to do anything: the right way and the official way. Let's go."

Feet moving away now, away from the doorway.

Soon other feet, shuffling leadenly across the floor outside the door. A woman sobbing. A man's voice saving: "Don't take it so hard, lady. You didn't get shot, did you? And neither did the girl." Woman sobbing louder. "And they might not even execute you. Life in a public brothel's not all that bad, so they tell me."

"What's—what's that?" asks a voice that might be that of a child, but isn't; it is the voice of the replicate of AkweNema's daughter.

"Don't you worry none, baby," the man's voice says. "It ain't no public whorehouse for you. Captain says he's gonna take you home for himself."

Girl and woman sobbing together.

Feet shuffling off into the distance.

Now 11:40:35. There is no sound in the Underground, save for the *shush-shush-shush* of air circulating through the vents somewhere above me, the buzzing of the recorder as it still operates, the hiss of tape across the recording heads.

Now I almost wished they had shot me. If I couldn't get out of the straps when the drugs wore off—and I was very much afraid that I couldn't; the straps were well made and MaLarba had done a good job fastening them—if I couldn't get out, then I might well die of thirst before the inspectors came to investigate the place, if the policemen I'd heard knew what they were talking about, and I was afraid they might. I might die of thirst, but I stood a pretty good chance of going out of my mind first.

I looked up as high as I could toward the ceiling, up toward the surface world so far away, and again I said to myself, Damn you, Shadowy Man, damn you to the deepest hell. . . .

14
Opening Corridors

I looked again at the chronometer—12:04:56—then down at the bloody, quiet, lifeless thing on the floor beside me, its sightless eyes turned toward the lighting strip that ran across the ceiling, as if during their final moments of vision they had sought the comfort of that glow. Forty minutes before it had been a human being, a technician, a young man named MaLarba; maybe his girl friend, GweZa, was dead too. Maybe KaphNo and ThefeRa and SkorTho and GrelLo and all the others were dead as well. And EnDera and AkweNema and perhaps even the lord DessaTyso were prisoners of the police and the state, if they weren't dead.

Once again I found myself alone, my friends dead around me, but there was a difference this time. I might be joining them soon. A few days at the most. I did not think my chances of getting out of that chair to be very good at all, and it would be some time yet before the drugs wore off enough for me even to make a probably futile attempt. So . . .

I wouldn't say that I became unhinged then, but for a while my grasp on reality slackened, a reality I could contact now only with my eyes and ears; and my eyes could see little, a narrow cone of vision; my ears could hear even less. For a moment I stood on the brink of something I couldn't grasp, couldn't understand, and then with an angry, silent scream, a curse thrown toward all the gods of all the Earths and toward the Shadowy Man, a curse that was mingled with a plea for help from those same malevolent forces, I plunged downward, inward, toward blackness, darkness, insanity, fear, terror . . . and fell all the way through and outward again, rushing upward, expanding into vast and empty corridors, chambers, halls. . . .

Of this I can speak only in analogies, for there are no words for what I experienced, not in any language I have ever known. If anyone has ever experienced this before, and if he has found a way of expressing it, I wish I could learn the way from him. As it was, no words. But it was *something* like this:

I had fallen into the darkness, screaming for help, and in some unconscious, unknowing way, that call had been answered, not by gods or by the Shadowy Man but by my replicates, my clones; through resonance they knew that I had asked something of them, though they did not know what, and they answered the only way they could: they opened themselves for me.

For the first seconds—read *years,* read *centuries*—I plunged, twisted, tumbled, turned, flew, soared. Out of the dark and fear-filled corridors of my own brain, I—whatever it is that is *I*, is *me*—swept into 337 sparkling new places, empty, virginal, untouched, waiting to be inhabited, waiting to be filled with sight and sound, with experience and memory.

I recoiled, drew back into the dark caverns of my own skull, found them not so dark now, not so frightening, yet crowded full, filled with memories aching to be freed, with thoughts waiting to be thought, dreams to be dreamed, fantasies to be conjured up, nightmares to be screamed at. They all wanted out—and now, for the first time in my life, maybe for the first time in anyone's life, there was a place for them to go, many places to go.

I reached out cautiously, gently, trying to narrow the mental probe I extended, trying to use the theories taught me by KaphNo and SkorTho and GrelLo, tried to exercise response control and select a single brain of a single replicate. Somehow, I did it.

On one level I knew, saw, felt, and sensed the organic brain of the replicate, the cerebral matter that provides the matrix from which the mind is built—from which a mind could be built, for as yet there had not evolved a mind from this raw cerebral material. This replicate had been deprived of all sensory data except on the lowest, most basic levels. The soil was fertile, rich, but no seeds had yet been planted.

On another level: again, vast and empty corridors, halls and chambers of potential consciousness, potential awareness. Corridors crying to be filled, begging for my entry, as if my slightest touch had made them aware, if but barely, of the vast and remarkable world outside.

I did not commit my next act volitionally. Perhaps if I'd wanted to I couldn't have accomplished it intentionally. But what happened, happened. . . .

My eyelids opened and I peered out of the murky liquid in which I half floated, felt the flow of it around my naked flesh, tasted the strange, comforting flavor of it in my mouth and took oxygen from it as I breathed it in through my lungs, heard it carry into my ears the sounds of the machines that kept me alive and growing.

Yet at the same time my eyes—my *other* eyes—looked around the recording room, saw the motionless corpse that had been MaLarba, saw out of their corners that the chronometer read only 12:05:02. Six seconds? And heard low rumblings that could have been only the swish of the air from the overhead vents and the slowed buzzing of the mnemonic recorder. It was something like being in X5 augmentation, but now the world was slowed by a factor much greater than five, slowed by powers of ten, by exponential factors.

And beyond either set of scanty sensory data, through the crowded corridors of my own brain and the empty ones of the replicates, I felt . . . I felt . . . Even analogies fail me here. As if I had expanded?

As if I had grown to twice my size? As if a portion of godhood had touched me and become a part of me? Or as if I had become a portion of the godhood?

I did expand—I am sure of that, if of nothing else. And out of the dim, dark rooms of my brain, out of the attics and cellars and closets of forgetfulness and of never having known, memory and unformed thoughts leaped free, dreams and visions jumped and gamboled across the connections, the junctions, the nexuses, spilling over, dancing free, running with the winds of a new freedom through fresh neural impulses.

For a thousand years I basked and shivered alternately in all the experiences of my life, seeing everything I'd ever seen before, everything I'd ever heard, ever felt, ever thought . . . yet with a clarity and a detail of vision I'd never before experienced or even imagined possible.

If not the fringes of godhood, then something terribly close to it.

I felt more fully realized than a human being has ever felt before.

But this was only one of them, only one of the replicates. And there were over 330 more of them. . . .

After another thousand years of reviewing only the most pleasurable of my life's experiences, I reached out again, probed with a more careful, wiser, more experienced touch. And there was another of the virginal brains, potential minds, more bright and empty corridors, and all waiting for me. I spilled into those empty places.

I had the same sensations as before, but this time I could experience them more critically, know them more intimately, all the beauty and ugliness, all the pain and pleasure. And again there were those feelings of expansion, of power. Again there were sensations of new, empty expanses of consciousness opening up before me, to be filled as fully as possible from the wells of my memory.

Now I was three. Not exactly HarkosNor/Eric Mathers anymore, but perhaps something bigger, better than he had ever been, something with at least the potential of being wiser, more intelligent, more able to grasp and understand the vastness of the worlds of my past experience.

I resonated between my own body and the bodies of the two replicates. Awaiting me were 335 more brains, more possible minds.

I reached out again.

And again.

And again ...

15
Genesis

All I have now is my own memory, a memory confined
and shackled by my very finite limitations. I am only
one man now, as I record these things out of the past,
and I can speak of them only as remembrances of once
having been a part of that creation, a part of that existence, a part of that being who came into the universe
when my mind and the personalityless minds of the
replicates resonated together, operated as a single,
thinking entity.

I am not that amalgam. But I was once a part of it.

And since I am not what *it* was, I cannot continue
to use the first-person singular. I, Eric Mathers, will
speak of it, of *him,* what I can still recall of him and
of that existence.

All but one of the replicates were now joined in
psionic resonance with the entity that had been their
senior—*had been,* for now they were one, with 337
bodies, one of them drugged, strapped into a chair, the
others still half floating in the solutions that filled their
encanters. They comprised a single mind that was then
the mind of Eric Mathers; during those first few moments, at least, it was the mind of Eric Mathers, for
all his memories, his experiences, his opinions, and his
beliefs had not yet changed; it was merely that there
were more vessels to carry him, and like a gas under
high pressure he had expanded to fill them, although in
that very process he had begun to become something
other than what he had been, something that no man
had ever been before.

Of the 337 replicates, all but one were now component parts of this new yet nameless entity. One of the replicates, the victim of previously undiscovered brain damage, was incapable of entering into the union, was little more than a vegetable whose autonomic nervous system kept his body alive, but who had virtually no capacity for cerebral growth, for consciousness, for thought. That body was left alone, to continue its maturation as best it could.

The others that were now one: After aeons of wonder and visions, he paused for what seemed to him to be still more aeons, though now he had lost all contact with the outside material world and had no real means of reckoning the passage of external time, if the passage of time had any real meaning for him then, of which he was not yet certain. Time was something about which he would speculate, he told himself. There was much he could learn about the nature of time, much to be drawn from the experiences of the past, things Eric Mathers had seen and heard and read and done that related to the nature of time itself. He decided he would do that, determine the nature of time. But not just yet. There was no hurry.

He rested then, gathered his strength, composed mental forces the immensity and nature of which he had hardly begun to comprehend. He pondered that strength and found himself almost frightened by it. In a sense, he thought, the doors of the universe might be open to him. Some of the doors at least. But not all of them, perhaps.

He remembered, in clarity and detail he still found startling:

Back across time and space, to a Timeline called KHL-000 in the month of February, over a year before . . . The Palace of the Tromas. The Place wherein Dwell the All-Wise Mothers.

And of the Tromas themselves: female Kriths, a

dozen of them, ancient, deformed, scarcely hominid in their obesity.

In the air about them was an almost electrical aura, a sensation of power held in tight check, of vast forces unseeable and perhaps unknowable, psionic powers that the Tromas and their ancestors had utilized to build the power of the Krithian race, to allow them to expand across the Timelines, to bend even time itself to their uses.

Now he recognized the Tromas for what they were. In some ways he was very much like them. But he had many more bodies, many more brains than their dozen —but they had centuries of experience and accumulated skill behind them. How great were the similarities? How great the differences?

As with the questions he had raised about time itself, he left these questions about the Tromas hanging, filed away in a place from which they could easily be retrieved when the time came to fully investigate.

Now, like the playful child he was, the composite mind of the man and his replicates began to search again, to explore, to probe outside itself, to see what it could find outside the complex universe it was building for itself in the resonance patterns that existed between its members.

He probed outward this time, not inward, out into the vast gulf of psionic darkness, out into an empty universe lighted only here and there by remote brilliances, galaxies far away in the darkness of that emptiness, quasars on the very limits of observation.

He reached out across the expanses . . . and touched another mind.

He recoiled for a moment, held back, for he was not certain whether he wanted to enter this mind, whether he could if he wanted to, whether the resonance patterns there coincided enough for there to be the full response control of level three. He paused, held, pondered, decided: response-level two would be sufficient, might be the best he could do no matter how hard he tried. He moved forward, looked. . . .

*Lieutenant Colonel Eric Mathers sat on a bunk, a cigarette between his lips, an energy pistol disassembled in his lap. He was the only person in the room.

*For furniture there was the bunk he sat on, another, similar bunk, a desk between them, a battered old dresser opposite the desk, on the dresser a pile of soiled clothing. Beside the dresser was a lavatory, above the lavatory a shelf on which sat two sets of shaving gear, folded towels, a cracked mirror.

*As he slowly put the weapon back together, apparently bored with the operation, apparently finding it merely something to do while he waited, Lieutenant Colonel Mathers could hear from outside the room, from outside the small, frame building, the passage of motorized vehicles on a dirt road, the rumbling of laboring engines, the complaining of metal, the yells and curses of tired men.

*Then there was a knock on the door. Mathers looked up, said, "Yes?"

*The door opened just enough to allow the head of a young soldier to slip through. His mouth said, "Colonel, he's on his way here now. The Krith, sir." The language the young soldier spoke was Timeliners' Shangalis.

*"Very good, Corporal. Thanks."

*"Right, sir."

*The head retreated; the door closed.

*Lieutenant Colonel Mathers completed reassembling the energy pistol, snapped its power cartridge into place, slipped the weapon into the holster on his hip, rose to his feet, brushed off his clothing, and stuffed his shirttails into his pants. After taking a quick glance around the room, he snuffed out his cigarette and went toward the door.

*He opened it just in time to see a naked, ugly,

brownish, alien Krith come around the back of the jeep in which he had arrived, his brown-marble eyes bright, his long tail swinging in the air like an interrogation point.

*"Eric, my friend," the Krith said.

*"Mar-masco," Mathers said in reply, bowing in Krithian fashion as the alien did the same. "Come in," Mathers said, gesturing toward the doorway behind him.

*The Krith nodded and followed him.

*Mathers had seen the brown folder in his hand. The Krith had brought what Mathers was hoping he would bring.

*Inside, Mar-masco sat down on one of the beds, Mathers on the other.

*"I have brought exactly what you wanted of me, Eric."

*"Exactly?" Mathers asked.

*"Exactly," the Krith repeated, opening the folder and then spreading sheets of paper out on the rough woolen blanket on the bed. "The new contract confirms your rank and pay scale and bonus, all in order. I have a check here too."

*"Very good."

"You will be granted a month's leave on one of the Rajaian Lines, as you requested, expenses paid— that part took some doing, I grant you, but we felt that your services to the Timeliners warranted it. Your next assignment, when your leave is up, will be to . . ."

He withdrew, pulled back into the psionic darkness, reviewed things for a moment.

That was *me*, he thought, a version of Eric Mathers, a parallel Eric Mathers . . . still working for the Kriths as a Timeliner mercenary, as *I* once did, still loyal to them, still unquestioning of them, still waging their wars for them and helping them alter the histories of the parallel Earths so that they would fit into whatever master plan it was the Kriths had for the universe.

There were other stars in the darkness; he sought out one of them, found . . .

*Pain and darkness, one eye seeing dimly the walls of the hospital room to which he was confined. Eric Mathers tried to stir on his bed, tried to use the stump of an arm to relieve the pressure on the sores on his back, caused himself only more pain, fell back, groaned, tried to remember what it was like when he had been a whole man, when every moment was not one of agony, but found that he could not.

With that same grotesque stump, he fumbled, pushed a button that rang a remote bell, sent current pulsing through a distant, incandescent bulb. A nurse would hear the bell, see the light, and eventually would come to see what he wanted. A bedpan? A bath? A drink of water? And then he would try to tell her, try to make her understand, for the nurse on duty now was one of the new ones and had not yet learned to decipher the gagged sounds that passed for speech, the noises that came from the twisted throat of Eric Mathers, ex-Timeliner, hopelessly injured beyond repair, another casualty of the endless wars across the Lines of Time. . . .

Again he withdrew into the darkness of psionic space, shuddering within the resonance patterns of himself. The horror had been too great; he was not ready for *that* yet, for he knew exactly what *it* was . . . himself, a parallel version of Eric Mathers, so seriously injured in the explosion that had wrecked a place called Staunton on Line RTGB-307, where *he* had discovered the presence of a second alien race moving across the Timelines, altering worlds to suit *their* purposes, that he was now little more than a basket case, a painful distortion of a man confined to a hospital bed for the rest of his life. Mercifully, it would be a short one.

He rallied himself, collected the various components of himself, looked across the darkness once more at other points of psionic light, hesitant at first about approaching another, finally doing so, reaching out, probing, seeing. . . .

This was not quite as bad as the last one, though bad enough. . . .

*A tall blond man who appeared to be in his sixties, but who was actually less than forty years old, his face covered with a full beard, his emaciated frame covered with filthy prison garments, huddled in his gray stone cell, chewing a crust of bread, gazing up at the narrow window above his head, which was the cell's only source of light. A bright beam of sunlight passed through the window, illuminating motes of dust in the air, splashing a narrow rectangle of light, bright and yellow, against the far wall, obscuring the wall's many scribblings, executed over the years with bits of charred wood.

*The man in the cell was named Thimbron Parnassos; that was the only name he had ever known in his life. He had never been approached by the Timeliners, had never joined them, had never moved across the Lines of Time, waging the wars of the Kriths to change tomorrow, had never been given the name Eric Mathers during an assignment in an English-speaking country on a Line labeled by the Kriths RTGB-307.

*Parnassos continued to stare at the beam of sunlight, wondering what the world was like outside the prison now, for it had been more years than he could remember since he had seen anything outside the four gray walls that enclosed him. He did not think of it now, but the memory was always there, just below the surface, the memory of the last time he had seen the outside world: it had been a gallows yard, where he and a dozen other students waited for their turns to come, their turns to mount the steps and place their heads within the sweat-stained nooses, for the traps to be opened under them and for their bodies to fall, for their necks to be snapped as the ropes burned into their flesh. They had been convicted of sedition and treason against the government of North Ionia, and they were to die. But they did not die. A cruel quirk of fate. In celebration of a major victory over the rebellious forces, the governor of North Ionia had commuted their sentences to life imprisonment, solitary confinement, no chance of parole. Death would have been preferable. The boys were taken back into the gray prison, never to see the outside world again.

Parnassos rocked on his knees on the floor of the cell, his crust of bread eaten, his stomach still empty. He rocked on his knees and hummed to himself an old, old song his father had taught him as a child. His father had been very lucky. He had been hanged. But he didn't think of that very often either. He didn't think of very much at all. . . .

He withdrew in pain and confusion. He found it hard to believe that the huddled figure was himself, was Eric Mathers, another parallel of the man he had been. But it was. It was.

Across the darkness again, seeking still another pinpoint of luminance, another fragment of consciousness in the emptiness.

Touching. Contacting . . .

*The big blond man was dressed conservatively, his clothing unsuited for his frame, the cravat around his neck loosened. Under his coat and his shirt, his shoulders slumped and his back bent; it was as if he were trying to diminish his size, to appear smaller than he actually was, as if he did not wish to bring attention to himself, which was true.

*He stood behind a lectern, this man named Thimbron Parnassos, and behind him was a large map of North Ionia, labeled in Greek characters. Before him was a room filled with students, and he was lecturing to them in a variant of the Greek language about the period of troubles in North Ionia, the time, nearly two decades before, when a handful of anarchists and misguided students had risen in revolt against the lawfully established government, and how the government had ruthlessly but righteously put down the revolt, how all sedition in North Ionia had been done away with, and how the governor, in his wisdom, had established what Professor Parnassos could not call a "police state" but which was exactly that.

*Thimbron Parnassos, professor of post-Hellenic history, did not mention the fact that his own father had been among those rebels. Of course, all that was in the files of the Astefee—the secret police—and had caused him many an uneasy moment. But, of course, the police knew that he, Professor Parnassos, was a loyal subject of the state, had rejected his father, had denied any allegiance to the older man's involvement in rebellion, and even had been instrumental in helping to arrest the group of which his father had been a member. Over the years since adolescence he had proved himself loyal, dependable, and trustworthy, never one to say a word out of line.

But still he had nightmares sometimes, and there was a portion of himself he could not trust. One day, he knew, that mad side of himself would break free, would reveal itself, and then the Astefee would come for him. . . .

Repelled, he withdrew, pulled back into darkness.

Were they all like this? All the versions of Eric Mathers/Thimbron Parnassos? Were all the rest of *him* traitors?

Farther and farther back he pulled, across the darkness, across the Timelines, back toward the Earth of the BrathelLanza and the Underground and the laboratories that held the forms of Eric Mathers and his

336 replicates that were the source of the response patterns that were himself.

And as he came back and drifted into the corporeal bodies, he thought he was beginning to understand exactly what the Shadowy Man really was. Who he was. And what he had to do.

16

A Shadow Visits

Through 674 now-opened eyes he saw 337 different scenes. One of them was a mnemonic-recording chamber, brightly lighted, in which lay the body of a dead technician named MaLarba and the living form of Eric Mathers, still strapped into a reclining chair, the body still incapacitated by drugs. The other 336 views were essentially the same: looking out through murky fluids that were in constant motion before the eyes, looking out of the transparent encanter cylinders, across a space, an aisle, to another cylinder in which floated the naked form of a young boy, perhaps fourteen years of age, whose eyes were now open, who looked out of his own cylinder into his own eyes, and in the eyes that looked and in the eyes that looked back was a strange, uncertain, excited, and very curious consciousness.

Carefully now he forced 672 eyelids to close, shutting off the nearly identical scenes they saw. Finally he saw only one scene. That of the recording room. He commanded the single pair of eyes through which he looked to move. Reluctantly they did.

Nothing appeared to have changed in the room. It was exactly as he remembered it. There was no indication that the drug had worn off the body that called itself Eric Mathers. Nor was there indication that corruption had begun to dissolve the body that had been MaLarba. Yet it seemed that days, even weeks, had gone by. There should have been signs of *something*. Time could not have stopped. Could it?

Leftward the eyes moved, seeking the chronometer and the digits in its face that displayed the passage of time. The eyes stopped, and the composite mind of the senior and his replicates considered the data.

The chronometer read 12:09.31.

Five minutes. Less than five minutes. How was it possible?

Or had a full twenty-four or a full forty-eight hours passed?

No, that was not possible.

Although it seemed that he had been roving through paratime for days, for weeks, and before that more days or weeks integrating himself, it had been less than five minutes since he had come in contact with the first of the replicates and begun his expansion, his creation.

Only minutes . . .

Or was it that his composite mind now had command of chronological time as well as parallel time, of vertical time as well as horizontal time? Had he actually spent days—or years—in his own creation and in his quest, and then returned from out of time to place his consciousness in this particular present, less than five minutes after his beginning? Or did he perhaps exist in a unique sort of chronological time, a subtime, so to speak, which progressed toward the future in a linear fashion, but at a different rate?

Could these things be so? And if so . . .

The Shadowy Man could command time. The Tromas had said so.

And I . . .

For a while he rested, in real time, feeling the breathing of the body of Eric Mathers, hearing the *swish-swish-swish* of air circulating through the room, the hiss of tape across recording heads above and behind him, seeing the digits that represented seconds clicking one after another across the chronometer's face.

When the chronometer read 12:11:17 he began to withdraw from the body, to fully reintegrate himself, to divorce himself from all the corporeal bodies. He was going to try an experiment.

There were now within his mind vague bits and pieces of data, odd and long-forgotten remembrances, sensations he had collected during the time of his own existence as the composite mind. He thought he knew what to do, how to do it, but he was yet uncertain— and there is no way I can put into words these feelings and hunches he felt then. Again: there are no words in any language; it is an experience beyond the finite concepts of finite beings. But he did it.

Into the psionic darkness again, searching, seeking, finding . . .

A bright point of awareness, of consciousness, similar to the others he had encountered, yet also different, far more familiar than they had been, a stronger sense of kinship. Here was another Eric Mathers, another Eric Mathers there in the Underground, a conscious, living, breathing Eric Mathers who was terribly similar to the Eric Mathers who was now a part of the composite resonance pattern.

He did not actually *touch* that mind. That was not his plan, to enter into a second- or third-level resonance. He was going to try to do something else, something wild, fantastic—impossible, perhaps; yet, if *he could* do it . . .

Focusing all his attention on that spot of light that was the consciousness of *an* Eric Mathers, he began to formulate within himself the position of that spot of light in time and in space, at least four frameworks of reference, at least four sets of coordinates: and he saw that it was a roving, wandering, three-dimensional tube of light passing through space/time from a direction that could be labeled past toward a direction that could be labeled future. He narrowed his references. Selected a space/time. Again he focused his attention, isolated one particular fragment of space/time, and propelled himself toward it.

Frozen time. Frozen space. A universe stopped dead in its tracks. Almost. Now he could do it.

In spatial frameworks he selected a spot a few feet from where the consciousness was located. He moved toward that position, into it, projecting *something* of himself into the particular tiny fragment of all continuua, all-space, all-time. He focused and focused again, grasping molecules of air, photons of light, adjusting them, bending them, twisting them, altering them, making out of them something that had not been there before. Not a significant thing, perhaps. No great alteration of the matter/energy of that place/time. But enough.

Some portion of himself was in the same room with the other consciousness. He could now see, or do something akin to seeing, and he sensed a series of overlapping images broken from bits of the high end of the electromagnetic spectrum: an infrared image here, a yellow one there, an ultraviolet one at another place. And he sensed the twisting of the fabric of the universe, minor though it was, and the aura of power, the crackling of something not unlike electrical tension that filled the small concrete room. And he was aware of how *he*, this force he projected, would appear to the room's physical occupant: hazy, smoky, wraithlike, a shadowy form with the figure of a man, no more than that.

And he saw this: A small room with damp concrete walls; moisture; a dimly glowing strip of light ran across the ceiling; a cot was the only article of furniture in the room; Eric Mathers, *aka* HarkosNor, dressed in a robe that was an appropriate costume for the city of VarKhohs of NakrehVatee, sat on the cot, a pained expression on his face, a lump on the back of his head; the medicine given him by RyoNa had begun to do its work, but all the pain was not yet gone.

The *presence* he had created out of light and air waited for Mathers to become aware of it, of him.

Then Mathers *was* aware of the forces at play within

the room; he looked up toward the center point of those forces and saw the shape forming in the air.

There was silence in the room for long, dragging moments. He knew that Mathers was waiting for him to speak. He would do so; he thought he knew how. Grasping molecules of air, he took them in hand and set them to vibrating, to pulsing at carefully determined frequencies and amplitudes, to forming waves in the air that passed from his focal point toward that of Mathers. Yes, this seemed to be the right way. The sounds he created were: "Well, Eric, I hope you're not feeling too badly now."

The Eric Mathers who sat in the room and awaited the coming of RyoNa's "very important people" looked a little puzzled but not totally surprised. "I'm okay," he said at last. "I was afraid the Tromas had destroyed you back in KHL-000."

He could not suppress his feelings. That was *his* future of which Mathers spoke, something he was yet to encounter. But to Mathers, *this* Eric Mathers, it was something that had occurred some months in the past. Involuntarily he chuckled; the air carried his chuckle in waves across the room. How could he ever explain this to Mathers? "Damn," he made the air say more expertly, focusing the sounds across the room, sounds identical with those the vocal cords and mouth and lips and tongue of Eric Mathers would have made, "this could get confusing."

"What do you mean?" Mathers asked, still puzzled.

"What you're talking about is in your past, you see," he made the air say, "but it's in *my* future. It hasn't happened to *me* yet, so I don't know the outcome of our fight with the Krithian ladies any more than you do." He wanted to tell Mathers a great deal more, but he knew he dared not.

"I see," Mathers said.

"I hope you do, though I'm not positive I do. As I said, it *could* get confusing." It already was, but perhaps he was beginning to understand more and more of it.

"Yeah." Mathers grunted, that was all he did in way of reply.

He created sounds again: "Your head's not hurting now, and don't worry, you don't have a concussion. The lump will go away in a few days."

"That's comforting," Mathers replied grudgingly, unhappily.

More sounds he created, projected across the room: "And I suggest that the best thing for you will be to cooperate with the members of the BrathelLanza when they come to visit you."

"The what?" Mathers asked.

"BrathelLanza. You'll find out what it is in due time. For now, cooperate with them as fully as possible, for from cooperating with them will come answers to the questions you want to ask of me, and a means of action."

"A means of action?" Mathers asked stupidly.

"Yes, a means of action, the action that will bring . . ." How much could he tell him? How much had *he* been told when he was Eric Mathers? "Well, you'll see." He could not repress another chuckle he created. There was some degree of humor in the situation. Mathers would see it. When he got here himself. In time.

He had said all he could. He had told Mathers enough. Now Mathers would do the rest of it himself. Mathers would do what had to be done so that the proper sequence of events would take place, so that months in the "future" Mathers would find himself in the recording studio when the police raided the Underground, so that he would be left alone and, with the aid of sense-altering drugs and mnemonic amplification, he would be forced to establish rapport and then resonance with the replicates and . . .

And the Shadowy Man would be born.

The Shadowy Man withdrew from the damp cell that contained Eric Mathers, withdrew into the blackness that is both outside space and time and is the very stuff upon which they are built.

For moments during which the word "time" was a meaningless noise, the Shadowy Man hung suspended, thinking, understanding, knowing. There it was. All laid out before him. There were things he would have to do. Within himself he chuckled, remembered words spoken by the Tromas of KHL-000, words that had seemed like madness to the Eric Mathers who had heard them, words that now the Shadowy Man understood.

The Tromas had said: "What we see is some great power behind this Shadowy Man, some great power that may not yet have even come into existence, that is reaching back through time to alter events—perhaps it is altering events in order to bring itself into existence."

The Tromas had said: "This is a universe of probabilities, Eric. *Probabilities*. Higher orders and lower orders of probability. It is a universe in which the *future* can reach back into the past in order to increase its *probability*. Lower orders of probability can become, through their own manipulation, higher orders of probability. This is so. Kriths know that."

The Tromas had said: "This power is reaching back in time, we believe, in order to manipulate you and those you come in contact with toward some dark future end that is involved with, in some way we do not yet fathom, the *possible* destruction of the entire Krithian race!"

The Tromas had said: "Your Shadowy Man is trying to kill us, Eric."

Yes, the Tromas had known, had understood.

Now *he* did too. He knew what he must do: bring about the past as he knew it, had experienced it as Eric Mathers, to force the past to bring about the present, to force the past to create the Shadowy Man so that he could . . . undo other pasts.

There are no paradoxes in time, he told himself. It is just that no one before me has had any conception of what it is. Though the Tromas do have a glimmering, I have a little more than that.

He set out to do what he knew he would have to do to assure his own creation. . . .

17

Downtime

Through a universe that earlier had seemed to be a blackness but now did not seem so black, for now he could discern in it more and more detail, various shades of blackness and innumerable fragments of light, pinpoints and glows of three-dimensional light as they had made/did make/would make their way through time and space; a void that was the very stuff of which continuua are made. Moving in it, through it, was everything that ever had been, everything that ever would be, everything that ever might have been.

The Shadowy Man moved himself, his awareness, his consciousness backward in time, outward in paratime, searching for a particular point in the multidimensional matrices of time and space and paratime, searching, finding. . . .

A plush villa outside a French town named Beaugency on Timeline RTGB-307, the early morning of 6 April 1972.

During the night the Kriths had sent a contingent of their own Timeliners and local British forces up the River Loire toward the villa presently inhabited by Imperial Count Albert von Heinen and his wife. Under cover of darkness and a surprise British attack, the Timeliners were to capture Von Heinen and his American wife and return them to the Kriths for questioning.

All had gone well enough at first. The Timeliner mercenaries had captured Von Heinen, though only after wounding him, and had gotten his wife without injuring her. But a paratime craft of strange design and capabilities had moved against them, had forced them into a pitched battle that required retreat back to RTGB-307 and the villa.

Now there was gunfire in the distance, the rapid sounds of automatic weapons, the slower noises of semiautomatic ones, the sound of a remote internal-combustion engine dwindling in the distance. Some of the Timeliners had escaped, and in doing so had drawn away the unknown attackers.

As the light of dawn spread across the villa and the stables behind it, figures were moving toward the stables in which there were no horses now, but three staff motorcars of the army of the Holy Roman Empire, brightly polished and immaculately clean, ready for instant use by the officers should they be needed.

One of the figures was a tall blond man in British uniform, who staggered slightly under the weight of the wounded man he carried. There was a determined, half-angry expression on his face, and now and again he glanced at the woman who accompanied him.

Dressed only in a heavy robe, she was a fair-haired woman of medium height, an attractive woman whose green eyes flashed anger and hatred, who glanced at the blond man with bitter lines around her eyes and mouth. She was doing as he told her, but reluctantly.

The man in the British uniform stopped just short of the stables, lowered the wounded man to the ground, ordered the woman to stay with him, and went into the stables to investigate. After a few moments of searching, he found the three motorcars, each decked out with the flag of a *Feldmarschall* of the Imperial Army. He smiled to himself for a moment before going back to where the woman and the wounded man waited.

The Shadowy Man once again took bits of material substance, molecules of air and pieces of floating dust, took them and shaped them with psionic force to create the hazy form that Mathers would later come to know so well. Back in the shadows of the cavernous stables, he bent waves of light, photonic particles, created *himself*, and waited.

When Eric Mathers got back to where Sally Beall von Heinen sat on the ground beside the still figure of the man who was nominally her husband, he holstered his pistol and bent to lift the unconscious man to his shoulder again. Then to Sally he said: "Go on. Get in the first car."

With resignation on her face, the young countess preceded the mercenary along the front of the stables to where the cars were parked.

"Can you drive?" Mathers asked.

"No," Sally von Heinen replied.

"I don't believe you," Mathers said with annoyance. "Get in front. Are the keys in it? Don't lie again."

"Yes, they are."

Mathers dumped the unconscious Von Heinen in the back seat and climbed in beside him. "Okay, let's go," he said.

The motorcar started at once. The Shadowy Man knew that Mathers was pleasantly surprised by this, considering the state of the art of motorcars on this Line. Sally shifted into gear and slowly pulled out of the stables and onto the driveway that led back around the villa's main structures.

"Head toward Beaugency for the moment," commanded the Timeliner mercenary.

He did not speak again for a moment, his eyes going back into the stables, a strange, puzzled expression on his face. For a few moments he peered at the smoky, hazy form in the shadows at the rear of the stables, seeing the image of a human form that the Shadowy Man had built out of air and dust and light. Something that may have been fear went over Mathers' face and his hand reached for the weapon on his hip.

The Shadowy Man loosened his grip on the air, dust, and light. A movement of breeze. The hazy shape was gone.

"What is it?" Countess von Heinen was asking.

"Nothing. Go on."

The car moved on, away from the stables, around the main house, away.

The Shadowy Man smiled within himself, and withdrew. . . .

He moved. Not far through space and time now: a few miles across space, a few hours uptime, no motion at all across paratime. He would not speak yet, would not interfere. There was no need for interference yet. The crucial moments of time and paratime were yet to come. Now he would observe. And let Mathers gradually begin to become aware of him. Later he would speak, when it was necessary. For now . . .

Under Mathers' direction, Sally had driven the German motorcar to a rural wooded area of wartorn France remote from the scene of the battle of the night before. Leaving Sally and the wounded Count tied with ropes, Mathers had then slipped away into the forest, where he had assembled a compact radio transceiver and made contact with the Krithian-Timeliner base of operations in the Outer Hebrides.

"Eric?" asked a Krith's voice from the radio earphone.

"Yes, Kar-hinter, late, but reporting."

"Are you safe?"

"For the moment."

"Count von Heinen?"

"Alive, the last time I looked. I don't know how long he'll last, though." Then he asked about the other Timeliners who had survived the firefight with the strange men from the alien skudder.

"Safe. They managed to get through the Imperial lines just after dawn. Hillary is in a field hospital now. He will be fine, the doctors say."

"Good. Did they tell you what happened?"

"Yes, but they could give no explanations. Can you?"

The Shadowy Man was nothing more than a *pres-*

ence now, a focalization of mental forces at a spot near Mathers. There was nothing visible of him, but Mathers seemed to become aware of him anyway. He looked up, curious, puzzled, worried.

Within himself the Shadowy Man was satisfied. That was sufficient.

"No," Mathers finally said into the transmitter microphone. "It doesn't make any sense. I've never seen a skudder like the one they were in."

"Nor I, from the descriptions." The Krith paused. "Can you tell me where you are?"

"Somewhere in France."

Kar-hinter advised Mathers to take Von Heinen and his wife into hiding if he could find a suitable place and then wait while radio triangulation determined their exact location. Then a skudder would be sent in to retrieve them.

The Shadowy Man withdrew, moved himself uptime, across space. All was going well, exactly as he remembered it. As yet he would not have to interfere. In a few hours, as seen by Eric Mathers, the people who had already made an attempt to rescue Sally and Von Heinen would try again—and this time they would be successful, and would take Mathers their captive. That is how it would happen; that is how it must happen.

Then he, the Shadowy Man, would come to watch, to assist when it was time to assist.

He moved toward a particular point in time, caught it, froze it, moved carefully into it. . . .

He forced matter and energy to form again the hazy figure, this time in the rear of a large hangar on the surface of the earth, above the underground complex called Staunton.

Now Mathers had escaped from Sally and had entered the hangar, where he hoped to gain access to a radio that he could use to once again contact Kar-hinter in the Outer Hebrides, to inform him of the existence of Staunton and the Paratimers.

What the Shadowy Man saw was: Eric Mathers holding a gun on a uniformed technician, forcing him before him across the floor of the hangar toward a craft shaped like a flattened egg, a sautierboat, a machine much like the skudders of the Kriths and Timeliners, yet in some ways very different.

The technician opened the hatch of the large craft and stood for a moment, waiting for Mathers to tell him what to do.

"Get in," Mathers said, gesturing with his weapon.

Then, as the technician obeyed, Mathers' eyes opened wider, for he had caught sight of the hazy figure in the deep shadows at the end of the hangar. Fear went across his features. He spun toward the image, leveling his pistol.

The Shadowy Man released his grip, and the air and light ceased to form the smoky image.

Mathers looked into the shadows, more puzzled than ever, then shook his head and entered the sautierboat behind the technician, to use the radio inside the craft. . . .

Only minutes uptime now, the Shadowy Man moved, the same point in space. . . .

Though now the appearance of the hangar had greatly changed: the Paratimers had discovered what he was doing, and had rushed forces into the hangar to deal with him before it was too late, with hand-weapons of astonishing power.

Now the egg-shaped sautierboat was a mass of ruined, smoldering, twisted metal, and something flammable inside the craft was burning, giving off clouds of smoke that boiled out into the hangar. Men moved about, some carrying fire extinguishers, attempting to put out the fire.

Other men stood above the torn, bloody figure they

had dragged from the wreckage, a mutilated thing that was Eric Mathers, who might be dying.

"Listen to me, bastard," said the man called Scoti who knelt beside him. "If you hurt Sally, I'll see that you live. You'll live so that I can slowly take you apart piece by piece."

Scoti rose, his fists knotted in anger, kicked the inert form savagely, then turned away when a man yelled from near the open front of the hangar: "Scoti, look up there!"

"What is it?" He moved toward the hangar's open doors.

"Airships. British airships."

"Call Mica! Full alert!"

The men dispersed, seeking shelter and more weapons. From the approaching airships, silvery, cigar-shaped, rigid and metallic, gondolas extending almost the full length of their undersides, bombs began to fall, machine guns began to chatter.

The hangar suffered a few near misses and one direct hit that rained fragments of steel and burning wood down over the ruined sautierboat and the still form of Eric Mathers.

The Shadowy Man moved, grasped air between psionic hands, shaped it, moved it, made a voice speak into Mathers' ear, a voice that was very much like Mathers' own voice, and what the voice said was:

"Stay alive, Eric. For God's sake, man, hang on just a little while longer. They're coming to help you. The pain won't last long. You can stand it, Eric. *I did.*"

This crucial point had been reached, achieved. The Shadowy Man had done what he could, now, here. The British airships would land, Mathers' Timeliner confederates would rescue him, find Sally, and take them both from Staunton before the Paratimers who defended the underground city saw that the situation was hopeless and destroyed it. The Shadowy Man withdrew. . . .

Upward in time to the next day, across space to another place, from North America to South Africa, to a hospital room in which Eric Mathers, drugged and bandaged, lay in uneasy sleep, nightmares passing through his mind.

The Shadowy Man touched the mind of the sleeping man, established a brief resonance, spoke to him without words, but tried to tell him that in time he would have the answers, in time he would be able to see through all the shams, the lies, the deceptions, the facades that the Kriths had built, would build, and the facades that the Paratimers had also built. In time he would see, but to do that he would have to survive.

He knew that little of this would get through to Mathers, and that much of what did would be mixed and confused with the nightmares he was experiencing. But some of it would remain, aiding and reinforcing other things that were slowly coming into his mind, awarenesses that would only later blossom into realizations. For a while now Eric Mathers would be on his own, would have to begin finding some of the truths for himself.

Again he withdrew across time and space and paratime . . . to a place months later in chronological time, worlds away in parallel time. . . .

Now a battle raged in a moving skudder. Mathers fought to escape from the Krith named Tar-hortha and the men with him who had captured him and Sally, had separated them, and now carried him across the Timelines toward a destination they had not revealed to him. He fought back.

Feigning drugged unconsciousness, he had slipped into augmentation and had taken a weapon from an unsuspecting guard, had swept the interior of the moving skudder with furious blasts of energy, set off an explosion that had blown away the hand of a giant named Marth, killed a guard named Sulla, and with an energy pistol he had burned to pieces a half-man named Mager.

Now he stumbled over broken flesh and writhing bodies and reached the skudder's hatch, undogged it, jerked it open—and was hit by something like a wind that was blowing out of the inner regions of a frozen hell.

"You did it before," he said aloud to himself, "and it didn't kill you. Dammit, man, you can do it again." But other expressions raced across his face, consternation, disbelief, fear. . . .

The Shadowy Man forced a nucleus of energy into the skudder, held with it as it flickered from world to world. Now he would have to interfere again, would have to act, would have to make certain that when Eric Mathers leaped from this skudder, it was at exactly the right moment, the right place along the Lines. If he failed to do that . . . Well, he couldn't fail.

As Mathers stood uncertainly in the open hatch, looking out at the flickering nothingness of rapidly passing worlds, the injured Krith within the cabin behind him began to move; he reached out a sable-brown hand to grasp Mathers' left ankle. The sounds that came from the Krith's full-lipped mouth were not English, were not Shangalis, were not even coherent. Mathers glanced back at the Krith and saw the mouth open in savage rage, rows of sharp teeth like those of a great cat coming to tear at his flesh.

And his gaze went on beyond the Krith to the shadowy, almost formless figure of the Shadowy Man's focuses of energy.

Now! the Shadowy Man yelled wordlessly to Mathers, exerting a force against him that steeled Mathers' mind and blew like a chill wind against his back.

Mathers jerked his ankle from Tar-hortha's grasp, plunged, leaped, and fell into nothingness right in the middle of a *flicker!*

He was gone. But the Shadowy Man knew exactly where he was, and went to join him.. . . .

Hours uptime now, on the world into which Mathers had leaped from the skudder.

It was dark and it was raining. Drugged, battered, beaten, the beginnings of fever in his body, Mathers lay on the sodden ground, no longer caring whether he lived or died.

The Shadowy Man created a voice out of the air and made it speak the same words he had spoken to Mathers before, another time, another place:

"Stay alive, Eric. For God's sake, man, hang on just a little while longer. They're coming to help you. The pain won't last long. You can stand it, Eric. *I did.*"

He remained there for a while, watching the slow breathing, the rain falling, hearing a distant booming across remote hills. They would come. He would live. . . .

Uptime again, some weeks, across space, some miles . . .

This one too would be critical. . . .

A place called Tapferkeitenhaven, a miniature medieval German castle transported to the New World and the Imperial Colony of Sclavania, a few miles south of the New East Anglia border: Von Heinen slept quietly but Mathers could not sleep; there was too much on his mind. He lay back on the soft bed, staring at the white ceiling, and he wondered how many plots were going on in this castlelike home of the Sclavanian Herr Jurgen, how many different webs were being spun and broken, how many. . . .

A point of energy moved through the corridors of Tapferkeitenhaven, observed the stealthy approach of two figures, a man and a woman, both with energy weapons in their hands. They were coming to do some killing.

The nucleus of energy flows moved into the room where the two men lay, not quite forming into the shadowy figure Mathers had seen before, but allowing a tension to build in the air that would bring Mathers out of his reverie, would bring him to full wakefulness so that he might know of the approaching assassins.

Mathers stirred, was aware. He moved, alerted his combat augmentation, slipped from the bed to the floor, knelt and drew a pistol from the drawer of the nightstand between the two beds, then rose to his feet. Outside, the assassins spoke in whispered Shangalis. Now Mathers was certain that Timeliner agents were coming to kill him. He was ready. He went into augmentation. The world slowed, reddened.

The door slowly opened and a heavy man named Otto and a woman named Fredericka stood framed in the yellow torchlight from the hall. Mathers could see Timeliner energy pistols in their hands.

Mathers pulled the trigger. The pistol loudly threw a heavy leaden slug into the face of the heavyset man. As his skull dissolved under the impact of the spreading lead, Mathers cocked the single-action pistol, pulled the trigger again, and put the second slug into the left breast of the pretty little blonde. Fredericka staggered backward, living seconds longer than Otto, long enough to pull the trigger of her own weapon and send a burst of furious coherent energy coruscating across the room, above Mathers' left shoulder.

He was temporarily blinded as he fired the third slug, but was later to find that it had hit the girl just above the navel, exiting through a shattered spine.

As he came out of augmentation, Von Heinen was coming up from the floor, to which he'd rolled during the shooting, crying, "What the hell's going on?"

"Timeliners," Mathers told him quickly. "They tried to kill us." He shoved the smoking pistol into Von Heinen's hand. "Tell them you did it."

"Why?"

"I'll explain later. Take the credit now."

Then Anglianers and liveried servants of Herr Jurgen began rushing into the room.

That's sufficient, thought the Shadowy Man, and disengaged himself from this moment of time, this fragment of space. . . .

The raid was in progress when the Shadowy Man again froze a slice of time and entered it. . . .

Then a firefight was raging in the Krithian skudder pool at Fort Lothairin. Devoto Baugh, Mica, Kjemi Stov and a handful of Paratimers attempted to prevent Mathers' theft of a skudder. Anglianers and Albert von Heinen had died, but Mathers had made his way through blood and flame to take command of a skudder. And as Mica took mortal wounds, bullets from his weapon penetrated the base of Mathers' skudder, damaging it, slowing its escape.

The skudder pool's lights surged to full brilliance, illuminating the broken, bloody tableau. Kjemi Stov—whom Mathers had believed to be a Paratimer, but who was something else—was now in augmentation and charged toward the skudder with a cry of insane rage on his lips, the words he yelled in the Shangalis of the Timeliners.

And into the bright and bloody skudder pool charged the troop that had waited until this moment to spring their trap, a troop of blue-clad Timeliners with energy weapons, olive-clad Sclavanians firing slug throwers, all led by a sable-skinned Krith with a look of fury and of triumph on his flat features, Tar-hortha!

He too was in X5 augmentation and he yelled above the roar, screaming in Shangalis—Mathers thought he could hear him even through the skudder's dome: "You have lost, Eric. You have lost again."

Still moving as only a man in augmentation can, though wounded twice, Mica fired his submachine gun once more before he died, not into the Anglianers so much as through them toward the Krith and his augmented Timeliners. Energy weapons replied to his slug

thrower—and Mica's mutilated body seemed to explode in their blaze.

Kjemi Stov, untouched by the lead and energy
bursts that swept the shed, had almost reached the
skudder. Now Tar-hortha was close behind him.

And as Mathers screamed out his fury at Mica's
dying retaliation, the Shadowy Man reached out with
a mental probe into the wrecked circuits of the skudder's base, examined the circuits, analyzed them, and
drew out of his Mathers-memory schematic diagrams
and wiring charts. The circuits were not destroyed,
though nearly so. And to repair them, if but briefly
and barely, would require a great deal more of him
than the mere forming of a shadowy figure or the
creation of sound vibrations in the air. The Shadowy
Man was not a material being, but he could produce
limited effects on matter. So, he applied force here,
then there, twisting atoms and molecules, grabbing
flowing electrons and moving them. . . .

Mathers knew that something was happening in the
circuits, the wiring, the generators of the skudder under
him. A scream to match his own, a yell, a roar of
mechanical pain, came from them. Lights flickered
erratically across the panels. His hands fell to the controls, but he did not know what to do.

Ignoring Kjemi Stov, Tar-hortha had come to a stop
only a short distance from the skudder, and looked at
Mathers through the glasslike dome, a strange expression on his alien features.

Even as one portion of the Shadowy Man's mind
worked to provide some small repair to the damaged
skudder, to get it moving at least across a few Lines
of Time, another portion of his mind again took air
and light and formed them in a smoky, hazy form, a
wraithlike shape between the skudder and Tar-hortha.

The Krith showed momentary terror, stepped back,
struggled with himself.

From inside the skudder Mathers saw the Shadowy

Man, but also felt the skudder's attempts at moving out of this Line. Then, suddenly, the world outside the skudder grayed. It did not exactly flicker, but the world outside was gone—the Krith, his Timeliners, the bloody skudder pool—and for a few moments there was nothing, nothing at all but grayness.

Mathers was moving across the Lines, but . . .

The Shadowy Man withdrew. The skudder would not go far in paratime, but far enough. And the Krith would move with it, self-skudding until the skudder reached the Line that both Tar-hortha and the Shadowy Man knew it would reach, must reach, or both memory and precognition were wrong. As would the Krith after him, the Shadowy Man went there, across paratime, uptime a matter of minutes to . . .

A large room in a huge building on a world known only to the Kriths, a secret kept even from their Timeliners. Into the room came Eric Mathers, forcing Tar-hortha before him, a pistol at the Krith's back. With them were six machines of grayish metal, the building's guardian robots, watching Mathers in a way that could almost be called suspicious. Inside the room they had entered were some half-dozen large cargo skudders.

"We are here now, Eric," Tar-hortha said, stopping and gesturing toward the skudders. "I suggest that you allow me to set the controls of one of them for you. It will carry you to our destination."

"I'll do my own control setting," Mathers said calmly.

"It would be very unwise for you to do anything other than what I suggest."

"Your robots?" Mathers asked.

"They will see that no harm comes to me."

Three of the devices moved closer to Mathers, raising their metal arms in a manner that could have been menacing.

"Put the foolish pistol away and come with me," Tar-hortha said.

The robots moved closer.

"I'm going to have some answers," Mathers told him.

"Of course you are, but killing me will not give them to you."

"And if I do as you say . . . ?"

"You will be my prisoner, of course."

"I won't put myself in that position again, Tar-hortha."

"I believe you already have."

A metal hand shot out from one of the faceless machines and clamped down suddenly on Mathers' right wrist. He tried to jerk away, to pull himself out of its grasp, but another of the machines came up be-hind him, grasped both his arms above the elbows, and pulled him backward.

"Tar-hortha!" Mathers screamed in anger. Pain reddened his vision as he fought against the machines that held him, as he willed his right hand to move against the pain, as he swung the barrel of the pistol a few inches to the left, as he pulled back on the trig-ger. . . .

The roar of the pistol was sudden and loud in the room's near silence, unexpected and terrible.

Mathers felt the bone snap in his wrist and saw his fingers release their hold on the pistol. But, dammit, I've done something! he thought.

Tar-hortha was screaming shrilly, staggering away, clutching at an arm broken between the wrist and elbow, red, manlike blood gushing from the open wound. He slowly dropped to his knees; in his eyes were only fear and horror, for he had been hurt, hurt by a human being, and that was something that never, never happened to a Krith.

"You will die, Eric!" he cried, resting now on his knees, blood pooling below him. "You will die!"

And with the words, the four gray robots moved toward Mathers to aid the two that held him, one by his upper arms, one by his broken wrist.

The pain was coming to him now, and along with it vertigo and nausea. So he'd never know. Now he'd . . .

A grayness came over the room, which for a moment he thought was caused by the pain, by the coming loss of consciousness. He thought he was going under and would probably never awaken again. Yet . . .

The Shadowy Man did not force air and light into the shape of a spectral figure. There was no need for that this time. The vibrations he had set up in the air would have to be sufficient, for there were other things he had to do.

"This isn't the way it should be done, Eric," he forced the air to say, "but there's no other way now."

Mathers attempted to speak; his mouth worked, but no sounds came from it.

The Shadowy Man formed six projections of himself and aimed them toward each of the six machines. The repairs he had performed on the damaged skudder had been difficult enough, but this . . . he had never done anything like this before, dividing himself into so many parts. He was uncertain of how to go about it, uncertain of how long he could remain so fragmented and still coordinate the six separate sets of activities. But there was nothing else he could do.

Each psionic extension found a robot, slipped through its metal skin, sought out its central control system, its computer, its brain, studied it, examined it, tried to find ways of deflecting flows of electrons, of creating pathways within the solid-state modules, of finding a means of temporarily incapacitating the various devices. He found them, the ways of doing what he wished, and the six fragments of his composite personality pushed subatomic particles into places where they had not been before, made electrons flow in pathways not designed for them. But he had not imagined how difficult it would be.

"Quickly now," he forced the air to say. "I can hold them only for moments!"

Mathers extricated himself from the machines as they stopped, then reversed their motion. He dragged himself to his feet, looked at his limp right hand dangling from the broken wrist, then looked at the Krith who knelt in a pool of his own blood.

"The gun, Eric!" the Shadowy Man said with vibrations of air.

Mathers nodded, seemed to regain some control of himself, and bent to grasp the gun in his left hand.

"Hurry!" the air said. "We haven't long."

Mathers stood up, holding the pistol awkwardly. "Into that skudder," he told the Krith, shaking his head to clear it as he moved toward Tar-hortha.

The Kirth shook his head in a very human fashion.

Mathers pointed the revolver at the Krith's face, only inches away. Tar-hortha sighed deeply through wide, wet lips, then he slowly came to his feet.

For a few moments more the Shadowy Man held the six machines immobile, long enough for Mathers to force the wounded Krith into the skudder and then climb in himself. That was long enough. Mathers could make it now. He let the robots go.

With a mental sigh, he relaxed for a moment, watched as the robots approached the skudder, as the skudder hummed and then, with a clap like thunder, slipped out of that universe and into another and then another, skudding across the Lines of Time.

The Shadowy Man relaxed, but not for long. There was one more encounter, one more place in time and space where his destiny was fixed, where he must go, for the memory of Eric Mathers told him that he must go there, must do things there, must fight and perhaps . . . Well, there was no knowing the outcome. He would learn.

Summoning his strength, he pulled himself out into the speckled blackness of Notever, Nowhen, and prepared to move uptime again, across the Lines to KHL-000 and the confrontation with the Tromas, who ruled the race of Kriths.

18

The First Confrontation

KHL-000. The Krithian Homeline. The most prime of all the Prime Lines. The fountainhead from which issued the decisions and the commands that altered uncounted worlds across the Lines, that affected billions upon billions of human beings across those worlds. The seat and source of the power of the Kriths. And the residence world of the Tromas, the twelve females of the race who were its guiding force.

It was toward KHL-000 that the Shadowy Man moved, toward a place in time where Eric Mathers was now a captive of the Kriths. In exchange for answers to his questions and his reunion with Sally, the Tromas expected him to lure the Shadowy Man to KHL-000. In truth, the Shadowy Man knew, they wished him to come to KHL-000 so that they might hold him and destroy him, forever ridding themselves of the danger to their plans that he represented.

Yet he went there. There may have been fear in him, but if there was he submerged it, pushed it away from himself. There was no time for fear now. He knew that he *must* go to KHL-000: his going there was in Mathers' memory, his going there had enabled Mathers and Sally to escape the Kriths, had allowed Mathers to complete the circuit that had brought the Shadowy Man into existence. He had no choice but to go there and risk exposing himself to the Kriths. And if there existed in Mathers' memory something that indicated the defeat and destruction of the Shadowy Man, there was not absolute certitude in it; Mathers had not *known* that the Shadowy Man was destroyed, but merely that his presence, after a terrible battle with the Tromas, was no longer there upon KHL-000. What might have become of him then, Mathers had not known, had had no way of knowing. So there was the hope in him, as he pushed his intelligence across time and space and paratime once more, that his defeat might not be total. Perhaps Mathers had known nothing of the *final* outcome of the battle between the Shadowy Man and the Tromas. He felt deep within the essence of himself that there was a great deal more to come that neither Mathers nor himself had yet suspected. He would see. . . .

Now: A room in a towering building, a spire that climbed toward the sky; a bedroom that was part of the suite that the Kriths had given Sally Beall von Heinen after bringing her across the Timelines and using her as bait to bring Eric Mathers to them.

Within the room was a bed on which lay Mathers and Sally, now sensing the approach of *something*.

In a far corner of the bedroom, a manlike shape formed, a thing only half visible in the gloom, hazy, ghostly, half immaterial, but it was a *presence* and the two people in the room were aware of it.

He collected himself, forced concentrations of himself into the modified air, the bending light. It had been harder to enter KHL-000 than he had anticipated; it had been farther across the Lines than he had realized, and there were forces here, powers and protections, that he had not realized could exist. But he had overcome them and he was there. He made the air speak:

"It was very difficult this time, getting here. I didn't think it would be that hard."

"Eric!" Sally cried, as she dropped the sheet she had pulled around herself and drew herself toward Mathers.

"It's okay," the man said. "I know who it is."

"That—that's your voice, Eric," Sally stammered, whispering.

The Shadowy Man again made the air speak for him: "There is little time. And the forces involved in this are beyond your present comprehension. In moments, if not already, the Tromas will know I'm here, and then . . . Well, you've got to get out of here, the two of you."

"Out of here?" Mathers asked stupidly.

In exasperation the Shadowy Man said: "That's why I came—to rescue the two of you! There's a way to escape, and if you'll listen to me I'll tell you how to do it."

"We're listening," Mathers replied from the bed.

"Very well," the Shadowy Man said; and, selecting fragments from the Mathers-memory he held, he told them how to get from Sally's apartment to the roof of the towering spire, of a half-secret stairway that would take them up to where there would be "a means of escape" awaiting them—best not yet to further confuse them with the nature of their escape route, which the Shadowy Man himself did not yet fully understand. He told them that there would be guards and obstacles before them but that he would do everything he could to pave the way for them.

"And then what?" Mathers asked, an awkward, strained sound to his voice.

"You escape. What you do after that is up to you, Eric, and you, Sally. I can't tell you what to do once you escape this Line. I've already done far more than I should have. I'm not yet certain just where in the orders of probability—or improbability—" He found that he could not help but chuckle at the confusion he felt in himself and was passing on to Mathers and Sally. "—all this lies anyway—we may one day find out that none of it has happened anyway."

"What do you mean?" Mathers asked in confusion.

"Nothing," answered the Shadowy Man, now becoming certain that the Tromas were aware of his presence in KHL-000, and that they would certainly be doing something about it soon, terribly soon.

Even as he prepared to speak again he could feel something moving in the world outside the apartment, a force swelling, expanding, probing toward him, carefully at first, hesitant, then more certain of itself.

"Now you must work out some simple ruse to distract the guards outside the doors of the apartment," he told them quickly. "Sally, you can help in this. Draw them into the room. Get their attention. Then perhaps Eric can do something. And remember, they have no women of their own." He thought briefly of the Magers, as Mathers had called them, not Kriths in disguise as he had once believed, but something else, almost men, but not quite men, something more, or perhaps something less, maybe a hybrid of man and Krith, certainly not the product of any known evolutionary process. But then neither were the Kriths. "And remember, they have no women of their own," he had said; "they're drawn to human women, some of them."

Sally made a motion as if to speak, but then did not, suddenly aware of a second *presence,* a new and terrible force gathering around the Shadowy Man.

He felt it too, a touch, lightly at first, no more than a brushing, then a first contact, a quick and ruthless examination. A pause. A flickering of fire across an endless sky. A swelling of anger and hatred. A rushing toward him. A further swelling. Then the lash of a whip of great psionic force across his consciousness.

He almost lost control of the air for a moment, then made it speak for him: "They know!"

The lash came again, and with it the swelling of pain, psychic pain of an intensity such as he had never before known or imagined. Then a momentary pause. He looked within himself to see what defenses he had, what weapons with which to strike back.

And with it all was a momentary sense of resonance

with the Eric Mathers who was still on the bed with Sally. A brief sharing of pain and awareness.

Mathers gasped aloud in that common pain.

"Eric!" Sally cried.

A momentary respite, the raising of a mental shield. The Tromas withdrew for instants, preparing to strike again, and harder.

"You're me," Mathers said.

The Shadowy Man made the air speak again: "In a sense. You might be me. You might become me, given time."

Mathers was there with him for instants more: Mathers looking forward in time, backward through the Shadowy Man's own memories. Fear!

Then he pushed Mathers away, out of him, knowing that Mathers could never withstand what he could feel sweeping toward him across space from the palace of the Tromas.

Lightning flashed in the bedroom, leaping from some point near the ceiling toward the focus of his consciousness. And with it the blow of a psionic ax, the cutting, ripping, tearing through him of a sharpened blade of mental force. He erected his shields, strengthened them, struggled to hold himself together until the swift and terrible pressure subsided.

Blazing with a halo of light and invisible radiation, the Shadowy Man made the air say: "I will fight them as long as I can, but I don't know how long that will be. I'm a long way from home. . . ." Another blow was coming. Lightning crackled through the room. "Hurry!" the air cried.

Mathers pulled himself from the bed, drew Sally after him, and, both of them naked, they stumbled from the bedroom as forces swept through it, blasting, shattering, rending.

"Come on," Mathers called, his voice dwindling as the blow came toward the Shadowy Man, sweeping toward him, then across him, battering again at his

shield, being partly held this time, only portions of
the psionic attack bursting through to shatter, to shake
him, to rip through him and fill him with pain.

He forced the shields up once more, swung them
forward to deflect streams of psionic flame, sought
again for weapons, found them, curled balls of coruscating energy within himself, outside the universe, and
sucked them into space/time to hurl them at the Tromas.

With the shields before him he advanced, feet, miles,
light-years; the terms are meaningless. He advanced
toward the Tromas.

The Krithian females drew together their own
strength, united again, raised their own shields, and
moved forward to meet him.

Through space and time he hurled the particles/
waves/balls/stars/novas/quasars of psionic force toward the advancing Tromas . . . who caught them and
hurled them back at him, splashing across his shields,
sending him reeling backward, ripping again through
his consciousness.

The Shadowy Man, stunned by the sudden reversal,
retreated. The nucleus of his energy floated, drifted,
moved relative to spatial frameworks.

Into the living room of the suite came the form of
the Shadowy Man, his smoky, ghostly form now clothed
in flickering lightning and halos of incandescence;
sheets of auroral flame surrounded him, flickering in
neon colors across the spectrum from the edges of infrared to the margins of ultraviolet. The air around
him was becoming ionized; carpeting and woodwork
smoldered as he brushed across them, moving ever
more slowly and ponderously, struggling to halt his
retreat, to turn back toward his enemies, to again try
to find weapons to use against them.

Other weapons he did find, and hurled the strength
of them outward, but with ease the Tromas seemed to
catch them and throw them back against his shields.

They were powerful, unimaginably powerful, these females of the Krithian race. How had he ever thought he could equal them in combat?

But he could not yield, not yet. For a while he must hold. He must give Mathers and Sally time to escape, for if they did not escape, there would never be a Shadowy Man. The universe looped and looped within itself. What was it Mathers had once said? "The universe is a can of worms, and each worm is bending back upon itself to eat its own tail. . . ."

For a moment there was respite again. For an instant the Tromas did not hurl wave after wave of psionic energy against him. He gasped within himself, drew himself together, welded back together the shattered margins of his consciousness, tried to find additional means of strengthening his shields, for now he knew that all he could hope to do was hold, for just a bit longer, hold and give Mathers and Sally time. He could not defeat the Tromas. He could barely even strike back at them.

And then there it was, sweeping across space and time again, a tsunami of psionic force, greater than all the others before, a cresting wave of hatred, anger, and destruction; burning, shattering mental forces rushing toward him. The Tromas had gathered all their power in one great field and threw it with all their strength at the conflux of forces that was the Shadowy Man.

He braced himself for the swelling tide of flame.

It came, splashed against his shields, tore against them and then through them, one after the other, ripping them away and plunging deeper and ever deeper toward the remote core of his consciousness.

How do I relate it? How do I tell what it was like to be . . . smashed and battered by psionic blows of tremendous, godlike, unimaginable power, to be struck and struck again and to be almost overwhelmed by the waves of hate and anger from the female Kriths, to feel your composite mind torn to shreds by psionic forces infinitely greater than your own, ancient and more wise in their use of power, to be beaten to your figurative knees and then, screaming in psionic pain, withdraw, fall upward through time, inward across the Lines, back into the subterranean laboratories where your own physical body and those of your replicates are contorted with pain.

How do I tell it? I don't know.

But with that last assault the Shadowy Man could endure no more; he knew that his consciousness was being destroyed and in instants more he would no longer exist and his physical bodies would be nothing more than vegetables with burned-out brains.

With an effort that took more strength than he knew he had, the Shadowy Man disengaged himself, not knowing at the time how he was able to accomplish even that. Mortally wounded, he felt himself, dying, himself and the physical bodies upon whose brains he was built. He fell upward, inward, screaming in the pain he could no longer tolerate, seeking the safety of the underground shelter so that he might die in some semblance of peace.

19

Downtime Again

But he did not die.

The wounds were not mortal. Painful and soul-shattering, yes, but not mortal. The blasts had hurt him, the Shadowy Man, but they had not moved far enough across time and space and paratime to touch the brains of which he was the composite mind.

He fell back to those cerebral cortexes, resonated among them, rested, wept, shuddered in remembered pain, and then, at last, for the first time in his existence, he slept.

When the consciousness of the Shadowy Man again had self-awareness, he knew that he would recover from the ordeal through which he had gone. He would recover and he would do more than that. There was a great deal that he could learn from the experience, a great deal that he could put into practice the next time he encountered the Tromas, for he was certain that he would again encounter them in combat, though exactly where, exactly when, he was yet to know.

He rested, studied, analyzed, gained knowledge and regained strength, and then, for a brief moment, cut himself away from the bodies of the replicates, now relaxing with the passing of the pain they too had felt, and entered complete third-level resonance with the superior of the replicates, the physical Eric Mathers of Here and Now.

The body was still drugged, was still without the ability to move itself, other than to rotate its eyes within their sockets and raise and lower its eyelids.

The Shadowy Man had anticipated this, and was not disturbed.

Through those eyes he again looked out into the recording room within the Underground of the Brathel-Lanza, saw once more the bloodstained body of the dead technician on the floor near the chair, and Mathers' immobile figure, what he could see of it. With the eyes of that body he swept leftward and found once more the chronometer. The digits read 12:42:01. Just over thirty minutes of chronological time had elapsed since he had last looked at the chronometer, before he had begun his series of flights across space and time.

There was, he realized, a definite correlation between time as he experienced it and time as the still body of Eric Mathers experienced it, a correlation, but one of extremely high ratio. There was a linearity to time, he was certain, although time was not linear in the sense that he had once believed it to be. Nor, he suspected, would it be possible for him, the Shadowy Man, to occupy a point in space/time already occupied by himself. Why, he was uncertain, but he believed it to be so. He would have to hold these things in mind and work them into the concepts of the nature of time as he was gradually developing them.

Thirty minutes. Then MaLarba had been dead nearly seventy-two minutes. An hour and twelve minutes had passed since the raid on the Underground had taken place. That still gave him ample time before the drugs began to wear off the body of Eric Mathers.

The drugs had begun to become a matter of concern to him. He was certain that, at least in part, his creation was based on the condition of this physical body, which had been his starting point. The drugs had altered the mind of Eric Mathers, had made that mind more capable of digging into itself, of bringing forth unconscious memories, had made it more sensitive and more receptive to union with the replicates. And the mnemonic recorder, he felt, was also a factor: the electrodes were still attached to Eric Mathers, his so-called brain waves were still being detected by them, passed on to the amplifiers of the recorder, and in the fact of their amplification lay something of the secret of the creation of the Shadowy Man. Many factors had gone into his genesis.

Now he was uncertain of how the wearing off of the mnemonic drugs might affect the resonance patterns between the senior and the replicates. There would be some effect, of that he was certain. But how great? Was it possible that with the passing of the drugs, it would be impossible to maintain the total resonance between the 337 bodies? Might it be that he would disintegrate into merely a senior and a cluster of replicates, a single conscious mind, that of Eric Mathers, and the nearly unconscious minds of the replicates? Would, he was asking, the Shadowy Man cease to exist once the drugs no longer held their sway?

He was not certain. Despite the data that had swelled up out of the unconsciousness of Eric Mathers, there still was not enough information to answer that question. Perhaps there was not enough data anywhere. Who had ever researched this sort of thing? Such a condition had never before existed in all the universes, he believed, outside of the existence of the Tromas themselves, and he was uncertain how close an analogy he could draw between them and himself. Again, too little data.

But that time was centuries away as time was experienced by the Shadowy Man, and there was a universe of things he could do before that much time had gone by.

He set out to do them.

Once again he divorced himself from the physical bodies upon which he was built, existed as a resonance pattern between the senior and the replicates, and once more moved into a psionic void where none of the conventional human senses had any validity, although he had awareness, more awareness than any mere human being could ever have had.

Again he moved outside the framework of ordinary dimensions, outside length, breadth, height, outside chronological time, outside parallel time. Now these terms were all but meaningless, save that he could move about and select whatever dimensional coordinates he might wish, pick out a spot in the continuua, touch it, freeze it, place himself there.

But he did not yet choose to do that. For a while, which could not be measured in terms of the passage of time, he remained without motion, without time, and once more assessed what knowledge he had gained since he had come into existence.

Most of what went through his composite mind could not be expressed in words, perhaps could not be expressed by the symbols of any human mathematics, but one line of thought, the conclusion of his mentation, might have been something like this, had he been using words:

It is obvious that I cannot defeat the Tromas on their own ground, on their own terms. Another encounter such as the last, even with what I have learned, could destroy me. So, I must find a way to meet them on more nearly equal terms. I must find conditions more favorable to me, find the Tromas less ready to fight back against me, find them ignorant of the threat I am to them and ignorant of the powers I possess, perhaps ignorant even of the powers they themselves possess. But where? When?

There were other hazards, he knew. The farther he moved from his time/place of origin, the more tenuous would become the link between himself and his corporeal bodies and weaker would become the powers he could summon. He could not move too far away, but . . .

The Shadowy Man moved outward in space, across paratime, backward in chronological time, downtime to . . . KHL-000 in the chronological past . . . pausing along the way to freeze a fragment of the continuua, to reach into four-dimensional space/time and touch the electronic workings of a vast library computer on a world dominated by the Kriths and their Timeliners. It took him moments or aeons to learn the computer's language, and more moments or aeons to seek out the data he wanted, to separate the truth from the lies. Then, satisfied that he knew what he wished to know—for the moment, at least—the Shadowy Man once more moved downtime. . . .

Years downtime now, centuries into the past as Eric Mathers would have understood the structure of time, back to the year A.D. 1610.

Eric Mathers had visited KHL-000 and had spoken with the ruling females of the Krithian race in the month of February, A.D. 1972, as the calendar was kept on some worlds.

Yet, in some spacio-temporal frameworks, from certain viewpoints, the Kriths themselves did not come into being until the year A.D. 2214, the product of genetic engineering on a Timeline the coordinates of which the Shadowy Man had not yet discovered. The Kriths had been "grown" from human genetic material, engineered to survive on a world very different from any of the Earths across the Lines, a planet of another star, light-years remote in space.

And it had been nearly two centuries later, A.D. 2404, before the descendants of the colonists of UR-427-51-IV fully assessed the power that resided within themselves, commandeered a spaceship and returned to Earth, then self-skudded across the Lines until they found a world to their liking, an Earth they could take over as their own, which they called KHL-000, their first headquarters in paratime.

Close to a century had gone by before the Kriths had decided to go downtime. After finding KHL-000, the few thousand members of the race had lived there for nearly a century before they became aware of the enormity of what would happen when the parachronal potential of the universe would be forced to reorder itself toward simplicity, or cease to exist. Around A.D. 2500 the Kriths somehow brought a chronal-displacement device to KHL-000. And from the KHL-000 of circa A.D. 2500, the entire Krithian race had migrated downtime to circa A.D. 1600, still on KHL-000. And from this vantage point in the "past" they had begun gradually increasing their strength, recruiting humans and then forming the Timeliners to do their work for them. Three and a half centuries later, a vast number of worlds lay under their sway, and more were poised to fall into their orbit.

The Shadowy Man knew his destination: in para-time, KHL-000, once more, in chronotime about the year A.D. 1610. The Kriths would be there, nearly every member of their race, just now beginning to move across the Lines of Time. This would be the place/time to strike, before they had begun their remodeling of tomorrow, perhaps before the Tromas had matured sufficiently to be fully cognizant of their powers.

As he moved through the darkness that he no longer considered black, as he swept across the multidimensional fabric of the universes and neared a destination that could only have been expressed in five or more separate sets of coordinates, certain things for which he was not looking impinged on the Shadowy Man's awareness, things he sought now to ignore—for he did not wish to be distracted from his goal—but which he found he could not totally disregard:

There was a distortion of the universal matrix through which he passed, a confusion, a series of anomalies; in terms of human senses, if such analogies are justifiable: shrieking sounds came out of the stillness, rising along an alien musical scale to vanish and then reappear; splashes of light and color coming and then going, yellows and oranges, explosions of bloody crimson; a flow here of space/time that seemed to turn about upon itself, moaning as it did so, leaking yellows and greens into the blackness, a loop in the stuff of the universe, or perhaps becoming a spiral, a purple, sighing whirlpool. And there was another, spinning off from the first, flashing silver and gold, touched with red, screaming and moaning, creating new and different, unknown and unexpected currents through the non-matter/nonenergy of the continuua. And farther on downtime, still another: vortexes of color and light, of infrared and ultraviolet, of sound and motion, vortexes of confusion wherein time and space and paratime followed not the multibranched, quasilinear progression, but doubled back, meeting themselves again, producing still more eddies in space/time. Then there was a wavefront sweeping forward in time, black and silvery, roaring as does an avalanche, spreading out from a single point in the five-dimensional context, producing still more confusion.

For a few moments, caught up in the bending, looping, swirling stuff upon which the universes are built, he lost his bearings, was unable to pinpoint himself within the five-sided references, felt a weakening not so much of himself as of the medium through which he swam, found it difficult to propel himself through the miasma, as if here, in this Nonplace, Nowhen, there was something that might be described as a tear, a flaw in the matrix.

A kind of fear swept through him. For a moment he was near panic. Was it possible that he might get caught in one of these eddies and be unable to escape, captured forever in a loop in time that had no beginning and no end, that forever doubled back on itself meaninglessly?

Then he regained control of himself, steadied, studied as well as he could the forces at work, and the lack of working forces in other places. For an infinite moment he paused, then charted himself a path. Drifted for a moment. Then propelled himself again across the Nothingness, the Everything.

He was free, and again paused, wondered, speculated. What had happened, what could possibly have taken place here to so disturb the basis of all time and space and paratime? And did he have time to try to determine the answers?

Although "time" was very largely a meaningless term in this context, there was a subjective passage of time to the Shadowy Man, an urgency within him. There were things he had to do, and the sooner he got them done, the better. He realized that despite the powers he had gained in evolving from Eric Mathers into the Shadowy Man, he was still very much a human being in his psychology, still very much hampered by a psychological point of view that saw time as a steady progression from past to present to future, and his consciousness still continued to function as if that progression were true. Perhaps that was the only way a human or human-evolved mind could function. But then, perhaps, once his quest was completed, once his mind was at ease, he could more fully explore this, could come to *feel* as well as *know* that such terms as "past," "present," and "future" really have very little meaning at all.

Later, he told himself, later—and realized that it would be a difficult thing indeed, even for him, to ever fully comprehend a nonlinear view of time.

Again he oriented himself, established once more his five-dimensional position, moved toward his goal, KHL-000, A.D. 1610.

Through the Nowhere, Nowhen, he moved again, passing out of the worst of the confusion and entering into relative blackness, relative silence, across time, space, and paratime, and arriving. . . .

Now, with a mental sigh of relief, the Shadowy Man once more was able to freeze a point in space/time, to focus himself on a single place/event, to involve himself with three-dimensional space, the passage of chronological time.

The spatial viewpoint that the Shadowy Man initially established for himself was akin to that of a low-orbiting satellite above Earth as it existed on Line KHL-000. Below him, the planet turned slowly, a cloud-whitened world, a world of oceans and land, rivers and mountains, forests and deserts.

For a long while he drank in with pleasure the sight of this Earth below him, reveling in the beauty of it. From this height it appeared to be a virgin world, an untouched, unspoiled near-paradise. He was still very much a human being, he thought, as he considered his love for this planet.

Then he began to move his viewpoint, the focus of his consciousness, his vision. Like a spaceship returning from a trip to the stars, he lowered himself toward the planet, entered the atmosphere, and approached the landmasses below.

Even as he came in and then momentarily held himself still, poised but a few miles up, he could see no signs of human habitation—or, in this case, Krithian habitation. Yes, he told himself, they have been here but a few years now, they will have only a few centers of their culture, for theirs is still a very small race, a few thousand individuals now. Their works would hardly be visible from any great distance.

And on Sally's world of A.D. 1610, what works of man would have been visible from this altitude? The Great Wall of China, perhaps. A few of the largest cities, their dim nighttime lights, their daytime smoke, London, Paris, Berlin, Moscow, Peking perhaps, few more, little else.

As he swept closer, now moving like a great-winged bird of prey above the virgin landscape, he wondered where the Kriths would have established their initial settlements. He delved into his memories, the memories of Eric Mathers, and sought.

Remembered . . . that when Mathers had arrived on KHL-000 of A.D. 1972 he had been in North America and it was there that he had been taken captive by the Kriths and their companions, the Mager-types, as he had called them. But a period of unconsciousness had followed his capture and during it he could have been taken just about anywhere on the planet. But had he been?

He dug further into the Mathers-memories. There was no reason to believe that he had been taken from North America, so for the moment he would assume that he had not been. Then what had been the weather, the climate, when Mathers awoke? Warm, pleasant, a day in spring or summer it had seemed, although it should have been late winter, the month of February. Therefore, if he had still been in North America, it must have been in the southern part, perhaps in one of the areas known as Florida or Mexico or California on some worlds.

Poised above the great landmass of Asia, the Shadowy Man turned his consciousness eastward, swept across the Pacific Ocean, approached North America, angled toward the southern coastline. As the water gave way to land, he slowed, stopped, poised, hovered again. Then he slipped a portion of himself out of the electromagnetic spectrum, entered into the semidarkness of psionic awareness, and probed for consciousness: dozens of minds, not the kinds of minds with which he was more familiar, but minds nonetheless— Krithian minds.

And were they aware of him as well, some of them?

He probed again, and found one particular cluster of minds shining more brightly than the others, eleven of them, glowing with psionic awareness, dimly conscious of his presence, he was now convinced, yet not knowing what he was.

With electromagnetic vision again he looked, and correlated this viewpoint with his psionic one. Then he knew where they were.

South he moved along the coastline. Saw them.

Not far from the sandy, rocky shore was a clearing in the trees and brush, not a city by any standards he cared to recall, hardly more than a village, a series of primitive, temporary structures in jumbled, unplanned arrangement. Only two of the structures appeared to have been built with any permanence in mind, and these were hardly more than crudely baked brick, with rough-hewn wooden beams and windows glazed with glass of poor quality. Hardly the majestic cities of KHL-000 that Eric Mathers had envisioned.

But then, he reminded himself again, they were but newly come to this world and as yet had not recruited their vast armies of human assistants. Kriths were a people never given to the building of technological things—a very unmechanical people, the Kriths—and he knew that the cities and the great landscaped parks of KHL-000 that Eric Mathers had seen would not come into being until large numbers of humans worked for the Kriths, until their companions—the semihuman, semi-Krithian Magers—were among them. Now the Kriths dwelt on a technologically primitive level. But, he told himself, it would be very unwise to underestimate them just because they did not have the artifacts of high technology. They had their minds, their ability to self-skud from Line to Line, and they had the Tromas—not yet so ancient and wise in their powers, but the powers were there, and could be used.

He quickly probed toward the two more-permanent-appearing structures.

What he found in the first of them was surprising, though it should not have been. He should have anticipated something like this. It would have been their first order of business.

Inside the structure, which had a primitive look from

the outside, he found ample evidence of the technology
he had seen before. The low, rambling, brick and
wooden structure reminded him very much of some
portions of the Underground of the BrathelLanza.
Rooms here and there were filled with white-smocked
figures—humans! Microscopes and centrifuges, incuba-
tion units and culture containers, equipment for the
analysis and study of unicellular life, row after row of
liquid-filled containers that brought to his mind the
term "encanters," for in these vessels embryos almost
human in their appearance developed outside the
wombs of their mothers. Within this building, as unpre-
possessing as it was, human scientists and technicians,
supervised by adult male Kriths, were growing clones,
Krithian replicates.

Of course, he said to himself, the very first thing
they would do is see to it that their numbers increase:
a race that numbers but a few thousand is hardly ready
to begin remodeling hundreds and hundreds of parallel
Earths. And he remembered the words that the Tromas
had spoken to Eric Mathers once he had realized how
terribly few there were of the female Kriths: "We all
are pregnant. We each give birth at least once a year.
Yet still we are few, terribly few to maintain a race
as widely spread as ours. . . . There are other means of
maintaining our race, of propagating our species. . . .
Once our chances of survival were minimal. You
might find it a wonder that there are Kriths in this
universe at all."

For the first time, the Shadowy Man realized that
the majority of the members of the Krithian race must
be replicates. Perhaps a dozen new individuals would
be born each year, but millions would be needed for
the ever-increasing number of worlds they dominated.
Cloning would be the only answer.

But in a race numerically dominated by clones, he
thought, had there ever occurred a situation analogous
to his own? But then, he thought not. The conditions

that conspired to create the Shadowy Man were, perhaps, unique in all the universes.

He withdrew from the first structure, turned his attention to the second, probed, entered.

Eleven female Kriths, gross, fat, ugly, sat in wheeled chairs in a circle facing inward, carrying on a silent conversation among themselves, when the Shadowy Man entered the room they occupied.

For an instant he was aware of bits of their silent conversation: *For the fifth Line to the Temporal-East of the first Indus Line, I would suggest . . . Would be a very wise move, for our initial objectives there are . . . What we shall call a "Prime Line," the first of many that we must . . .*

Then the conversation ceased in midstream. Before, they had been dimly, vaguely aware of a presence outside themselves, but had not concerned themselves greatly with it. Now they knew *he* was there. Their attention, now focused into what might be considered a single consciousness, turned to him.

Who are you? the Tromas asked.

You don't know? the Shadowy Man asked them.

We do not know. Answer us, who are you?

Have you not looked into your own future? Have you not scanned far uptime?

We have, and . . .

A pause in the voiceless reply. Then what could be described as a soundless cry, an astonishment, a gasp. A babble of separate mental voices: *. . . It cannot be . . . It is him . . . But the orders of probability are so low . . . Those probabilities can be altered, we know this . . . Then is it? . . . It is!*

The Shadowy Man realized his mistake. He had waited too long; he had given them an opportunity to recognize him for what he was, could be, would be.

Together, sisters! . . .

Now he was forming a psionic bolt, a mass of furious energy to use against them; he drew it back, launched it toward the clustered female Kriths.

The atmosphere within the building was charged with tension. Balls of lightning skittered across the floor. The smell of ozone grew thick in the air.

The psionic blast slapped against the Tromas, but already their shields were coming up, deflecting most of the energy, converting it to other forms, radiating heat, light, X-rays, and microwave radio energy back into the air, into the sky, into space.

The Shadowy Man dodged backward, prepared another bolt of psionic energy, brought up his own shields . . . only to feel the lash of the Tromas striking out against him, splashing against his shields, sending him reeling.

His shields came up again and once more he rushed toward them, launching his bolts and finding them met by bolts of even greater strength hurled at him by the Tromas.

A second time he retreated, pulled farther away, and felt the Tromas seeking him, probing outward, upward, across time and space. As yet he had suffered no pain, for no significant energies had gotten past his shields, but he could weigh his power against theirs, and he saw that, despite the comparative youth of the Tromas as a psionic entity Here and Now, it was still far older and more experienced than he. Even Here and Now, the Tromas had the capability to defeat him.

It was not cowardice but wisdom that led the Shadowy Man to make his decision to withdraw not only from the direct confrontation with the Tromas but from that space/time itself.

Another place, another set of circumstances more to his liking, would have to be found. He was still meeting the Tromas on their own ground, their own terms, and there was no way he could hope to best them there.

He fled outward, upward, across time and space, toward . . .

He was not yet certain. He would think, consider, decide, and then . . .

Before him, as he moved in the direction he called "uptime," he was again aware of the flux of space/time that he had encountered before, the vortexes and loops, the spirals and pinwheels, the shades of blackness that became great splashes of mingled colors, the sounds of a maddened symphony orchestra, the wavefront of confusion, now followed by still another such wavefront that engendered still more confusion, more loops and swirls in the universal substance.

He paused in his flight, considered, then probed. He reached out, grasped one particular piece of space/time, froze it, peered into it, then sought another and did the same, trying as he did to build within his composite mind some picture of what was taking place within this area of madness in the universal matrix.

What he found was a multitude of conflicting and confusing worlds lying side by side in paratime.

One world, a KHL-000 a century or more uptime from his conflict with the younger Tromas, a place in time that could perhaps have carried the label A.D. 1740 had anyone been able to place the world within the framework of a calendar: a world without intelligent life at all; a world on which men had once lived, long before, but from which they had been removed by forces not totally comprehensible even to the Shadowy Man; a world where forests engulfed ruined castles and hamlets, while the bones of men were dust within ancient tombs.

And beside this world in paratime, a world that would have had the same calendrical label: it was the focus of a conflict, yet not a conflict between men but between Kriths. The Shadowy Man found himself rocked by the improbability of it: Kriths do not fight among themselves. Yet there it was—a Krith who had a large red disk painted on his chest and whose genitals were painted the same color stood silently, with his back to a tree, his eyes scanning the forest before him. Silently another Krith appeared, one with blue-painted genitals and a blue star on his chest, skudding in from another Line (or from another place on this Line? the Shadowy Man wondered), then making a sudden, deadly leap, planting a sharpened stick in the throat of the red-painted one. The victorious Krith gave out a great war whoop; but, as suddenly as he had appeared, two more self-skudded into this place, their genitals and chests painted red. They saw the slain Krith, one of their own kind, and his slayer, decorated with blue, and they pounced on him, driving him to the ground with wooden staffs, battering him until his arms were broken and his skull cracked and a reddish gray muck spilled onto the ground beneath the trees.

Still other worlds, as insane and improbable, in wild juxtaposition, seeming to have no relation to one another as did normal worlds in paratime. He saw worlds where men fought rearguard actions against numerically inferior but technologically superior Kriths; armies of men with muskets and crossbows being wiped out by a single Krith with an energy rifle! Worlds where Krithian overlords, with no apparent desire to dominate other worlds, worked human slaves in vast plantations that grew esoteric crops such as no Earth had ever seen before. Worlds where semibarbaric humans worshiped the sole survivor of the Krithian race, an ancient, nearly senile, alien god-king who knew that when he died, with him would die all the dreams of his vanished race.

An uncountable multitude of worlds branching, splitting, proliferating.

And other worlds of encapsulated time: a world whose history began about A.D. 1610 and would end about A.D. 2500, looping back upon itself and begin-

ning again, meaninglessly; a world so isolated from
the rest of the universe that its Krithian inhabitants
could not even skud away from it to places of sanity,
but were doomed to repeat that slice of 890 years forever.

Another encapsulation: frozen time, no movement
at all. There is no life on this Earth. Barren stone,
frozen water, unimaginable gulfs of loneliness. Not
death. Just nonlife.

The Shadowy Man shuddered in terror, and asked
himself how it was possible for such worlds to be. Then
realized. As the Kriths should have realized. At least
part of it.

The Kriths had come across the parallel worlds and
settled on KHL-000 and for a time had lived there,
then had decided to go downtime to begin their remak-
ing of the histories of the parallel worlds as early as
possible. From their decision to pluck themselves out
of space/time and hurl themselves, as a race, backward into the historical past had come this fragmentation. Moving backward in time, passing themselves, as
it were, moving through already established historical
eras of solely human habitation, they had brought into
being a fragmentation of paratime, the waves, the whirl-
pools, the eddies in space/time that had brought about
further fragmentation, further duplication, further mul-
tiplication of world after world after world. The Kriths
had done a lot of it themselves.

And yet, he realized, as he prepared to move uptime again, some of it was *his own* doing: in going
downtime, in challenging the Tromas on KHL-000 in
A.D. 1610, he had set into motion still another "new"
set of probabilities, more *possible* ways that things
could have been. In the chronological period A.D. 1610–
2500, a vast and still increasing number of possible
worlds had come into being, and as each moved forward in time, approached still more possible alternatives, they fragmented further, moving further and

still further from probability into improbability, demanding more and more from the substance of space/time, drawing the fabric of the universe thinner and thinner, ever closer to its bursting point.

The fear was still in him as he launched himself uptime again. And as he moved he continued to scan the worlds around him, he found the Lines more and more confused, the fabric of space/time thinner and thinner still. How much more would it take to tear it? he wondered. And what would happen if it tore?—when it tore? What would a hole in the universe, in the universe of the universes, become?

The Tromas had once had an answer to that too, he thought.

He paused again in his movement uptime, and scanned the parallel worlds.

Some calendars would have recorded the date in time as A.D. 1920.

A world here: KHL-000 much as Mathers had known it, a highly civilized world of cities and landscaped parks, of Kriths and their companions; yet, for all that, it was a world over which hung the pall of doom, dark and heavy, eminently menacing.

And beside it in paratime: a blasted, desolate world, created like the moon, seething with radioactivity.

And beside it: a world of men and women huddled in caves, looking with incomprehension at the night sky in which there was no moon, but a series of glittering bands that looked much as the rings of Saturn might look to an observer on that planet.

And beside it: a world where Kriths were the ones who huddled in foul caves, fearful of the sounds in the night, unaware of the powers their ancestors had once possessed.

And beside it: a world dominated by humankind, building a technological culture, a world where airplanes were beginning to take to the sky and iron rails spanned continents, where radio was more than just a curiosity, and where a savage world war loomed on the horizon of history, a war in which biological and chemical weapons might well destroy the human race.

And beside it: a world in which strange, unhuman, unholy figures stalked the forests, alien, asymmetrical things out of nightmares and drug-distorted hallucinations, monstrous things with only the barest glimmerings of intelligence in their grotesque eyes.

And beside it: a world dominated not by humans or by Kriths or by nightmare monsters, but by mammalian humanoids whose skin had a bluish tinge and who had the mastery of a high order of technology, who had craft capable of going to the stars and other craft capable of crossing the Lines of Time . . .

The Shadowy Man felt another chill enter the fear that already filled him. From out of Eric Mathers' memory came these words:

"Their heads and faces were half hidden by transparent helmets, but I saw enough, more than enough: their eyes were too big and their noses too flat and their jaws hinged wrongly and there was an unmistakable tinge of blue to their skin. Oh, they were about the size and shape of men, as far as I could tell from the bulky suits they wore, but there the resemblances ended."

These were the beings whom Mathers had believed to be the founders and the coordinators of the Paratimers, the beings who had called themselves Albigensians when they disguised themselves as humans, the beings who appeared to hate all things human and Krithian and had set out across the Lines, much as had the Kriths, to change the parallel worlds—or to destroy them—to suit their own enigmatic purposes.

But Albert von Heinen, who had worked for them and had once seen them in their natural, undisguised state, had said they came from the far Temporal-West, the products of laboratories, not wombs, artificial beings, androids who had risen to destroy their human masters and then to destroy all humankind on all the Lines. That was what Von Heinen had believed them to be. But . . .

Could it be, the Shadowy Man asked himself, that the Paratimers were not as alien as he had believed? Could it be that they are some variant of the Kriths themselves? Or some alternative race brought into being by the same people who molded the Kriths from human genetic material? Or could they be in a way analogous to the Magers, the companions of the Kriths, some sort of halfway point between human and Krith? Or are they, perhaps, a wild variation of natural evolution, a quantum leap in mutation that created a whole new species on a single, improbable Timeline in this maelstrom of paratemporal madness? Or . . . ?

And if these were the true Albigensians, the true Paratimers, as they certainly appeared to be, then what were they doing exactly here? Had they skudded into this world? Or had they, as he had just speculated, come from this world originally and then gone to the far T-West to begin their work from there?

And how did all this figure into the disruption of the Timelines he was witnessing, the fragmentation of Line after Line after Line into multiplicities of worlds? Were they part of the cause, as he was? Or were they merely an effect of it?

There was too much here for even the Shadowy Man to begin to comprehend at once, though there was an overriding concern in his mind that came back to him, an awareness of the eventual consequences of such universal fragmentation.

He remembered a part of the conversation that Eric Mathers had held with the Tromas. As he again moved uptime toward decision and further action, this came to him:

The Tromas had said: "In the beginning, when the universe came into being, when there was only one master Timeline and it existed in and of itself, it contained in itself all the chronal or parachronal energy, all the temporal potential that would ever exist. Then as the Lines began branching, as the various alternative worlds came into being, that temporal potential began being divided among them."

The Tromas had said: "Each succeeding Timeline, as history progresses, is lower in potential than those which had existed earlier. . . . And . . . the universe *is* limited. Something is either infinite or it is finite. . . . If it is infinite, there is no end *ever*. If it is finite, there is a limit that sooner or later must be reached."

The Tromas had said: "The probability energy, one might say, of the universe is large, large beyond imagining, yet it is not infinite, and for billions of years it has been spreading itself thinner and thinner as more and more Timelines come into being to further subdivide that potential."

Mathers had asked: "Are you saying then that there will come a time when the potential is spread between too many Timelines?"

The Tromas had said: "Exactly, Eric, and when that time comes, the laws of conservation of energy—or something very like them—will come into play to rearrange the probability indices of the Timelines.

"In order to maintain itself—though not exactly in the forms to which we have become accustomed—the universe will have to make major readjustments within itself.

"Timelines vary in their probability. . . . Some are *more likely* than others, more *probable,* and possess, even now, greater values of parachronal energy than do Lines of lesser likelihood.

"Those with lesser likelihood, with lower orders of probability, will *cease to exist,* and their parachronal energy will be redistributed among the Lines of higher orders of probability. That is to say that a vast number of Timelines will cease to exist in order that a smaller number, with greater likelihoods, will be able to continue to exist."

When the universe reordered itself and the lesser Lines ceased to exist, among them would be the Line that had spawned the Kriths, unless they were able to do something to increase their *probability*—which was exactly the purpose of their spreading across the Lines.

But, the Shadowy Man asked himself, were they correct in their projections of when the reordering would come? They had said hundreds or thousands of years uptime. But . . . but did they fully realize how thinly the fabric was already stretched in some areas of space/time? Did they realize how much they themselves had done to weaken the matrix from which *everything* was built?

Farther uptime he moved, crossing the twentieth century and then the twenty-first.

Ultimate questions about the future of all the Timelines would have to wait, he told himself. That was not the immediate problem. The Tromas were. And the problem of *their* existence, and his own, must be settled before he could allow himself the luxury of such metaphysical speculation.

And he thought he now knew where and how he could challenge the Tromas, the time and the place where they would be weak enough, inexperienced enough for him to hope to defeat them—if he had not stretched himself too far when he reached that place in space and time.

That he would see.

Uptime he plunged, into the future far beyond the point where he had come into existence, out into space and far away from the planet called Earth that circled a star called Sol. Into interstellar space . . .

20
UR-427-51-IV

Had an observer been watching the Shadowy Man, had it been possible for human eyes to see him then and to follow the swiftness of his motion in some sort of coherent space/time framework, it would have appeared to the observer that the Shadowy Man moved away from Earth, toward the constellation of Gemini, the Twins.

And had the observer's eyes been able to follow him out of the solar system and into the limitless blackness between the stars, he would have seen the Shadowy Man aiming himself directly toward the second-brightest star in that constellation, Beta Gemini, an orange K0 star that had an absolute magnitude of $+0.8$, a star somewhat brighter than Earth's Sol, a star often called Pollux on a number of Earths, but known by other names on other worlds, a star listed in the fabled Breston Survey Catalog as UR-427-51.

Had the observer, like the Shadowy Man, been able to step outside the conventionally understood configurations of space and time, had his eyes been able to transcend lightspeed by means of some nonphotonic vision, had he seen by tachyons, perhaps, and had he in this fashion followed the Shadowy Man across the twelve parsecs that separated Sol from Pollux, he would have eventually seen that a host of planets revolved around that orange sun: five of them so-called terrestrial planets, Earthlike in that they were primarily cold balls of stone and perhaps had cores of molten nickel-iron, two of them with gaseous envelopes sufficient to warrant the name "atmosphere." Beyond them, farther out from the star, five more planets revolved on their axes, followed long elliptical orbits around their primary, though these planets were of the type often called "gas giants," worlds not greatly unlike Jupiter or Saturn, though none was as large as Jupiter; in the planetary system of UR-427-51, the total mass of the outer planets was more evenly distributed among the five bodies.

The observer would have seen that the Shadowy Man paid scant attention to the large, gaseous worlds, but swept past them across the plane of the ecliptic and centered his attention on the planet that lay fourth from its sun, a world more distant from Pollux than Earth is from Sol, but at such a distance that it received only a little less heat and light, at least in its upper atmosphere.

The observer would have seen that the nucleus of mental concentration that was the Shadowy Man slowed as he approached UR-427-51-IV, slowed and then swept around it in a great spiraling orbit, examining the planet as the first interstellar probes must have examined it when they discovered the star's planetary system.

The Shadowy Man was in no hurry now, or so he insisted to himself. He must approach slowly, carefully, examining the world below him and determining as much about it as possible before actually pushing his focus of consciousness toward the surface. No hasty rushing in this time. He must be careful; he must be certain, absolutely certain, of everything before he once again challenged the Tromas, or what might now be the proto-Tromas, for as yet he doubted that the Krithian females had full awareness of their potentially enormous power.

In terms of Earth's calendars, one particular calendar that Eric Mathers had often had reference to, it was sometime in the twenty-fourth century, he believed, though he was uncertain of the exact year, perhaps between 2340 and 2350, although the exact year was not a matter of great importance. The Kriths had been here for about a century, genetically modified colonists sprung from human stock, and adapted, by the scientists and technicians of their particular Earth, to survival in the unpleasant environment of the world he saw below him. It would be another fifty or sixty years, as time was measured on Earth, before they would be ready to commandeer a supply ship and in it return to the planet that had created them and then sent them out here.

Now they would be wondering, asking questions, growing within themselves a bitterness toward Earth-norm humans that they would probably never fully express. At least the Kriths had never shown the fullness of their hatred, as far as he knew. But then they had never shown great love toward normal humankind either.

(And what of the blue-skinned ones? he asked himself. If they were akin to the Kriths, if their origin was similar to or identical with that of the Kriths, had they not shown their hatred toward mankind? And he remembered the horrible desolation of world after world among the Albigensian Lines, worlds blasted by thermonuclear hell to lifeless balls of burning stone. Compared to them, the Kriths actually seemed beneficent.)

Around the planet and around again he orbited, each circuit of the planet bringing him closer to the surface. From this distance, UR-427-51-IV was a beautiful world, yet unlike Earth, a dazzling radiance under Pollux, not greatly unlike Venus as seen from a distance, although its cloud cover was less than that of Venus, greater than that of Earth. Beneath those clouds, which did show occasional breaks through which the surface was visible, the greenhouse effect had been at work for long ages, though not with the cataclysmic kind of temperature building Earth's sister world had seen. Enough breaks existed in this cloud cover, sufficient forces were at work to allow at least some of the infrared of the lower atmosphere to leak back into space. Had this not been so, even Kriths could not have survived here. To the best of the Shadowy Man's knowledge, no one on any Line had ever been able to survive unprotected on Venus' surface, no matter how greatly his genes had been modified.

Below the almost but not quite perpetual covering of clouds, the planet was hot, far too hot for Eric Mathers or his kind to have endured for long without extensive refrigeration and air-conditioning facilities. Kriths, or the proto-Kriths who dwelt there now, could endure it, though they might not have found it the most pleasant of climates.

It was a world with an axial tilt greater than Earth's, a world where winds of high velocity swept through the atmosphere, where great storms boiled, where thunder played a nearly continual tune and lightning frequently illuminated the underside of the dark, heavy clouds. It was a world where rain fell as often as it did not, where great oceans spread across most of the surface, untroubled by lunar tides, churned only by the pull of Pollux and its companion planets and by the frequent storms that lashed across uncounted leagues of water. Where there was land on UR-427-51-IV, it was mostly swamp, forever wet to a greater or lesser degre, for whatever volcanism the planet had, whatever slipping continental plates might have crushed together, whatever mountain ranges might once have reared toward the dark skies, constant rain and wind had quickly eroded them, tumbling stone and earth and mud back into the sea from which they had come.

It was not a pleasant world, either to the humans who had discovered it and its potential value or to the colonists they had adapted from their own flesh and blood, their own fertilized ova, to dwell here, doing tasks that unmodified men and women of Earth did not wish to do. It had been largely a cold, economic decision, he suspected, to send genetically modified colonists here rather than send unmodified Earth-norms who would have required elaborate life-support systems, complex protection from the environment, insulated, bubble-enclosed housing, and much more. It was simply cheaper to send the genetically modified, who could get by without these things.

The Shadowy Man moved still closer to the surface, noting in his passage the observation satellites strung across the skies, satellites with electronic eyes, with cameras and antennae that constantly watched the turning world below.

And he noted the single inhabited platform that circled the world in a polar orbit. Not a large station by any means, but sufficient to hold four Earth-norm humans in some degree of comfort and safety. It was the four inhabitants of this platform who monitored the world of the colonists below, who directed their tasks, who sent down to the planet robotic cargo shuttles to carry supplies to the colonists, matériel essential to their survival that they could not produce themselves, and to carry back into orbit for transshipment to Earth the results of the colonists' labor: a particular and rather esoteric drug manufactured by a plant that grew in the shallow swamps; the lovely, multicolored fur of a near-mammal that looked something like an otter and something like a cat, but differed from both; the beautiful gemlike stones created inside the bodies of certain deep-sea crustaceans, amphibious creatures that returned to the shore annually to breed, and to be captured by the colonists.

While still outside of all but the most rarefied portions of the atmosphere, the Shadowy Man began to probe into the psionic world, into the darkness that was something other than the absence of light, the absence, rather, of intellect, and within that darkness began to search out the bright points of consciousness, of self-awareness.

On the surface of the planet below he found those points of light, a familiar kind of mind now, the Krithian mind. He found clusters of these lights, apparently strung out along an archipelago, clusters that in most cases consisted of no more than a few dozen individuals each, though toward the center of the curved line they formed was a larger cluster, and within that cluster was a group of ten minds that glowed more brightly than the others, that were more aware, more powerful, that reinforced one another through psionic interchange, through something that might have been called resonance but was not quite the same as that.

In their total, the Shadowy Man thought as he lowered his focus of consciousness still closer to the surface, as he withdrew his probes so that the ones below would not yet become aware of his presence, there were no more than a few hundred of the colonists, and knowing what great handicaps had been placed on their reproduction, he wondered how it would be possible for so small a group to survive even the next fifty or sixty years, much less commandeer a spaceship to carry them to Earth. But they would do that, both survive and eventually leave this world, he was certain. The histories of hundreds of Timelines bore ample witness to that.

With electromagnetic vision but remotely akin to human sight, the Shadowy Man looked as he lowered himself through the perpetual overcast and saw below him the dark world under the clouds, saw the wind-whipped rain charging in near-torrents across the far southern archipelago, as thunder rolled across the sky and great bolts of lethal lightning crackled between the clouds and the stunted growths of trees that huddled close to the damp land.

On one of those islands, amid a cluster of supple reeds that bent with the force of the wind, a dozen or more naked Kriths, bigger and physically stronger than most men, were struggling in the downpour to draw in a net that contained a score or more large crustaceans, lobsterlike animals with bulging eyes and long, dangerous-looking pincers that snapped at the ropes that held them and at the fingers that held the ropes. More than one of the Kriths was missing a finger or two from each of his hands.

As the Shadowy Man watched, one of the struggling Kriths lost his footing on the muddy soil as he tugged at the net, stumbled, fell, then slid, foundering into the water, flailing about with his arms and prehensile tail, to no avail. His companions saw what had happened, but none of them dared release his grip on the net. The struggle was already so awkwardly balanced that the loss of another pair of hands would have certainly meant the loss of the net and its contents. They fought to pull the net from the water, perhaps hoping their companion could regain land without their help.

The Krith who had fallen into the water surfaced, gasped for air, and fought to stay afloat. He did not cry out for help. He seemed to know that his companions would help him if they could, but now could not. For a few moments he seemed to have gained some control over the situation. It appeared that he might be able to make his way back to land without help. But that changed in moments. As he half swam, half crawled toward the higher ground, an expression of astonishment, then pain, crossed his flat features. He flailed again and fell backward, the water around him turning to a muddy crimson. He screamed, again screamed, again struggled awkwardly toward land.

Now the other Kriths had managed to conquer the struggling crustaceans within the net, exerted an enormous final effort, and drew the net from the water onto the soggy land. While three of them hurried to secure the net to pegs driven into the ground and hold the crustaceans within their fibrous prison, the others dashed back to the edge of the water, formed a living ladder of themselves, moved toward the weakening, wounded Krith, touched hands with him, and pulled him to safety.

When at last they had him out of the water and he lay on the damp earth, gasping for air, sobbing in pain, the Shadowy Man could see what had happened. Teeth or pincers, claws or tentacles, he could not tell which, had fastened onto the Krith, had torn away most of his tail, the toes and most of the flesh of one foot, strips of flesh from both calves and thighs, and had left his genitals an unrecognizable mass of mangled flesh. He probably would live, had not poison been introduced into his system, did not infection enter the wounds. But whether he would wish to live in such a fashion was another question.

There was perhaps in the Shadowy Man a new understanding, a new appreciation of the Kriths, as he moved his consciousness away from that spot. It had not been easy, nor had it been pleasant, that first century or two of their racial existence. Mere survival had been a hard-won prize. And along with that understanding there came to him a glimmering of admiration. Under such conditions could another sapient race have survived at all? Could humankind have done as well as the Kriths had?

Above the islands he moved again, across them, toward the center of the long, slightly curving archipelago, toward the place where he had detected the largest cluster of minds, where he had detected the brighter points of psionic light, the more intense concentrations of mind that were the Tromas, or the proto-Tromas, the ten females of the race. And he asked himself: With such attrition as I have just seen, how can *they* even maintain the race, much less increase it?

One of the islands jutted a little higher above the level of the sea, provided a greater slope for the runoff of rain water, and was a bit dryer than the other islands. And on the highest point of the curving, dome-like island stood a cluster of rude huts, jerry-built affairs of reeds and vines, thatched with the broad leaves of some low-growing plant, huts without windows, but with doors covered with the colorful hides of some semiaquatic mammal-like creatures.

At first sight there was no indication that these people were the product and the agents of a civilization with the capability of crossing twelve parsecs of space in huge, plasma-powered spaceships. But on closer examination, in the center of the cluster of huts there stood something that could have come only from a highly advanced technology. A metal cylinder just slightly taller than the largest of the huts, of gleaming metal and glass that would have sparkled brightly had there been sunlight rather than this perpetual gloom, that did reflect brilliantly the flashes of lightning across the sky, an artifact from distant Earth that could have been nothing less than a communications center, a radio/video/laser transceiver of great power, a holographic tank that would display images sent down from the orbiting platform, from the overseers who commanded from many miles above in the comparative safety of their metal cocoon.

Not far from the cluster of huts was a cleared area where the dirt had been packed firmly, then covered with broken bits of stone and shell, obviously the landing field for the cargo shuttles that passed between the islands and the orbiting platform. But it was not the landing field that attracted the Shadowy Man's attention.

Rather, it was the largest of the huts, the one nearest the communications cylinder. Even without probing, he was aware that in that hut dwelt the females of the race, who had already, even this early in their history, become the directors of the actions of the proto-Kriths, the givers of wisdom, and who might now have some glimmerings of tomorrow and the awesome powers they and their people would one day wield. . . .

Would wield, unless the Shadowy Man could stop them now.

Now he paused, hovered, analyzed. He was far, far from home, in frames of reference that encompassed space and time and paratime. The nexus that connected him with his corporeal bodies was now a tenuous one, stretched across great five-dimensional distances. And he was aware of the lessening of his powers, of how far across the continuua he would have to draw the forces with which he was to do battle.

Yet, he was not pitting his strength against the Tromas of KHL-000 on their own world, their own time, with centuries of experience behind them. He was pitting himself against ten tired female Kriths who huddled in a rain-drenched hut, who had never had enough to eat, who had never received proper care or medical attention, who were lashed by weather and heat and parasites, who did not yet fully comprehend the potentials within themselves.

He could defeat *them*.

Couldn't he?

And as he took a brief glance at them, as he flashed his electromagnetic vision into and then out of the hut, as he saw them huddling in the semidarkness of the hut's interior, illuminated feebly by two sputtering oil lamps, he felt a great sense of pity, of sympathy, even of concern for their wretched condition. Could he bring himself to strike against *them*, these pitiful half-humans who had been born to suffer and to die as lonely, hopeless castaways over 19×10^{12} miles from the homeworld Earth?

Yes, he could.

Now they were exactly as he saw them. But . . . looking across time and space and paratime, he saw other things through the vision of Eric Mathers' memory: he saw the vast armies of Timeliners moving from parallel Earth to parallel Earth to alter the histories of uncounted worlds in accordance with a plan the Tromas had developed in order to increase *their* chances of survival, heedless of what their meddling might do to millions upon millions of innocent human beings; he saw wars and death and destruction; he saw the deaths of a girl named Kristin and of a girl named Marissa, of a man named Hillary Tracy and a man named Jock Kouzenzas, of the men and women of New Anglia, and of so many, many others that he could not distinguish all of them; he saw the dark-uniformed bodyguards of the Kriths, men like Pall and Marth, no longer human except in their bodily forms, more Krith than man in their minds; he saw armies of the Mager-types, the Companions, who were not men at all but something the Kriths themselves had created or had had created for them; he saw all the lies and deceptions that the Kriths had perpetrated over the years; and most of all he saw the Tromas in their "palace" on KHL-000 and sensed the power they possessed and would use to destroy the Shadowy Man and anyone else who stood between them and the future as they envisioned it, a future that, when the universe had reordered itself toward greater simplicity, would have the Kriths supreme on all the Lines of Time.

Yes, he would do it. He would attack and destroy these pitiful wretches. He had no other choice if man was ever to be free of them and be allowed to seek his own multiple destinies across the Lines of Time.

From remote distances across time and space he drew toward him energies, forces, powers, shaped them into lances of fire and spears of fury. He drew them back, tensed, and then for a moment, before he launched his attack, he projected out of the sky and into the hut this mental construction:

If you can see into tomorrow, you will know who I

*am and why I have come. I do not do this for pleasure,
but because it must be done. . . .*

And he was briefly aware of their astonishment,
their fear.

Then his probe was gone, his shields were up, and
toward and into the hut he hurled his psionic blasts.

The inside of the hut shimmered with auroral brightness, sparks and streams of lightning flickered across
the interior walls, the dryer reeds inside smoldering
and then beginning to burn. The ten females of the
proto-Tromas writhed in agony, curled into balls, tumbled grotesquely across the floor, screaming in pain
and terror.

For an instant he lowered his shield and peered into
the hut.

Sisters . . . A mental voice was crying out of its
pain. *Sisters, rally to me, to me. . . .*

Incoherent mentations. Pain climbing toward the sky.
One figure ceasing its horrible writhing, falling still,
silent, the brightness of its mind fading to blackness,
nothingness, death.

*Sisters, he has come. Rally to me. We can still fight
back. . . .*

Nine consciousnesses now, through their pain seeking one another, converging, melting, blending, becoming one.

The Shadowy Man reached out into space/time, a
minor sensation of triumph in him. He had killed one
of them; their collective strength would not be as
great as it could have been. Their collective strength
was . . .

Now, sisters! . . .

As he gathered new energies into himself, as he
forged new weapons to dash against them, the females
as a single entity struck, battered against his not fully
sustained shields, broke through them, hurled him backward.

Damn you! he cried to himself, now feeling pain as

they did, pushing away their force, bringing his shields back up, completing the manufacture of his weapons, deploying them, using them.

The invisible shields of the females shimmered with furious incandescence. Around them, the walls of the hut began to catch fire.

Outside, the male Kriths of the village, who had some awareness of what was happening, rushed to offer what help they could to their females, their guardians.

Tear down the walls, brothers/husbands, they cried. *Keep the fire away from us. . . .* Out of their pain and their fury they screamed.

With bare hands, two dozen or so male Kriths attacked the burning hut, ripped away portions of it, threw them across the damp earth, and let the rain do its work.

The females were hurt, were in pain both psionic and physical, for the males had not acted quickly enough, despite their swiftness, and the flames had licked across them, embers had scorched their flesh. But still they had repelled the blasts he had thrown at them, had held their shields.

Damn you! the Shadowy Man said to himself again, throwing up his own shields to ward off the flames and fury they cast at him. Now the pity and the sympathy were gone from him; now there was only his own fury and a desire to destroy them.

Again he reached out, again sought raw energy from which to build more weapons, groped across darkness, found . . . found dwindling supplies. He was too far away. Too far. And the females were rallying again.

Know this, thou force from out of time . . . they cried at him. *Know this: you cannot now defeat us, now or ever. Have done with it. Let us be. . . .*

What energy he could he took and brought it to this place, molding it, shaping it, propelling it against the shields of the females, which again flickered and burned brightly. Once again they held off the bulk of his attack, swept it away, felt only minor pain. The nine of them still held, and prepared to lunge against him.

The Shadowy Man sought to strengthen his shields once more, found them weaker still and weakening more. His reserves were almost gone. Across the light-years, across the centuries, he tried to drag replacement powers, reinforcement energies, but the gulf was too great, too great.

Again the Krithian females struck against him, battering his shields again and again, smashing through them, tearing them down one after the other, forcing piercing lances of psionic force through them and into him.

The Shadowy Man screamed, felt the last of his defenses fall, felt himself being rocked backward in space, in time.

No, damn you, no! he cried silently, but that was all he could do. They had defeated him again. Before they could strike against him once more, before they could drive more bolts of hellish fury into him and through him across time and space into the bodies that were his component parts, he disengaged, withdrew, fled, hung suspended Nowhere, Nowhen.

They had beaten him. And they had been right: *You cannot now defeat us, now or ever. . . .*

He had lost again.

Perhaps for the last time.

21

The Sundering of Time

Still feeling the agony inflicted upon him by the blows
of the proto-Tromas, still tasting in his mind the gall of
defeat, the Shadowy Man slowly propelled the focus
of his consciousness backward through time, across
space and across paratime toward the physical bodies
in the Underground of the BrathelLanza. Along with
the pain there was confusion and a sense of hopeless-
ness.

He had done what he had been able to do. There
seemed no other avenues to pursue. Even in their infancy the Tromas were more than a match for him.
And although he thought that he could have beaten
them had he not been so thinly drawn, he knew that to
be only academic. The facts being what they were,
there was no way he could hope ever to meet the
Tromas with an advantage over them. Perhaps there
was, after all, a measure of predestination in the universe; perhaps it had been preordained that the Kriths
would dominate all the Lines of Time, the bastard children of humankind, perhaps, but better suited for rule
of the continuua of Earths.

So, despite his efforts, by and large the future would
be as the Tromas had always seen it. When finally,
centuries hence, the Timelines had multiplied so greatly
that the universe would be forced to reorder itself to
greater simplicity, the Kriths would most likely have
had ample opportunity to assure their continued existence after that reordering. Then what? Once they had
accomplished their racial goal, what would they do
next?

The Kriths had no great love for their parent race, humankind, he knew, and would probably feel no significant obligation toward whatever portion of that race still existed after the reordering, whatever human Lines still remained, which should be a considerable number, considering the vast number of Lines spawned by mankind's decisions when facing Either-Or. Would the Kriths finally take their vengeance on the race that had created them and then sent them off to the living hell of UR-427-51-IV? Or would they by then have gained sufficient insight to no longer hate humankind for being what it was? Would they allow the race of Eric Mathers and his kind to go on living, developing, perhaps to one day live up to the standards it sometimes tried to set for itself but seldom met? If the Kriths did let humankind go on, then in what status? As slaves of the Kriths? As inferior people to do their bidding, to further advance the Kriths and further assure *their* continued survival during any future universal catastrophe? He did not know, could only speculate, but there was still enough of the human in him, enough of Eric Mathers, for him to feel a great concern, a fear for the future of man.

But what could he do?

He drifted back in space and time and paratime toward the Underground and the place of his physical existence as the senior of his resonating replicates. Now he could not even assure the survival of the physical body of Eric Mathers, though perhaps something could be done to help him. Perhaps.

As he came closer in space/time, as he moved through the nothingness that is everything, new perceptions came to him, sensations that impinged on his withdrawn consciousness. He looked out of himself, felt, probed, sensed.

Downtime, he thought, downtime there is *something*. What, he could not have said, could not have even guessed, but he was aware of something that had happened/was happening/would happen, something that did have/was having/would have great consequences for all the Lines of Time.

With a growing sense of anxiety, forgetting momentarily the pain and humiliation, he thrust himself through nothingness with greater force, swept downtime toward the space/time of Eric Mathers and the replicates, then past them and farther into the "past."

Then he saw, felt knew. . . .

He had encountered it before, but then it had been farther downtime, more remote in the chronological past as Eric Mathers would have conceived it. And *it moved*. . . .

A great wavefront was coming uptime, sweeping forward, fracturing and sundering as it came, spawning world after world after world, an ever-growing multiplicity of Timelines. The meddling of the Tromas, their flitting through and past themselves in retrograde time, their being/not being in duplication of themselves in the same relative space/time—all this, multiplied by the activities of the Shadowy Man in his own movements through time and his added manipulation of spatio-temporal events, had brought into being this *something* that was the wavefront, *something* that was a swelling tide of rupturing paratime, duplicated, quadrupled world after world: worlds twinned, spawned, modified, and mutated, spreading the fabric of all the universes, all the continuua, thinner, thinner, ever thinner. . . .

And in the midst of this wavefront, spreading like a second cancer across the multiplicity of worlds, were the bluish-tinted creatures who were the true Paratimers, the beings truly behind Staunton and the raid on Fort Lothairin and who, perhaps, had been behind the destruction of the BrathelLanza, the nonhumans, non-Kriths who were the actual operating force behind so much that had been done in opposition to the Kriths—and in opposition to mankind as well.

Like the Kriths, the Paratimers sought to subvert a
vast number of Earths, to bring them under their
control, to alter the master plans of the Kriths and
create futures more to their own liking.

But why? the Shadowy Man wondered. And what
are they?

As he moved backward in chronological time, the
Shadowy Man paused only briefly, snatching an image
here, another image there, putting together in his composite mind a backward-running motion picture film
that led him to the devastated Albigensian Lines of the
far Temporal-West, to the dead, blasted worlds Eric
Mathers and Sally had found when they had fled from
Kar-hinter and sought Mica's world. Still farther back
in chronotime: balls of thermonuclear flame and towering mushrooms of dark smoke; missiles climbing on
tails of fire from hidden silos, from submerged sub-
marines, falling from orbiting stations: a war that
spanned a dozen parallel Earths and more, a war
fought by the Kriths and their human servants who
weren't yet Timeliners against the Paratimers.

Kriths! the Shadowy Man wondered. On worlds this
far to the T-West? But the Kriths had never come this
far to the T-West, had they? But perhaps they had.
Perhaps they had—originally.

Still farther back in time: the Kriths consolidating
their hold on a world, a single world; Kriths without their Great Lies and their Timeliner mercenaries
and their vast propaganda machines to convince humans
of their beneficence; Kriths who had established a tyran-
nical rule over the race who had created them and
sent them to a hell among the stars; a beleaguered
humanity fighting a losing war against its creation, then
turning to fight with fire, unleashing against the Kriths
a second subspecies created in the laboratories of genetic engineers, a second subspecies as different from
the Kriths as the Kriths were different from their an-
cestral humans, a second subspecies that turned against

its embattled creators and destroyed them before taking up the war against the Kriths and their human servants.

Insanity! the Shadowy Man cried within himself. And wondered if any of what he was witnessing had any reality at all or was just some vague, fanciful twist of probability/improbability as the universe of universes grew near sundering, as the maddened wavefront swept uptime, spawning a phantasmagoria of worlds and drawing thinner yet the fabric of totality.

He looked again at the wavefront that moved forward in chronological time and thought: in such a condition the universe cannot long endure. If the wavefront were to spread much farther uptime, increasing the number of existing Lines by exponential powers, the universe would have to crumble to its very foundations, or reorder itself.

The concept of godhead, of deity, had little place in his mind, in his thoughts, as he considered the restructuring of the universe to greater simplicity. Yet there was about it, almost, the feeling of a directing intelligence, a guiding force that would see to it that the universe remained intact, did not crumble into an infinite number of bright but meaningless fragments. Something, mind or force or basic structure, would not let this happen, would step in and see to it that the now almost incoherent multiplicity was reordered into sanity and greater simplicity. What it was even the Shadowy Man did not know. He did not call it God, though perhaps that name could have been applied. Whatever the name, he knew *it* was there and *it* would act. Soon. Very soon.

The Tromas had been right in their judgment of the coming necessity of universal reorganization. But their time scale had been off, very far off. Not hundreds or thousands of years from the moment Eric Mathers stood in the palace of the Tromas and learned of it from them, but only months ahead in time.

But then they couldn't have known all that the

Shadowy Man now knew, couldn't have foreseen it, could they?

There was a great deal more he knew now, and he realized that the Tromas had not even begun to fully understand the nature of time, nor had he. Perhaps it was incomprehensible. Perhaps it did take a universal godhead to fully comprehend what time was/is/will be, how it is an aspect of the same thing of which paratime is an aspect, of which all energy and matter too are aspects.

As wrong as was the viewpoint of time being a linearly progressing thing, so was it equally wrong to consider time an all-existing thing, the future, the present, and the past already in final shape and unchangeable. Time was not such a simple thing. It was far more complex than that—or perhaps far less so: or both at once. And it existed not by the rules laid down by men or Kriths or any other finite intelligences. It, and all the universe, existed by its own rules, regardless of whether anyone knew those rules.

What the Tromas had told Eric Mathers about the nature of time had not been *wrong*, no more than Newtonian physics were *wrong*. Just incomplete. If he carried the analogy forward: his present knowledge of time was Einsteinian to their Newtonian, and just as Einstein had superseded Newton, had explained more of the workings of the universe, so too had his viewpoint been incomplete and would one day be replaced by another viewpoint that more nearly comprehended it all.

How ignorant we will always be! he said to himself. And "looked" at the wavefront that swept glittering and screaming uptime, the wavefront that he had abetted. Unwittingly, unknowingly, by means he had not intentionally devised, but because of what he had done, the sundering of the universe would come long before the Kriths were ready for it, long before they had become so entrenched in the Timelines that nothing could dislodge them. They had greatly increased their probability, of course. But not enough. Though they commanded hundreds of Timelines, there were millions more they had not touched, and for each they had touched, for each Line they had manipulated and altered, there stood beside it its parallel, which they had not touched, perhaps could not touch, for by their very touching of a Line they engendered its alternative, a Line they had not influenced. Had they realized this? That their very manipulation, too, had twinned each Line they had reached, had created its duplicate—one world manipulated, one not—so that no matter how many worlds they entered, altered, they could never hope to encompass even a small fraction of all the Lines of Time, Lines they themselves helped to multiply at an ever-increasing rate. Would they ever have been able to keep up with it?

Did it matter now? he asked himself, pausing in space/time, observing the wavefront that "moved forward" at a rate of its own, creating a subtime within the totality of time.

When the universal catastrophe came, when the majority of Timelines with lower orders of probability winked out of existence, *would never have been,* so too would the Kriths cease to exist, so too would they never have been. Neither they nor the Paratimers, whatever they were, nor all the works they had set out to do would ever have existed.

He watched the wavefront, calculated, saw the coming of the limits, the final sundering when catastrophe would occur.

He fixed a date in his mind. The year A.D. 1973 as the calendar was reckoned on the world of Sally's birth. Early in the year. What day? The sixty-third day of that year. The month of March. The fourth day of that month, on Sally's calendar.

Then it would be over. All of it. No more Kriths. No more Timeliners. No more Paratimers.

He had won; in a very real sense he had accomplished what he had set out to do. . . .

And what of himself?

He too was a creature of the Kriths—Eric Mathers was a creature of the Kriths, so thus was he. And so was Sally. So were . . .

Amid the numbness that spread across his consciousness, amid the questions and the fear, there came another realization. . . .

He himself had come/would come into being on 4 March 1973. Before that there had been no Shadowy Man.

Then . . . did he/would he exist?

Feeling a terror that could only be called mortal, the Shadowy Man hurled himself through nothingness, uptime, toward the Underground and the immobile body of Eric Mathers, the motionless replicates, his very existence. . . .

22

The Last Encounter

Once more the Underground of the BrathelLanza enveloped the Shadowy Man. He settled into the individual bodies and into the resonance patterns that existed among those bodies, feeling almost as a human might feel, returning to the comfort and security of his mother's womb, for this was the womb from which the Shadowy Man had been born.

The sense of terror partially slipped from him, receding from the front of his consciousness, although he did not forget that the end was approaching—the end of the universe as he had known it, the end of the Kriths and the Timeliners and all the things they had done, and the end of the mysterious Paratimers and their efforts across the Lines. How soon, he did not know. Now? An hour from now? Anytime . . . He could not calculate the time of sundering with that precision; yet, within the next six to eight hours at the most, he thought.

And still there were things he had to do, things that might be totally futile now, but he must make every effort to complete the past as Eric Mathers had experienced it—if he did not, he suddenly asked himself, how would that affect things? If the universal reorganization came before he had completed his work, what would that do to his participation in the chronological past? Wipe it out? Alter things in the Kriths' favor? Paradoxes . . .

He was not certain of any of this, but he could take no chances. He knew that he must complete Eric Mathers' experiences, down to the last detail he could

cull from his memory, and then—if at all possible—
make some provisions for the continued existence of
Eric Mathers, should he still exist after the reordering
of the universe. The continuation of his own existence,
that of himself as the Shadowy Man, he knew to be
considerably unlikely. But if he could save at least the
Eric Mathers portion of himself, that would be enough.
If the universe didn't destroy *him* . . .

Once again he looked out through the eyes of
Mathers and saw the chronometer in the recording
room. More time had gone by, to the motionless figure
strapped in the chair—over an hour since he had last
looked out through those eyes. The chronometer read
13:50:17. Early afternoon. Perhaps the universe still
had a few hours before it altered itself, before the
parachronal subtime wavefront swept this far uptime
and demanded that the universe reorder itself toward
greater simplicity, or cease to exist altogether.

A few hours, perhaps . . .

Now, he told himself, there are three things I must
do.

First: he must provide for the "parachronal convolution" through which Eric Mathers and Sally had
escaped KHL-000, the sphere of blackness that had
awaited them on the roof of the apartment building
toward which they had fled as the Shadowy Man battled the Tromas in their own place/time, the first and
perhaps the worst of his encounters with the Krithian
females. While Mathers was under attack by the
Tromas, after the Shadowy Man's defeat by them, Sally
had dragged him into the black sphere and through
it they had plunged across space and time, to the
Far World where they had lived for some time, where
Sally still lived on 4 March 1973, and from which
Mathers had begun the adventures, some eleven months
before, that had led him to the Underground of the
BrathelLanza and to evolution into the Shadowy Man.

Mathers and Sally had been told that they had

passed through a "parachronal convolution," a term that had meant nothing to them, though now the Shadowy Man was beginning to have some inkling of what it might be.

. Second: he must provide them with a skudder at their destination. It had been there and the Shadowy Man had provided it. So he must now do it; otherwise Mathers could never have left the Far World and come across the Lines to this place that the Shadowy Man presently occupied.

And finally: he must provide for the escape of the corporeal body of Eric Mathers, get him out of this place and into another, safer one; a place where he *might* survive the reordering, if it was possible for him to survive, if it was possible for him to *exist* once the Kriths no longer existed anywhere, on any Line.

Once more the Shadowy Man set out on quest, and in learning how to accomplish the first of his objectives he learned how to accomplish the others.

Time was lost, time that he could not regain, for, as he had suspected, he found that he could not return to the Underground in a time/place he already had occupied. But as time was lost, knowledge was gained.

The composite mind of the senior and his replicates swept back and forth across time and space, searching out bits and pieces of knowledge that the Shadowy Man was now capable of using, always terribly aware that he was in the moments of time just before the reordering of the universe.

He found: esoteric bits of knowledge; fragments of theories about the nature of space/time; ways of manipulating the unraveling of fabric of the universe; means of twisting that fabric into unusual and intricate shapes; processes through which one segment of space/time/paratime could be linked with another, momentarily, tenuously, but sufficiently for a material object to pass from one point to another in the five-sided references; learned how to bring into being a para-

chronal convolution, a tunnel through time and space
and paratime.

He was astonished by the powers he found he could
use, and wished that he had learned these tricks earlier,
or that the universe would give him more time to fully
exploit their value. But now there was a linear progression of subtime, or perhaps a paralinear progression of subtime—the holocaust of the moving wavefront
sweeping uptime—that even he could do nothing to
alter. He was caught in subtime as fully as any man
had ever been caught in the inexorable movement of
time in the conventional universe. He could not hold
back the hands of *that* clock.

But he could at least do what he had set out to do.

Returning briefly to the Underground, he rested,
went over what he had just learned, then launched himself outward again, backward in chronological time
and across paratime to the world of the Kriths, KHL-
000, A.D. February 1972.

For a moment he poised his consciousness above the
top of the apartment building that he had visited
before. It was night Here and Now, and from the top
of the spire the lights of the vast capital city of the
Kriths spread out below him toward the horizon on
one side, the dark sea on the other. In the building
below, from the open doorway at the top of the stairwell, he could already hear gunfire and the yells of the
Mager-guards who pursued Mathers and Sally as they
made their attempt to escape. Farther below, in the
apartment Sally had occupied, a great struggle had just
terminated. His previous self, an earlier Shadowy Man,
had just been vanquished by the Tromas and had
fled, screaming in pain, back toward the Underground.
For a few moments the Tromas would be occupied
with their own problems, assessing their victory, seeing to their own minor psionic wounds. If he acted
quickly enough, they would never become aware of
him. He thought they would not recognize the para-

chronal convolution for what it was, even if they were to notice it. He hoped.

Mathers and Sally, naked but not unarmed, firing behind them as they came, were about to reach the top of the stairs.

There was no more time for thought. With mental probes, with Waldos of psionic force, he reached out and grabbed a piece of the space/time stuff of Here and Now, held it in an unrelenting grasp; and then, with all the force he could muster, he tore a strand loose and withdrew with it across time and space and paratime, drawing the strand with him.

This is how it works, isn't it? he asked himself, and thought that it was.

Pulling a dimple of time/space/paratime deeper and deeper into nothingness, he drew it toward and finally to his destination, a few weeks downtime, a very short distance relative to spatial distances, but a long, long way across the dimension he called paratime.

There! He had reached it, pulled another pucker out of another world's framework, connected them together.

How long the connection would hold, in terms of chronological time, he did not know. Not long. Minutes at the most. But time enough. Mathers and Sally would see the blackness that the convolution presented to their senses, would realize it to be their means of escape, and, in desperation, would use it. Through it they would pass across to the Far World and there they would be safe. From there Mathers would later follow the path that led him, eventually, to the BrathelLanza and their underground laboratories.

Accomplished! he said to himself, a sense of relief coming over him. He had done this much. He could do the rest. And he could hope that in the end it all would have meant something.

Pausing only momentarily, he then moved to accomplish the second of his three objectives. Once again

he propelled himself into the future, leaped a few
Lines horizontally in paratime until he located a world
where the Kriths and the Timeliners had established
themselves, searched for a skudder pool or its equivalent on that world, and found one.

The year was A.D. 2004, as chronological time is
measured, a few miles from a place occupied by At-
lanta, Georgia, on some worlds, where the Timeliners
had set up a large, well-equipped base. Into this base
the Shadowy Man went, to a large depot building that
contained nearly a score of brand-new skudders, just
recently arrived there from the Line of their manufacture. Blue-clad Timeliner technicians were completing
their final checks of the craft before sending them out
into the field. One of these skudders would do perfectly for Mathers' future needs.

The Shadowy Man was feeling almost happy as he
moved into the fabric of space/time around one of the
new skudders, as he extended psionic appendages to
grasp that fabric. The fact that this was a "future" world
that would soon cease to exist, with the coming of the
universal reorganization, did not bother him in the
least; in fact, there seemed to be something very funny
about it. As long as the skudder stayed downtime of
4 March 1973, it would have *some* probability—
enough, at least, to serve his purposes and Mathers'.

And there was something very funny about the expressions on the faces of the technicians as the skudder
vanished before their eyes, as the depot reverberated
with the sound of imploding air, rushing in to fill the
vacuum left by the skudder's sudden and unexpected
departure.

With the skudder nestled in a capsule of detached
space/time, the Shadowy Man drew it across nothingness until he reached the Far World again and completed the convolution. The skudder then sat but a
short distance from where Mathers and Sally would
come out of their escape route.

There was a feeling within him that would have been a smile on a human face, a satisfaction with this stage of his work, when the Shadowy Man retreated back to the Underground for what he anticipated to be the next to last time, back to where he could check the passage of chronological time as seen by Eric Mathers and decide how to go about the last, final phase of his labors.

He was astonished at what he found there, though he knew he should not have been. He should have anticipated it. For all the vast mental powers he had, he knew that he was but an infant in his knowledge of their use. And it was very unlikely that he would be given the opportunity to complete his maturation.

Eric Mathers and the replicates were no longer alone in the Underground. People had entered, more than one kind of *people.* . . .

Through the eyes of Mathers the Shadowy Man looked, and with Mathers' ears he heard.

There was the sound of several pairs of feet moving in the corridor outside the recording room, and distant voices speaking a language Eric Mathers had heard before, a variation of Middle French as spoken by the so-called Albigensian Paratimers, male voices and female voices he soon recognized. One of those voices—one he had heard quite recently—was saying, as its owner approached the door of the recording room:

"In all likelihood, Scoti, he was in one of the mnemonic-recording rooms when the raid took place. If that is so, he may well still be in one of them, and alive. At least the police do not have him, and his body does not appear to be among the dead. I'm certain no one escaped."

"You said he might be under the influence of drugs, OrDjina," said a voice that Eric Mathers hadn't heard in quite some time, the voice of a man named Scoti Hauser Angelus, who had been the second in command of the Paratimers, Mica's lieutenant, in the place called Staunton.

"Yes, that's so," replied the lady OrDjina. "That must somehow be related to the phenomenon you described."

"That may well be," said the voice of another woman, a voice that was in Mathers' memory as well.

"Here," said OrDjina's voice. "This door does not appear to have been opened."

The Shadowy Man tensed, waited, listened, as a hand curled around the knob of the door, turned the knob, and tried to force open the bolted door.

"It's locked," said Scoti's voice. "That figures."

"Then kick it open," said a voice that the Shadowy Man did not recognize, a voice with an accent unknown to Eric Mathers, a voice that somehow did not sound like that of a human.

"Right," replied Scoti's voice; then he grunted as he kicked the door, rattling it and the wall.

"Kick it again," said the alien voice.

"Right," Scoti repeated, and once more the Paratimer kicked savagely at the door. This time there came with it the sound of wood splintering.

"Once more," said the voice that the Shadowy Man did not believe to come from a human mouth and throat.

With the third kick the lock broke and the door swung inward.

There were six individuals in the corridor, six who began to come into the room to look down at the unmoving form of Eric Mathers.

The first of these was the lady OrDjina, dressed in a black, tight-fitting gown more appropriate for a dinner party than for the charnel house that the Underground had become. There was an ugly pistol in her hand, and on her face a look of satisfaction, an expression that briefly turned to one of disgust when she saw the mutilated body of the technician MaLarba on the floor near Mathers' chair. Her eyes quickly went back to the figure in the chair and the look of satisfaction returned.

Immediately behind her was a stocky, dusky-skinned man, fairer than OrDjina, a man whom Mathers had once considered an improbable blend of Italian and Nipponese parentage. Scoti, also armed, was dressed in a blouse and slacks of pale green, and had a look of satisfaction similar to that of OrDjina's—a look that swept the gamut from revulsion, when he saw MaLarba's body, to astonishment, when he saw the face of the man in the chair before him, and finally to triumph.

"My God, OrDjina!" He gasped, glanced back at the others behind him for confirmation, then continued: "Do you know who your HarkosNor *really* is?"

"No. Should I?" OrDjina asked, puzzled.

Scoti laughed, then clenched his left fist and shook it toward the man strapped in the chair. "Dammit, we should have known who he was."

"This does sort of tie things together, doesn't it?" said a young, beautiful, black-skinned woman, who was the third to enter the room, and who was dressed similarly to Scoti, and armed as he was. Long, tempestuous nights with G'lendal came up out of Mathers' memory. She would have been difficult to forget.

"Oh, doesn't it!" Scoti gloated. "All of it begins to make sense now."

"Well, who is he?" OrDjina demanded.

Before Scoti could answer, the remaining three had filed into the room. Two of them, a black man and woman, were dressed in the long white robes of Paratimer physicians, with the badges of telepaths on their chests. As they came into the room, each was moving exactly as the other did, down to the most subtle gestures. The Shadowy Man knew who they were, something of a forerunner of himself: Sol-Jodala they/

it were called. And were probably among the finest,
most talented physicians in all the universes.

The sixth individual gave the Shadowy Man pause
as he—a male, surely—moved forward. The others
gave way, moved aside, so that this one could come
up to Mathers' immobile form and look down into
his open eyes.

"Can he hear me, OrDjina?" this one asked, human
vocabulary coming only with difficulty to his lips,
mouth, and tongue.

"Yes, sir, I believe he can," OrDjina answered, a
respect and a submissiveness in her voice that Eric
Mathers had never heard before.

"Hear me, then, you who are known by many
names. I am called Foraldar. Some call me the Inquisitor. You will know me as Master."

Through the eyes of Eric Mathers, and through his
own electromagnetic vision, the Shadowy Man looked
at the one who called himself Master Foraldar the
Inquisitor.

He was as tall as a man, taller than Scoti, equal in
height to Sol of Sol-Jodala, and, like a man, he had
two arms, two legs, a head on a neck above his shoulders, two eyes, a nose, a mouth, and two ears. He
looked much like a man, yet there was a coloring of
blue to his skin and his eyes were too large and his
jaw was hinged wrongly and he had six fingers on
each hand.

"We have many names," Foraldar said slowly, carefully articulating his words to the being he believed
to be Eric Mathers, who was he, but was also something more. "To you we are the masters. You will do
as we say. You will obey. You will answer. And you
will assist." The being glanced over his shoulder at
G'lendal and said, "With your mind, speak to him. Tell
him why we have come."

Foraldar stepped back a pace or two to make room

for the black woman, who approached the form of Mathers, extended her fingers, and touched his temples.

In the background he could hear OrDjina's whispering voice asking of Scoti, "Who is this man?"

"He called himself Eric Mathers when I knew him," Scoti whispered in reply.

"Eric Mathers?" OrDjina said with a gasp.

"Exactly," Scoti told her.

Inside Eric Mathers' head, inside the Shadowy Man's mind, came these words: *Eric, you know me, don't you? G'lendal, G'lendal from Staunton. We have come to help you, Eric. We know what you are and we wish to help you.*

Help me? the Shadowy Man asked, pretending to be the man who was but a single part of him. *How can you help me? What do you want of me?*

Eric, we know who you are. We know about the Shadowy Man and how he is fighting the Kriths. The Kriths are our enemies too. Together we can fight them and together we can defeat them.

Exactly who are you asking me to help? That thing over there?

He is not a thing, Eric. You would never give them a chance to explain themselves. They aren't our enemies. They're helping us fight the Kriths. They and mankind, together with you, can defeat the Kriths.

And then be what, G'lendal? A race of lapdogs for your masters?

That's just Foraldar's way of speaking, Eric. He's our leader, our unit's leader, and like any good leader he expects his people to follow his orders.

It sounds like a great deal more than that to me.

You don't understand, Eric. . . .

I don't even want to understand the mentality of a willing slave, G'lendal.

Eric! That's not the way it is at all.

Isn't it? Then tell me, G'lendal, what is he? What

*kind of creatures are they and where do they come
from?*

*There's no time for all that now, Eric. We will ex-
plain it to you later, when it's safe. . . .*

While this mental conversation passed back and
forth, the Shadowy Man formed a second mental extension, a fine and delicate psionic probe, which he
carefully pushed toward the creature who called himself Master Foraldar, toward the brightly glowing point
of alien mental light in the psionic darkness.

He probed, touched, entered into the brightness, and
found . . .

Even the Shadowy Man, a composite of 337 human
cerebral cortices and their mentation patterns, who had
entered into the minds of parallel Eric Matherses and
who had grappled with the minds of the female rulers
of the Kriths, could not deal with what he now encountered: below the glow of self-awareness, of consciousness, he found inside the mind of Foraldar a type
of mental process such as he had never encountered
before, had never even imagined. This was not a mind
like a man's, or even like a Krith's, or like that of the
composite Tromas, or even, by a stretch of the imagination, a mind like that of an electronic computer. There
were mental processes going on there, passages of
neural impulses, thoughts being created, but these were
being done in fashions totally incomprehensible to the
Shadowy Man. He found no way to equate these with
his own mental processes, no way to translate these
into anything he could understand. He could have
called them dark, evil, alien, malignant, but he was
not certain that would have been correct. Different,
they were. Alien, yes. But beyond that he could gather
almost nothing.

He formed words in the language Foraldar had
spoken, pushed them into the alien mind: *What are
you?*

The alien screamed, threw himself backward, clawed

at his face, then collapsed to the floor in a shuddering bundle.

The humans stood for a moment, transfixed. Then Scoti moved, turned away from the sobbing alien, faced the form of Eric Mathers, leveled his pistol, and asked, "G'lendal, what happened?"

"I don't know," the black girl said aloud, then turned back to Mathers and touched his temples again. *Eric, what have you done? . . .*

I just asked him who he was.

My God! . . . G'lendal's mind gasped. Then she said, angrily, *Leave him alone, Eric. Give us time. . . .* Aloud she said to Scoti, "He'll be okay in a minute. Get him outside and give him some water. Sol-Jodala can tend to him."

"G'lendal," Scoti cried, "we're running out of time."

"I know," she said, glancing back at Mathers. "But give me just a few more minutes. I've got to convince him."

"Maybe it would be better to kill him now," Scoti said.

"Foraldar wants him."

"Wanted him, you mean. He may be ready to kill him now too."

"Then he will have to decide that," G'lendal said. "See to him."

Angrily, reluctantly, with the help of the physician Sol-Jodala, Scoti carried Foraldar out of the room and into the corridor.

Well, Eric, G'lendal said into his mind, *do you see what you have done?*

It wasn't my intention to harm him.

You did, though. Their minds are very unlike ours, although I am surprised that even you have the power to cause him pain like that.

I've changed a lot since you knew me. . . .

I know that. That's why we're here.

Why?

As I said, we know of the Shadowy Man. We need him.

You won't get him until I know a great deal more.

And I told you we don't have the time.

What's the hurry?

Don't be a fool, Eric. If we know of the Shadowy Man, where he is, don't you think the Kriths do too?

Yes, I suppose they would. But how did you know?

We have no time for all that now. Just think on this: if we have come here, the Kriths are surely sending people too. They will be here soon. . . .

I imagine they will, G'lendal, but it will be too late for them, just as it's too late for you.

And what do you mean by that, Eric?

Answer my questions and I'll answer yours. What is this Foraldar of yours? Where does he come from?

A mental sigh. *Oh, very well, Eric. Foraldar's people, the people you know as "Albigensians," come from a Timeline on which there occurred a terrible genetic war.*

Explain that . . .

Very well. On Foraldar's Line of origin, the Kriths returned to Earth from UR-427-51-IV, as you know, but rather than moving across the Lines and establishing KHL-000, they remained and set out to exterminate the humans of that world. During the war that followed there were—

G'lendal's narrative was cut short by the sound of shouting voices, then the firing of weapons.

"Right over there, Cal-sarlin," said the first of the voices, a deep, masculine voice speaking in Shangalis. "Over . . . Look out!"

"Who . . ."

Guns began to fire.

"Paratimers!"

G'lendal screamed.

Through Mathers' eyes the Shadowy Man could not see what was happening, divorced himself from that body, threw psionic extensions into the corridor, then saw.

A band of men, led by a towering, naked, ugly Krith, was coming down the corridor, armed as were the Paratimers. The two men leading the Timeliners were tall and were dressed in harsh, black uniforms, and they had sighted the Paratimers outside the room clustering around the figure of Foraldar, had yelled a warning to their Krithian leader. Scoti had gotten his weapon up and had pulled off the first shot. As they dispersed, the Timeliners fired back.

Now energy weapons and slug throwers raked the hallway. A blast of coherent energy caught the kneeling Scoti full in the face, washed away flesh to blackened bone, kicked Scoti's still-writhing body backward against a wall. Leaden slugs tore through both members of the telepathic team Sol-Jodala, ripping apart Sol's arm and shoulder, almost cutting Jodala apart at the waist. Another bundle of slugs kicked into the still-prostrate Foraldar, puncturing his green uniform and the body wearing it, giving it some semblance of jerking life as the impact of the slugs knocked him against the crumpling form of Scoti.

OrDjina, who had been standing in the doorway, leaped back into the recording room, too frightened even to use the gun she held. G'lendal stood transfixed.

In moments the two black-clad men stood in the doorway, their energy pistols covering the two women and the immobile Eric Mathers.

The Shadowy Man recognized the towering men dressed in midnight black, Turothians, Eric Mathers had once heard them called. Humans, but . . . from worlds so far across the Timelines, the products of experiences so far outside the pale of Eric Mathers, that it had been hard for him to consider them humans.

One was named Pall, and the look he gave Mathers was one of intense hatred.

The second was named Marth, and he had but one

hand, and the look that he gave Mathers was of even greater hatred.

Both their energy pistols were now leveled at the motionless form, at Eric Mathers' chest, and it would have taken only a few ounces of pull on the weapons' triggers to reduce this corporeal body to charred organic ruin.

Neither of the men spoke.

Next into the room came the Krith, a tall, sable-colored being Mathers had known by the name Cal-sarlin, a minister to the Tromas back on KHL-000. He was naked, as his kind almost always were, and he smiled.

"Good afternoon, ladies," he said in the French-descended language of the Paratimers. OrDjina let her pistol fall from limp fingers. G'lendal now began to come out of her shock, though she looked at the Krith with incredulity. "And good afternoon to you, Eric." He smiled wickedly. "I can only say that I am glad we have caught you again—and saved you from your Paratimer friends. This time, well, we shall see that you do not escape us again."

Outside, in the corridor, above the four ruined corpses, now stood a stocky, redheaded man who could have been a caricature of an Irishman, but was anything but that. Mathers had known him by the name Kjemi Stov. And if there was hatred on his face, it was well hidden by a noncommittal look of Timeliner efficiency.

Cal-sarlin glanced over his shoulder toward Stov.

"Shall I go on?" the red-haired man asked in Shangalis.

"You know where they are, I believe," the Krith replied in the same language. "See that they are all destroyed."

Stov nodded curtly and went off down the hallway, and as he did so the Shadowy Man saw that he led half a dozen almost-men, Mager-types in dark, harsh uniforms, and each of them carried an automatic weapon.

"I regret what happened to your friends, ladies," Cal-sarlin said politely in the language of the Paratimers. "But they did present us something of a problem. If you can see your way clearly to cooperate with us, no harm will come to you."

OrDjina spoke an obscenity, then spit on the floor near the Krith's unshod feet.

G'lendal merely looked at the Krith's brown, marble-round eyes. Her face was devoid of expression, though there may have been hatred in her eyes.

"We do not customarily persecute women," Cal-sarlin told them. "But you must consider yourselves prisoners of war and conduct yourselves accordingly."

OrDjina repeated herself. G'lendal did nothing.

"And as for you, friend Eric," the Krith said carefully, "we are not yet certain what you are, or what you have become. Given time, the Tromas will be able to determine that, I am certain. But that will be after the fact, I am afraid. A postmortem, shall we say?"

He stepped closer to the motionless figure. The two Turothians, Pall and Marth, flanked him, the aim of their weapons never faltering.

"I know you can hear me, Eric," Cal-sarlin said, switching to Shangalis. "The Tromas at least know your physical condition and its relationship to your, ah, replicates. We will see to them. And to you."

He paused, ruminated, scratched himself, then said, "We do not think you can harm us, either you or your Shadowy Man. But even if you could, it would be useless. More of us will come here—are coming here already. So, if we fail, Eric, others who follow us will not fail.

"I do wish we had more time to speak with you, Eric, but . . ."

The Krith's voice was interrupted by the remote

chattering of automatic weapons, the sounds of shattering glass and spilling liquids.

"Your replicates, you know," Cal-sarlin said. "Pall, Marth, you may now see to his . . ."

Even while the fingers of the black-clad men were pulling back on triggers, the Shadowy Man felt himself dying, dissolving, disrupting as leaden slugs tore through the bodies of his replicates, felt the horrible agonies of their dying, a prelude to his own. . . .

One of the fourteen-year-old bodies was all but cut in half, its entrails spilling out, wet and bloody, through gashes in its abdomen. A huge, jagged sliver of glass tore into the chest of another replicate, slashing into heart and lungs as nutrient fluid, now reddened with blood, spilled out of the shattered encanter. A bullet pierced the eye of a third replicate, stunning it but not yet killing it, throwing it against the back of the cylinder, which shattered with the impact, impaling the body on stalagmites of glass. . . .

As the triggers of the Turothians' energy weapons completed their travel and electrical circuits closed inside the weapons, the Shadowy Man began what he knew to be the last act of his existence.

Psionic fingers grasped the fabric of space/time that surrounded the physical form of Eric Mathers, tightened, pulled, jerked, flexed, tore, retreated. One last parachronal convolution was opening, one last spot of blackness swelling to encompass the man who soon would be all that was left of the Shadowy Man.

He pulled the bubble out of its context, still not fully understanding how he was doing it, but knowing that he was doing it. The bubble crossed the nothingness of everything, touched another strand of space/time, and joined the convolution through which the skudder had recently gone. He released his grip on the bubble, left it to fall, twist, spin, and snap through the joined convolutions across time and space and paratime to the Far World. Eric Mathers was safe, as safe as he could be in a universe about to undergo cataclysmic reorganization.

Then he flickered his dying awareness back into the Underground, back to where enough replicates still lived to sustain some portion of himself, back to where the Krith and the two black-clad men and the two women who had worked for the Paratimers now stood, all in dumbfounded astonishment as they struggled with the after-effects of the implosion caused by the sudden disappearance of the physical matter of Eric Mathers' body. The sphere of blackness had appeared and then vanished so quickly that none of them could have really seen it.

"Damn you!" Cal-sarlin cried as he picked himself up off the floor, his Krithian dignity hurt more than anything else. "Damn you, Eric Mathers, damn you . . ."

Pall and Marth looked at each other with incomprehension on their faces. Their energy blasts had done nothing but sear the far wall.

The implosion had ripped OrDjina's thin gown, half torn it from her body, but she hardly seemed aware that her breasts were exposed and her beautiful coiffure destroyed. Her face showed only fear.

Against the console that housed the still-operating mnemonic recorder leaned G'lendal, gasping for breath, but on her face there was a tiny smile, as if she understood better than any of the others what had happened, and her smile was given to the common enemy of the Kriths and the Paratimers, who was winning this very last battle of them all.

Although his strength was fading rapidly, his existence winking out as replicate after replicate died under the bullets of Kjemi Stov and the Magers, the Shadowy Man found the strength within what was left of himself to make the air speak one last time.

"Cal-sarlin," said the voice out of the air, the voice of Eric Mathers, "we have come to the end of the road, all of us. There is not the strength within me now to tell you all of it, so this will have to do: you and your kind, and the Paratimers too, all of you have lost, lost now and forever. Tell your Tromas that. If there is still time."

Fear now replaced incomprehension on the Krith's face. His voice was weak and faltering when he said, "W-what do you mean?"

"The end of the world is at hand," the Shadowy Man said, and laughed, and died.

G'lendal laughed with him, a laughter that bordered on hysteria.

OrDjina screamed.

Cal-sarlin's hands made and then unmade fists. But he never had the time to begin to comprehend the meaning of the Shadowy Man's last words.

The reorganization of the universe had already begun. And in moments there was not/never would be any such thing as a Krith.

It was 14:07:21, 4 March 1973.

23

The Far World

It was morning, 15 January 1972, as time is recorded on some worlds, when I awoke and found out who I was.

Even as I started to pull myself to my knees and rise enough to observe my surroundings, once again wholly and only Eric Mathers, I was struck by an appalling sense of loss, a terrible poignancy, and a realization of my own human limitations. I, who had once been a part of the Shadowy Man—or would be, if you want to look at time that way—was now just a man again, and after the experience through which I had just passed, that didn't seem like a great deal to be: human and so terribly finite.

From my knees I finally drew myself to my feet, pulling myself up with my hands around the trunk of a slender, graceful tree, something a bit like a willow, which grew beside a small, quickly flowing stream. A breeze moved along with the stream, across my naked hips, and I realized that I had arrived there, wherever *there* was, without clothing. And this realization came too: I had arrived without the chair I had been in, without the straps that had held me in the chair while drugged. Somehow the Shadowy Man had discarded them along the way, along with my clothing. I silently thanked him for getting me out of the Underground alive and well, and found my eyes moving toward the sky, as if now I identified *him* with some sort of heavenly deity. But I knew he hadn't been that. Less than a god. But, if he'd had the time . . .

It was a morning sky that was above me. Somehow

I was certain of that. A clear blue sky with wispy patches of clouds here and there. In my nudity the sun was comfortably warm.

Around me were forest and meadow. Graceful, thin-leafed trees, not quite like any I'd ever known anywhere else, clustering clumps of grasses, scattered mushroomlike growths, some of which might have been as much as ten feet tall. Remotely, a birdlike creature sang from the limb of a tree, calling his mate or maybe marking the limits of his territory, I thought. And I now knew where I was. I'd been there before. And an earlier version of me, along with Sally, would be coming soon.

And I knew what the Shadowy Man had left for me to do. A couple of little things he hadn't been able to do himself, just to round out what *I* remembered of the past. I could do that much for him, couldn't I?

After a quick dip in the cold, clear water of the creek, I set out to do those things.

The skudder sat not far from the little stream, a few hundred feet, no more, a bright and untarnished craft, the product of a "future" world that would soon cease to exist, *soon* being March of next year. The skudder wouldn't be built until years after that, but that didn't matter. Until next March that future would exist, at least in potentiality, and for now that was enough for me. If the Shadowy Man hadn't been able to fully understand Time, how could I ever hope to?

I went into the skudder he had delivered there, and for a moment sat before the controls, wondering what would happen if I were to start it up and in it leave this world. What would have become of that other Eric Mathers if he had had no skudder? How could he ever have gone to the world of the BrathelLanza and become the Shadowy Man? But then, would it even be possible for me to use the skudder if I wanted to? Possibly. Probably. For this is a universe of probabilities, never of certainties.

Inside one of the skudder's lockers I found clothing, and dressed, and then had myself a quick meal from the skudder's provisions, which were decidedly better than skudder fare usually is.

As I ate, I thought: Some distance to the west of where the skudder sat was a small, rather primitive village inhabited by people who could have been called civilized. The village was on the frontier of a small kingdom of people who were just beginning to work iron into weapons and jewelry, the smelting of iron a newly discovered art Here and Now. Although semi-barbarians, they weren't a bad lot. I'd lived with them for a while—or I would. Sally and I hadn't been—wouldn't be—really uncomfortable there, but then they had treated us like godlings. They'd been expecting us, I remembered. And how had they known we were coming? I'd told them, I suppose. Or I was about to tell them.

The Shadowy Man was right. This business of time travel can be very confusing.

So my first order of business was to go to the village and give the people there a little speech; I knew their language, of course. I'd tell them I was an emissary of a pair of deities who would be arriving in a few days—and with an energy pistol and a couple of other gadgets from the skudder, it shouldn't be too hard for me to convince them that I was something of a god myself. Then I'd prepare them for the man and woman, dazed and battered, naked and tired, who would come into their village soon. By the time I was finished I'd have them convinced that they were about to have a major miracle occur in their hometown, something that would really put it on the map. And when the next (or first) Eric Mathers got there, with Sally along with him, there would be no problem. At least that's how it had been with Sally and *me* when I'd come here the first time.

Then, when that was done, I would go back to the skudder and compose a note for the two fugitives from the Kriths, a note to my previous self and to Sally, which would read something like this:

"Dear Eric and Sally,

"If you read this note you will have escaped from the Tromas and have found the refuge I selected for you." I would write "I," though perhaps it would have been more honest to write "he" or "the Shadowy Man." "You're safe here as long as you wish to stay." Which was true within certain limits.

Still using the first-person singular, I would go on to say:

"I know you're curious about your means of transportation from KHL-000 to here, and I would explain it to you if I could, but none of us has the proper mathematical background to really understand it." Which was very true. I certainly didn't understand it. "I could tell you it's a 'parachronal convolution,' but what would that explain? Labeling something doesn't necessarily define it.

"This skudder, from some decades into the future, as you two have been reckoning time, is yours. It's fully provisioned and ready to take you wherever you might wish to go, spatially or paratemporally. You may use it when you will.

"Some miles to the west of here you will find a village. It is an outpost of a kingdom barely out of the Bronze Age, though its inhabitants are friendly and pleasant people. You will find yourselves welcome there, though don't be too surprised if you're treated as something a bit more special than a pair of naked wanderers. They're expecting a couple of exiled godlings. Try to act the part.

"In time you're a few weeks downtime from our recent conflict with the Tromas. In the past, as you see it.

"In space, you're still in North America, the Florida peninsula.

"In paratime, well, you're one hell of a long way to

the T-East, far beyond the Line the Kriths call KHL-000. It's as safe a place as any you can hope for, but try not to be disturbed by the oddness of some of the things you find here. There are some aspects of the evolutionary process that have worked out differently here."

I'll say! Ten-foot-tall mushrooms and fat unicorns!

But I would scribble on, and finally conclude with something like:

"As for advice, I can give you none, as much as I would like to." That was true.

"The future is yours to do with as you wish.

"I think." And that was a kind of truth too.

"Yours"—and I would sign my own name—"Eric Mathers."

That's the note I would write, but first I had a couple of other things to do.

From the skudder's locker I got several packages of provisions, took them to a place near the stream, and placed them in a small, neat pile where they were sure to be found by the two I knew were coming. If some animal didn't get them first. But I was certain they'd be waiting for Eric and Sally when they got there. I remembered them having been.

Then, feeling much better than I could remember having felt in a long, long time, I set out toward the west, where there was supposed to be—would be! I'd been there—a village that would give Eric and Sally a warm reception.

And as I walked I thought about the things that the Shadowy Man had experienced, the inexplicable paradoxes of a probabilistic universe. Nothing really *was*. Everything was just *might be*. Maybe that was a hell of a way to run a railroad, but it did keep things interesting.

And I wondered what the universe would be like *afterward*, when there were no Kriths or Timeliners or Paratimers to foul things up even worse than human

beings fouled things up. Things might not be so bad.
Maybe . . .

And I made a few plans of my own. After I got
finished at the village and wrote my note, then I'd go
off by myself for a while, do a little wandering, see the
country, maybe finally get my mind together and try
to understand a little of it. Then, in a few months, in
late April, I'd go back to Sally and tell her what had
happened. To her I'd have been gone only a few days;
to me it would be more than a year.

Then . . .

Well, I wasn't certain then. I'd come back to her in
April 1972, and the reorganization of the universe
wasn't scheduled to happen until March 1973. We'd
have almost a year to do whatever we wanted, to eat
and make love and sing songs and recite poems and
tell stories and make love . . . to dream and wish and
hope and . . .

And wonder about 4 March 1973.

That day would come eventually.

We'd have to face it.

The Shadowy Man hadn't been certain what would
happen to us, so neither could I be. Maybe there was
a chance for us, way off here in the sidelines. Maybe,
somehow, when the universe reordered itself, it would
miss us. Maybe we could go on and have those babies
after all, and be the godlings the people here thought
us to be. There would be a lot of things we could do
to help these people: introduce them to the concept
of sanitation, tell them their world wasn't the center
of the universe and help them develop this world's
first constitutional monarchy. There was a lot we could
do. Like the poor Timeliners used to say of themselves:
they have a lot of history in front of them.

But maybe it wouldn't work out that way.

I wasn't going to be frightened about it. And I
wouldn't let Sally be frightened either. Even if we did

wink out of existence, come next March, it had been one hell of a life.

I wouldn't have missed it.

And as I walked toward the village, I actually felt happy.

What the hell!

I began to whistle.

And once I glanced over my shoulder in a non-direction that I imagined to be the Temporal-West and the Lines of Men, and I yelled to them:

"Good luck, you silly bastards. You're going to need it. I won't be there to help."

AUTHOR'S NOTE

The curious publishing history of *The Timeliner Trilogy*
made it difficult for most readers of the hardcover editions
to know where the various sequences of events began or
ended.

I would like to express my thanks to Playboy Press, and
especially to senior editor Sharon Jarvis, for giving the
three novels that make up the trilogy this opportunity to
exist as a concurrent series.

I also appreciate the opportunity given to me by Playboy Press to eliminate some of the errors, inconsistencies,
and redundancies that existed in the previous editions.

And I offer a special word of thanks to Russell Galen
of the Scott Meredith Literary Agency for his efforts to
gain for The Timeliner Trilogy this unique existence.

To all and sundry who have helped, again, my thanks.

Richard C. Meredith
Milton, Florida
September 1978

PUBLISHER'S NOTE

Richard C. Meredith did not live to see his trilogy published. He died in March of 1979. We will miss him.